THE *Pirate* AND THE PORCELAIN GIRL

WRITTEN BY **EMILY RIESBECK**

ILLUSTRATED BY **NJ BARNA**

LETTERED BY **LUCAS GATTONI**

SIMON & SCHUSTER BFYR

New York   London   Toronto   Sydney   New Delhi

An imprint of Simon & Schuster Children's Publishing Division

1230 Avenue of the Americas, New York, New York 10020

This book is a work of fiction. Any references to historical events, real people, or real places are used fictitiously. Other names, characters, places, and events are products of the author's imagination, and any resemblance to actual events or places or persons, living or dead, is entirely coincidental.

Text © 2023 by Emily Riesbeck

Illustration © 2023 by NJ Barna

Lettering by Lucas Gattoni

Cover design by Sarah Creech © 2022 by Simon & Schuster, Inc.

SIMON & SCHUSTER BOOKS FOR YOUNG READERS

and related marks are trademarks of Simon & Schuster, Inc.

For information about special discounts for bulk purchases, please contact Simon & Schuster Special Sales at 1-866-506-1949 or business@simonandschuster.com.

The Simon & Schuster Speakers Bureau can bring authors to your live event. For more information or to book an event, contact the Simon & Schuster Speakers Bureau at 1-866-248-3049 or visit our website at www.simonspeakers.com.

Interior design by Tom Daly

The text for this book was set in Benoda, Goth Chic, Herald, Origin Story, and Spicy Noodles.

The illustrations for this book were rendered digitally.

Manufactured in China

First SIMON & SCHUSTER BFYR Edition

2 4 6 8 10 9 7 5 3 1

Library of Congress Cataloging-in-Publication Data

Names: Riesbeck, Emily, author. | Barna, Nora J., illustrator.

Title: The pirate and the porcelain girl / Emily Riesbeck ; illustrated by NJ Barna.

Description: First hardcover edition. | New York : Simon & Schuster, 2023. | Audience: Ages 12 up. | Audience: Grades 7–9. | Summary: "Cursed with porcelain skin and on the run from a zealous knight, Ferra has no choice but to trust the disgraced pirate captain Brig to keep her safe and reunite her with her ex-girlfriend in a faraway city. Together, they bicker across the high seas, dodge nefarious obstacles, and accidentally fall in love"— Provided by publisher.

Identifiers: LCCN 2021047136 | ISBN 9781534487765 (hardcover) | ISBN 9781534487758 (paperback) | ISBN 9781534487772 (ebook)

Subjects: CYAC: Graphic novels. | Pirates—Fiction. | Blessing and cursing—Fiction. | Lesbians—Fiction. | Sea stories. | LCGFT: Graphic novels.

Classification: LCC PZ7.7.R554 Pi 2022 | DDC 741.5/6973—dc23/eng/20220114

LC record available at https://lccn.loc.gov/2021047136

TO EVERYONE WHO'S CHANGED TO SUIT SOMEONE
ELSE, ALL THE PEOPLE WE'VE CHANGED WITHOUT EVEN
KNOWING IT, AND TO ALL THE KIDS AND KIDS AT HEART
TO WHOM THE SPIRIT OF ADVENTURE CALLS

—E. R. & N. J. B.

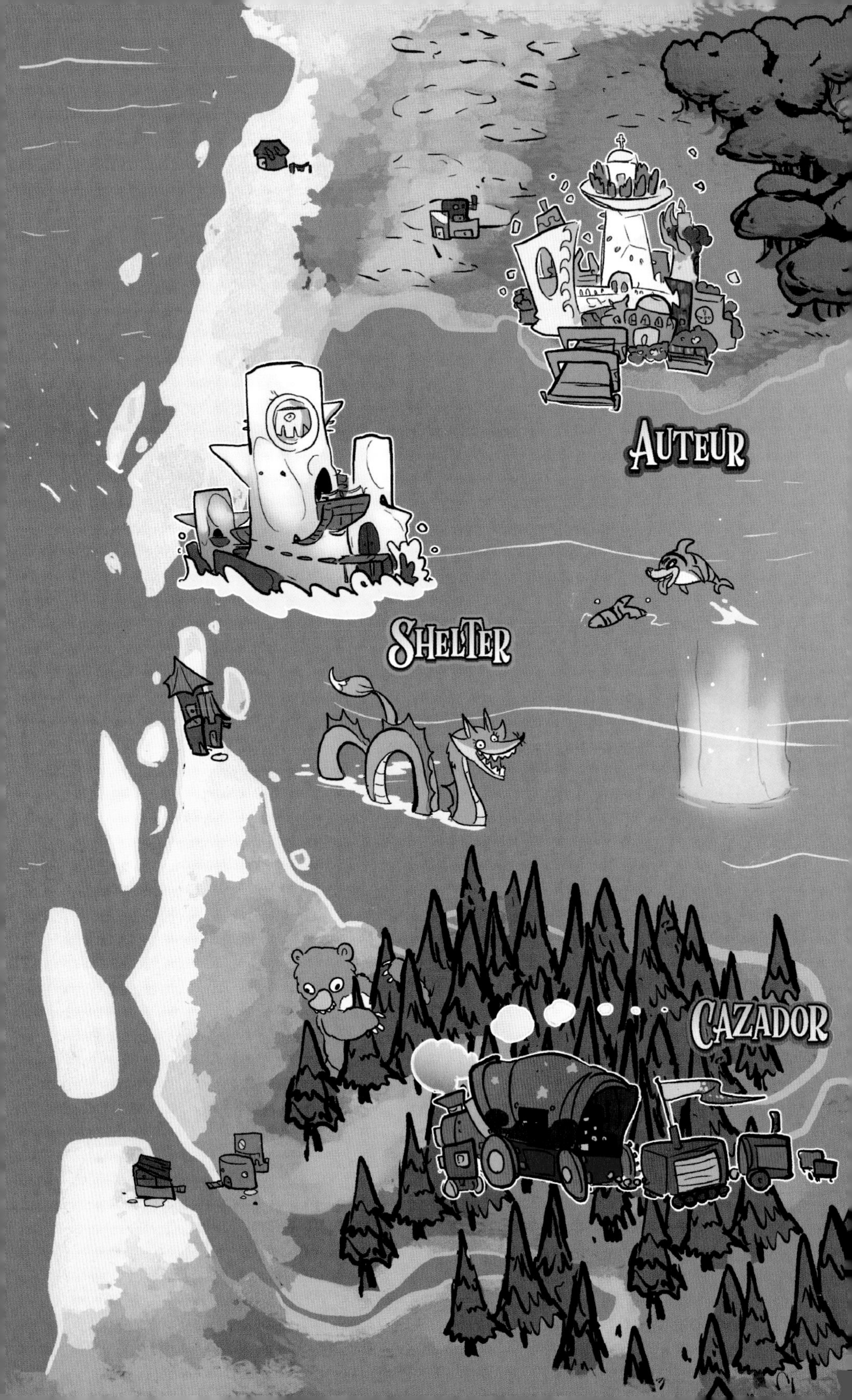
Auteur
Shelter
Cazador

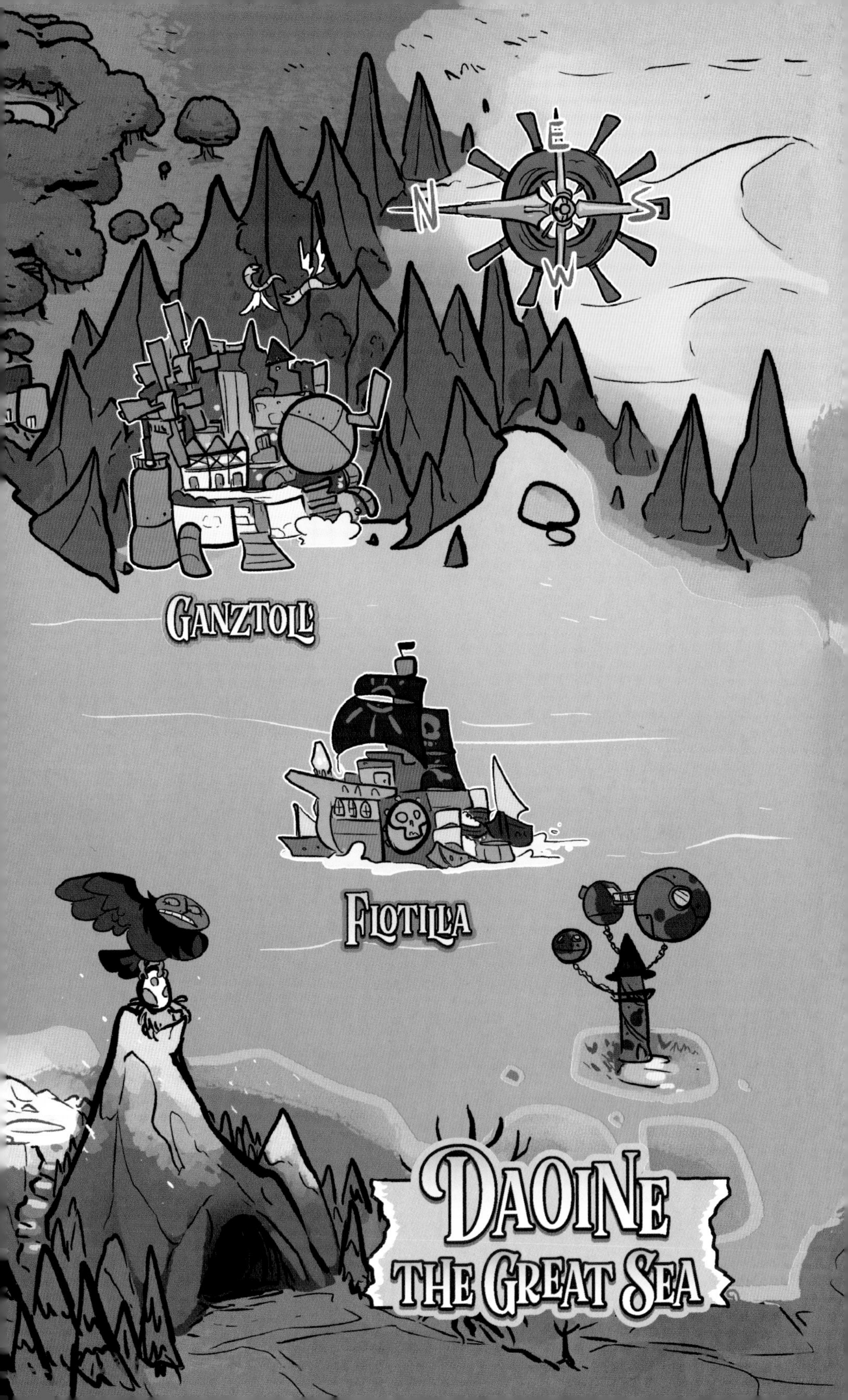
E
N
S
W
GANZTOLL
FLOTILLA
DAOINE
THE GREAT SEA

Chapter 1

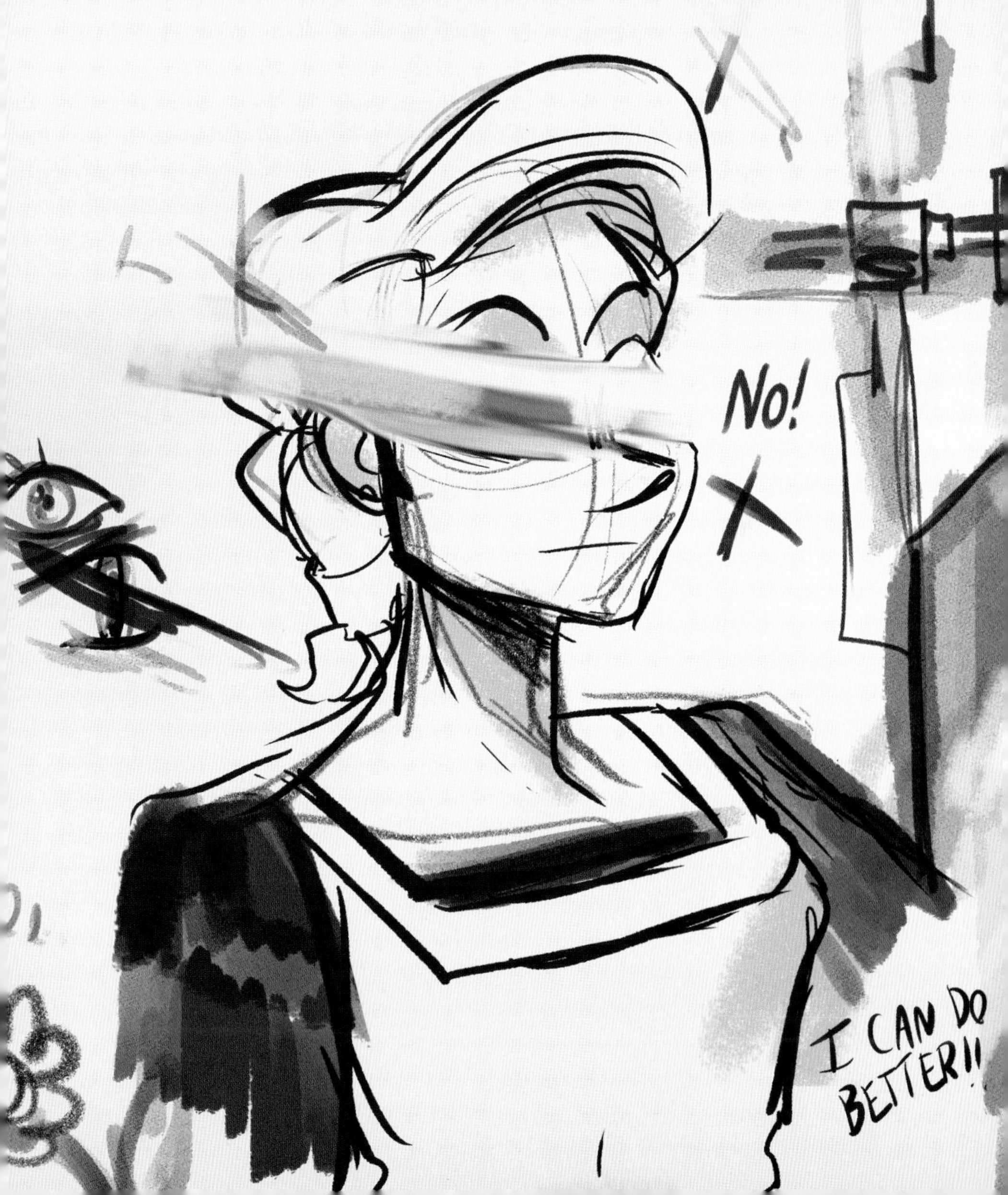
No!
I CAN DO BETTER!!

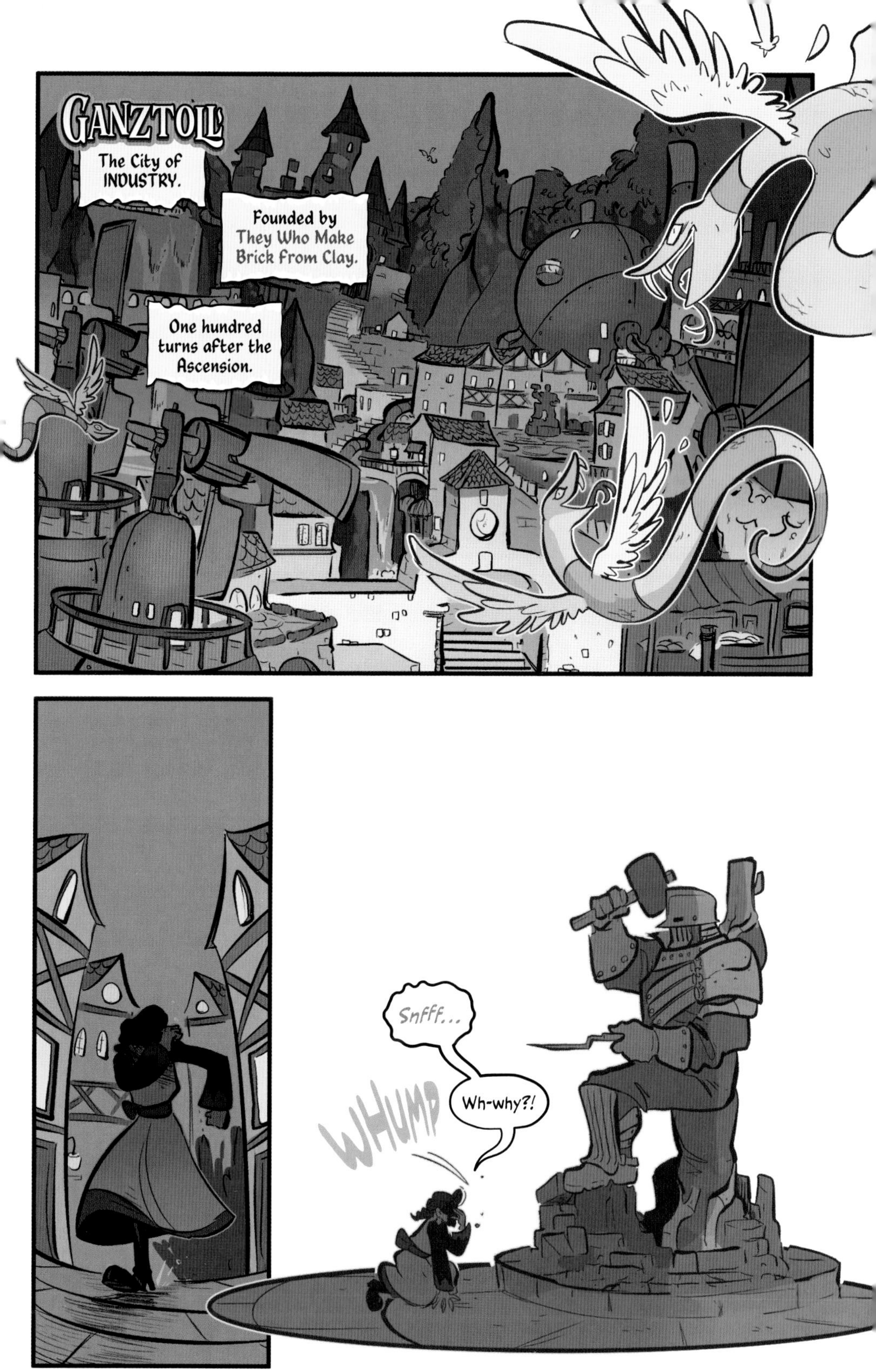
GANZTOLL
The City of INDUSTRY.
Founded by They Who Make Brick From Clay.
One hundred turns after the Ascension.
Snfff...
Wh-why?!
WHUMP

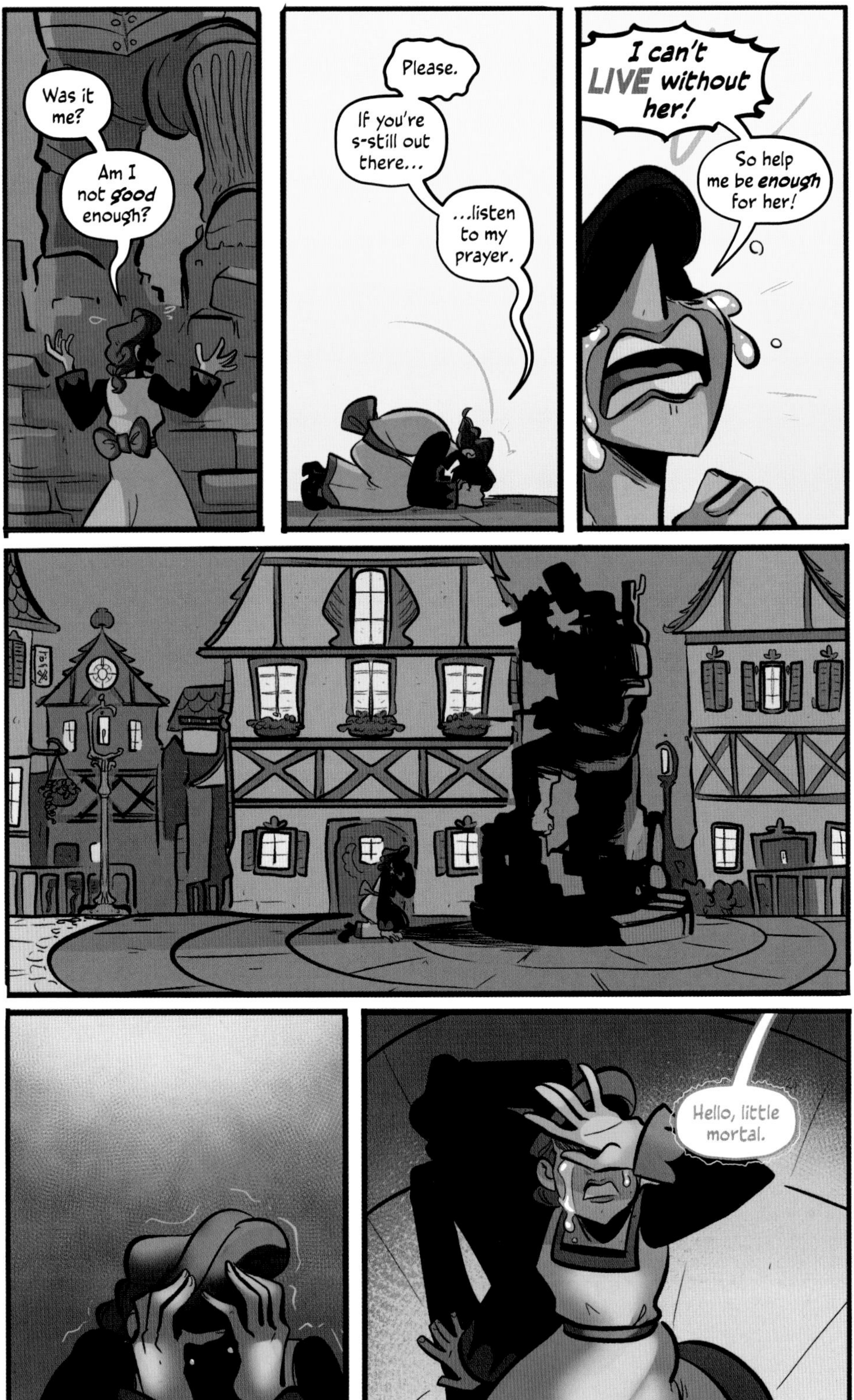

Was it me?
Am I not good enough?
Please.
If you're s-still out there...
...listen to my prayer.
I can't LIVE without her!
So help me be enough for her!
Hello, little mortal.

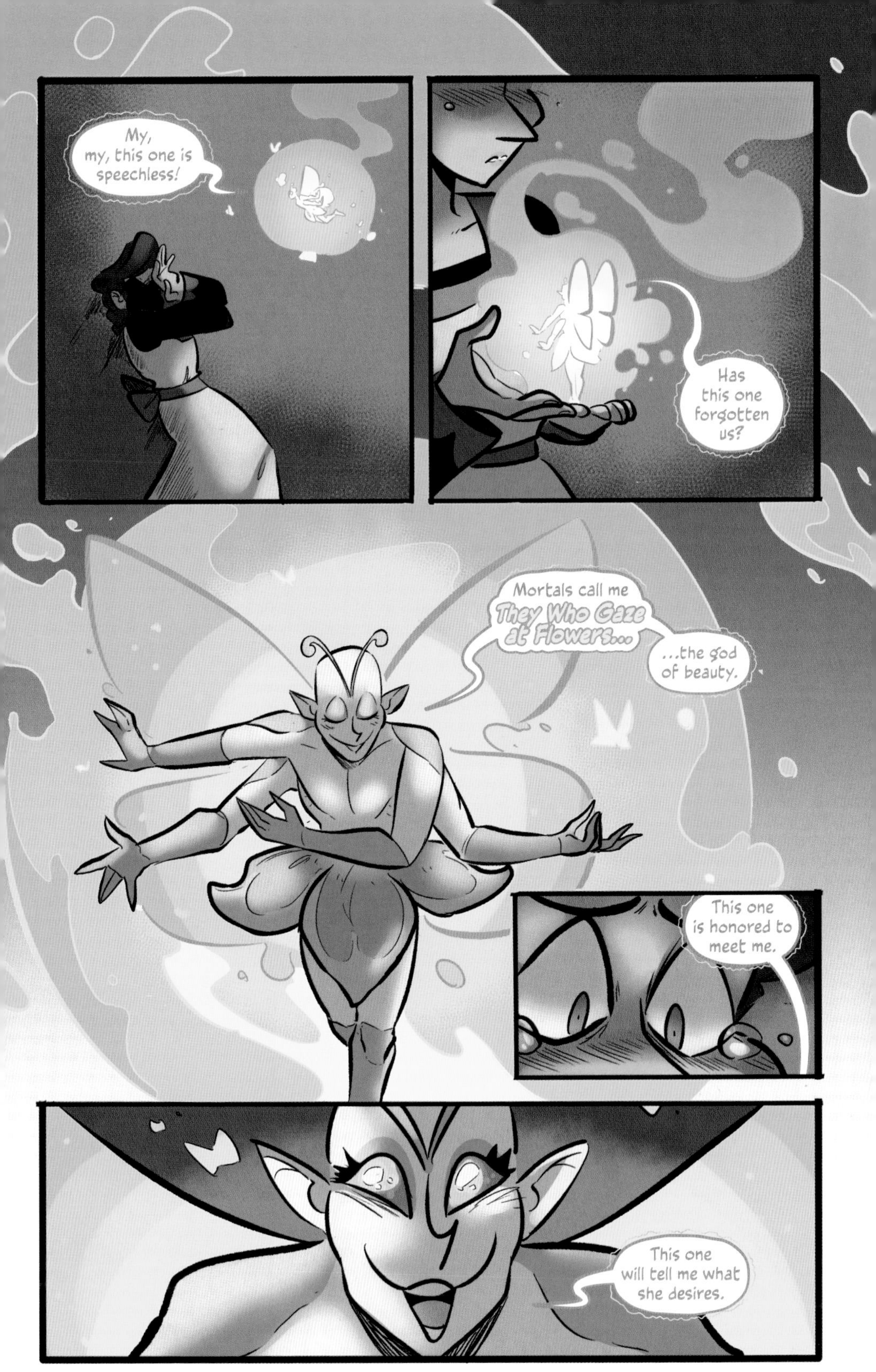

My, my, this one is speechless!
Has this one forgotten us?
Mortals call me They Who Gaze at Flowers...
...the god of beauty.
This one is honored to meet me.
This one will tell me what she desires.

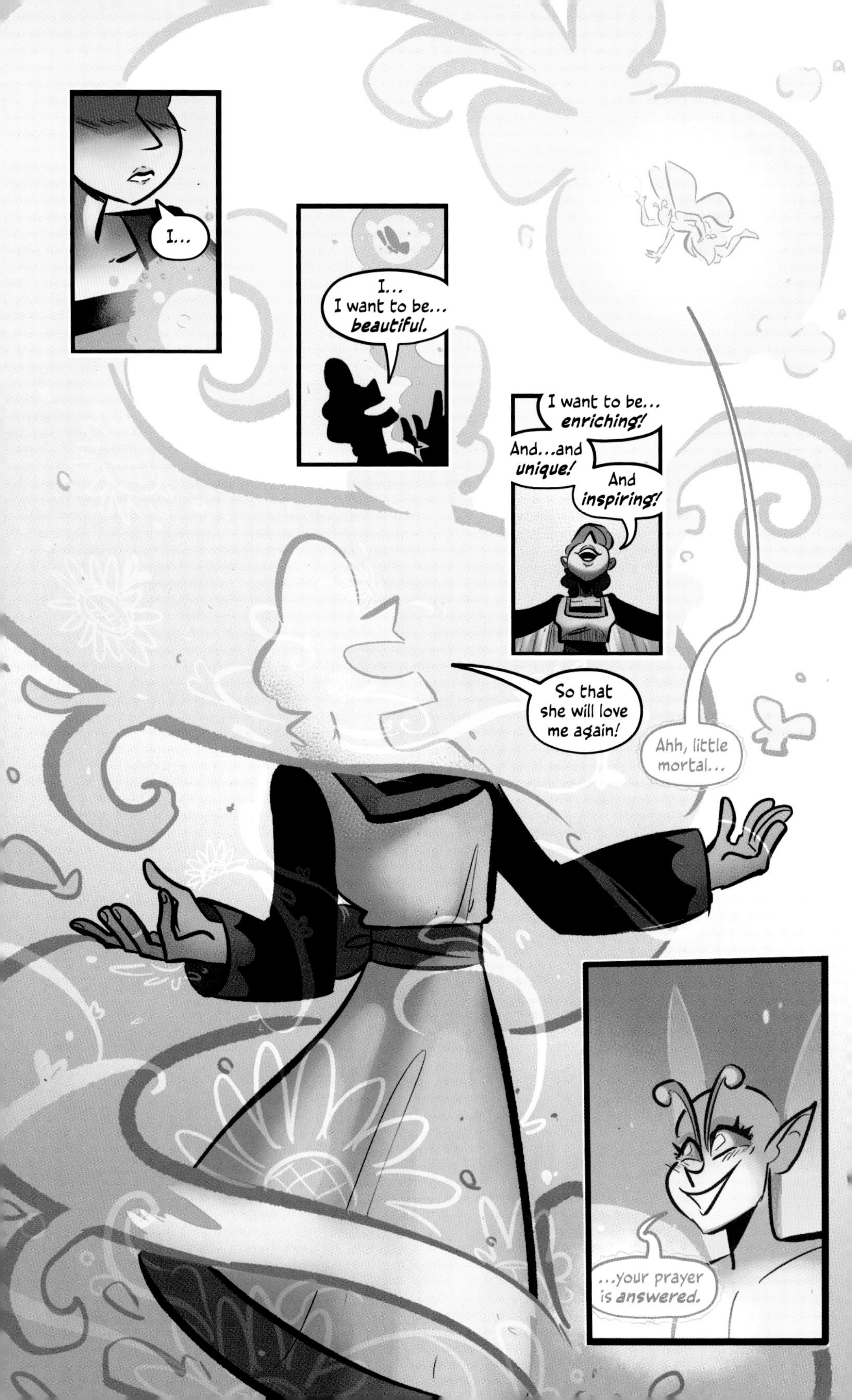

I...
I...
I want to be...
beautiful.
I want to be...
enriching!
And...and
unique!
And
inspiring!
So that
she will love
me again!
Ahh, little
mortal...
...your prayer
is answered.

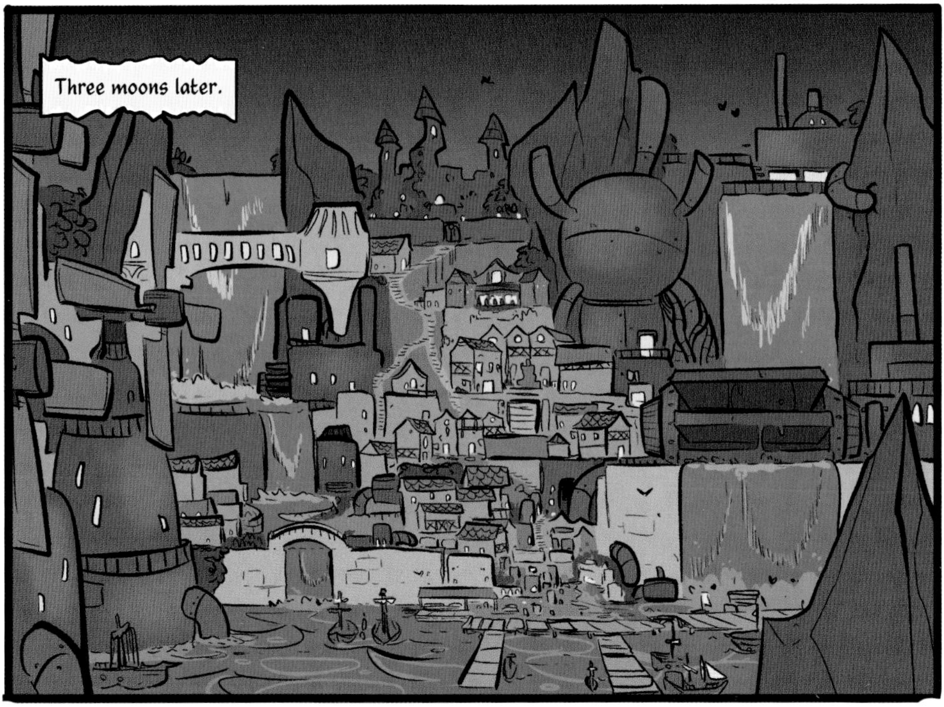
Three moons later.

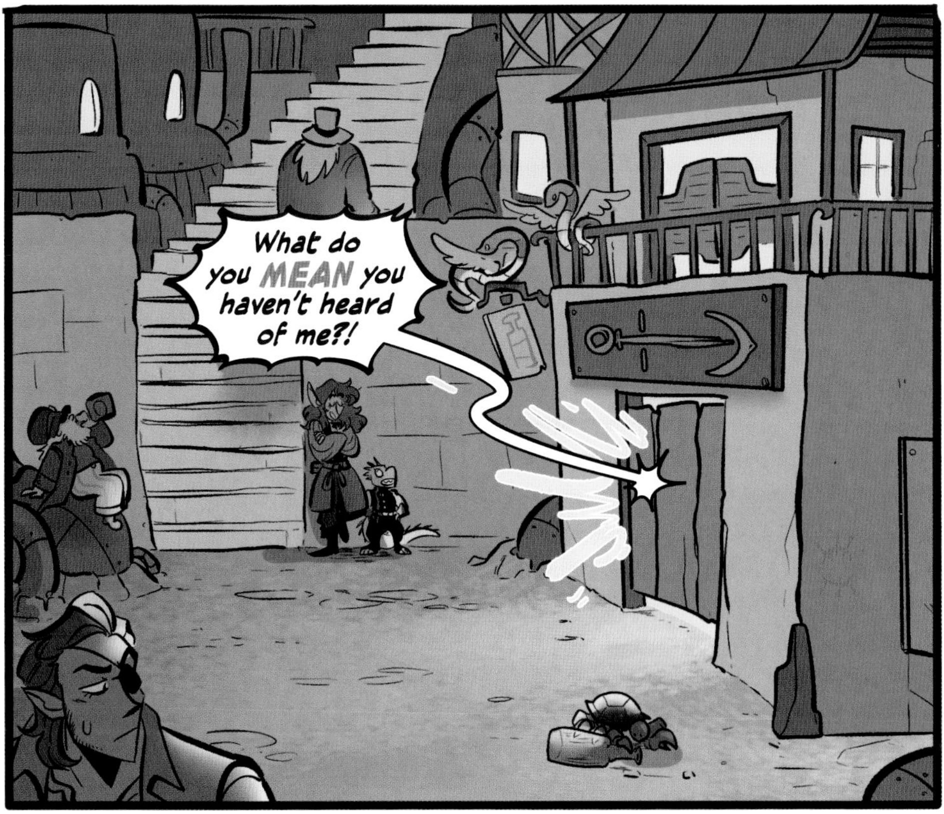
What do you MEAN you haven't heard of me?!

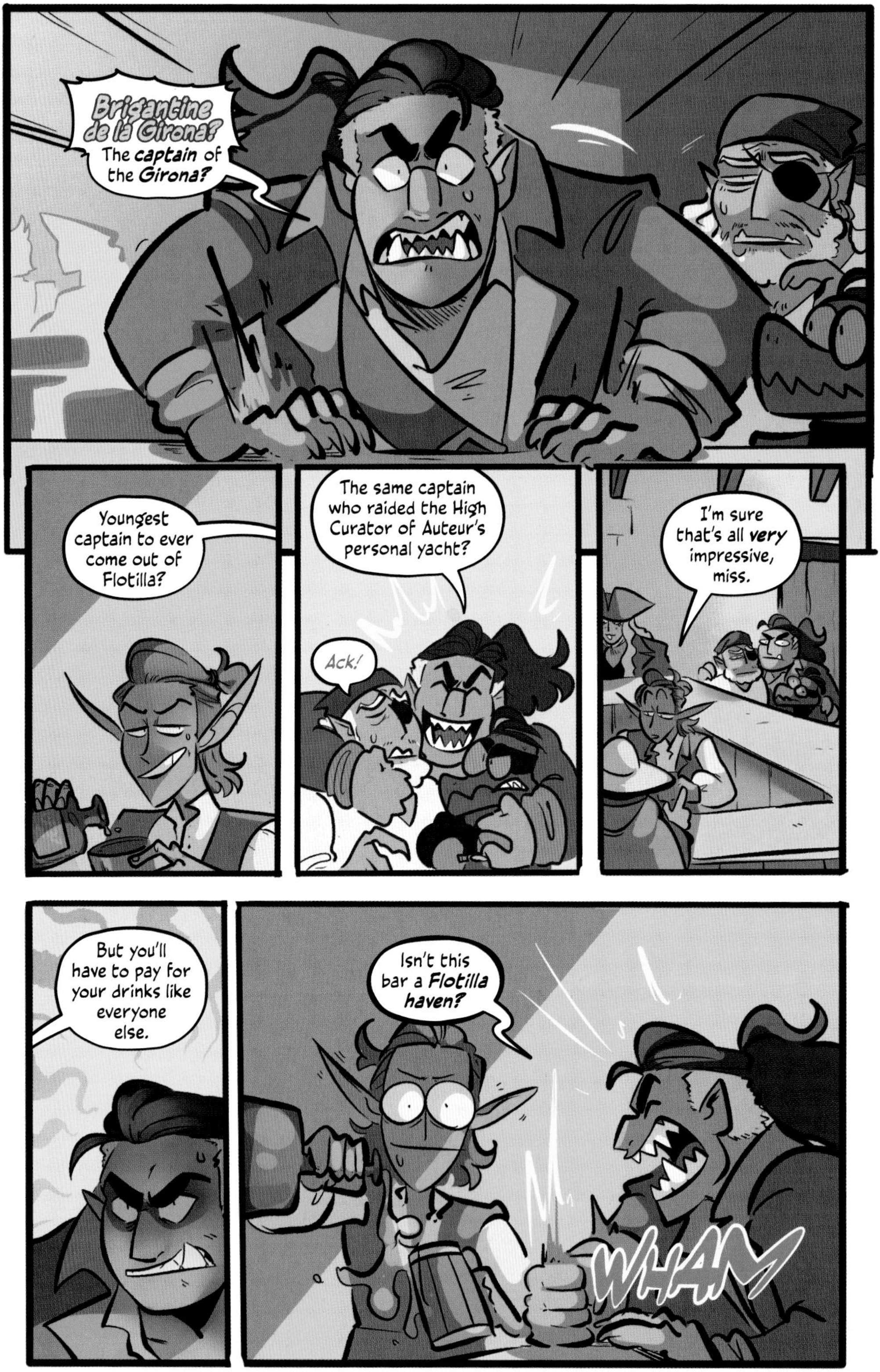
Brigantine de la Girona? The captain of the Girona?
Youngest captain to ever come out of Flotilla?
The same captain who raided the High Curator of Auteur's personal yacht?
Ack!
I'm sure that's all very impressive, miss.
But you'll have to pay for your drinks like everyone else.
Isn't this bar a Flotilla haven?
WHAM

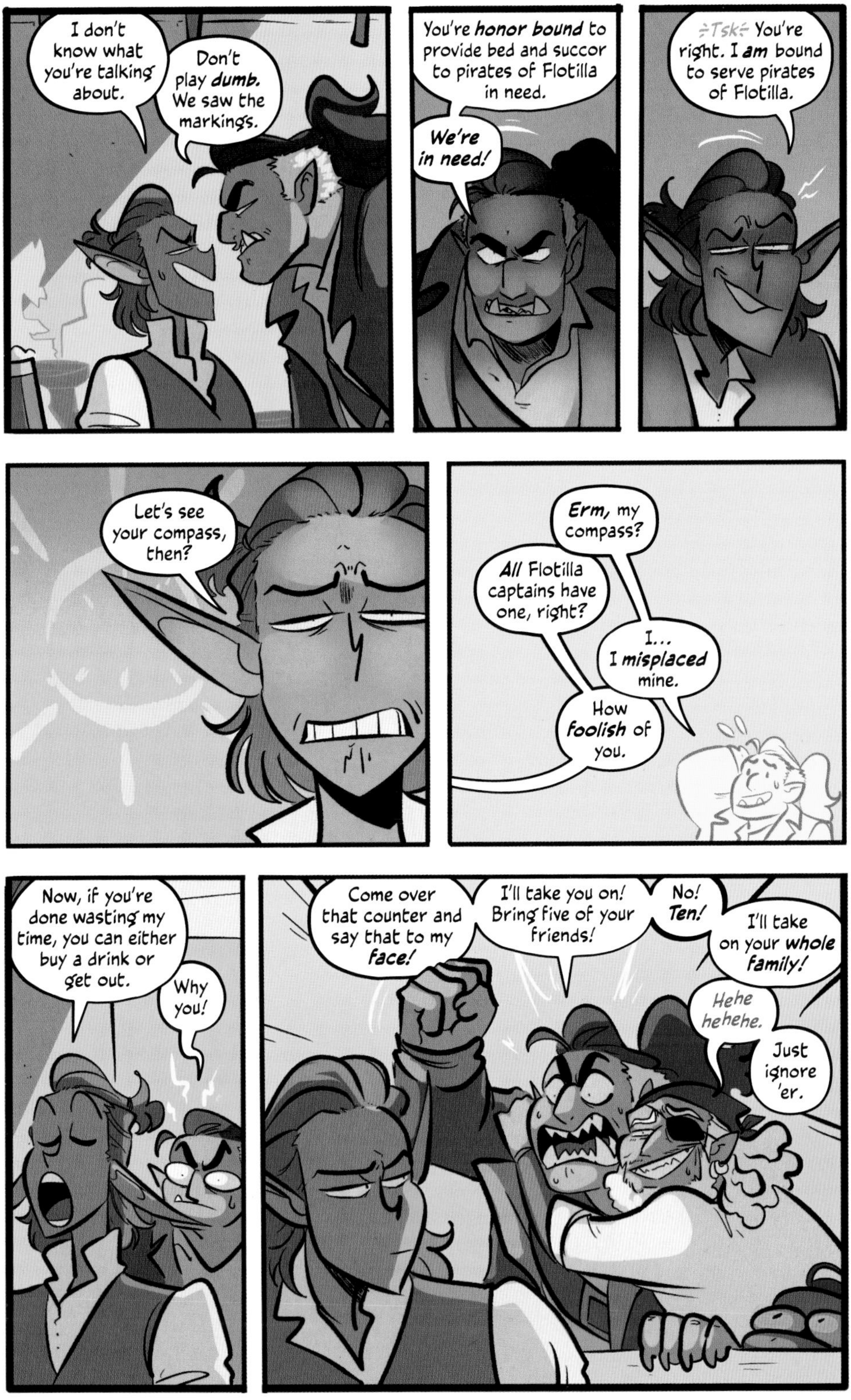
I don't know what you're talking about.
Don't play **dumb.** We saw the markings.
You're **honor bound** to provide bed and succor to pirates of Flotilla in need.
We're in need!
÷Tsk÷ You're right. I **am** bound to serve pirates of Flotilla.
Let's see your compass, then?
Erm, my compass?
All Flotilla captains have one, right?
I... I **misplaced** mine.
How **foolish** of you.
Now, if you're done wasting my time, you can either buy a drink or get out.
Why you!
Come over that counter and say that to my **face!**
I'll take you on! Bring five of your friends!
No! **Ten!**
I'll take on your **whole family!**
Hehe hehehe.
Just ignore 'er.

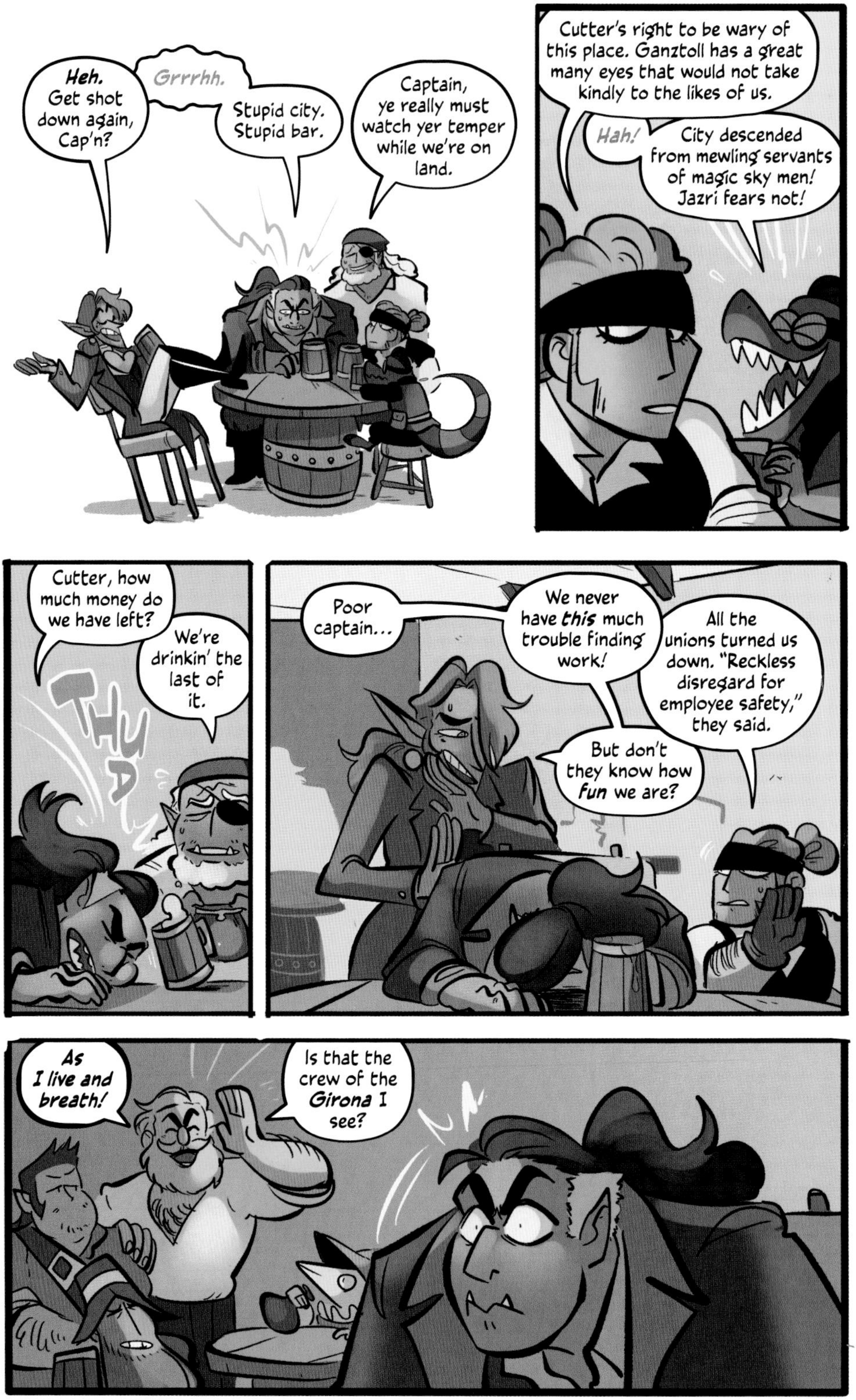
Heh. Get shot down again, Cap'n?
Grrrhh.
Stupid city. Stupid bar.
Captain, ye really must watch yer temper while we're on land.
Cutter's right to be wary of this place. Ganztoll has a great many eyes that would not take kindly to the likes of us.
Hah!
City descended from mewling servants of magic sky men! Jazri fears not!
Cutter, how much money do we have left?
We're drinkin' the last of it.
THUD
Poor captain...
We never have this much trouble finding work!
All the unions turned us down. "Reckless disregard for employee safety," they said.
But don't they know how fun we are?
As I live and breath!
Is that the crew of the Girona I see?

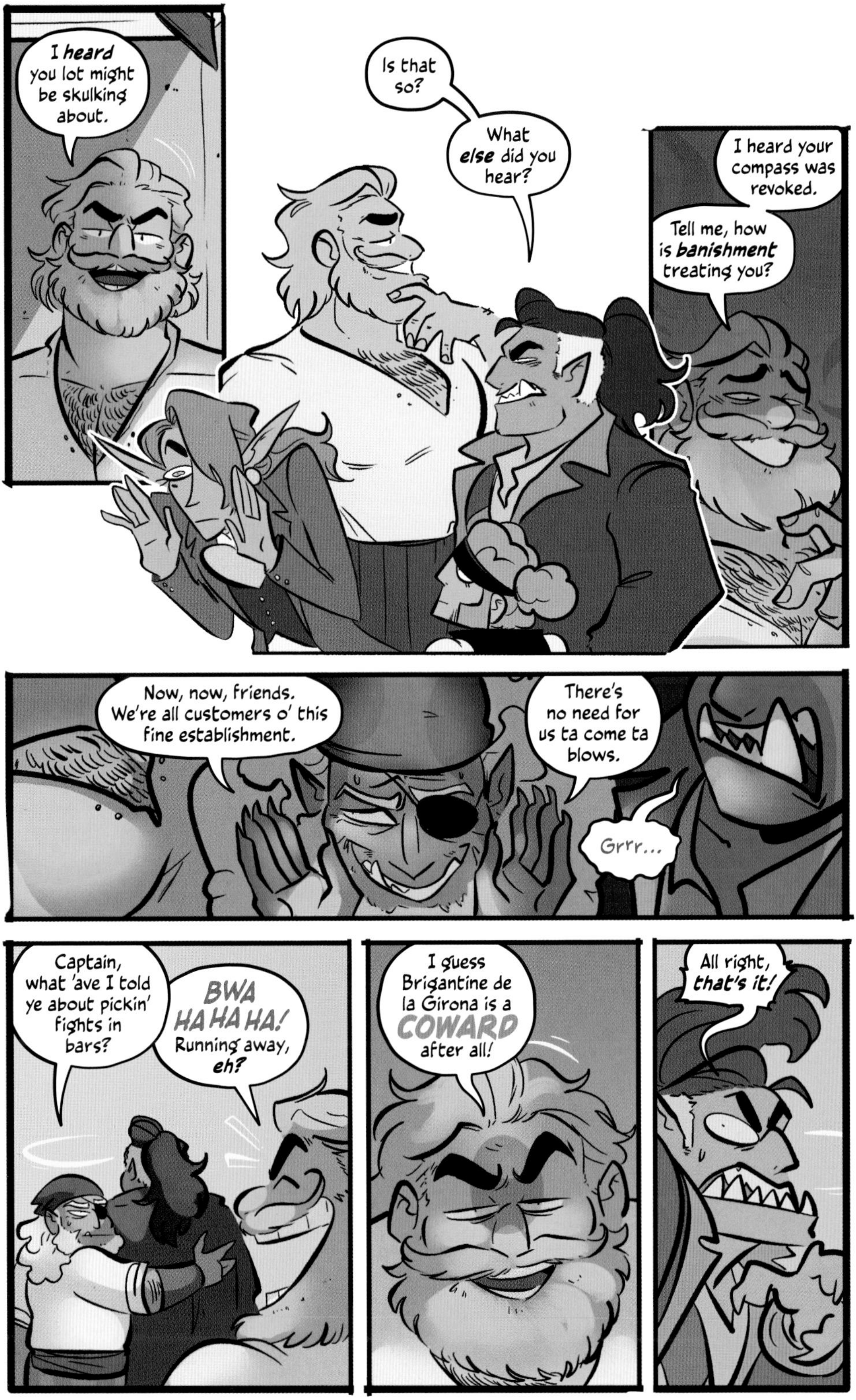
I heard you lot might be skulking about.
Is that so?
What else did you hear?
I heard your compass was revoked.
Tell me, how is banishment treating you?
Now, now, friends. We're all customers o' this fine establishment.
There's no need for us ta come ta blows.
Grrr...
Captain, what 'ave I told ye about pickin' fights in bars?
BWA HA HA HA! Running away, eh?
I guess Brigantine de la Girona is a COWARD after all!
All right, that's it!

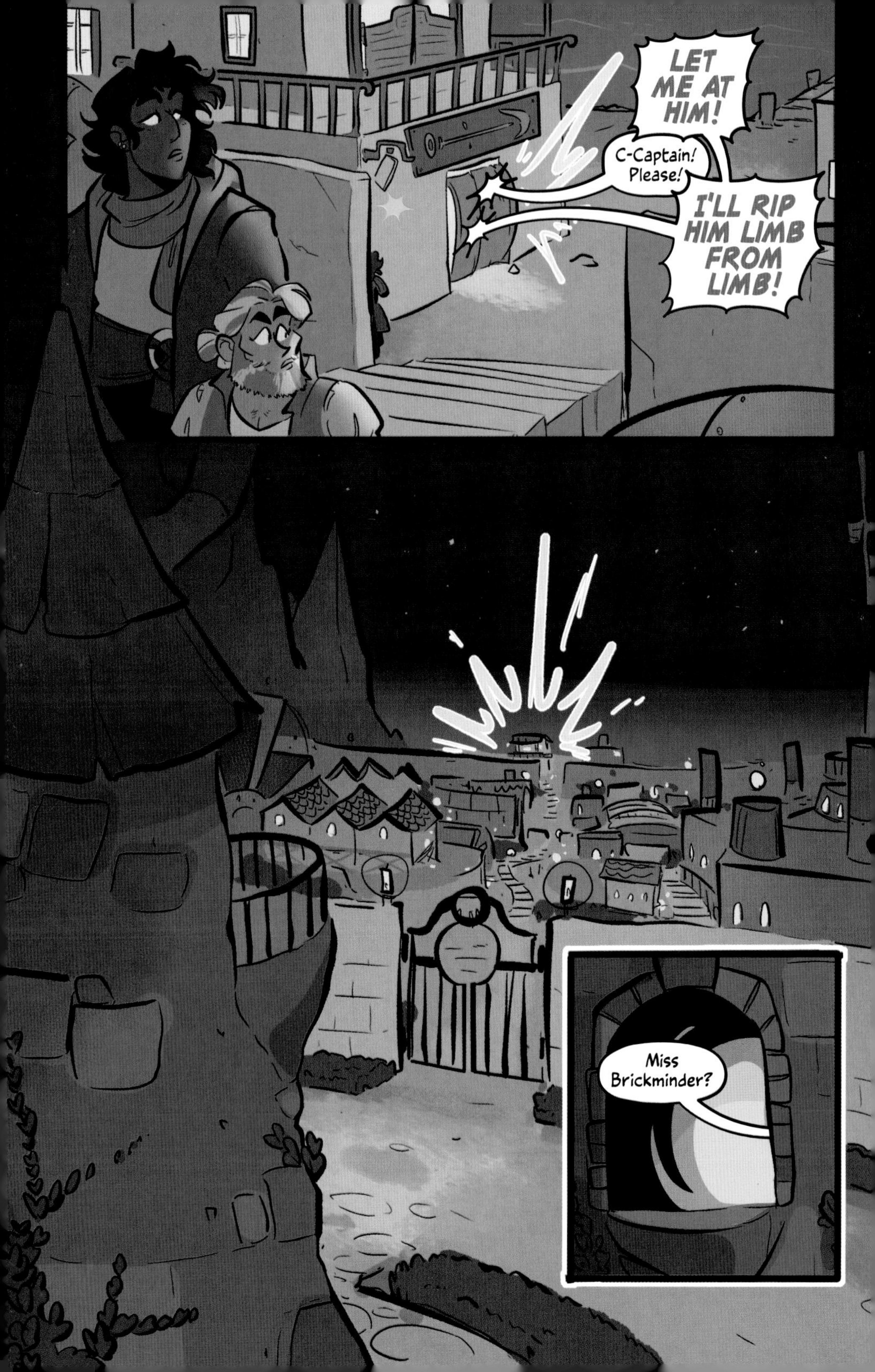
LET ME AT HIM!
C-Captain! Please!
I'LL RIP HIM LIMB FROM LIMB!
Miss Brickminder?

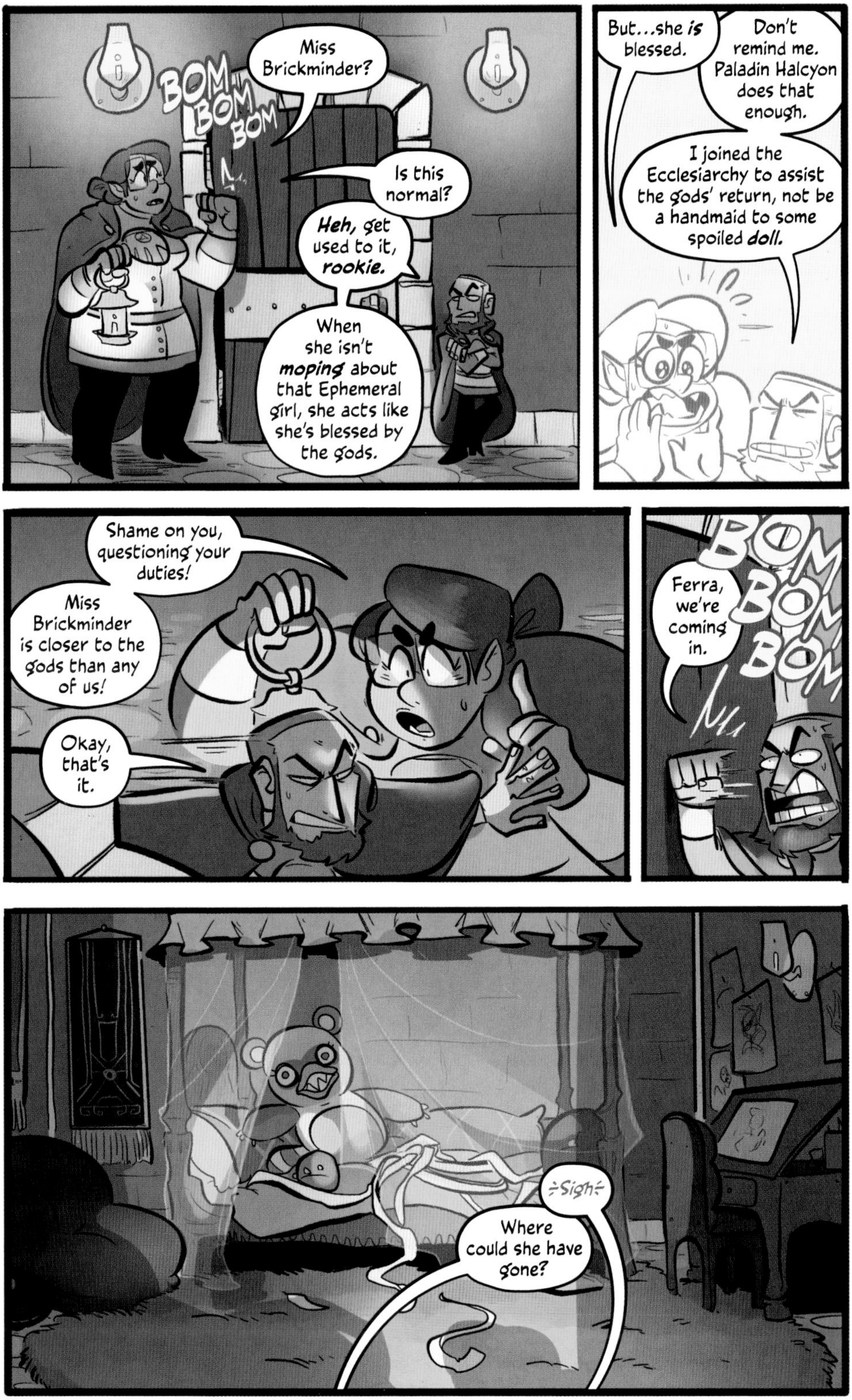
BOM BOM BOM
Miss Brickminder?
Is this normal?
Heh, get used to it, rookie.
When she isn't moping about that Ephemeral girl, she acts like she's blessed by the gods.
But...she is blessed.
Don't remind me. Paladin Halcyon does that enough.
I joined the Ecclesiarchy to assist the gods' return, not be a handmaid to some spoiled doll.
Shame on you, questioning your duties!
Miss Brickminder is closer to the gods than any of us!
Okay, that's it.
BOM BOM BOM
Ferra, we're coming in.
Sigh
Where could she have gone?

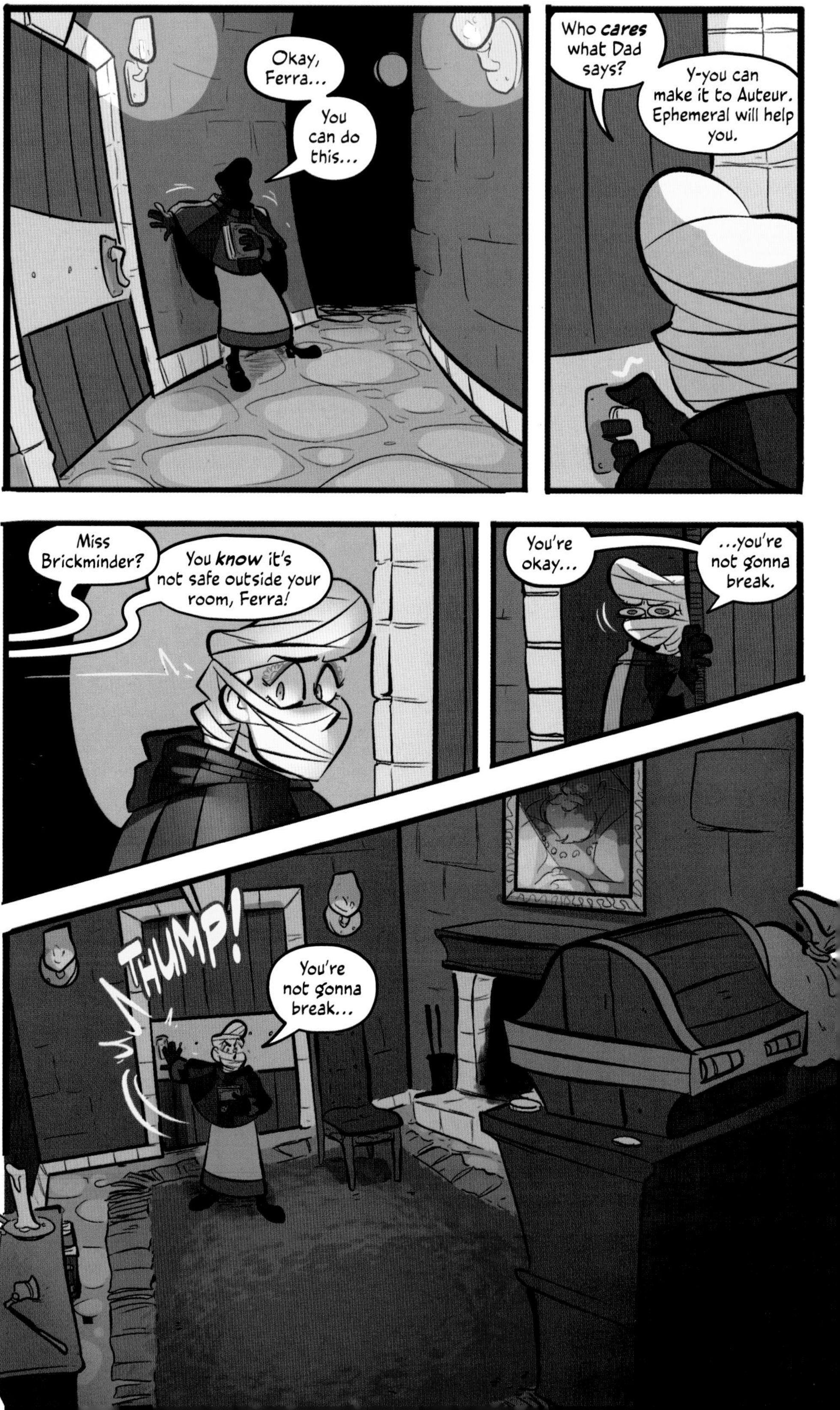
Okay, Ferra...
You can do this...
Who *cares* what Dad says?
Y-you can make it to Auteur. Ephemeral will help you.
Miss Brickminder?
You *know* it's not safe outside your room, Ferra!
You're okay...
...you're not gonna break.
THUMP!
You're not gonna break...

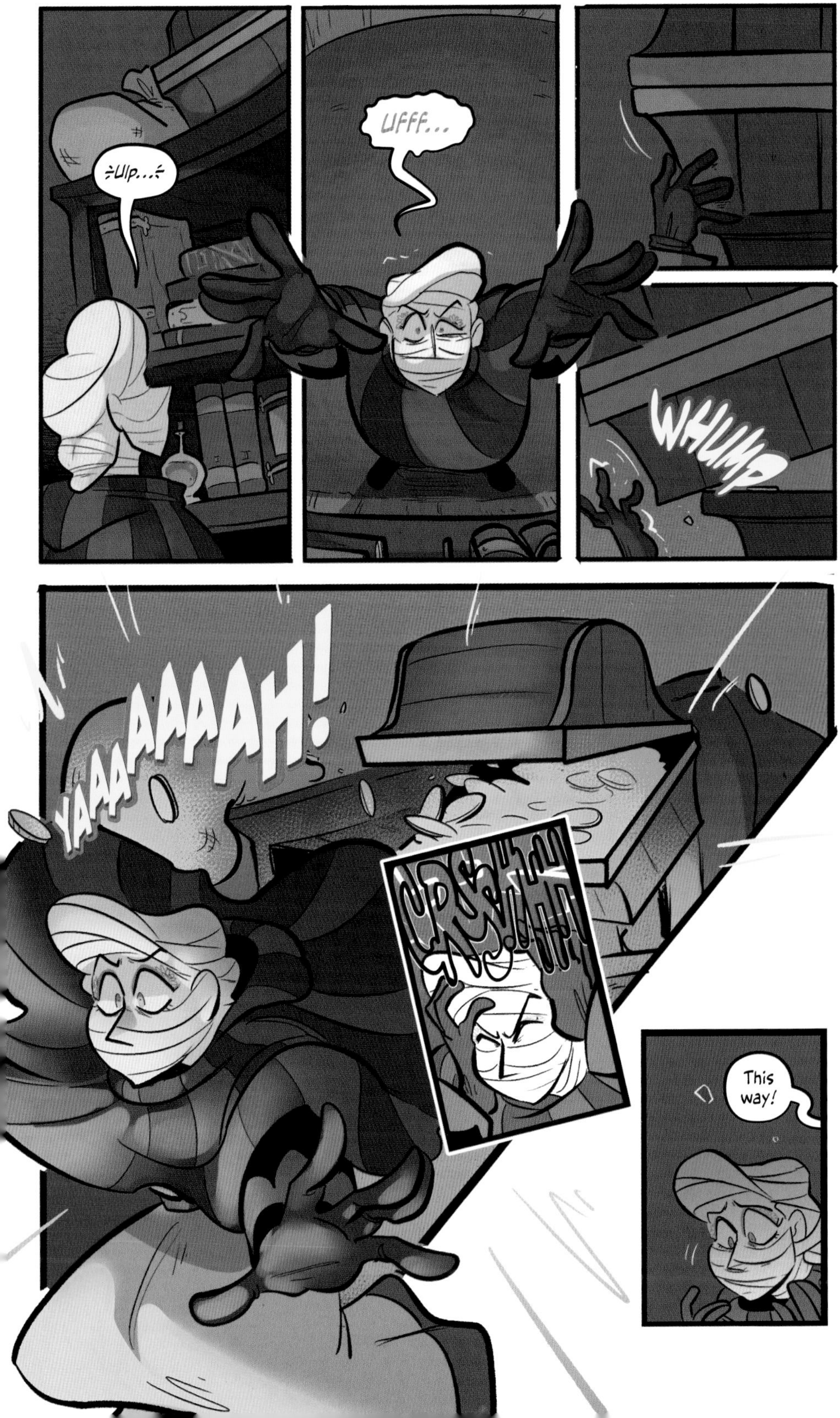

~Ulp...~
UFFF...
WHUMP
YAAAAPPPAH!
CRSHHH
This way!

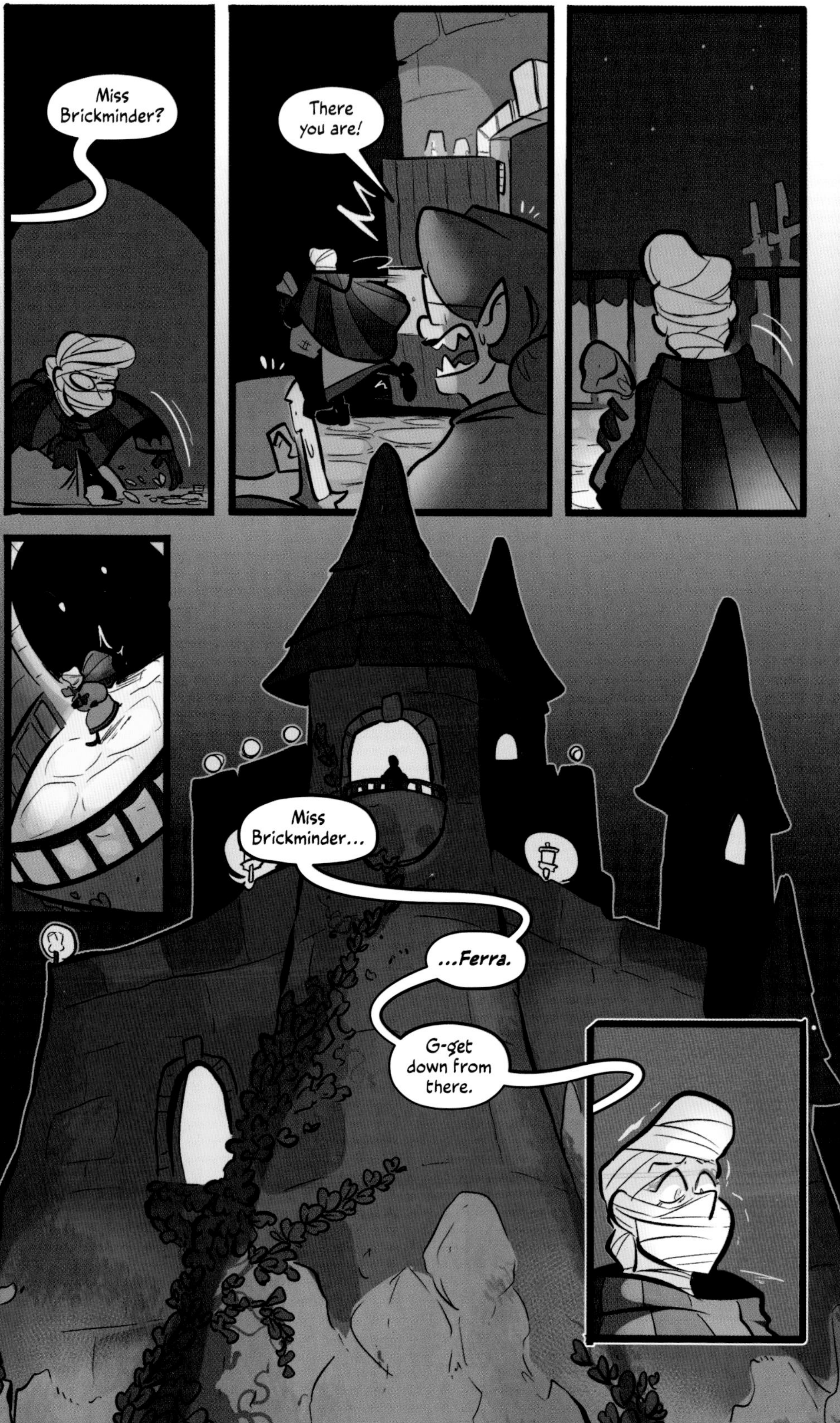
Miss Brickminder?
There you are!
Miss Brickminder...
...Ferra.
G-get down from there.

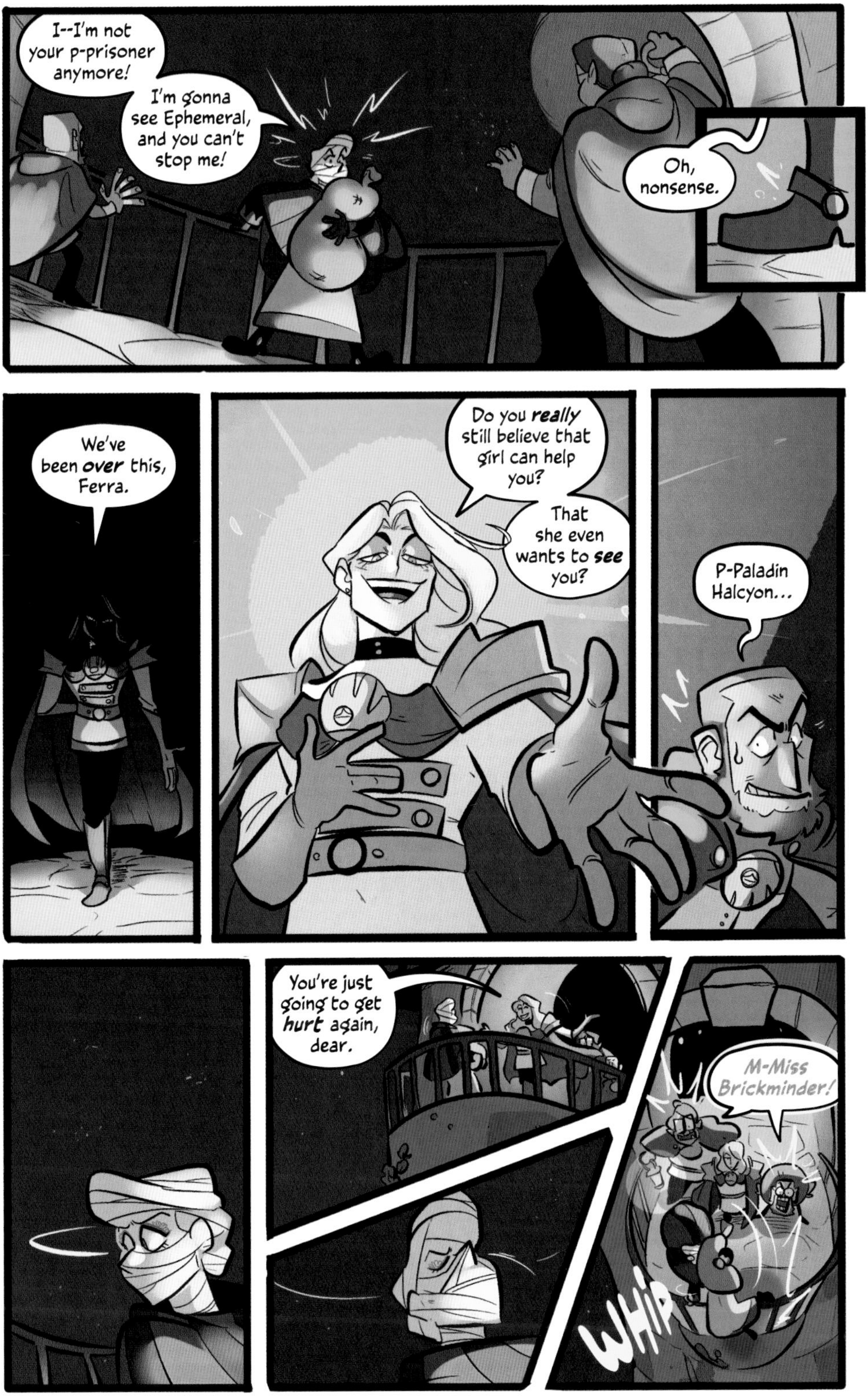
I--I'm not your p-prisoner anymore!
I'm gonna see Ephemeral, and you can't stop me!
Oh, nonsense.
We've been **over** this, Ferra.
Do you **really** still believe that girl can help you?
That she even wants to **see** you?
P-Paladin Halcyon...
You're just going to get **hurt** again, dear.
M-Miss Brickminder!
WHIP

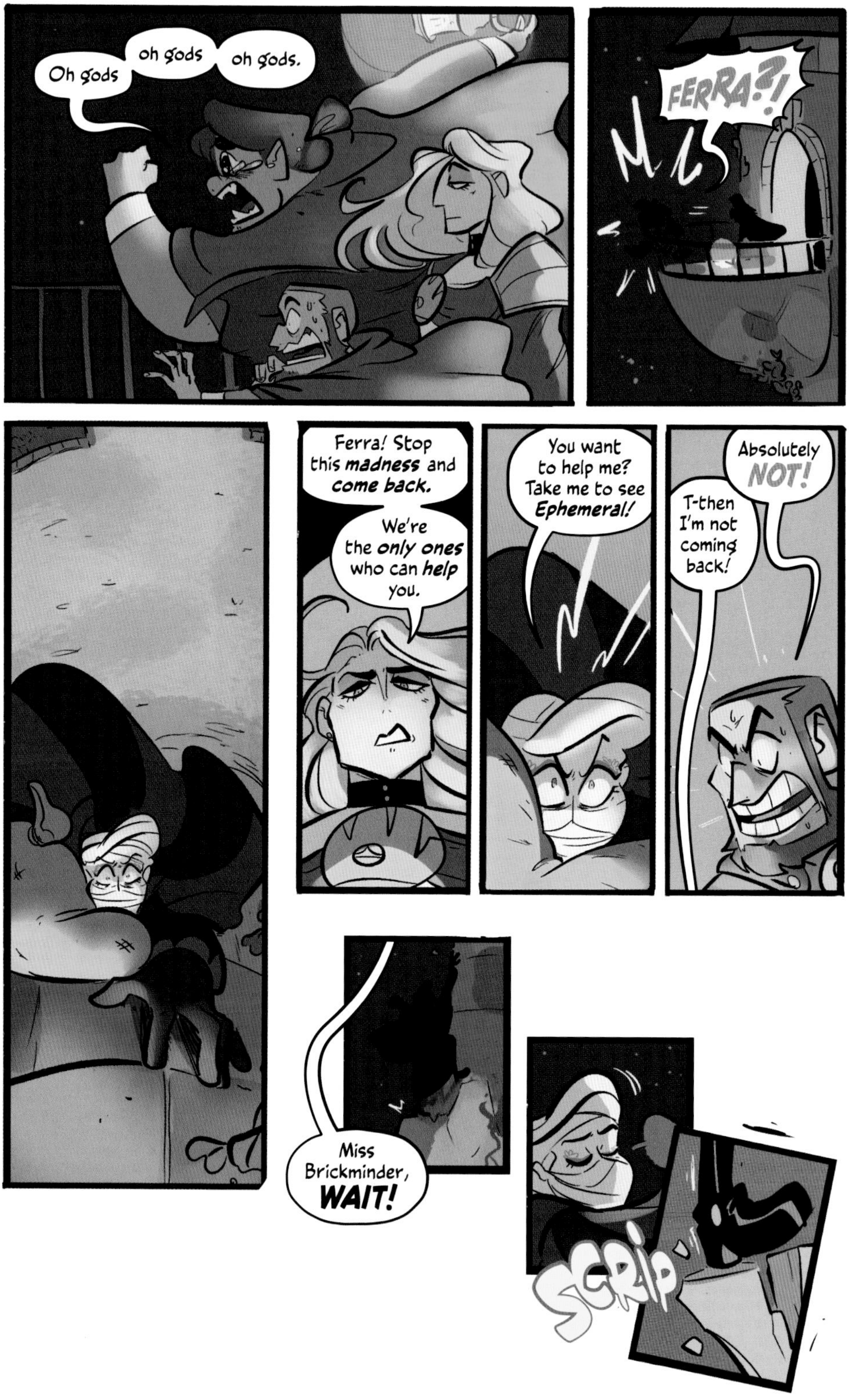

Oh gods
oh gods
oh gods.
FERRA?!
Ferra! Stop this *madness* and *come back.*
We're the *only ones* who can *help* you.
You want to help me? Take me to see *Ephemeral!*
T-then I'm not coming back!
Absolutely NOT!
Miss Brickminder, WAIT!
SCRIP

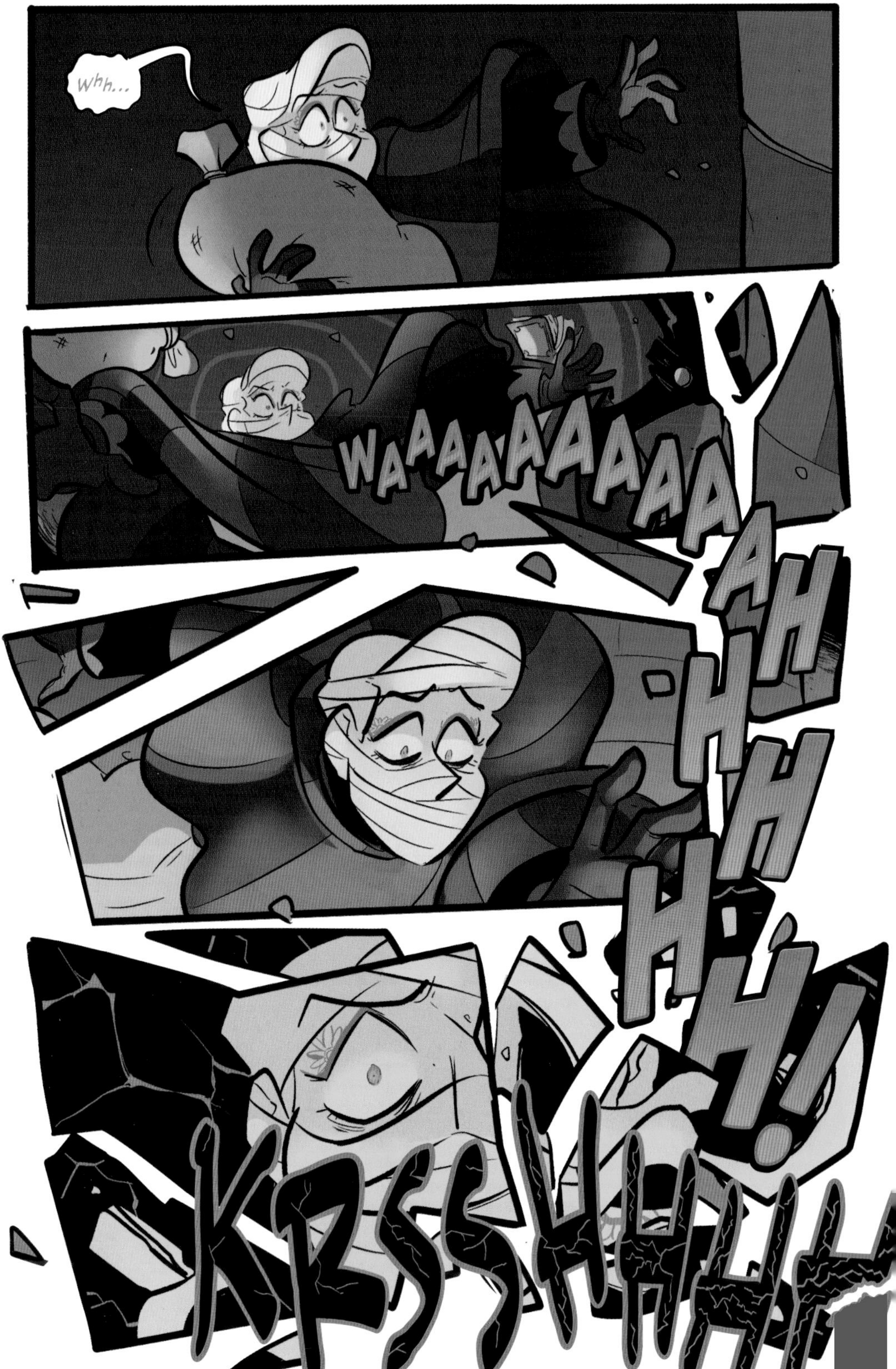
Whh...
WAAAAAAAAAAAAHHHHHHH!!
KRSSHHHHH

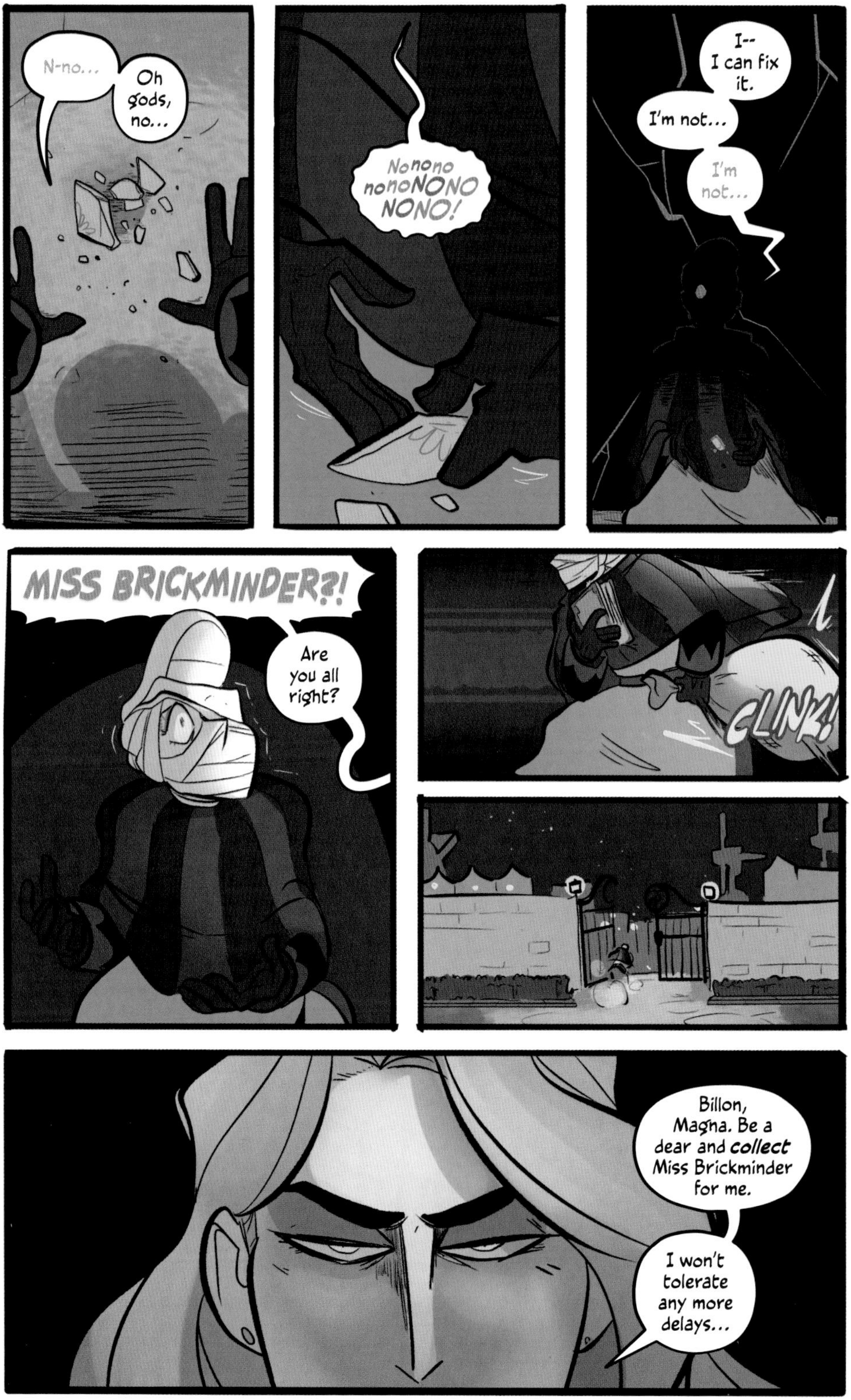

N-no...
Oh gods, no...
Nonono nonoNONO NONO!
I-- I can fix it.
I'm not...
I'm not...
MISS BRICKMINDER?!
Are you all right?
CLINK!
Billon, Magna. Be a dear and *collect* Miss Brickminder for me.
I won't tolerate any more delays...

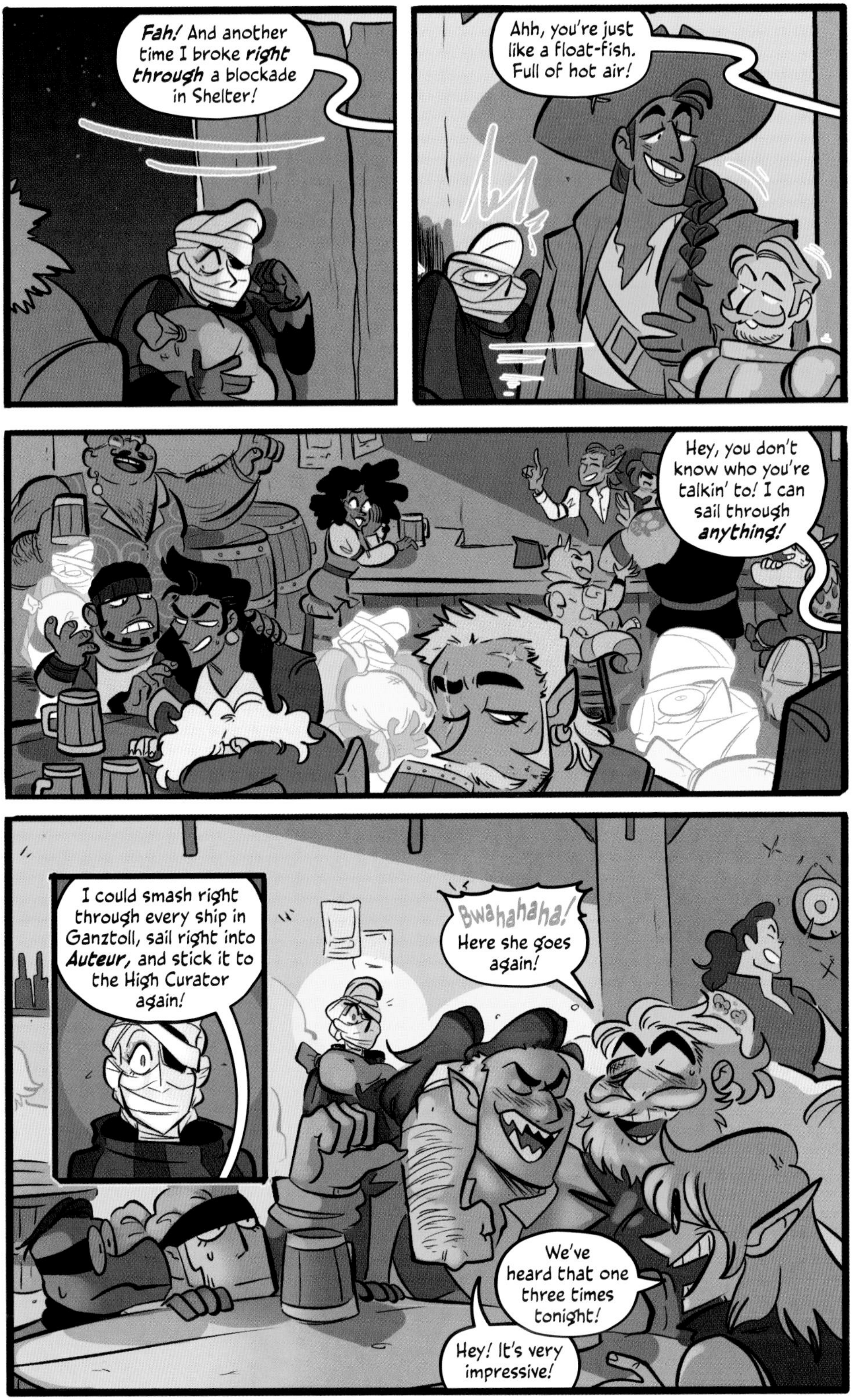
Fah! And another time I broke right through a blockade in Shelter!
Ahh, you're just like a float-fish. Full of hot air!
Hey, you don't know who you're talkin' to! I can sail through anything!
I could smash right through every ship in Ganztoll, sail right into Auteur, and stick it to the High Curator again!
Bwahahaha! Here she goes again!
We've heard that one three times tonight!
Hey! It's very impressive!

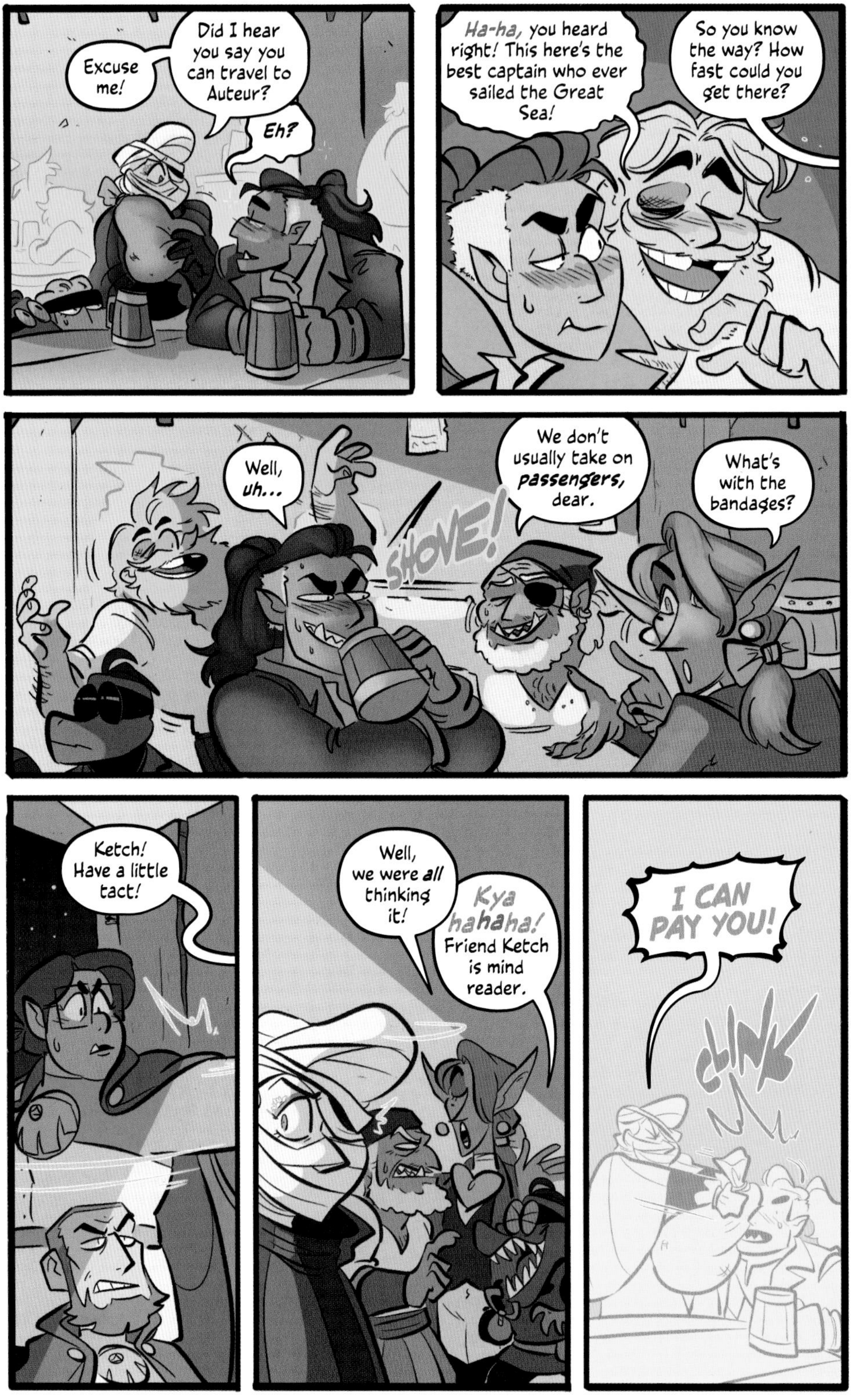
Excuse me!
Did I hear you say you can travel to Auteur?
Eh?
Ha-ha, you heard right! This here's the best captain who ever sailed the Great Sea!
So you know the way? How fast could you get there?
Well, uh...
SHOVE!
We don't usually take on passengers, dear.
What's with the bandages?
Ketch! Have a little tact!
Well, we were all thinking it!
Kya hahahaha! Friend Ketch is mind reader.
I CAN PAY YOU!
CLINK

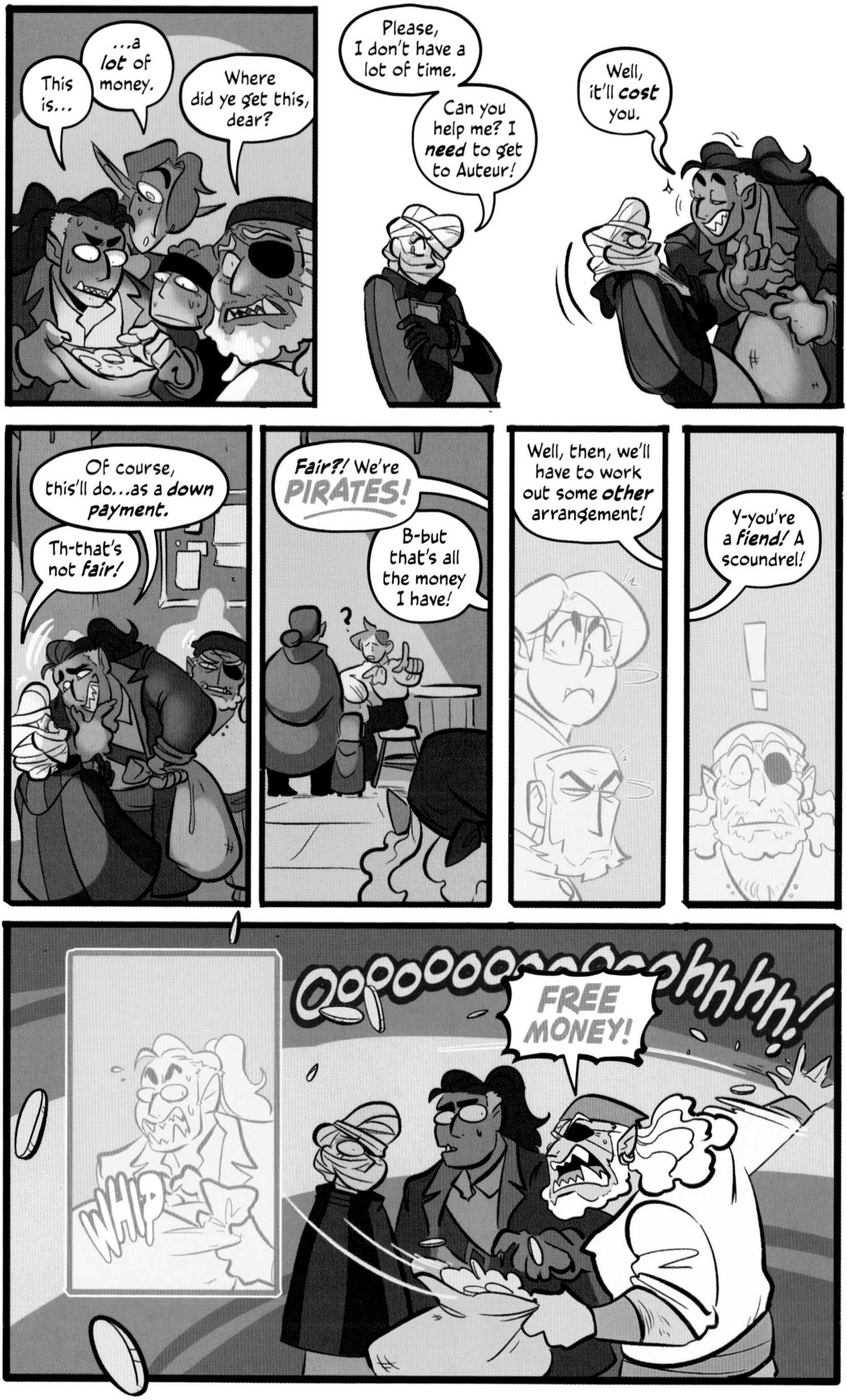
This is...
...a lot of money.
Where did ye get this, dear?
Please, I don't have a lot of time.
Can you help me? I need to get to Auteur!
Well, it'll cost you.
Of course, this'll do...as a down payment.
Th-that's not fair!
Fair?! We're PIRATES!
B-but that's all the money I have!
Well, then, we'll have to work out some other arrangement!
Y-you're a fiend! A scoundrel!
OOOOOOOOOOOOOhhhh!
FREE MONEY!
WHIP

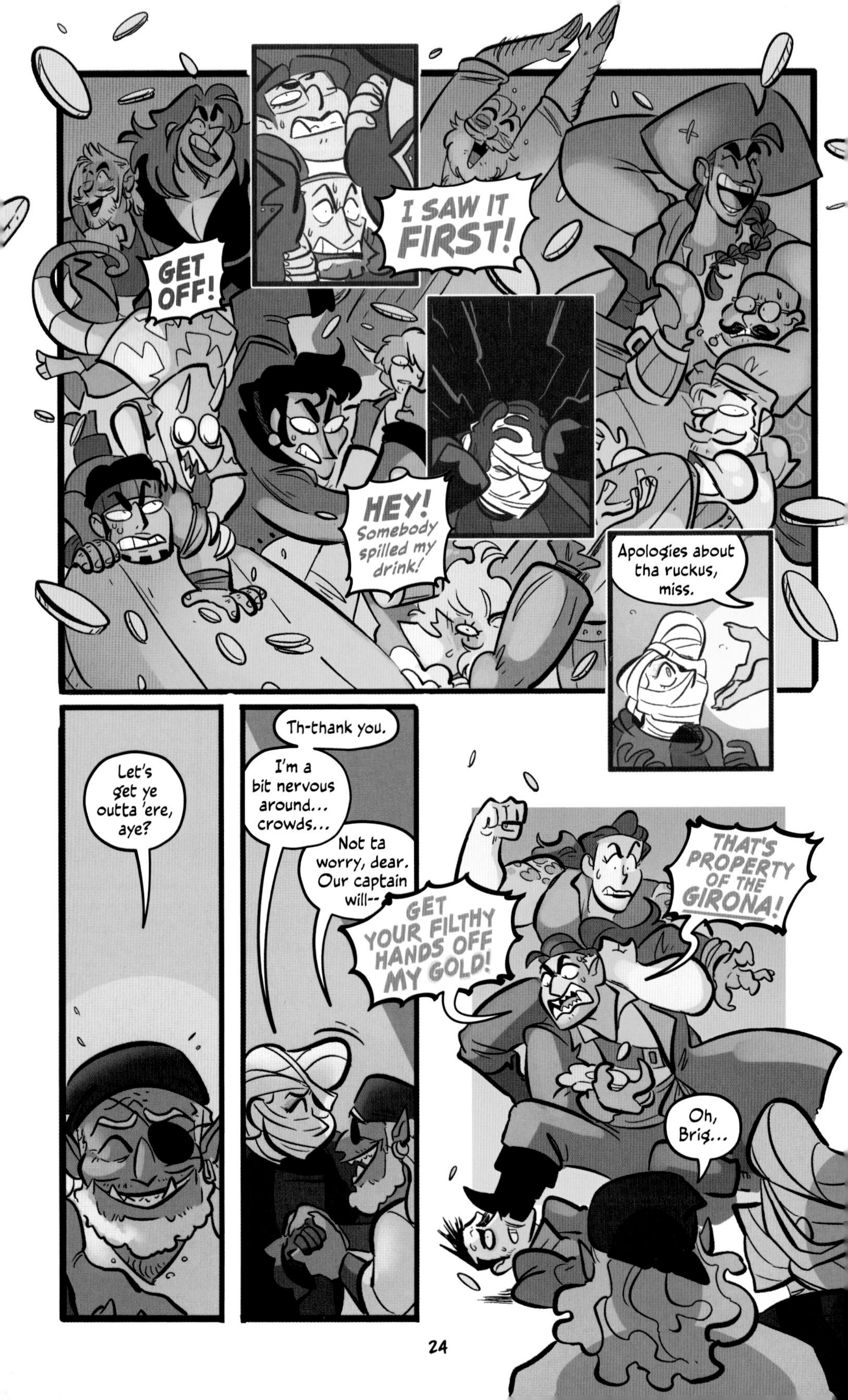
GET OFF!
I SAW IT FIRST!
HEY! Somebody spilled my drink!
Apologies about tha ruckus, miss.
Let's get ye outta 'ere, aye?
Th-thank you.
I'm a bit nervous around... crowds...
Not ta worry, dear. Our captain will--
GET YOUR FILTHY HANDS OFF MY GOLD!
THAT'S PROPERTY OF THE GIRONA!
Oh, Brig...

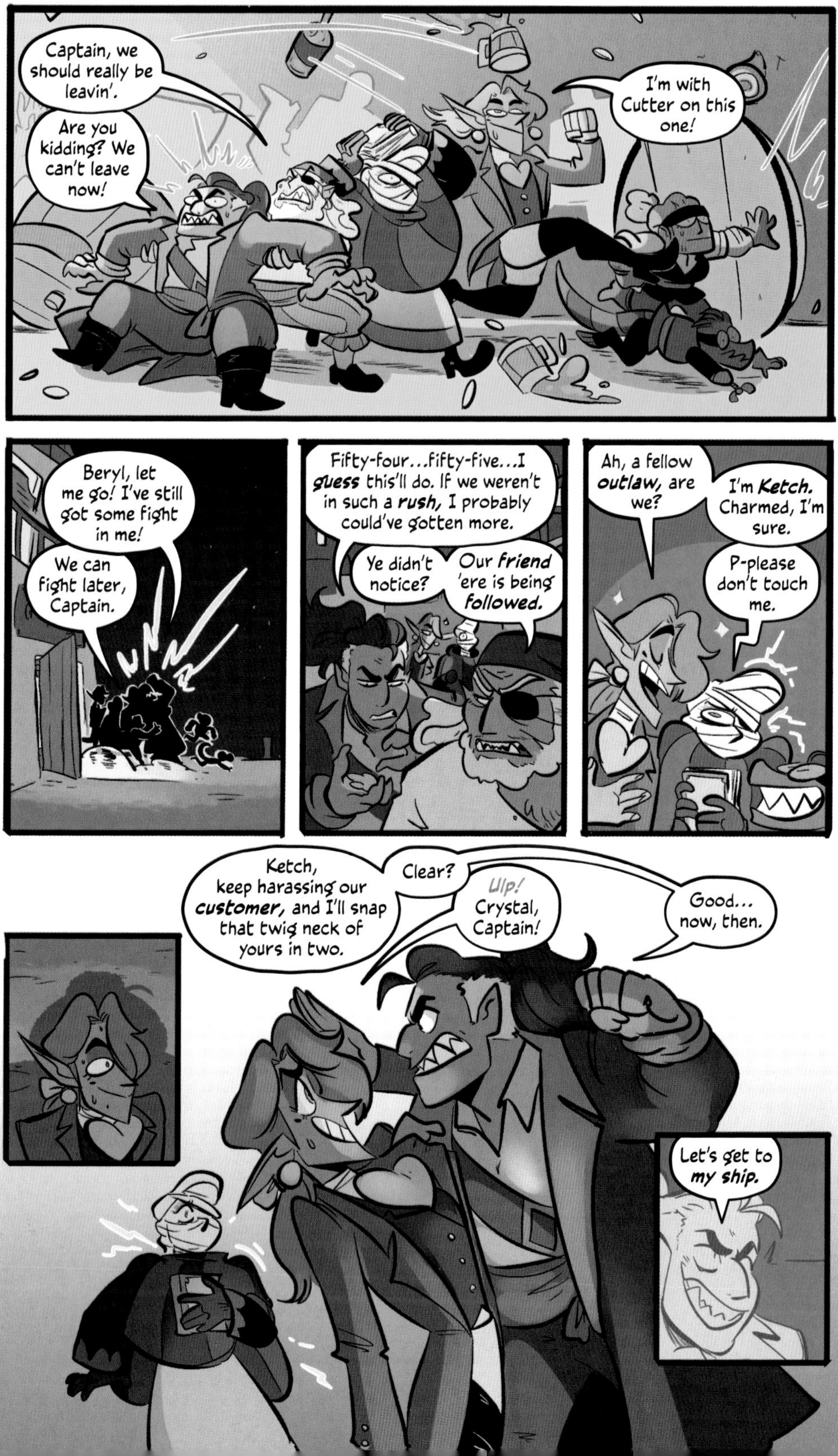
Captain, we should really be leavin'.
Are you kidding? We can't leave now!
I'm with Cutter on this one!
Beryl, let me go! I've still got some fight in me!
We can fight later, Captain.
Fifty-four...fifty-five...I *guess* this'll do. If we weren't in such a *rush,* I probably could've gotten more.
Ye didn't notice?
Our *friend* 'ere is being *followed.*
Ah, a fellow *outlaw,* are we?
I'm *Ketch.* Charmed, I'm sure.
P-please don't touch me.
Ketch, keep harassing our *customer,* and I'll snap that twig neck of yours in two.
Clear?
Ulp! Crystal, Captain!
Good... now, then.
Let's get to *my ship.*

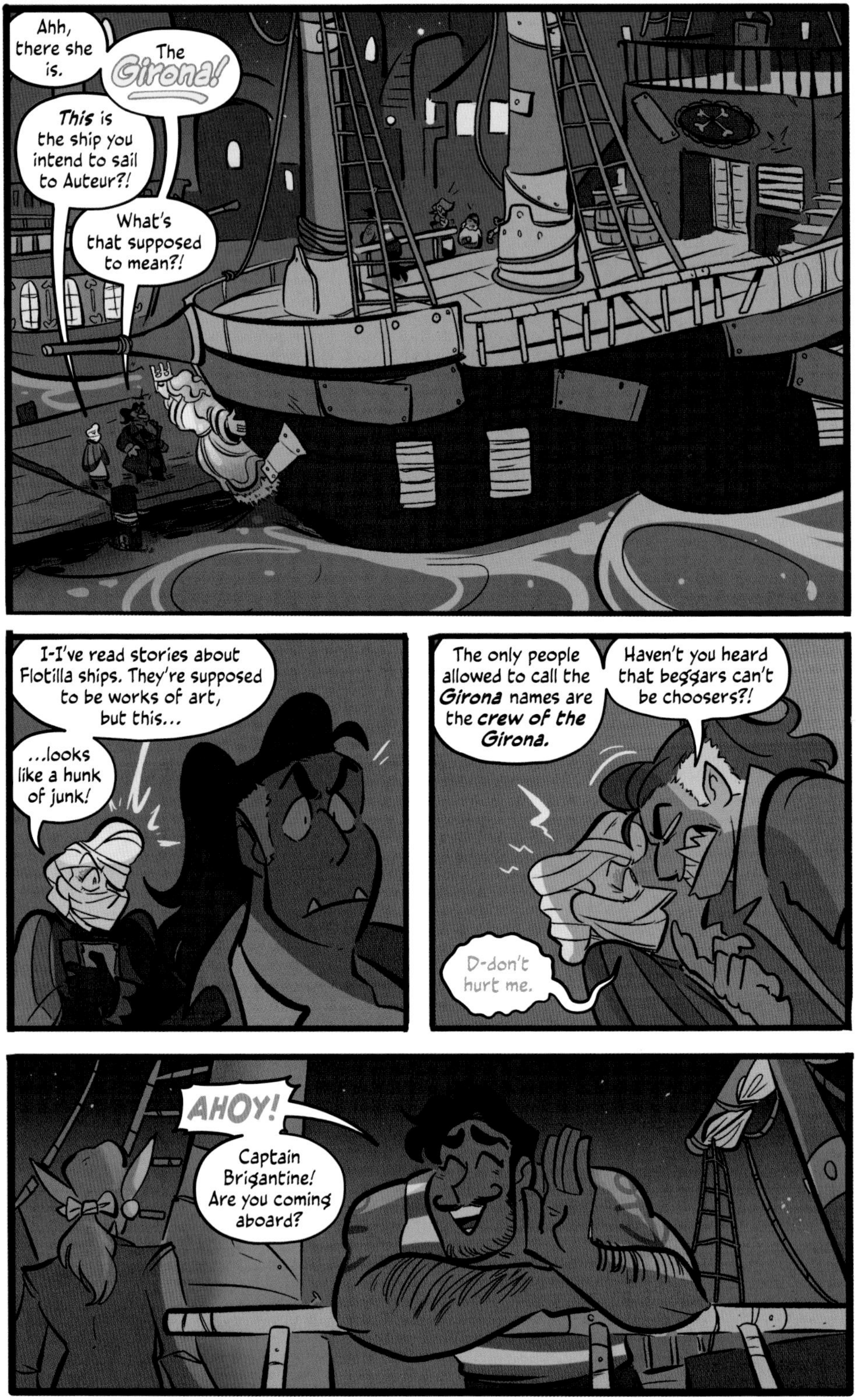
Ahh, there she is.
The Girona!
This is the ship you intend to sail to Auteur?!
What's that supposed to mean?!
I-I've read stories about Flotilla ships. They're supposed to be works of art, but this...
...looks like a hunk of junk!
The only people allowed to call the Girona names are the crew of the Girona.
Haven't you heard that beggars can't be choosers?!
D-don't hurt me.
AHOY!
Captain Brigantine! Are you coming aboard?

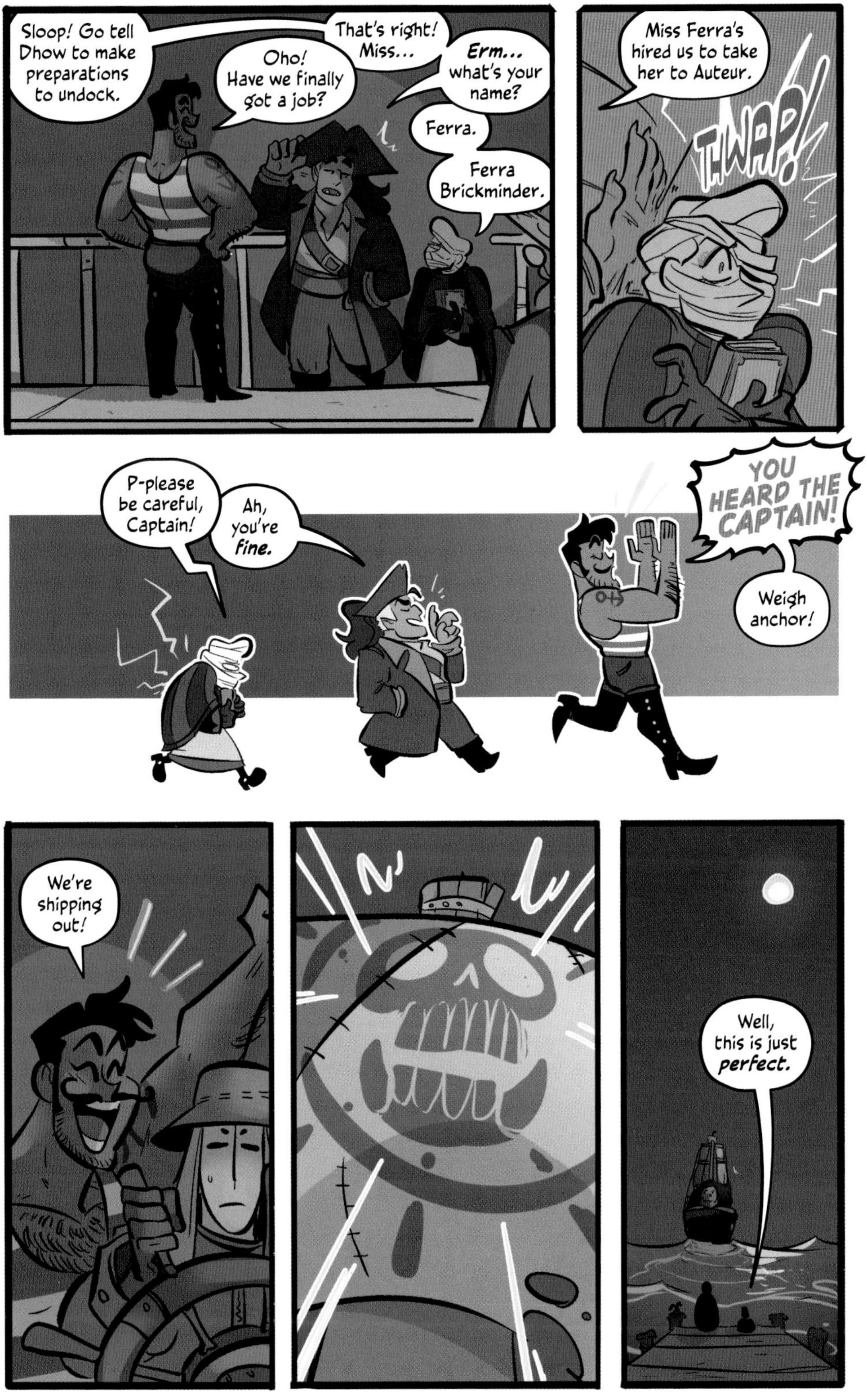
Sloop! Go tell Dhow to make preparations to undock.
Oho! Have we finally got a job?
That's right! Miss...
Erm... what's your name?
Ferra.
Ferra Brickminder.
Miss Ferra's hired us to take her to Auteur.
THWAP!
P-please be careful, Captain!
Ah, you're fine.
YOU HEARD THE CAPTAIN!
Weigh anchor!
We're shipping out!
Well, this is just perfect.

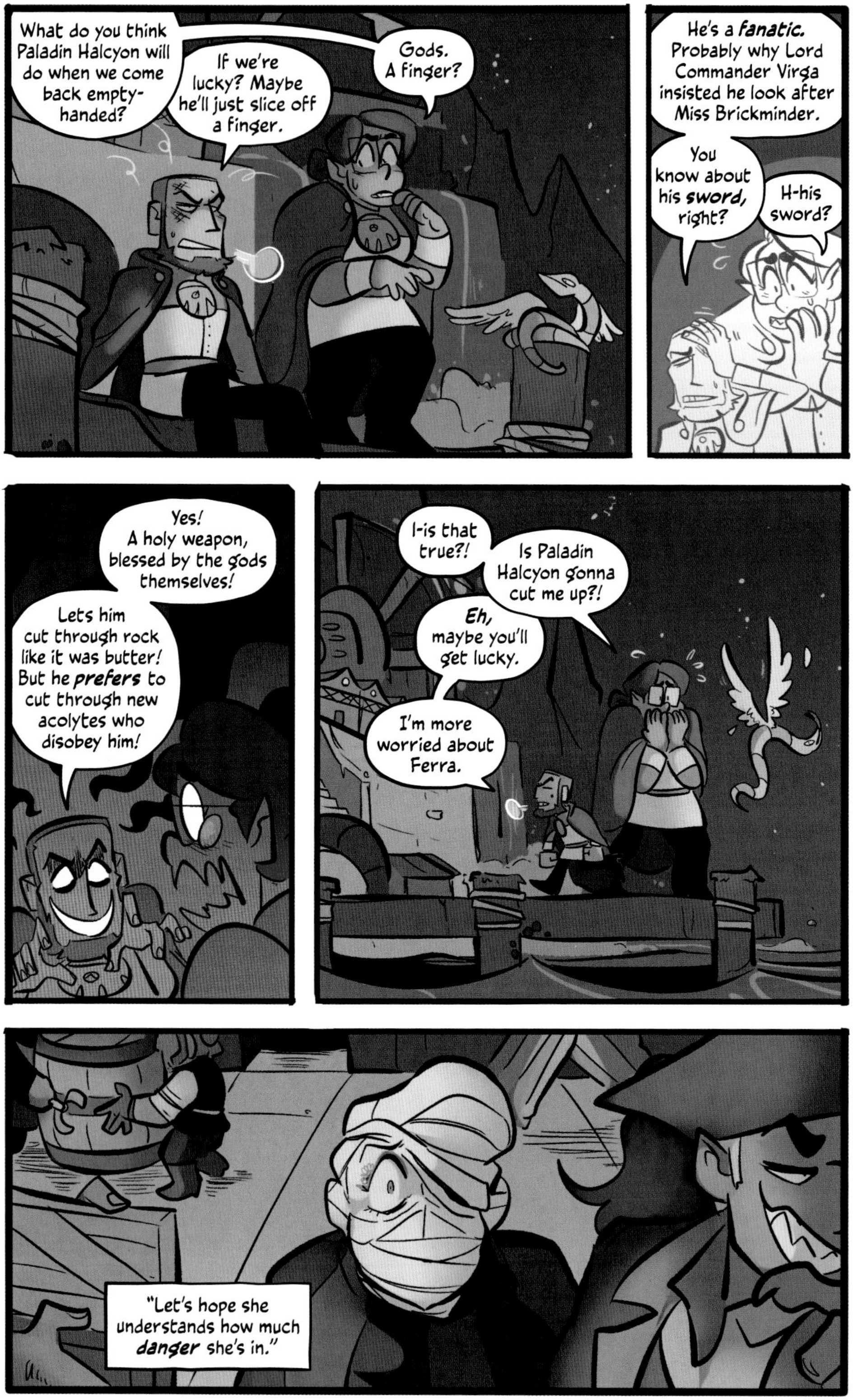
What do you think Paladin Halcyon will do when we come back empty-handed?
If we're lucky? Maybe he'll just slice off a finger.
Gods. A finger?
He's a ***fanatic.*** Probably why Lord Commander Virga insisted he look after Miss Brickminder.
You know about his ***sword,*** right?
H-his sword?
Yes! A holy weapon, blessed by the gods themselves!
Lets him cut through rock like it was butter! But he ***prefers*** to cut through new acolytes who disobey him!
I-is that true?!
Is Paladin Halcyon gonna cut me up?!
Eh, maybe you'll get lucky.
I'm more worried about Ferra.
"Let's hope she understands how much ***danger*** she's in."

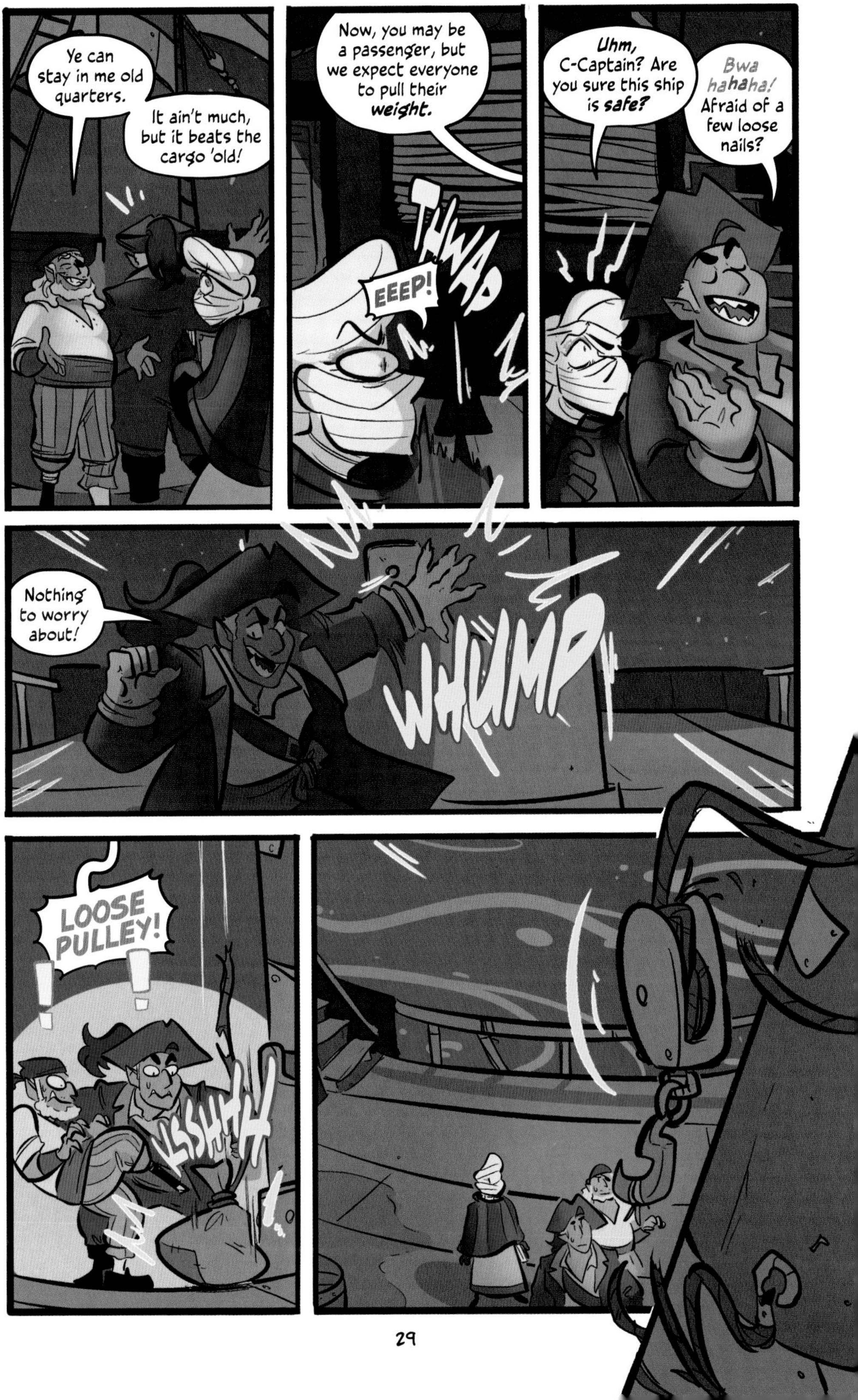

Ye can stay in me old quarters.
It ain't much, but it beats the cargo 'old!
Now, you may be a passenger, but we expect everyone to pull their *weight.*
THWAP
EEEP!
Uhm, C-Captain? Are you sure this ship is *safe?*
Bwa hahaha! Afraid of a few loose nails?
Nothing to worry about!
WHUMP
LOOSE PULLEY!
!
!

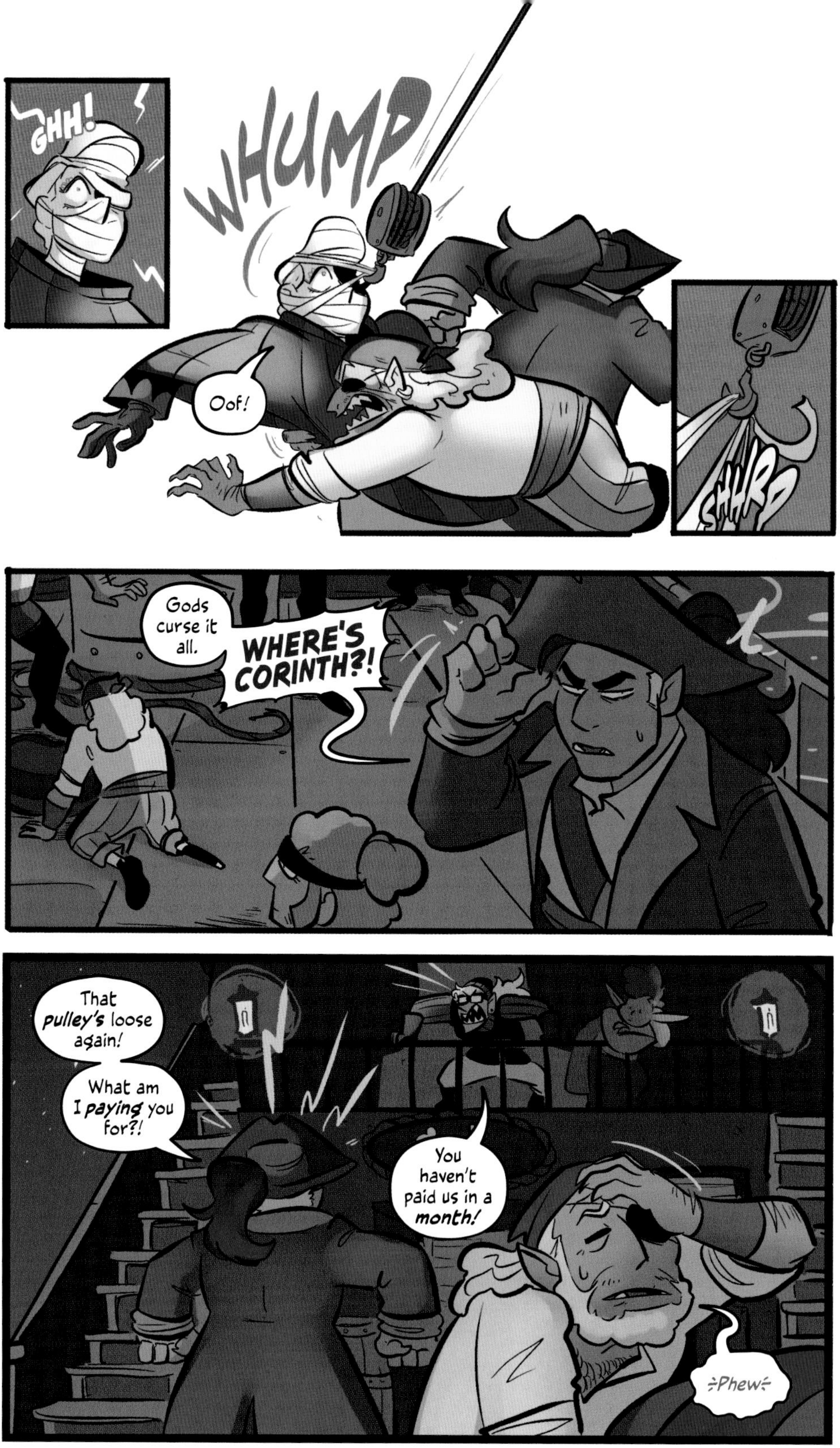
GHH!
WHUMP
Oof!
SHRP
Gods curse it all.
WHERE'S CORINTH?!
That pulley's loose again!
What am I paying you for?!
You haven't paid us in a month!
Phew

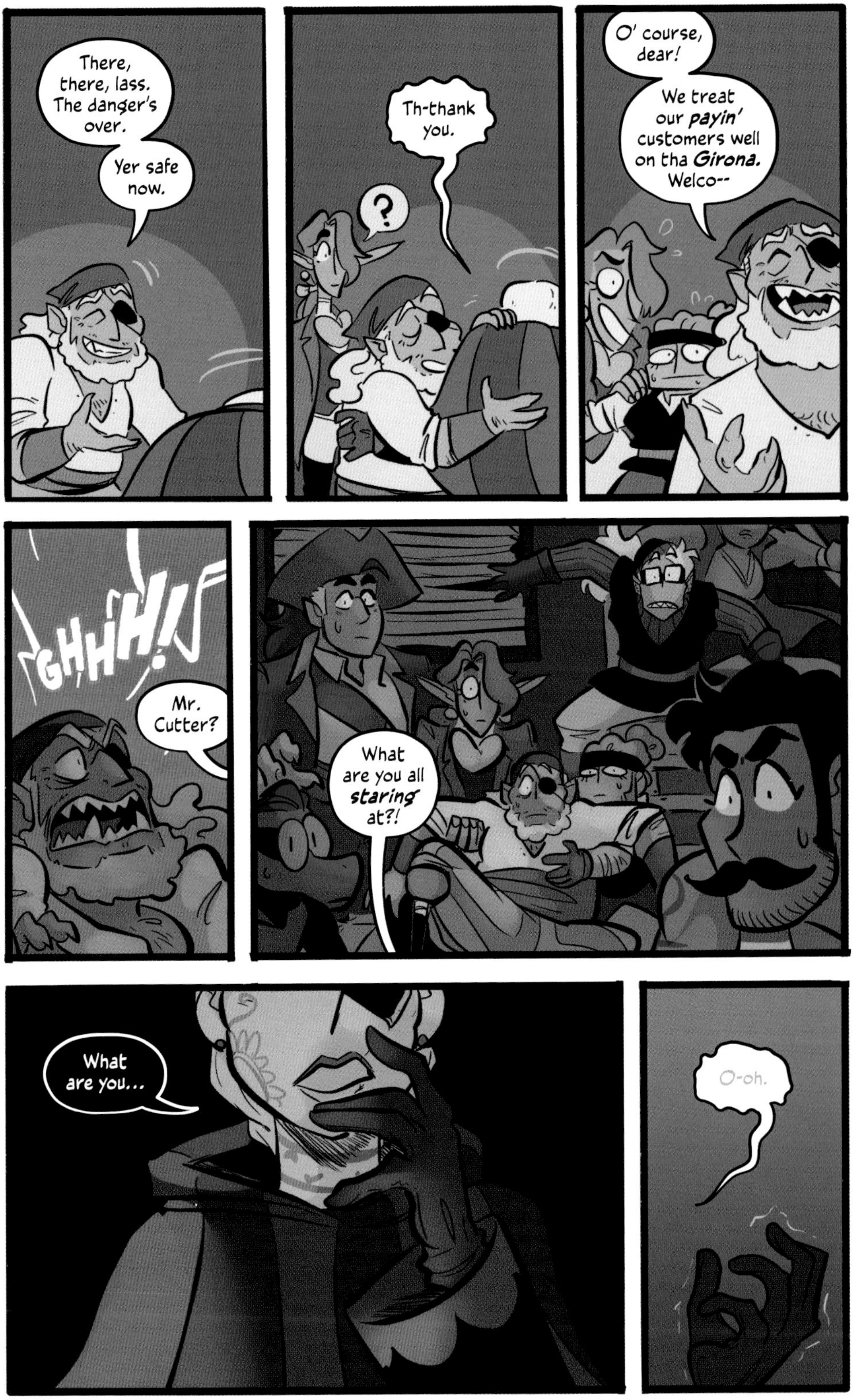
There, there, lass. The danger's over.
Yer safe now.
Th-thank you.
?
O' course, dear!
We treat our *payin'* customers well on tha *Girona.* Welco--
GHHH!
Mr. Cutter?
What are you all *staring* at?!
What are you...
O-oh.

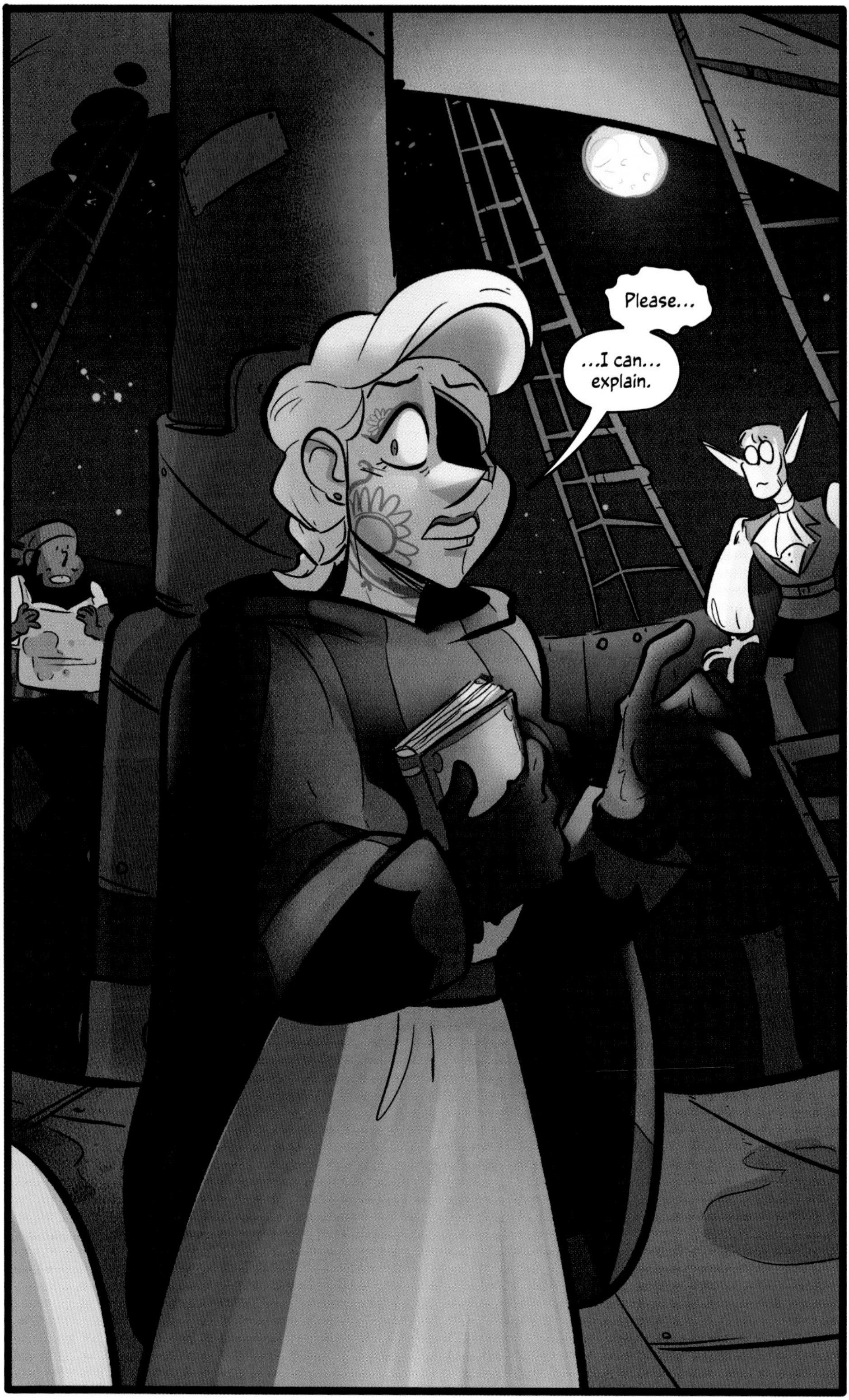
Please...
...I can... explain.

Chapter 2

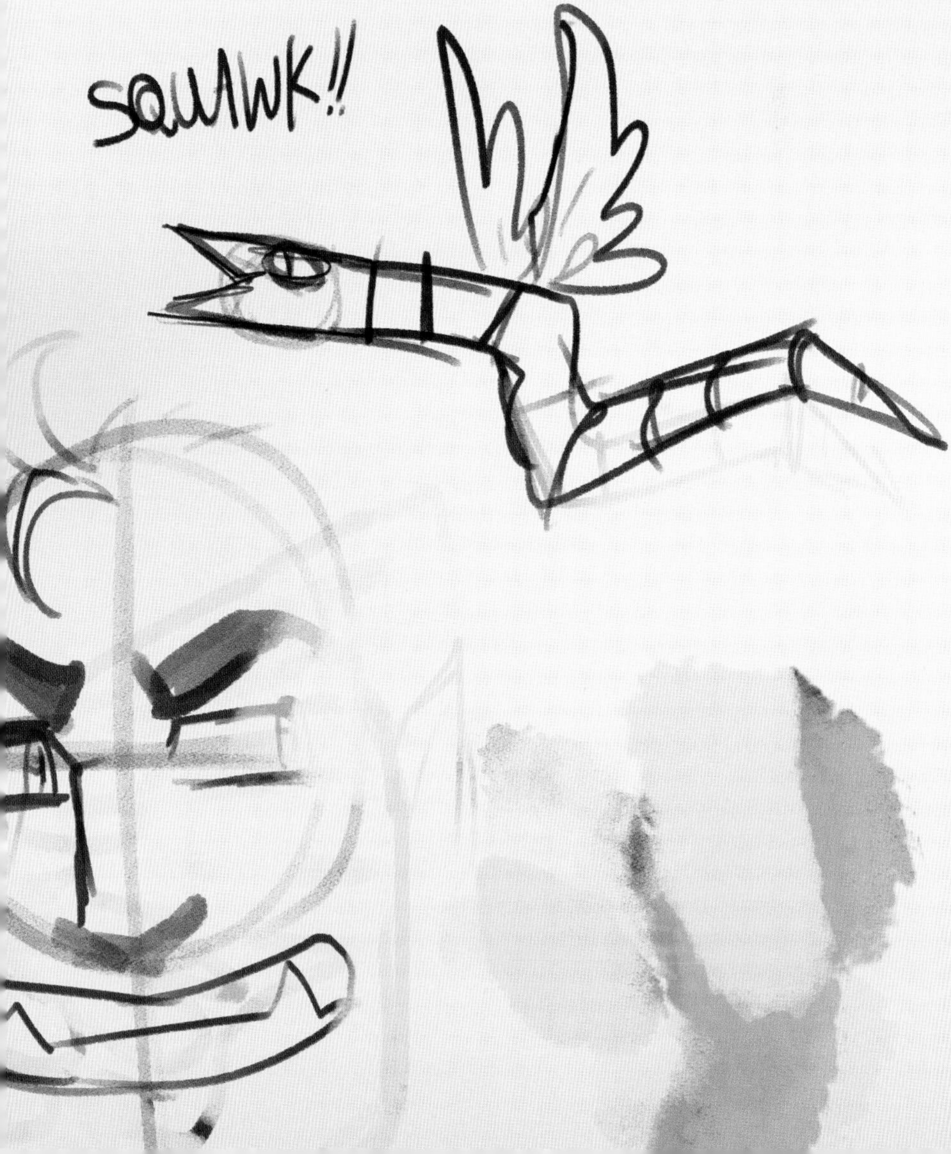
SQUAWK!!

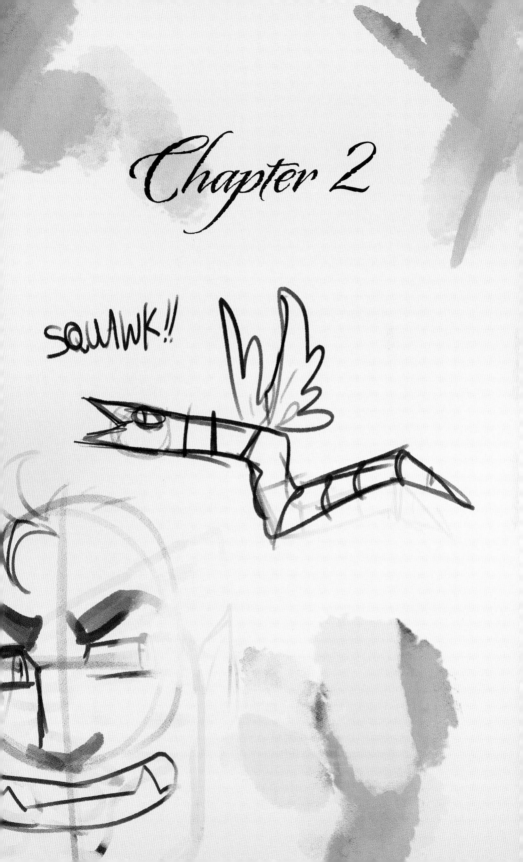

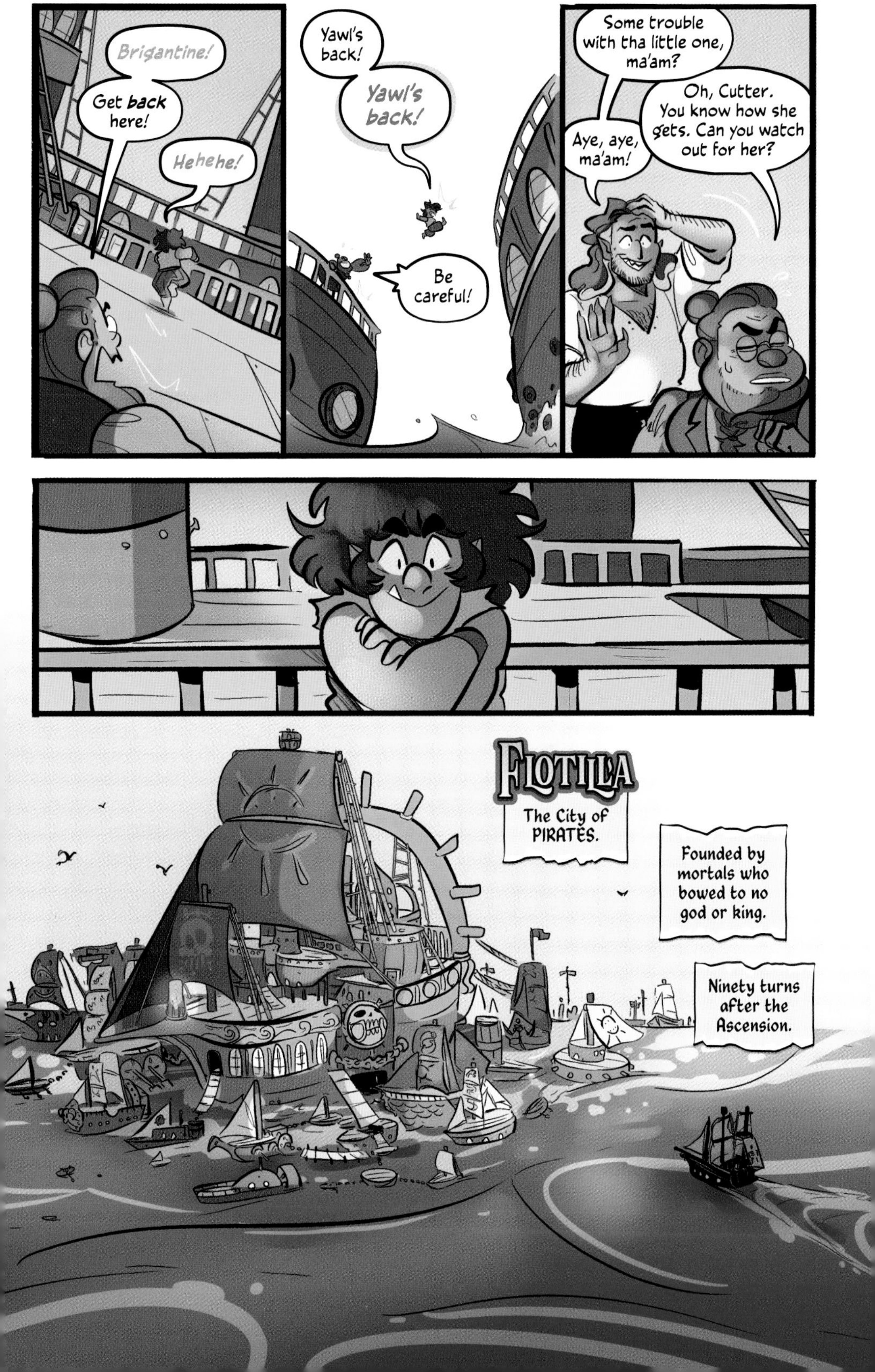
Brigantine!
Get back here!
Hehehe!
Yawl's back!
Yawl's back!
Be careful!
Some trouble with tha little one, ma'am?
Oh, Cutter. You know how she gets. Can you watch out for her?
Aye, aye, ma'am!
FLOTILLA
The City of PIRATES.
Founded by mortals who bowed to no god or king.
Ninety turns after the Ascension.

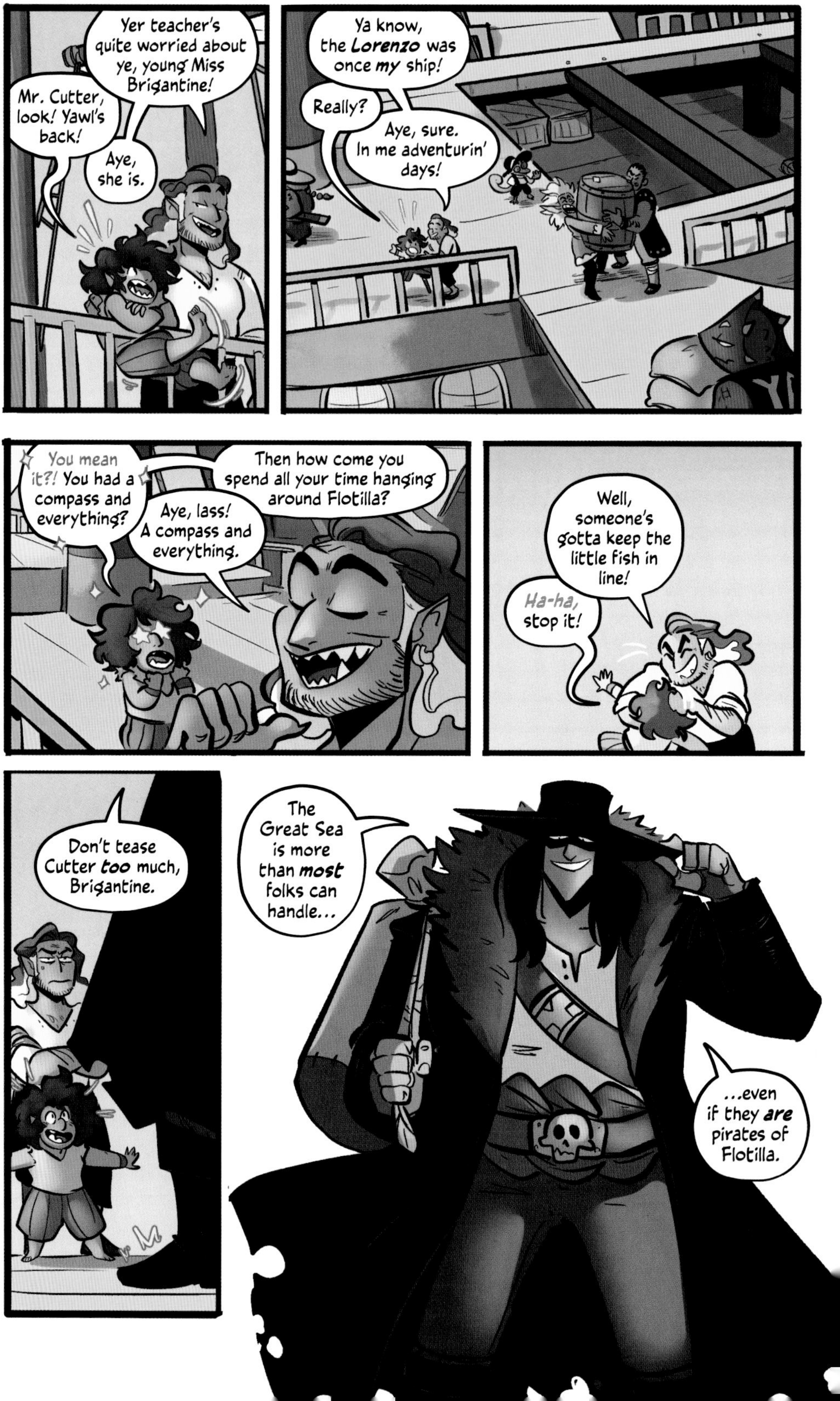

Mr. Cutter, look! Yawl's back!
Yer teacher's quite worried about ye, young Miss Brigantine!
Aye, she is.
Ya know, the Lorenzo was once my ship!
Really?
Aye, sure. In me adventurin' days!
You mean it?! You had a compass and everything?
Aye, lass! A compass and everything.
Then how come you spend all your time hanging around Flotilla?
Well, someone's gotta keep the little fish in line!
Ha-ha, stop it!
Don't tease Cutter too much, Brigantine.
The Great Sea is more than most folks can handle...
...even if they are pirates of Flotilla.

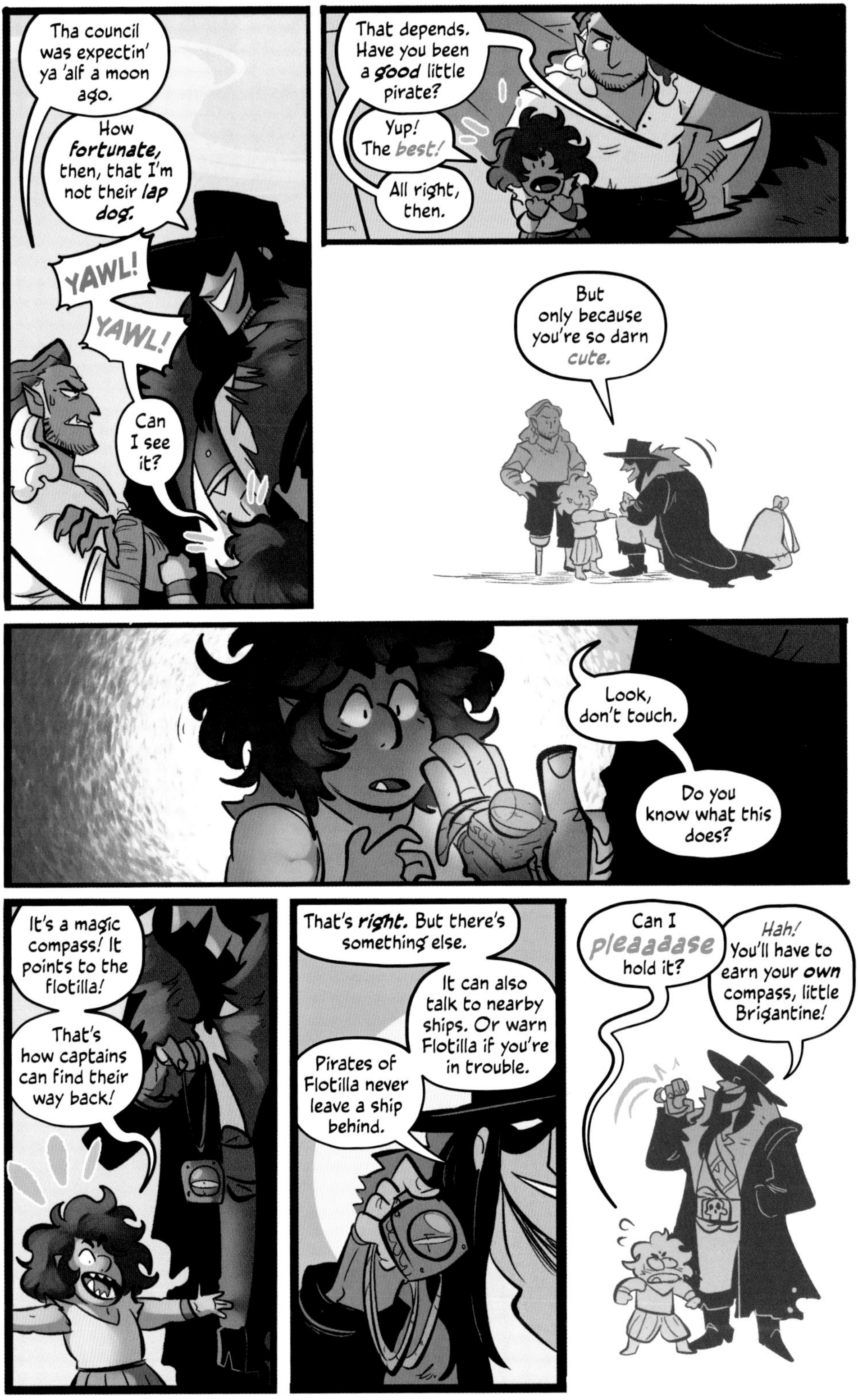

Tha council was expectin' ya 'alf a moon ago.
How fortunate, then, that I'm not their lap dog.
YAWL!
YAWL!
Can I see it?
That depends. Have you been a good little pirate?
Yup! The best!
All right, then.
But only because you're so darn cute.
Look, don't touch.
Do you know what this does?
It's a magic compass! It points to the flotilla!
That's how captains can find their way back!
That's right. But there's something else.
It can also talk to nearby ships. Or warn Flotilla if you're in trouble.
Pirates of Flotilla never leave a ship behind.
Can I pleaaaase hold it?
Hah! You'll have to earn your own compass, little Brigantine!

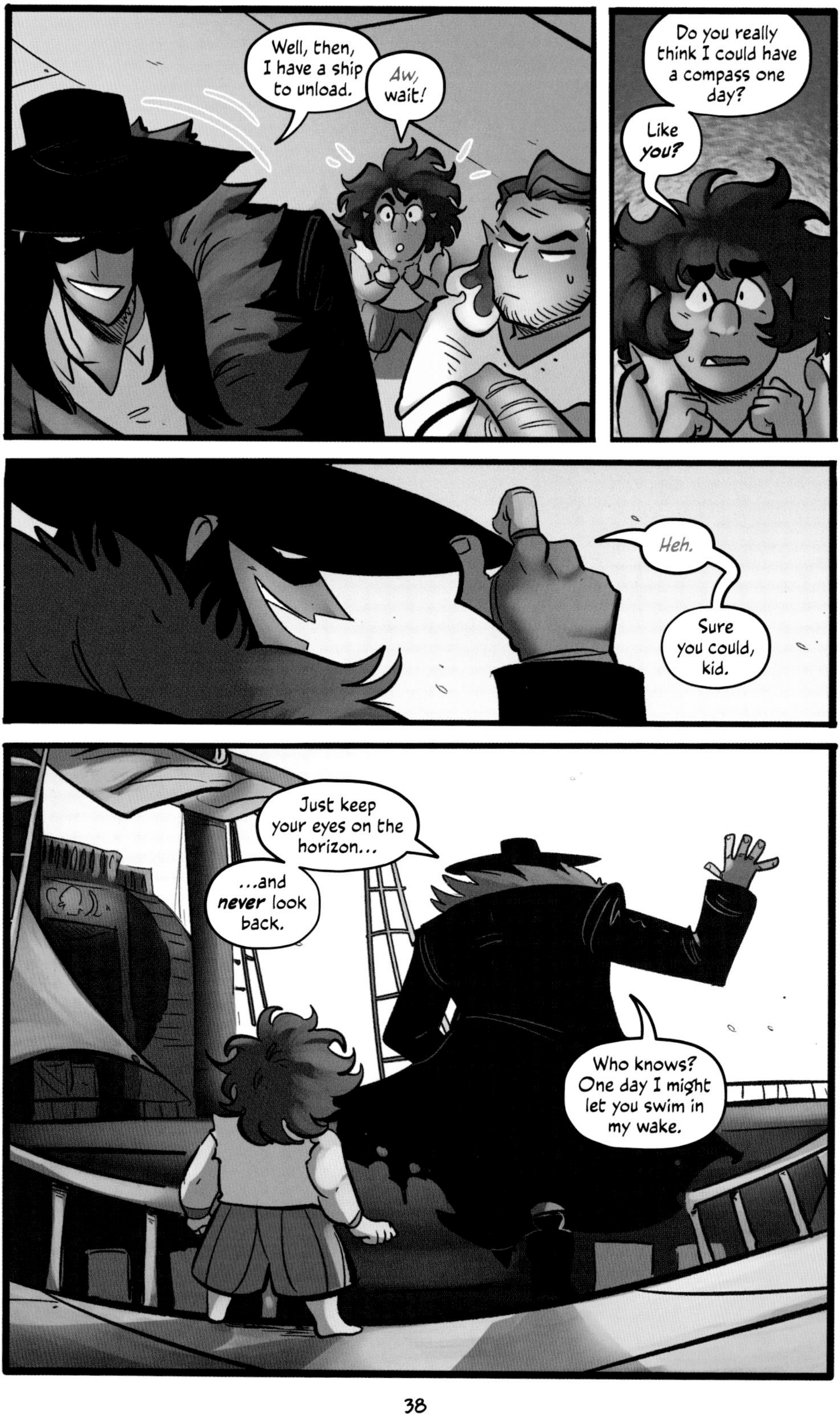
Well, then, I have a ship to unload.
Aw, wait!
Do you really think I could have a compass one day?
Like *you?*
Heh.
Sure you could, kid.
Just keep your eyes on the horizon...
...and **never** look back.
Who knows? One day I might let you swim in my wake.

GANZTOLL

Tower of the Ecclesiarchy.

Present day.

What do you mean you *lost* **HER?!**

Mr. Brickminder, I *understand* you are *concerned*, but--

Concerned?! I'm *terrified!*

My baby girl is out there somewhere, all **alone!**

My poor, sweet Ferra! She's always been **sensitive,** even before the...well, *you know.*

And I can assure you, we're doing *everything* we can to find her.

But every moment we tarry is a moment wasted.

The Ecclesiarchy has eyes in every city-state in Daoine. Have we *ever* steered you wrong?

Snff...

N-no. I suppose not.

Please, Palad Bring daugh *hom*

You have my word, Mr. Brickminder.

EPHEWS

Feeling relaxed, are we?

Eep!

39

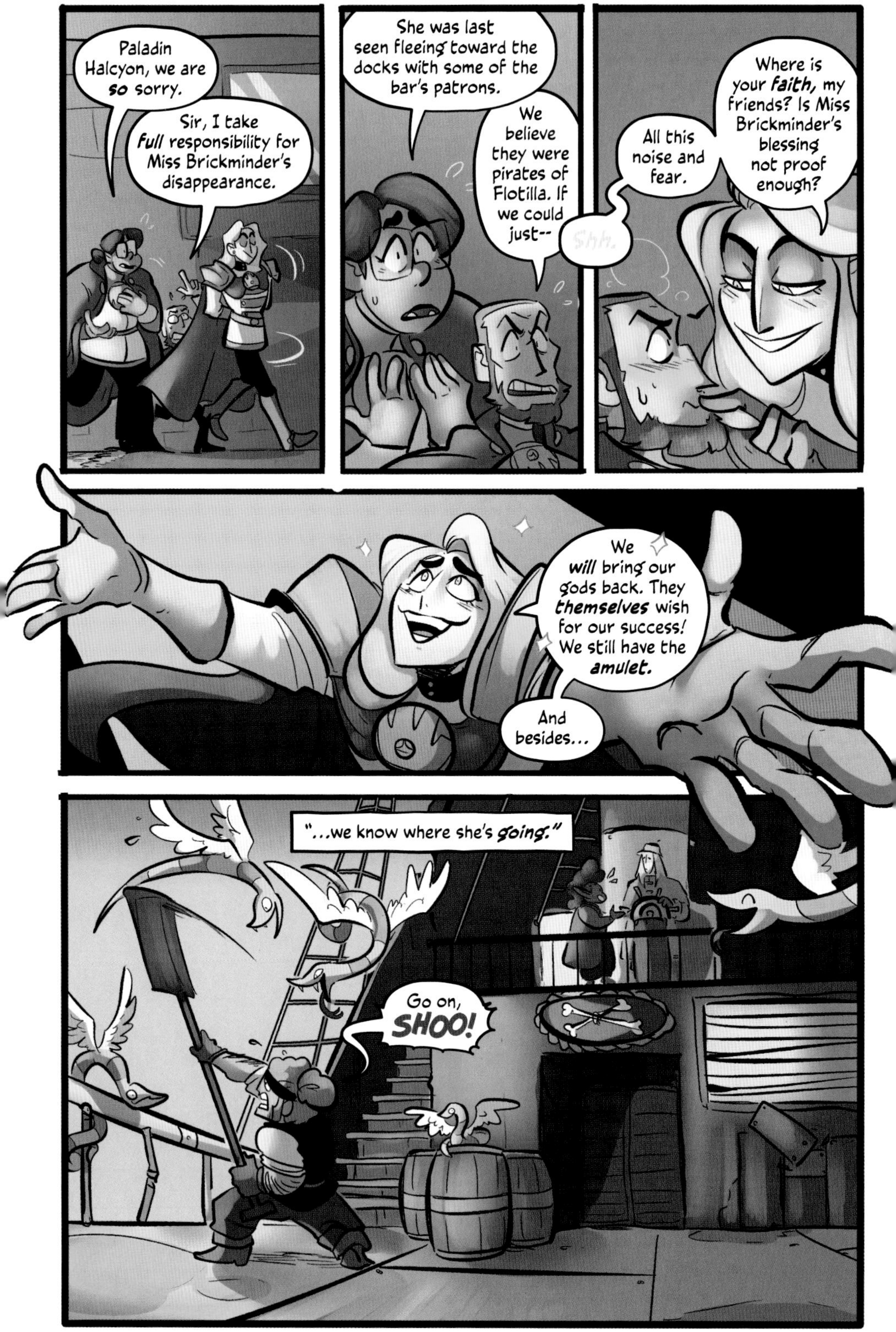
Paladin Halcyon, we are *so* sorry.
Sir, I take *full* responsibility for Miss Brickminder's disappearance.
She was last seen fleeing toward the docks with some of the bar's patrons.
We believe they were pirates of Flotilla. If we could just--
Shh.
All this noise and fear.
Where is your *faith,* my friends? Is Miss Brickminder's blessing not proof enough?
We *will* bring our gods back. They *themselves* wish for our success! We still have the *amulet.*
And besides...
"...we know where she's *going.*"
Go on, **SHOO!**

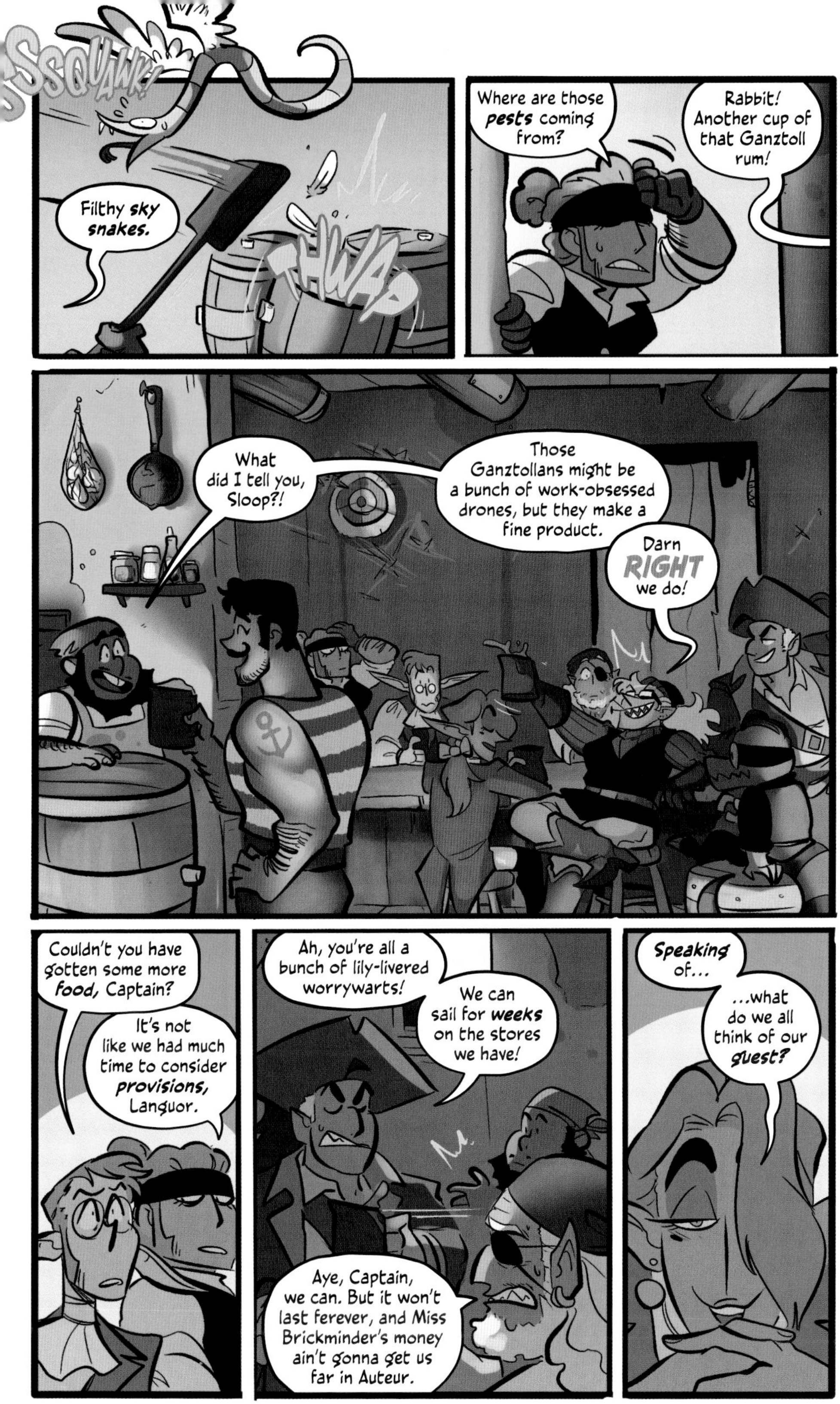
SSQUAWK!
Filthy sky snakes.
THWAP
Where are those pests coming from?
Rabbit! Another cup of that Ganztoll rum!
What did I tell you, Sloop?!
Those Ganztollans might be a bunch of work-obsessed drones, but they make a fine product.
Darn RIGHT we do!
Couldn't you have gotten some more food, Captain?
It's not like we had much time to consider provisions, Languor.
Ah, you're all a bunch of lily-livered worrywarts!
We can sail for weeks on the stores we have!
Aye, Captain, we can. But it won't last forever, and Miss Brickminder's money ain't gonna get us far in Auteur.
Speaking of...
...what do we all think of our guest?

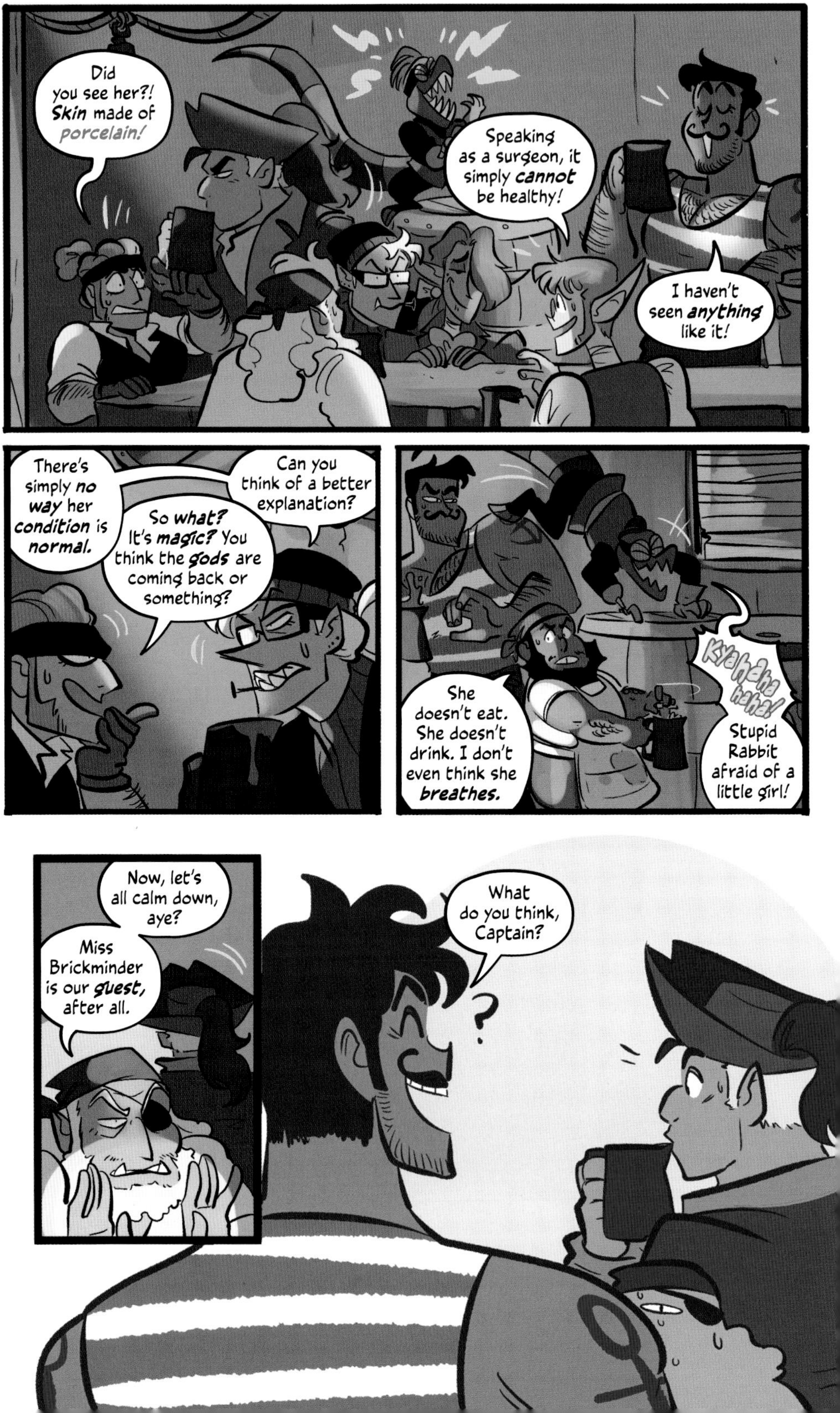
Did you see her?! Skin made of porcelain!
Speaking as a surgeon, it simply cannot be healthy!
I haven't seen anything like it!
There's simply no way her condition is normal.
Can you think of a better explanation?
So what? It's magic? You think the gods are coming back or something?
She doesn't eat. She doesn't drink. I don't even think she breathes.
Kyahahahaha!
Stupid Rabbit afraid of a little girl!
Now, let's all calm down, aye?
Miss Brickminder is our guest, after all.
What do you think, Captain?
?

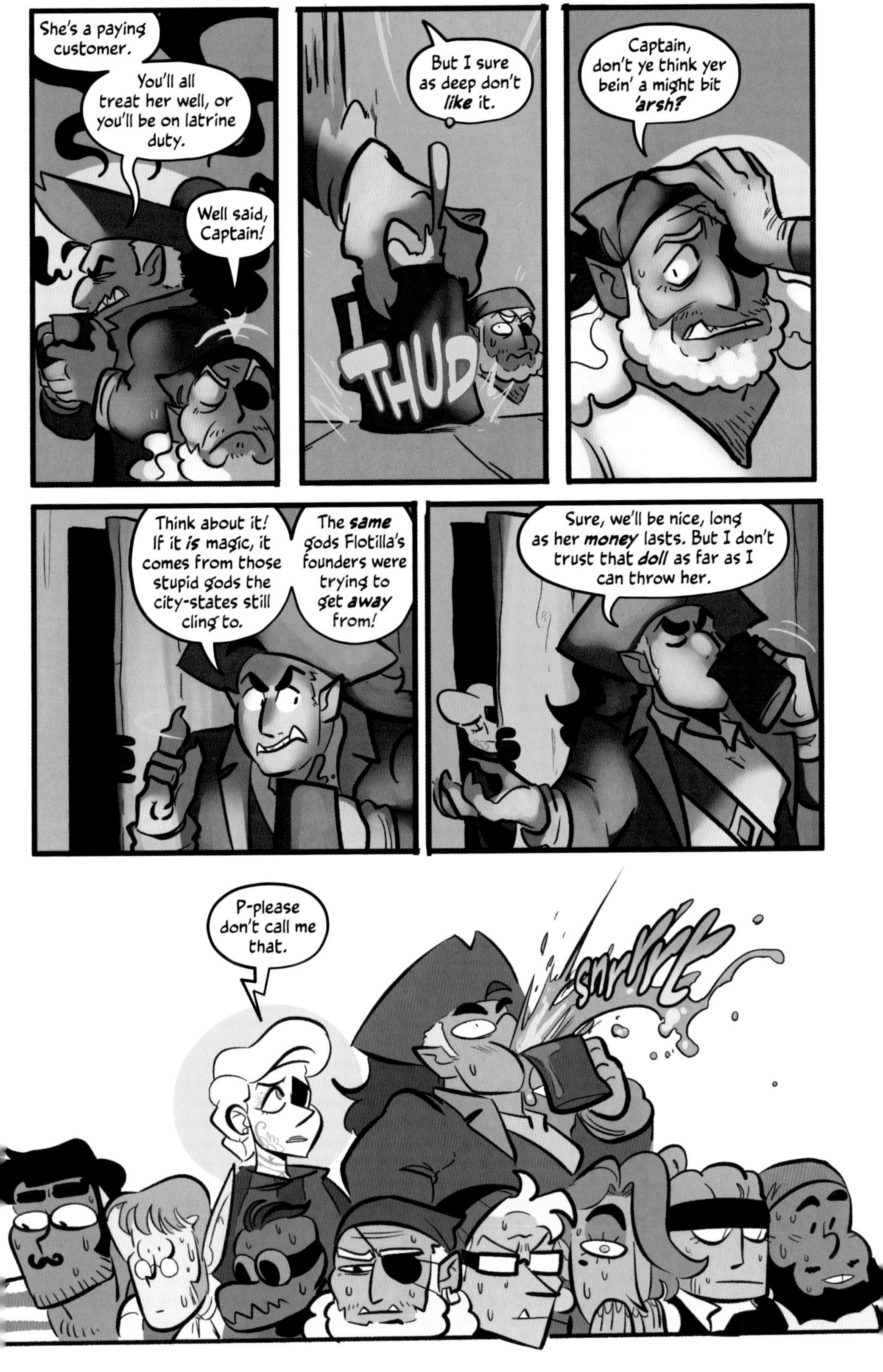
She's a paying customer.
You'll all treat her well, or you'll be on latrine duty.
Well said, Captain!
But I sure as deep don't *like* it.
THUD
Captain, don't ye think yer bein' a might bit *'arsh?*
Think about it! If it *is* magic, it comes from those stupid gods the city-states still cling to.
The *same* gods Flotilla's founders were trying to get *away* from!
Sure, we'll be nice, long as her *money* lasts. But I don't trust that *doll* as far as I can throw her.
P-please don't call me that.
SNRKKK

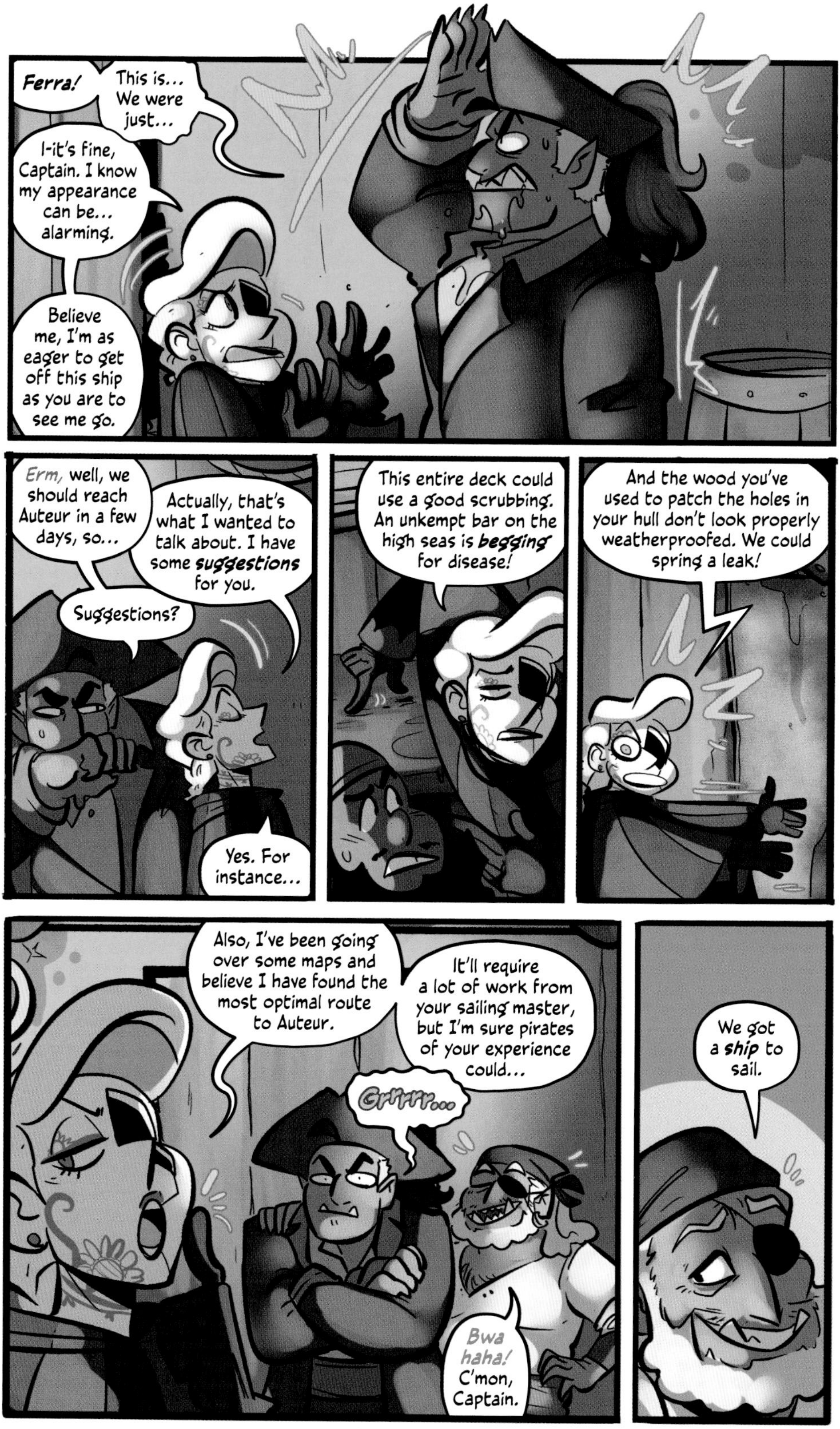

Ferra!
This is... We were just...
I-it's fine, Captain. I know my appearance can be... alarming.
Believe me, I'm as eager to get off this ship as you are to see me go.
Erm, well, we should reach Auteur in a few days, so...
Actually, that's what I wanted to talk about. I have some *suggestions* for you.
Suggestions?
Yes. For instance...
This entire deck could use a good scrubbing. An unkempt bar on the high seas is *begging* for disease!
And the wood you've used to patch the holes in your hull don't look properly weatherproofed. We could spring a leak!
Also, I've been going over some maps and believe I have found the most optimal route to Auteur.
It'll require a lot of work from your sailing master, but I'm sure pirates of your experience could...
Grrrrr...
Bwa haha! C'mon, Captain.
We got a *ship* to sail.

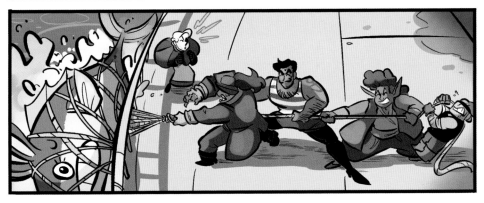

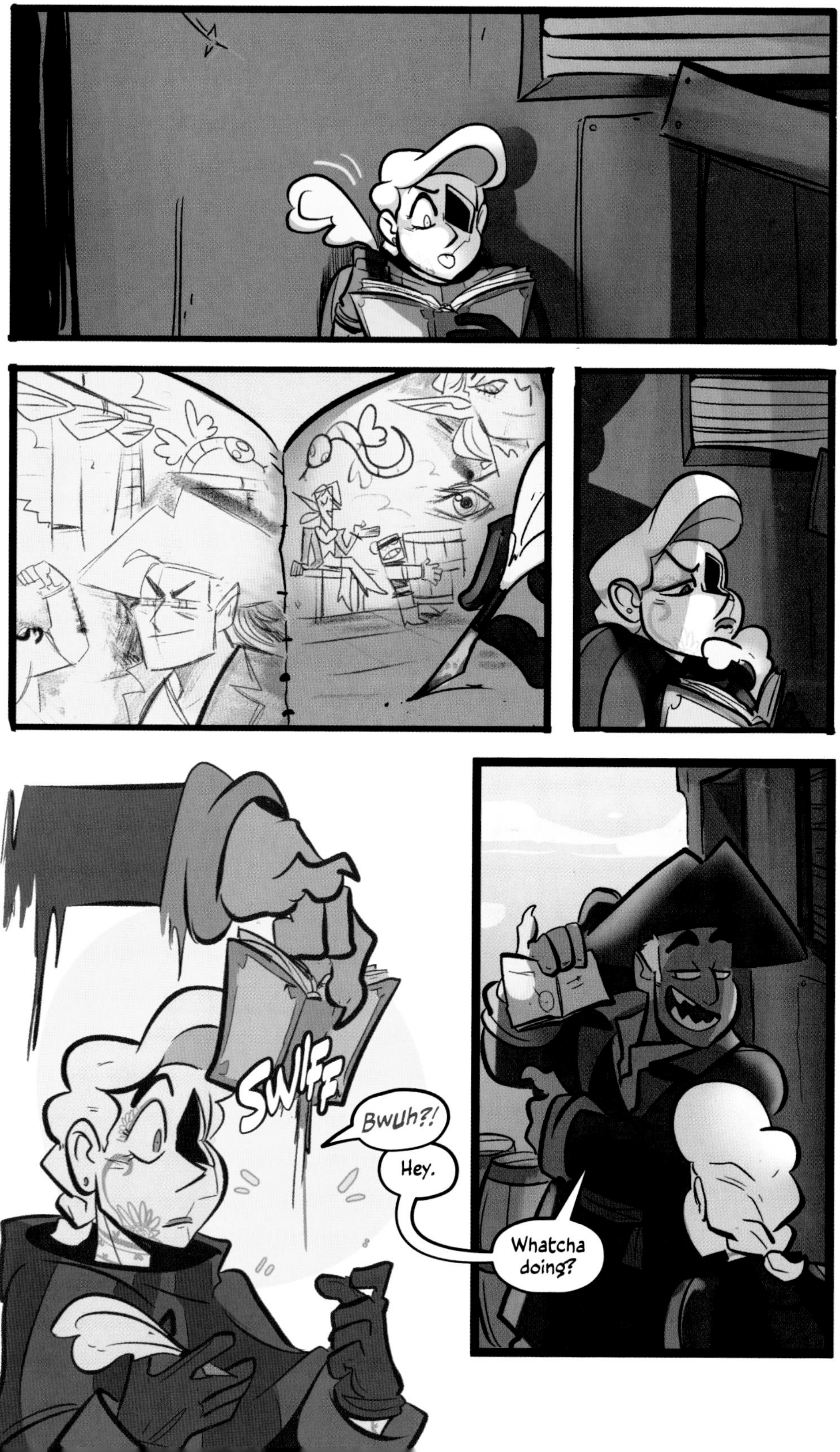
SWIFF
Bwuh?!
Hey.
Whatcha doing?

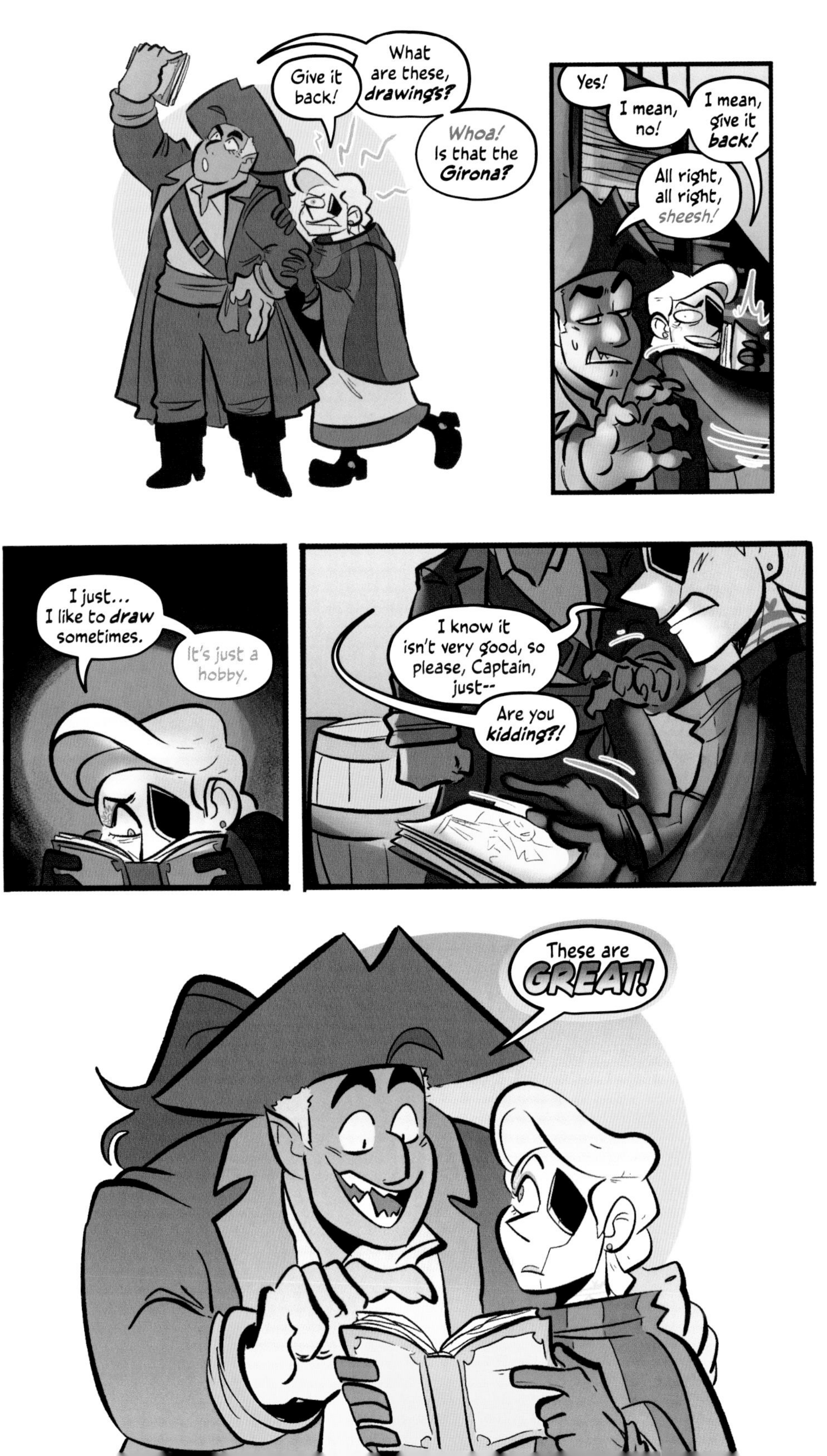
What are these, drawings?
Give it back!
Whoa! Is that the Girona?
Yes!
I mean, no!
I mean, give it back!
All right, all right, sheesh!
I just... I like to draw sometimes.
It's just a hobby.
I know it isn't very good, so please, Captain, just--
Are you kidding?!
These are GREAT!

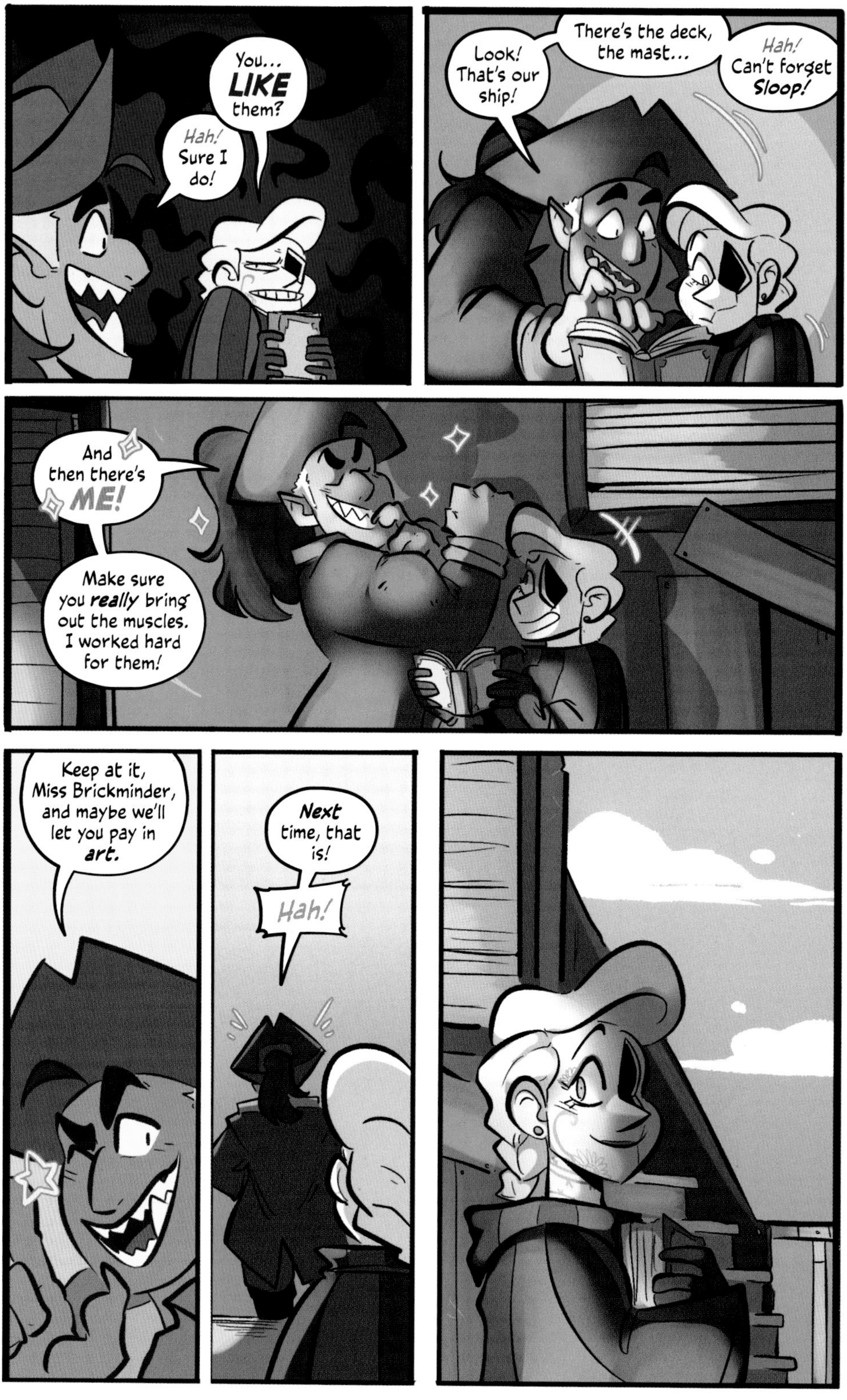
You... LIKE them?
Hah! Sure I do!
Look! That's our ship!
There's the deck, the mast...
Hah! Can't forget Sloop!
And then there's ME!
Make sure you really bring out the muscles. I worked hard for them!
Keep at it, Miss Brickminder, and maybe we'll let you pay in art.
Next time, that is!
Hah!

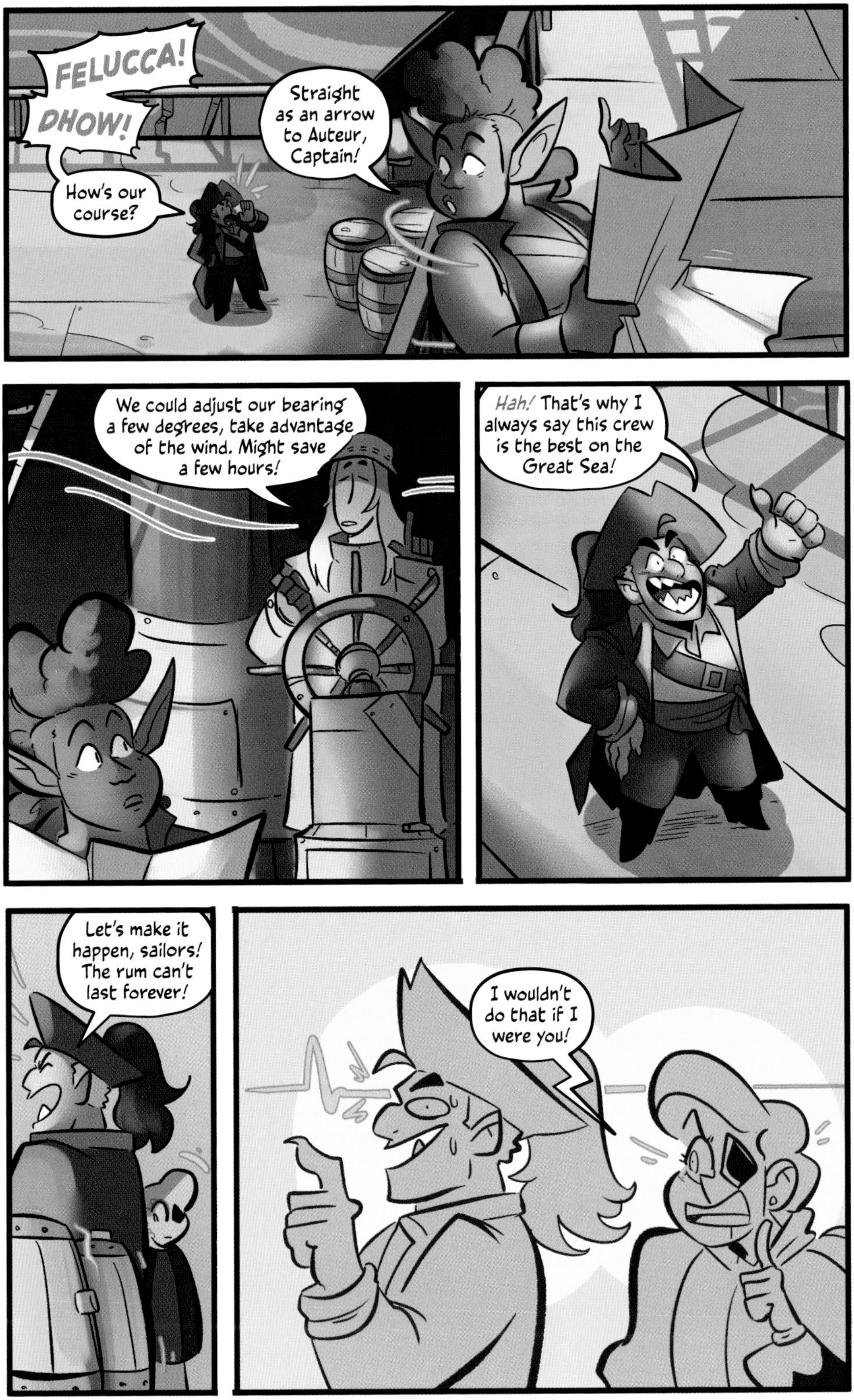
FELUCCA!
DHOW!
How's our course?
Straight as an arrow to Auteur, Captain!
We could adjust our bearing a few degrees, take advantage of the wind. Might save a few hours!
Hah! That's why I always say this crew is the best on the Great Sea!
Let's make it happen, sailors! The rum can't last forever!
I wouldn't do that if I were you!

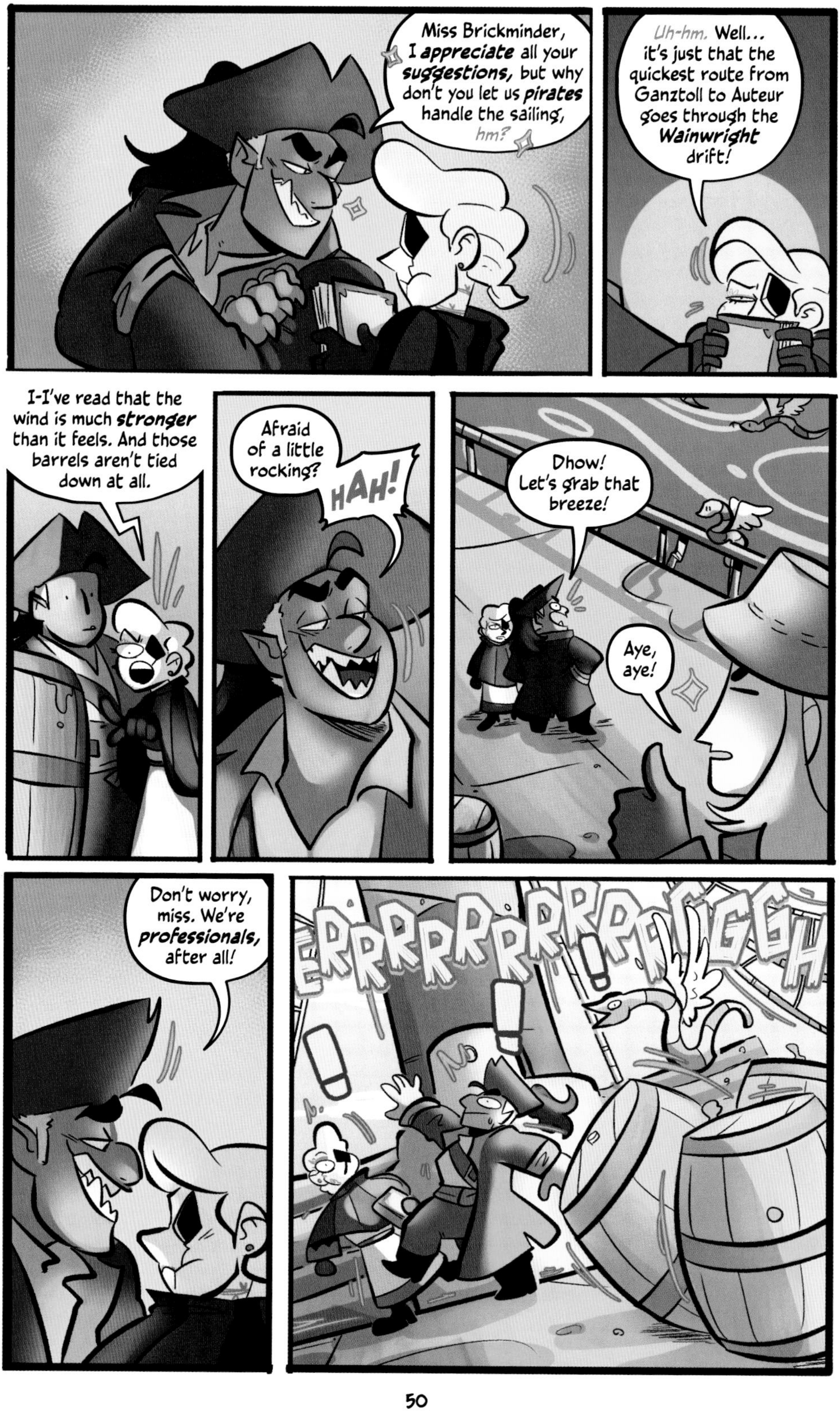
Miss Brickminder, I appreciate all your suggestions, but why don't you let us pirates handle the sailing, hm?
Uh-hm. Well... it's just that the quickest route from Ganztoll to Auteur goes through the Wainwright drift!
I-I've read that the wind is much stronger than it feels. And those barrels aren't tied down at all.
Afraid of a little rocking?
HAH!
Dhow! Let's grab that breeze!
Aye, aye!
Don't worry, miss. We're professionals, after all!
ERRRRRRRRRGGH

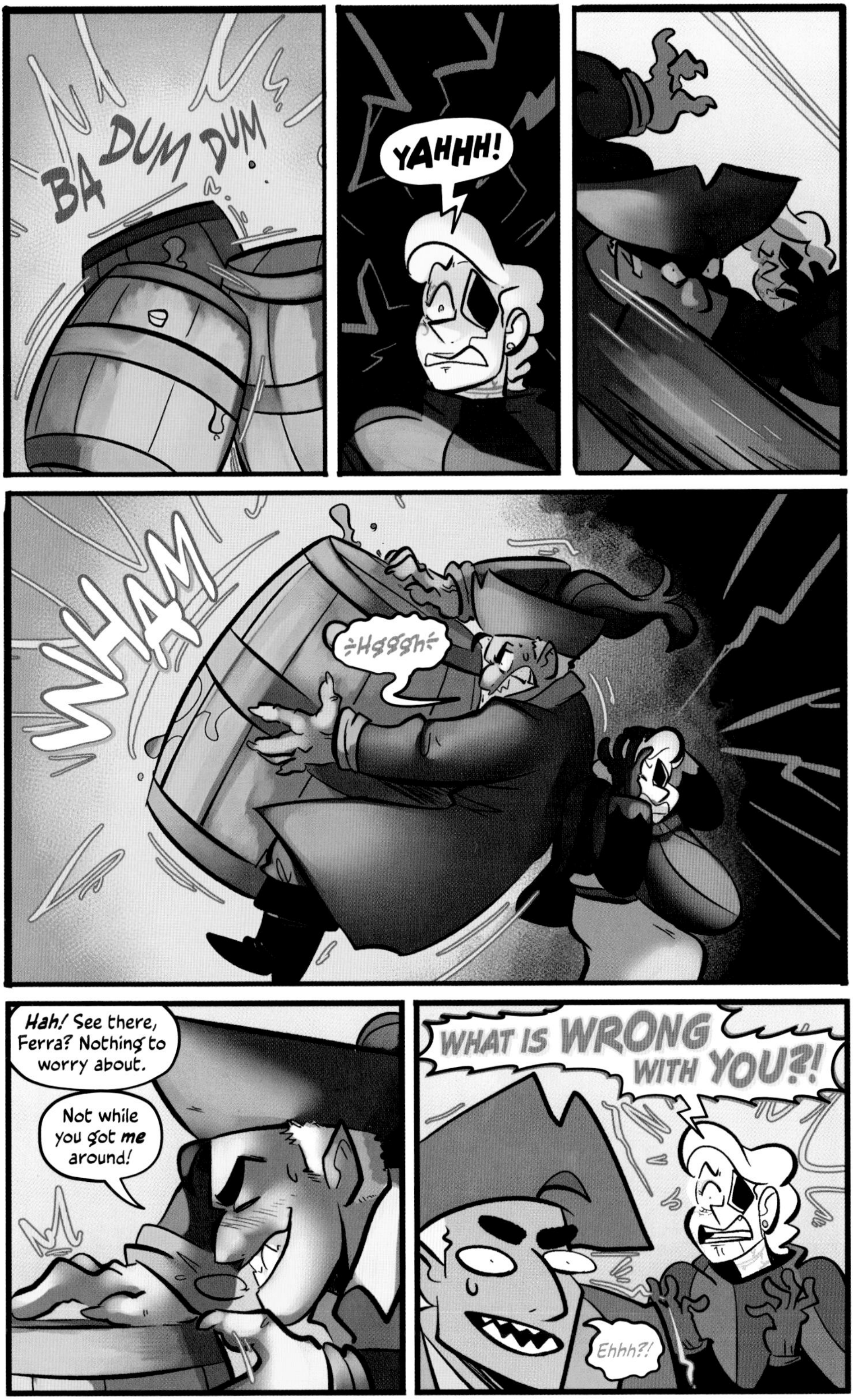
BA DUM DUM
YAHHH!
WHAM
Hgggh
Hah! See there, Ferra? Nothing to worry about.
Not while you got me around!
WHAT IS WRONG WITH YOU?!
Ehhh?!

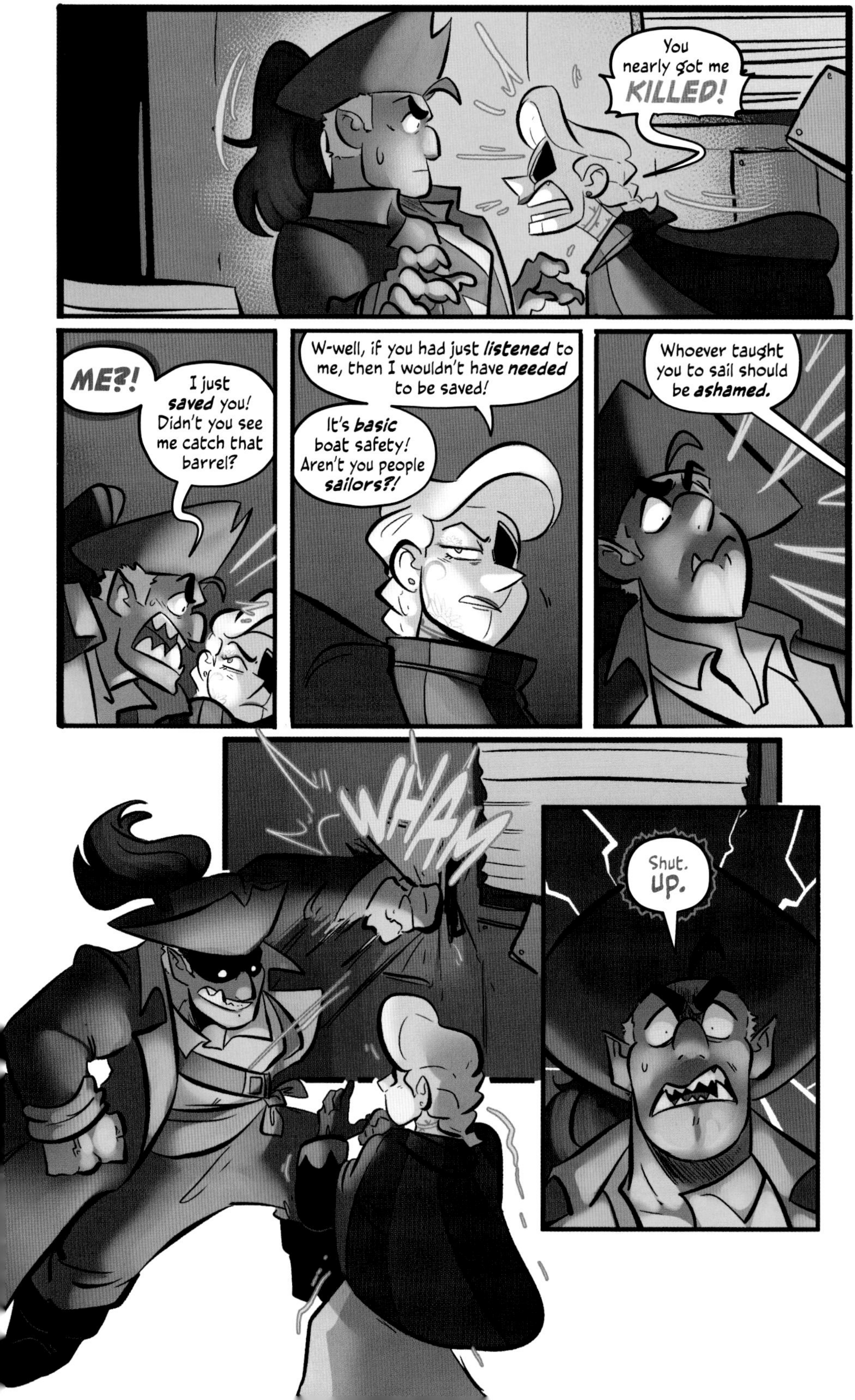
You nearly got me KILLED!
ME?!
I just saved you! Didn't you see me catch that barrel?
W-well, if you had just listened to me, then I wouldn't have needed to be saved!
It's basic boat safety! Aren't you people sailors?!
Whoever taught you to sail should be ashamed.
WHAM
Shut. UP.

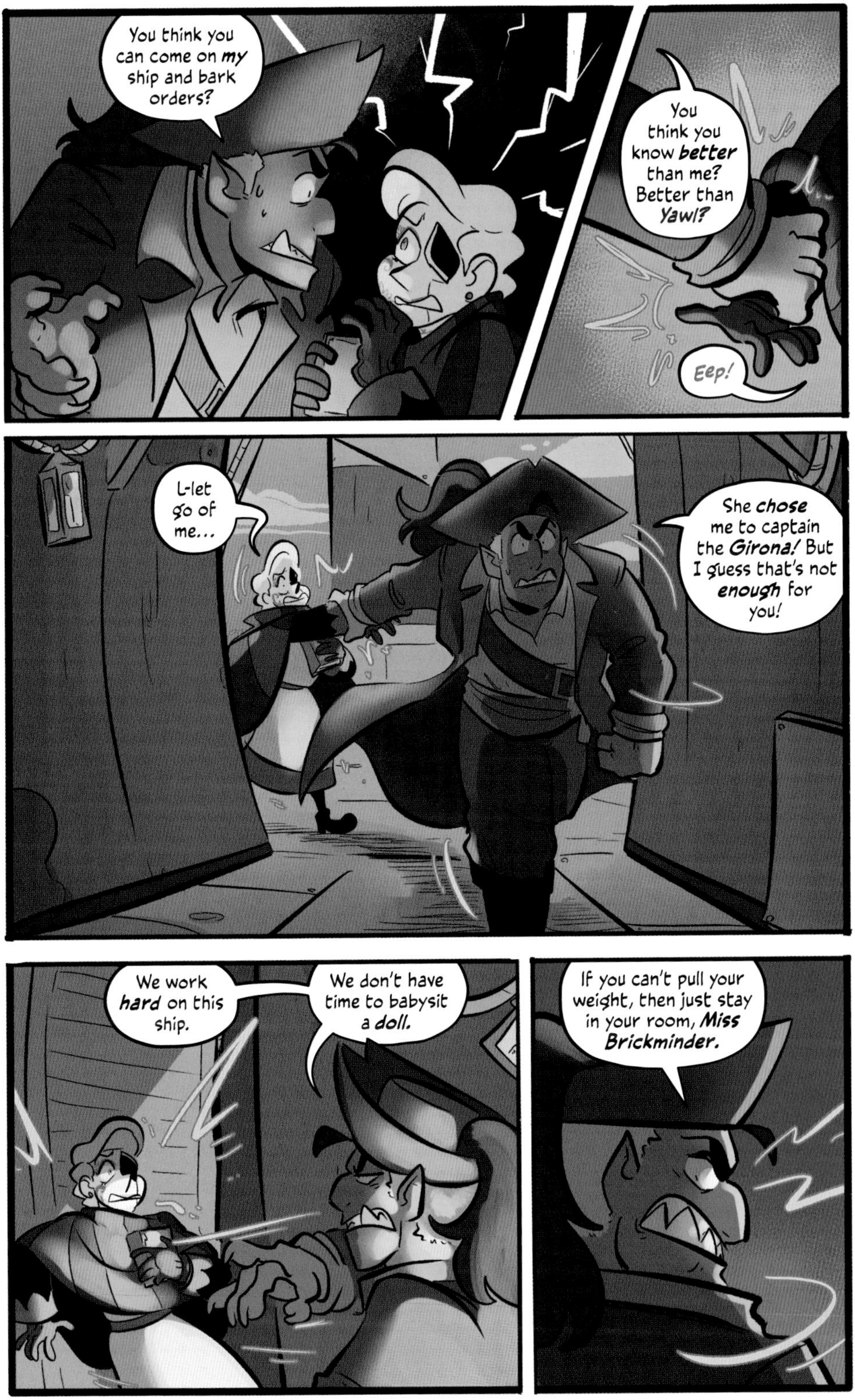
You think you can come on *my* ship and bark orders?
You think you know **better** than me? Better than *Yawl?*
Eep!
L-let go of me...
She **chose** me to captain the ***Girona!*** But I guess that's not ***enough*** for you!
We work ***hard*** on this ship.
We don't have time to babysit a ***doll.***
If you can't pull your weight, then just stay in your room, ***Miss Brickminder.***

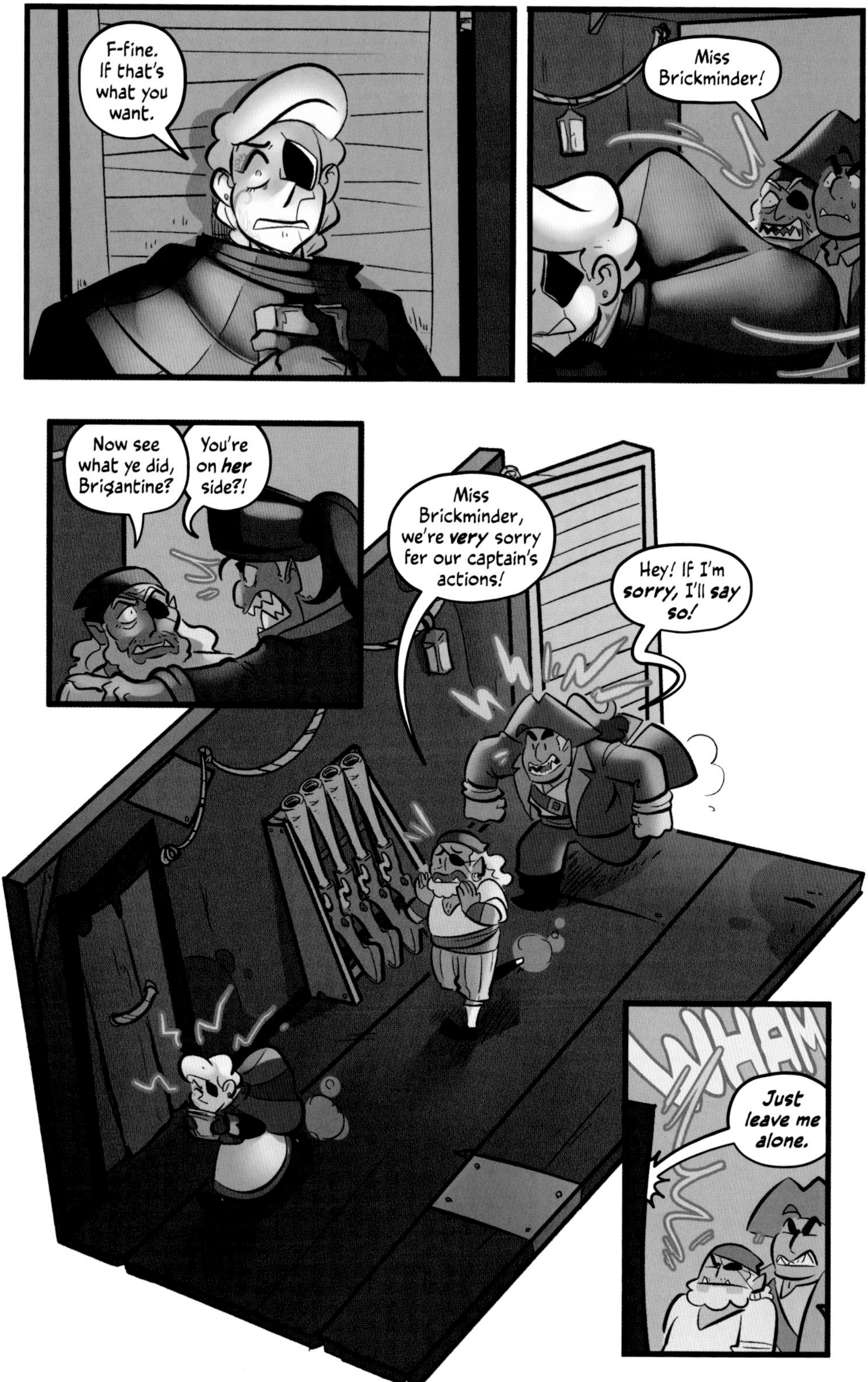
F-fine. If that's what you want.
Miss Brickminder!
Now see what ye did, Brigantine?
You're on her side?!
Miss Brickminder, we're very sorry fer our captain's actions!
Hey! If I'm sorry, I'll say so!
WHAM
Just leave me alone.

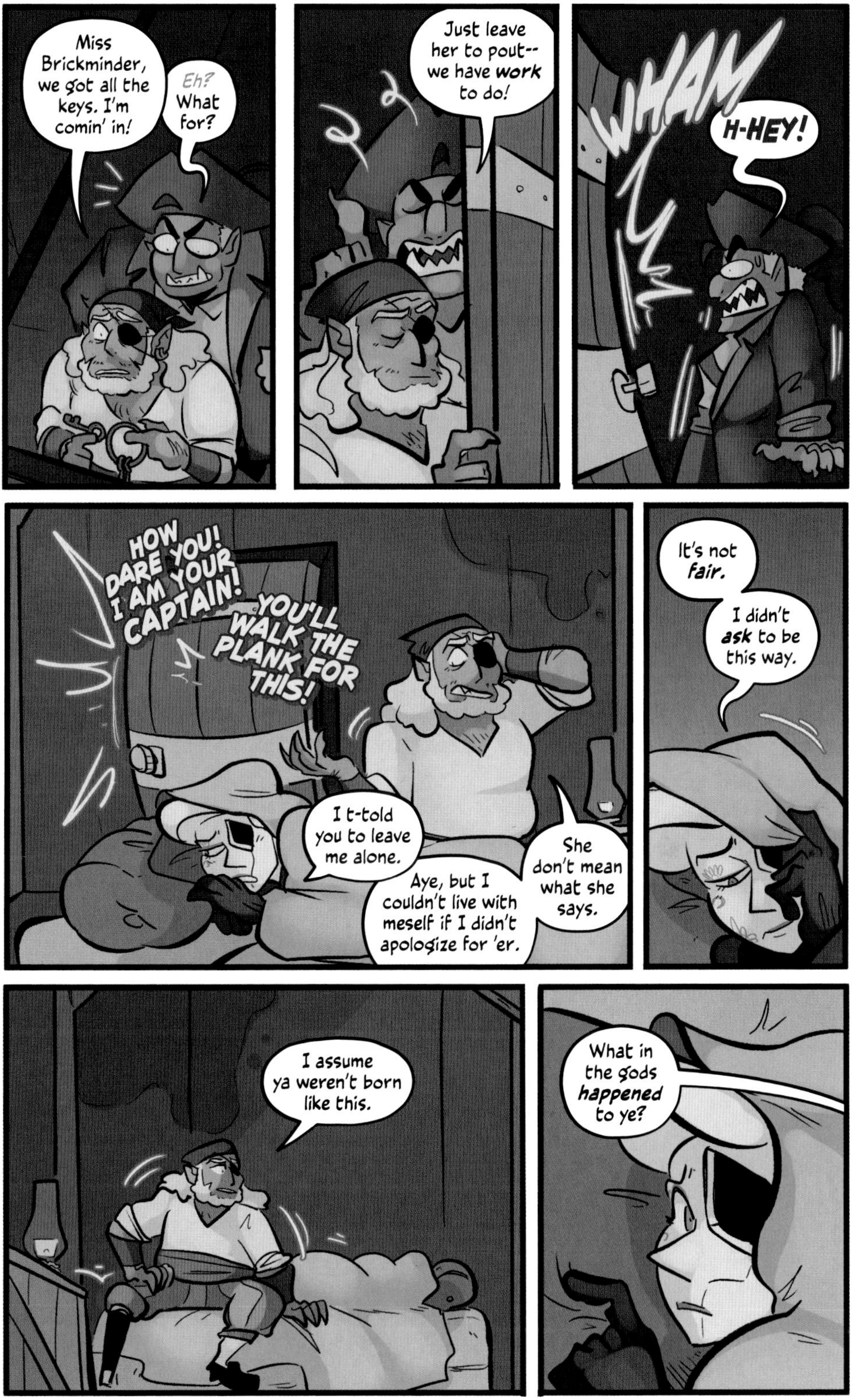

Miss Brickminder, we got all the keys. I'm comin' in!
Eh? What for?
Just leave her to pout-- we have **work** to do!
WHAM
H-HEY!
HOW DARE YOU! I AM YOUR CAPTAIN!
YOU'LL WALK THE PLANK FOR THIS!
I t-told you to leave me alone.
Aye, but I couldn't live with meself if I didn't apologize for 'er.
She don't mean what she says.
It's not *fair.*
I didn't *ask* to be this way.
I assume ya weren't born like this.
What in the gods *happened* to ye?

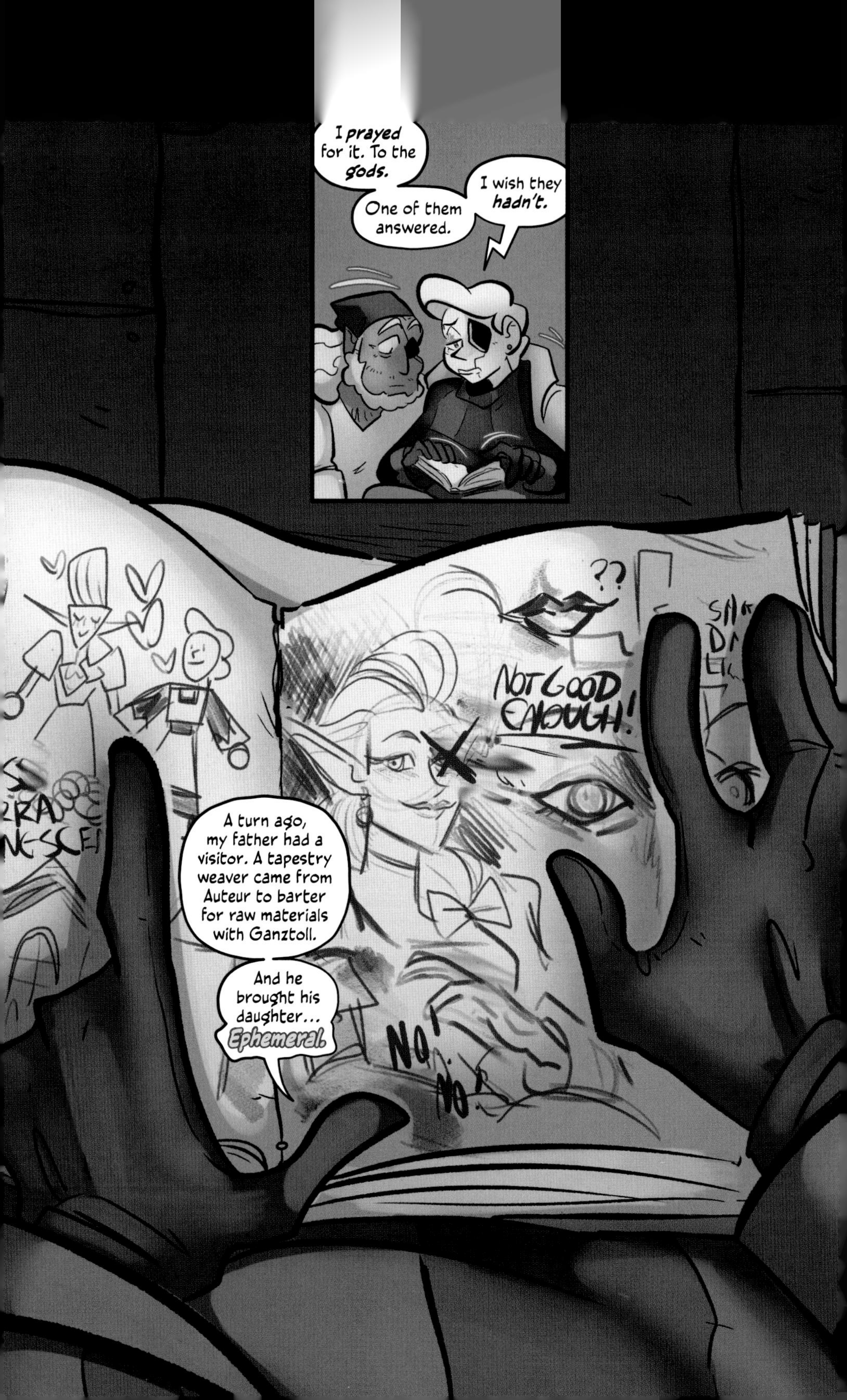
I prayed for it. To the gods.
One of them answered.
I wish they hadn't.
??
NOT GOOD ENOUGH!
A turn ago, my father had a visitor. A tapestry weaver came from Auteur to barter for raw materials with Ganztoll.
And he brought his daughter… Ephemeral.
NO! NO!

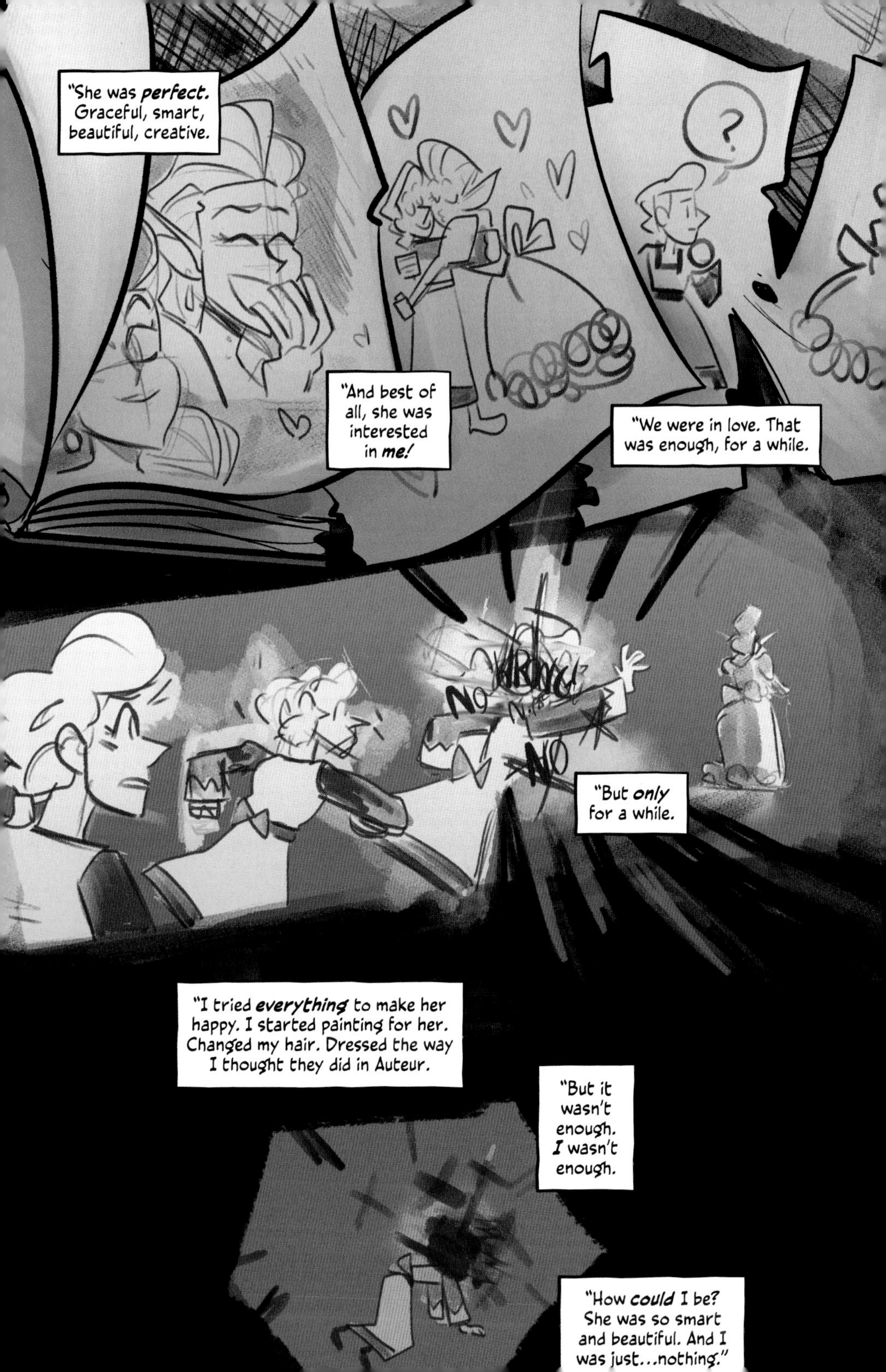
"She was *perfect.* Graceful, smart, beautiful, creative.
"And best of all, she was interested in *me!*
"We were in love. That was enough, for a while.
NO
NO
"But *only* for a while.
"I tried *everything* to make her happy. I started painting for her. Changed my hair. Dressed the way I thought they did in Auteur.
"But it wasn't enough. *I* wasn't enough.
"How *could* I be? She was so smart and beautiful. And I was just...nothing."

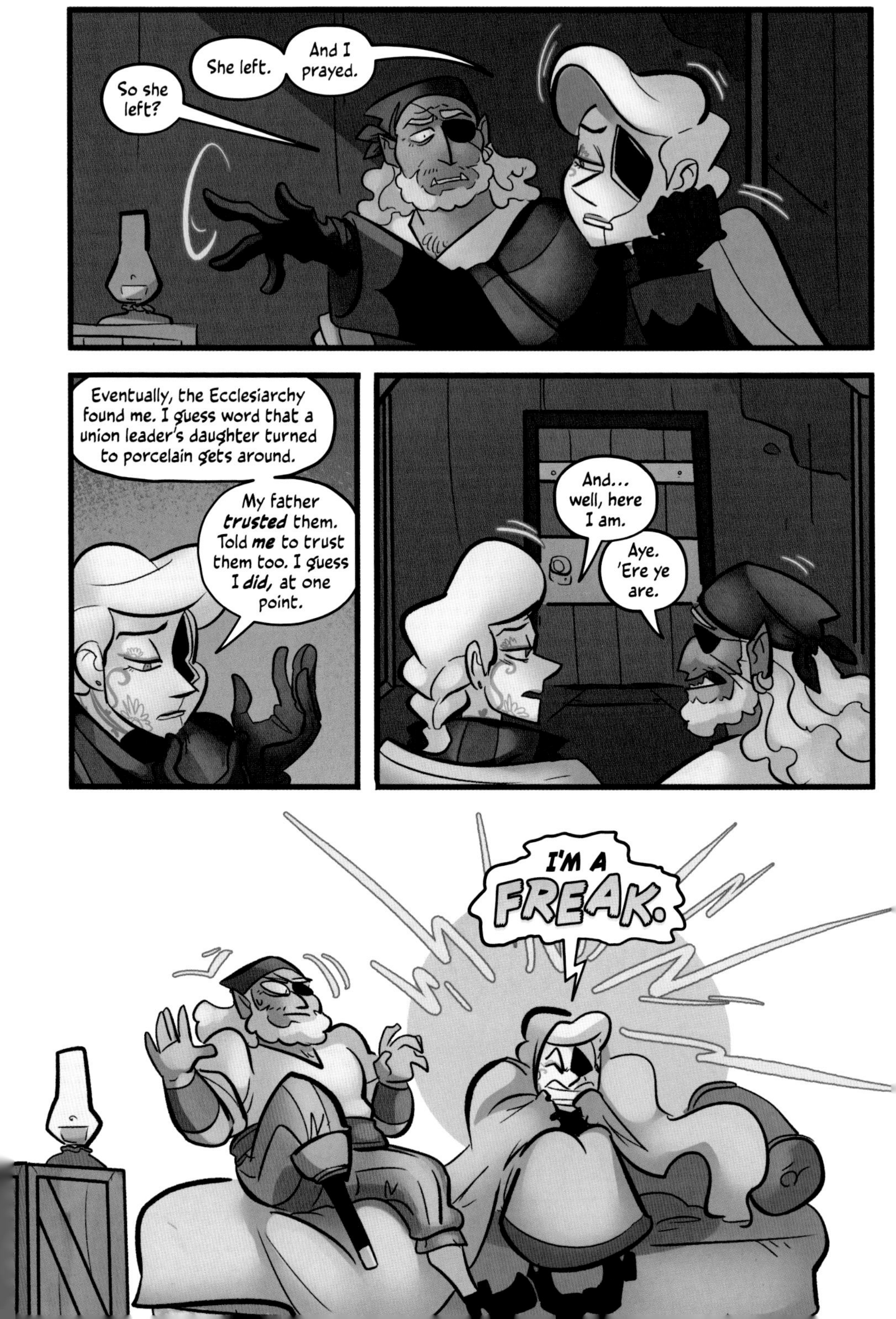
So she left?
She left.
And I prayed.
Eventually, the Ecclesiarchy found me. I guess word that a union leader's daughter turned to porcelain gets around.
My father *trusted* them. Told *me* to trust them too. I guess I *did,* at one point.
And... well, here I am.
Aye. 'Ere ye are.
I'M A FREAK.

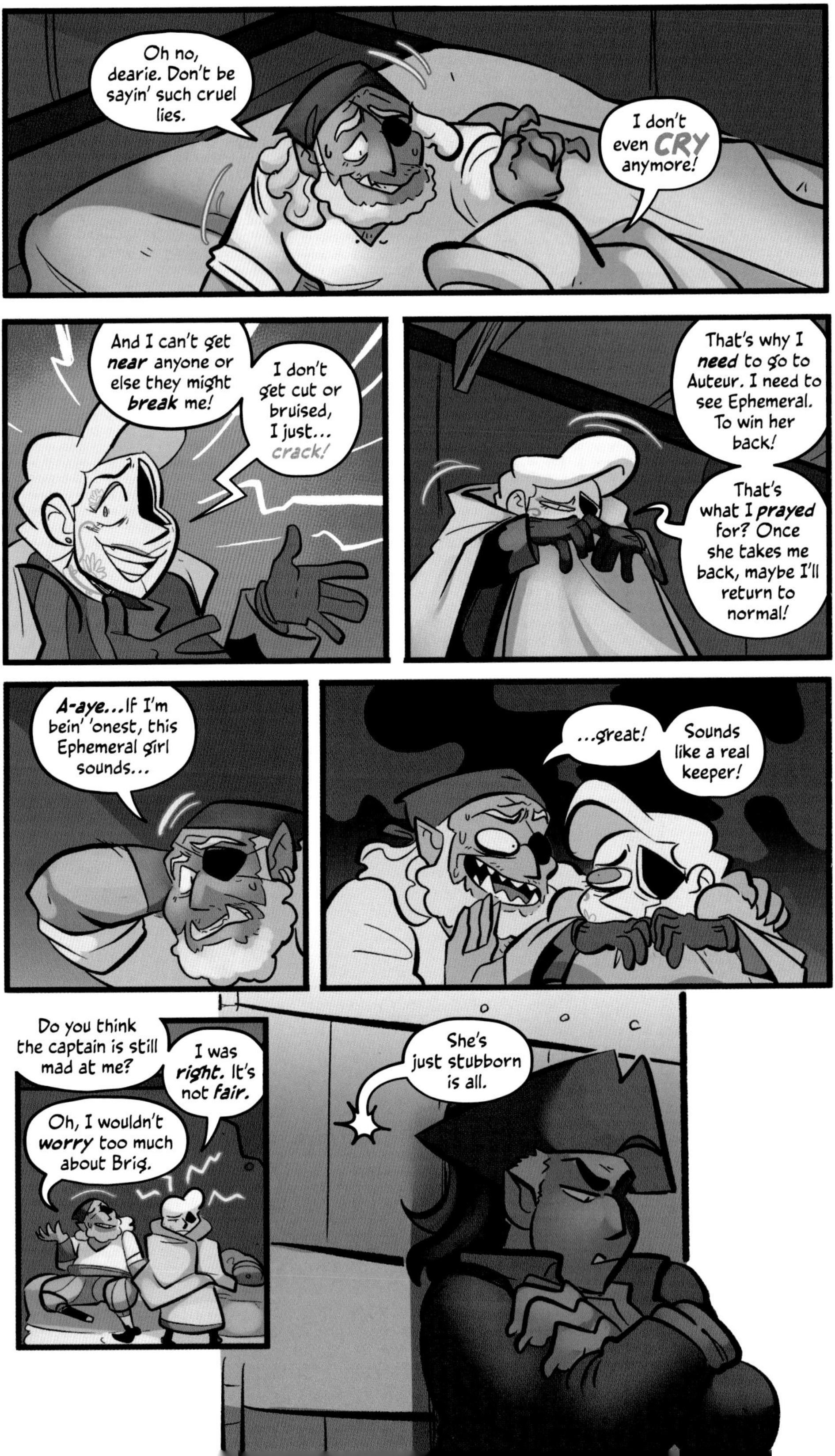
Oh no, dearie. Don't be sayin' such cruel lies.
I don't even CRY anymore!
And I can't get near anyone or else they might break me!
I don't get cut or bruised, I just... crack!
That's why I need to go to Auteur. I need to see Ephemeral. To win her back!
That's what I prayed for? Once she takes me back, maybe I'll return to normal!
A-aye...If I'm bein' 'onest, this Ephemeral girl sounds...
...great!
Sounds like a real keeper!
Do you think the captain is still mad at me?
I was right. It's not fair.
Oh, I wouldn't worry too much about Brig.
She's just stubborn is all.

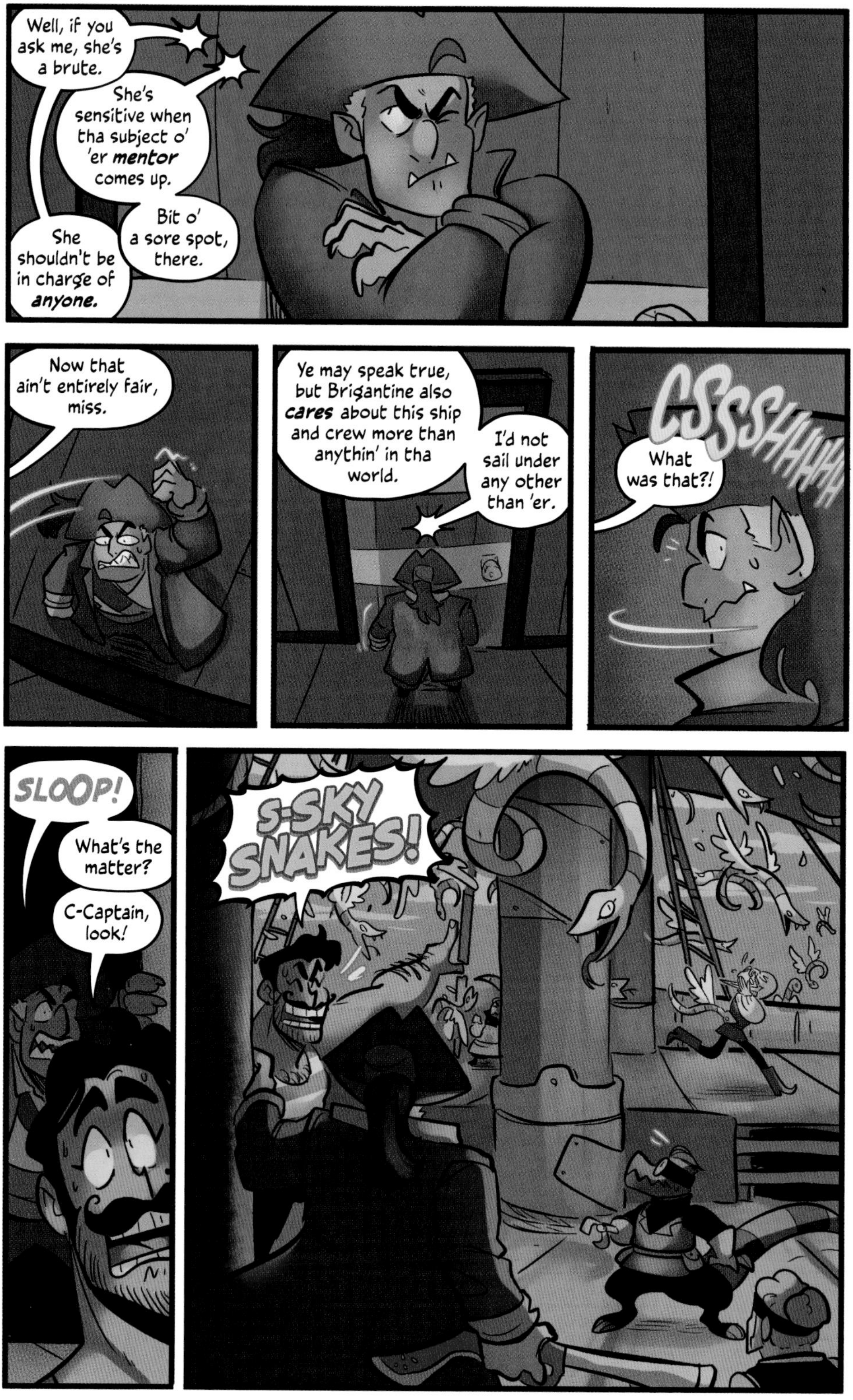
Well, if you ask me, she's a brute.
She's sensitive when tha subject o' 'er **mentor** comes up.
She shouldn't be in charge of ***anyone.***
Bit o' a sore spot, there.
Now that ain't entirely fair, miss.
Ye may speak true, but Brigantine also ***cares*** about this ship and crew more than anythin' in tha world.
I'd not sail under any other than 'er.
CSSSHHHH
What was that?!
SLOOP!
What's the matter?
C-Captain, look!
S-SKY SNAKES!

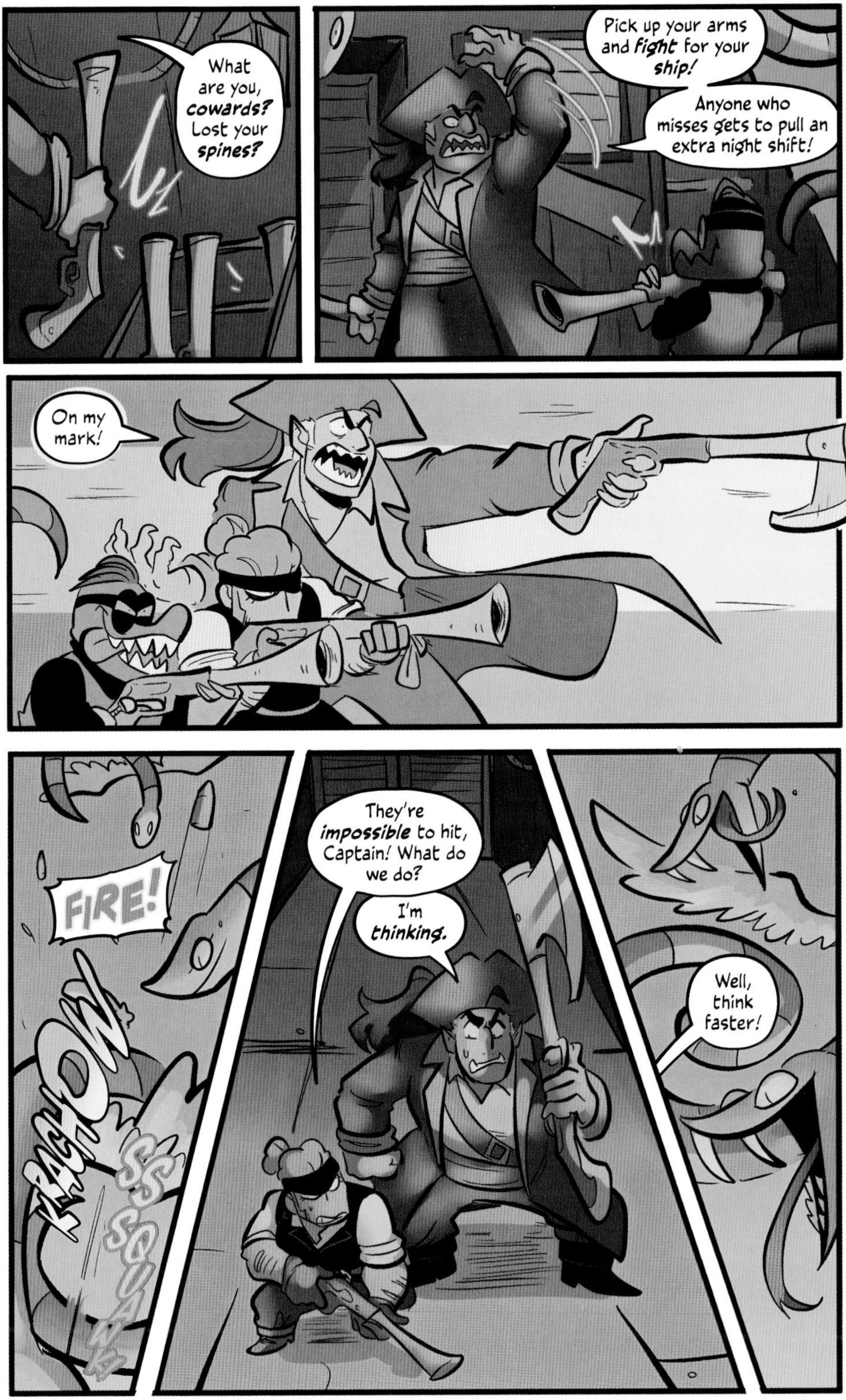
What are you, **cowards?** Lost your **spines?**
Pick up your arms and **fight** for your **ship!**
Anyone who misses gets to pull an extra night shift!
On my mark!
FIRE!
KRACHOW
SSSQUAWK
They're **impossible** to hit, Captain! What do we do?
I'm **thinking.**
Well, think faster!

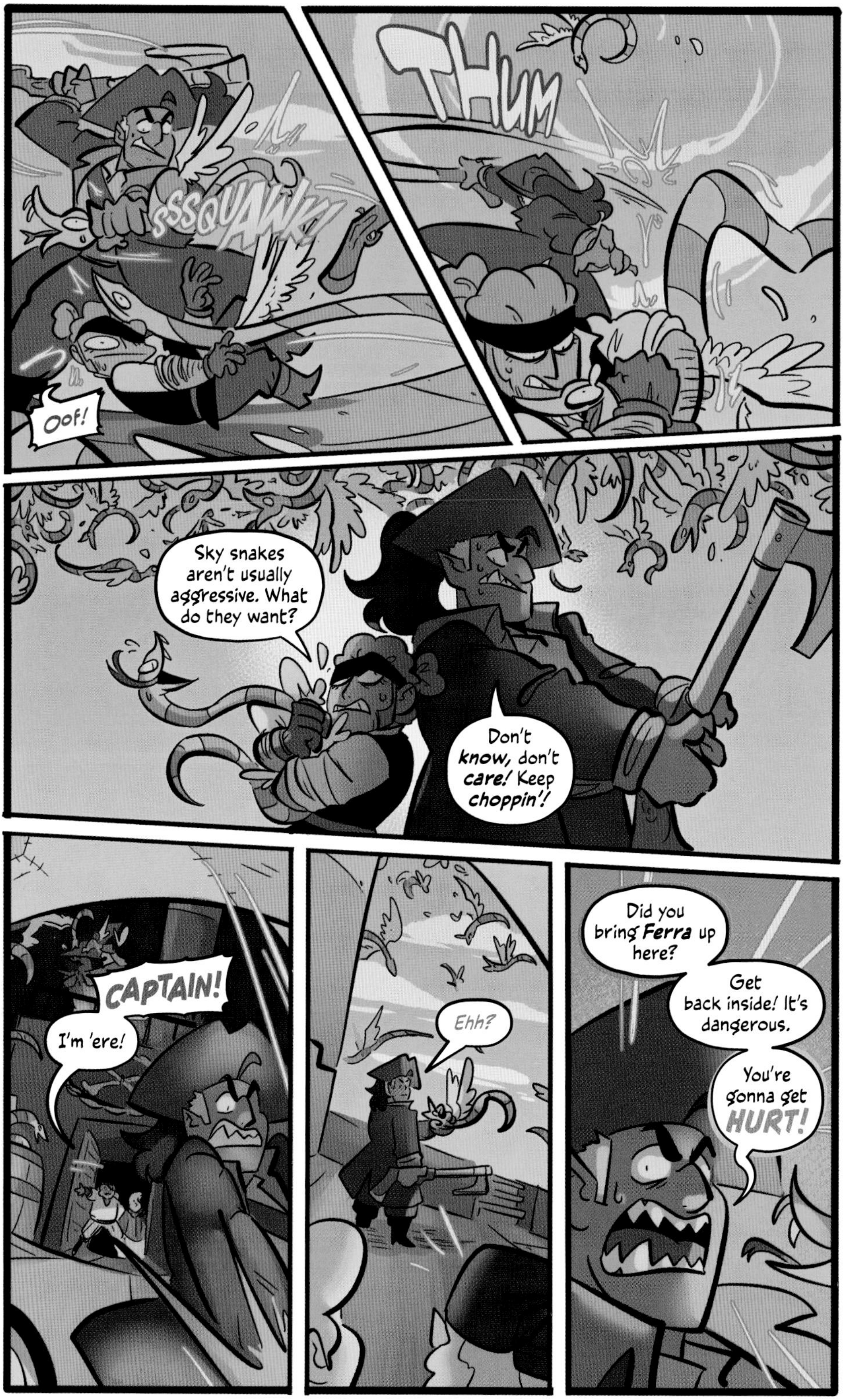
SSSQUAWK!
Oof!
THUM
Sky snakes aren't usually aggressive. What do they want?
Don't know, don't care! Keep choppin'!
CAPTAIN!
I'm 'ere!
Ehh?
Did you bring Ferra up here?
Get back inside! It's dangerous.
You're gonna get HURT!

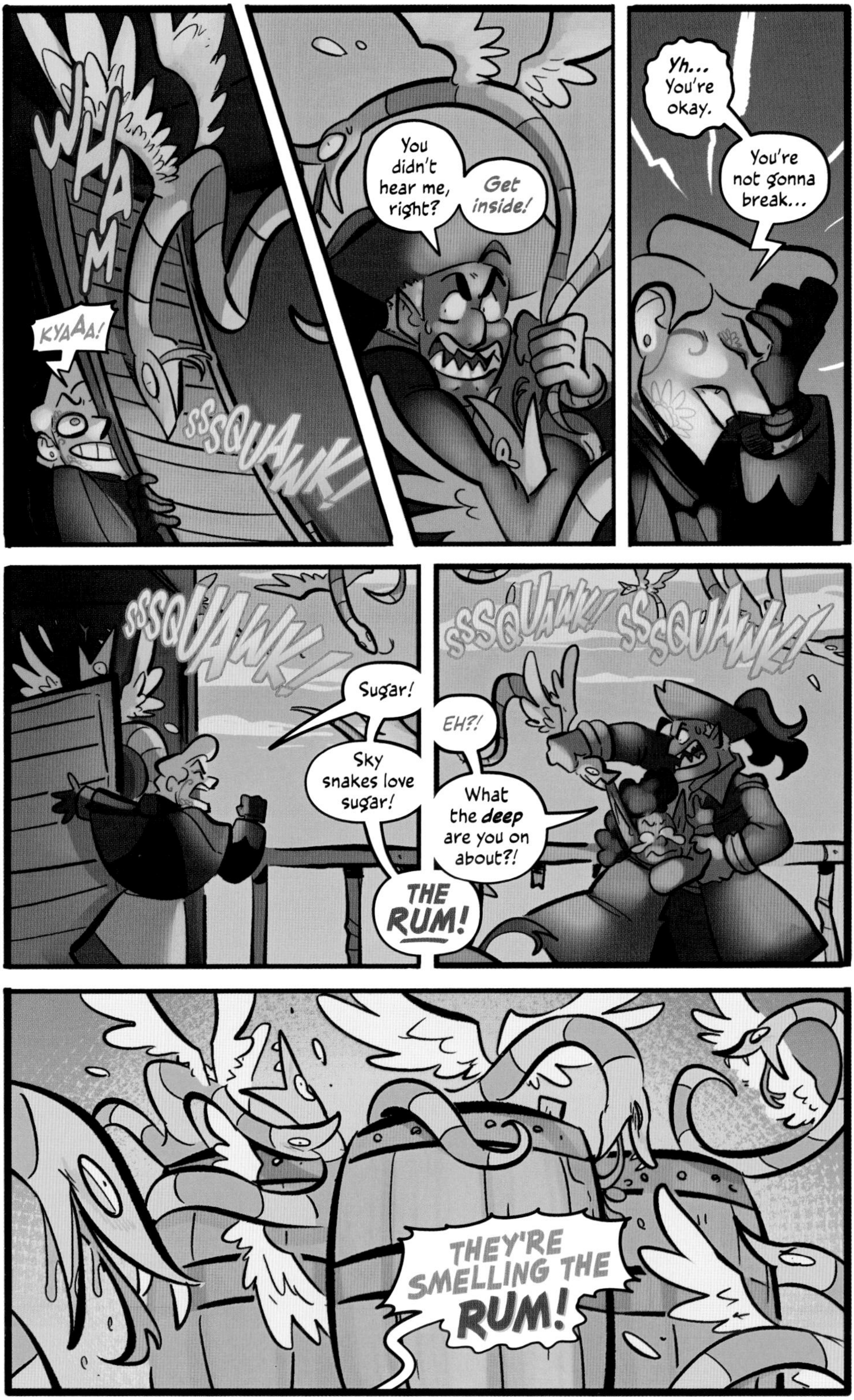
WHAM
KYAAA!
SSSQUAWK!
You didn't hear me, right?
Get inside!
Yh... You're okay.
You're not gonna break...
SSSQUAWK!
Sugar!
Sky snakes love sugar!
THE RUM!
SSSQUAWK! SSSQUAWK!
EH?!
What the deep are you on about?!
THEY'RE SMELLING THE RUM!

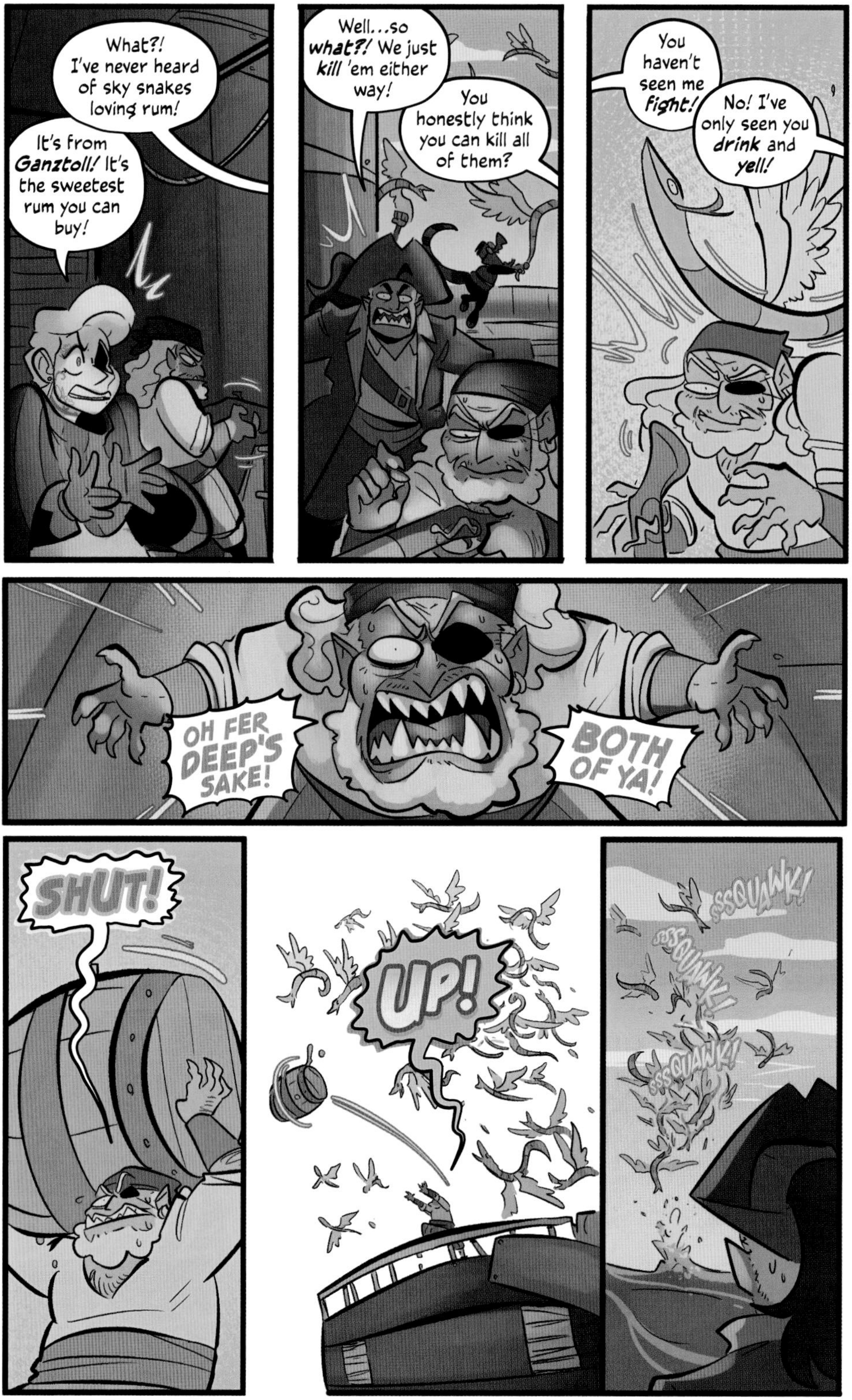
What?! I've never heard of sky snakes loving rum!
It's from Ganztoll! It's the sweetest rum you can buy!
Well...so what?! We just kill 'em either way!
You honestly think you can kill all of them?
You haven't seen me fight!
No! I've only seen you drink and yell!
OH FER DEEP'S SAKE!
BOTH OF YA!
SHUT!
UP!
SSSQUAWK!
SSSQUAWK!
SSSQUAWK!

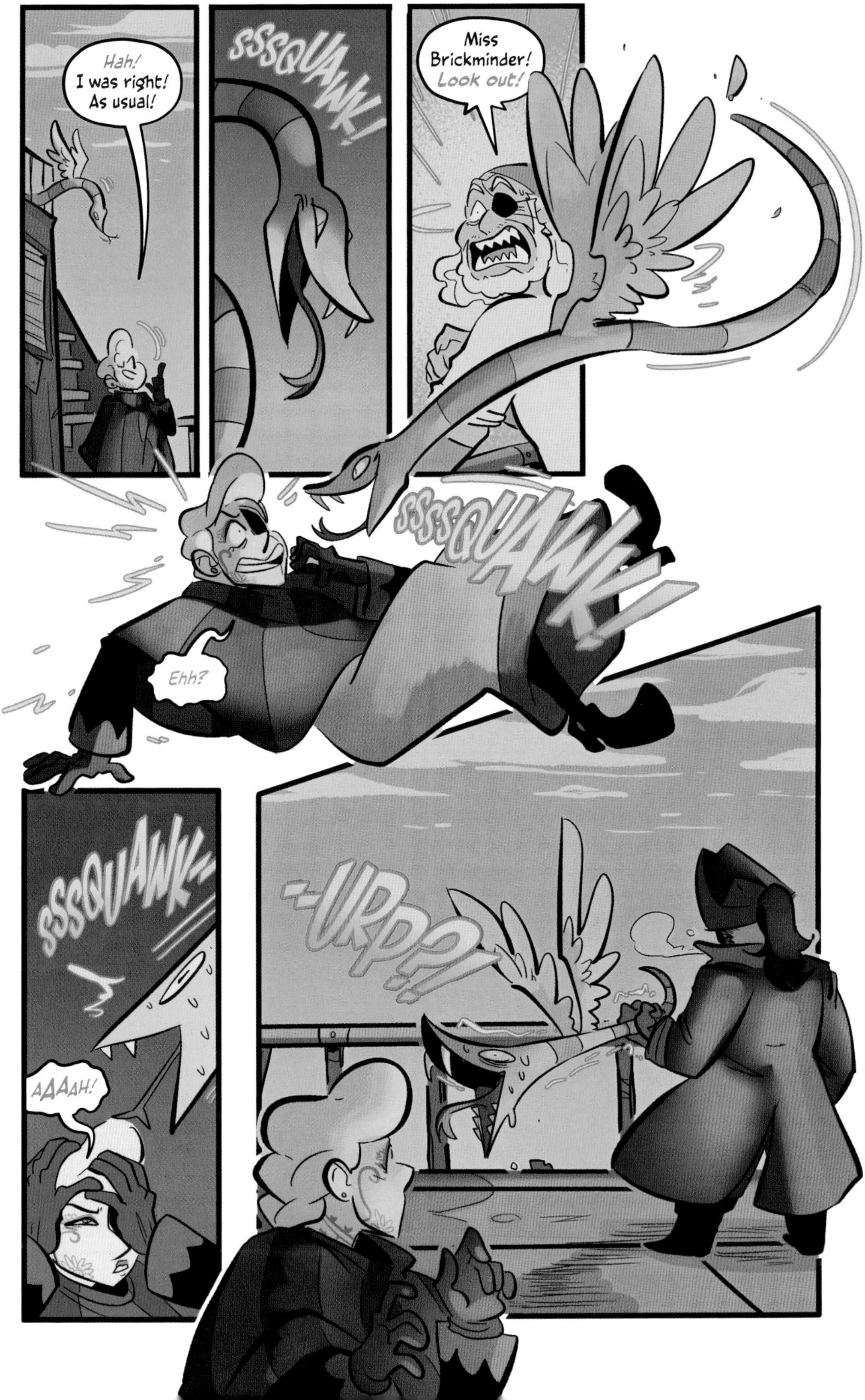
Hah! I was right! As usual!
SSSQUAWK!
Miss Brickminder! Look out!
SSSSQUAWK!!
Ehh?
SSSQUAWK--
AAAAH!
-URP?!

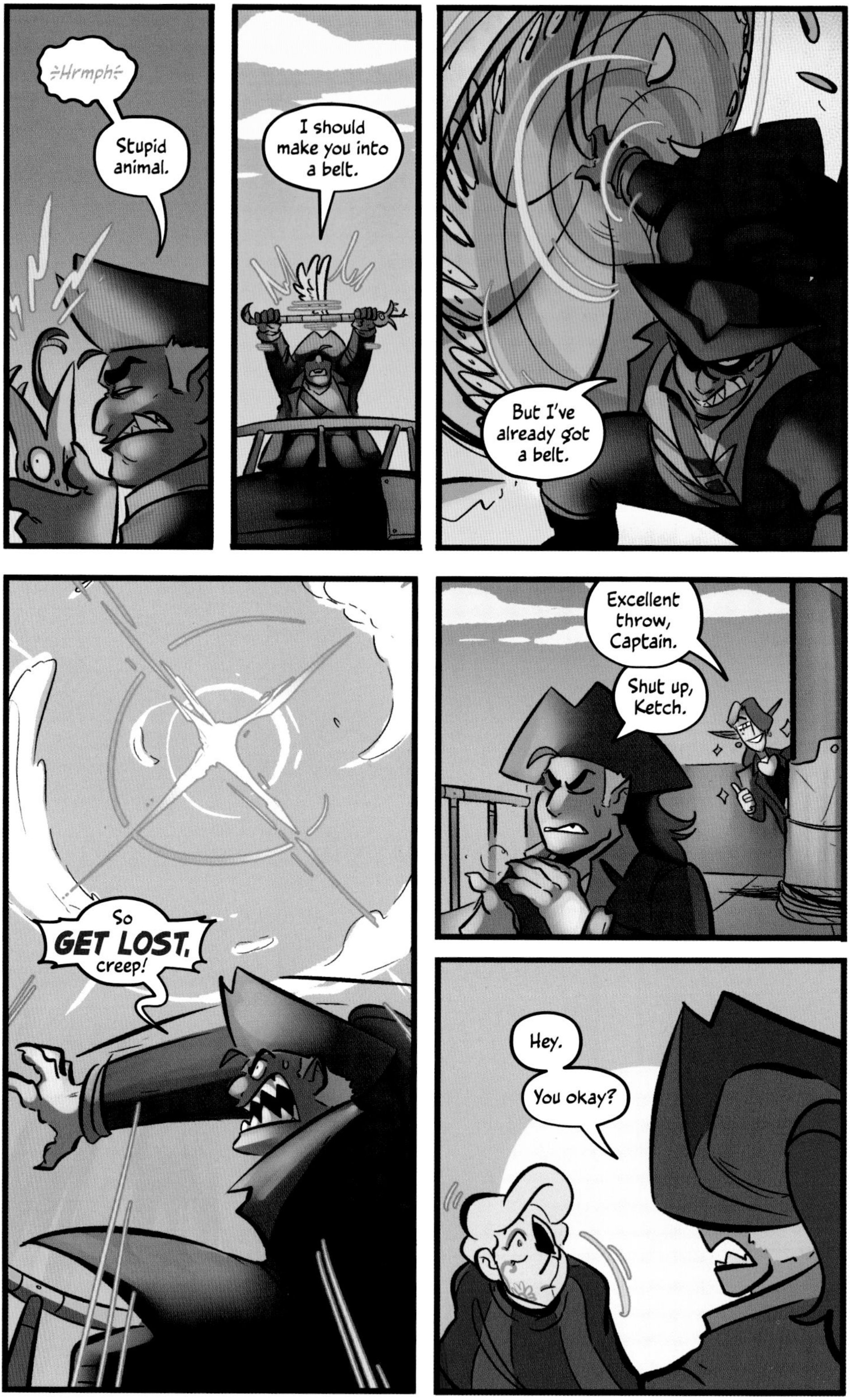
Hrmph
Stupid animal.
I should make you into a belt.
But I've already got a belt.
So GET LOST, creep!
Excellent throw, Captain.
Shut up, Ketch.
Hey.
You okay?

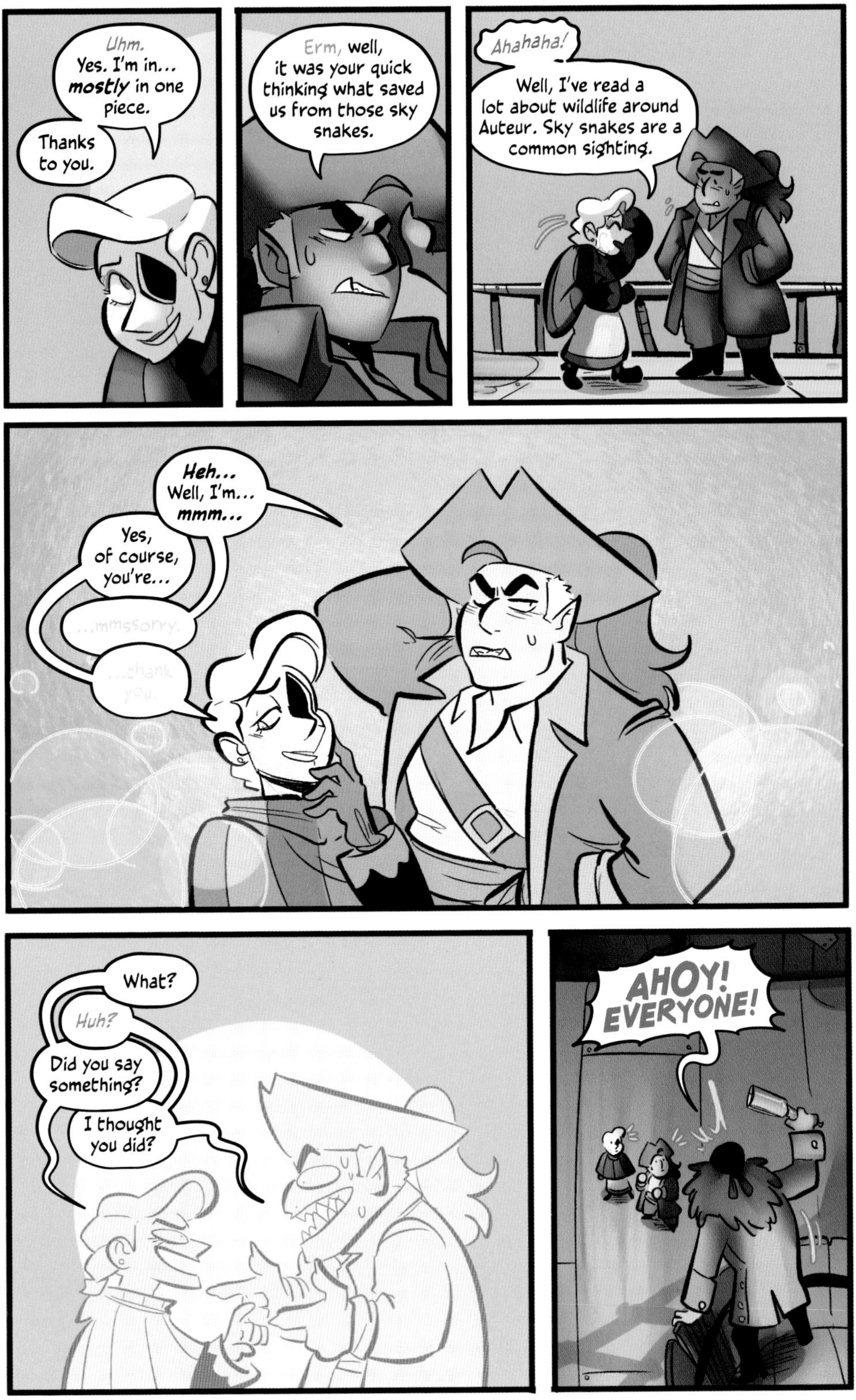
Uhm.
Yes. I'm in... *mostly* in one piece.
Thanks to you.
Erm, well, it was your quick thinking what saved us from those sky snakes.
Ahahaha!
Well, I've read a lot about wildlife around Auteur. Sky snakes are a common sighting.
Heh... Well, I'm... mmm...
Yes, of course, you're...
...mmsorry.
...thank you.
What?
Huh?
Did you say something?
I thought you did?
AHOY! EVERYONE!

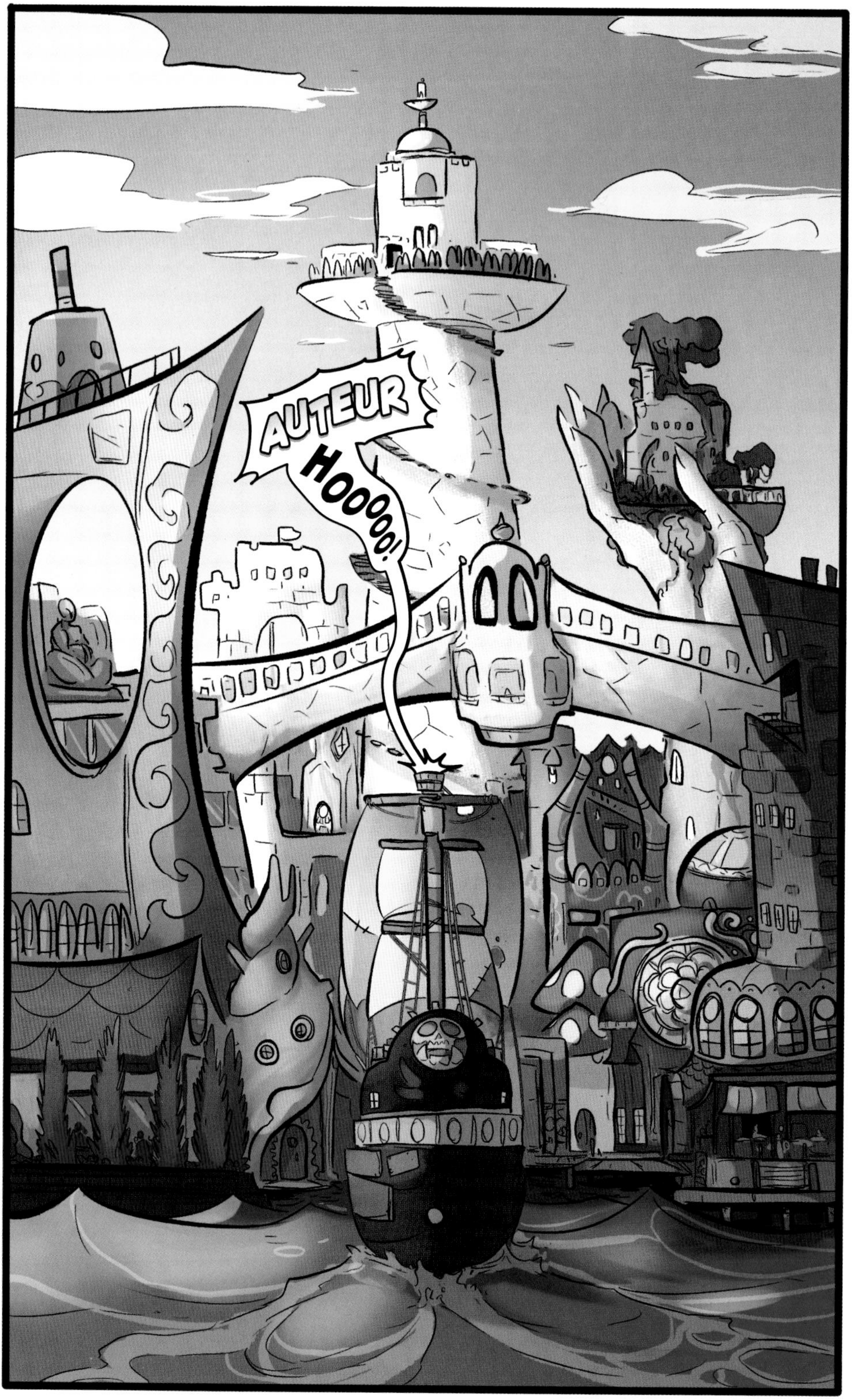
AUTEUR HOOOOOO!

Chapter 3

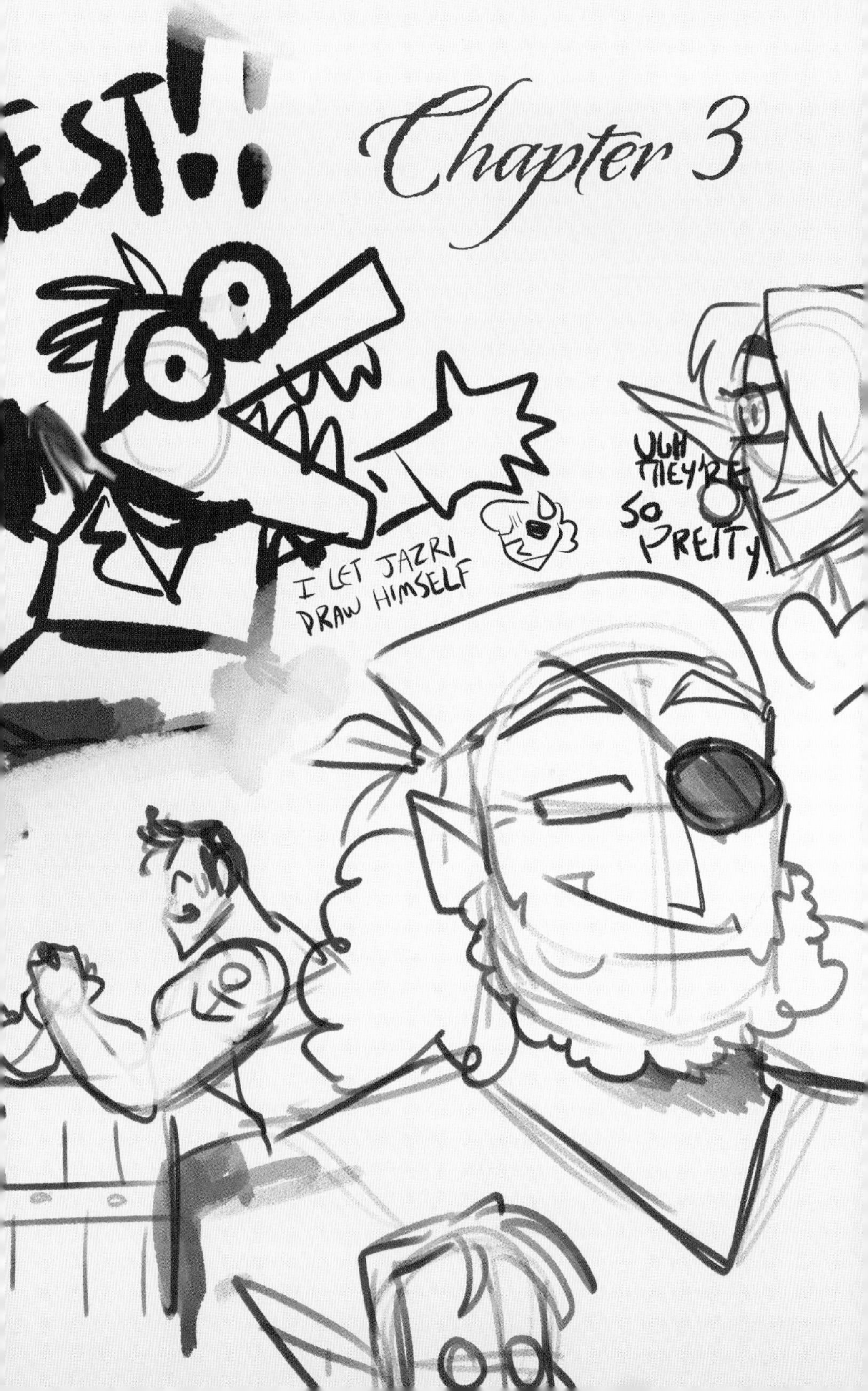
EST!!
I LET JAZRI DRAW HIMSELF
UGH THEYRE SO PRETTY.

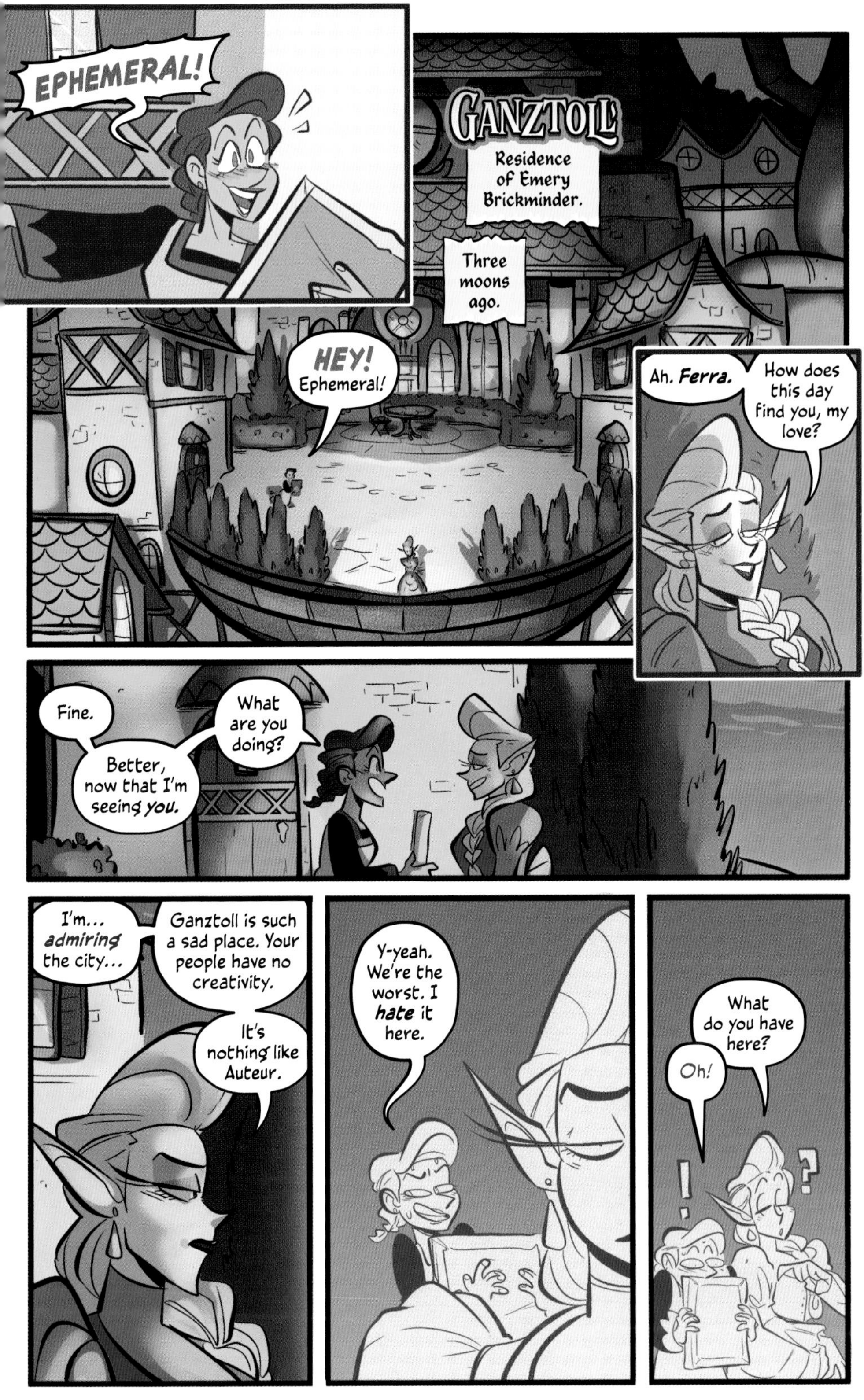
EPHEMERAL!
GANZTOLL
Residence of Emery Brickminder.
Three moons ago.
HEY! Ephemeral!
Ah. Ferra.
How does this day find you, my love?
Fine.
Better, now that I'm seeing you.
What are you doing?
I'm... admiring the city...
Ganztoll is such a sad place. Your people have no creativity.
It's nothing like Auteur.
Y-yeah. We're the worst. I hate it here.
Oh!
What do you have here?
!
?

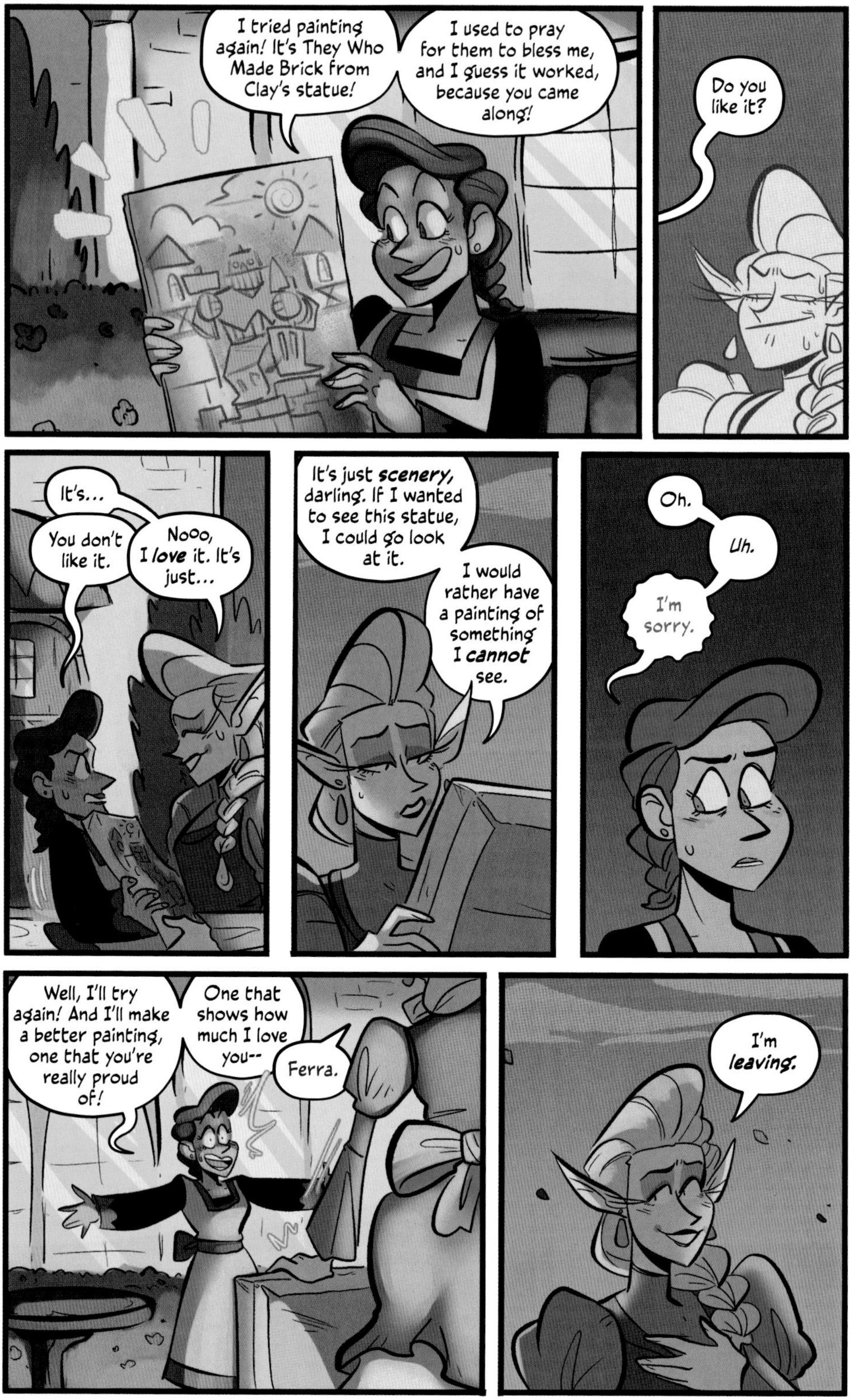
I tried painting again! It's They Who Made Brick from Clay's statue!
I used to pray for them to bless me, and I guess it worked, because you came along!
Do you like it?
It's...
You don't like it.
Nooo, I *love* it. It's just...
It's just ***scenery,*** darling. If I wanted to see this statue, I could go look at it.
I would rather have a painting of something I ***cannot*** see.
Oh.
Uh.
I'm sorry.
Well, I'll try again! And I'll make a better painting, one that you're really proud of!
One that shows how much I love you--
Ferra.
I'm ***leaving.***

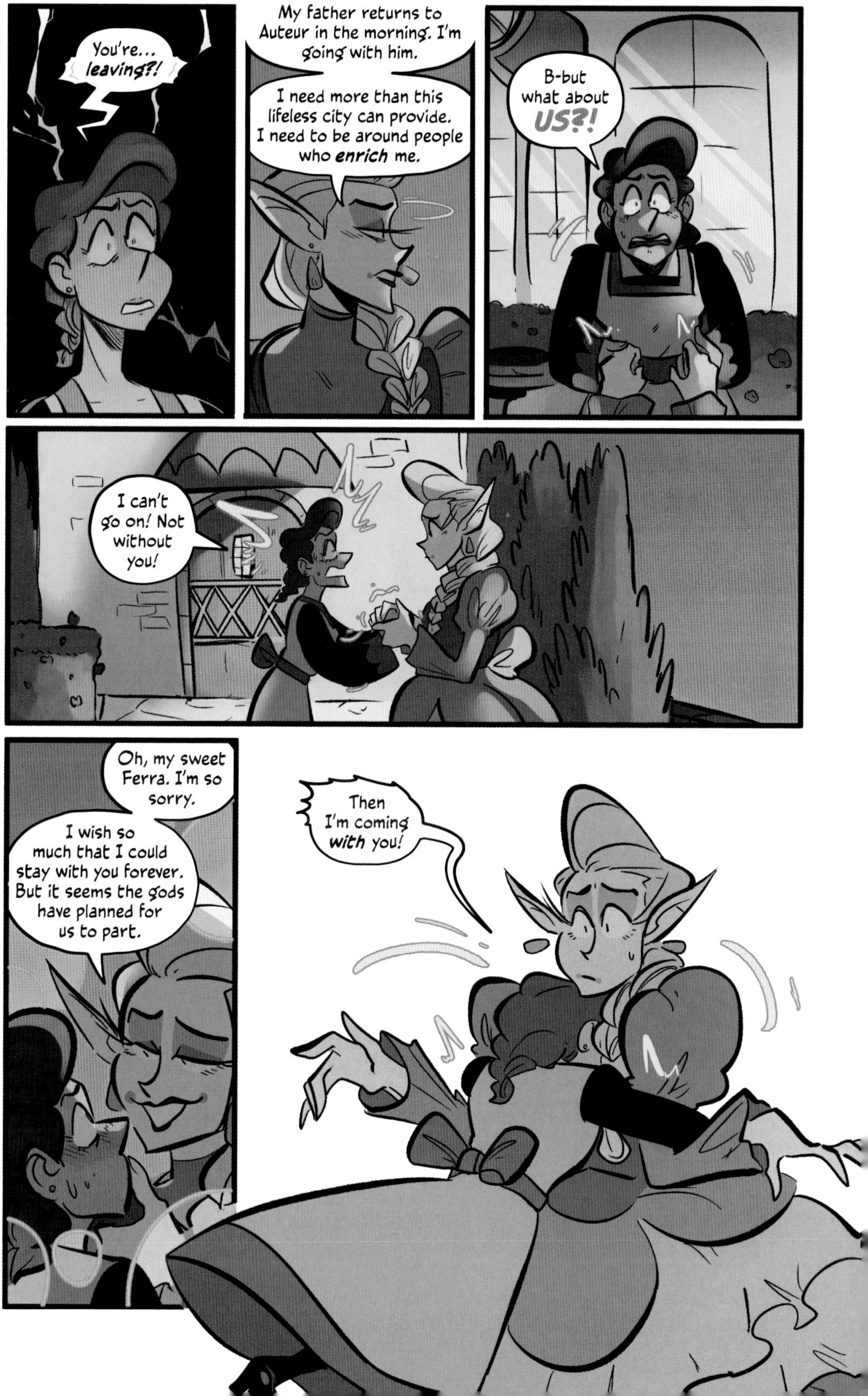

You're... leaving?!
My father returns to Auteur in the morning. I'm going with him.
I need more than this lifeless city can provide. I need to be around people who enrich me.
B-but what about US?!
I can't go on! Not without you!
Oh, my sweet Ferra. I'm so sorry.
I wish so much that I could stay with you forever. But it seems the gods have planned for us to part.
Then I'm coming with you!

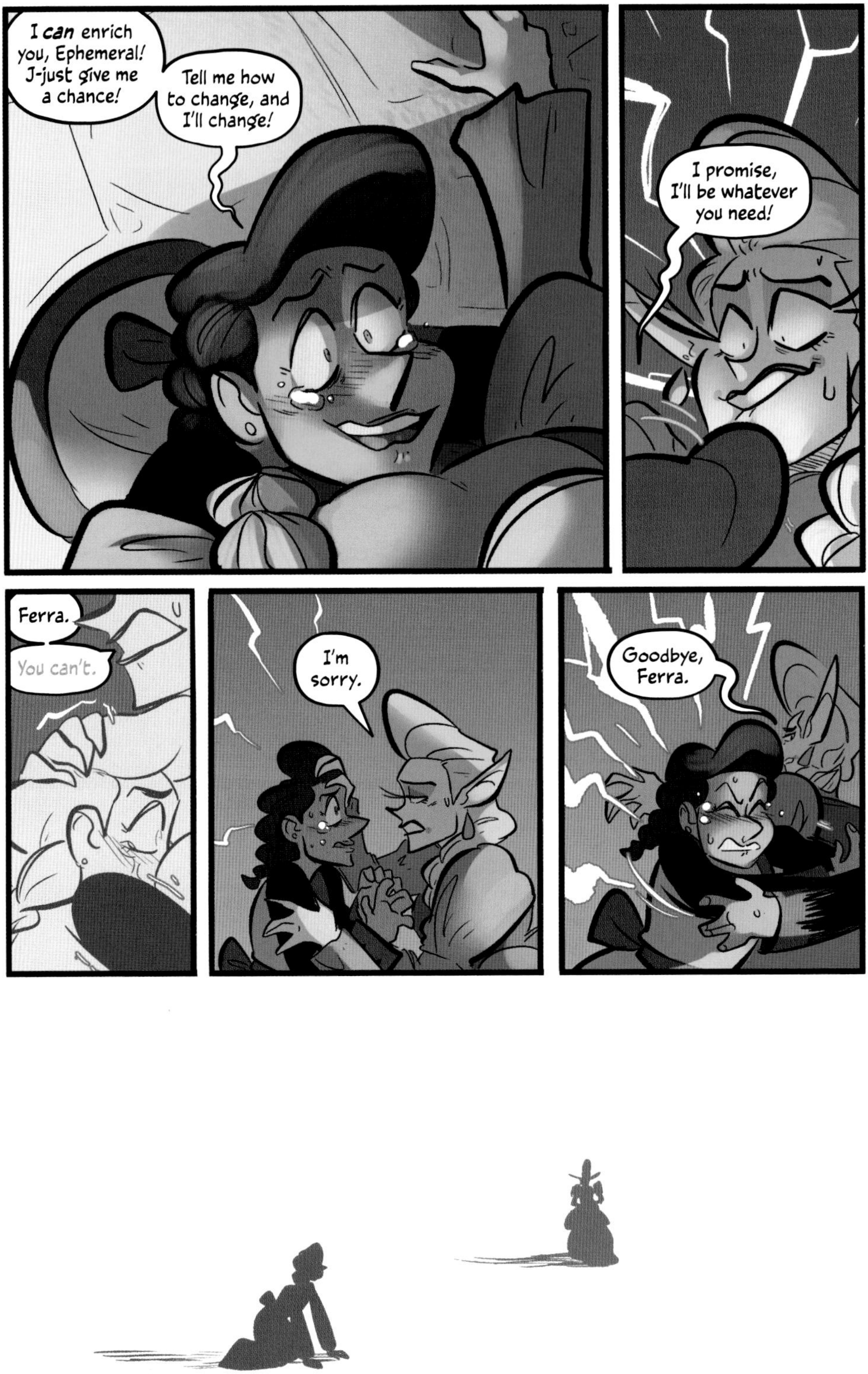
I can enrich you, Ephemeral! J-just give me a chance!
Tell me how to change, and I'll change!
I promise, I'll be whatever you need!
Ferra.
You can't.
I'm sorry.
Goodbye, Ferra.

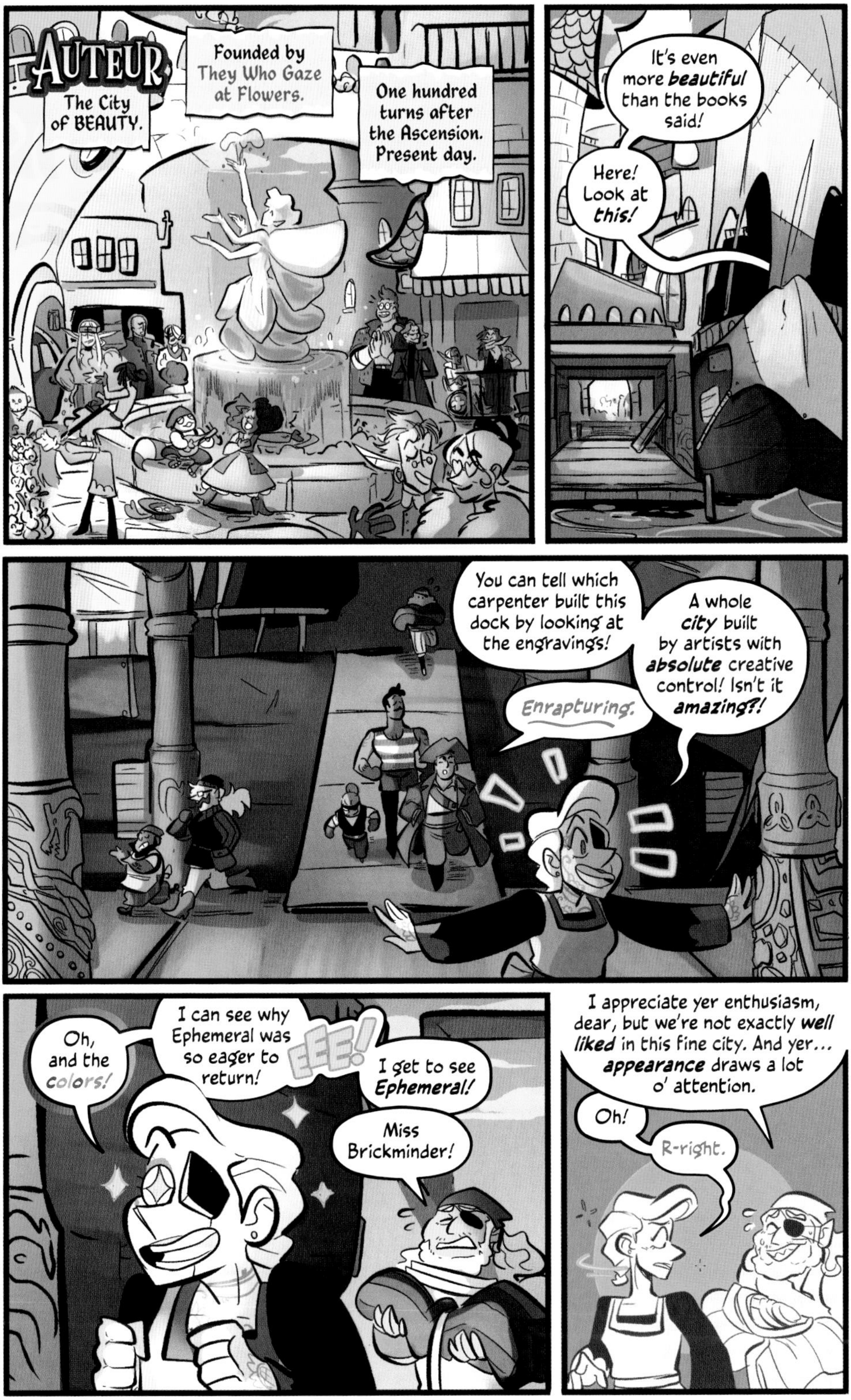
AUTEUR
The City of BEAUTY.
Founded by They Who Gaze at Flowers.
One hundred turns after the Ascension. Present day.
It's even more beautiful than the books said!
Here! Look at this!
You can tell which carpenter built this dock by looking at the engravings!
A whole city built by artists with absolute creative control! Isn't it amazing?!
Enrapturing.
Oh, and the colors!
I can see why Ephemeral was so eager to return!
EEE!
I get to see Ephemeral!
Miss Brickminder!
I appreciate yer enthusiasm, dear, but we're not exactly well liked in this fine city. And yer... appearance draws a lot o' attention.
Oh!
R-right.

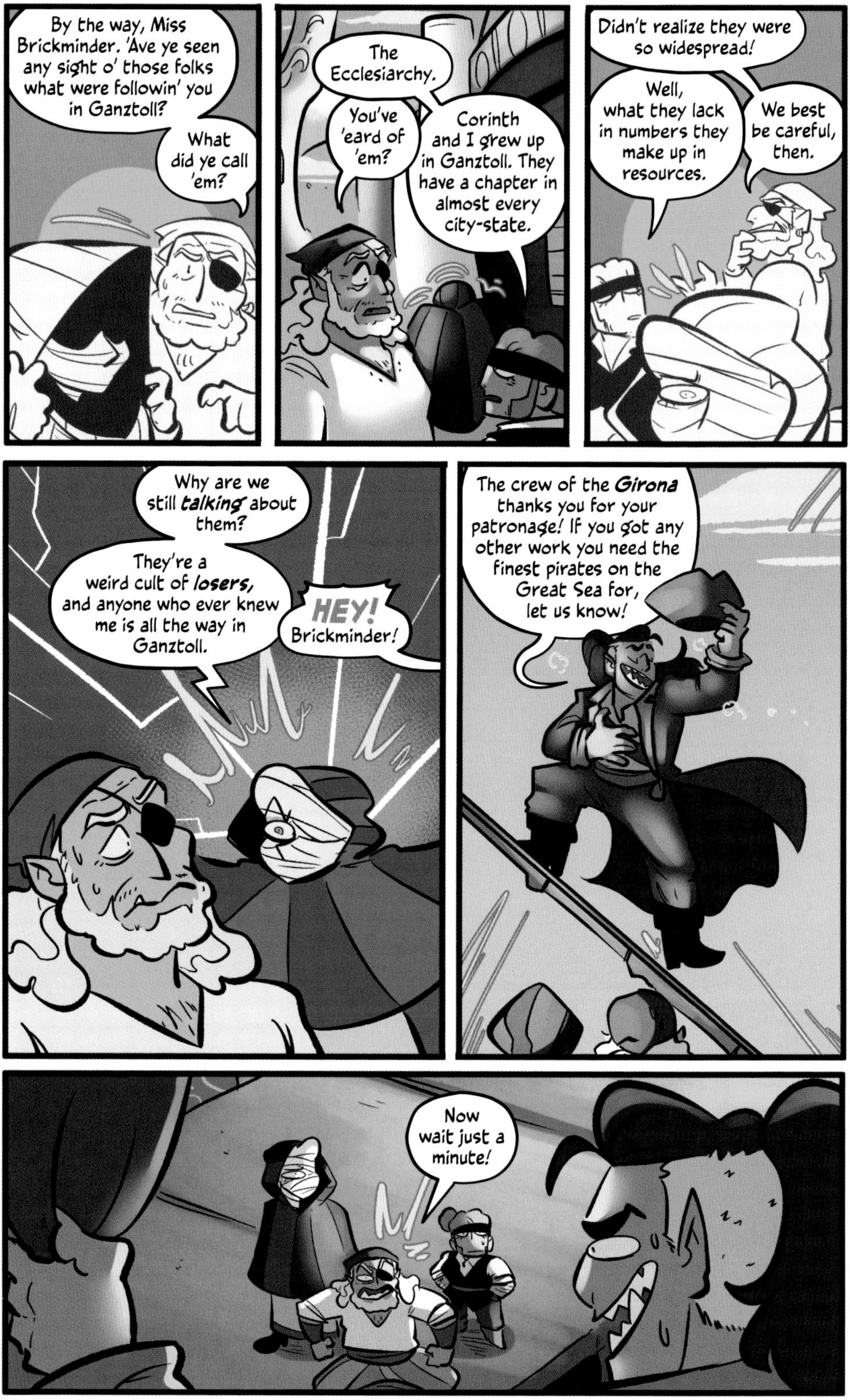
By the way, Miss Brickminder. 'Ave ye seen any sight o' those folks what were followin' you in Ganztoll?
What did ye call 'em?
The Ecclesiarchy.
You've 'eard of 'em?
Corinth and I grew up in Ganztoll. They have a chapter in almost every city-state.
Didn't realize they were so widespread!
Well, what they lack in numbers they make up in resources.
We best be careful, then.
Why are we still *talking* about them?
They're a weird cult of *losers,* and anyone who ever knew me is all the way in Ganztoll.
HEY! Brickminder!
The crew of the *Girona* thanks you for your patronage! If you got any other work you need the finest pirates on the Great Sea for, let us know!
Now wait just a minute!

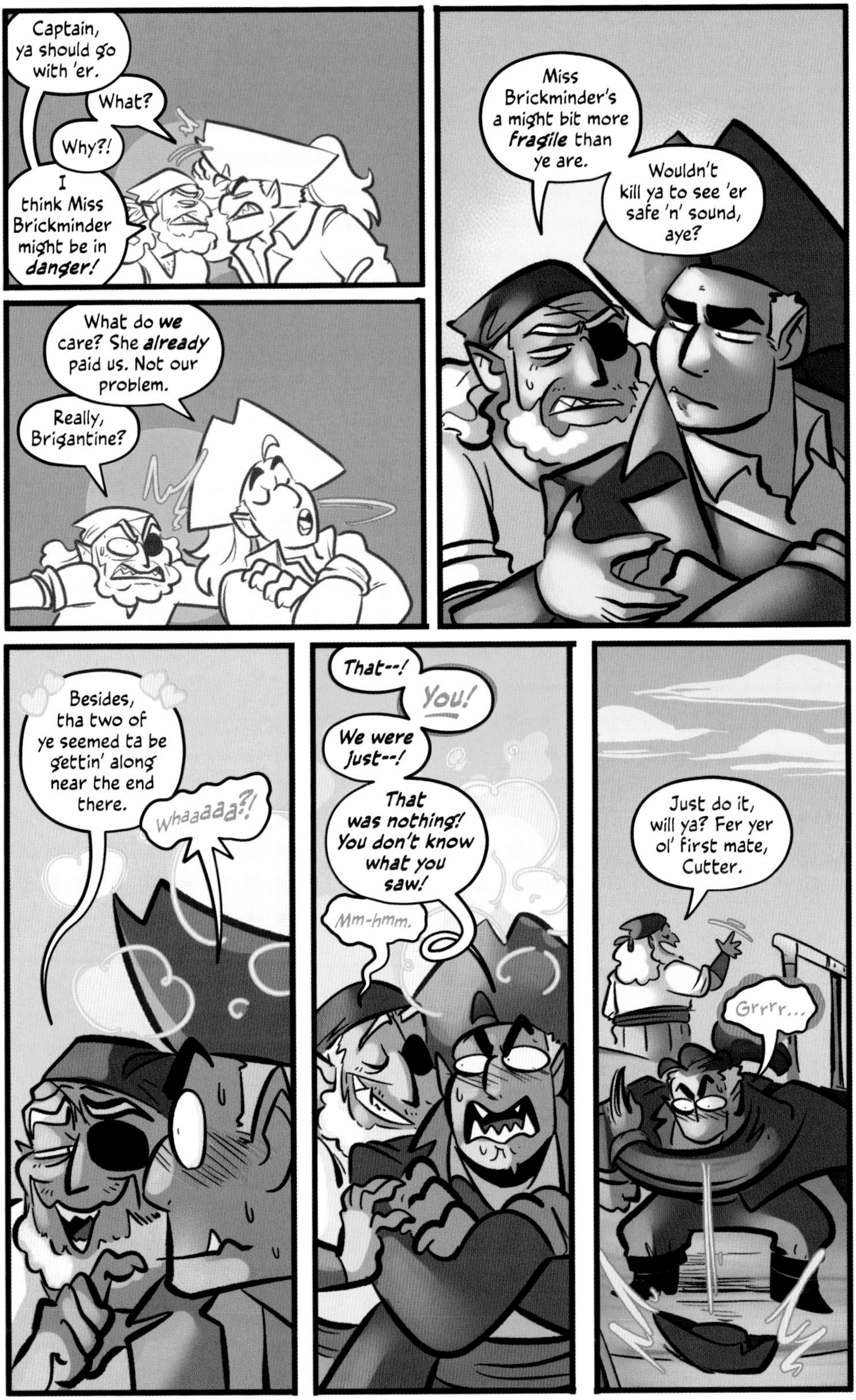

Captain, ya should go with 'er.
What?
Why?!
I think Miss Brickminder might be in *danger!*
Miss Brickminder's a might bit more *fragile* than ye are.
Wouldn't kill ya to see 'er safe 'n' sound, aye?
What do *we* care? She *already* paid us. Not our problem.
Really, Brigantine?
Besides, tha two of ye seemed ta be gettin' along near the end there.
Whaaaaa?!
That--!
You!
We were just--!
That was nothing! You don't know what you saw!
Mm-hmm.
Just do it, will ya? Fer yer ol' first mate, Cutter.
Grrrr...

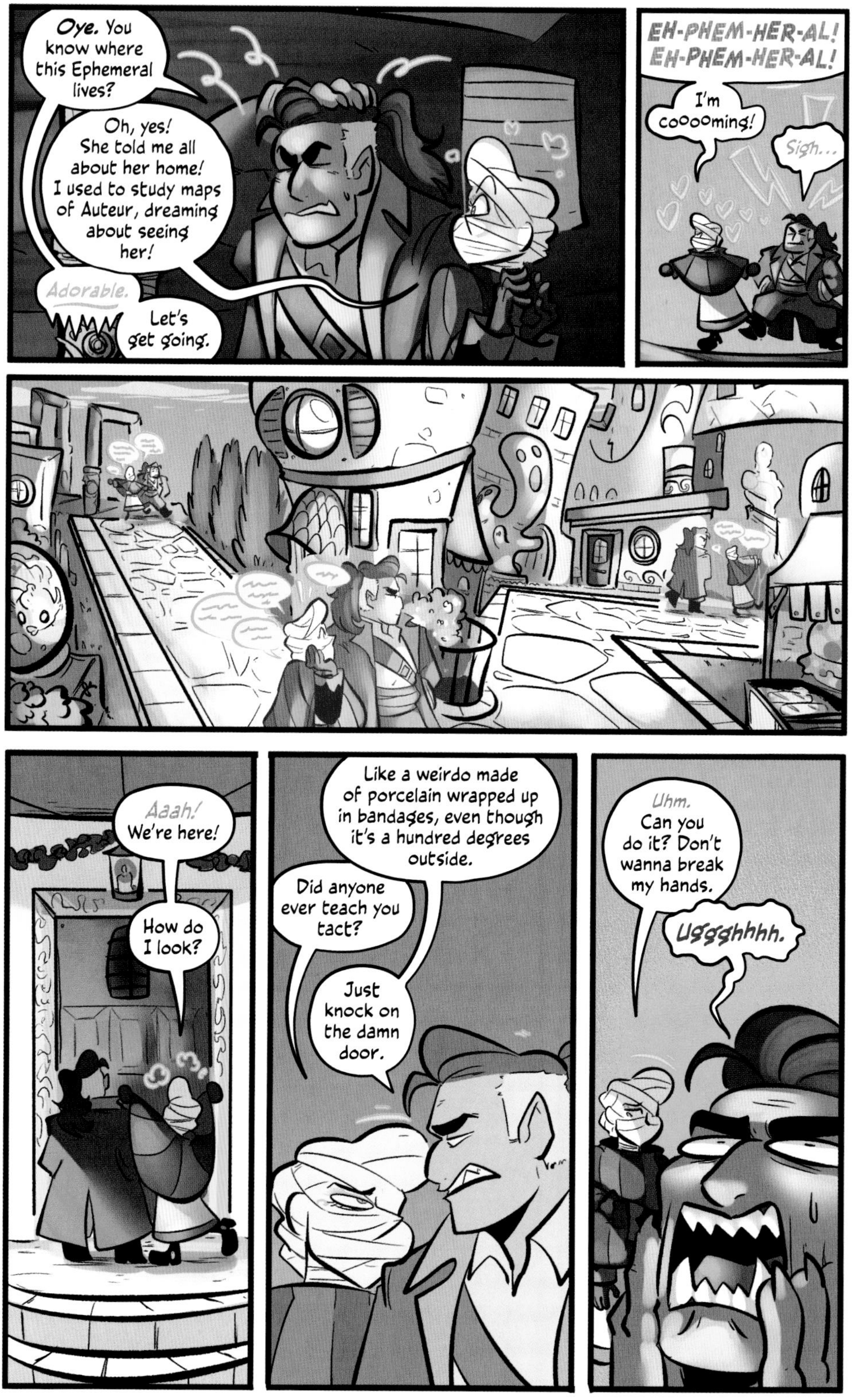

Oye. You know where this Ephemeral lives?
Oh, yes! She told me all about her home! I used to study maps of Auteur, dreaming about seeing her!
Adorable.
Let's get going.
EH-PHEM-HER-AL! EH-PHEM-HER-AL!
I'm coooming!
Sigh...
Aaah! We're here!
How do I look?
Like a weirdo made of porcelain wrapped up in bandages, even though it's a hundred degrees outside.
Did anyone ever teach you tact?
Just knock on the damn door.
Uhm. Can you do it? Don't wanna break my hands.
Ugggghhh.

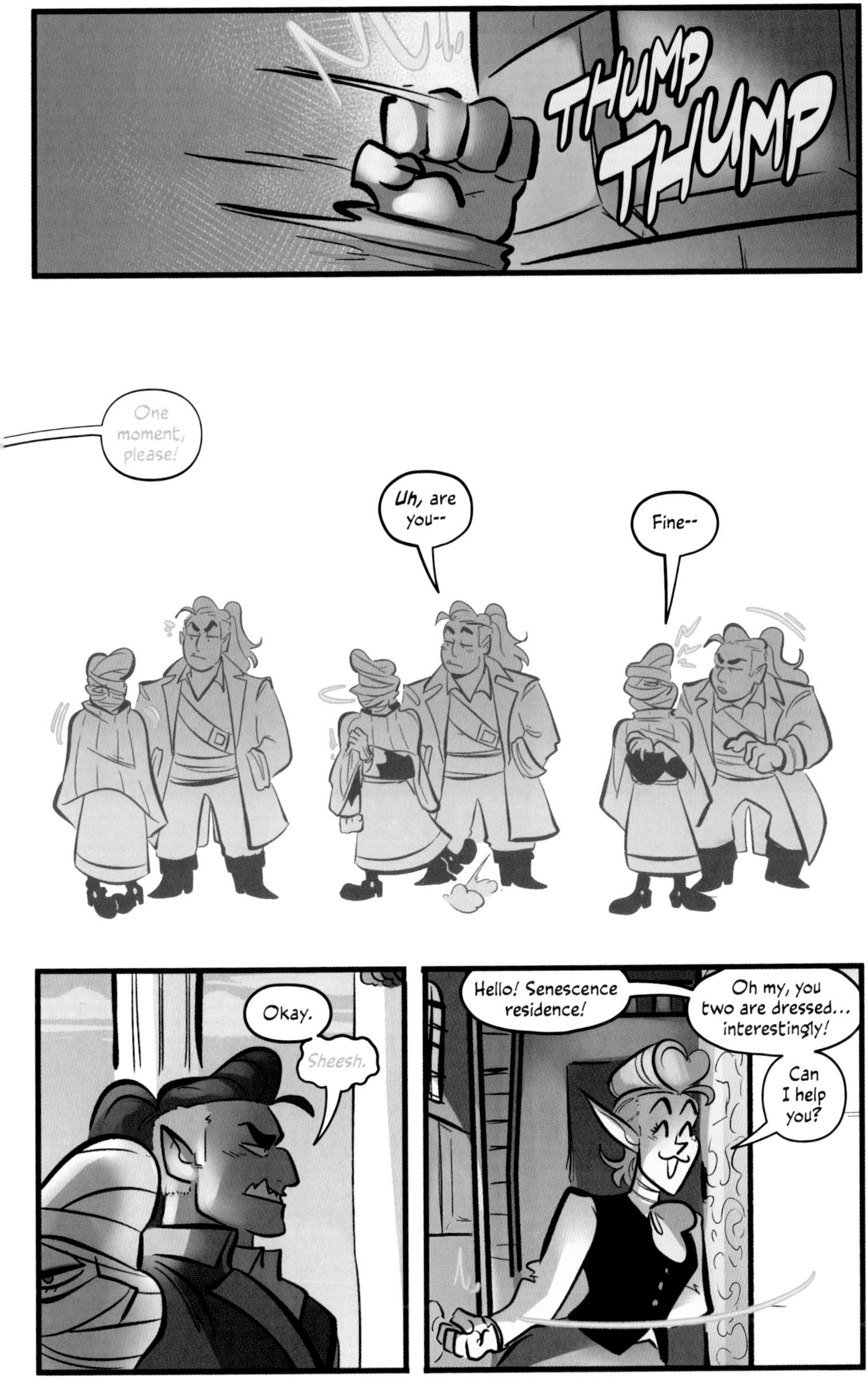
THUMP
THUMP
One moment, please!
Uh, are you--
Fine--
Okay.
Sheesh.
Hello! Senescence residence!
Oh my, you two are dressed... interestingly!
Can I help you?

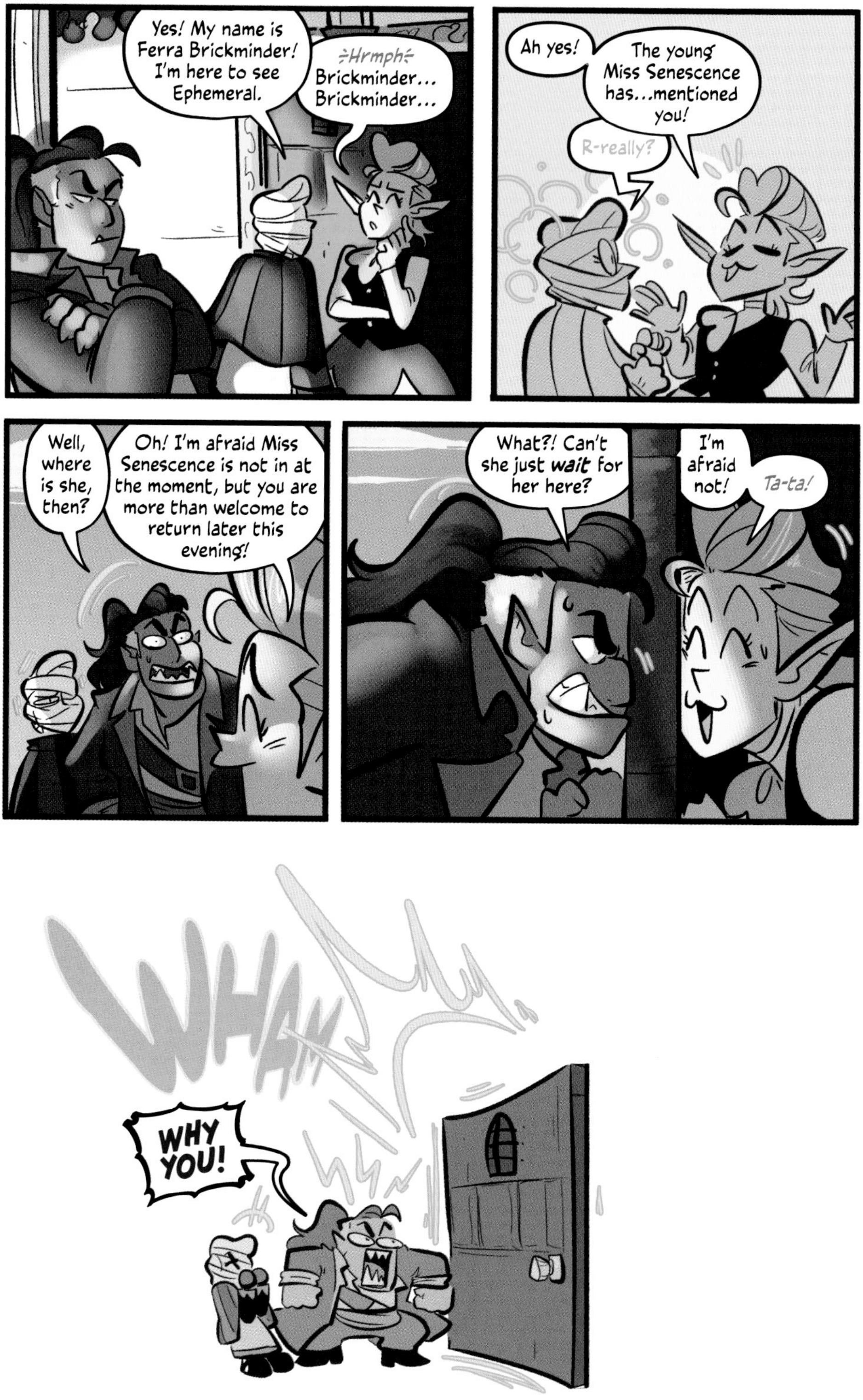
Yes! My name is Ferra Brickminder! I'm here to see Ephemeral.
≑Hrmph≑ Brickminder... Brickminder...
Ah yes!
The young Miss Senescence has...mentioned you!
R-really?
Well, where is she, then?
Oh! I'm afraid Miss Senescence is not in at the moment, but you are more than welcome to return later this evening!
What?! Can't she just **wait** for her here?
I'm afraid not!
Ta-ta!
WHAM
WHY YOU!

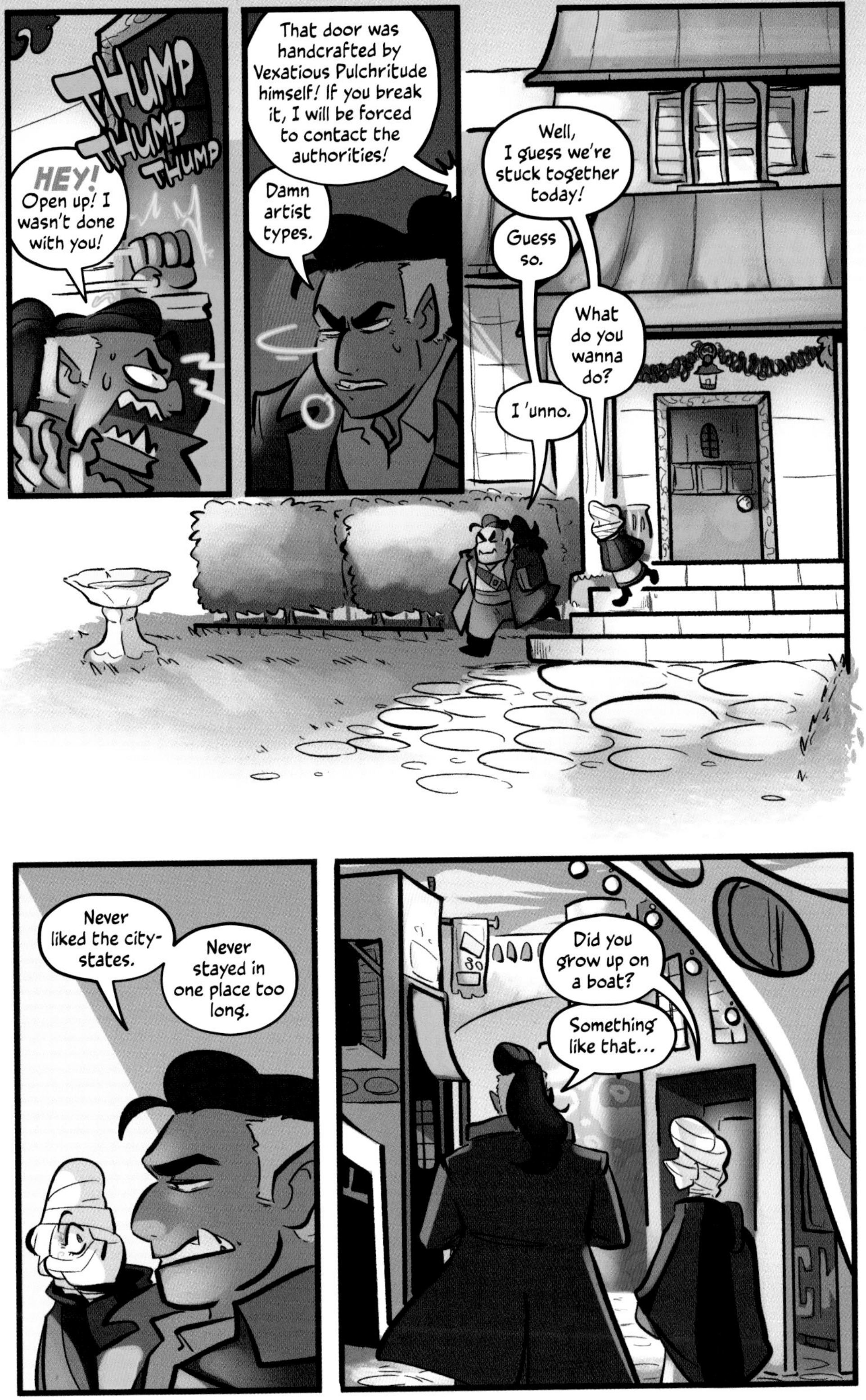

THUMP THUMP THUMP
HEY! Open up! I wasn't done with you!
That door was handcrafted by Vexatious Pulchritude himself! If you break it, I will be forced to contact the authorities!
Damn artist types.
Well, I guess we're stuck together today!
Guess so.
What do you wanna do?
I 'unno.
Never liked the city-states.
Never stayed in one place too long.
Did you grow up on a boat?
Something like that...

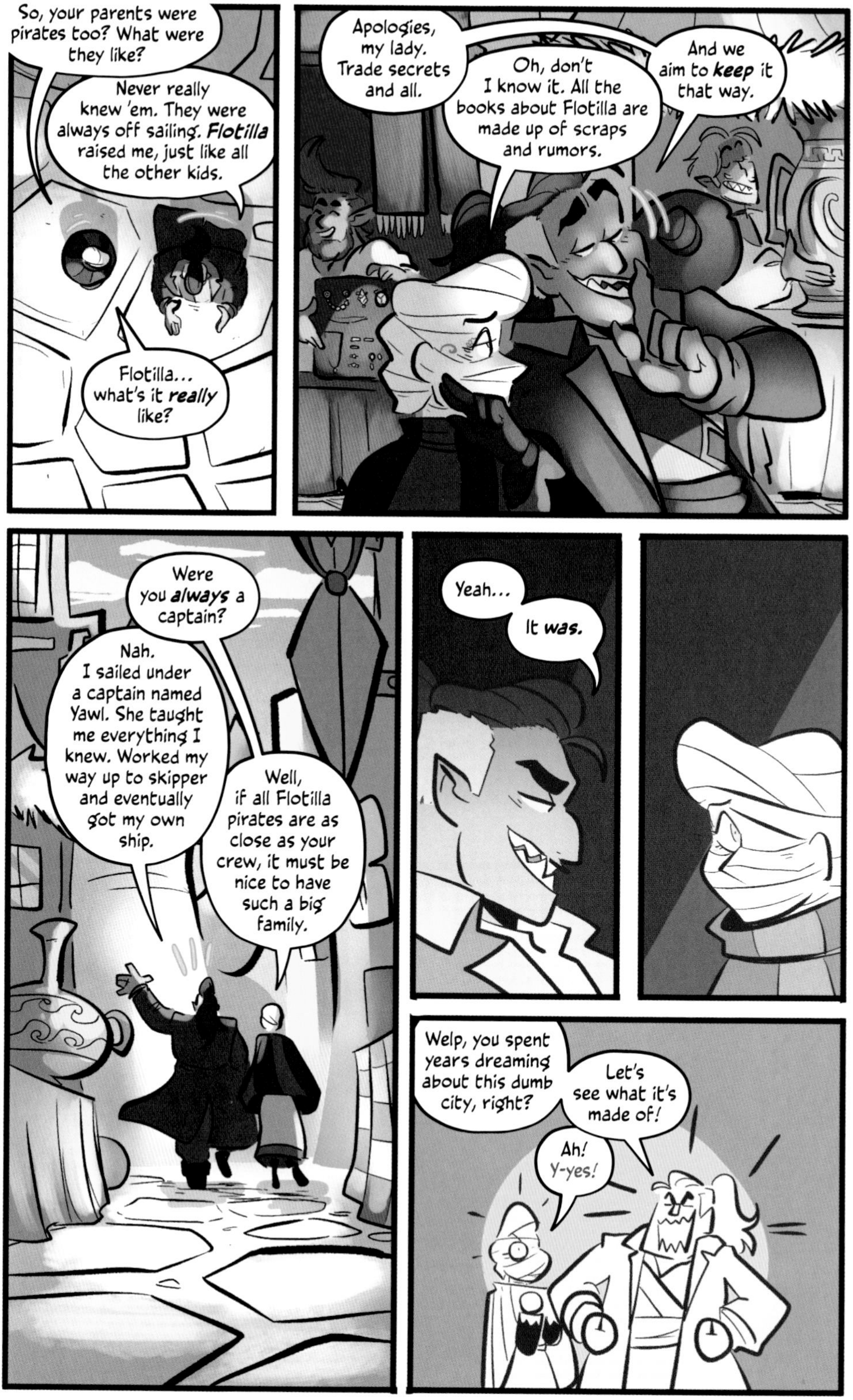

So, your parents were pirates too? What were they like?
Never really knew 'em. They were always off sailing. *Flotilla* raised me, just like all the other kids.
Flotilla... what's it *really* like?
Apologies, my lady. Trade secrets and all.
Oh, don't I know it. All the books about Flotilla are made up of scraps and rumors.
And we aim to *keep* it that way.
Were you *always* a captain?
Nah. I sailed under a captain named Yawl. She taught me everything I knew. Worked my way up to skipper and eventually got my own ship.
Well, if all Flotilla pirates are as close as your crew, it must be nice to have such a big family.
Yeah...
It *was.*
Welp, you spent years dreaming about this dumb city, right?
Let's see what it's made of!
Ah! Y-yes!

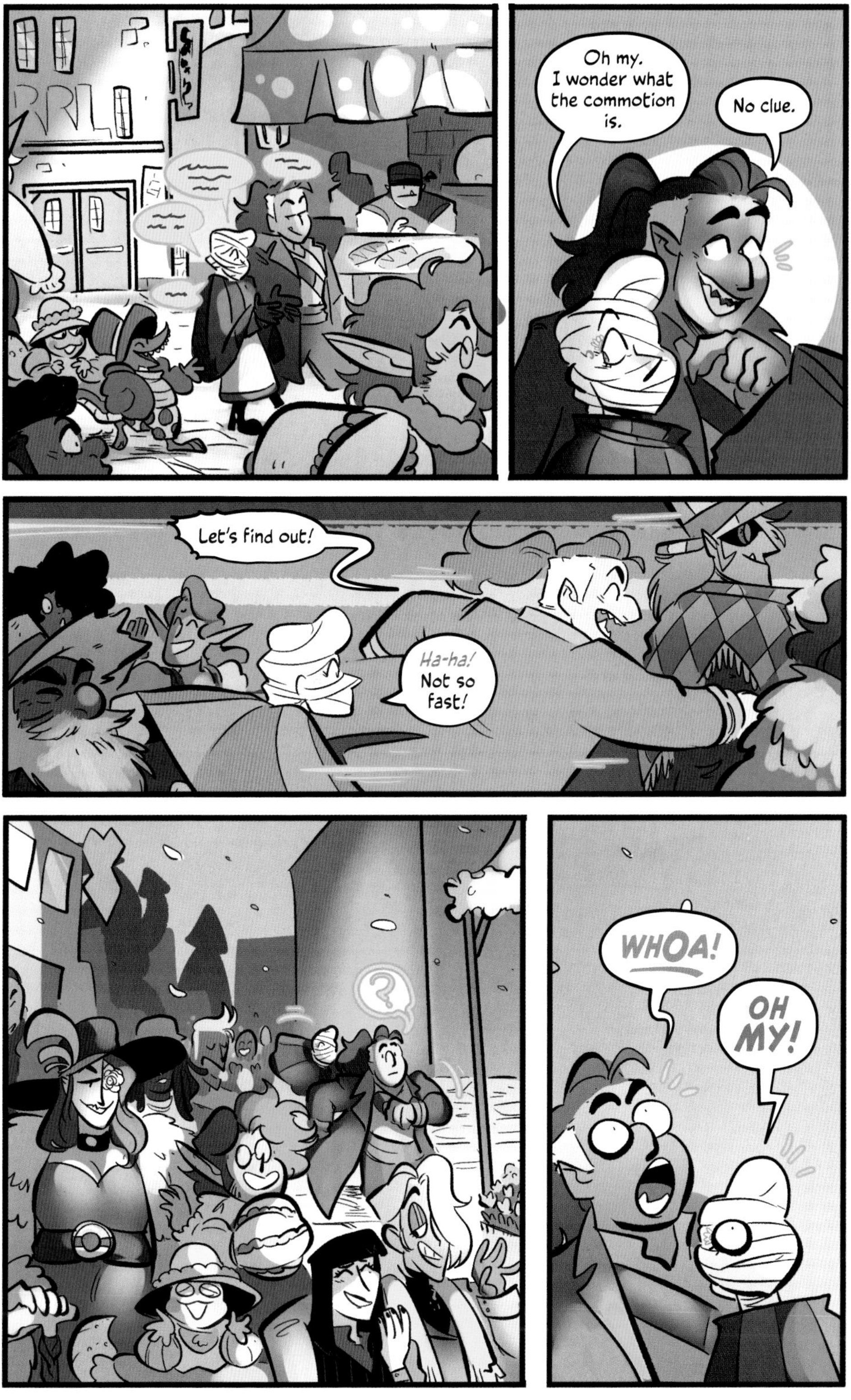
Oh my. I wonder what the commotion is.
No clue.
Let's find out!
Ha-ha! Not so fast!
WHOA!
OH MY!

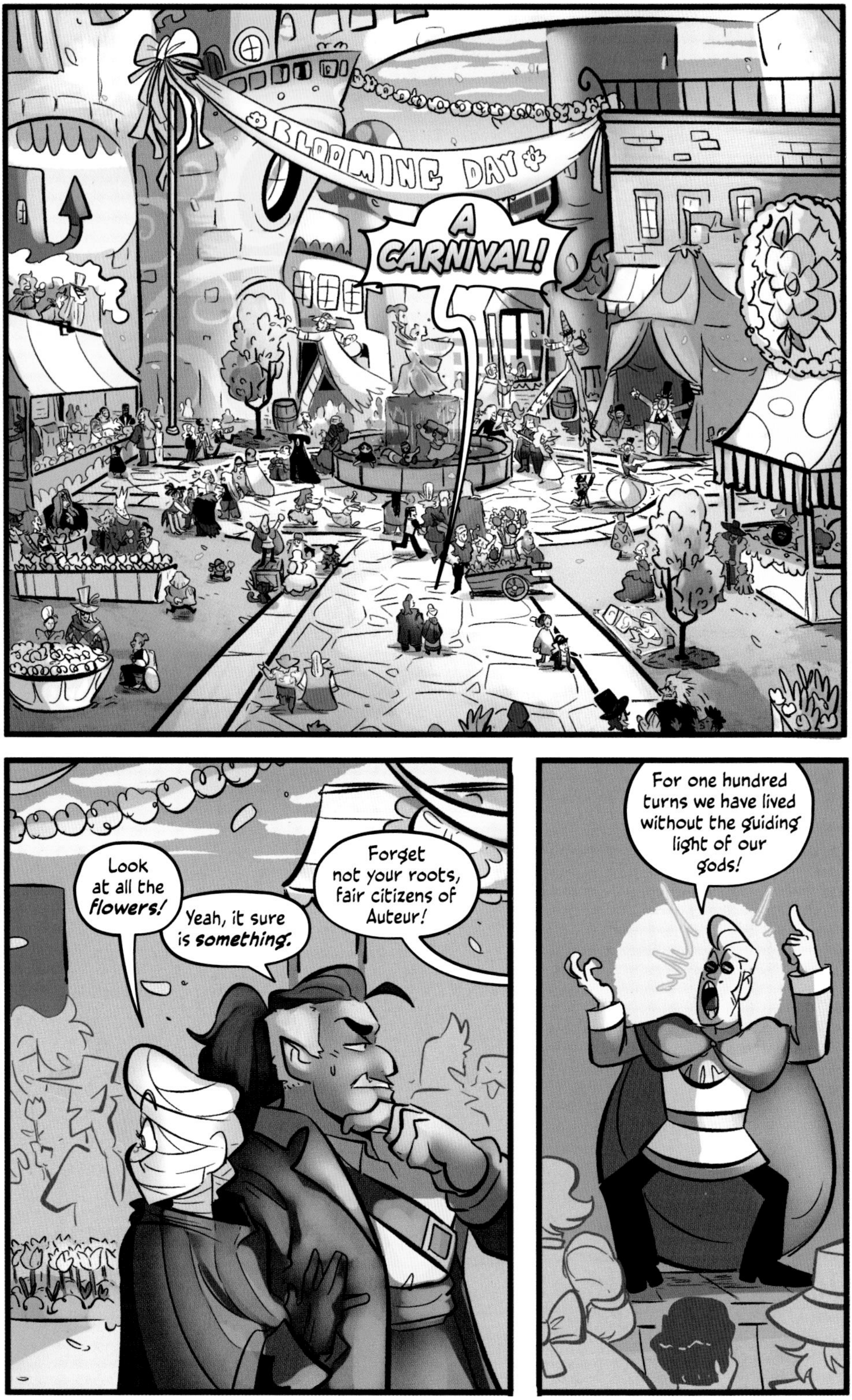
BLOOMING DAY
A CARNIVAL!
Look at all the flowers!
Yeah, it sure is something.
Forget not your roots, fair citizens of Auteur!
For one hundred turns we have lived without the guiding light of our gods!

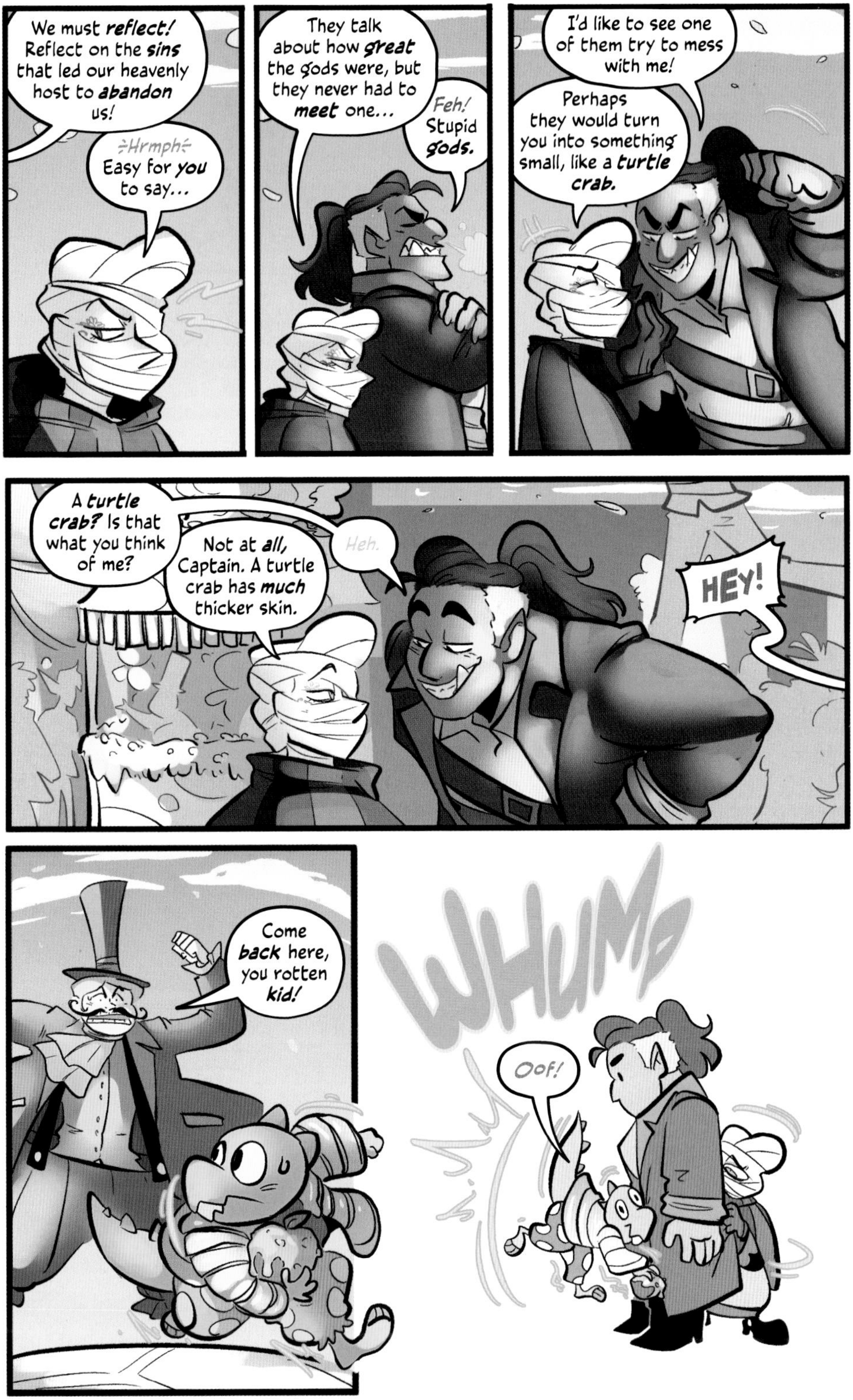
We must *reflect!* Reflect on the *sins* that led our heavenly host to *abandon* us!
-Hrmph- Easy for *you* to say...
They talk about how *great* the gods were, but they never had to *meet* one...
Feh! Stupid *gods.*
I'd like to see one of them try to mess with me!
Perhaps they would turn you into something small, like a *turtle crab.*
A *turtle crab?* Is that what you think of me?
Heh.
Not at *all,* Captain. A turtle crab has *much* thicker skin.
HEY!
Come *back* here, you rotten *kid!*
WHUMP
Oof!

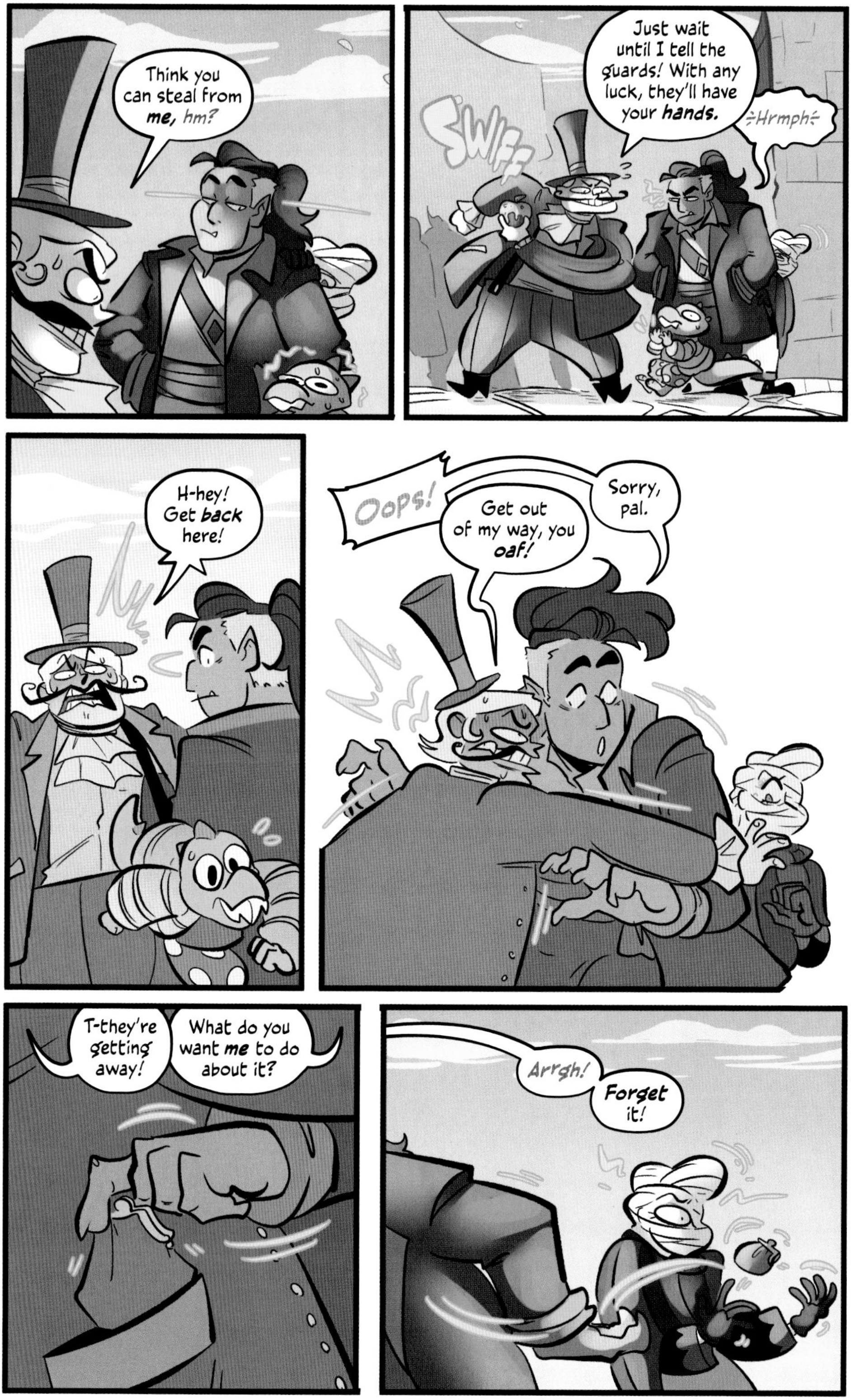
Think you can steal from *me*, hm?
SWIFF
Just wait until I tell the guards! With any luck, they'll have your **hands.**
Hrmph
H-hey! Get *back* here!
Oops!
Get out of my way, you *oaf!*
Sorry, pal.
T-they're getting away!
What do you want *me* to do about it?
Arrgh!
Forget it!

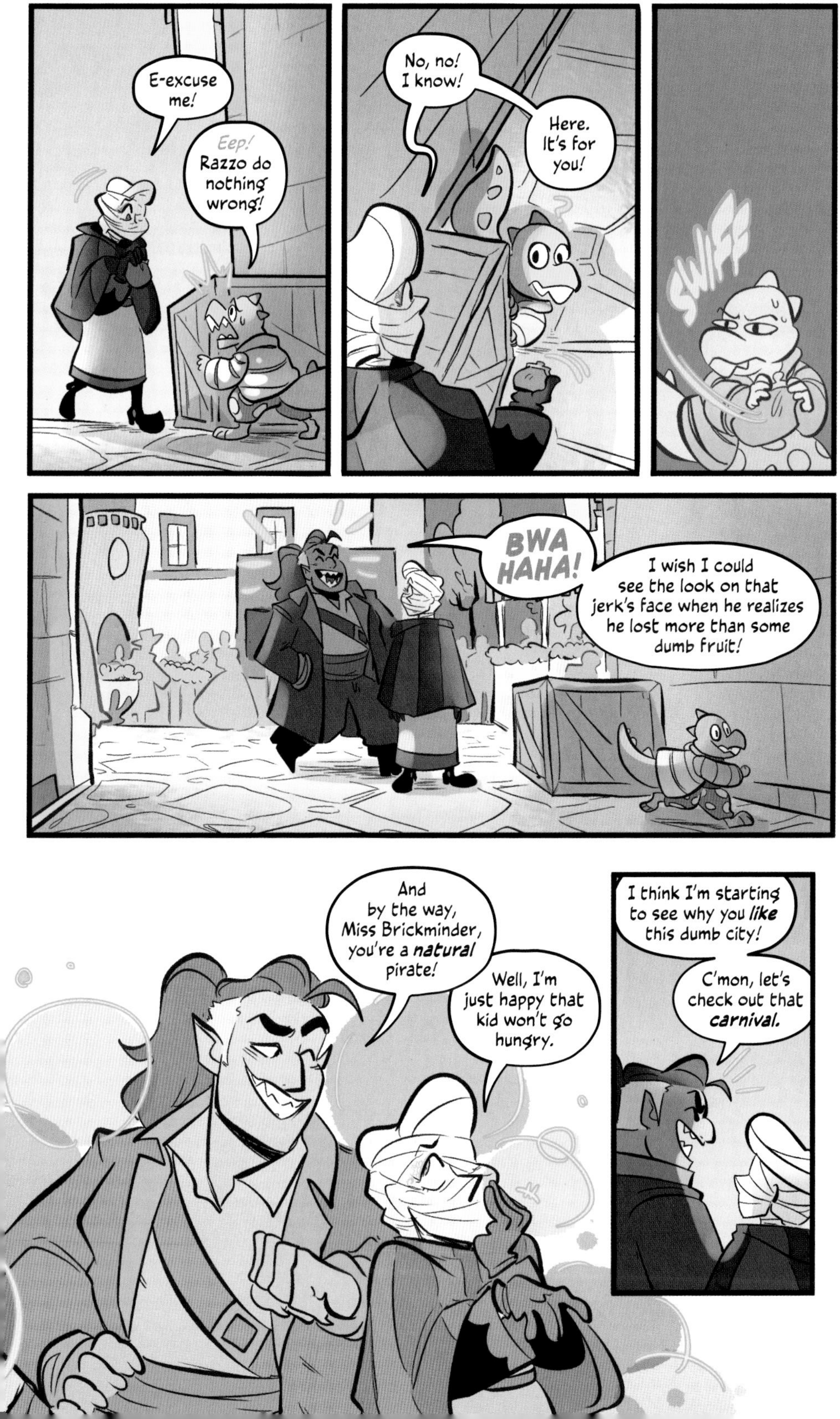
E-excuse me!
Eep! Razzo do nothing wrong!
No, no! I know!
Here. It's for you!
SWIFF
BWA HAHA!
I wish I could see the look on that jerk's face when he realizes he lost more than some dumb fruit!
And by the way, Miss Brickminder, you're a *natural* pirate!
Well, I'm just happy that kid won't go hungry.
I think I'm starting to see why you *like* this dumb city!
C'mon, let's check out that *carnival.*

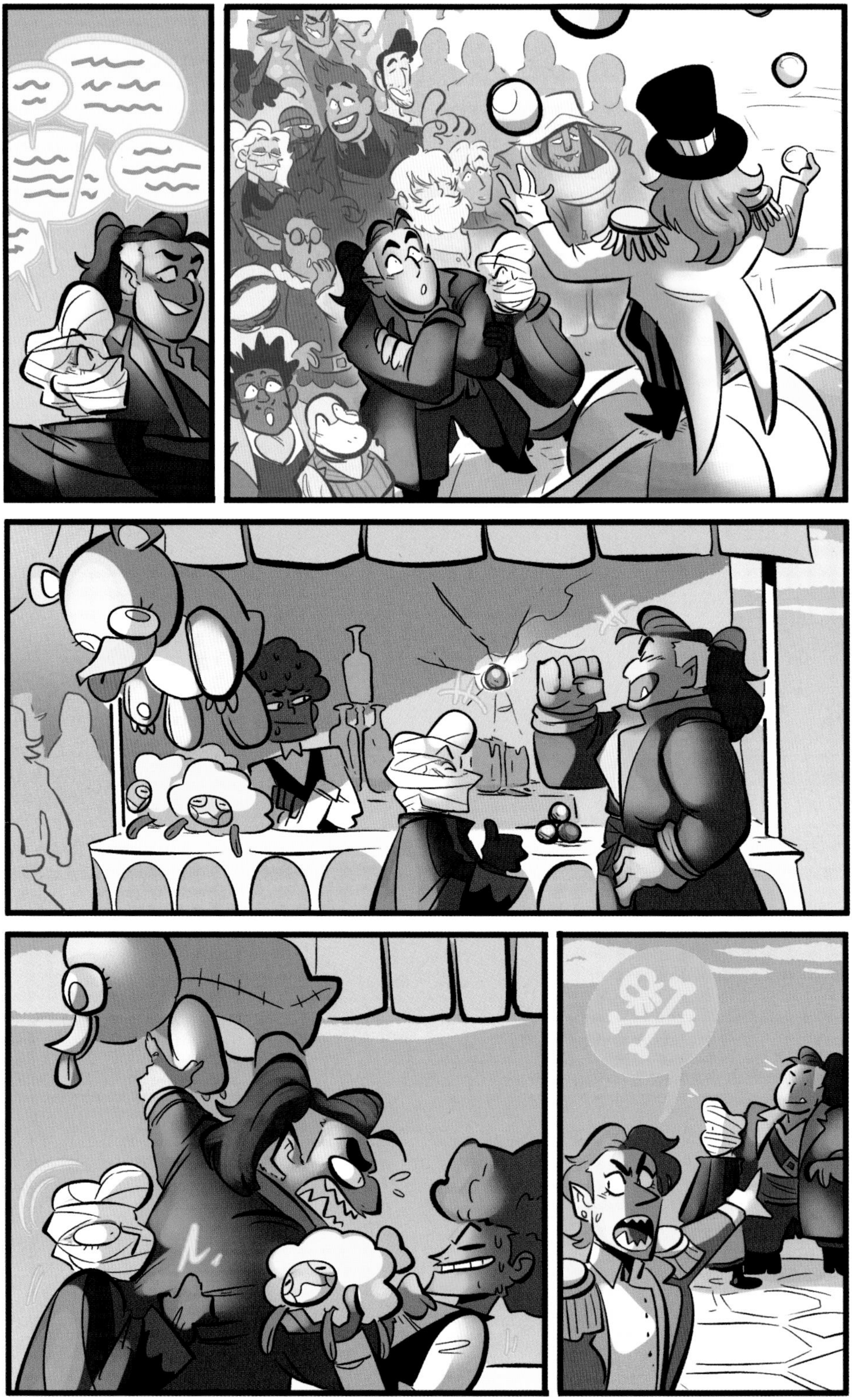

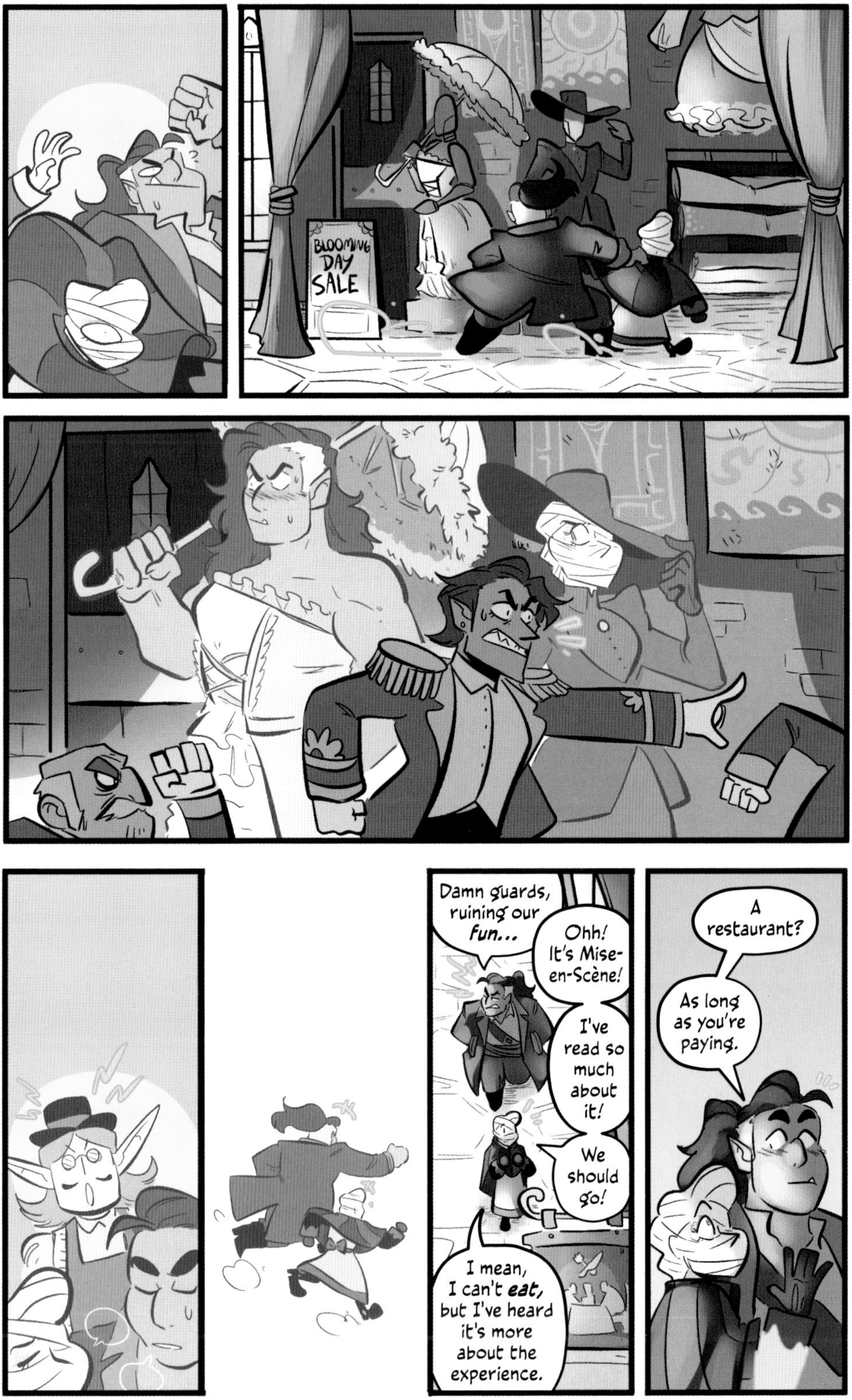
BLOOMING DAY SALE
Damn guards, ruining our *fun*...
Ohh! It's Mise-en-Scène!
I've read so much about it!
We should go!
I mean, I can't *eat*, but I've heard it's more about the experience.
A restaurant?
As long as you're paying.

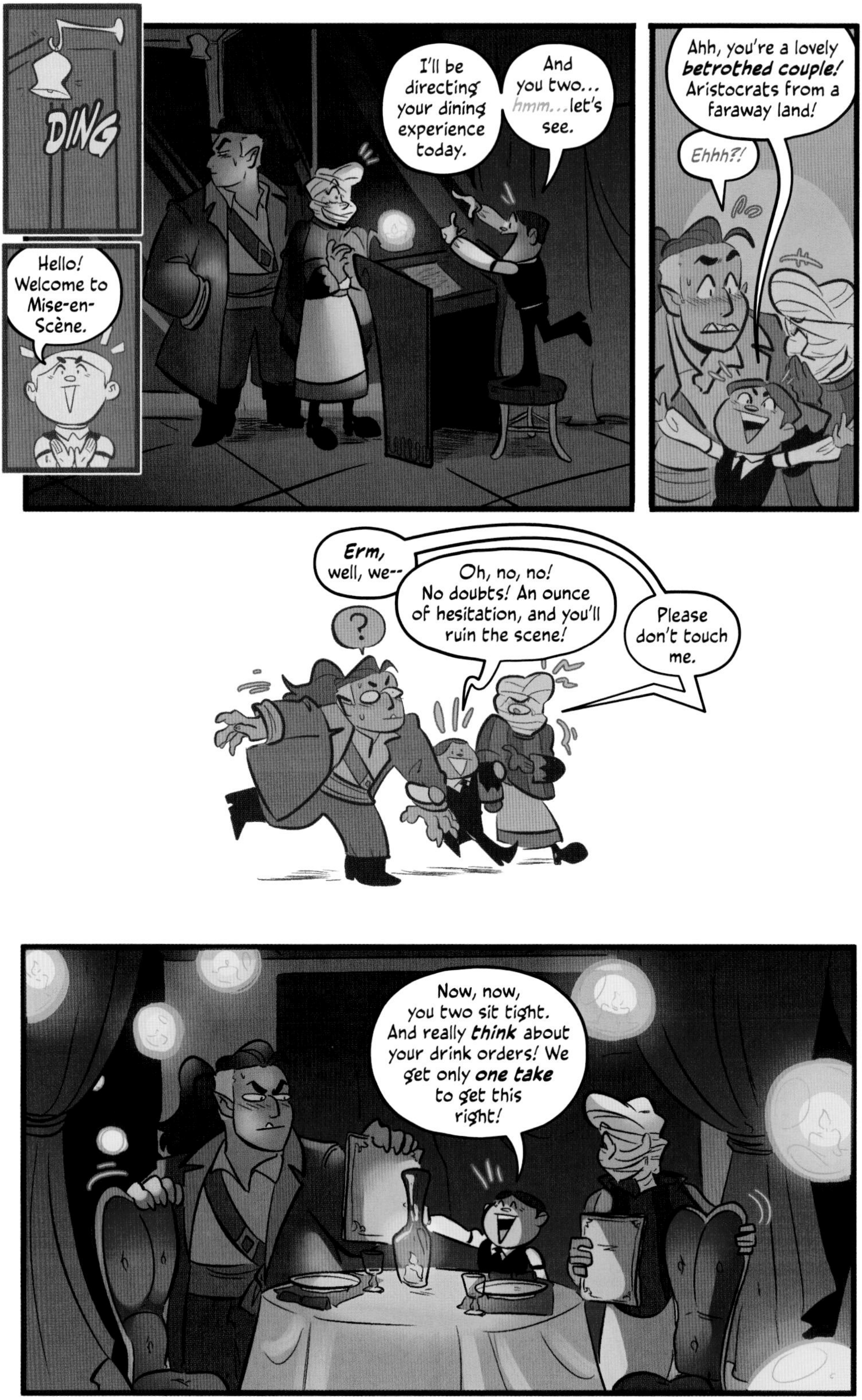
DING
Hello! Welcome to Mise-en-Scène.
I'll be directing your dining experience today.
And you two... hmm...let's see.
Ahh, you're a lovely betrothed couple! Aristocrats from a faraway land!
Ehhh?!
Erm, well, we--
Oh, no, no! No doubts! An ounce of hesitation, and you'll ruin the scene!
Please don't touch me.
?
Now, now, you two sit tight. And really think about your drink orders! We get only one take to get this right!

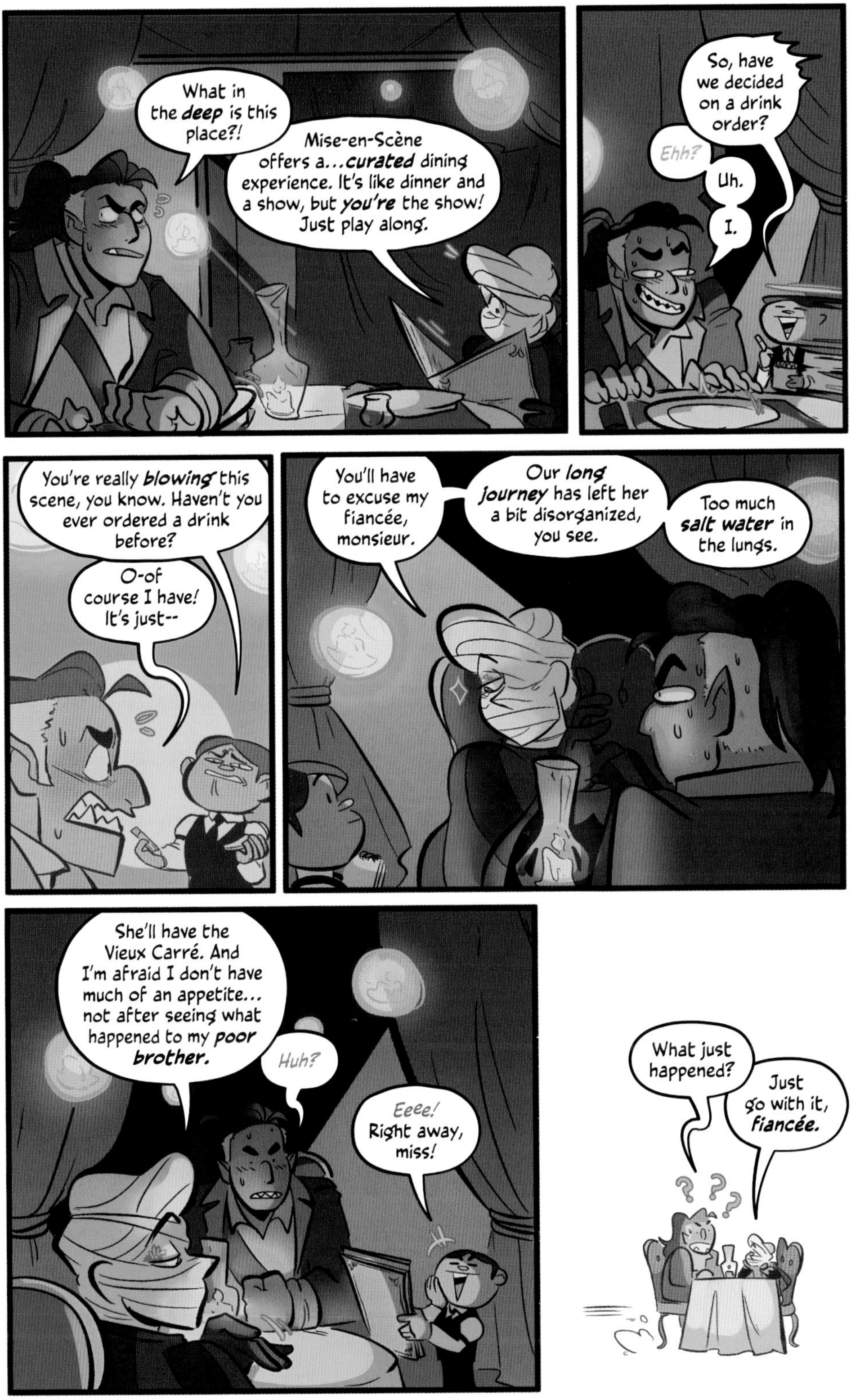
What in the *deep* is this place?!
Mise-en-Scène offers a...*curated* dining experience. It's like dinner and a show, but *you're* the show! Just play along.
So, have we decided on a drink order?
Ehh?
Uh.
I.
You're really *blowing* this scene, you know. Haven't you ever ordered a drink before?
O-of course I have! It's just--
You'll have to excuse my fiancée, monsieur.
Our *long journey* has left her a bit disorganized, you see.
Too much *salt water* in the lungs.
She'll have the Vieux Carré. And I'm afraid I don't have much of an appetite... not after seeing what happened to my *poor brother.*
Huh?
Eeee! Right away, miss!
What just happened?
Just go with it, *fiancée.*

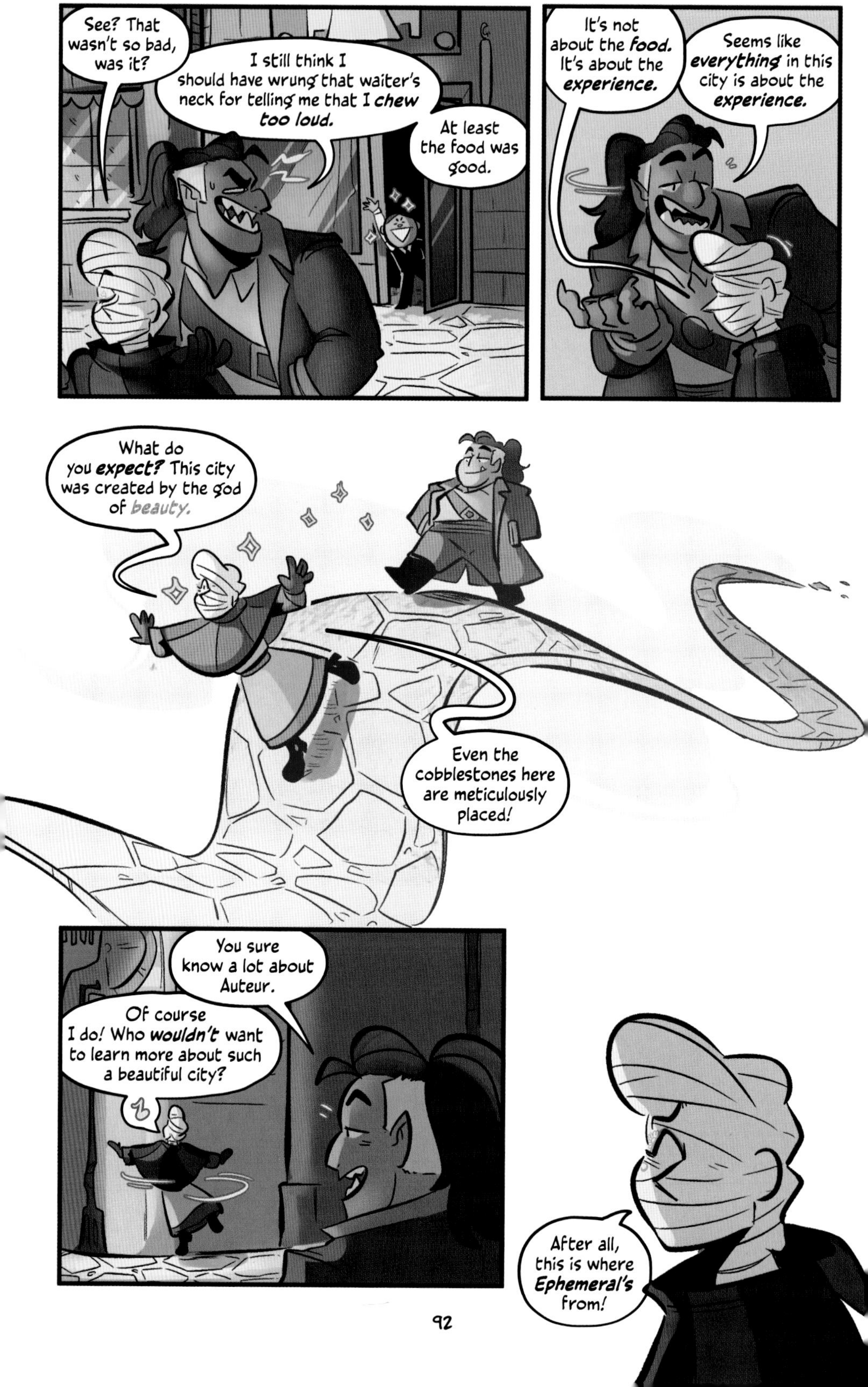
See? That wasn't so bad, was it?
I still think I should have wrung that waiter's neck for telling me that I *chew too loud.*
At least the food was good.
It's not about the *food.* It's about the *experience.*
Seems like *everything* in this city is about the *experience.*
What do you *expect?* This city was created by the god of *beauty.*
Even the cobblestones here are meticulously placed!
You sure know a lot about Auteur.
Of course I do! Who *wouldn't* want to learn more about such a beautiful city?
After all, this is where *Ephemeral's* from!

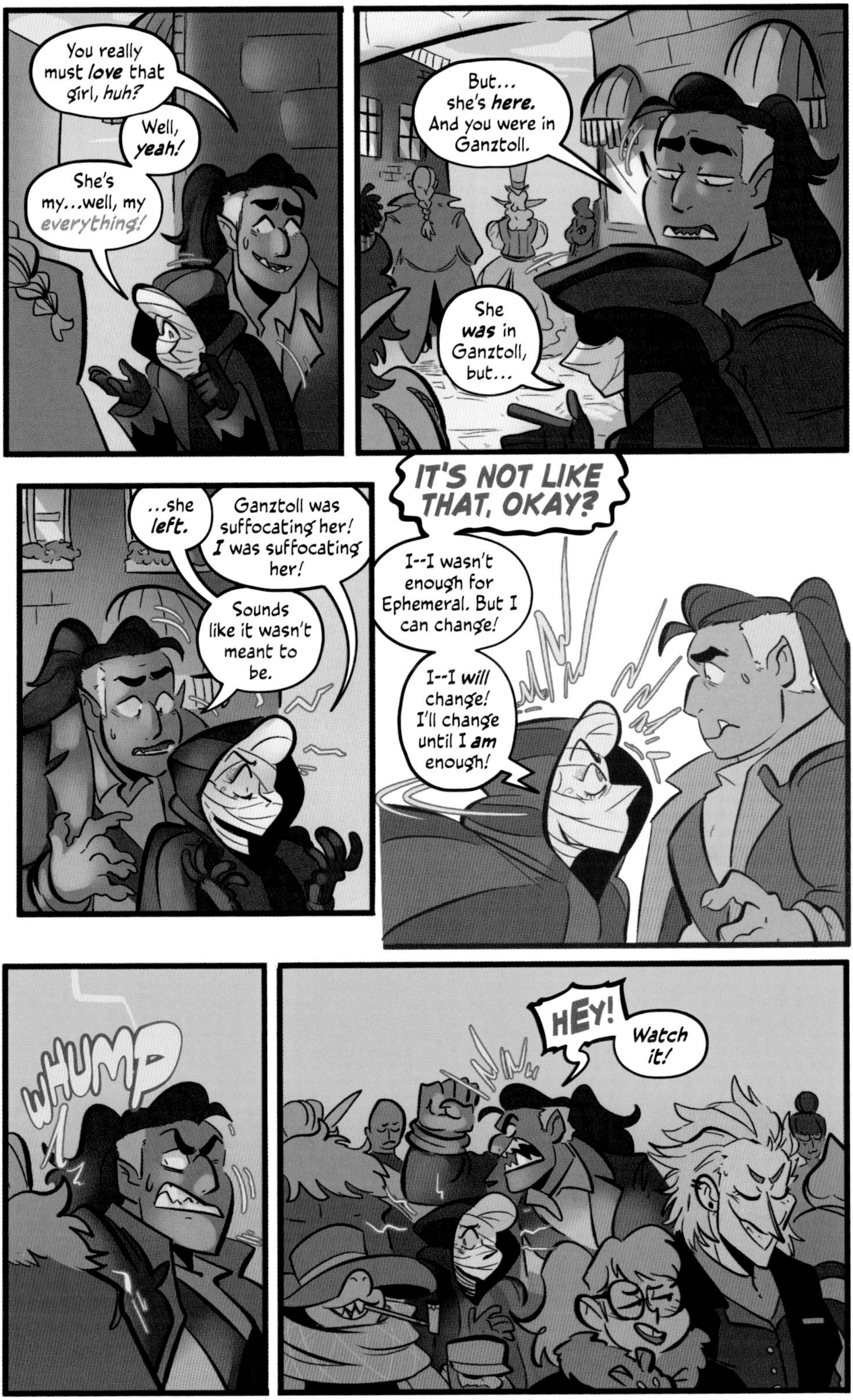
You really must love that girl, huh?
Well, yeah!
She's my...well, my everything!
But... she's here. And you were in Ganztoll.
She was in Ganztoll, but...
...she left.
Ganztoll was suffocating her! I was suffocating her!
Sounds like it wasn't meant to be.
IT'S NOT LIKE THAT, OKAY?
I--I wasn't enough for Ephemeral. But I can change!
I--I will change! I'll change until I am enough!
WHUMP
HEY!
Watch it!

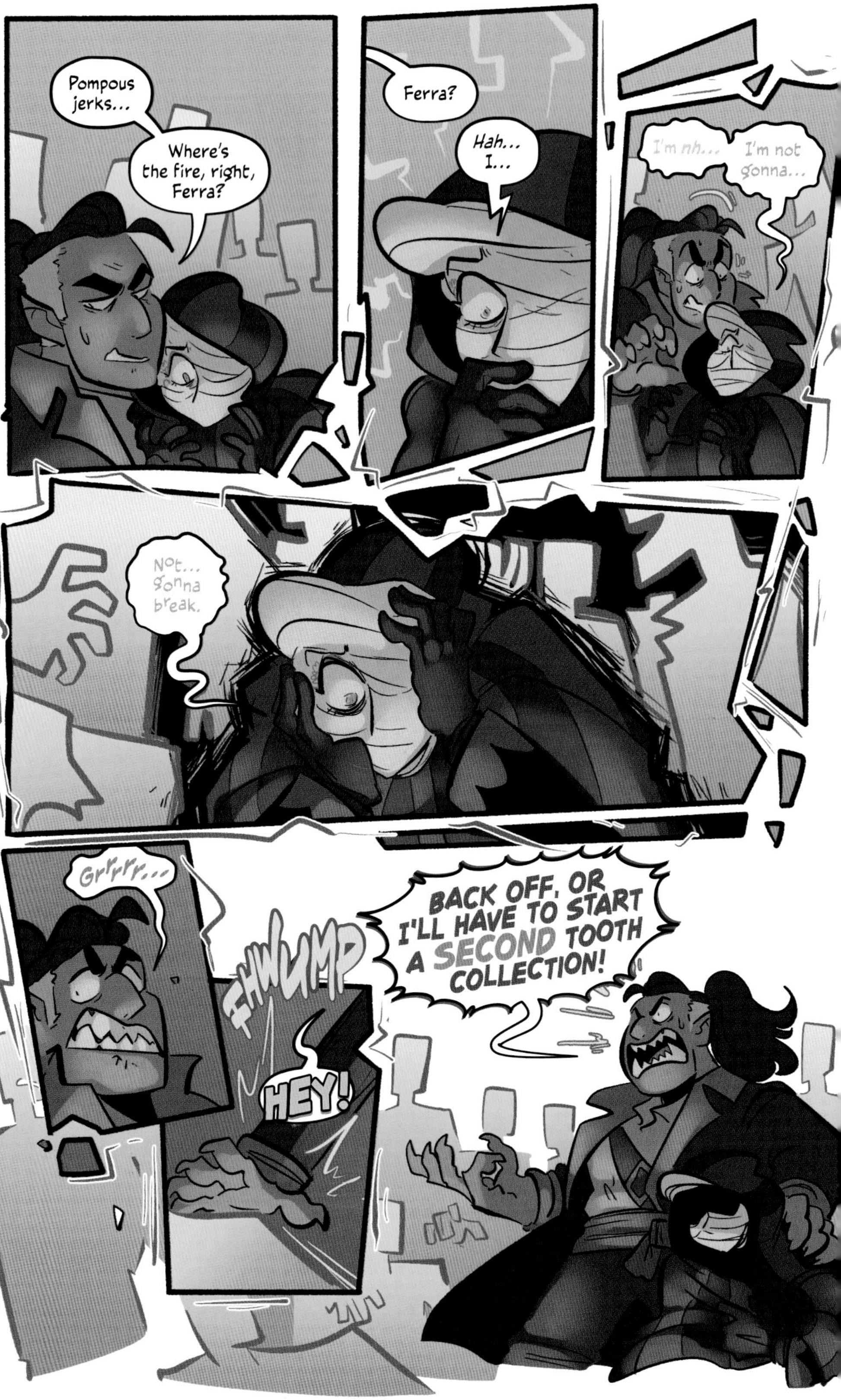

Pompous jerks...
Where's the fire, right, Ferra?
Ferra?
Hah... I...
I'm nh...
I'm not gonna...
Not... gonna break.
Grrrrr...
FHWUMP
HEY!
BACK OFF, OR I'LL HAVE TO START A SECOND TOOTH COLLECTION!

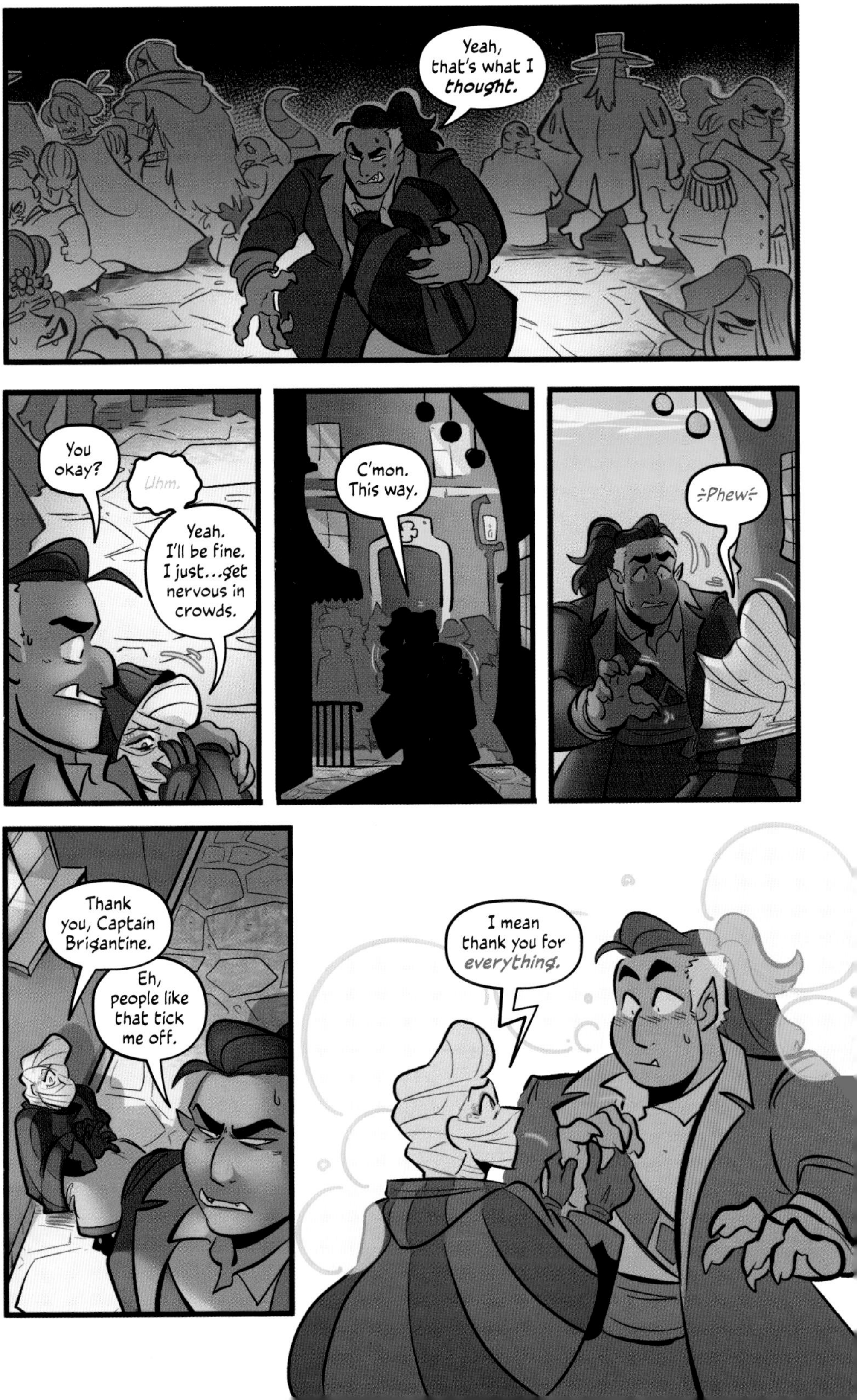
Yeah, that's what I *thought.*
You okay?
Uhm.
Yeah. I'll be fine. I just...get nervous in crowds.
C'mon. This way.
Phew
Thank you, Captain Brigantine.
Eh, people like that tick me off.
I mean thank you for *everything.*

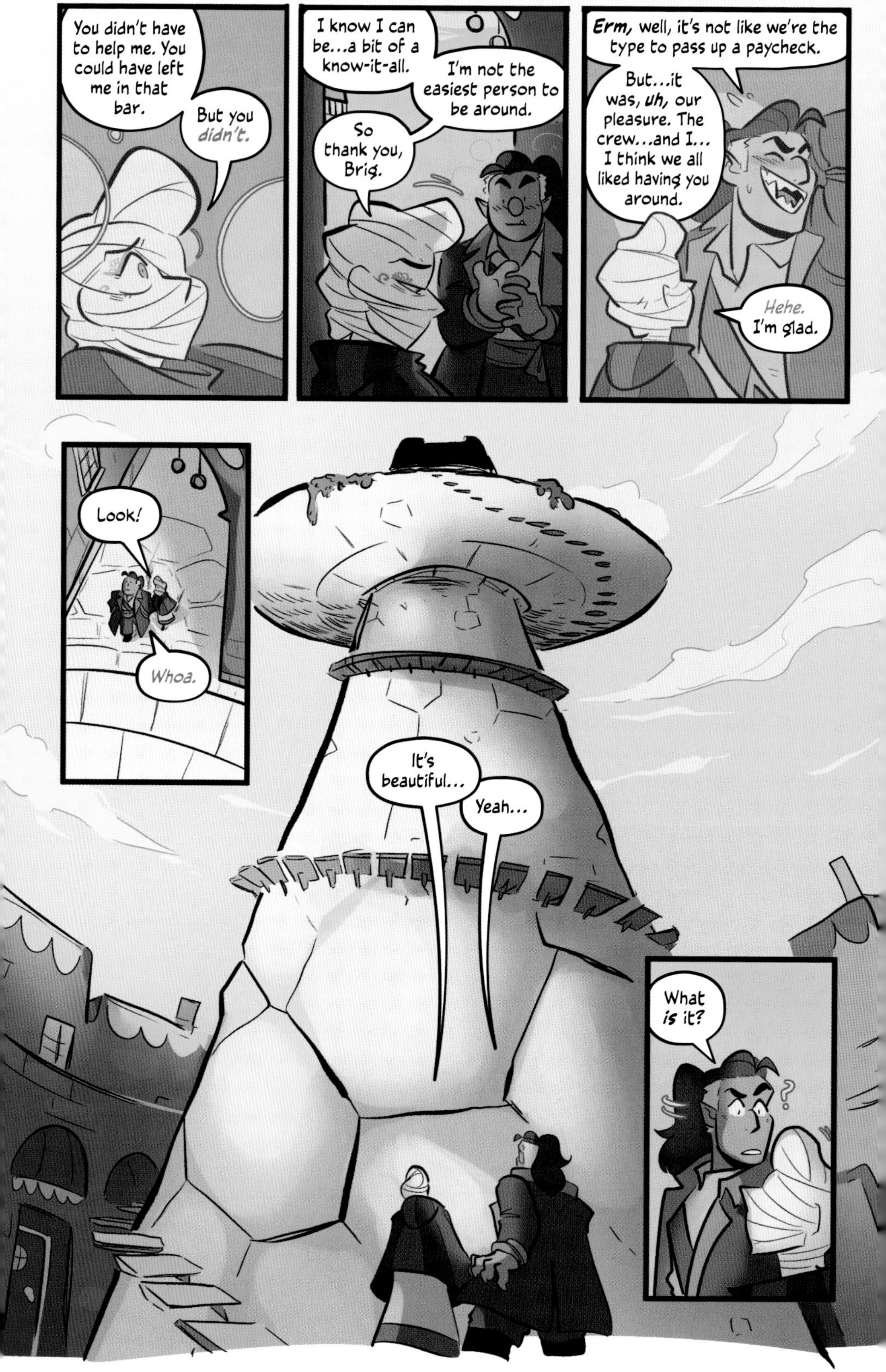
You didn't have to help me. You could have left me in that bar.
But you *didn't.*
I know I can be...a bit of a know-it-all.
I'm not the easiest person to be around.
So thank you, Brig.
Erm, well, it's not like we're the type to pass up a paycheck.
But...it was, ***uh,*** our pleasure. The crew...and I... I think we all liked having you around.
Hehe. I'm glad.
Look!
Whoa.
It's beautiful...
Yeah...
What ***is*** it?

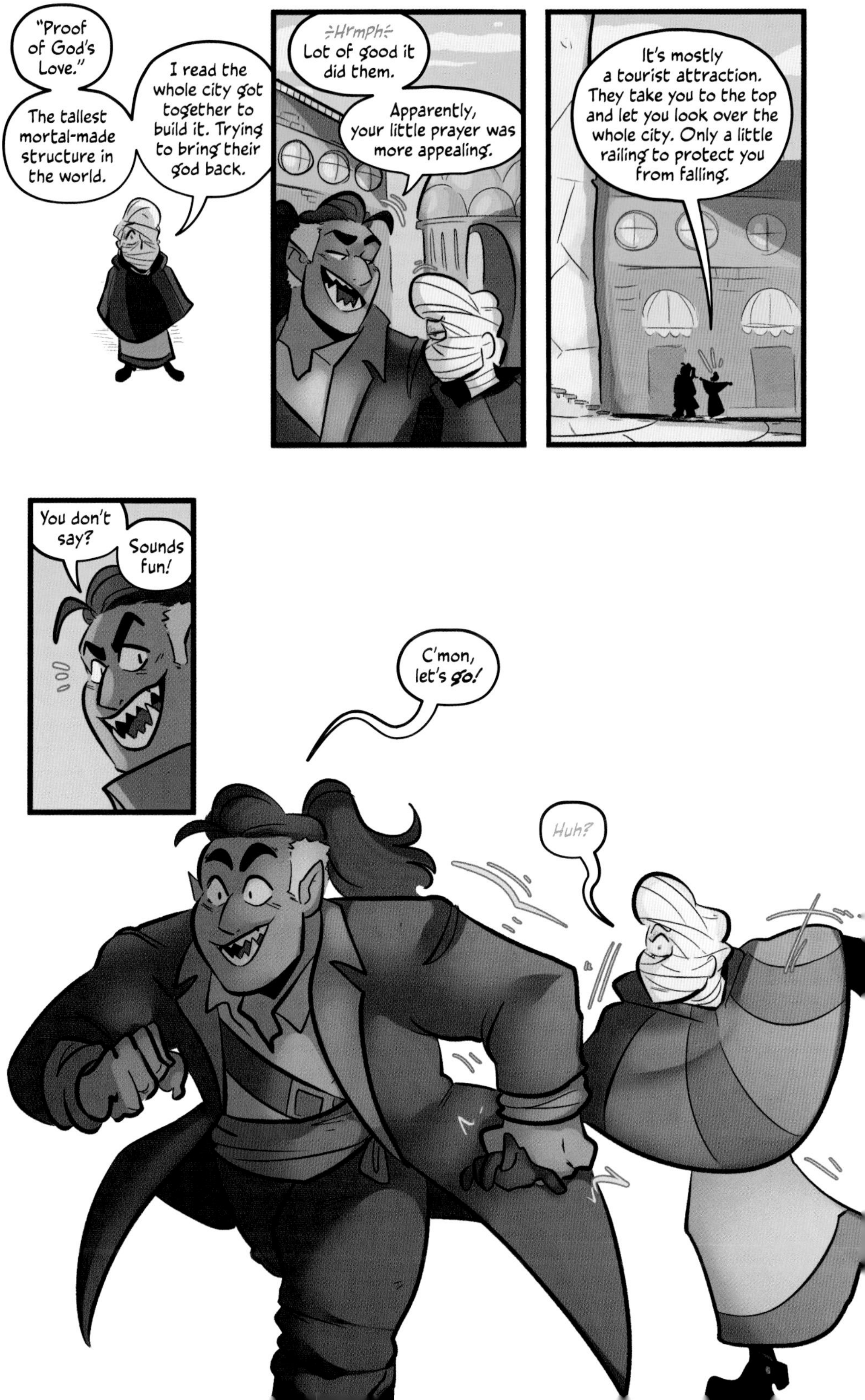
"Proof of God's Love."
The tallest mortal-made structure in the world.
I read the whole city got together to build it. Trying to bring their god back.
Hrmph
Lot of good it did them.
Apparently, your little prayer was more appealing.
It's mostly a tourist attraction. They take you to the top and let you look over the whole city. Only a little railing to protect you from falling.
You don't say?
Sounds fun!
C'mon, let's go!
Huh?

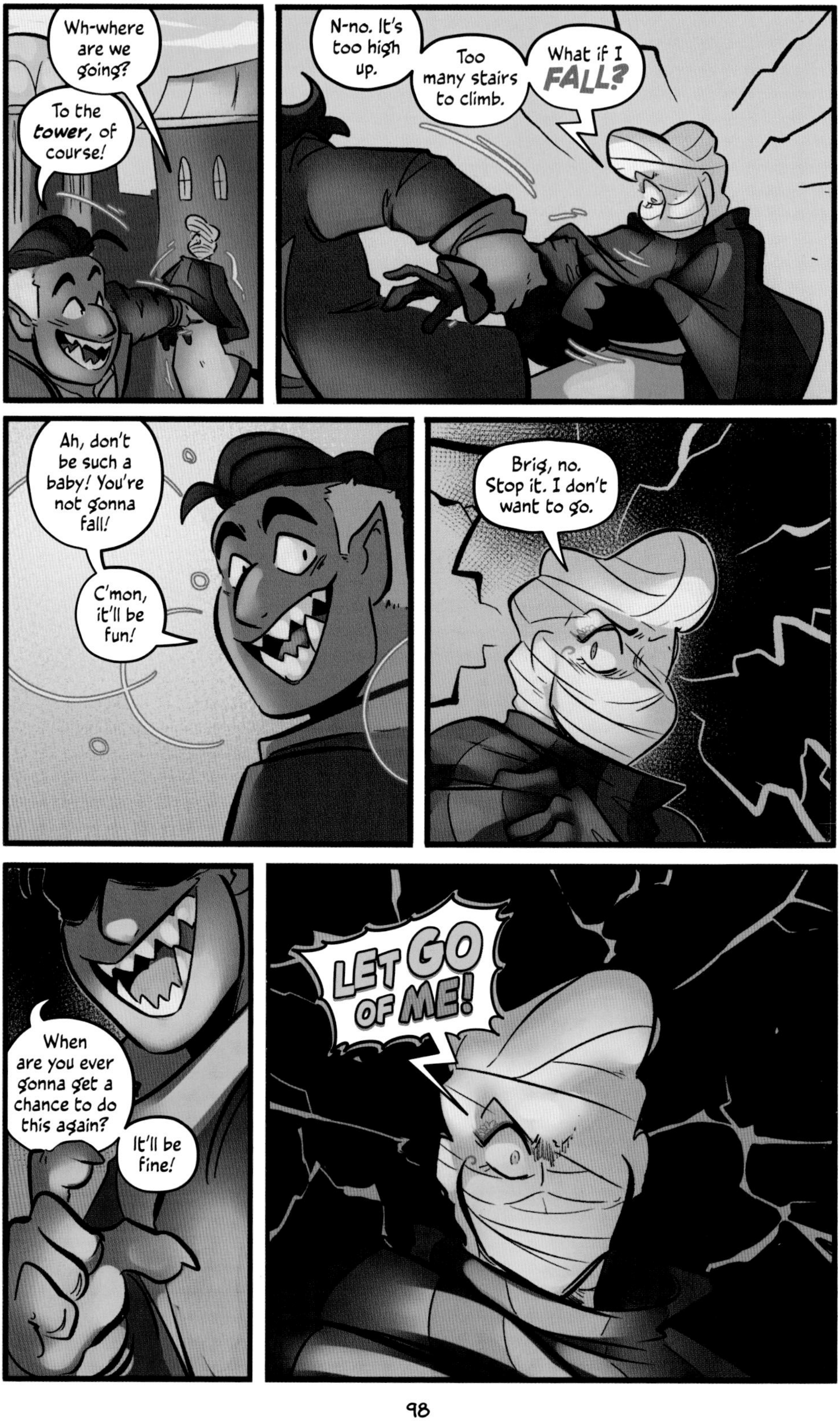
Wh-where are we going?
To the *tower,* of course!
N-no. It's too high up.
Too many stairs to climb.
What if I FALL?
Ah, don't be such a baby! You're not gonna fall!
C'mon, it'll be fun!
Brig, no. Stop it. I don't want to go.
When are you ever gonna get a chance to do this again?
It'll be fine!
LET GO OF ME!

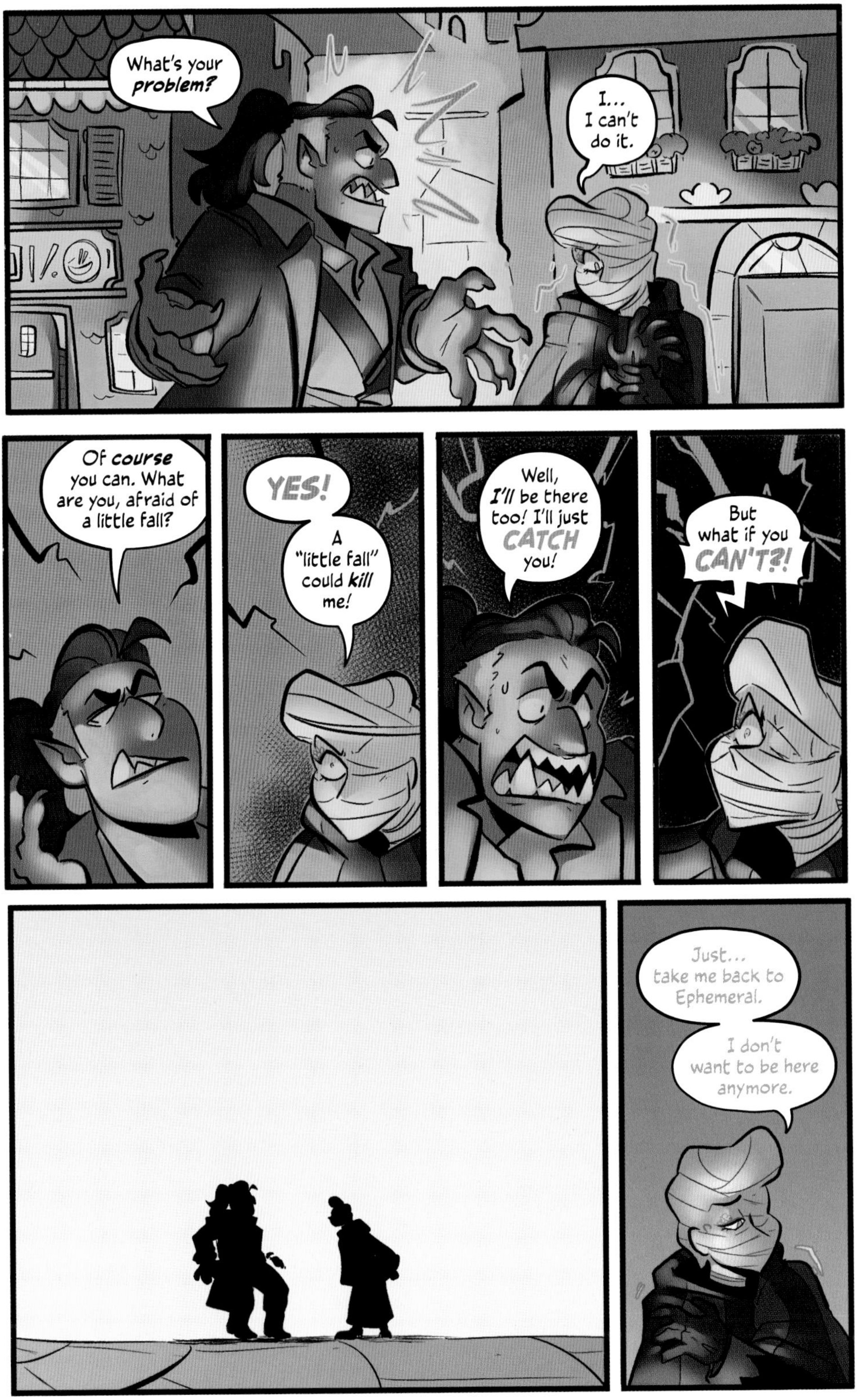
What's your *problem?*
I... I can't do it.
Of *course* you can. What are you, afraid of a little fall?
YES!
A "little fall" could *kill* me!
Well, *I'll* be there too! I'll just CATCH you!
But what if you CAN'T?!
Just... take me back to Ephemeral.
I don't want to be here anymore.

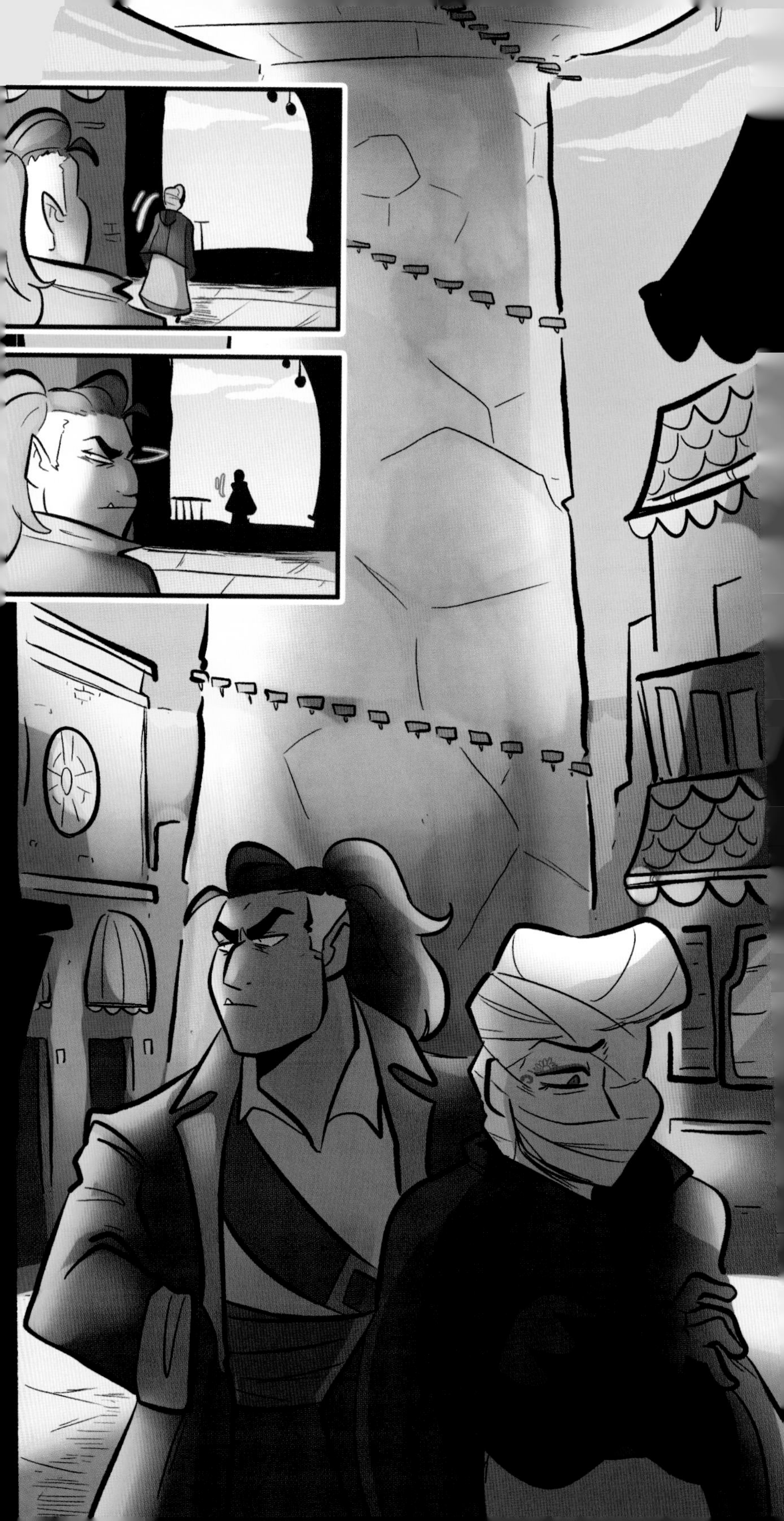

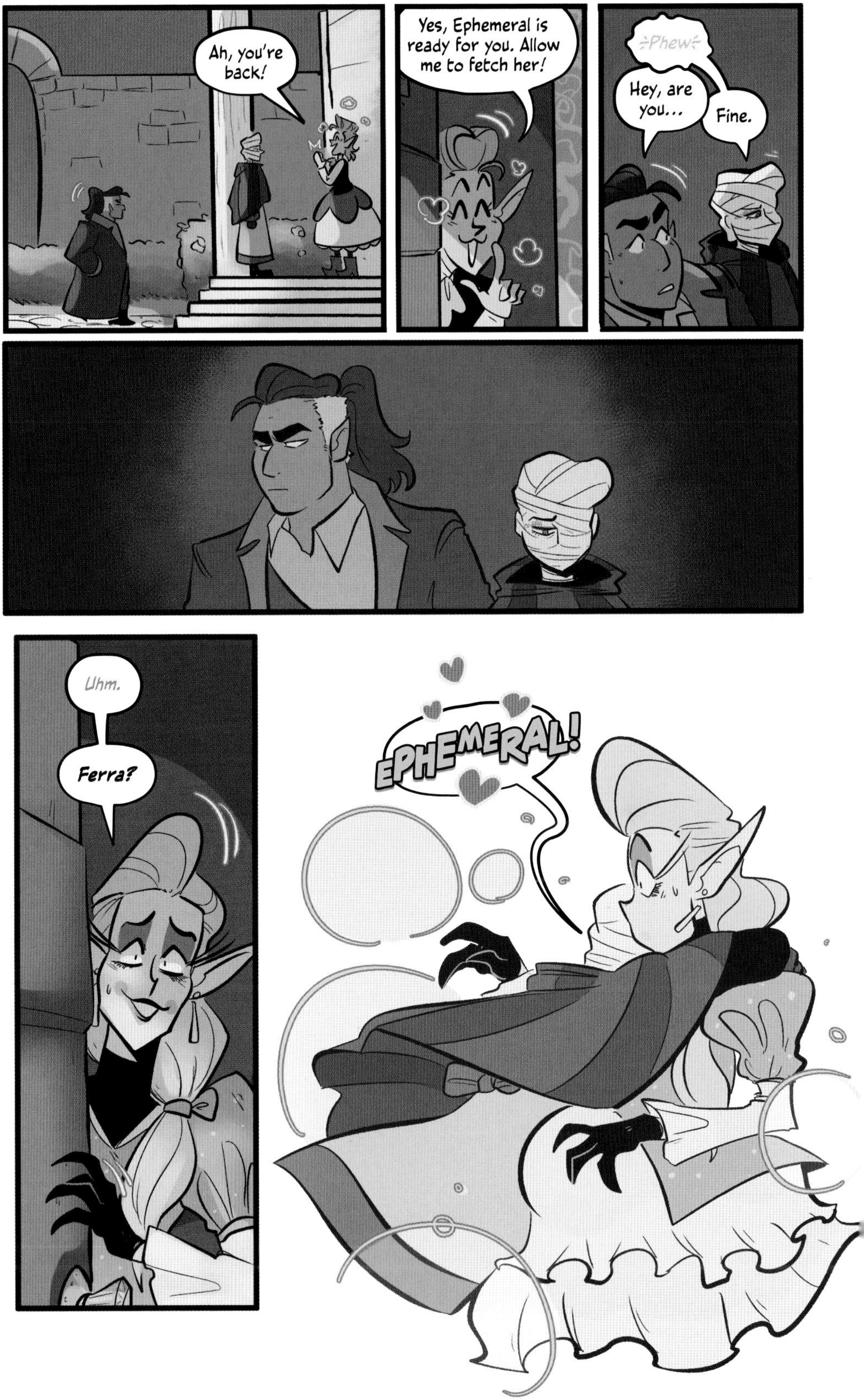

Ah, you're back!
Yes, Ephemeral is ready for you. Allow me to fetch her!
Phew
Hey, are you...
Fine.
Uhm.
Ferra?
EPHEMERAL!

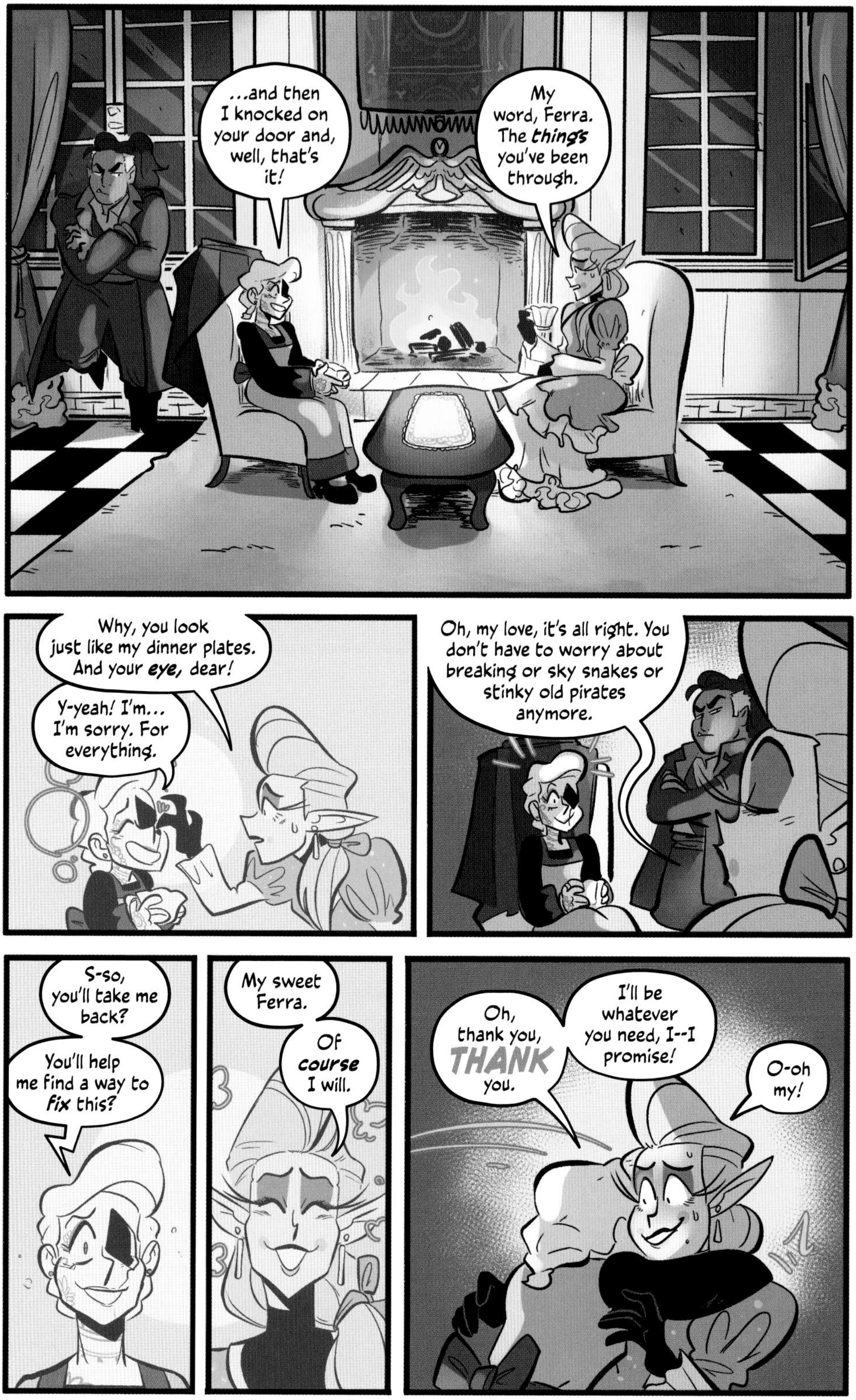
...and then I knocked on your door and, well, that's it!
My word, Ferra. The *things* you've been through.
Why, you look just like my dinner plates. And your *eye,* dear!
Y-yeah! I'm... I'm sorry. For everything.
Oh, my love, it's all right. You don't have to worry about breaking or sky snakes or stinky old pirates anymore.
S-so, you'll take me back?
You'll help me find a way to *fix* this?
My sweet Ferra.
Of *course* I will.
Oh, thank you, THANK you.
I'll be whatever you need, I--I promise!
O-oh my!

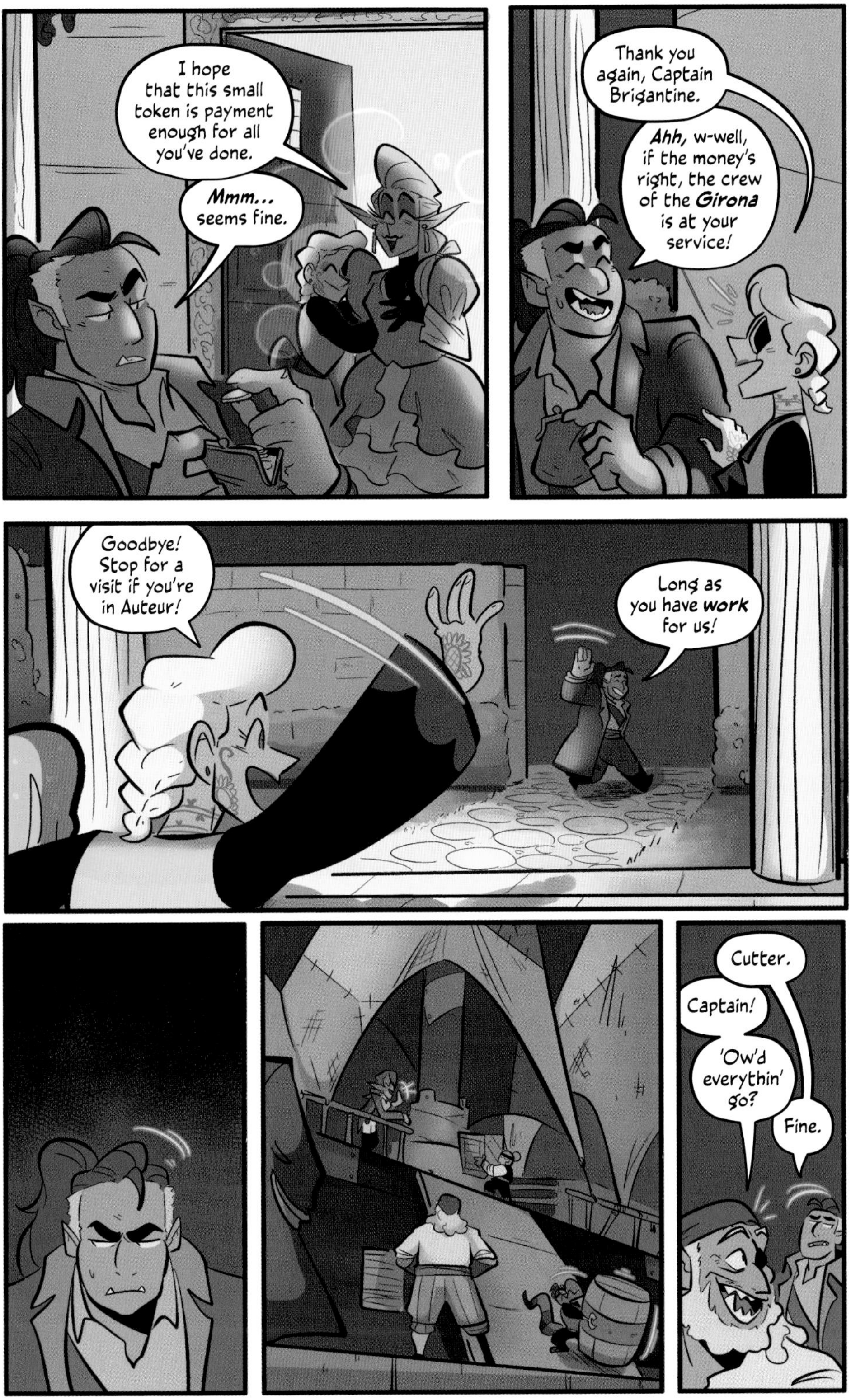
I hope that this small token is payment enough for all you've done.
Mmm... seems fine.
Thank you again, Captain Brigantine.
Ahh, w-well, if the money's right, the crew of the *Girona* is at your service!
Goodbye! Stop for a visit if you're in Auteur!
Long as you have **work** for us!
Cutter.
Captain!
'Ow'd everythin' go?
Fine.

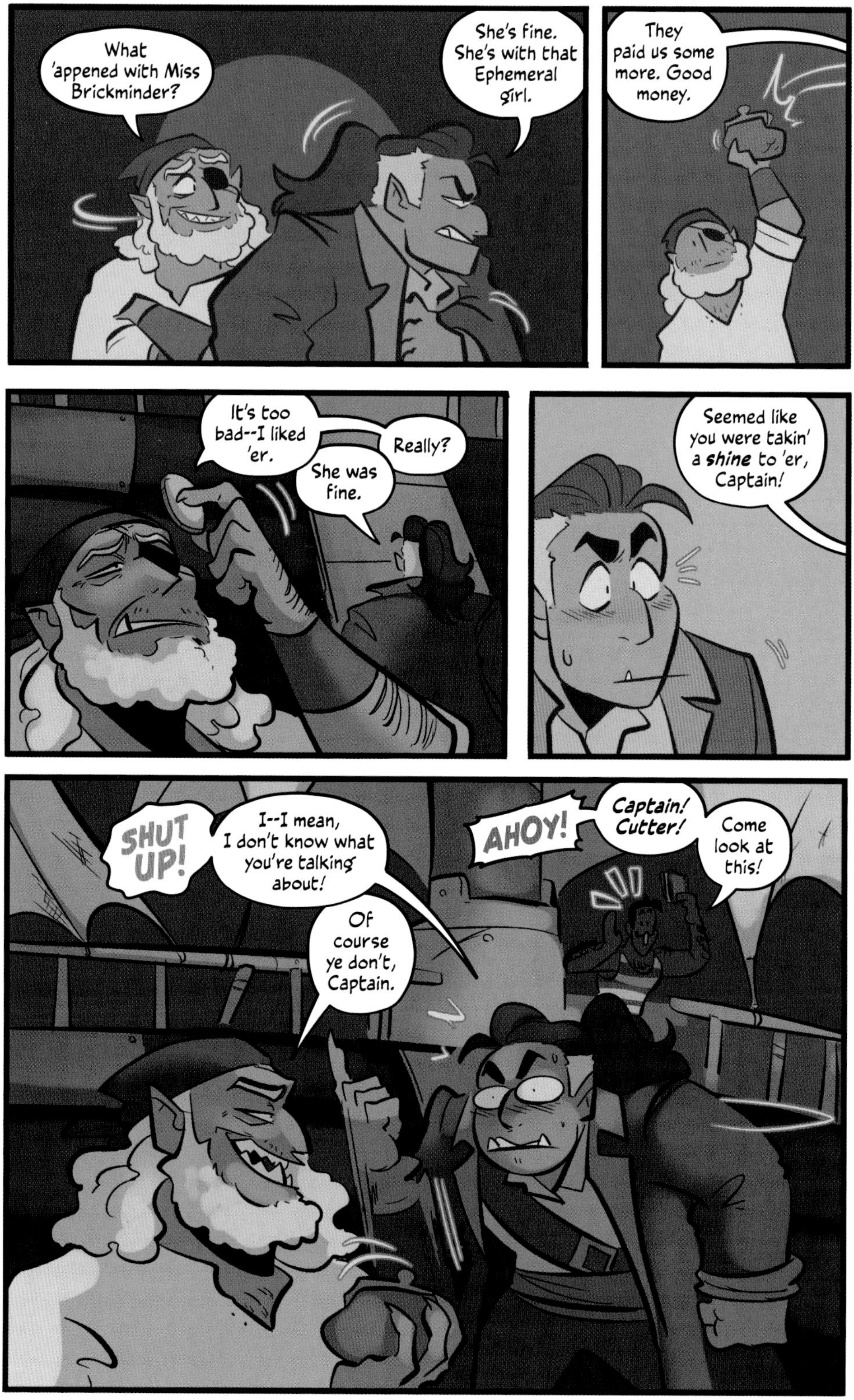
What 'appened with Miss Brickminder?
She's fine. She's with that Ephemeral girl.
They paid us some more. Good money.
It's too bad--I liked 'er.
Really?
She was fine.
Seemed like you were takin' a ***shine*** to 'er, Captain!
SHUT UP!
I--I mean, I don't know what you're talking about!
Of course ye don't, Captain.
AHOY!
Captain! Cutter!
Come look at this!

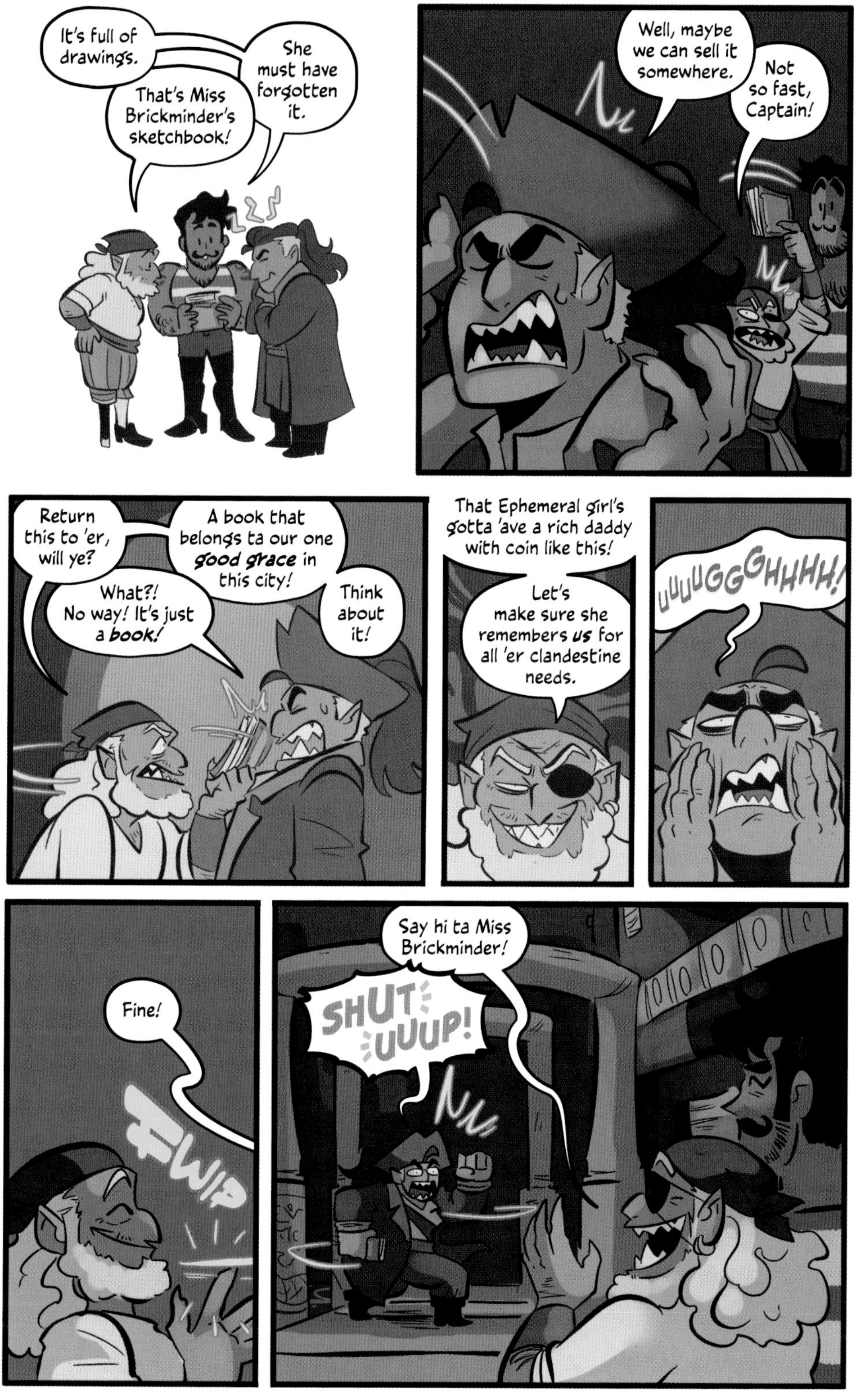
It's full of drawings.
That's Miss Brickminder's sketchbook!
She must have forgotten it.
Well, maybe we can sell it somewhere.
Not so fast, Captain!
Return this to 'er, will ye?
A book that belongs ta our one *good grace* in this city!
What?! No way! It's just a *book*!
Think about it!
That Ephemeral girl's gotta 'ave a rich daddy with coin like this!
Let's make sure she remembers *us* for all 'er clandestine needs.
UUUUGGGHHHH!
Fine!
FWIP
Say hi ta Miss Brickminder!
SHUT UUUP!

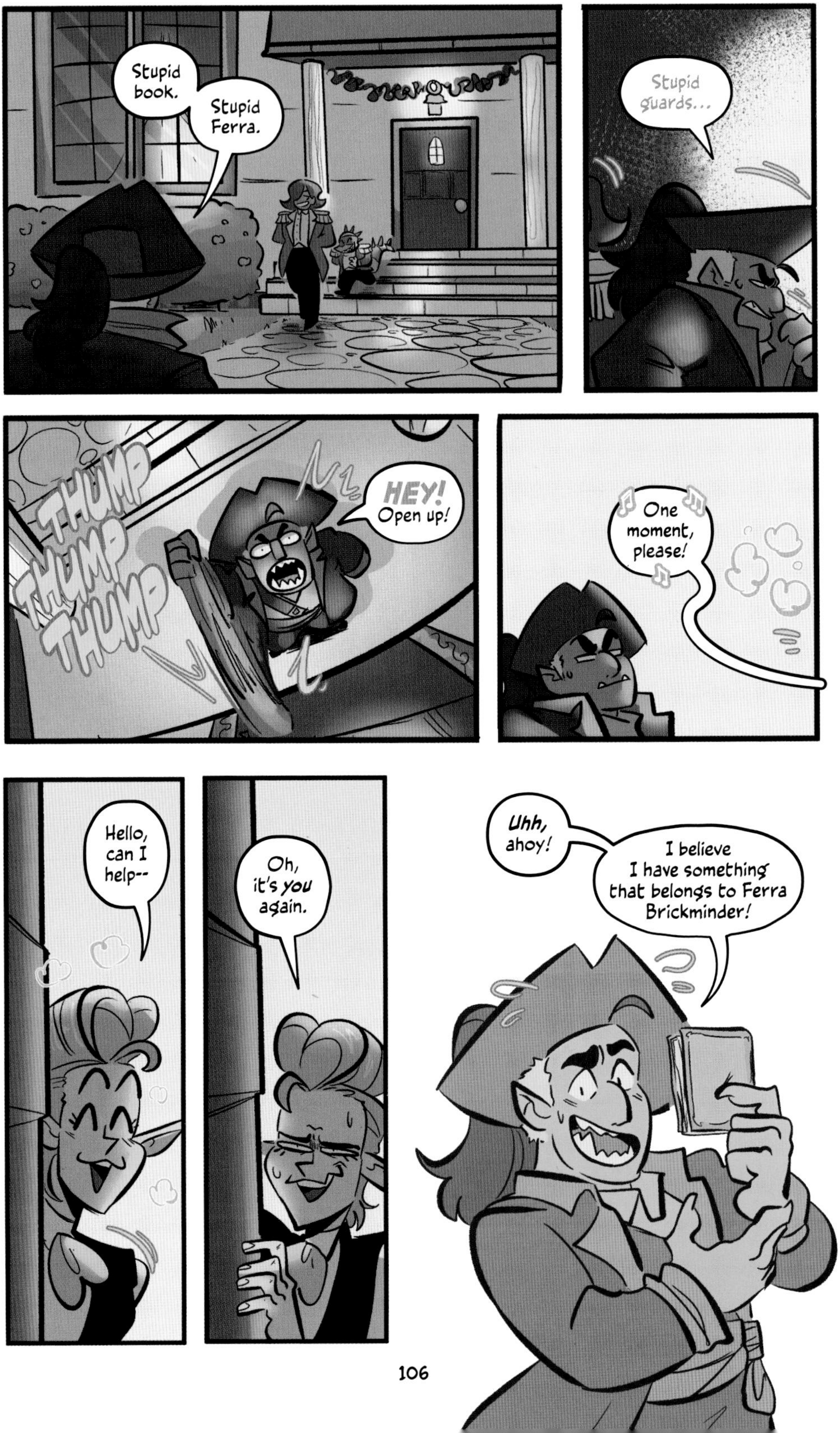
Stupid book.
Stupid Ferra.
Stupid guards...
THUMP THUMP THUMP
HEY! Open up!
One moment, please!
Hello, can I help--
Oh, it's *you* again.
Uhh, ahoy!
I believe I have something that belongs to Ferra Brickminder!

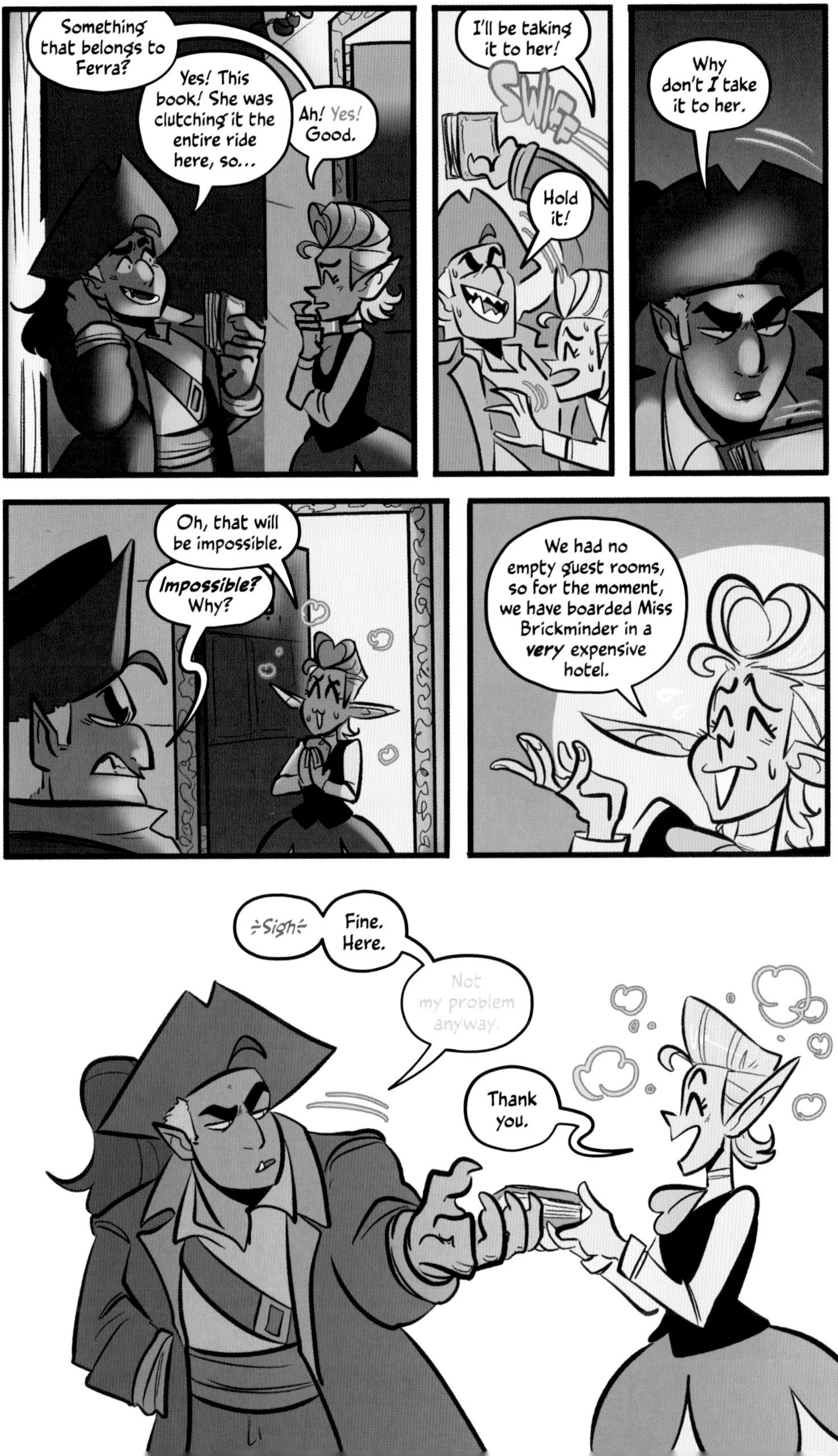
Something that belongs to Ferra?
Yes! This book! She was clutching it the entire ride here, so...
Ah! Yes! Good.
I'll be taking it to her!
SWIFF
Hold it!
Why don't I take it to her.
Oh, that will be impossible.
Impossible? Why?
We had no empty guest rooms, so for the moment, we have boarded Miss Brickminder in a very expensive hotel.
Sigh
Fine. Here.
Not my problem anyway.
Thank you.

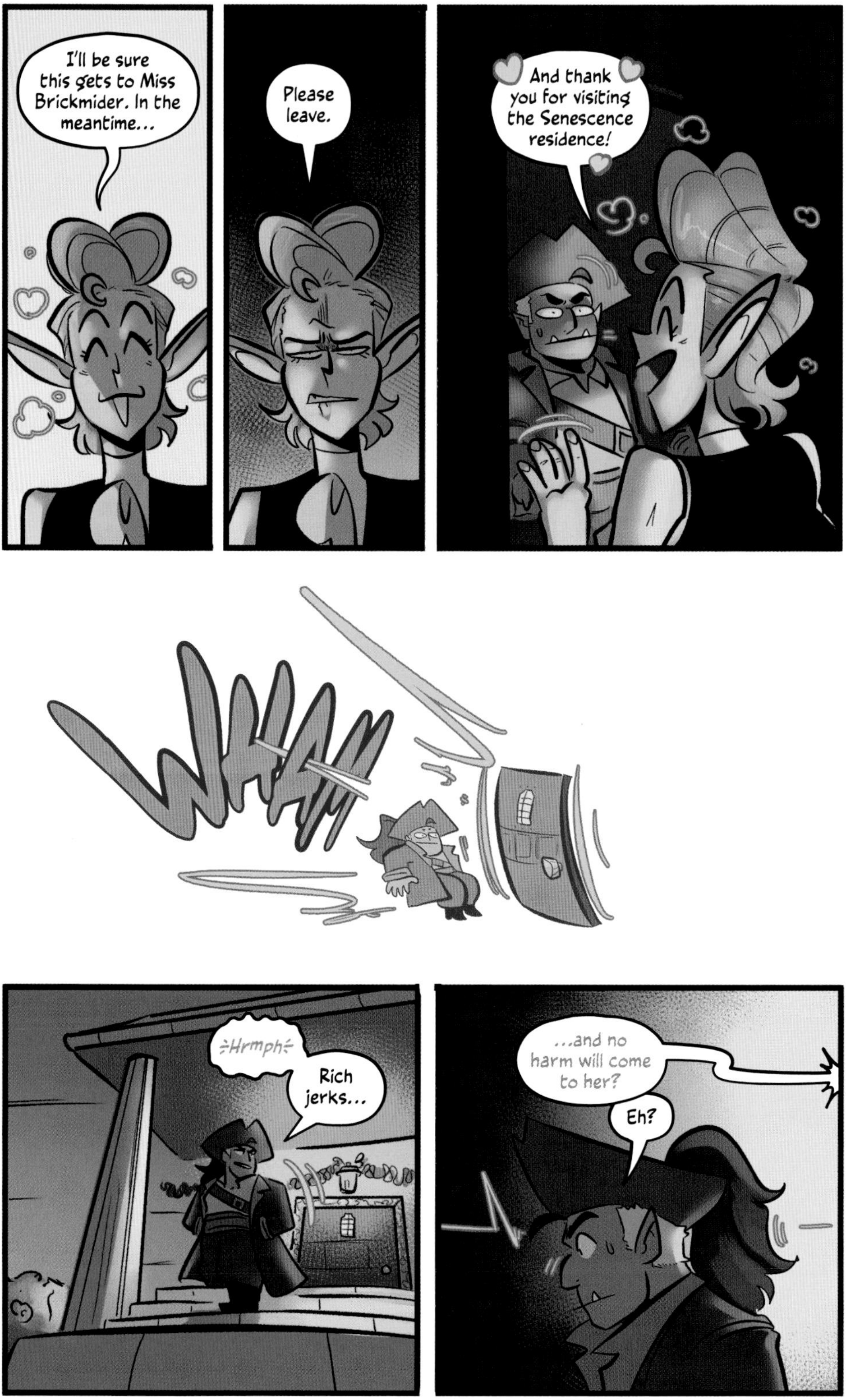
I'll be sure this gets to Miss Brickmider. In the meantime...
Please leave.
And thank you for visiting the Senescence residence!
WHAM
Hrmph
Rich jerks...
...and no harm will come to her?
Eh?

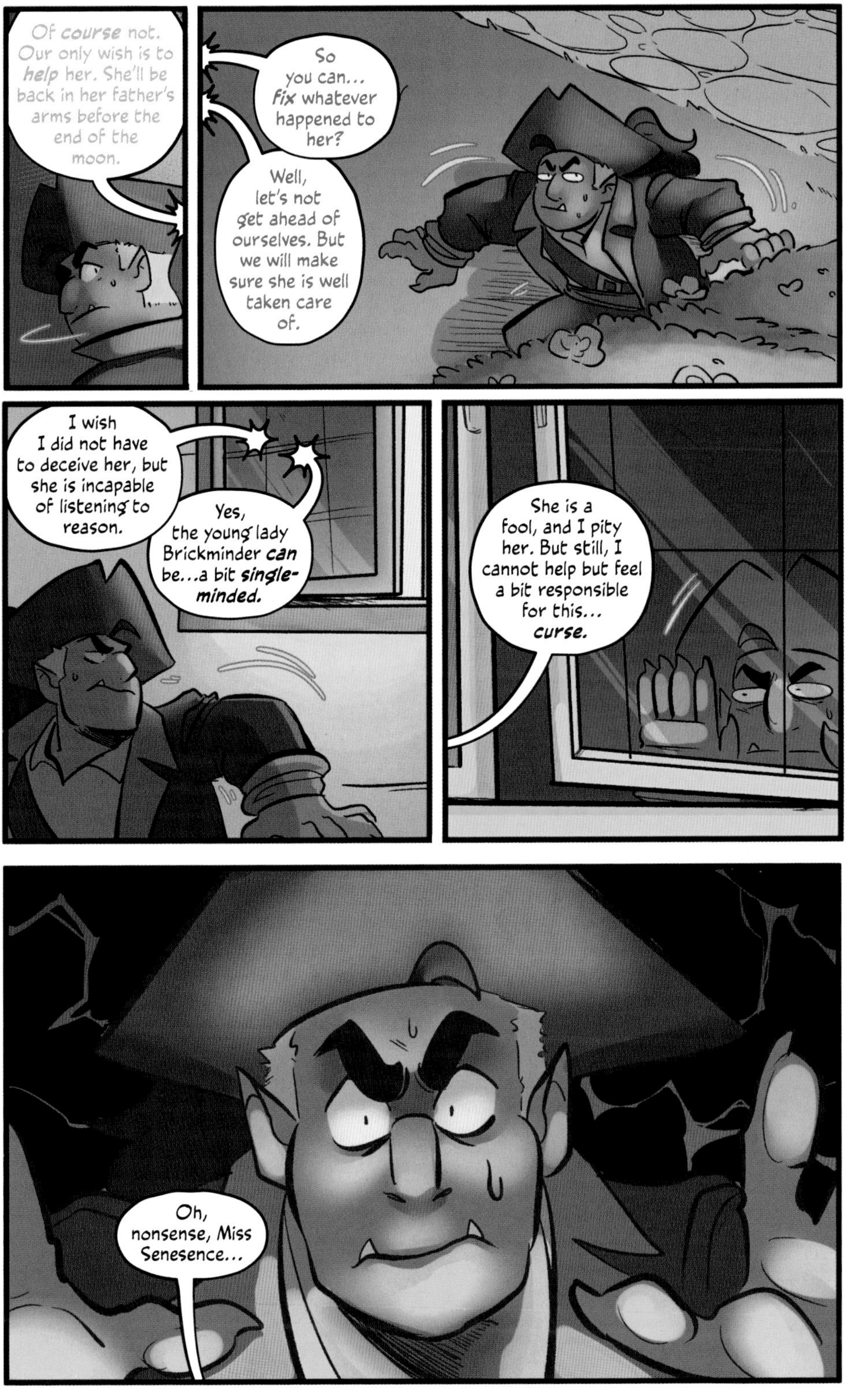
Of course not. Our only wish is to help her. She'll be back in her father's arms before the end of the moon.
So you can... fix whatever happened to her?
Well, let's not get ahead of ourselves. But we will make sure she is well taken care of.
I wish I did not have to deceive her, but she is incapable of listening to reason.
Yes, the young lady Brickminder can be...a bit single-minded.
She is a fool, and I pity her. But still, I cannot help but feel a bit responsible for this... curse.
Oh, nonsense, Miss Senesence...

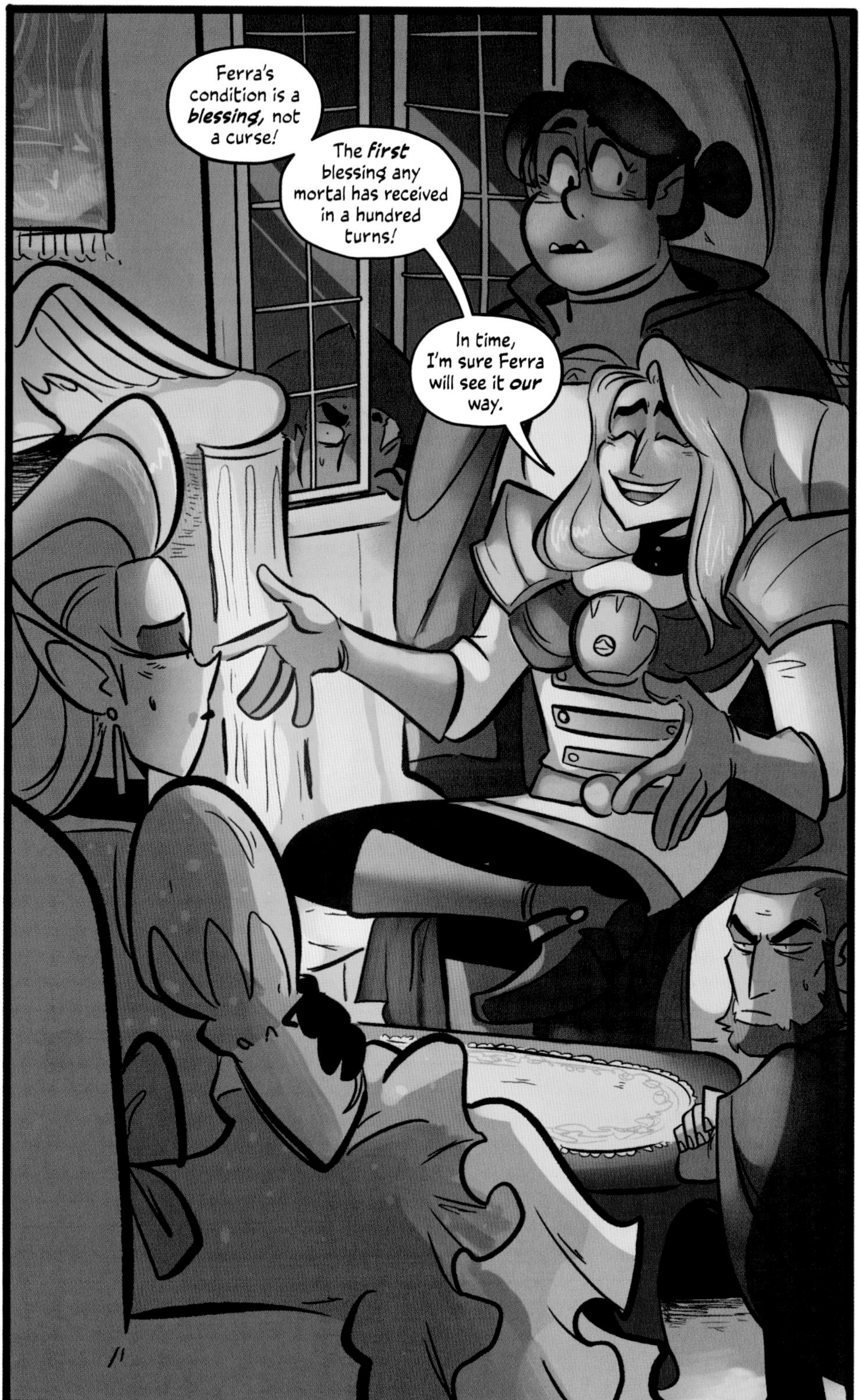
Ferra's condition is a ***blessing,*** not a curse!
The ***first*** blessing any mortal has received in a hundred turns!
In time, I'm sure Ferra will see it ***our*** way.

Chapter 4

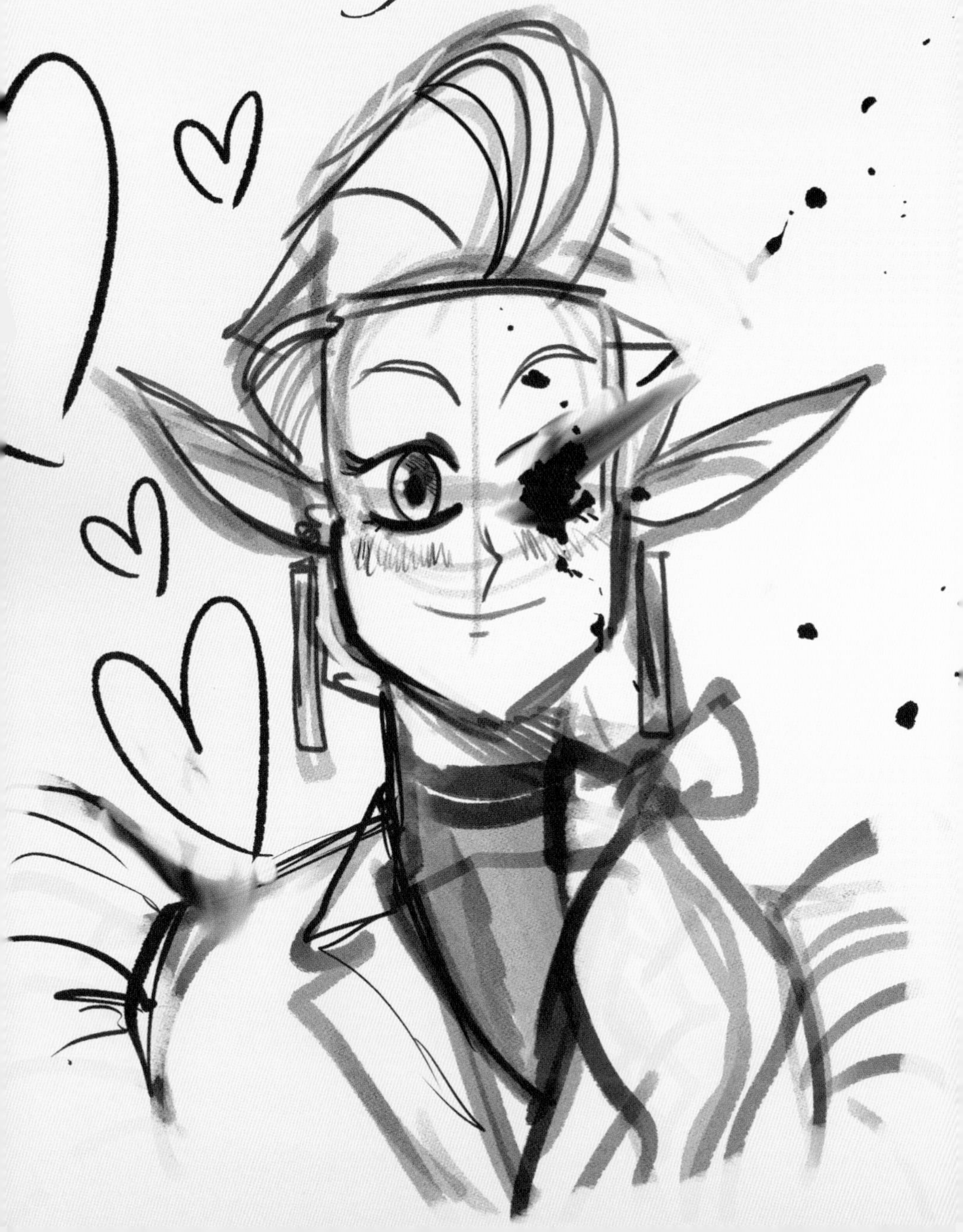

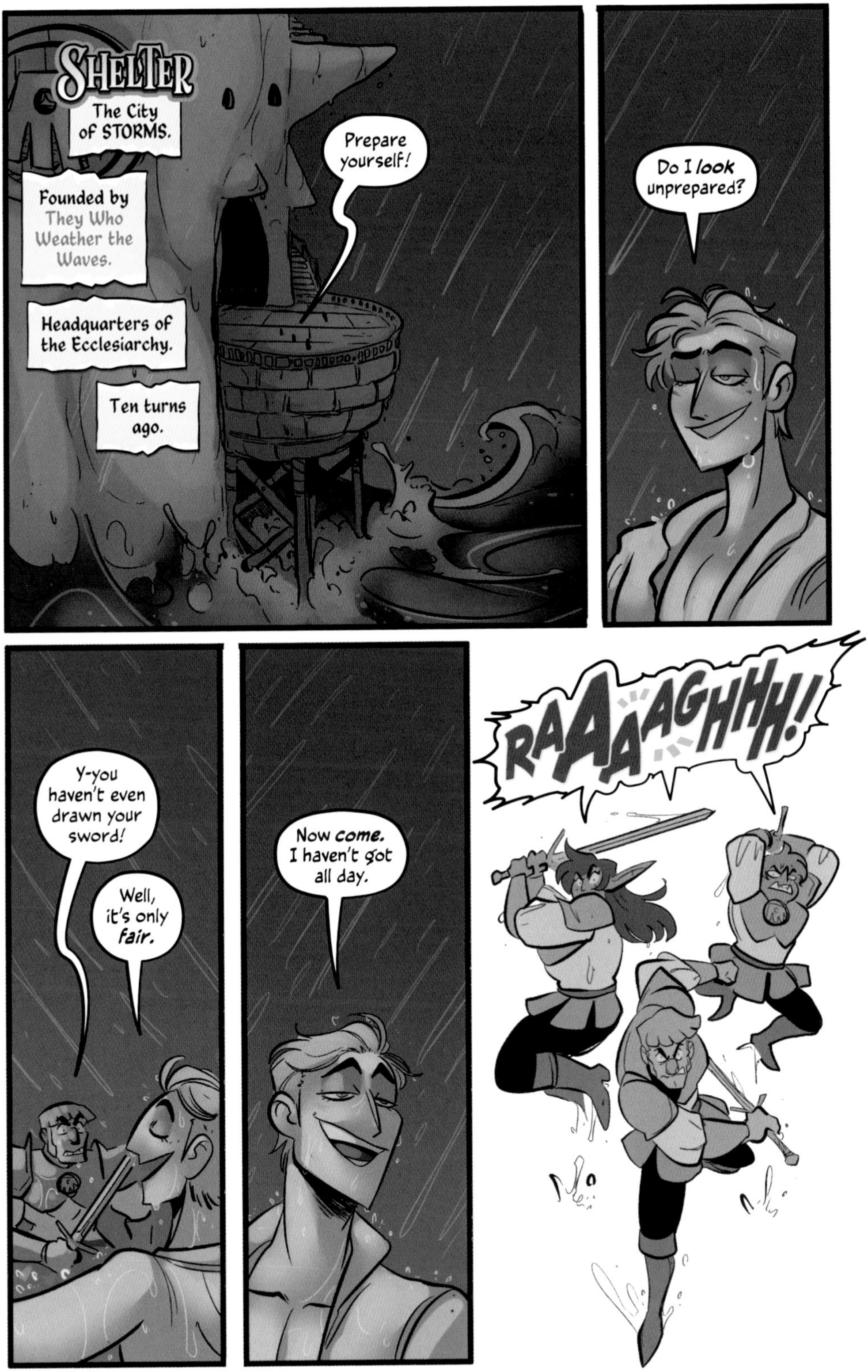
SHELTER
The City of STORMS.
Founded by They Who Weather the Waves.
Headquarters of the Ecclesiarchy.
Ten turns ago.
Prepare yourself!
Do I *look* unprepared?
Y-you haven't even drawn your sword!
Well, it's only *fair.*
Now *come.* I haven't got all day.
RAAAAGHHH!

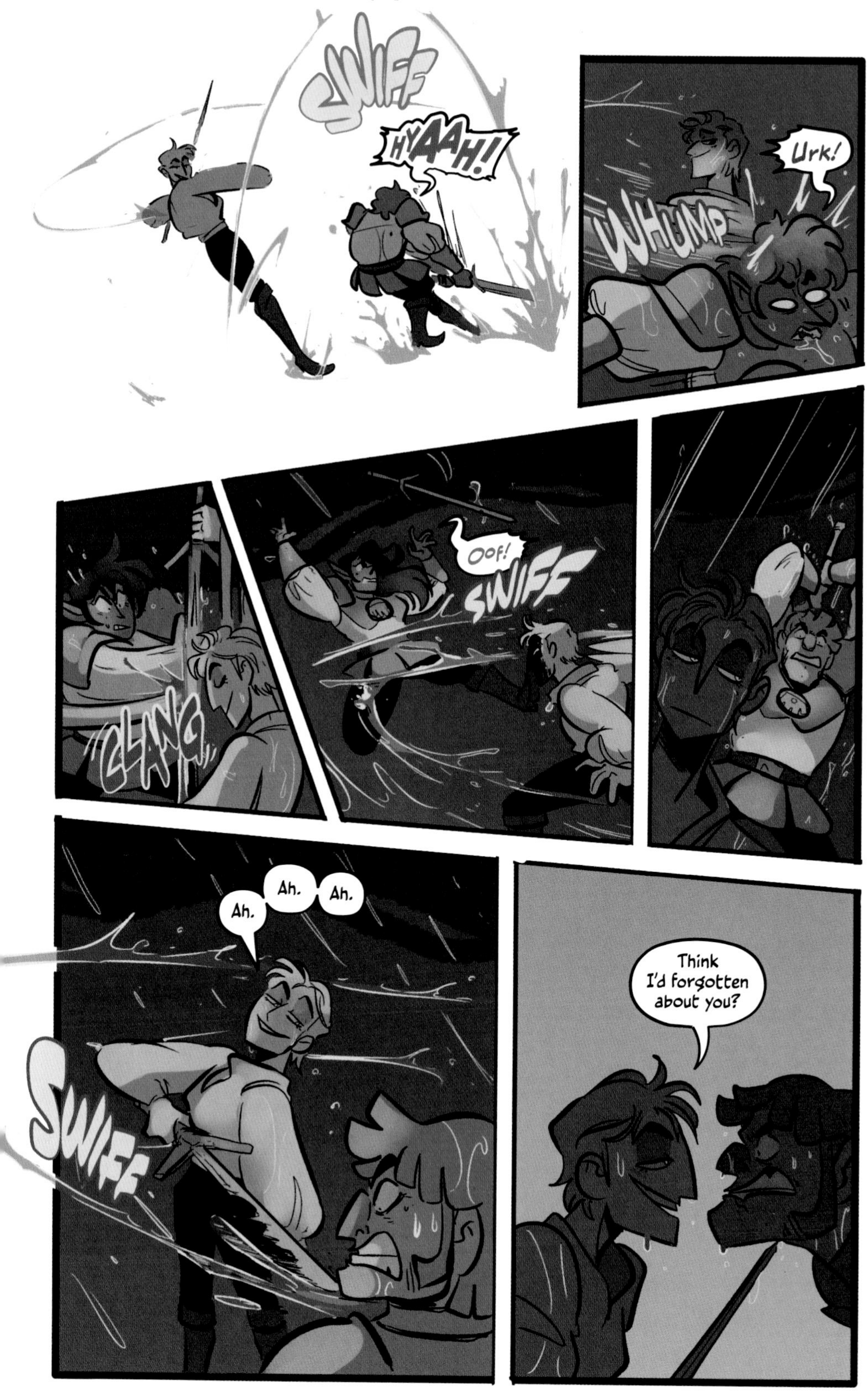
SWIFF
HYAAH!
Urk!
WHUMP
CLANG
OOF!
SWIFF
Ah.
Ah.
Ah.
SWIFF
Think I'd forgotten about you?

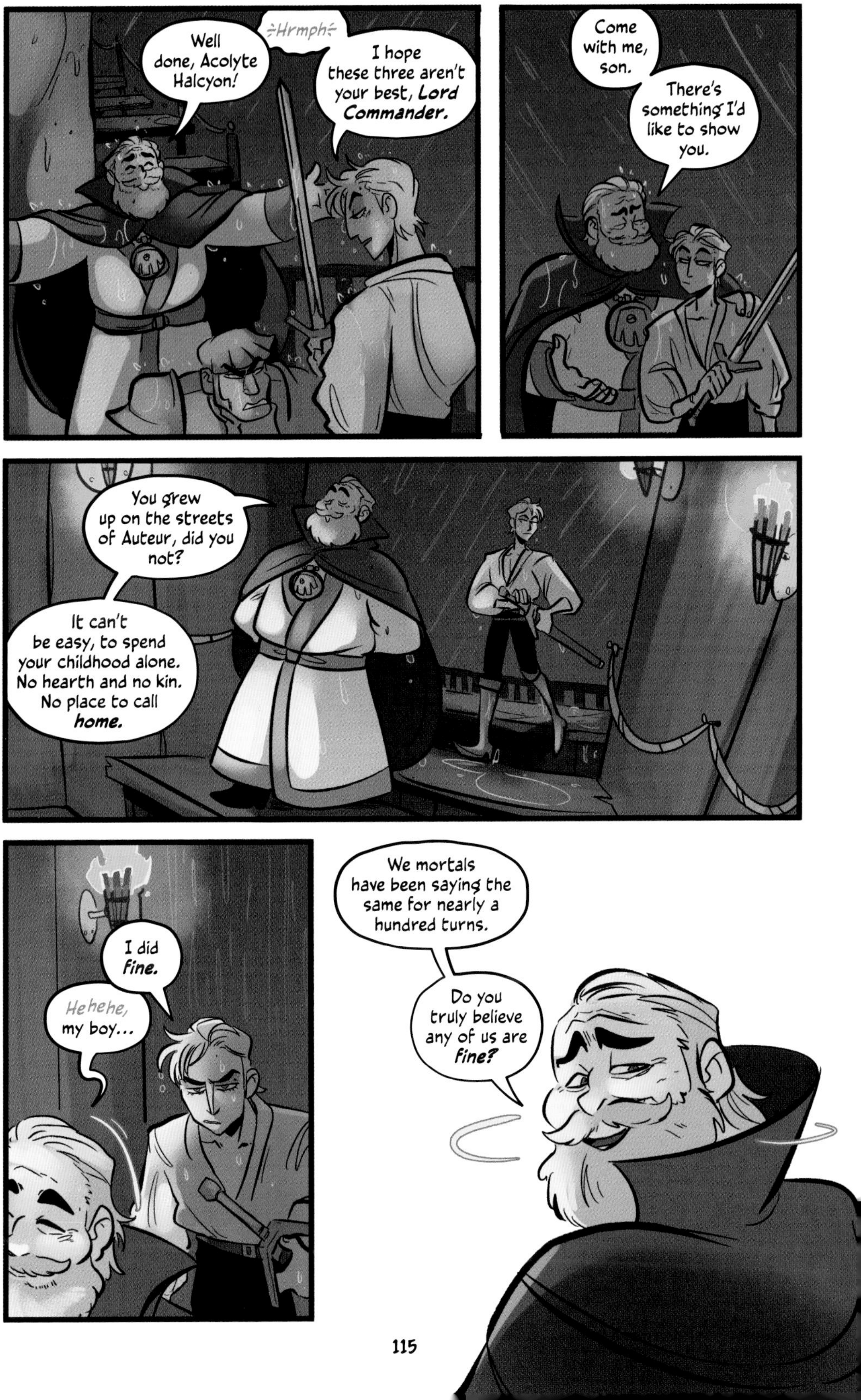
Well done, Acolyte Halcyon!
Hrmph
I hope these three aren't your best, Lord Commander.
Come with me, son.
There's something I'd like to show you.
You grew up on the streets of Auteur, did you not?
It can't be easy, to spend your childhood alone. No hearth and no kin. No place to call home.
I did fine.
Hehehe, my boy...
We mortals have been saying the same for nearly a hundred turns.
Do you truly believe any of us are fine?

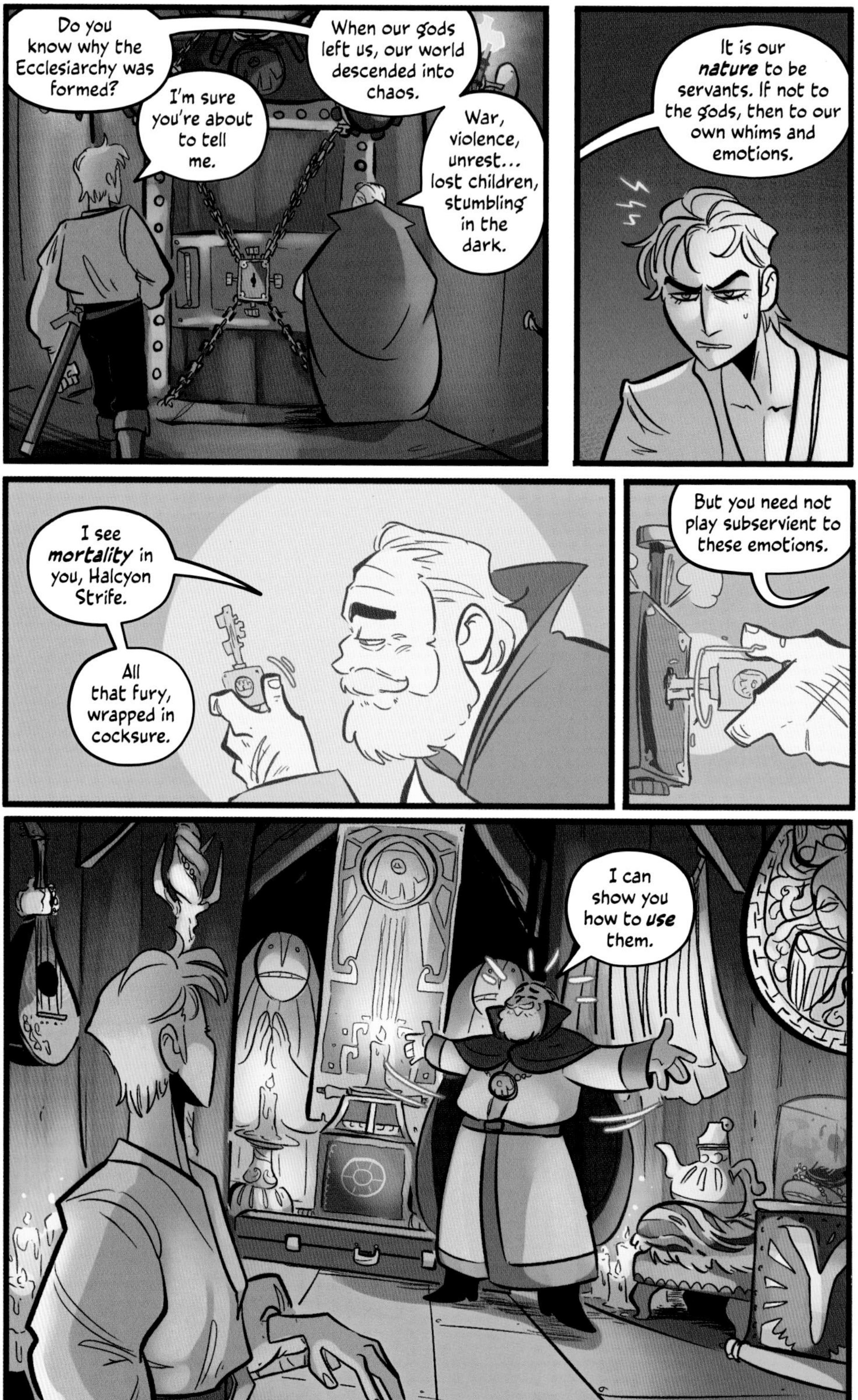
Do you know why the Ecclesiarchy was formed?
I'm sure you're about to tell me.
When our gods left us, our world descended into chaos.
War, violence, unrest... lost children, stumbling in the dark.
It is our *nature* to be servants. If not to the gods, then to our own whims and emotions.
I see *mortality* in you, Halcyon Strife.
All that fury, wrapped in cocksure.
But you need not play subservient to these emotions.
I can show you how to *use* them.

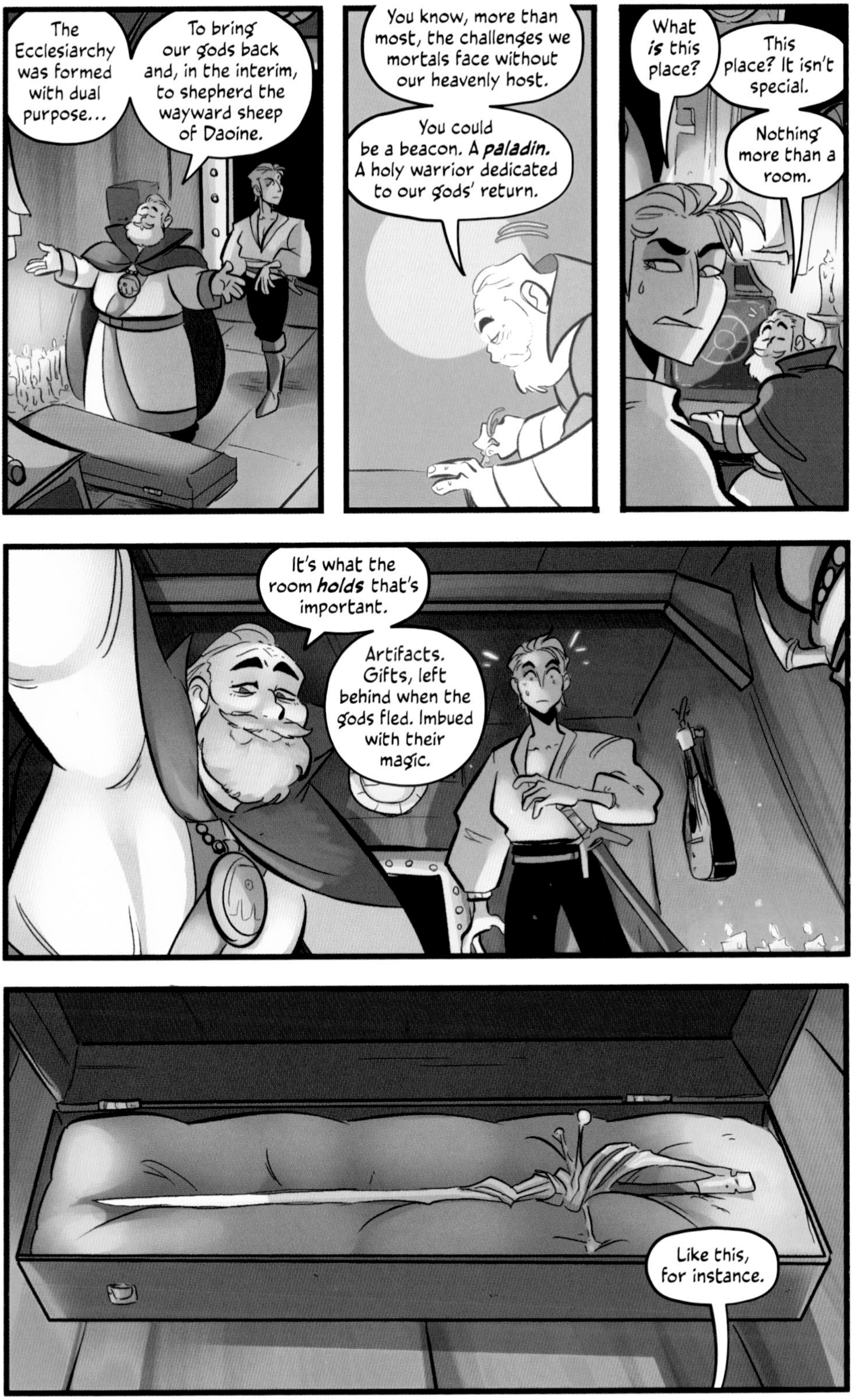
The Ecclesiarchy was formed with dual purpose...
To bring our gods back and, in the interim, to shepherd the wayward sheep of Daoine.
You know, more than most, the challenges we mortals face without our heavenly host.
You could be a beacon. A *paladin.* A holy warrior dedicated to our gods' return.
What *is* this place?
This place? It isn't special.
Nothing more than a room.
It's what the room *holds* that's important.
Artifacts. Gifts, left behind when the gods fled. Imbued with their magic.
Like this, for instance.

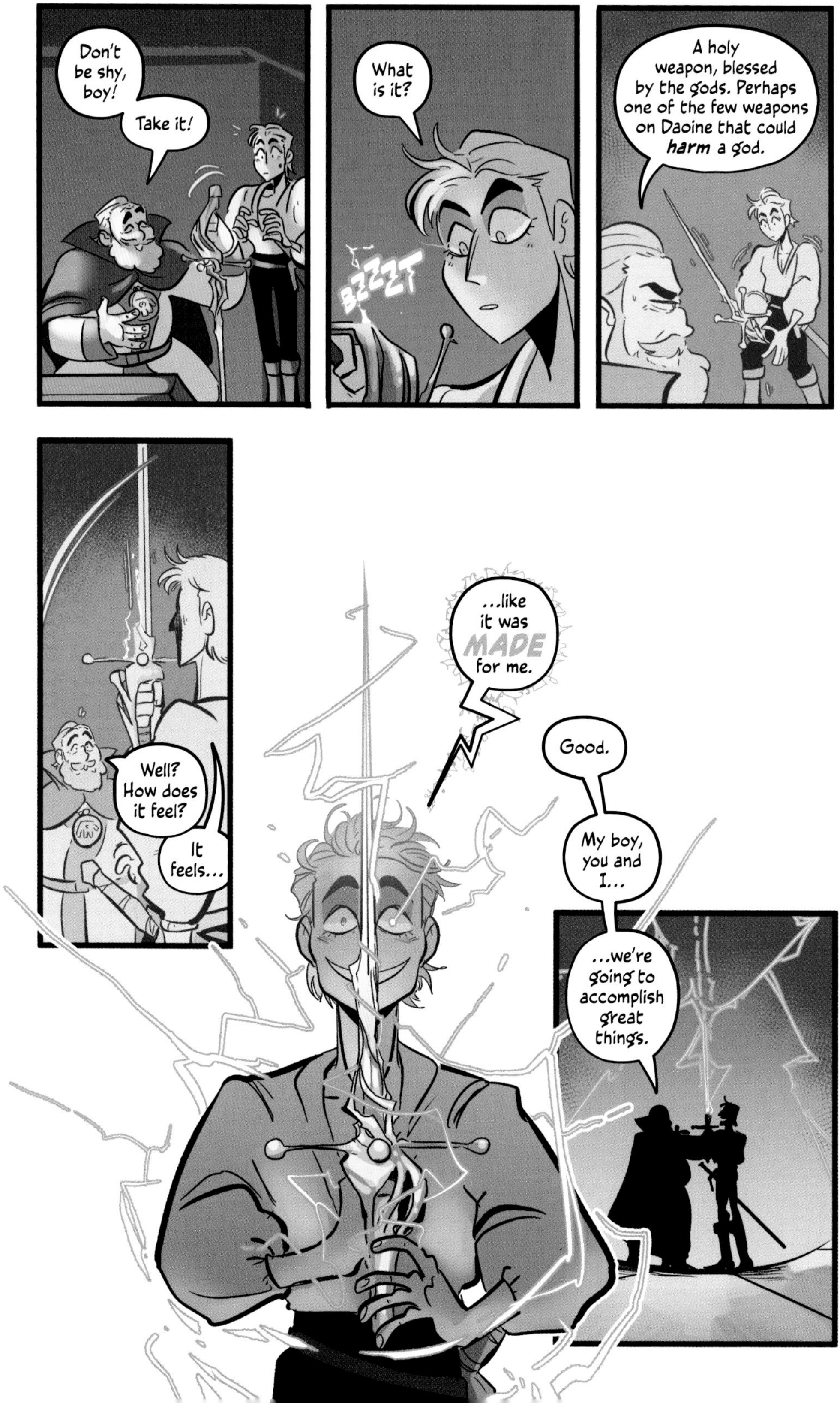

Don't be shy, boy!
Take it!
What is it?
BZZZT
A holy weapon, blessed by the gods. Perhaps one of the few weapons on Daoine that could **harm** a god.
Well? How does it feel?
It feels...
...like it was MADE for me.
Good.
My boy, you and I...
...we're going to accomplish great things.

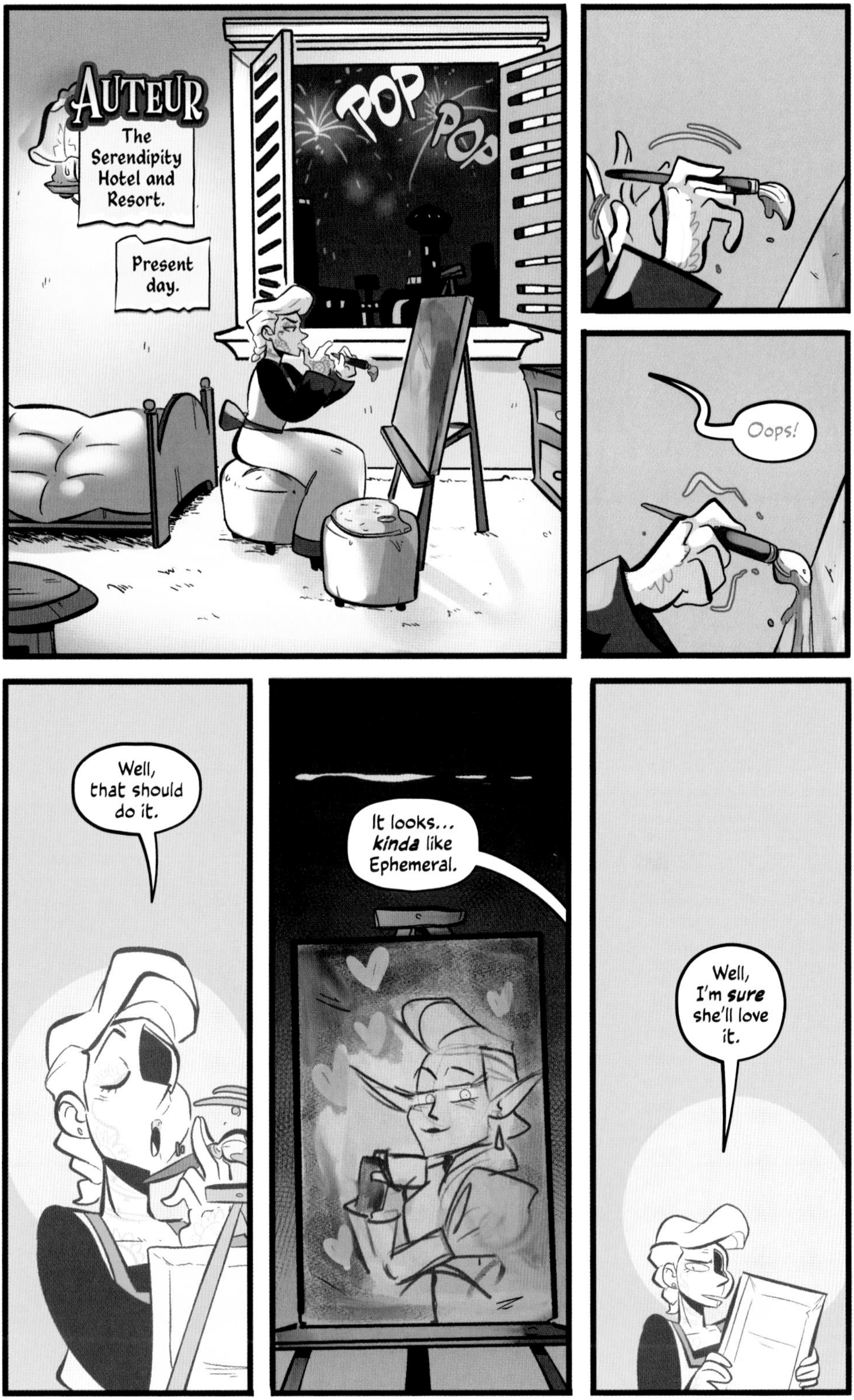
AUTEUR
The Serendipity Hotel and Resort.
Present day.
POP
POP
Oops!
Well, that should do it.
It looks... *kinda* like Ephemeral.
Well, I'm *sure* she'll love it.

--erraaaa!

That sounded like...

Ah, Ferra.

Hearing things.

FERRRAAAA!

BWAH!

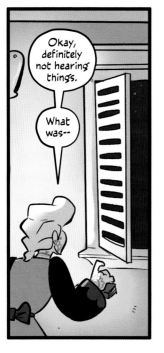

Okay, definitely not hearing things.

What was--

FERRAA!

YAAAH!

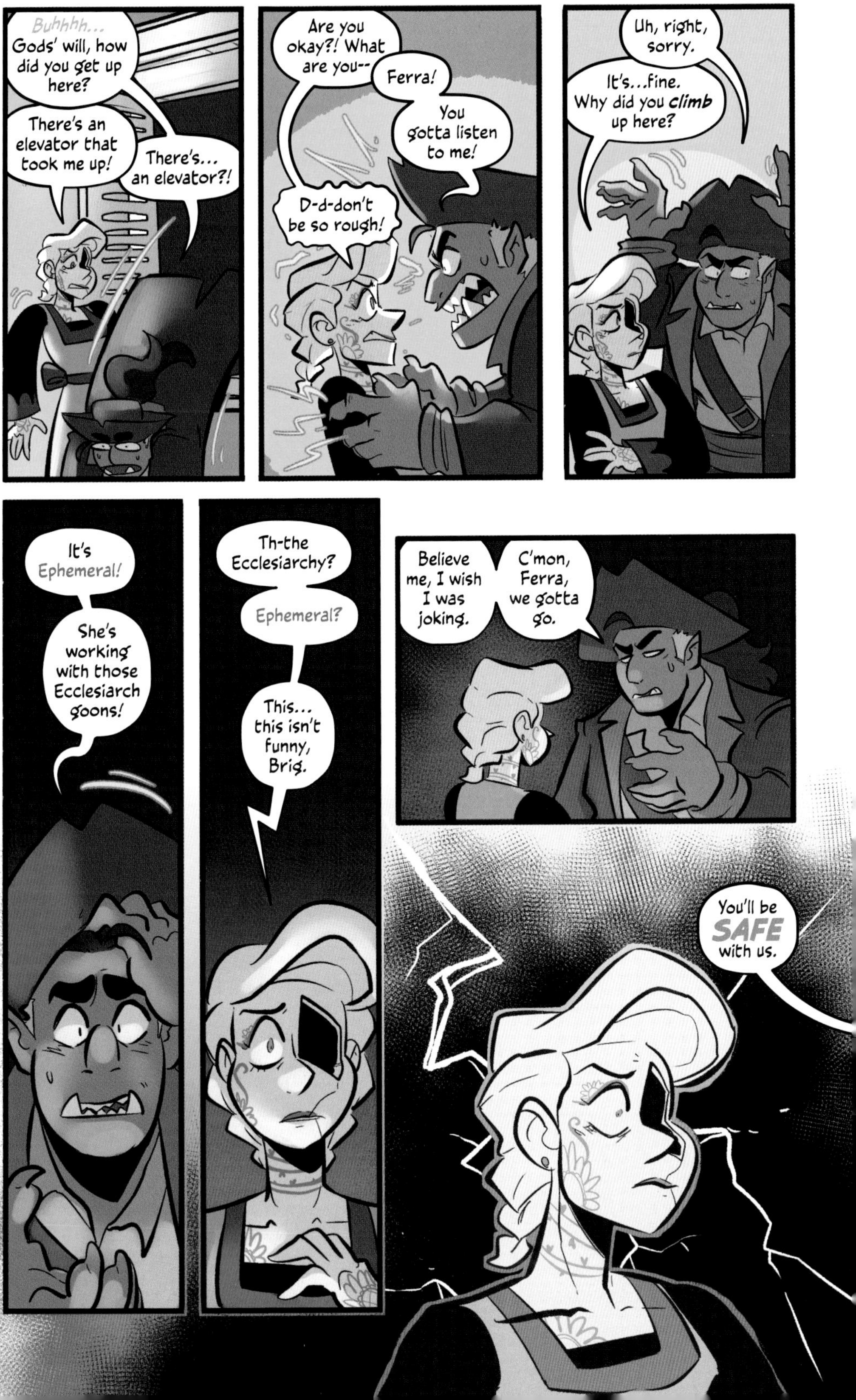
Buhhhh...
Gods' will, how did you get up here?
There's an elevator that took me up!
There's... an elevator?!
Are you okay?! What are you--
Ferra!
You gotta listen to me!
D-d-don't be so rough!
Uh, right, sorry.
It's...fine. Why did you climb up here?
It's Ephemeral!
She's working with those Ecclesiarch goons!
Th-the Ecclesiarchy?
Ephemeral?
This... this isn't funny, Brig.
Believe me, I wish I was joking.
C'mon, Ferra, we gotta go.
You'll be SAFE with us.

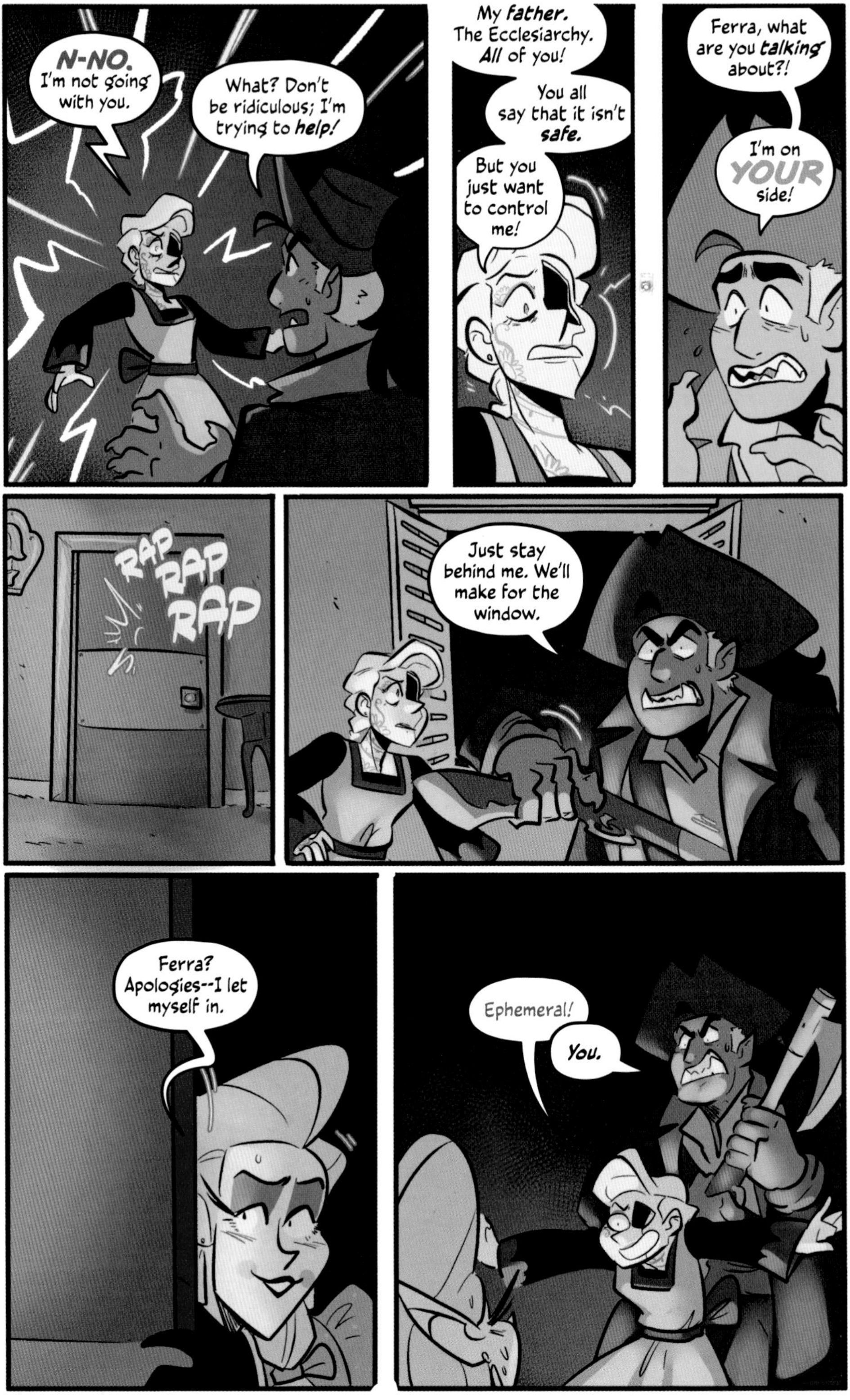
N-NO. I'm not going with you.
What? Don't be ridiculous; I'm trying to help!
My father. The Ecclesiarchy. All of you!
You all say that it isn't safe.
But you just want to control me!
Ferra, what are you talking about?!
I'm on YOUR side!
RAP RAP RAP
Just stay behind me. We'll make for the window.
Ferra? Apologies--I let myself in.
Ephemeral!
You.

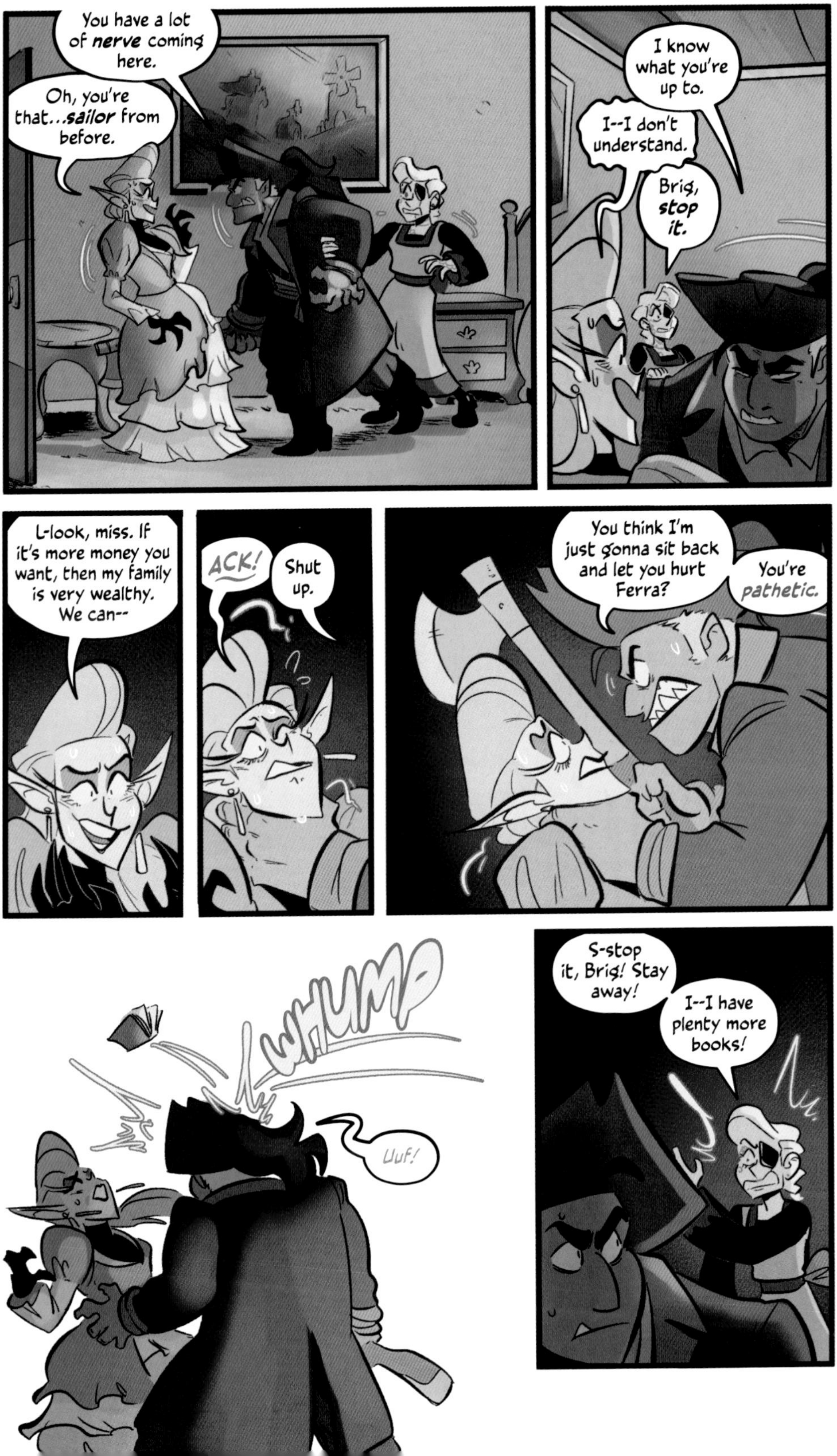
You have a lot of *nerve* coming here.
Oh, you're that...*sailor* from before.
I know what you're up to.
I--I don't understand.
Brig, *stop it.*
L-look, miss. If it's more money you want, then my family is very wealthy. We can--
ACK!
Shut up.
You think I'm just gonna sit back and let you hurt Ferra?
You're *pathetic.*
WHUMP
Uuf!
S-stop it, Brig! Stay away!
I--I have plenty more books!

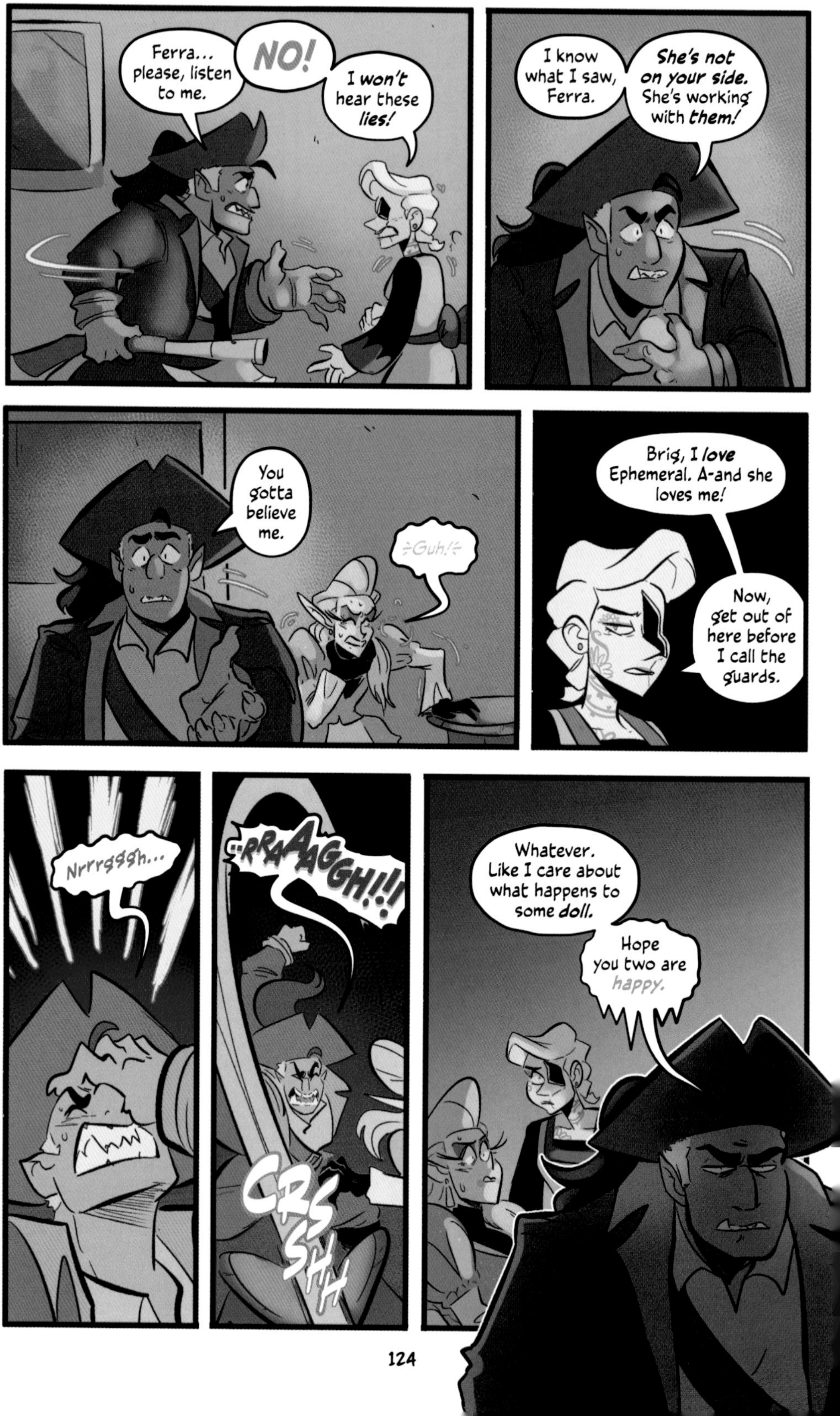
Ferra... please, listen to me.
NO!
I won't hear these lies!
I know what I saw, Ferra.
She's not on your side. She's working with them!
You gotta believe me.
Guh!
Brig, I love Ephemeral. A-and she loves me!
Now, get out of here before I call the guards.
Nrrrggh...
RRAAAGGH!!!
CRSSHH
Whatever. Like I care about what happens to some doll.
Hope you two are happy.

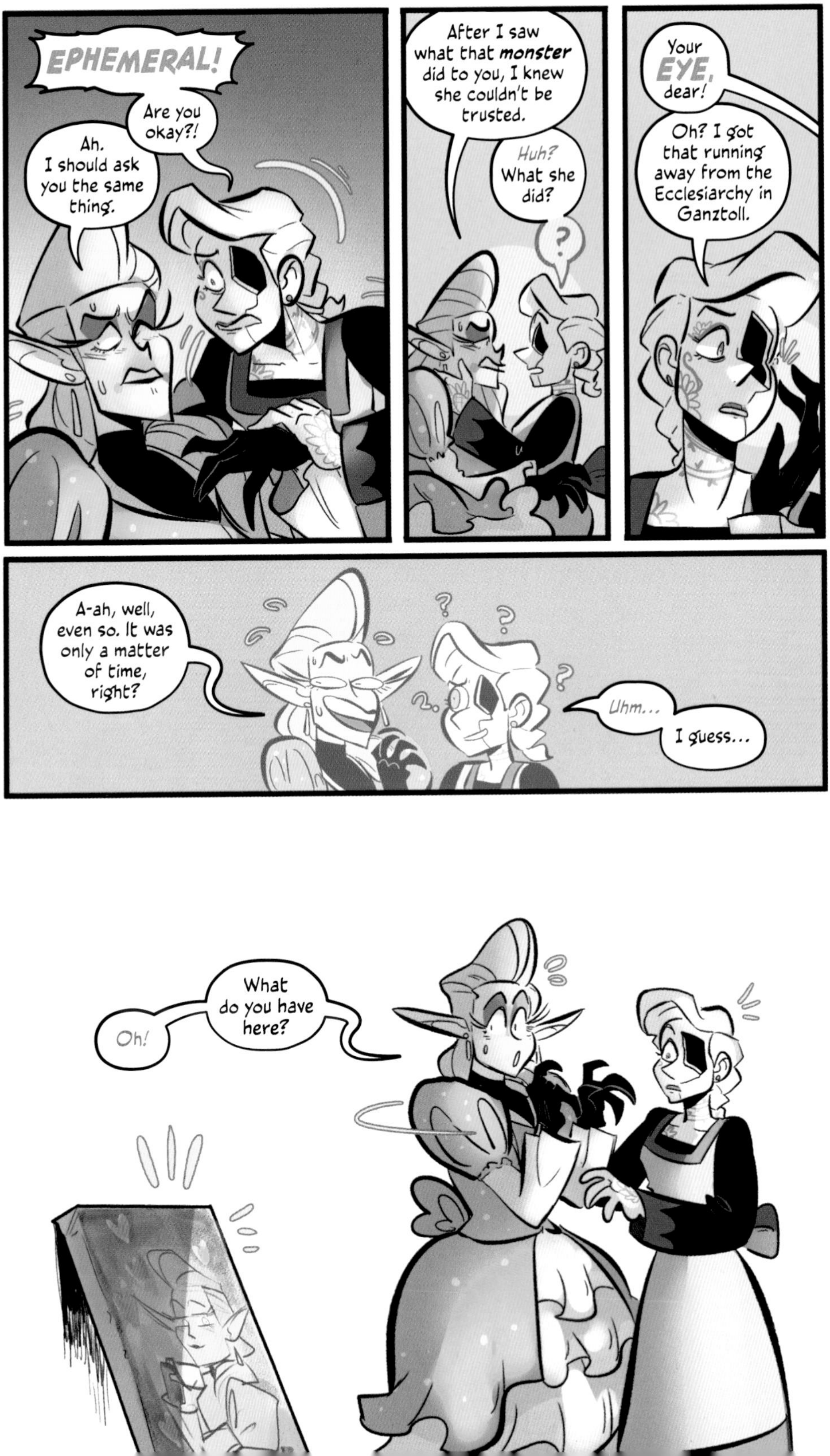
EPHEMERAL!
Are you okay?!
Ah. I should ask you the same thing.
After I saw what that monster did to you, I knew she couldn't be trusted.
Huh? What she did?
?
Your EYE, dear!
Oh? I got that running away from the Ecclesiarchy in Ganztoll.
A-ah, well, even so. It was only a matter of time, right?
Uhm...
I guess...
Oh!
What do you have here?

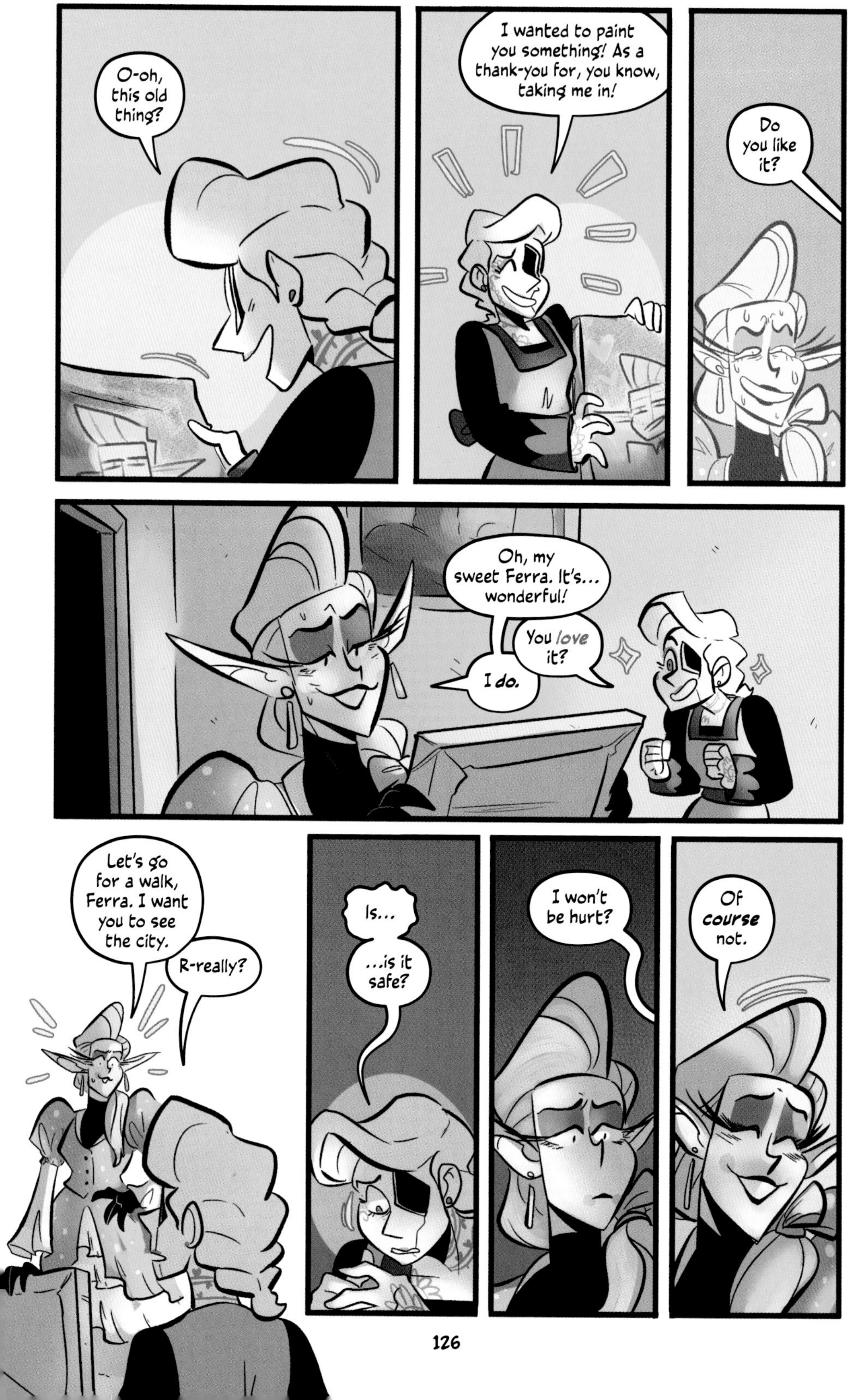
O-oh, this old thing?
I wanted to paint you something! As a thank-you for, you know, taking me in!
Do you like it?
Oh, my sweet Ferra. It's... wonderful!
You *love* it?
I *do.*
Let's go for a walk, Ferra. I want you to see the city.
R-really?
Is...
...is it safe?
I won't be hurt?
Of **course** not.

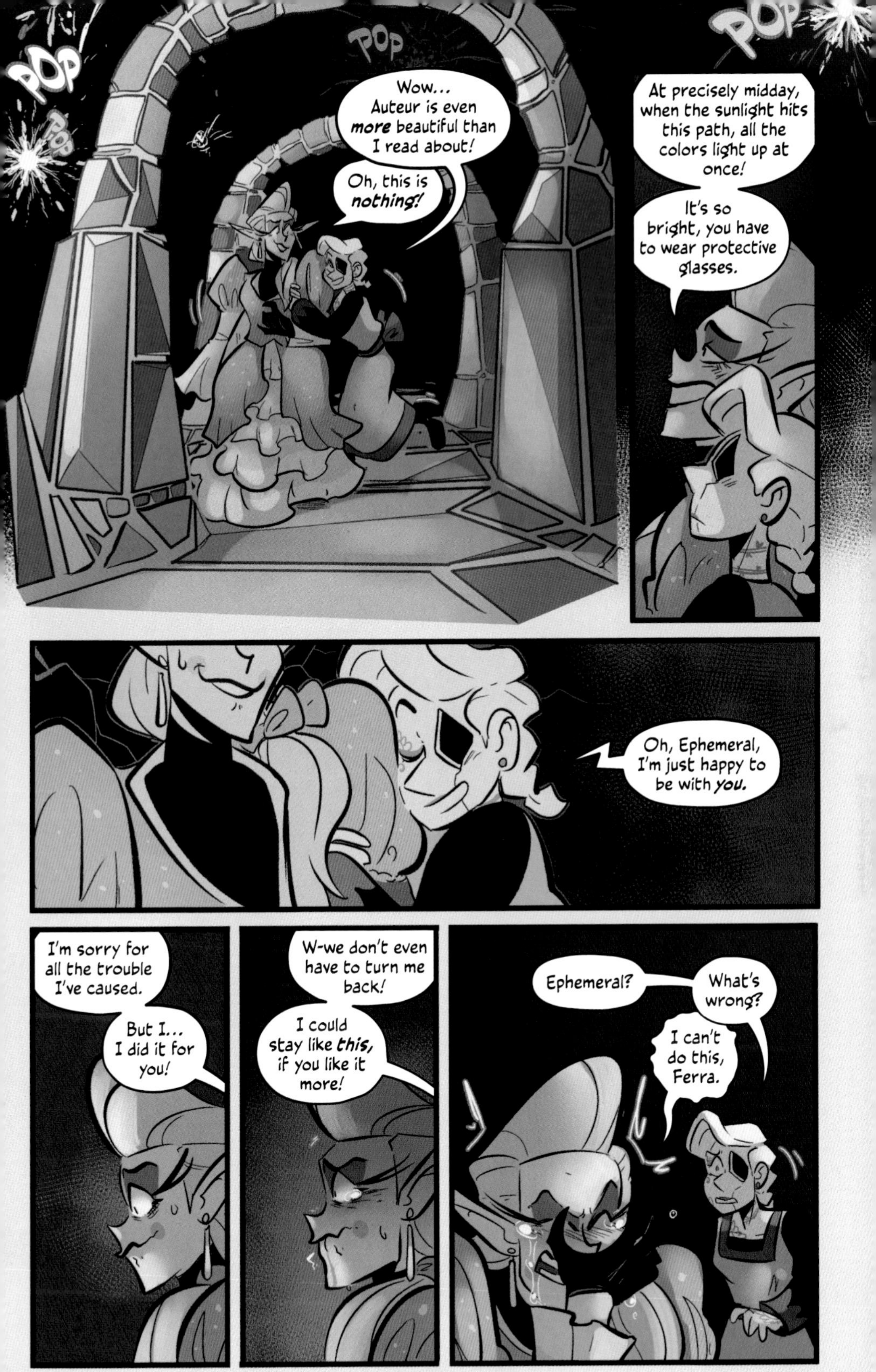
POP
POP
POP
POP
Wow... Auteur is even ***more*** beautiful than I read about!
Oh, this is ***nothing!***
At precisely midday, when the sunlight hits this path, all the colors light up at once!
It's so bright, you have to wear protective glasses.
Oh, Ephemeral, I'm just happy to be with ***you.***
I'm sorry for all the trouble I've caused.
But I... I did it for you!
W-we don't even have to turn me back!
I could stay like ***this,*** if you like it more!
Ephemeral?
What's wrong?
I can't do this, Ferra.

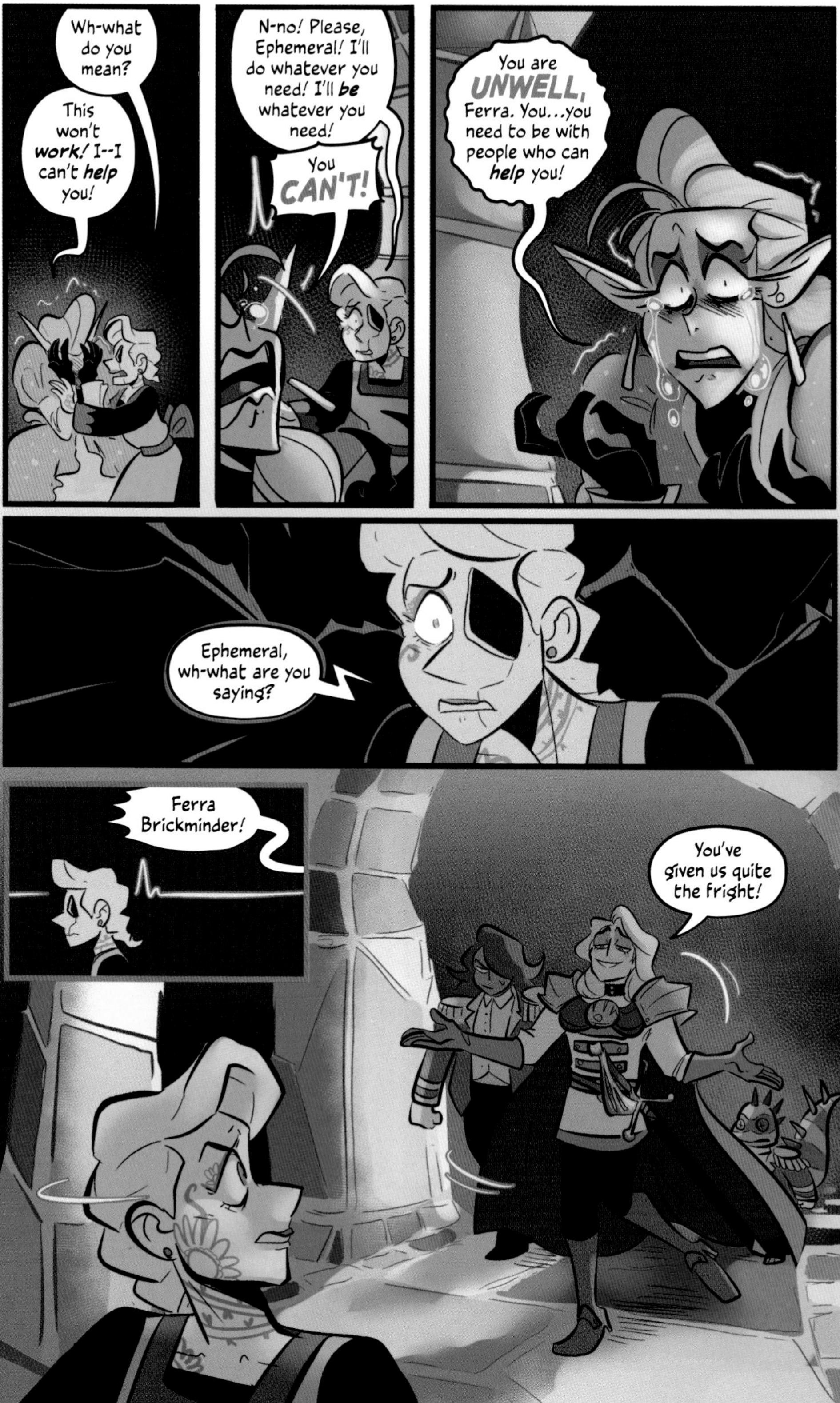
Wh-what do you mean?
This won't *work!* I--I can't *help* you!
N-no! Please, Ephemeral! I'll do whatever you need! I'll *be* whatever you need!
You CAN'T!
You are UNWELL, Ferra. You...you need to be with people who can *help* you!
Ephemeral, wh-what are you saying?
Ferra Brickminder!
You've given us quite the fright!

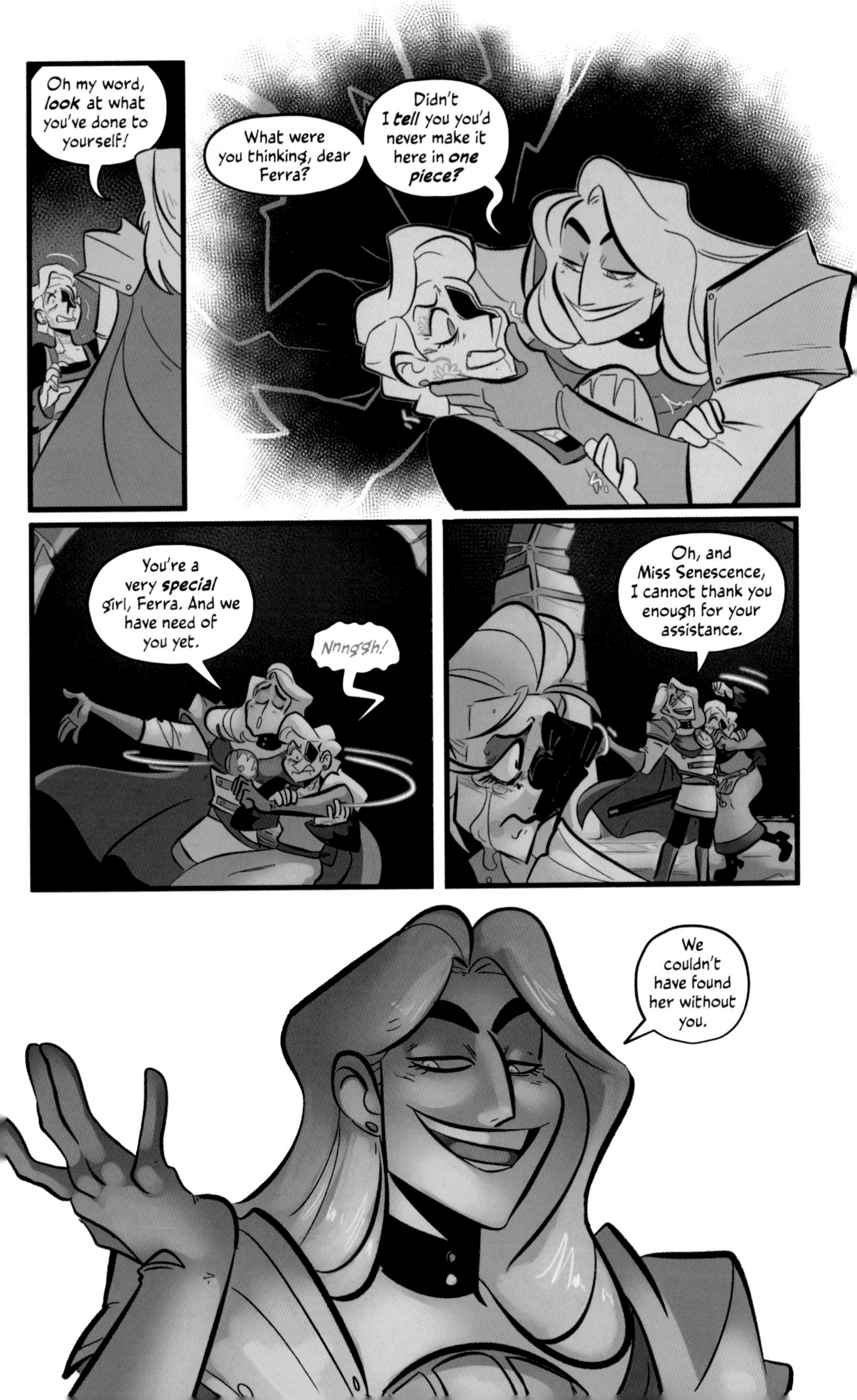

Oh my word, *look* at what you've done to yourself!
What were you thinking, dear Ferra?
Didn't I *tell* you you'd never make it here in *one piece?*
You're a very *special* girl, Ferra. And we have need of you yet.
Nnngggh!
Oh, and Miss Senescence, I cannot thank you enough for your assistance.
We couldn't have found her without you.

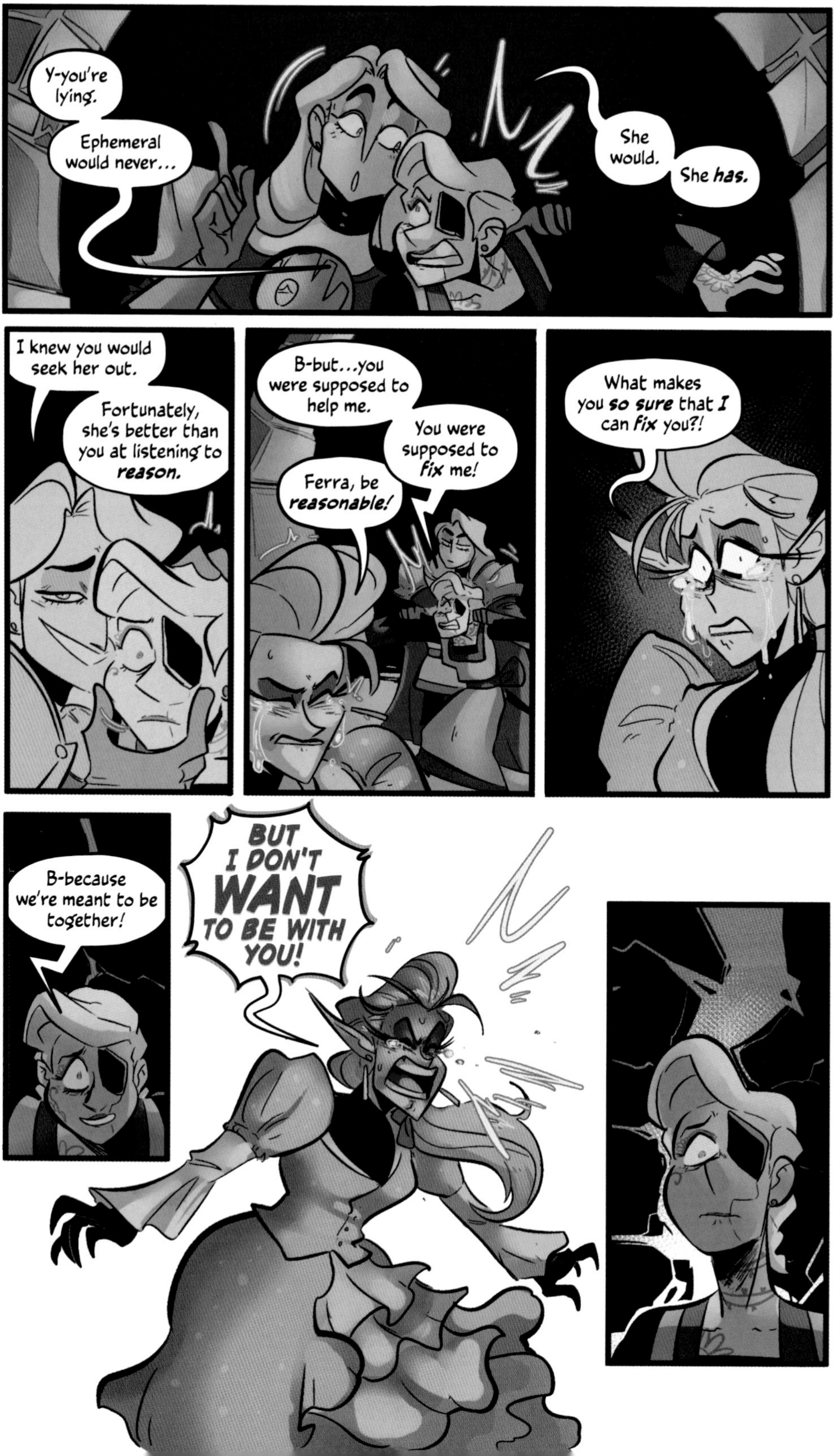
Y-you're lying.
Ephemeral would never...
She would.
She has.
I knew you would seek her out.
Fortunately, she's better than you at listening to reason.
B-but...you were supposed to help me.
You were supposed to fix me!
Ferra, be reasonable!
What makes you so sure that I can fix you?!
B-because we're meant to be together!
BUT I DON'T WANT TO BE WITH YOU!

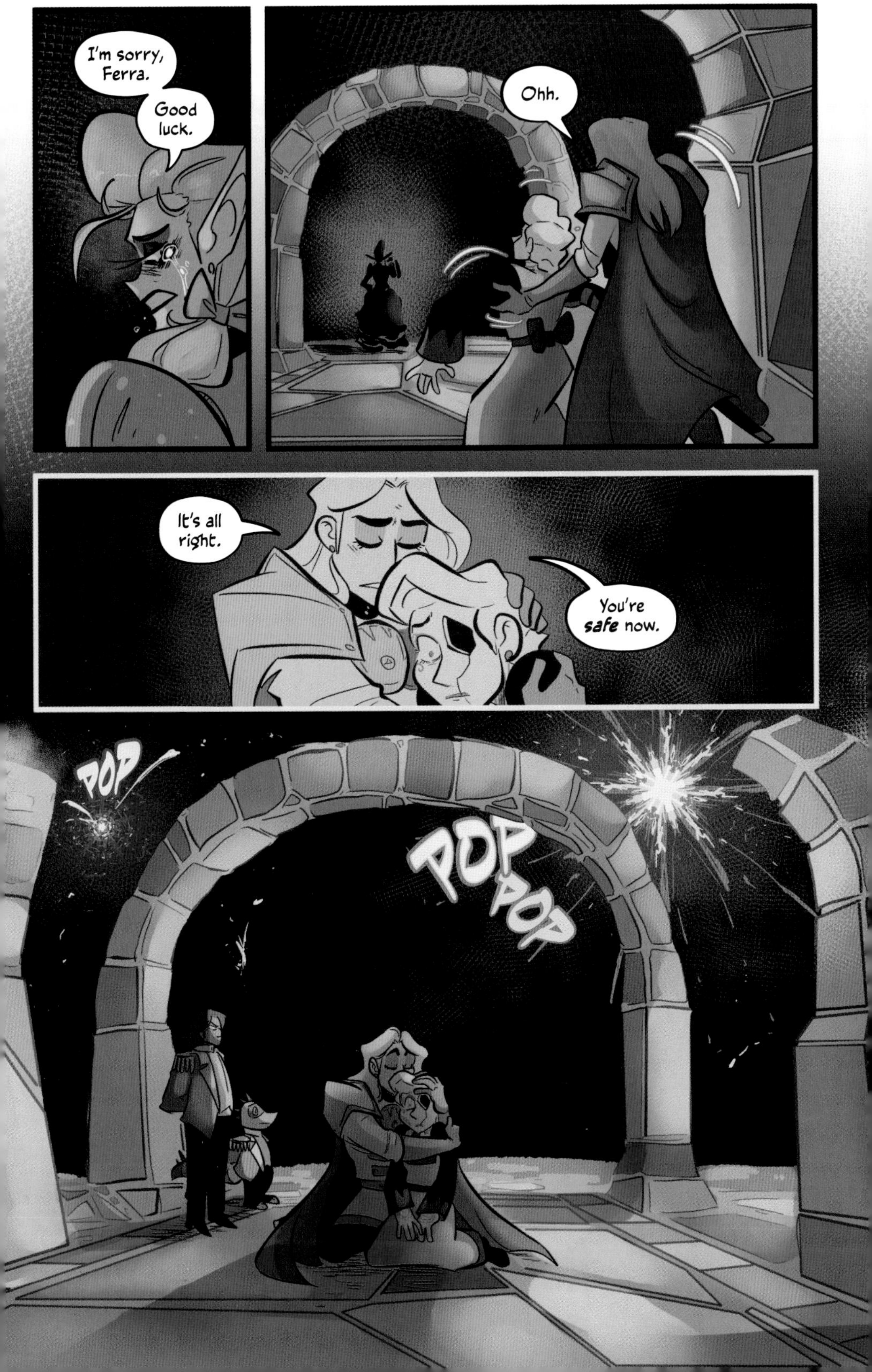
I'm sorry, Ferra.
Good luck.
Ohh.
It's all right.
You're *safe* now.
POP
POP
POP
POP

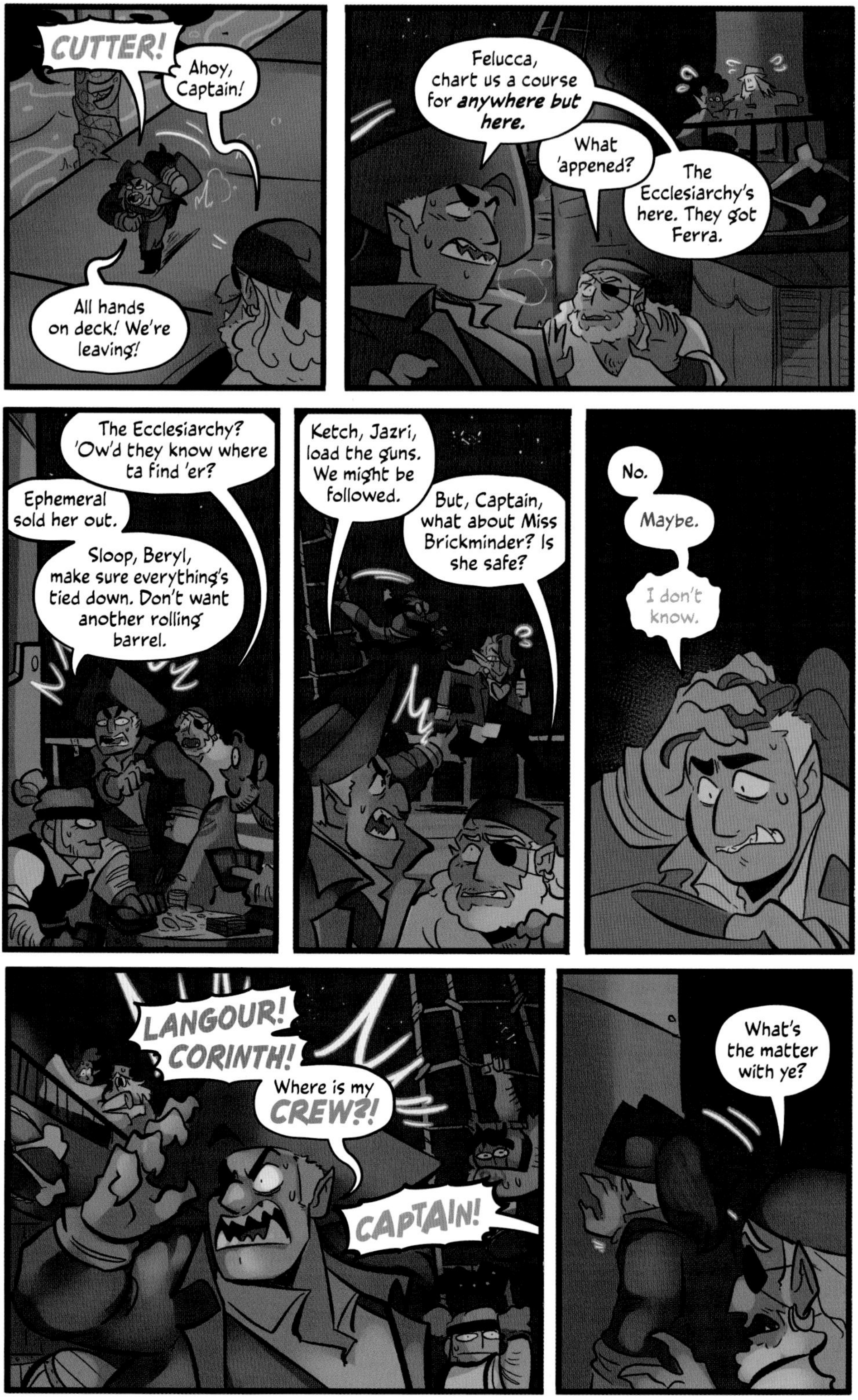
CUTTER!
Ahoy, Captain!
All hands on deck! We're leaving!
Felucca, chart us a course for *anywhere but here.*
What 'appened?
The Ecclesiarchy's here. They got Ferra.
The Ecclesiarchy? 'Ow'd they know where ta find 'er?
Ephemeral sold her out.
Sloop, Beryl, make sure everything's tied down. Don't want another rolling barrel.
Ketch, Jazri, load the guns. We might be followed.
But, Captain, what about Miss Brickminder? Is she safe?
No.
Maybe.
I don't know.
LANGOUR! CORINTH!
Where is my CREW?!
CAPTAIN!
What's the matter with ye?

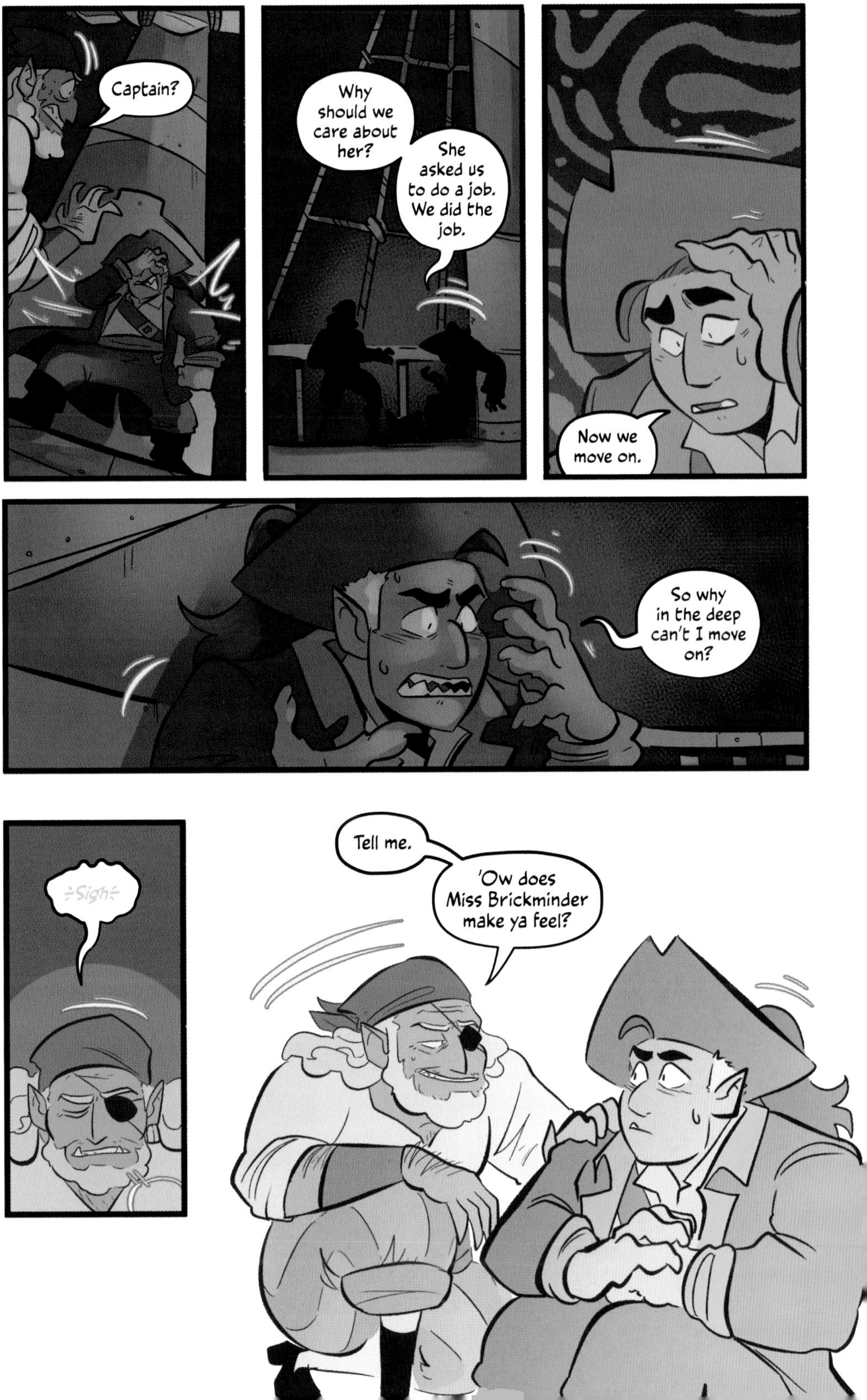
Captain?
Why should we care about her?
She asked us to do a job. We did the job.
Now we move on.
So why in the deep can't I move on?
Sigh
Tell me.
'Ow does Miss Brickminder make ya feel?

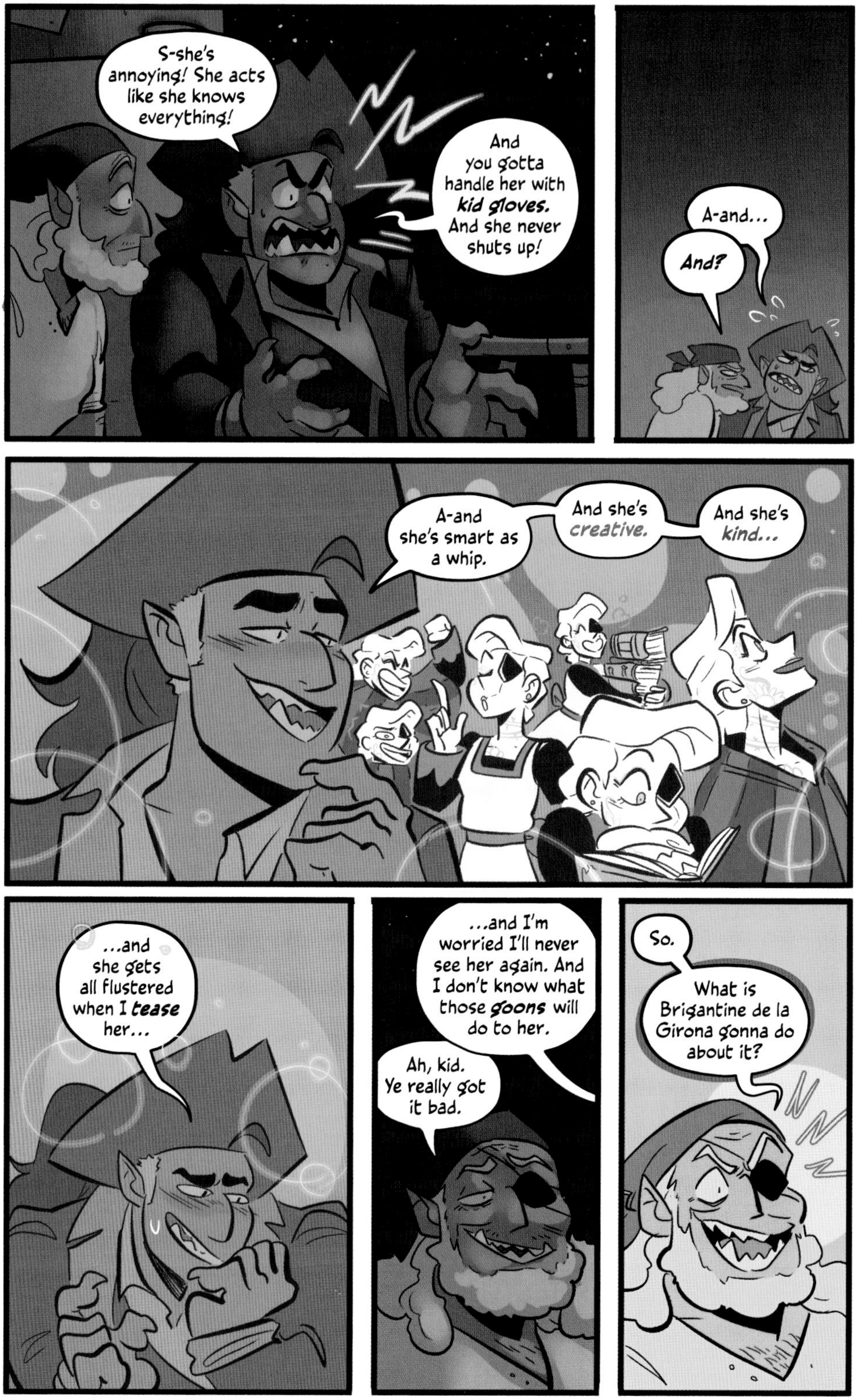
S-she's annoying! She acts like she knows everything!
And you gotta handle her with *kid gloves.* And she never shuts up!
A-and...
And?
A-and she's smart as a whip.
And she's *creative.*
And she's *kind...*
...and she gets all flustered when I *tease* her...
...and I'm worried I'll never see her again. And I don't know what those *goons* will do to her.
Ah, kid. Ye really got it bad.
So.
What is Brigantine de la Girona gonna do about it?

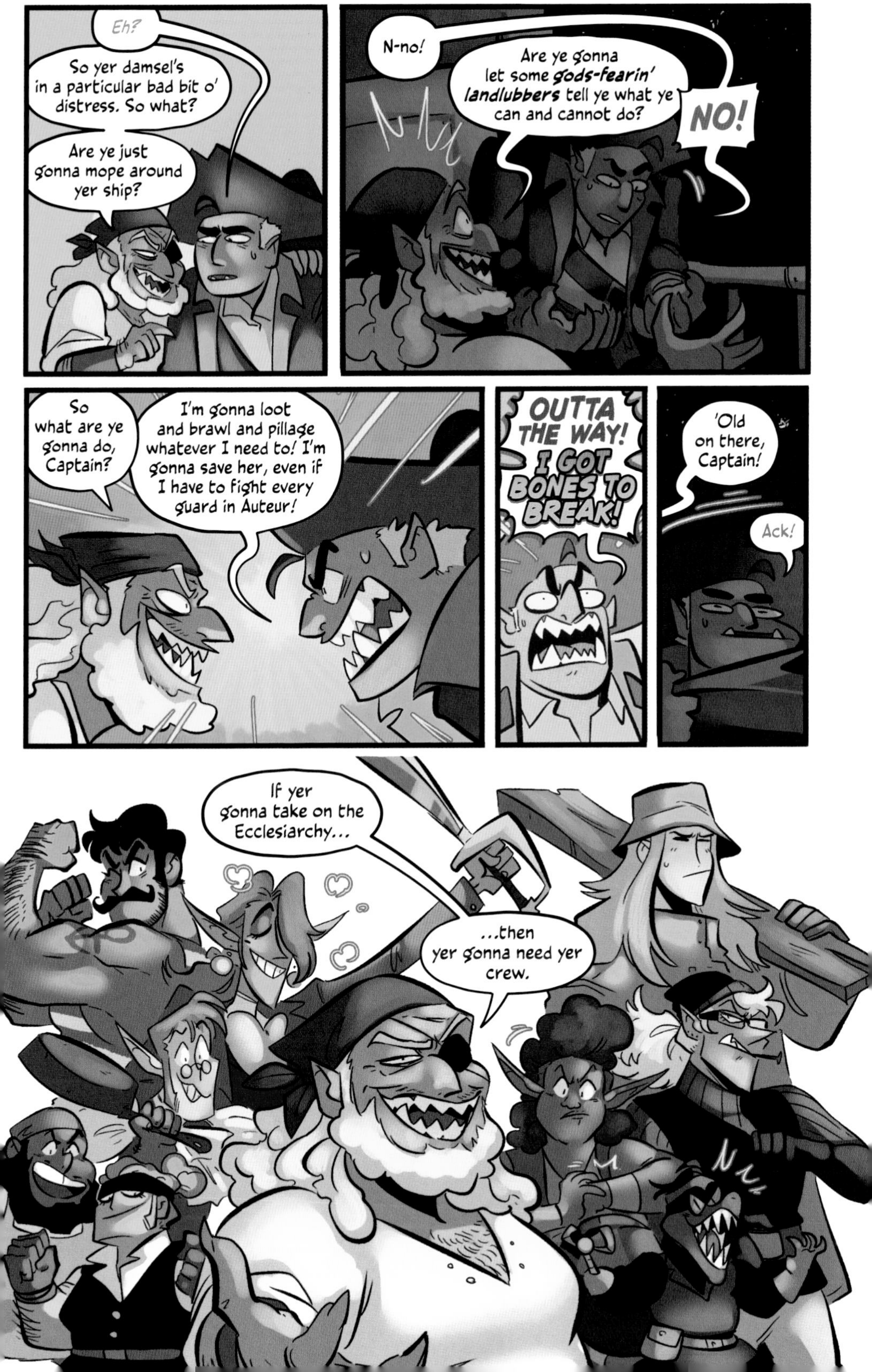
Eh?
So yer damsel's in a particular bad bit o' distress. So what?
Are ye just gonna mope around yer ship?
N-no!
Are ye gonna let some gods-fearin' landlubbers tell ye what ye can and cannot do?
NO!
So what are ye gonna do, Captain?
I'm gonna loot and brawl and pillage whatever I need to! I'm gonna save her, even if I have to fight every guard in Auteur!
OUTTA THE WAY! I GOT BONES TO BREAK!
'Old on there, Captain!
Ack!
If yer gonna take on the Ecclesiarchy...
...then yer gonna need yer crew.

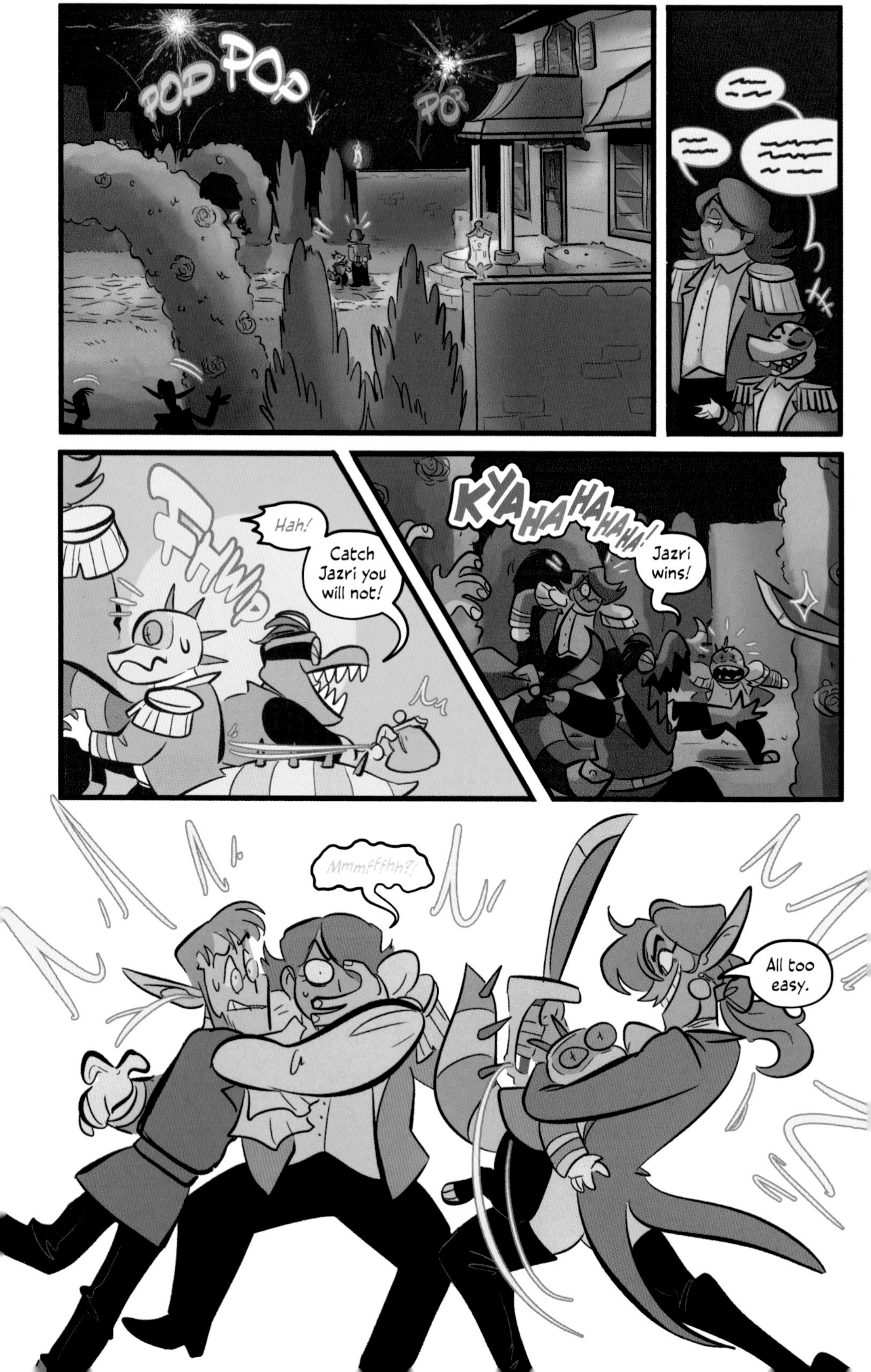
POP POP
POP
Hah!
Catch Jazri you will not!
FWUMP
KYAHAHAHAHAHA!
Jazri wins!
Mmmffhh?!
All too easy.

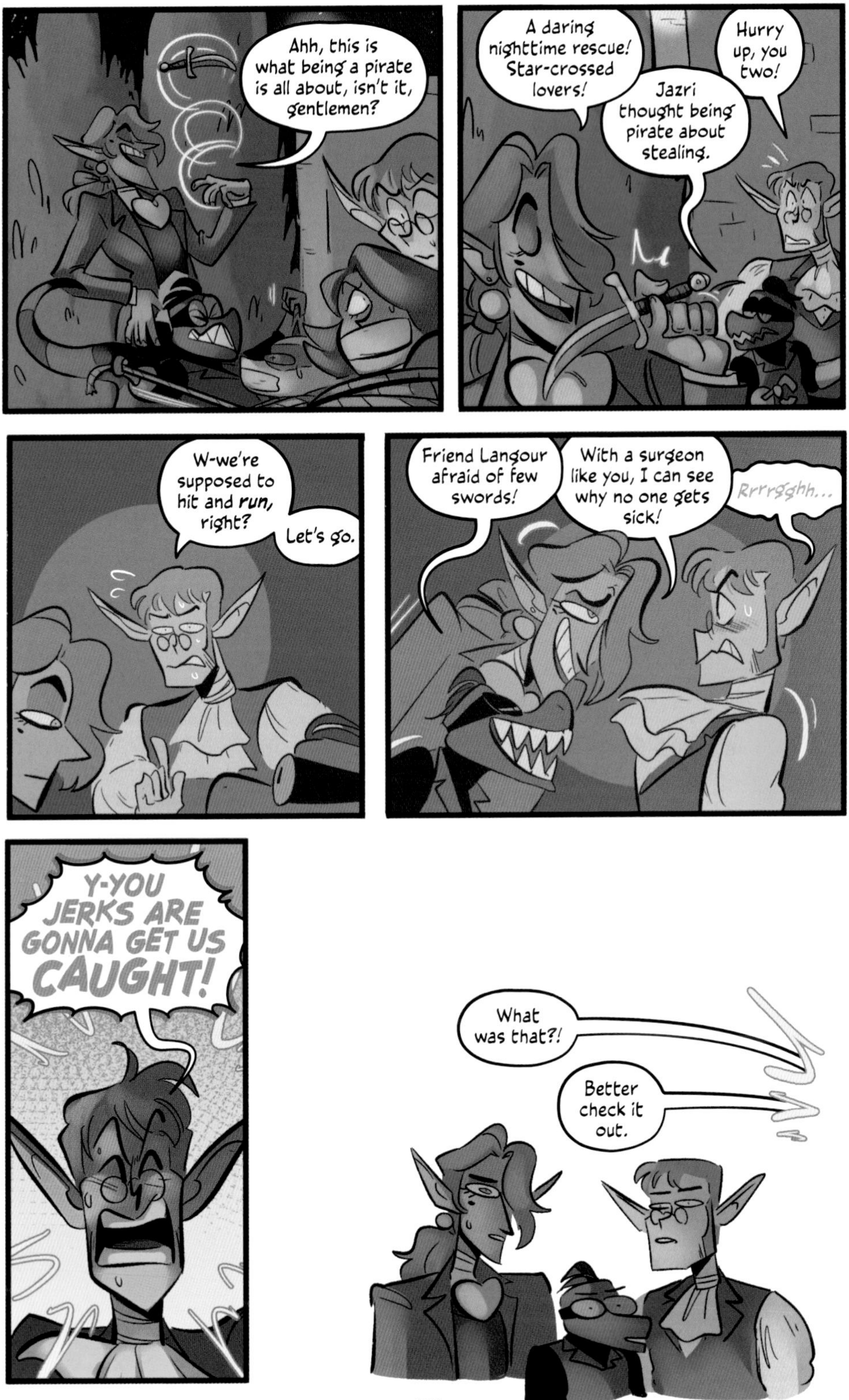
Ahh, this is what being a pirate is all about, isn't it, gentlemen?
A daring nighttime rescue! Star-crossed lovers!
Jazri thought being pirate about stealing.
Hurry up, you two!
W-we're supposed to hit and *run*, right?
Let's go.
Friend Langour afraid of few swords!
With a surgeon like you, I can see why no one gets sick!
Rrrrgghh...
Y-YOU JERKS ARE GONNA GET US CAUGHT!
What was that?!
Better check it out.

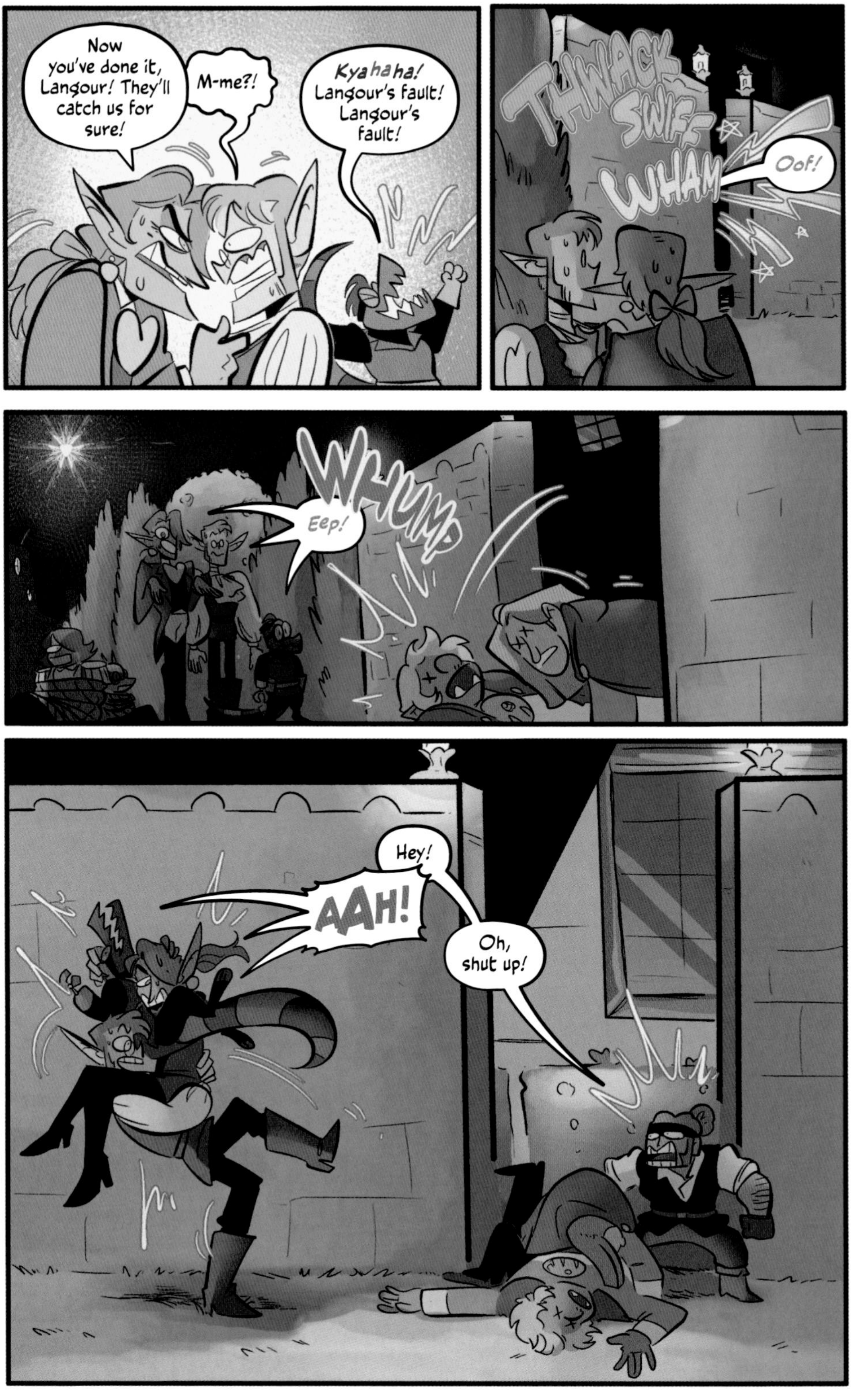
Now you've done it, Langour! They'll catch us for sure!
M-me?!
Kyahaha! Langour's fault! Langour's fault!
THWACK
SWIFF
WHAM
Oof!
WHUMP
Eep!
Hey!
AAH!
Oh, shut up!

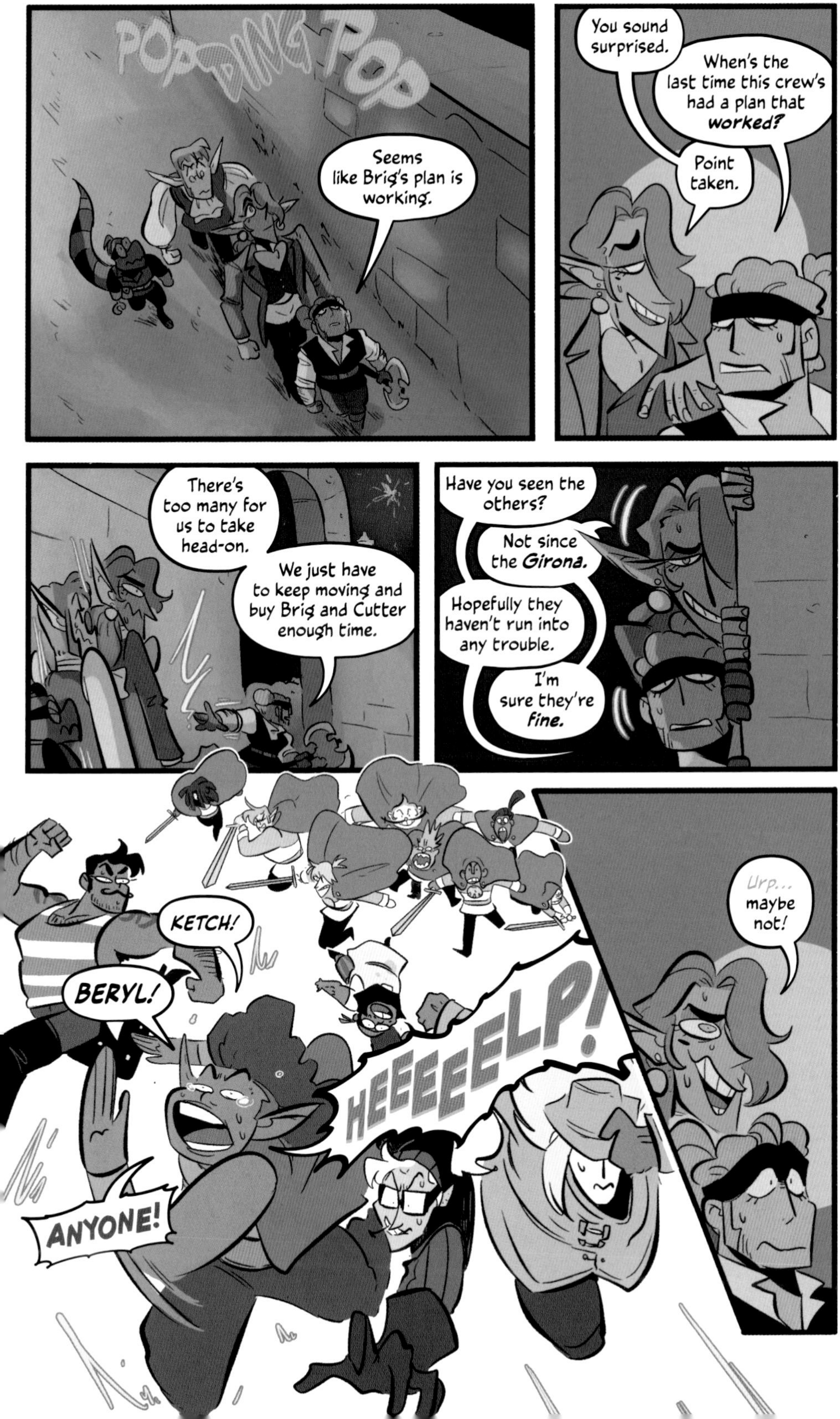
POP DING POP
Seems like Brig's plan is working.
You sound surprised.
When's the last time this crew's had a plan that *worked?*
Point taken.
There's too many for us to take head-on.
We just have to keep moving and buy Brig and Cutter enough time.
Have you seen the others?
Not since the *Girona.*
Hopefully they haven't run into any trouble.
I'm sure they're *fine.*
KETCH!
BERYL!
HEEEEEELP!
ANYONE!
Urp... maybe not!

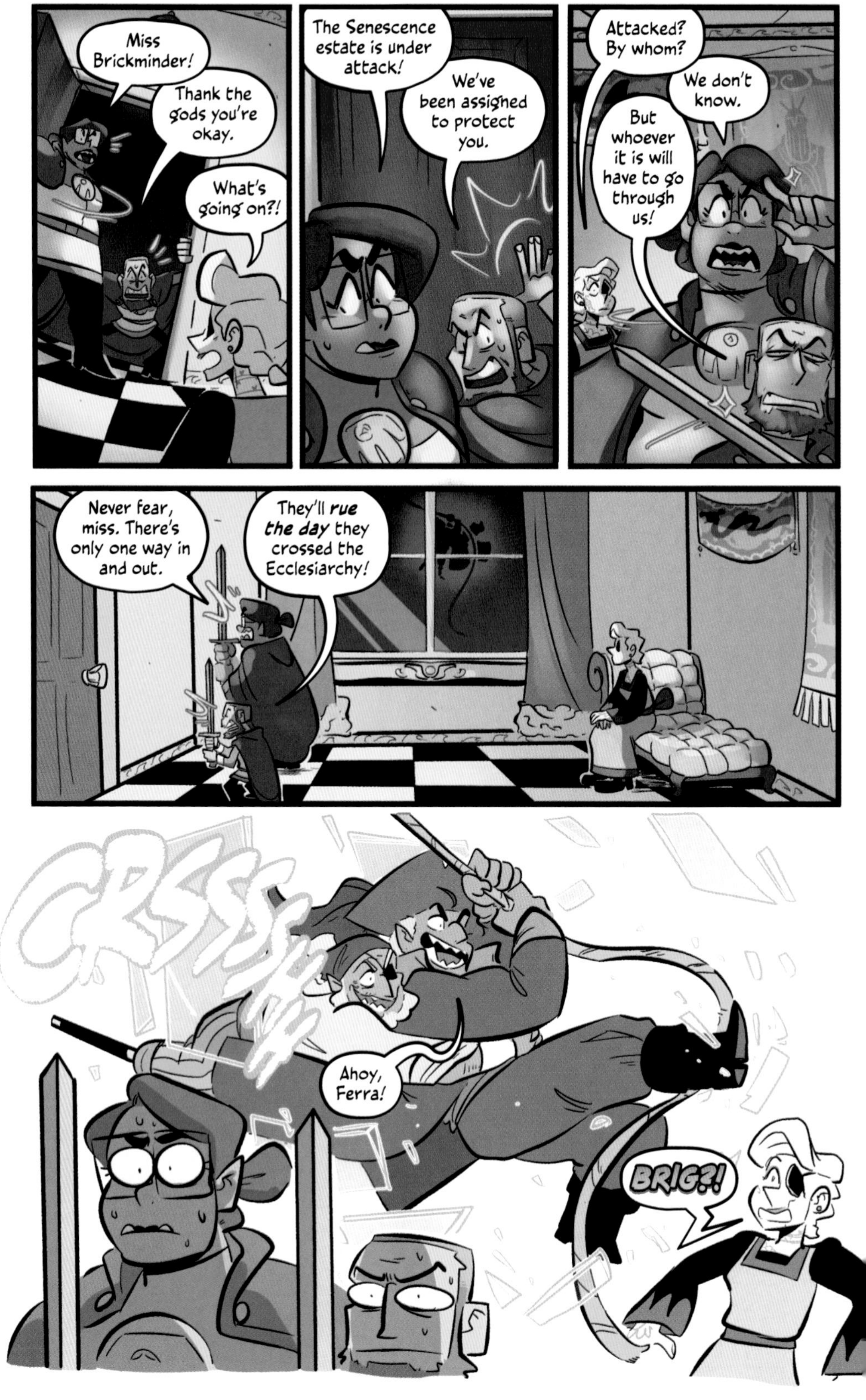
Miss Brickminder!
Thank the gods you're okay.
What's going on?!
The Senescence estate is under attack!
We've been assigned to protect you.
Attacked? By whom?
We don't know.
But whoever it is will have to go through us!
Never fear, miss. There's only one way in and out.
They'll *rue the day* they crossed the Ecclesiarchy!
CRSSH
Ahoy, Ferra!
BRIG?!

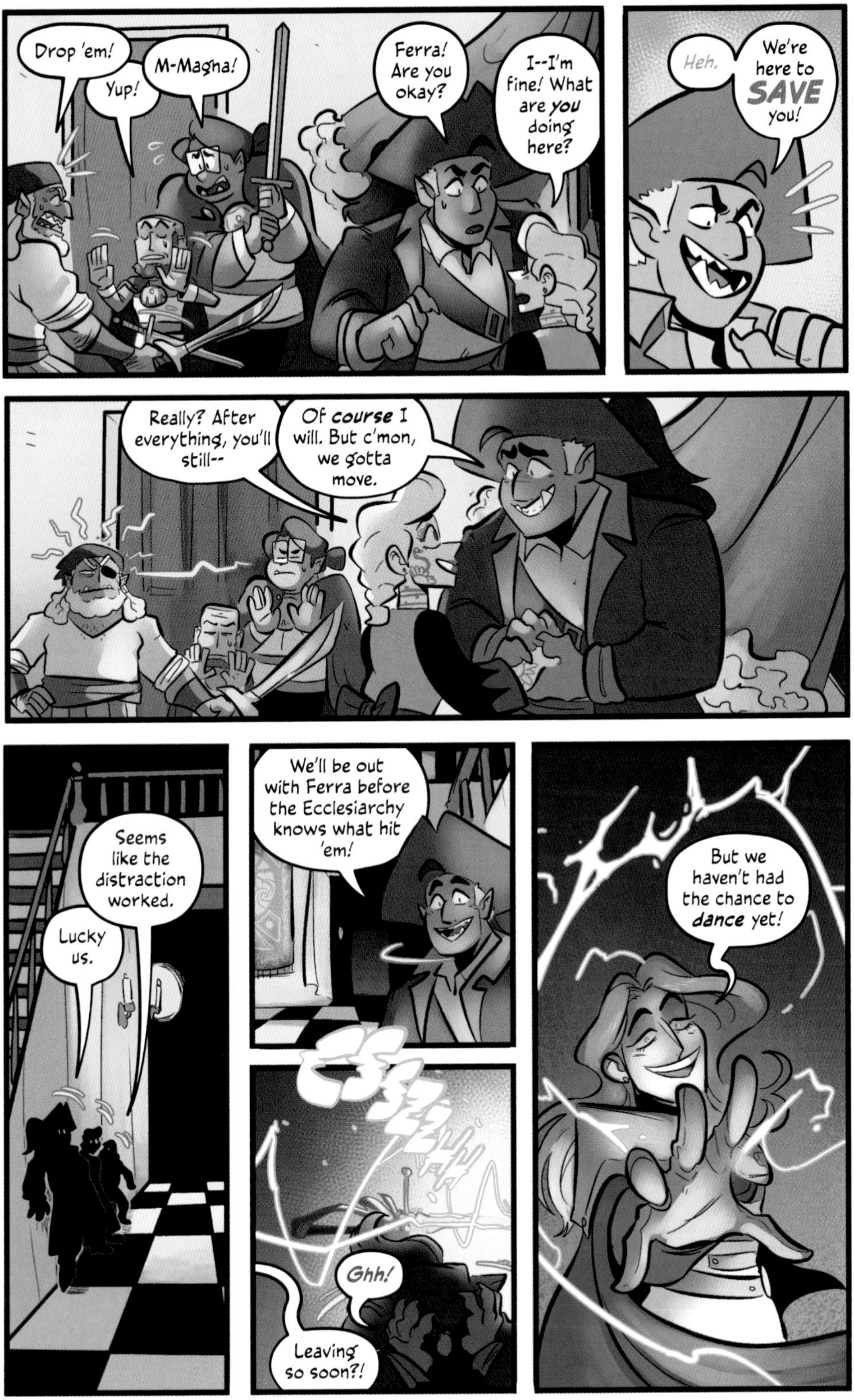
Drop 'em!
Yup!
M-Magna!
Ferra! Are you okay?
I--I'm fine! What are you doing here?
Heh.
We're here to SAVE you!
Really? After everything, you'll still--
Of course I will. But c'mon, we gotta move.
Seems like the distraction worked.
Lucky us.
We'll be out with Ferra before the Ecclesiarchy knows what hit 'em!
Ghh!
Leaving so soon?!
But we haven't had the chance to dance yet!

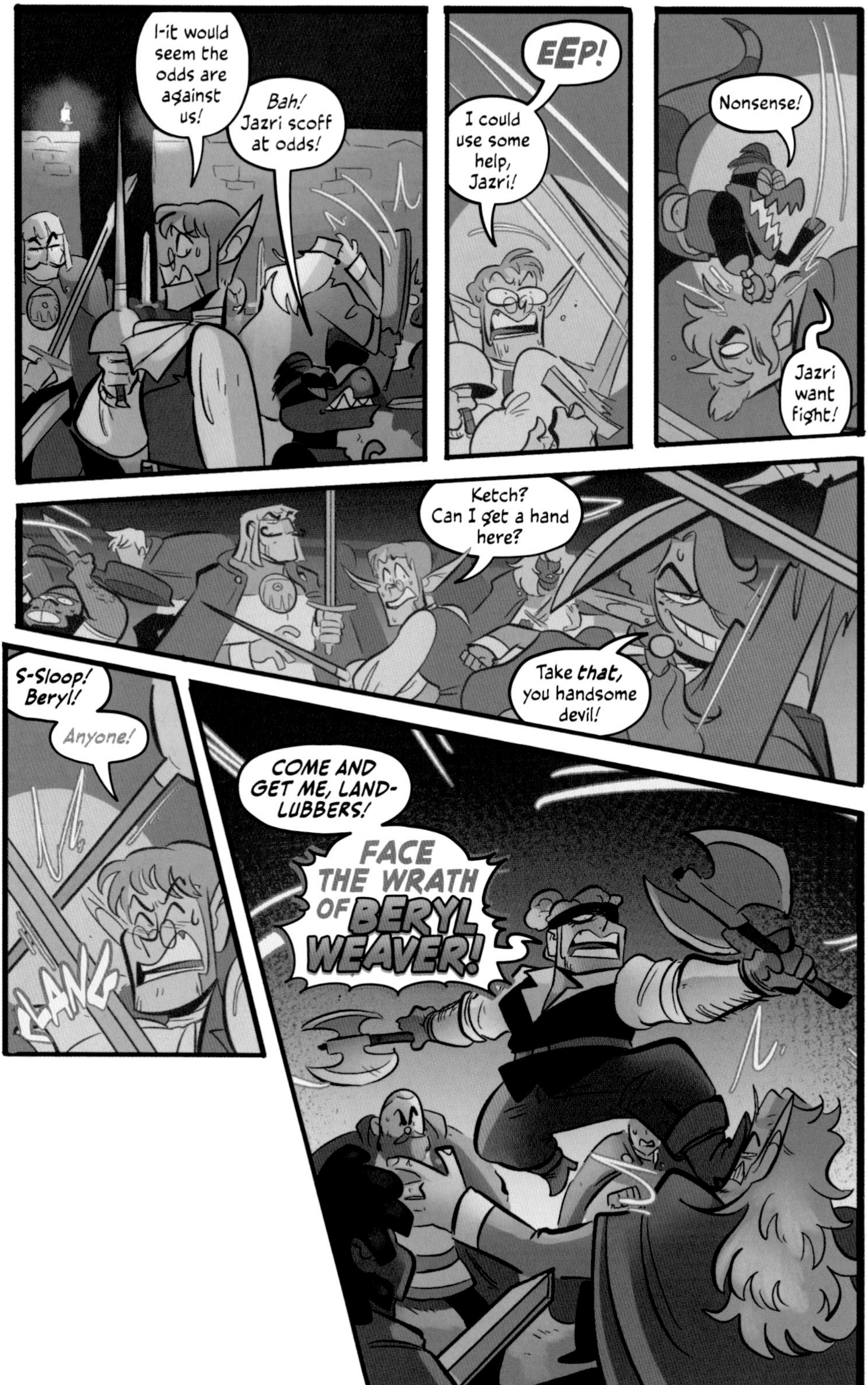
I-it would seem the odds are against us!
Bah! Jazri scoff at odds!
EEP!
I could use some help, Jazri!
Nonsense!
Jazri want fight!
Ketch? Can I get a hand here?
Take that, you handsome devil!
S-Sloop! Beryl!
Anyone!
CLANG
COME AND GET ME, LAND-LUBBERS!
FACE THE WRATH OF BERYL WEAVER!

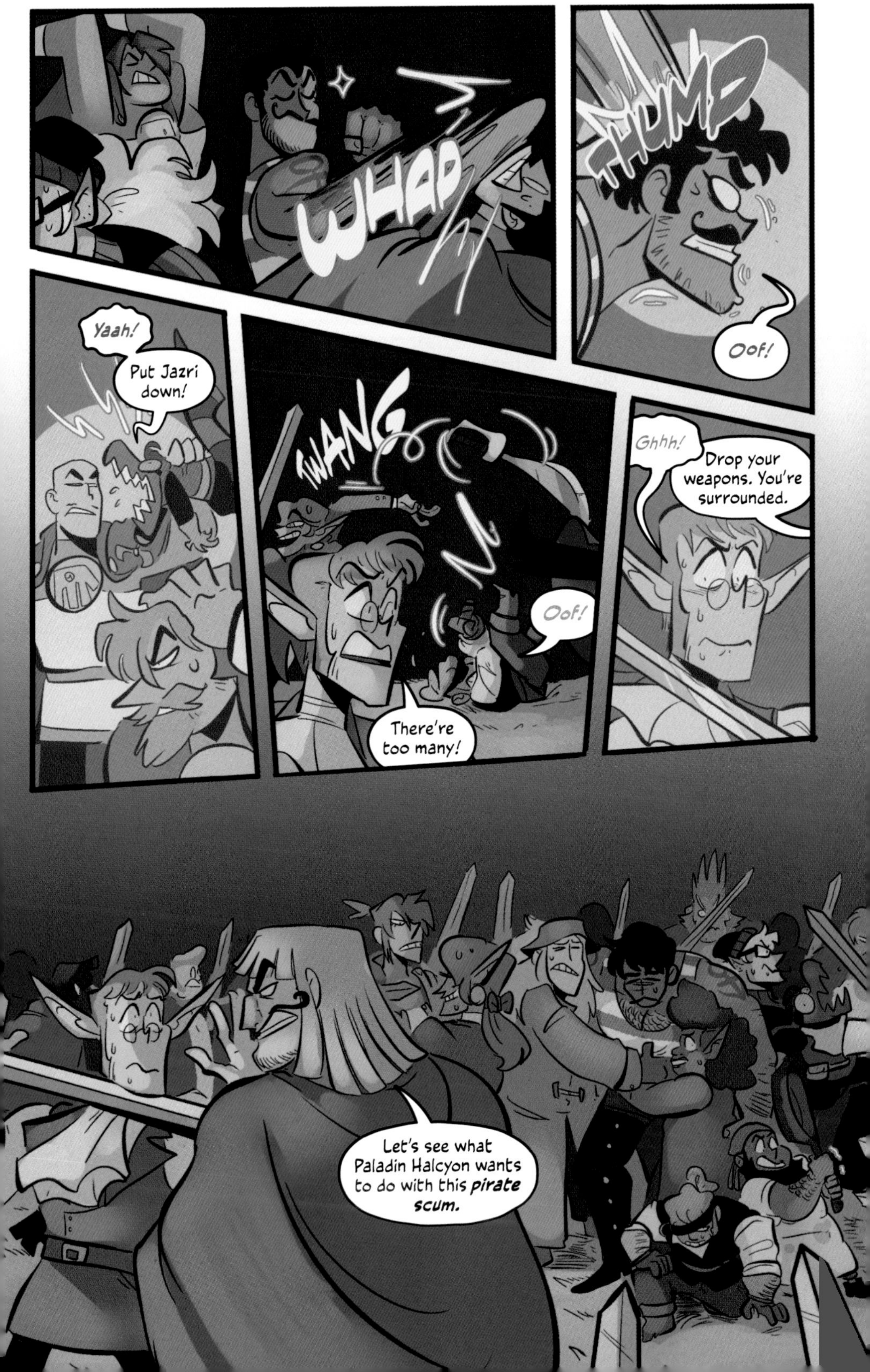
WHAP
THUMP
Oof!
Yaah!
Put Jazri down!
TWANG
Oof!
There're too many!
Ghhh!
Drop your weapons. You're surrounded.
Let's see what Paladin Halcyon wants to do with this *pirate scum.*

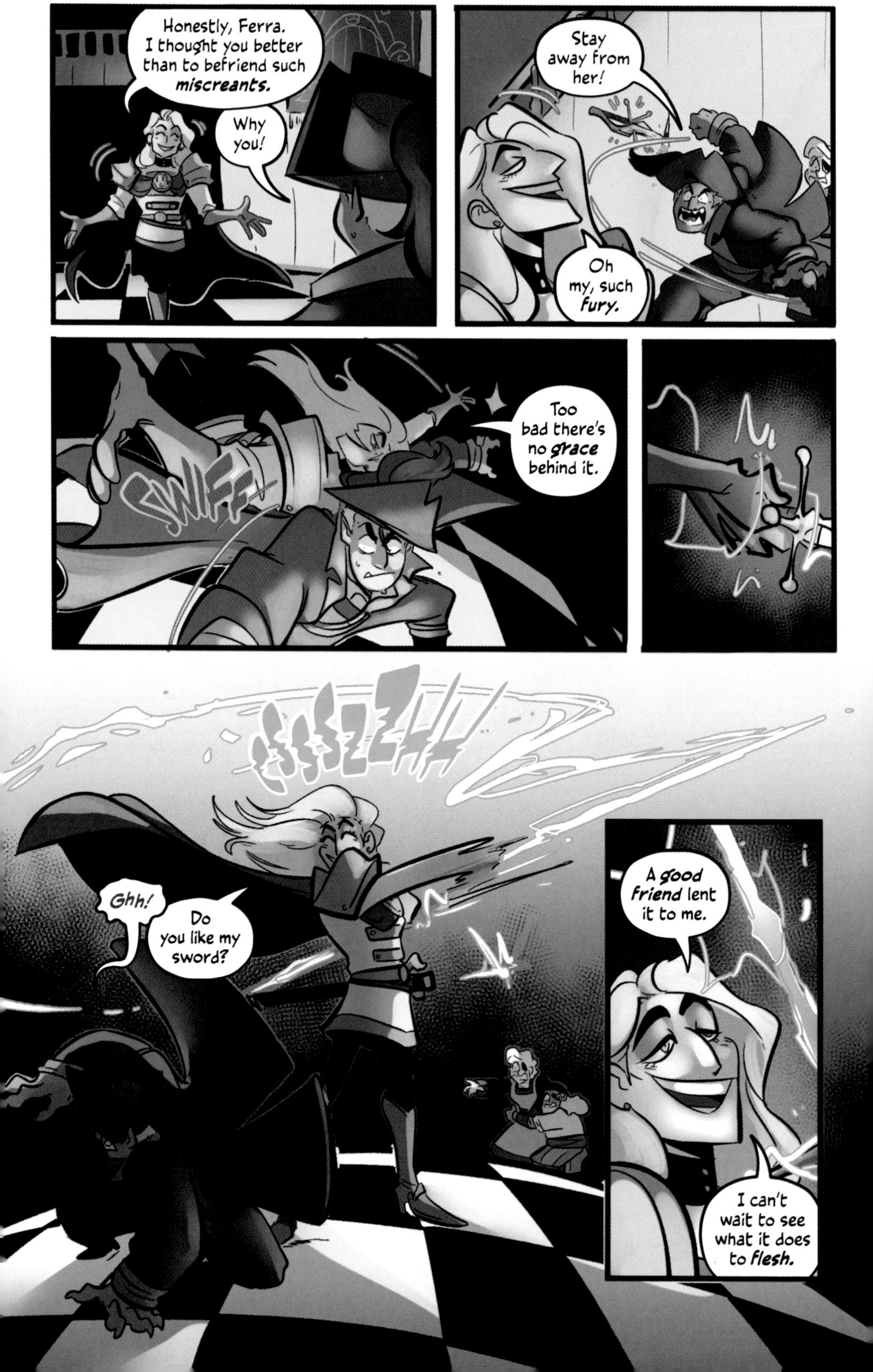
Honestly, Ferra. I thought you better than to befriend such miscreants.
Why you!
Stay away from her!
Oh my, such fury.
SWIFF
Too bad there's no grace behind it.
SSSSZZHH
Ghh!
Do you like my sword?
A good friend lent it to me.
I can't wait to see what it does to flesh.

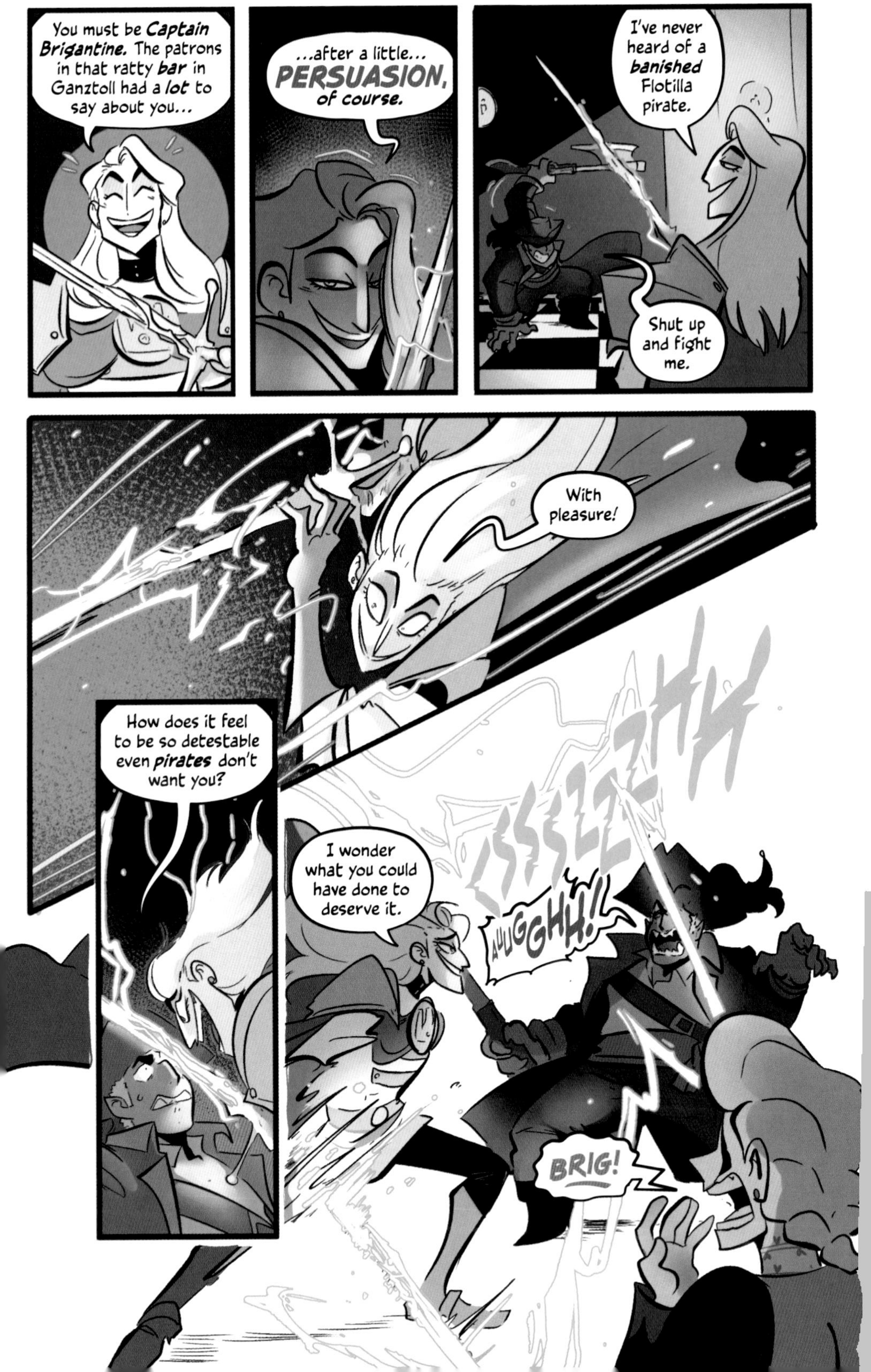

You must be Captain Brigantine. The patrons in that ratty bar in Ganztoll had a lot to say about you...
...after a little... PERSUASION, of course.
I've never heard of a banished Flotilla pirate.
Shut up and fight me.
With pleasure!
How does it feel to be so detestable even pirates don't want you?
I wonder what you could have done to deserve it.
SSSSZZZZHH
AUUGGHH!!
BRIG!

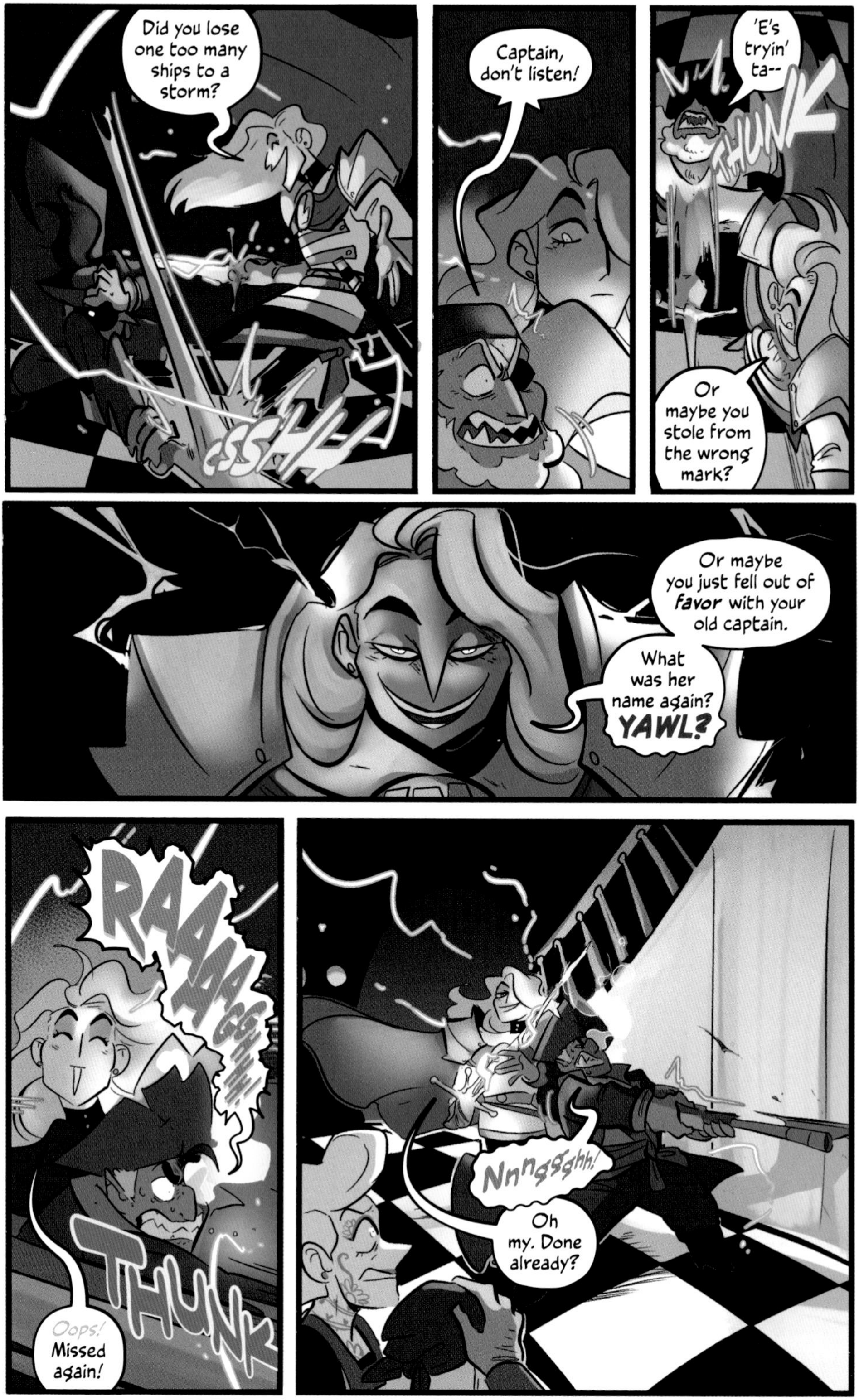

Did you lose one too many ships to a storm?
CSSHH
Captain, don't listen!
'E's tryin' ta--
THUNK
Or maybe you stole from the wrong mark?
Or maybe you just fell out of *favor* with your old captain.
What was her name again? **YAWL?**
RAAAAAGGHHH!
THUNK
Oops! Missed again!
Nnngggh!
Oh my. Done already?

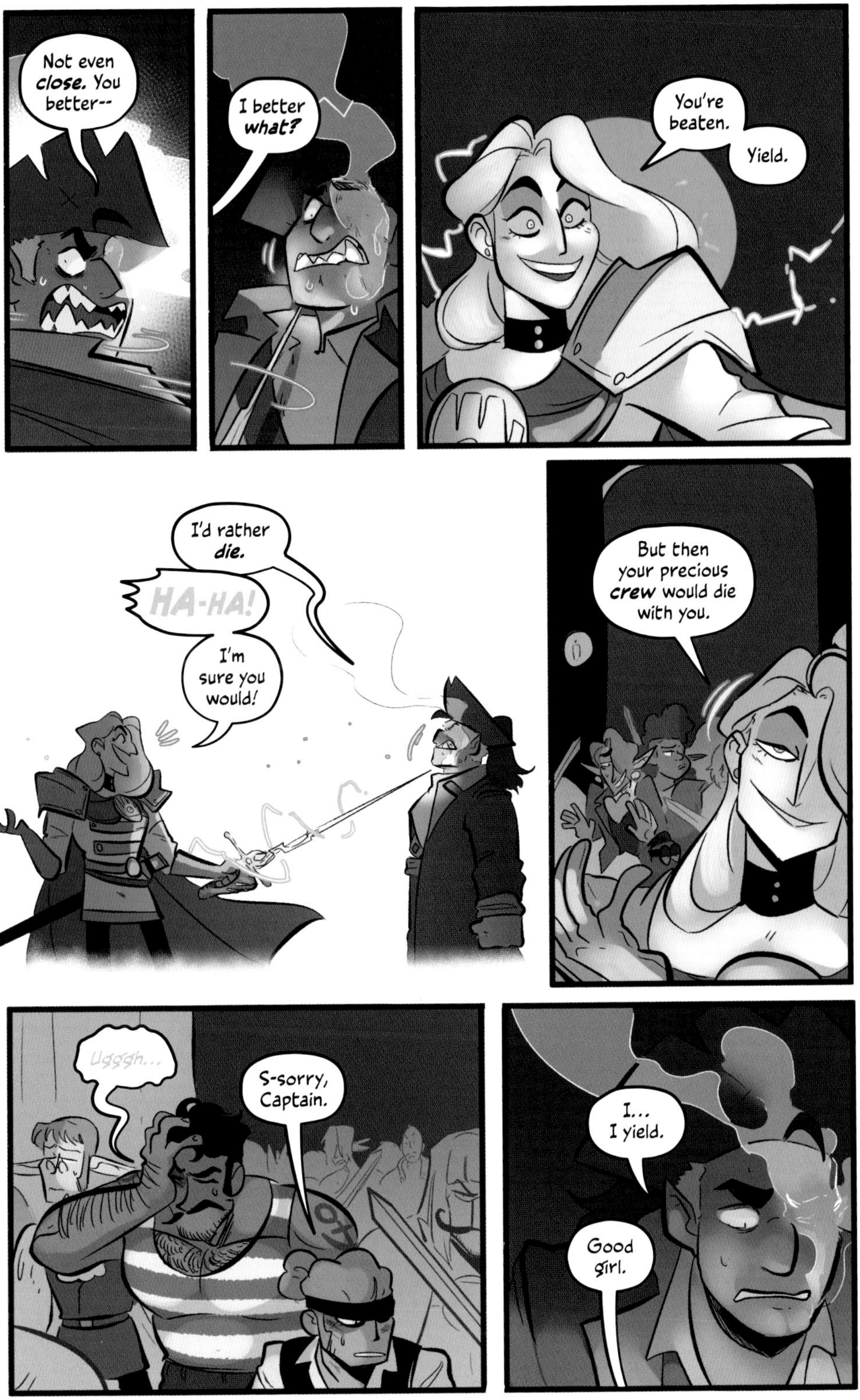
Not even *close.* You better--
I better *what?*
You're beaten.
Yield.
I'd rather *die.*
HA-HA!
I'm sure you would!
But then your precious *crew* would die with you.
Ugggh...
S-sorry, Captain.
I... I yield.
Good girl.

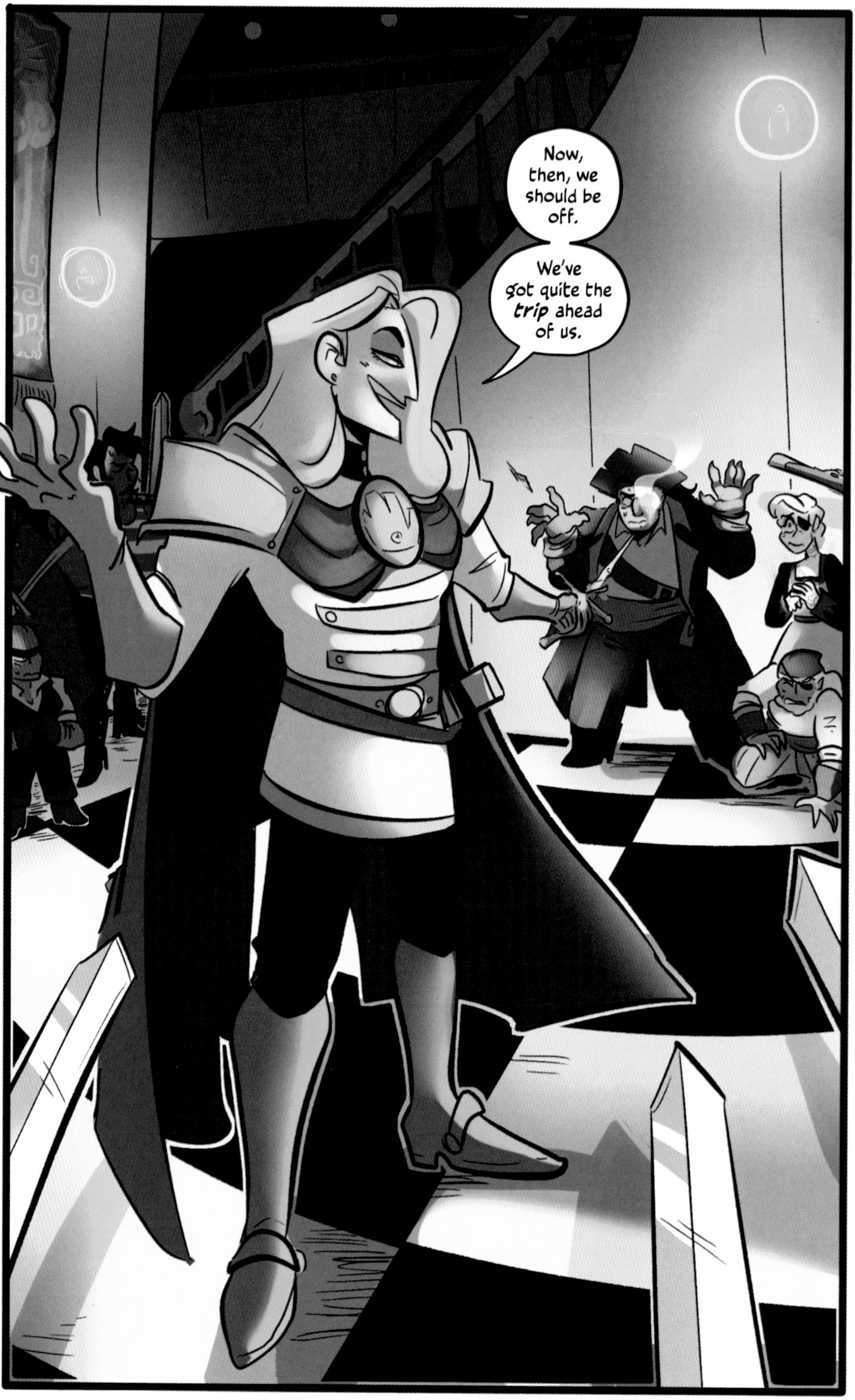
Now, then, we should be off.
We've got quite the *trip* ahead of us.

Chapter 5

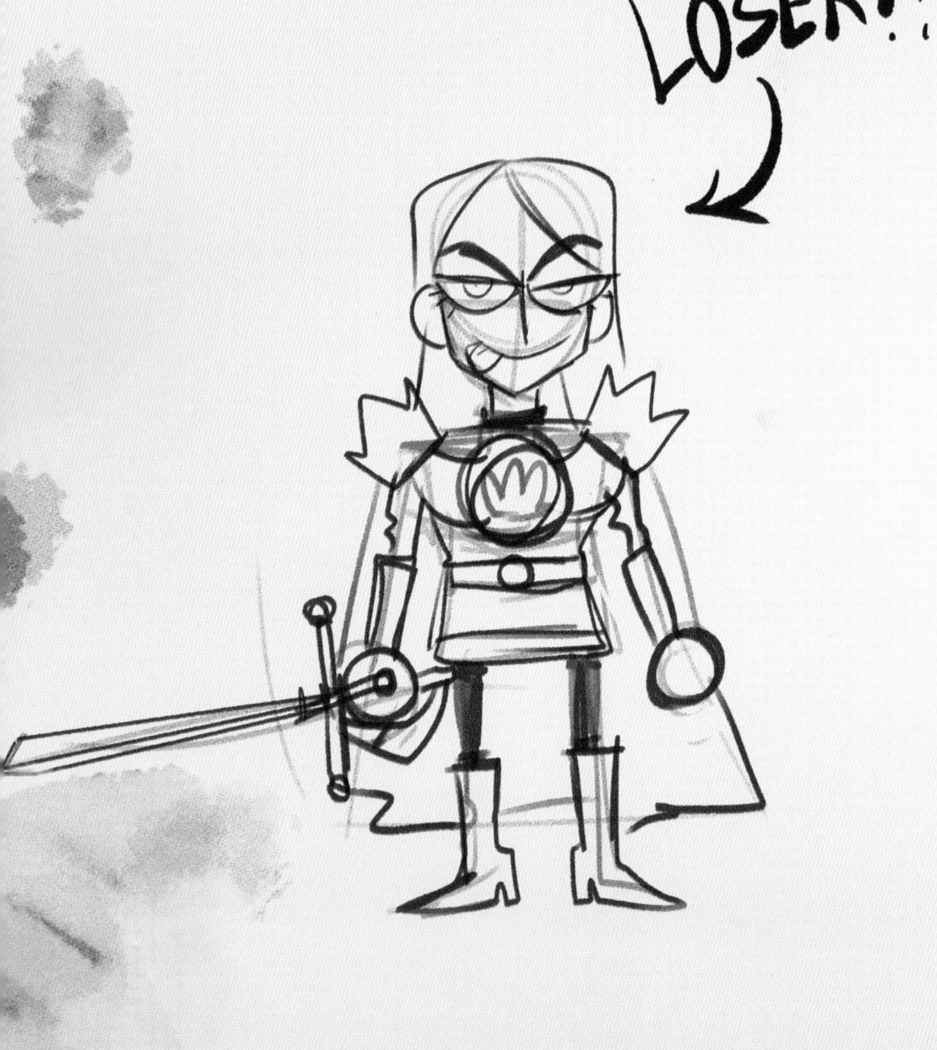
LOSER!!

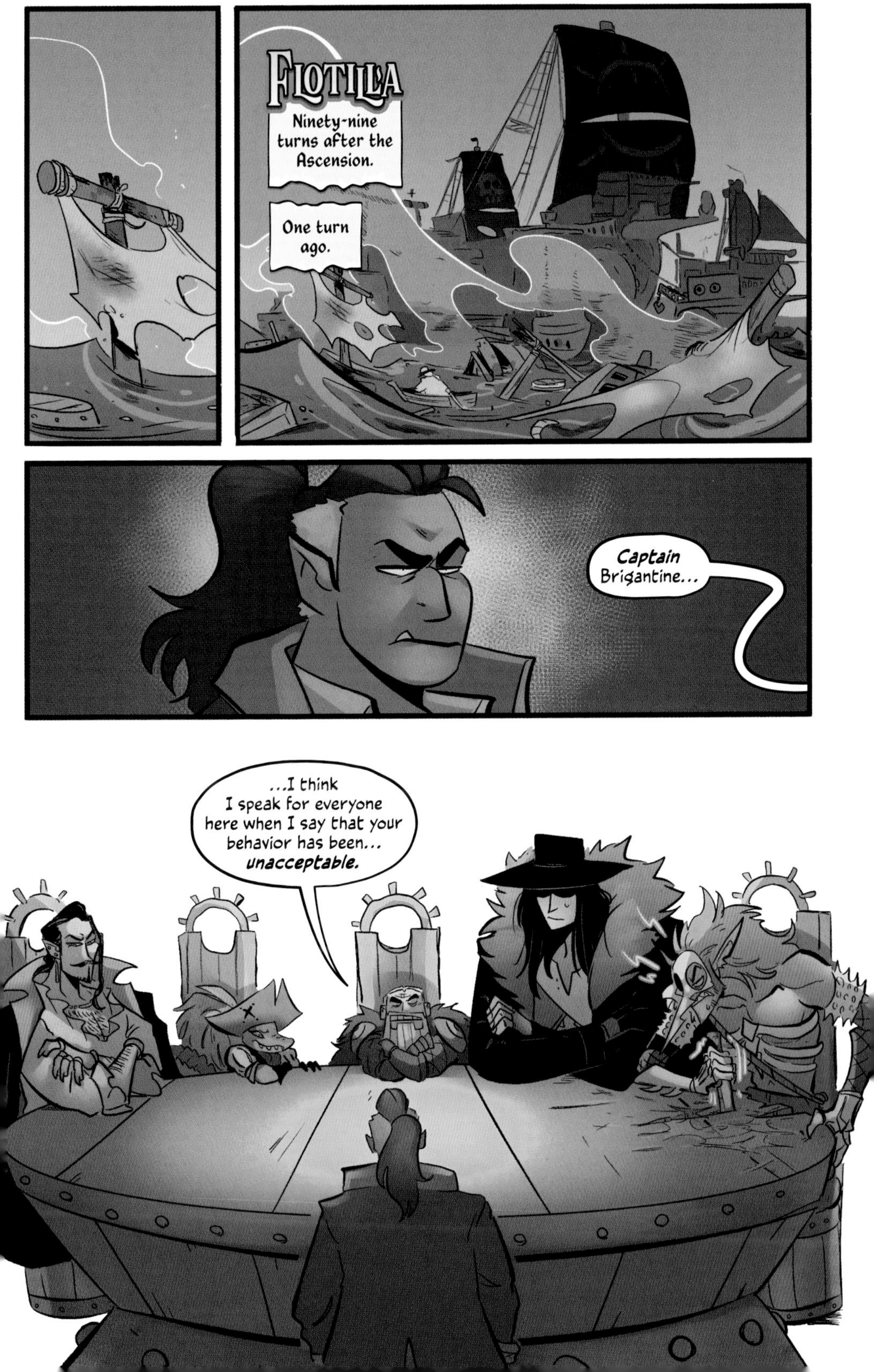
FLOTILLA
Ninety-nine turns after the Ascension.
One turn ago.
Captain Brigantine...
...I think I speak for everyone here when I say that your behavior has been... unacceptable.

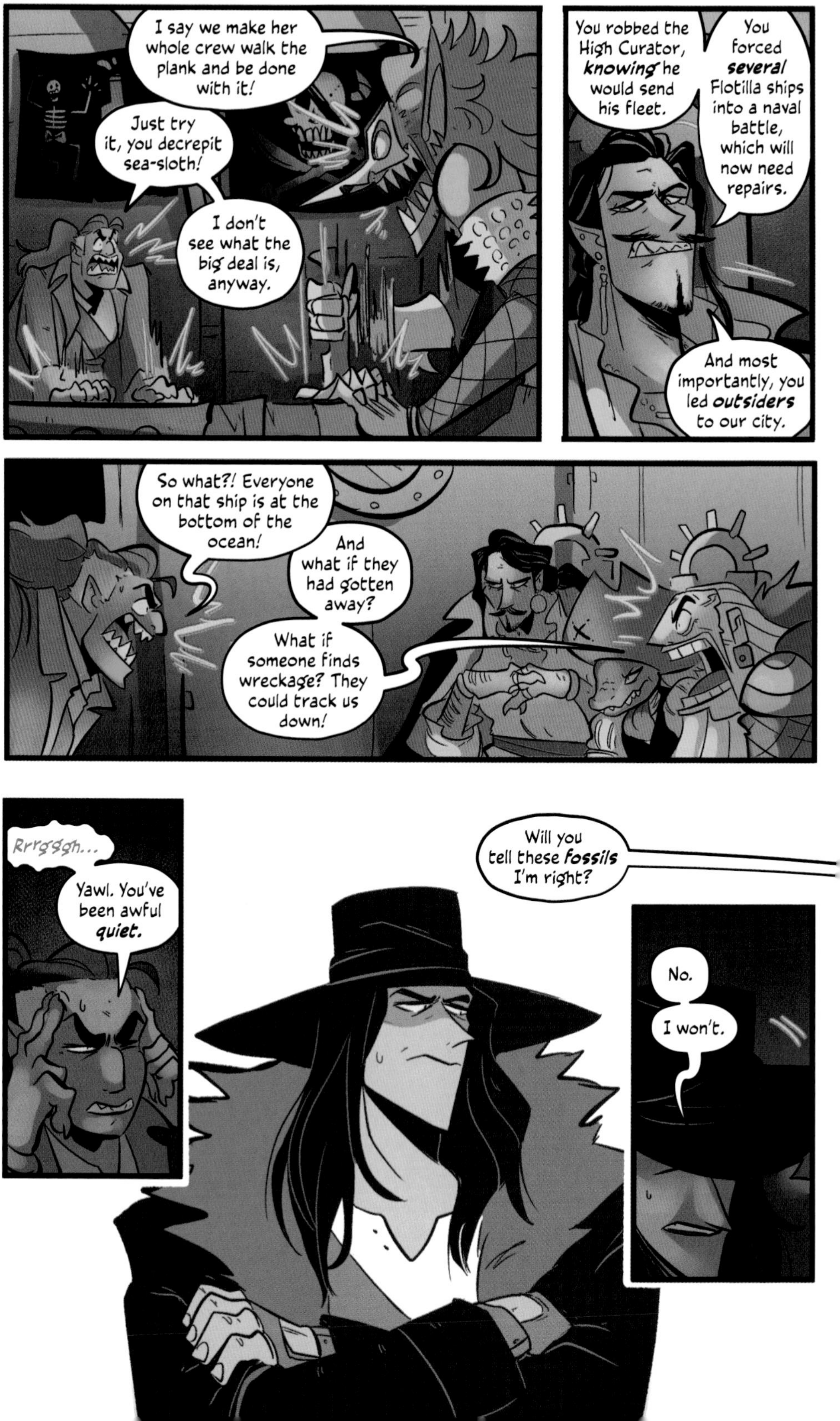

I say we make her whole crew walk the plank and be done with it!
Just try it, you decrepit sea-sloth!
I don't see what the big deal is, anyway.
You robbed the High Curator, *knowing* he would send his fleet.
You forced *several* Flotilla ships into a naval battle, which will now need repairs.
And most importantly, you led *outsiders* to our city.
So what?! Everyone on that ship is at the bottom of the ocean!
And what if they had gotten away?
What if someone finds wreckage? They could track us down!
Rrrgggh...
Yawl. You've been awful *quiet.*
Will you tell these *fossils* I'm right?
No.
I won't.

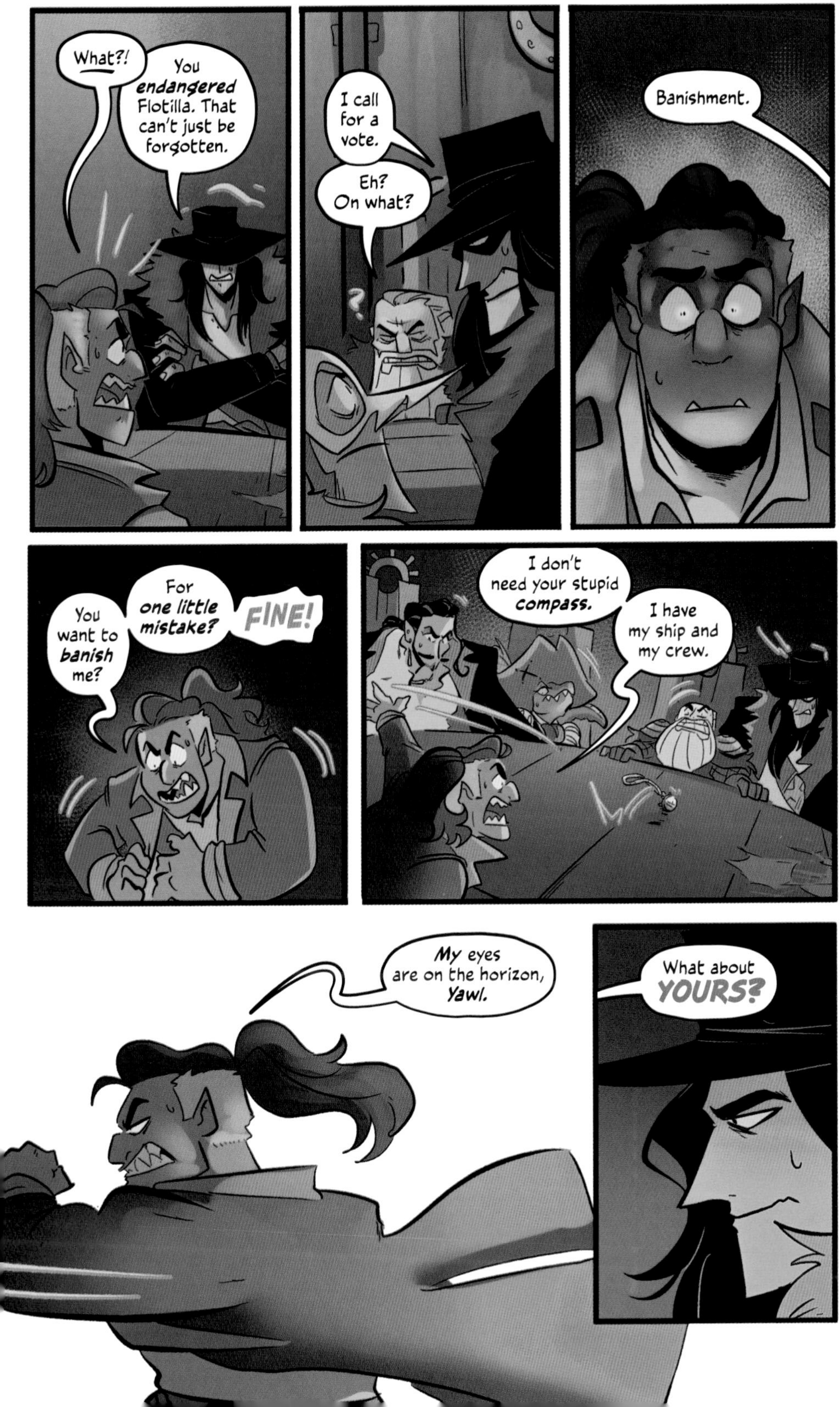

What?!
You endangered Flotilla. That can't just be forgotten.
I call for a vote.
Eh? On what?
Banishment.
You want to banish me?
For one little mistake?
FINE!
I don't need your stupid compass.
I have my ship and my crew.
My eyes are on the horizon, Yawl.
What about YOURS?

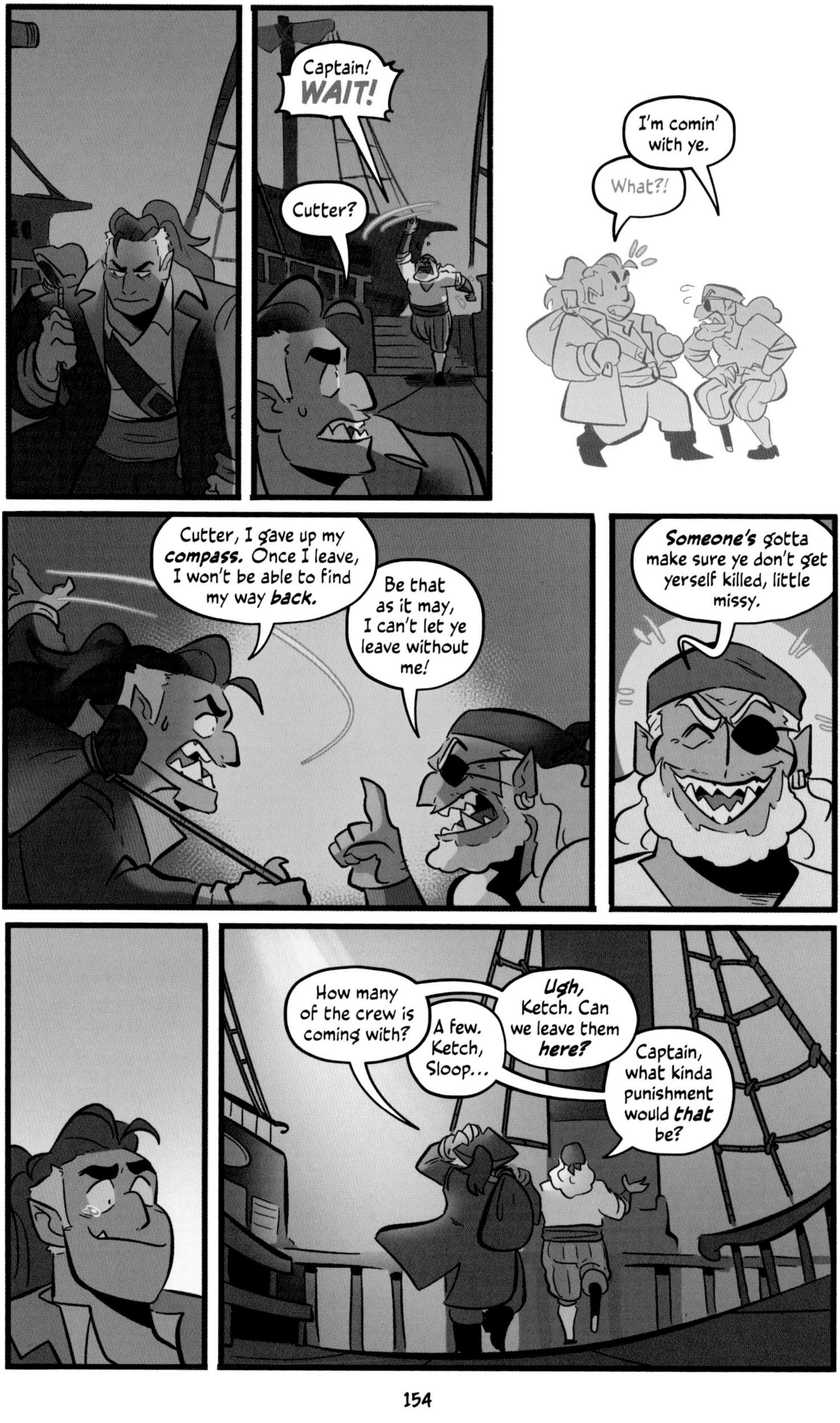
Captain! WAIT!
Cutter?
What?!
I'm comin' with ye.
Cutter, I gave up my ***compass.*** Once I leave, I won't be able to find my way ***back.***
Be that as it may, I can't let ye leave without me!
Someone's gotta make sure ye don't get yerself killed, little missy.
How many of the crew is coming with?
A few. Ketch, Sloop...
Ugh, Ketch. Can we leave them ***here?***
Captain, what kinda punishment would ***that*** be?

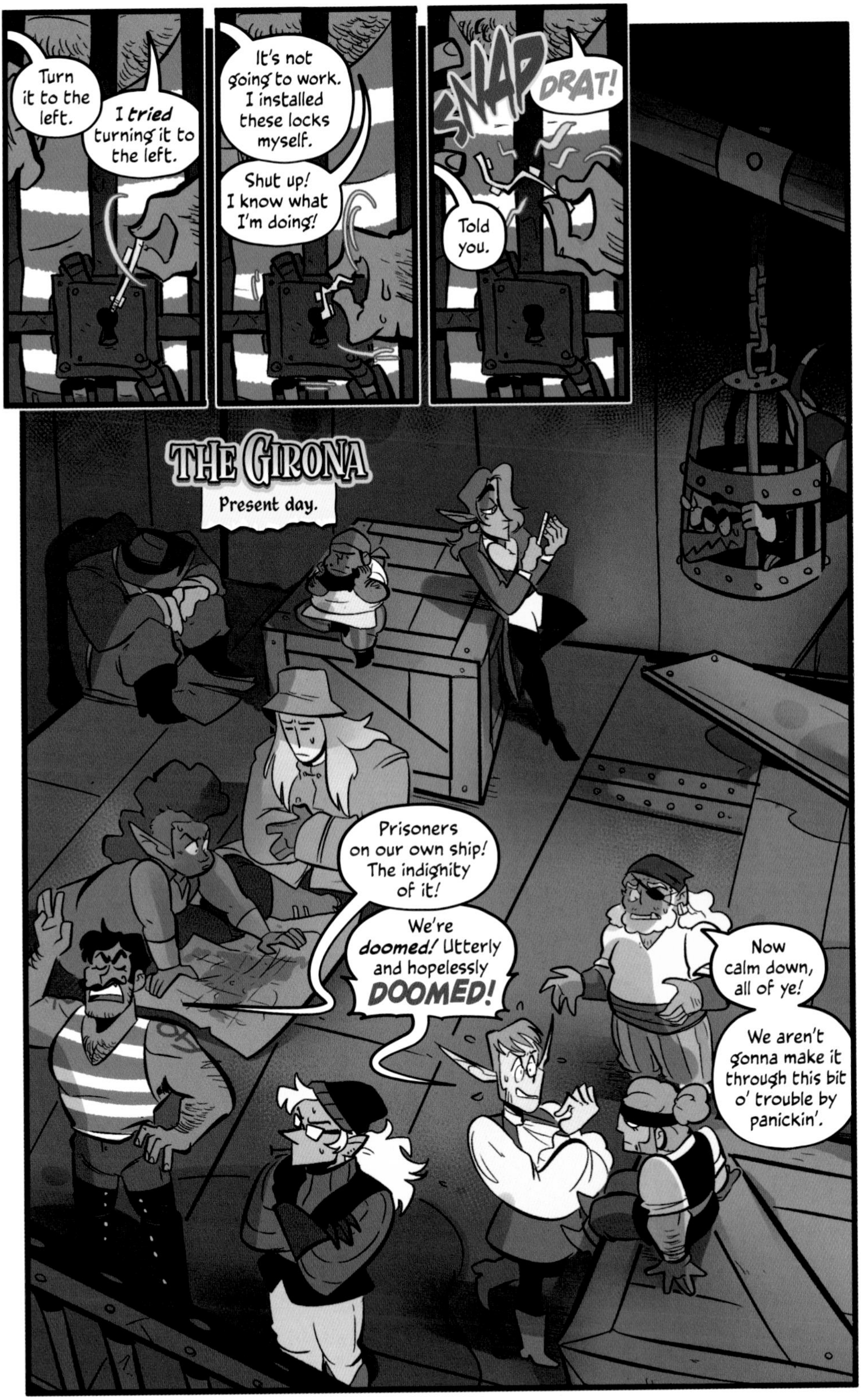

Turn it to the left.
I *tried* turning it to the left.
It's not going to work. I installed these locks myself.
Shut up! I know what I'm doing!
SNAP
DRAT!
Told you.
THE GIRONA
Present day.
Prisoners on our own ship! The indignity of it!
We're *doomed!* Utterly and hopelessly **DOOMED!**
Now calm down, all of ye!
We aren't gonna make it through this bit o' trouble by panickin'.

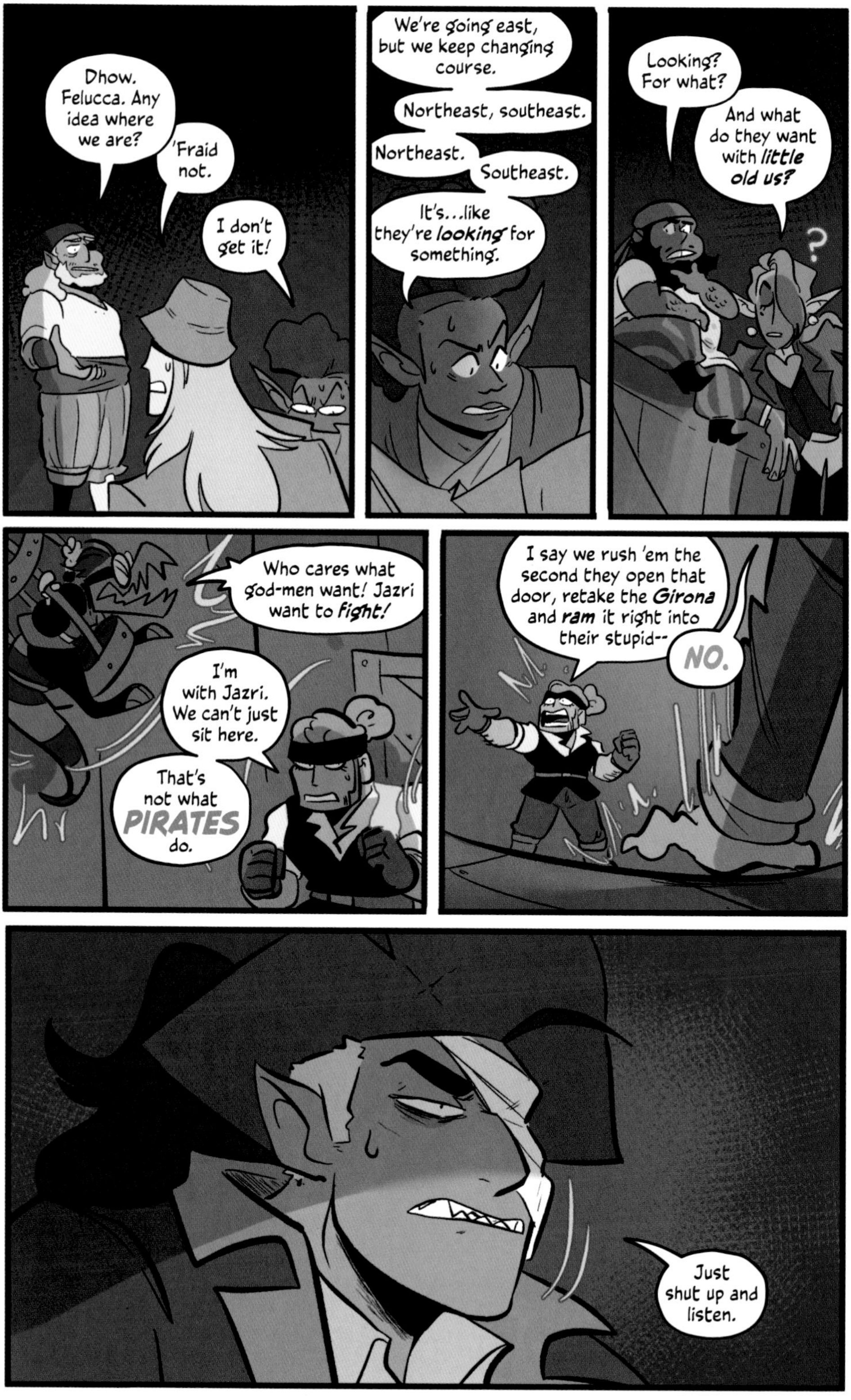
Dhow. Felucca. Any idea where we are?
'Fraid not.
I don't get it!
We're going east, but we keep changing course.
Northeast, southeast.
Northeast.
Southeast.
It's...like they're *looking* for something.
Looking? For what?
And what do they want with *little old us?*
?
Who cares what god-men want! Jazri want to *fight!*
I'm with Jazri. We can't just sit here.
That's not what PIRATES do.
I say we rush 'em the second they open that door, retake the *Girona* and *ram* it right into their stupid--
NO.
Just shut up and listen.

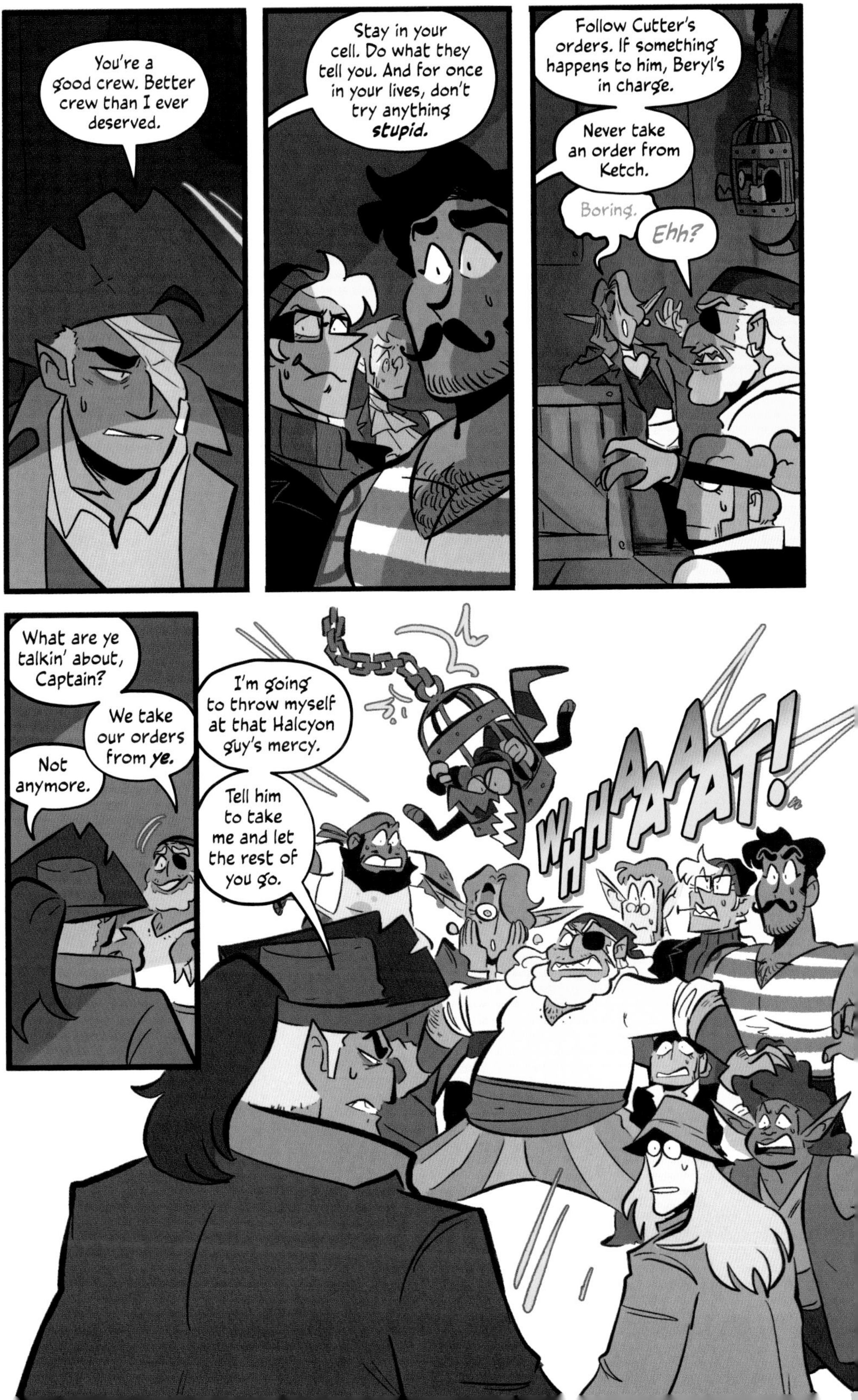
You're a good crew. Better crew than I ever deserved.
Stay in your cell. Do what they tell you. And for once in your lives, don't try anything ***stupid.***
Follow Cutter's orders. If something happens to him, Beryl's in charge.
Never take an order from Ketch.
Boring.
Ehh?
What are ye talkin' about, Captain?
We take our orders from *ye.*
Not anymore.
I'm going to throw myself at that Halcyon guy's mercy.
Tell him to take me and let the rest of you go.
WHHAAAAT!

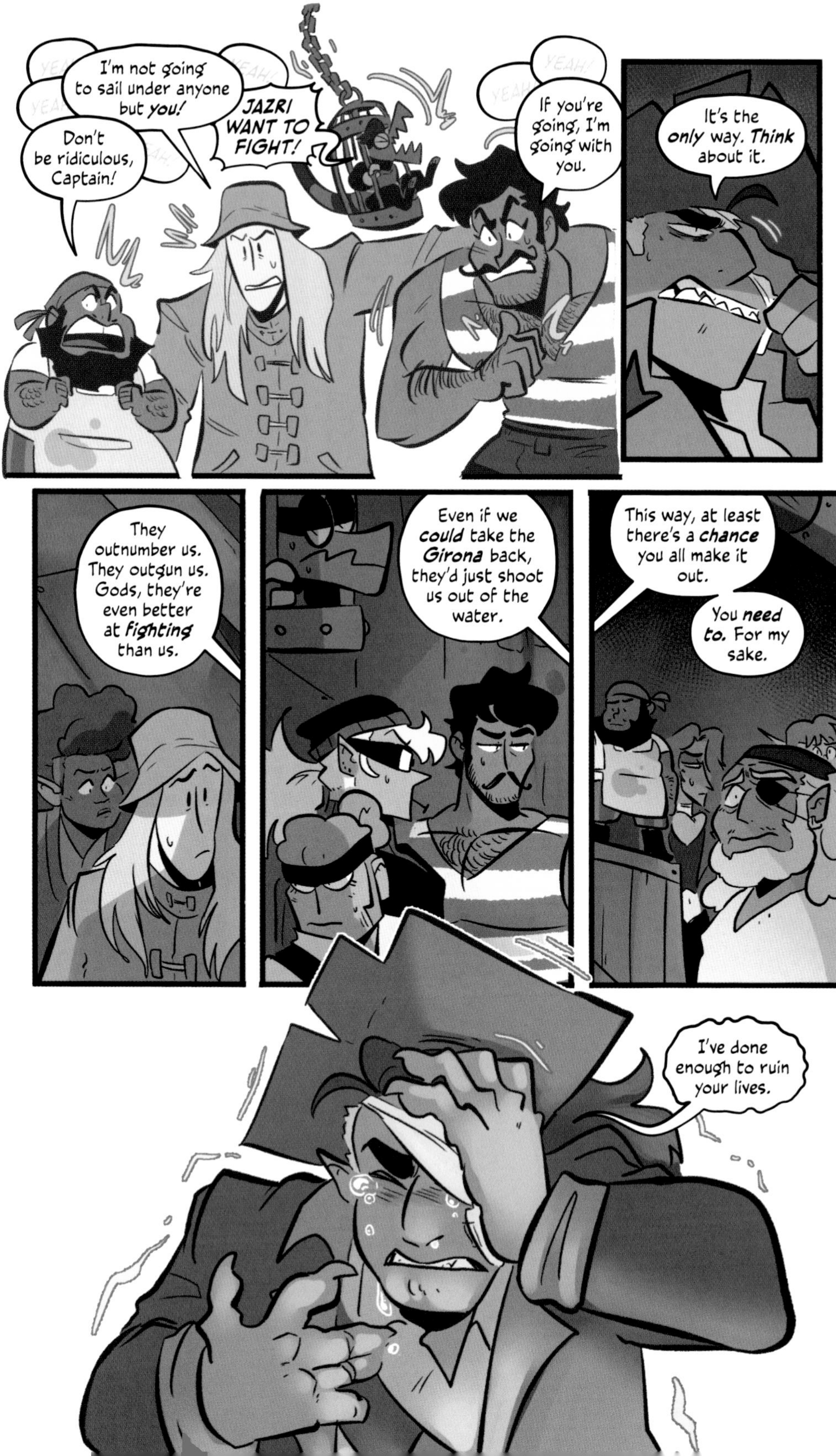

YEAH!
YEAH!
Don't be ridiculous, Captain!
I'm not going to sail under anyone but *you!*
JAZRI WANT TO FIGHT!
YEAH!
YEAH!
If you're going, I'm going with you.
It's the *only* way. *Think* about it.
They outnumber us. They outgun us. Gods, they're even better at *fighting* than us.
Even if we *could* take the *Girona* back, they'd just shoot us out of the water.
This way, at least there's a *chance* you all make it out.
You *need to.* For my sake.
I've done enough to ruin your lives.

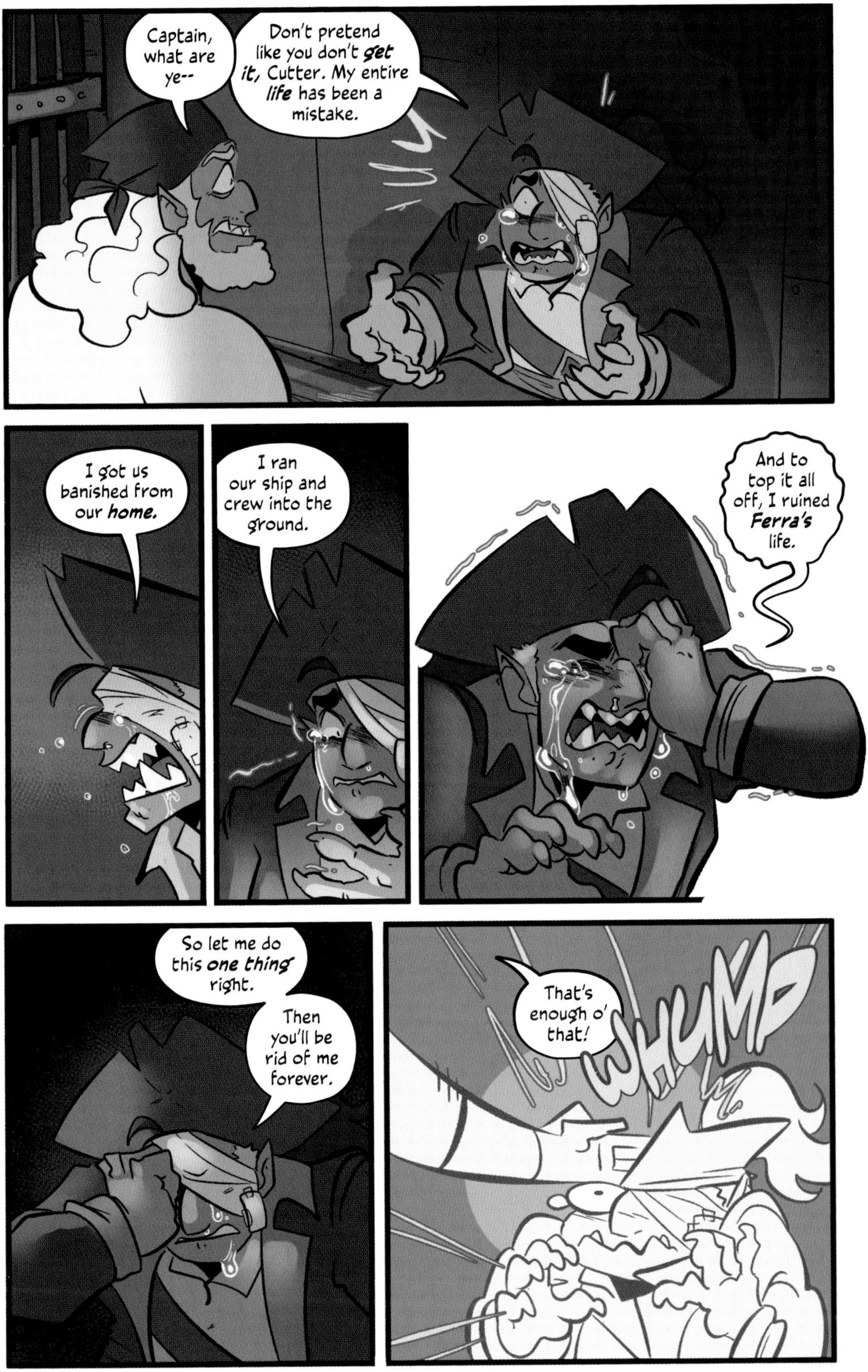
Captain, what are ye--
Don't pretend like you don't ***get it,*** Cutter. My entire ***life*** has been a mistake.
I got us banished from our ***home.***
I ran our ship and crew into the ground.
And to top it all off, I ruined ***Ferra's*** life.
So let me do this ***one thing*** right.
Then you'll be rid of me forever.
That's enough o' that!
WHUMP

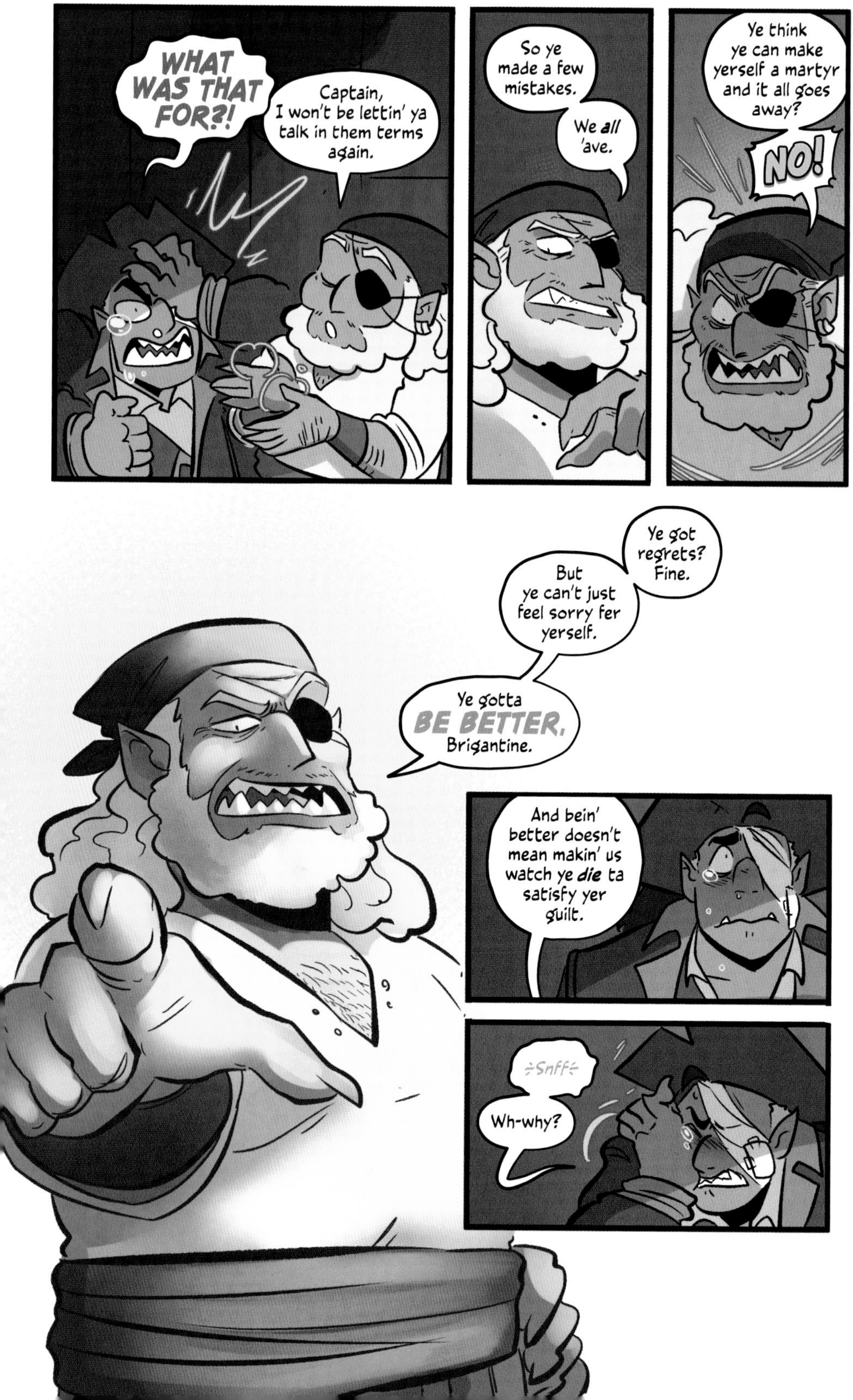
WHAT WAS THAT FOR?!
Captain, I won't be lettin' ya talk in them terms again.
So ye made a few mistakes.
We *all* 'ave.
Ye think ye can make yerself a martyr and it all goes away?
NO!
Ye got regrets? Fine.
But ye can't just feel sorry fer yerself.
Ye gotta BE BETTER, Brigantine.
And bein' better doesn't mean makin' us watch ye *die* ta satisfy yer guilt.
Snff
Wh-why?

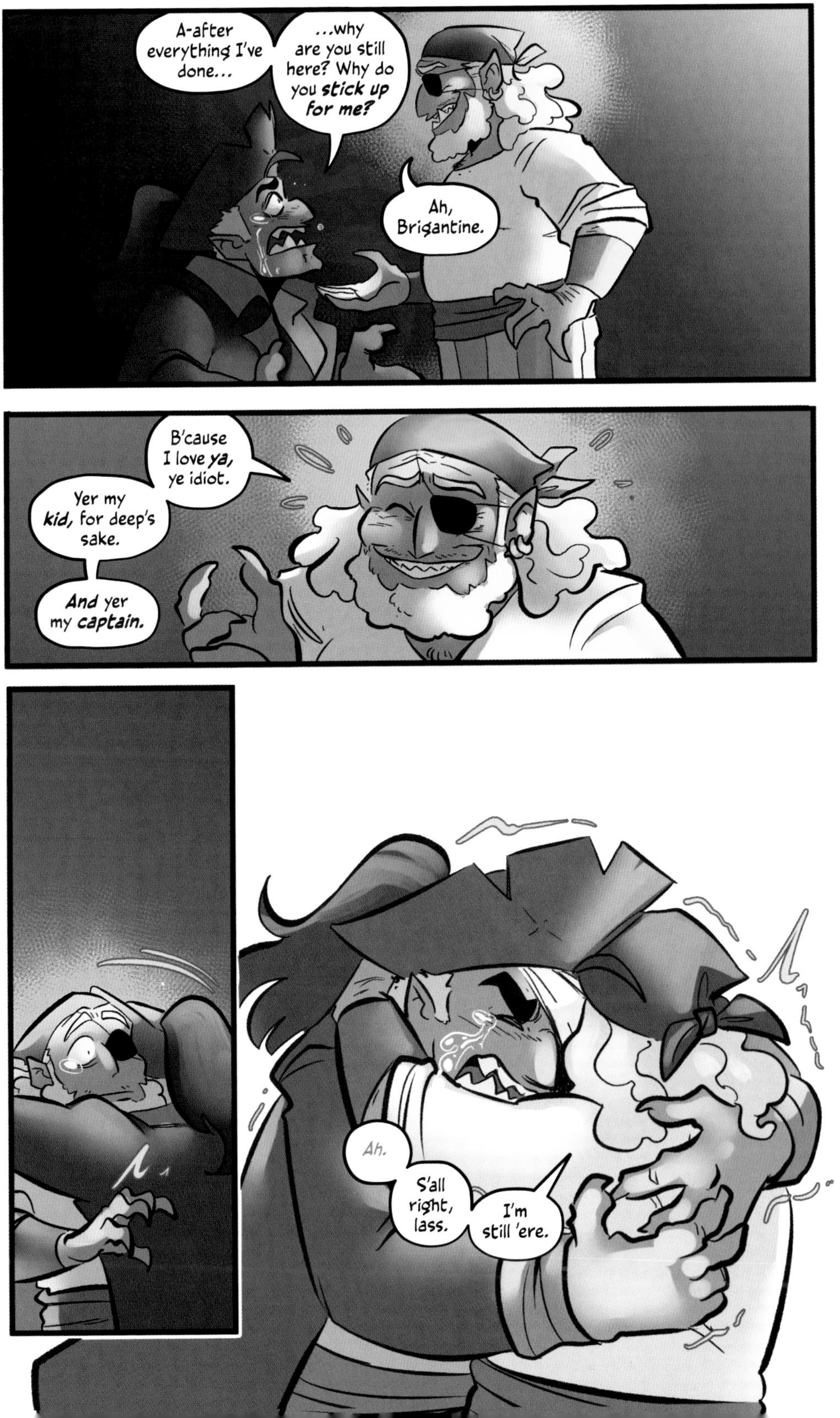
A-after everything I've done...
...why are you still here? Why do you stick up for me?
Ah, Brigantine.
B'cause I love ya, ye idiot.
Yer my kid, for deep's sake.
And yer my captain.
Ah.
S'all right, lass.
I'm still 'ere.

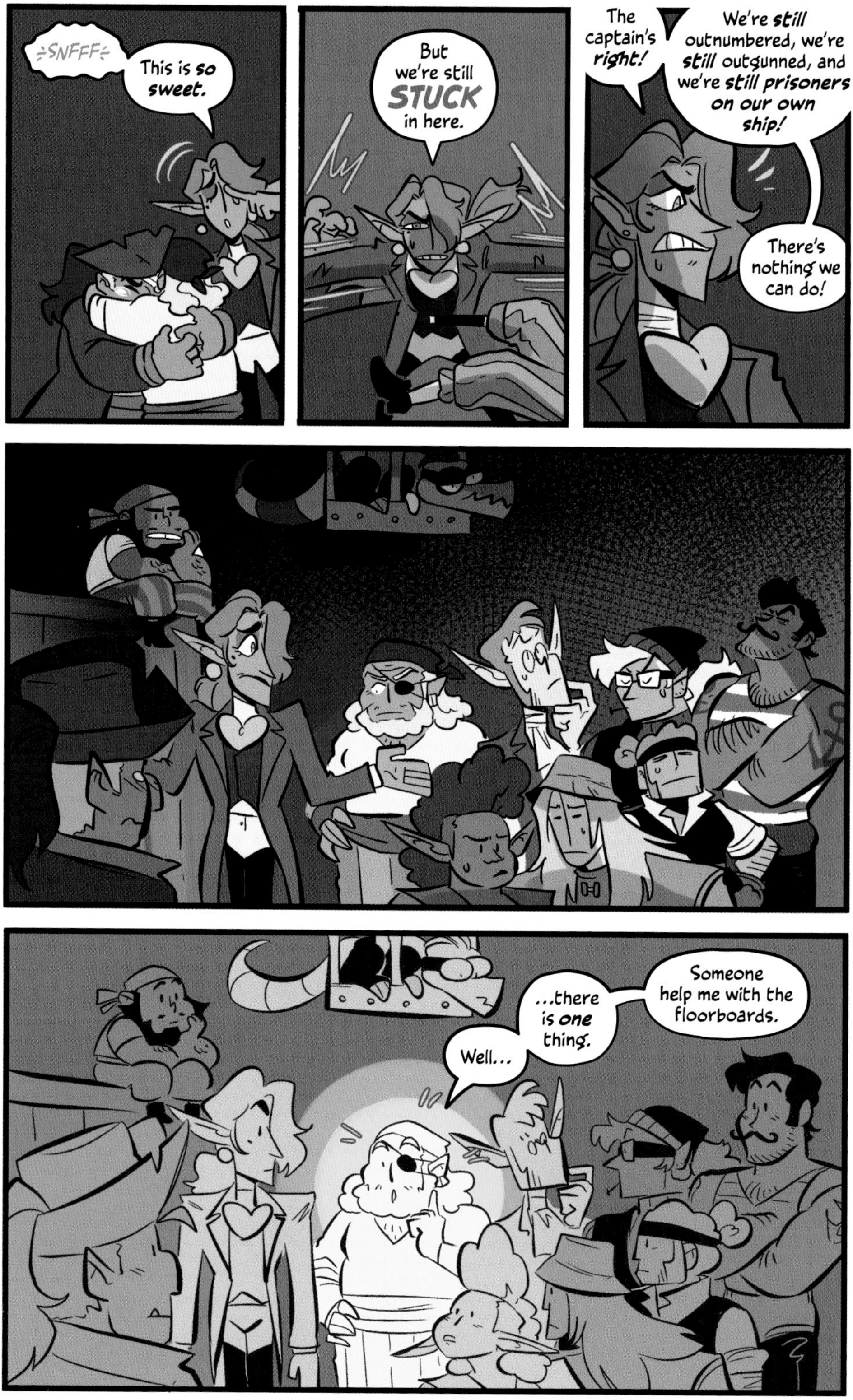
SNFFF
This is so sweet.
But we're still STUCK in here.
The captain's right!
We're still outnumbered, we're still outgunned, and we're still prisoners on our own ship!
There's nothing we can do!
Well...
...there is one thing.
Someone help me with the floorboards.

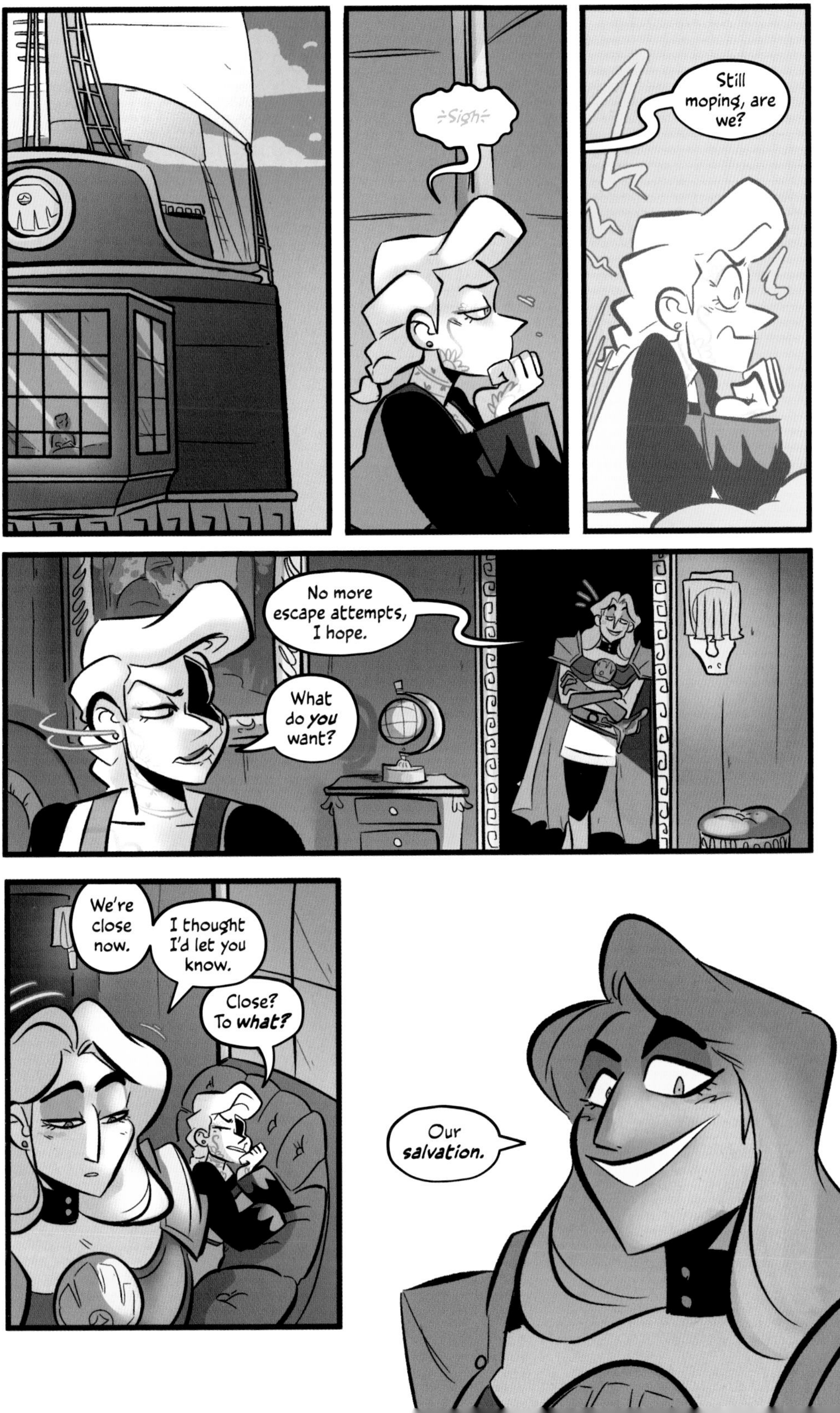
Sigh
Still moping, are we?
No more escape attempts, I hope.
What do you want?
We're close now.
I thought I'd let you know.
Close? To what?
Our salvation.

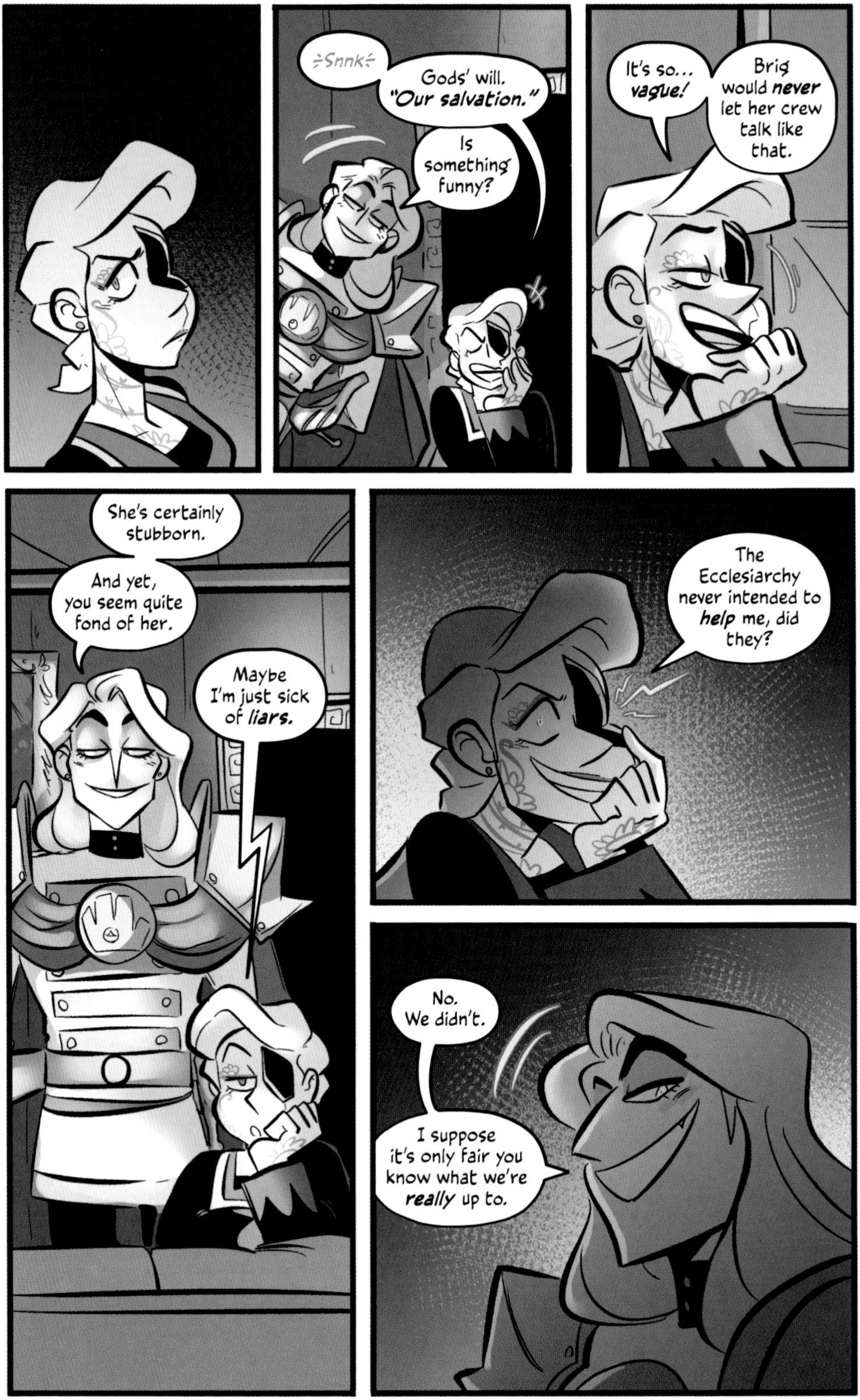

Snnk
Gods' will. "Our salvation."
Is something funny?
It's so... vague!
Brig would never let her crew talk like that.
She's certainly stubborn.
And yet, you seem quite fond of her.
Maybe I'm just sick of liars.
The Ecclesiarchy never intended to help me, did they?
No. We didn't.
I suppose it's only fair you know what we're really up to.

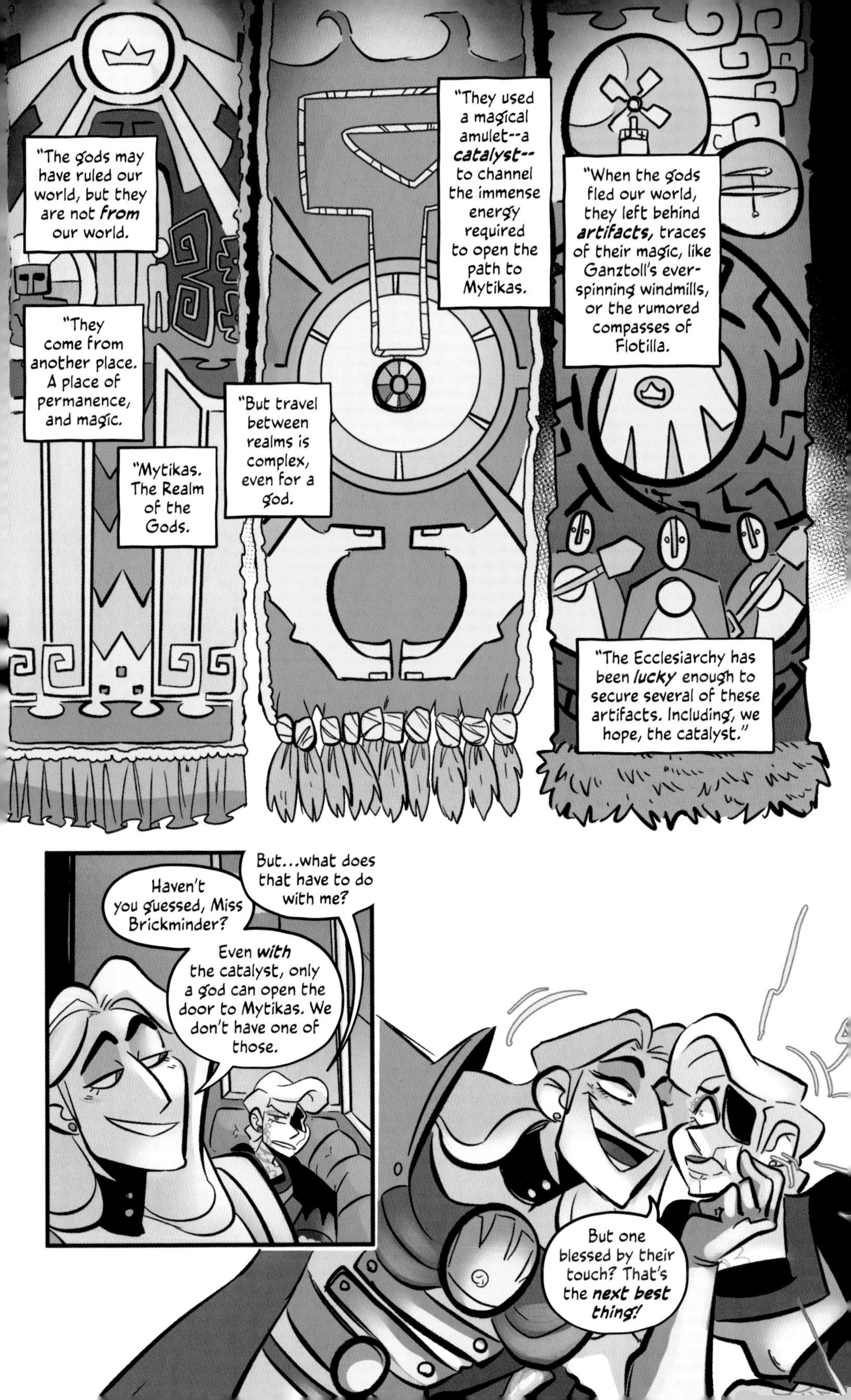
"The gods may have ruled our world, but they are not *from* our world.
"They come from another place. A place of permanence, and magic.
"Mytikas. The Realm of the Gods.
"But travel between realms is complex, even for a god.
"They used a magical amulet--a *catalyst--* to channel the immense energy required to open the path to Mytikas.
"When the gods fled our world, they left behind *artifacts,* traces of their magic, like Ganztoll's ever-spinning windmills, or the rumored compasses of Flotilla.
"The Ecclesiarchy has been *lucky* enough to secure several of these artifacts. Including, we hope, the catalyst."
But...what does that have to do with me?
Haven't you guessed, Miss Brickminder?
Even *with* the catalyst, only a god can open the door to Mytikas. We don't have one of those.
But one blessed by their touch? That's the *next best thing!*

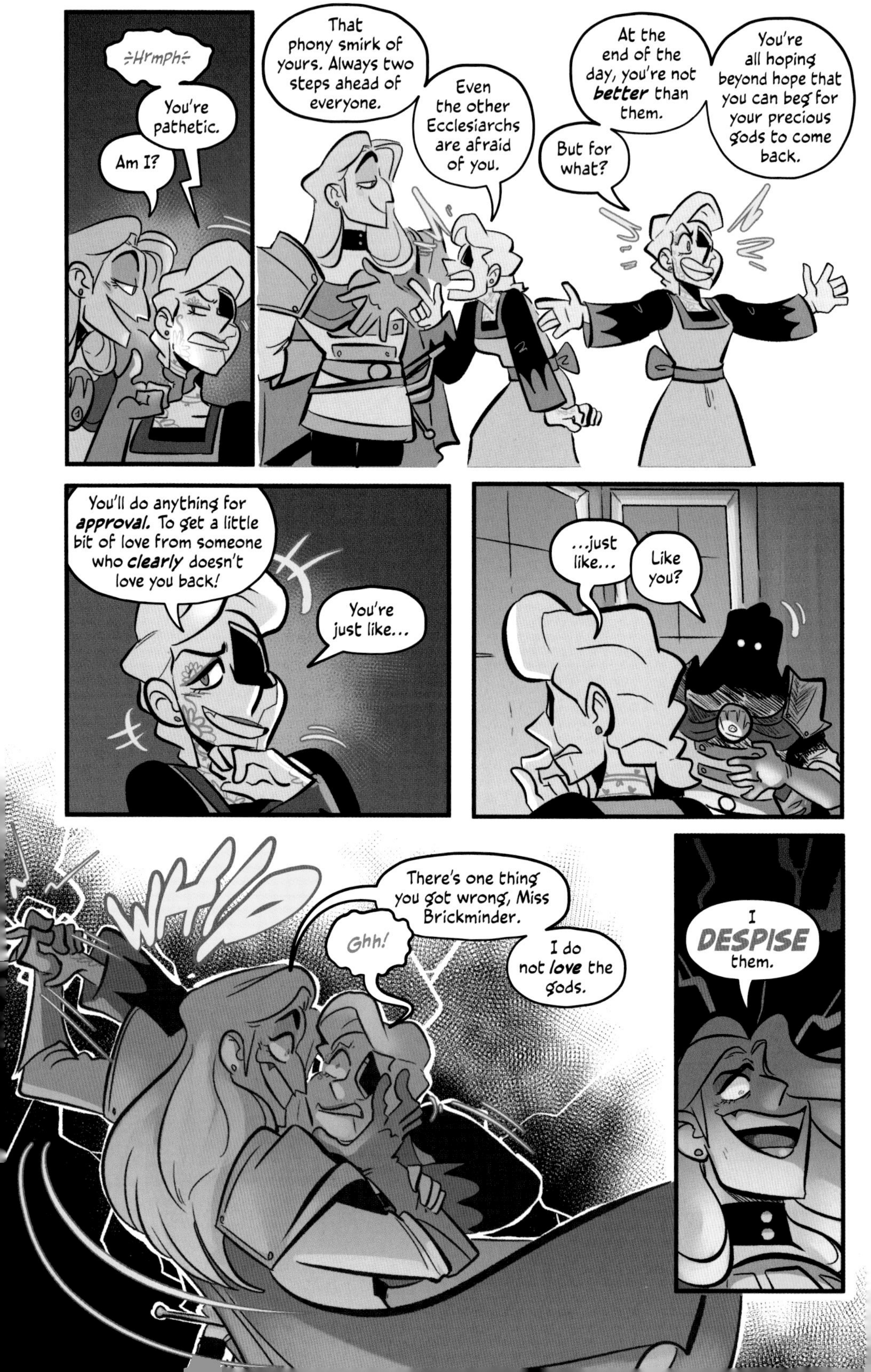

Hrmph
You're pathetic.
Am I?
That phony smirk of yours. Always two steps ahead of everyone.
Even the other Ecclesiarchs are afraid of you.
At the end of the day, you're not better than them.
But for what?
You're all hoping beyond hope that you can beg for your precious gods to come back.
You'll do anything for approval. To get a little bit of love from someone who clearly doesn't love you back!
You're just like...
...just like...
Like you?
WHIP
There's one thing you got wrong, Miss Brickminder.
Ghh!
I do not love the gods.
I DESPISE them.

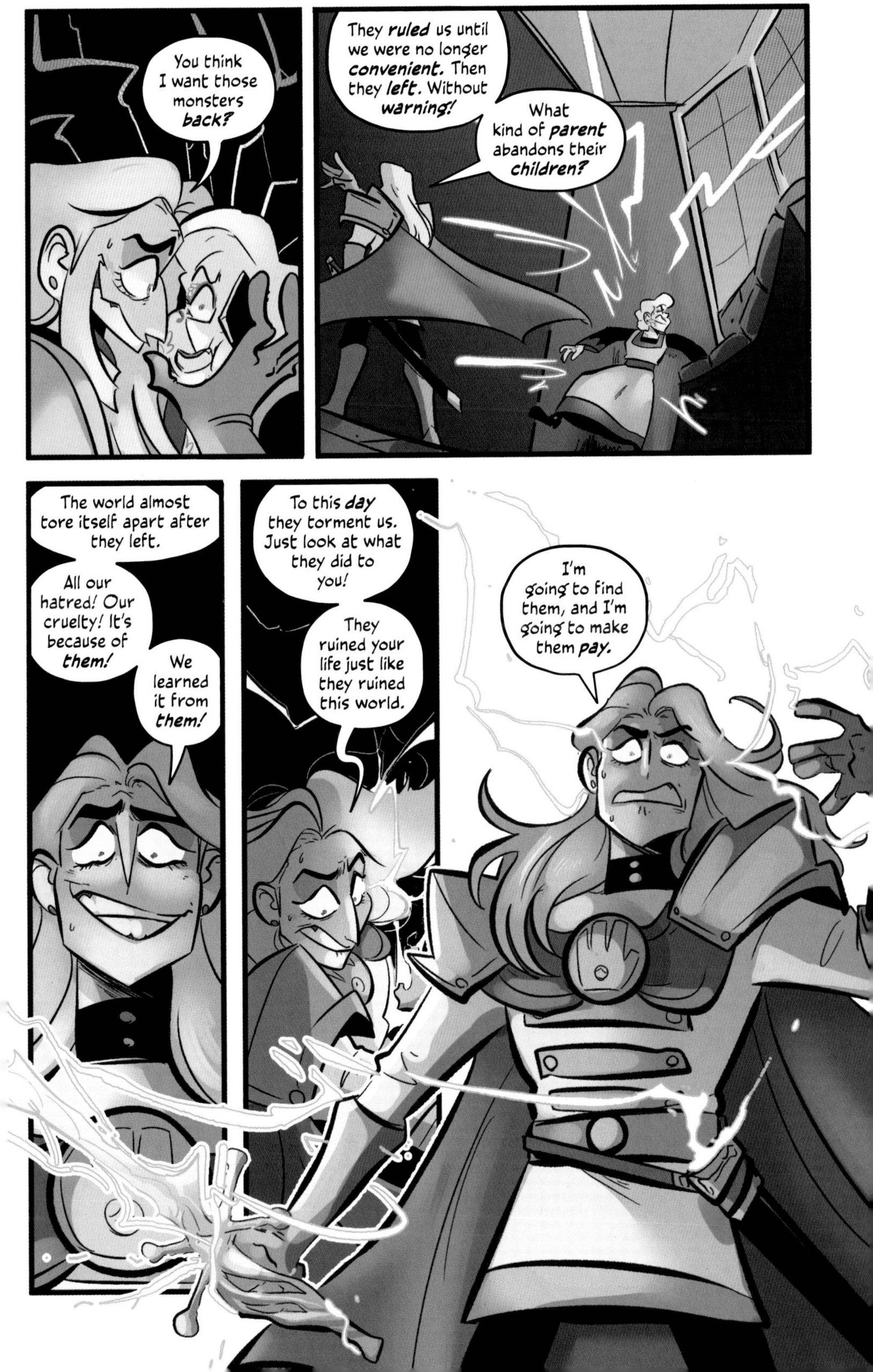
You think I want those monsters *back?*
They *ruled* us until we were no longer *convenient.* Then they *left.* Without *warning!*
What kind of *parent* abandons their *children?*
The world almost tore itself apart after they left.
All our hatred! Our cruelty! It's because of *them!*
We learned it from *them!*
To this *day* they torment us. Just look at what they did to you!
They ruined your life just like they ruined this world.
I'm going to find them, and I'm going to make them *pay.*

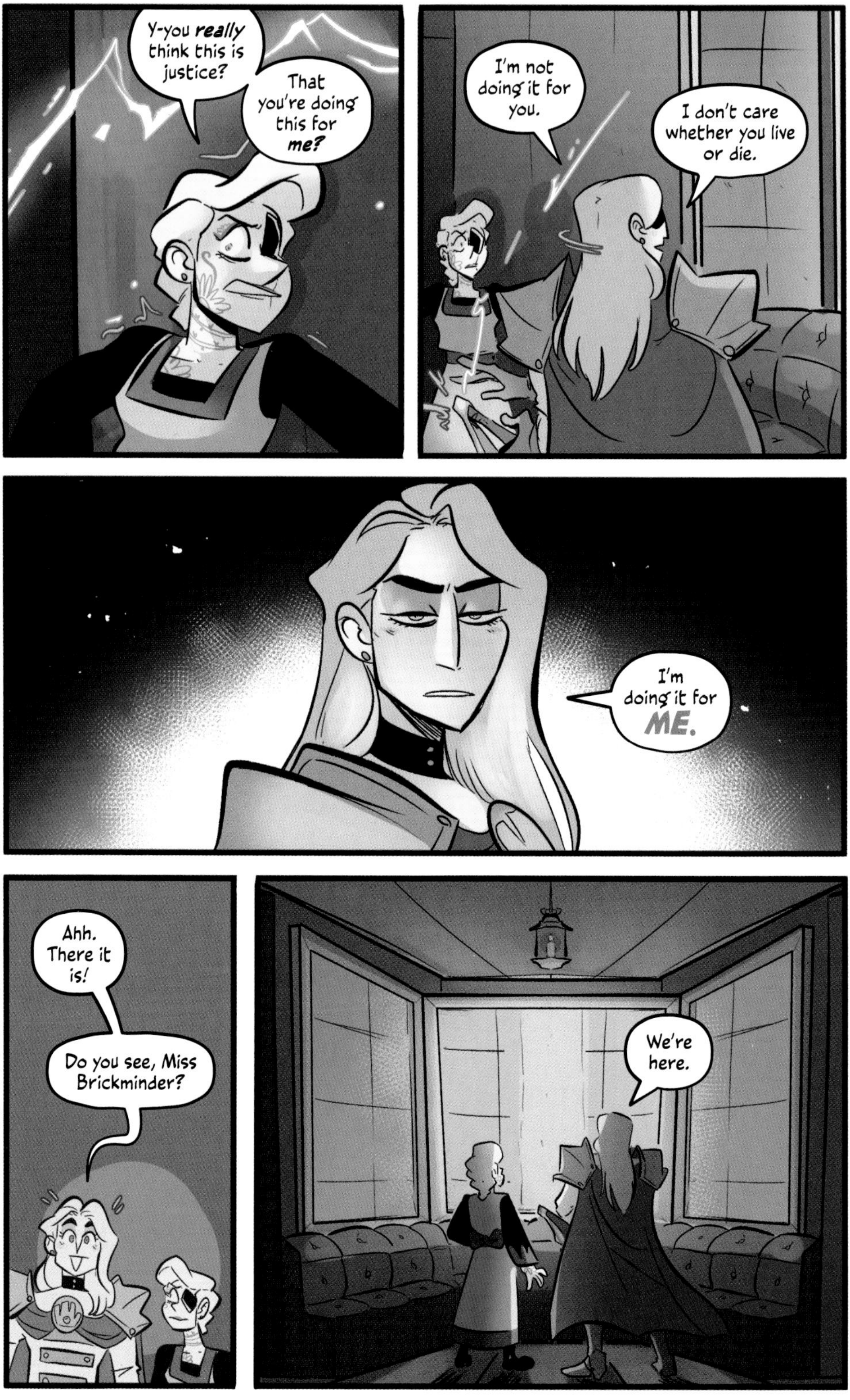
Y-you *really* think this is justice?
That you're doing this for *me?*
I'm not doing it for you.
I don't care whether you live or die.
I'm doing it for **ME.**
Ahh. There it is!
Do you see, Miss Brickminder?
We're here.

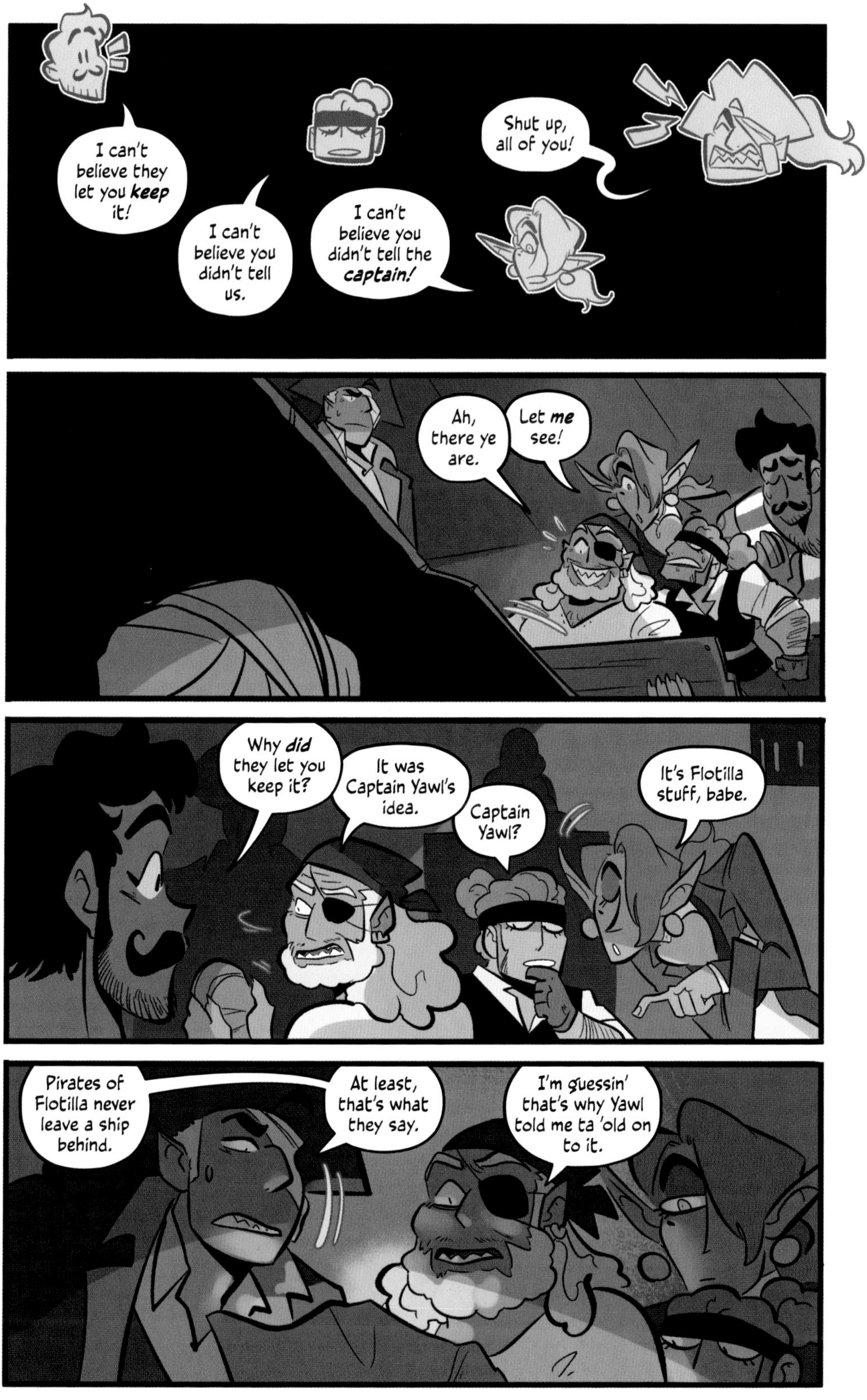
I can't believe they let you *keep* it!
I can't believe you didn't tell us.
I can't believe you didn't tell the *captain!*
Shut up, all of you!
Ah, there ye are.
Let *me* see!
Why *did* they let you keep it?
It was Captain Yawl's idea.
Captain Yawl?
It's Flotilla stuff, babe.
Pirates of Flotilla never leave a ship behind.
At least, that's what they say.
I'm guessin' that's why Yawl told me ta 'old on to it.

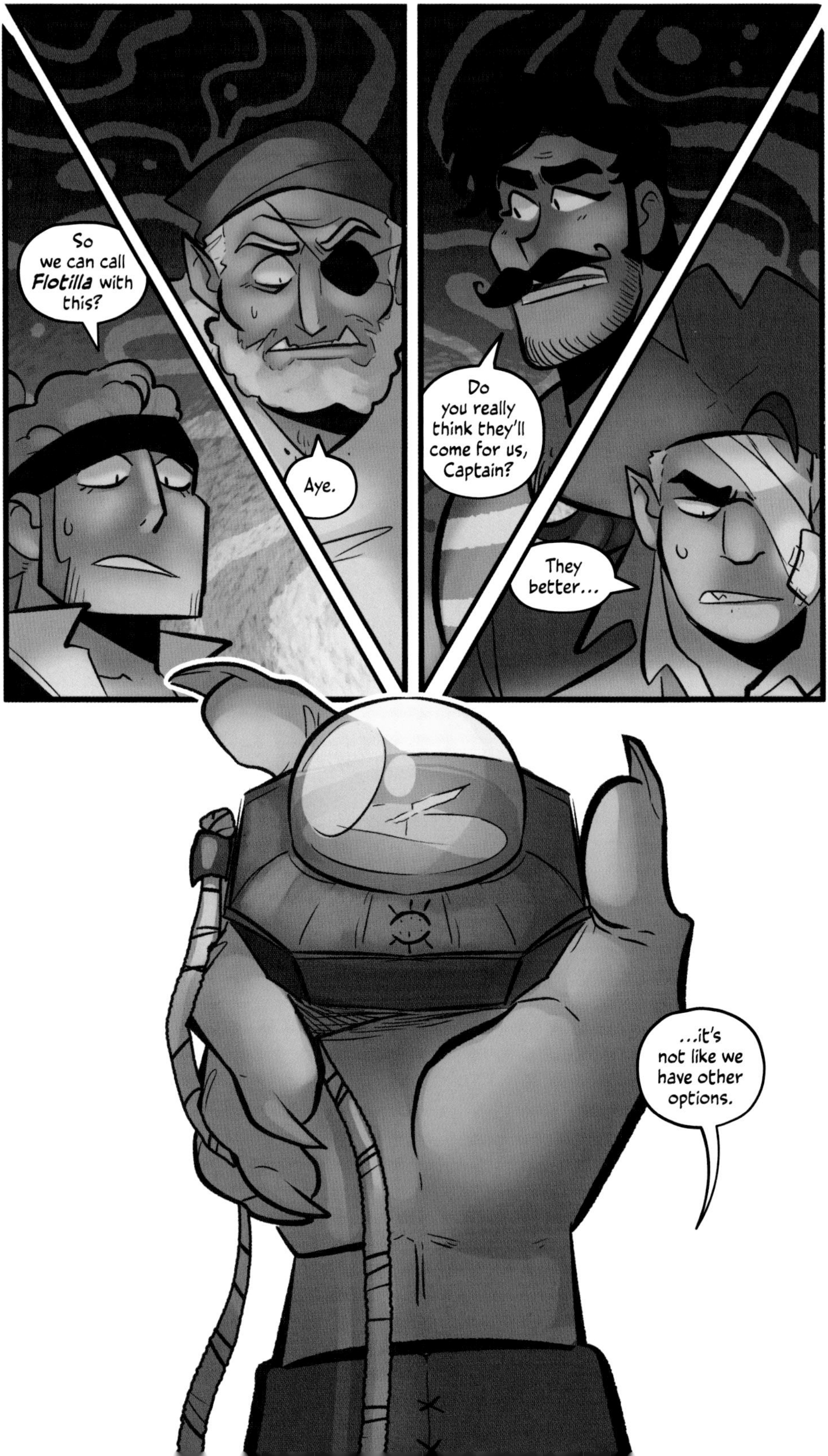
So we can call *Flotilla* with this?
Aye.
Do you really think they'll come for us, Captain?
They better...
...it's not like we have other options.

Chapter 6

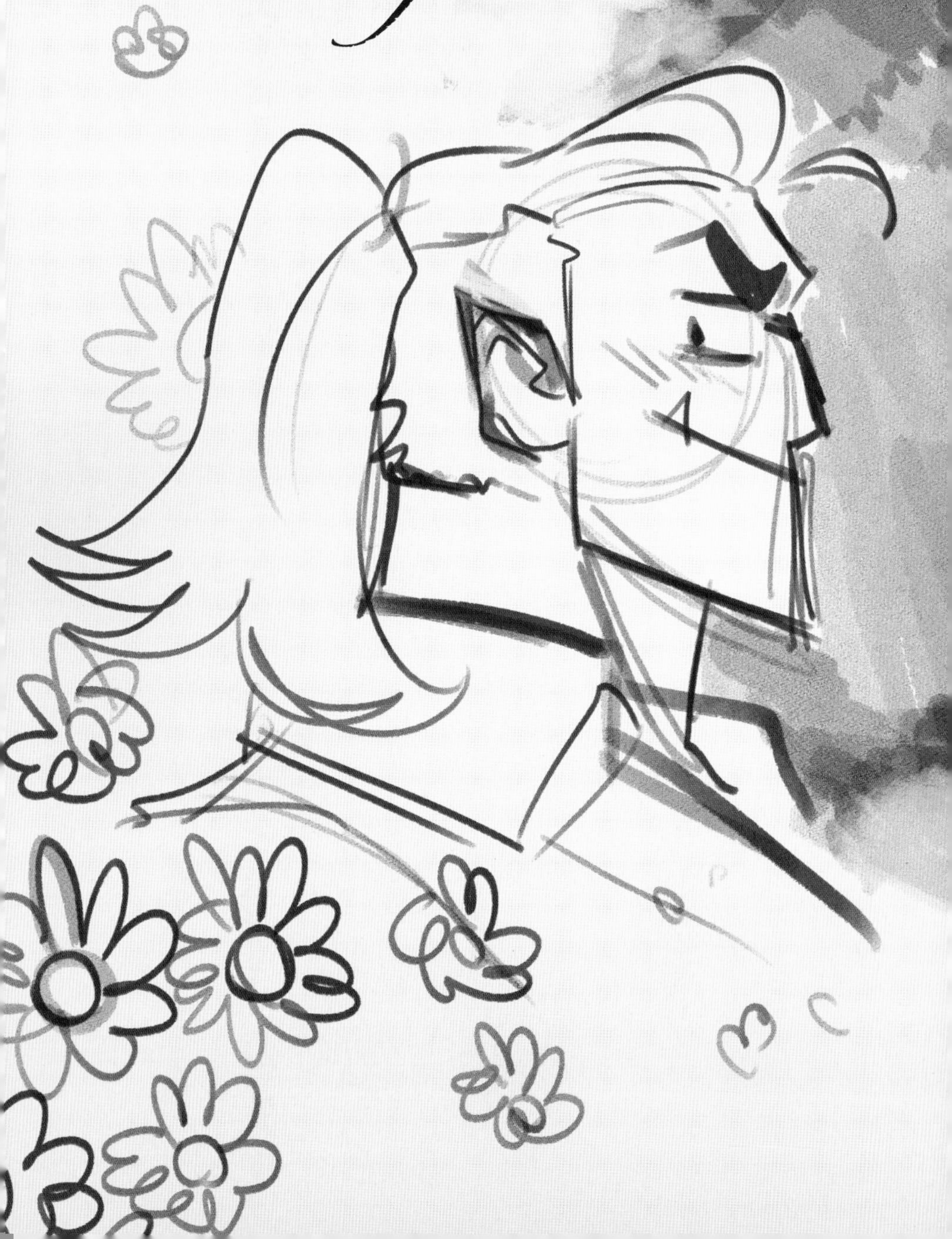

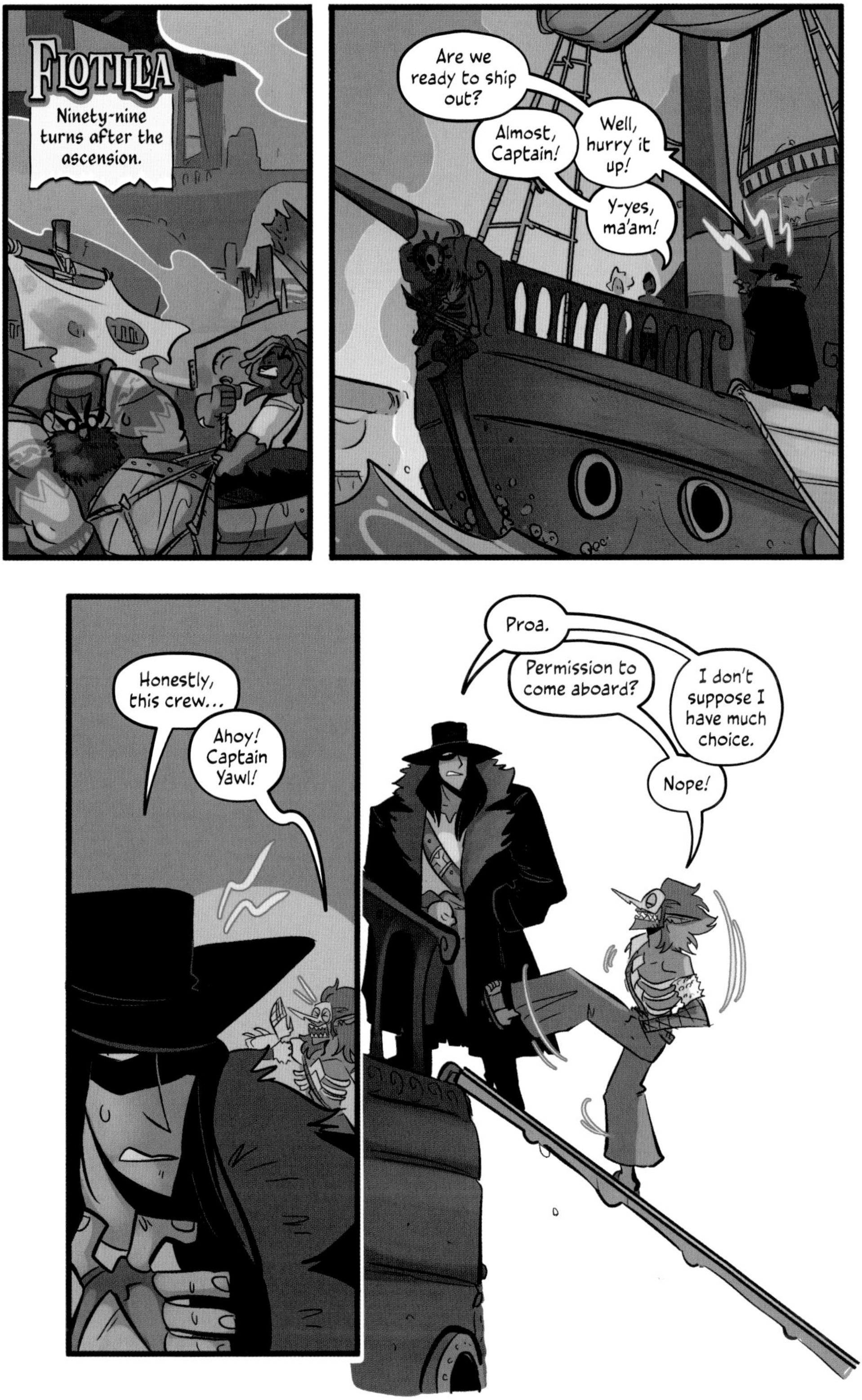
FLOTILLA
Ninety-nine turns after the ascension.
Are we ready to ship out?
Almost, Captain!
Well, hurry it up!
Y-yes, ma'am!
Honestly, this crew...
Ahoy! Captain Yawl!
Proa.
Permission to come aboard?
I don't suppose I have much choice.
Nope!

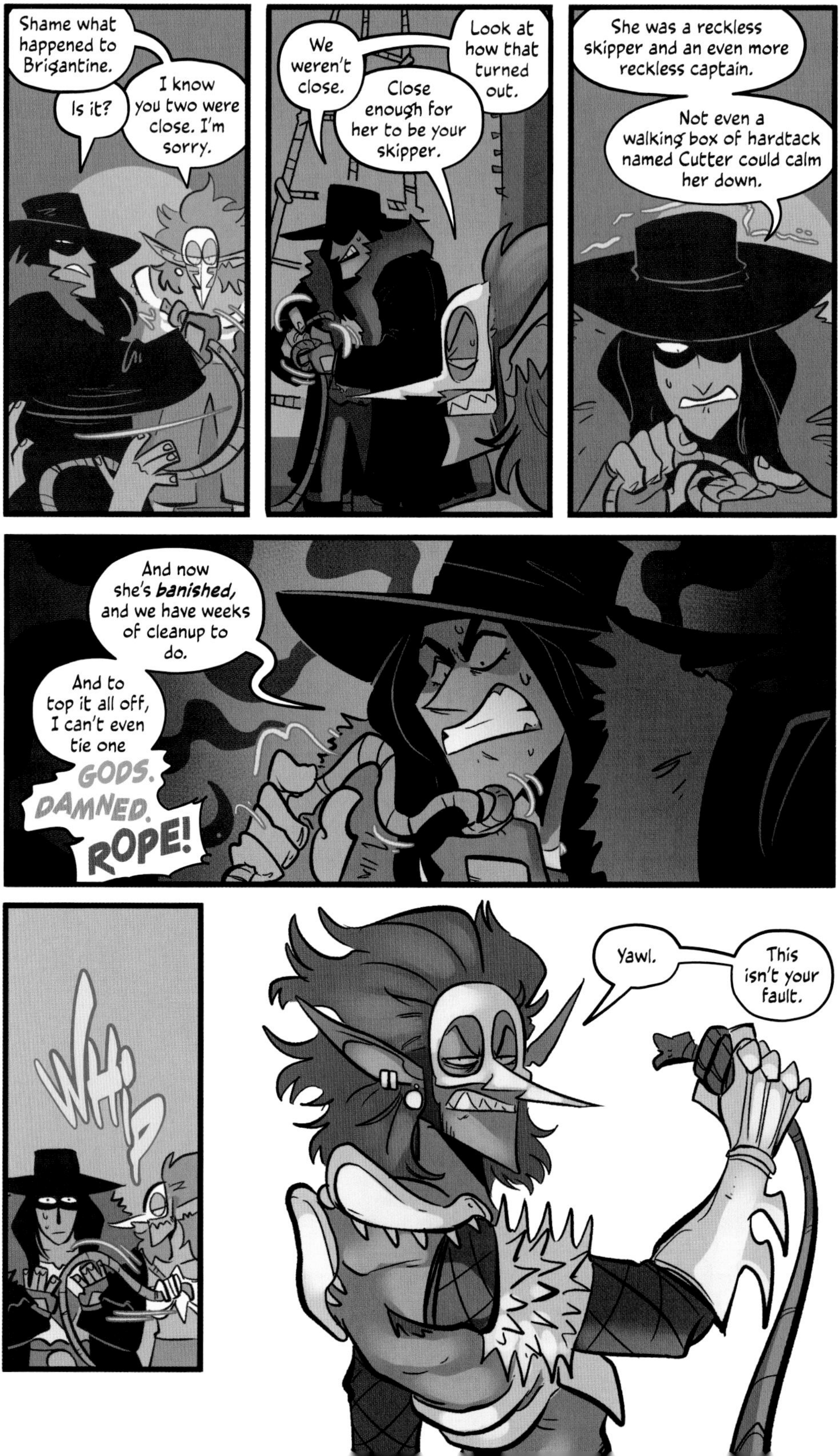

Shame what happened to Brigantine.
Is it?
I know you two were close. I'm sorry.
We weren't close.
Look at how that turned out.
Close enough for her to be your skipper.
She was a reckless skipper and an even more reckless captain.
Not even a walking box of hardtack named Cutter could calm her down.
And now she's ***banished,*** and we have weeks of cleanup to do.
And to top it all off, I can't even tie one
GODS. DAMNED. ROPE!
WHIP
Yawl.
This isn't your fault.

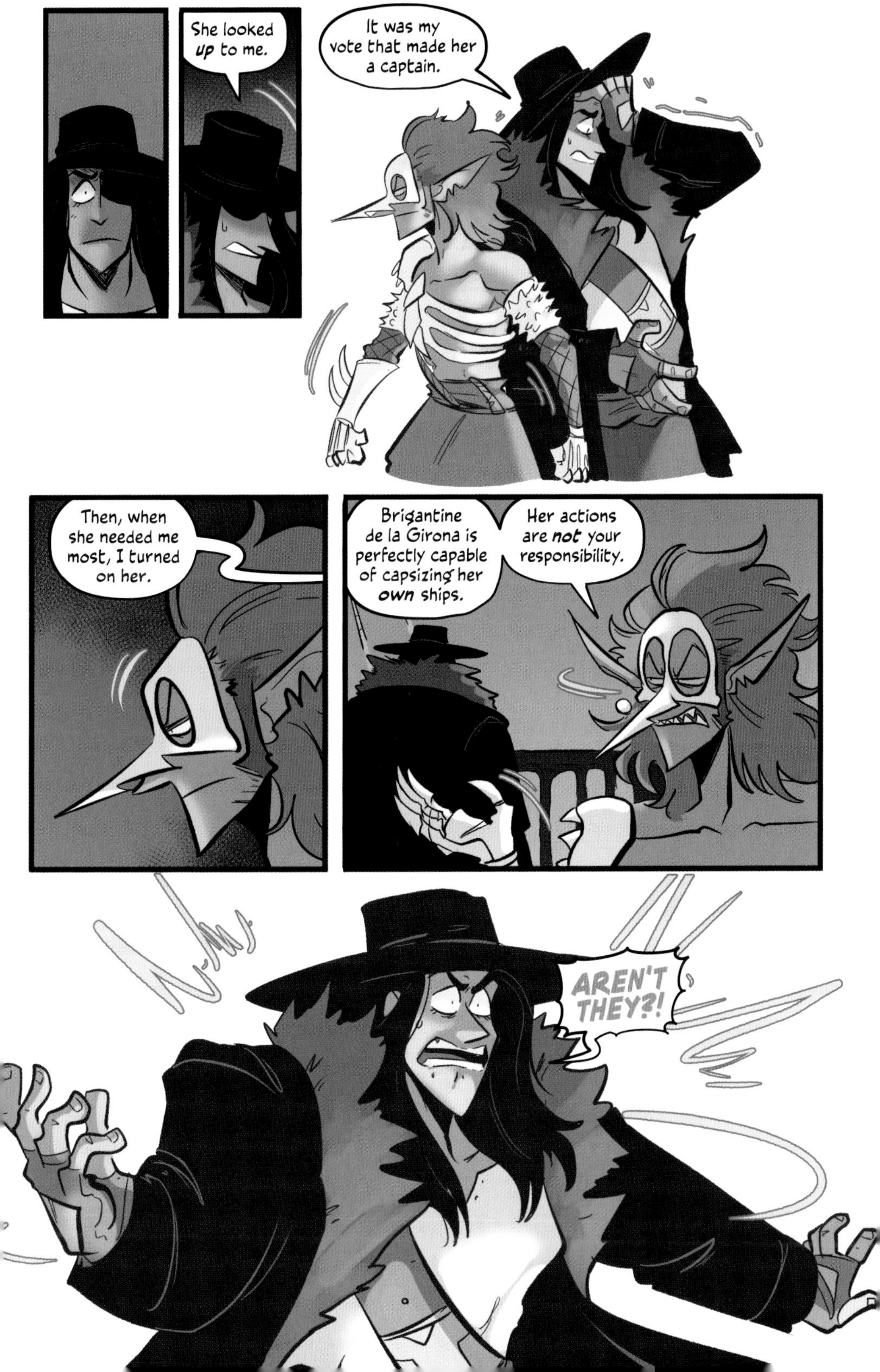
She looked *up* to me.
It was my vote that made her a captain.
Then, when she needed me most, I turned on her.
Brigantine de la Girona is perfectly capable of capsizing her *own* ships.
Her actions are *not* your responsibility.
AREN'T THEY?!

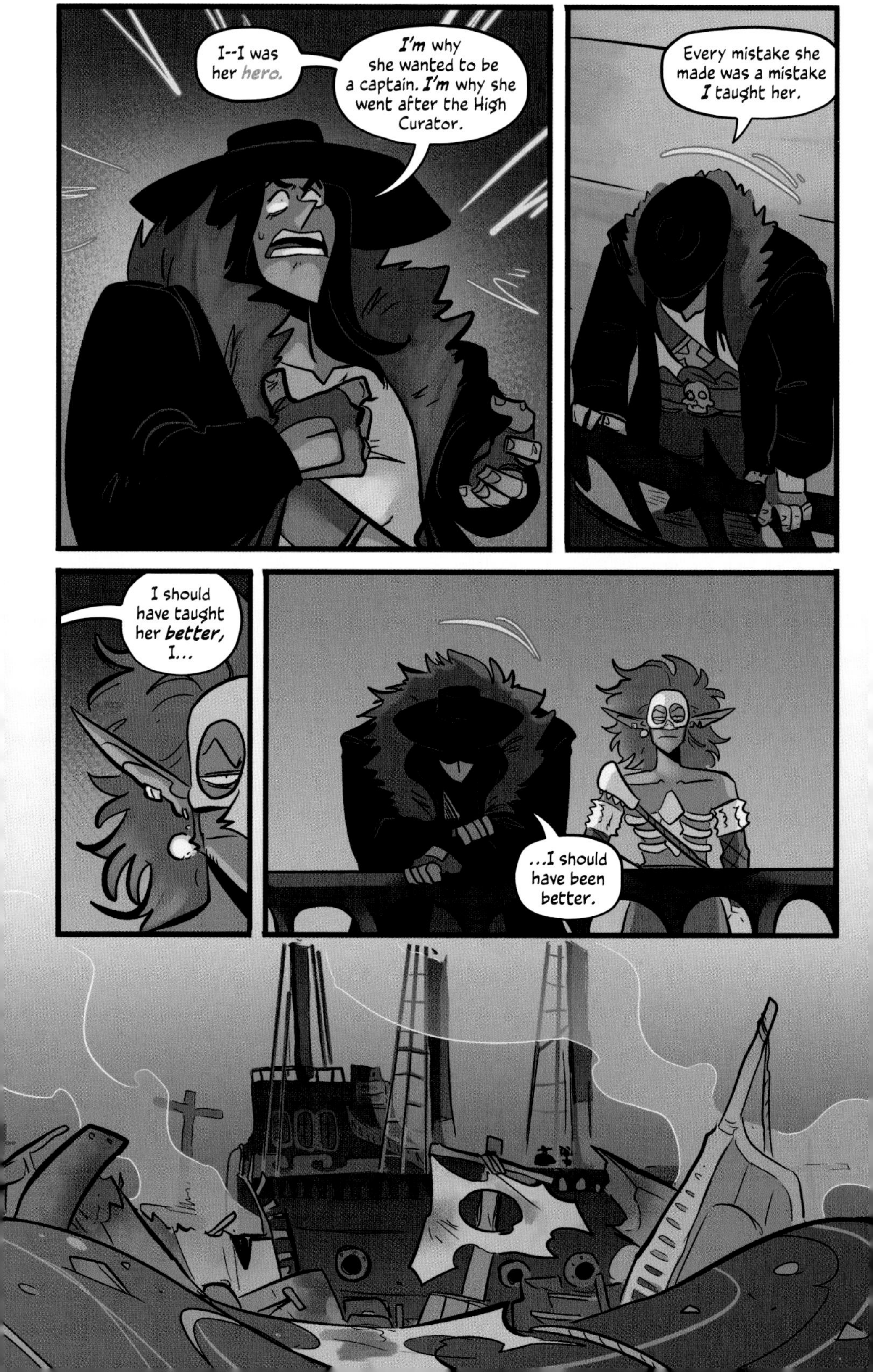

I--I was her *hero.*
I'm why she wanted to be a captain. *I'm* why she went after the High Curator.
Every mistake she made was a mistake *I* taught her.
I should have taught her *better,* I...
...I should have been better.

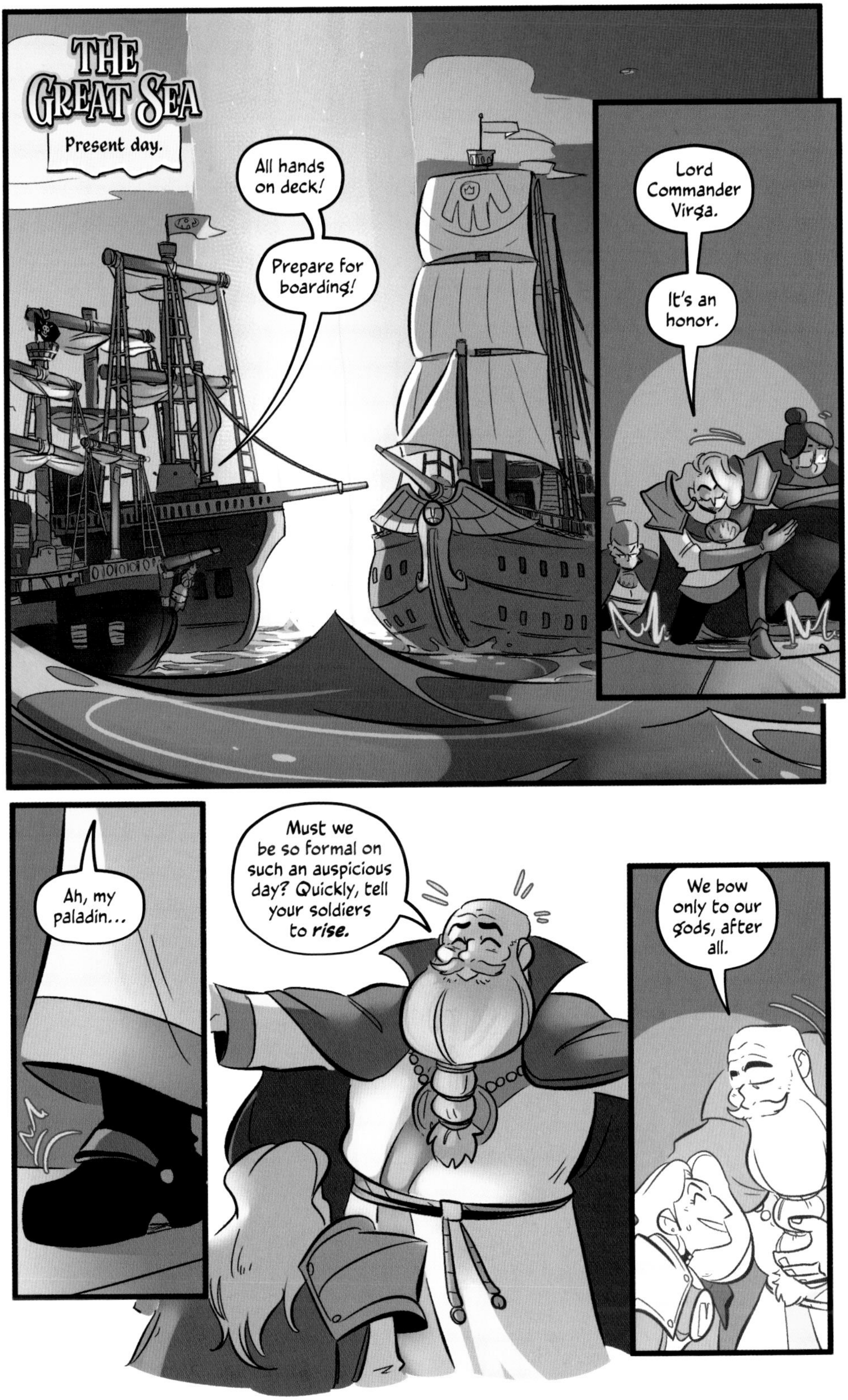

THE GREAT SEA
Present day.
All hands on deck!
Prepare for boarding!
Lord Commander Virga.
It's an honor.
Ah, my paladin...
Must we be so formal on such an auspicious day? Quickly, tell your soldiers to *rise.*
We bow only to our gods, after all.

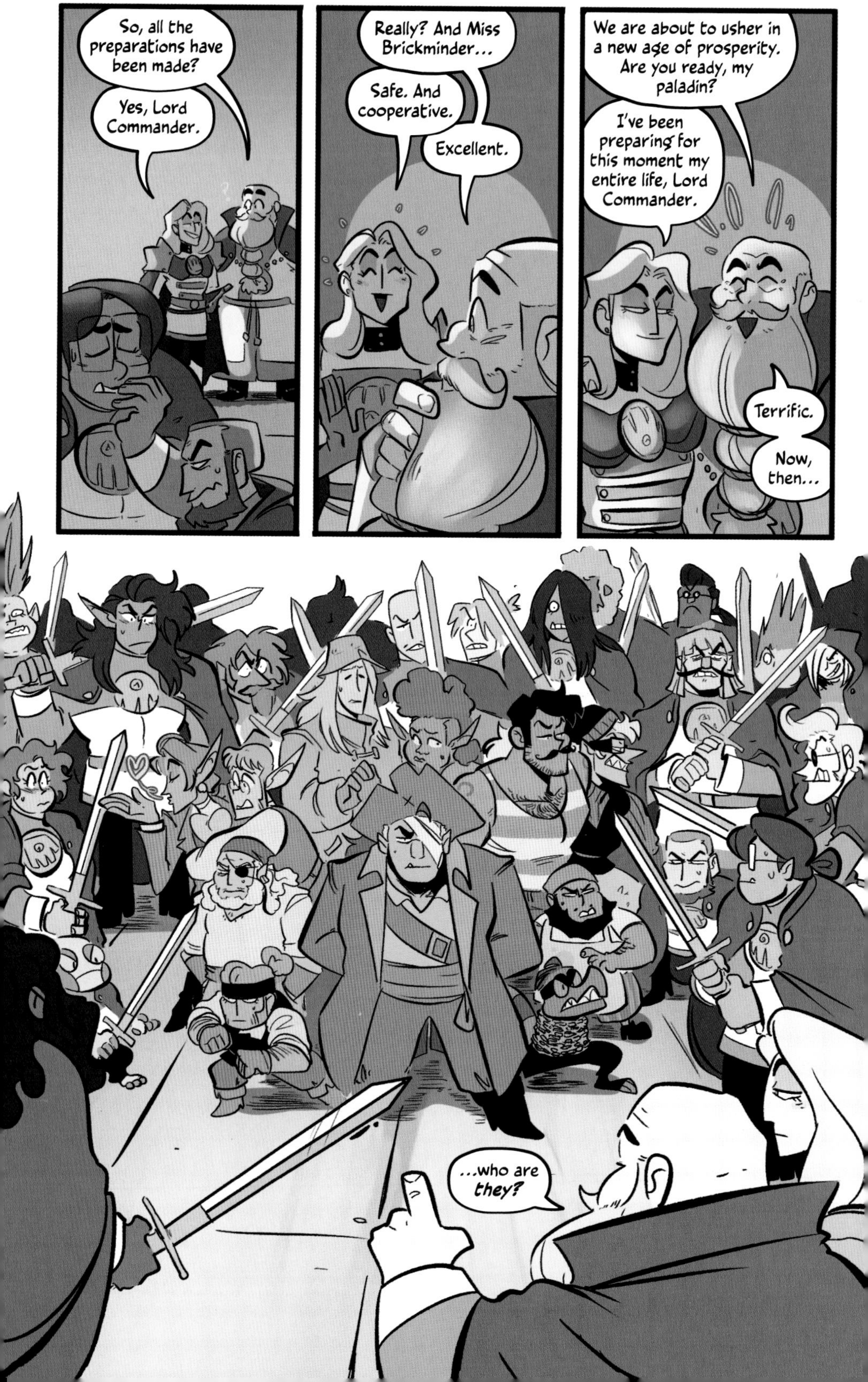
So, all the preparations have been made?
Yes, Lord Commander.
Really? And Miss Brickminder...
Safe. And cooperative.
Excellent.
We are about to usher in a new age of prosperity. Are you ready, my paladin?
I've been preparing for this moment my entire life, Lord Commander.
Terrific.
Now, then...
...who are *they?*

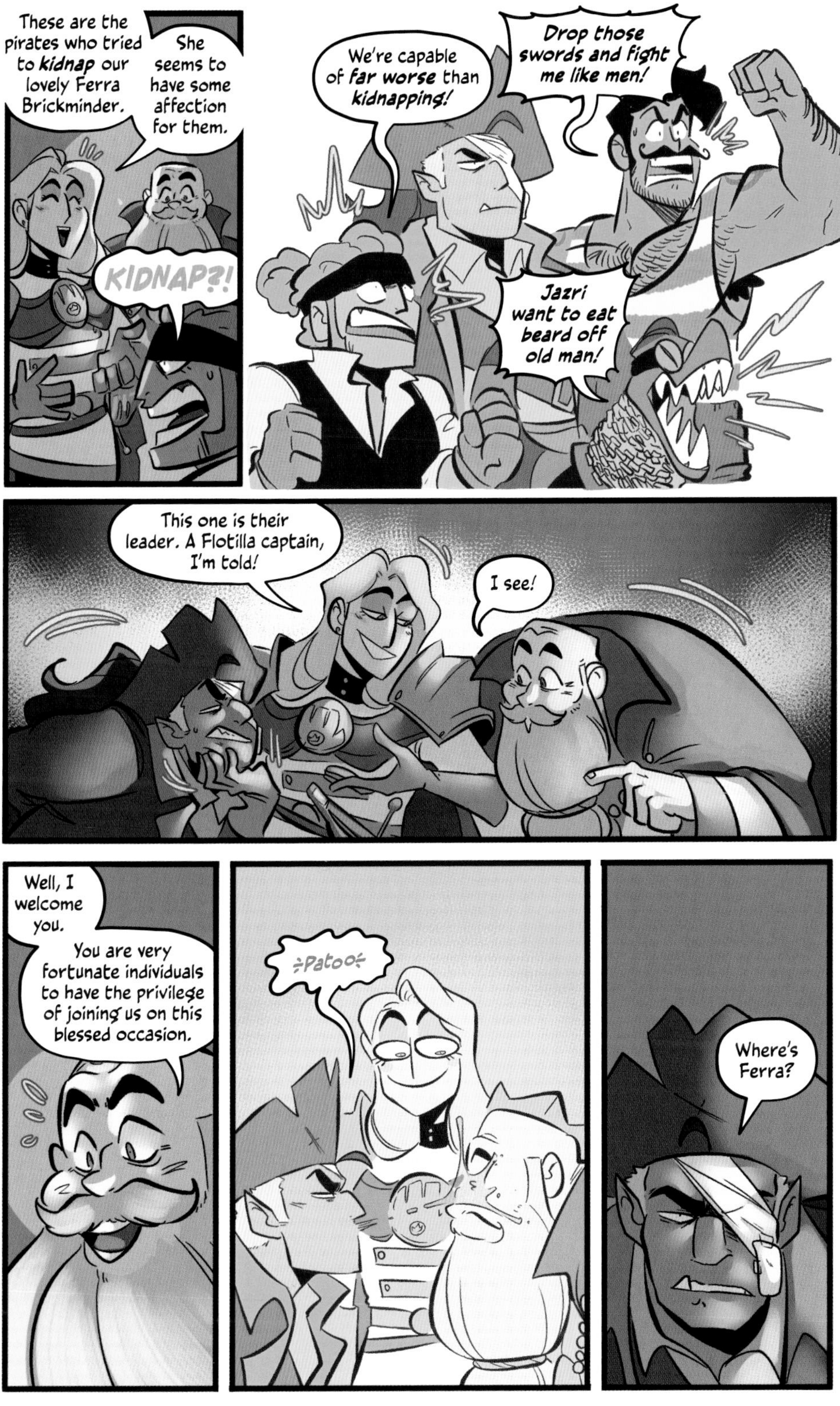

These are the pirates who tried to *kidnap* our lovely Ferra Brickminder.
She seems to have some affection for them.
KIDNAP?!
We're capable of *far worse* than *kidnapping!*
Drop those swords and fight me like men!
Jazri want to eat beard off old man!
This one is their leader. A Flotilla captain, I'm told!
I see!
Well, I welcome you.
You are very fortunate individuals to have the privilege of joining us on this blessed occasion.
÷Patoo÷
Where's Ferra?

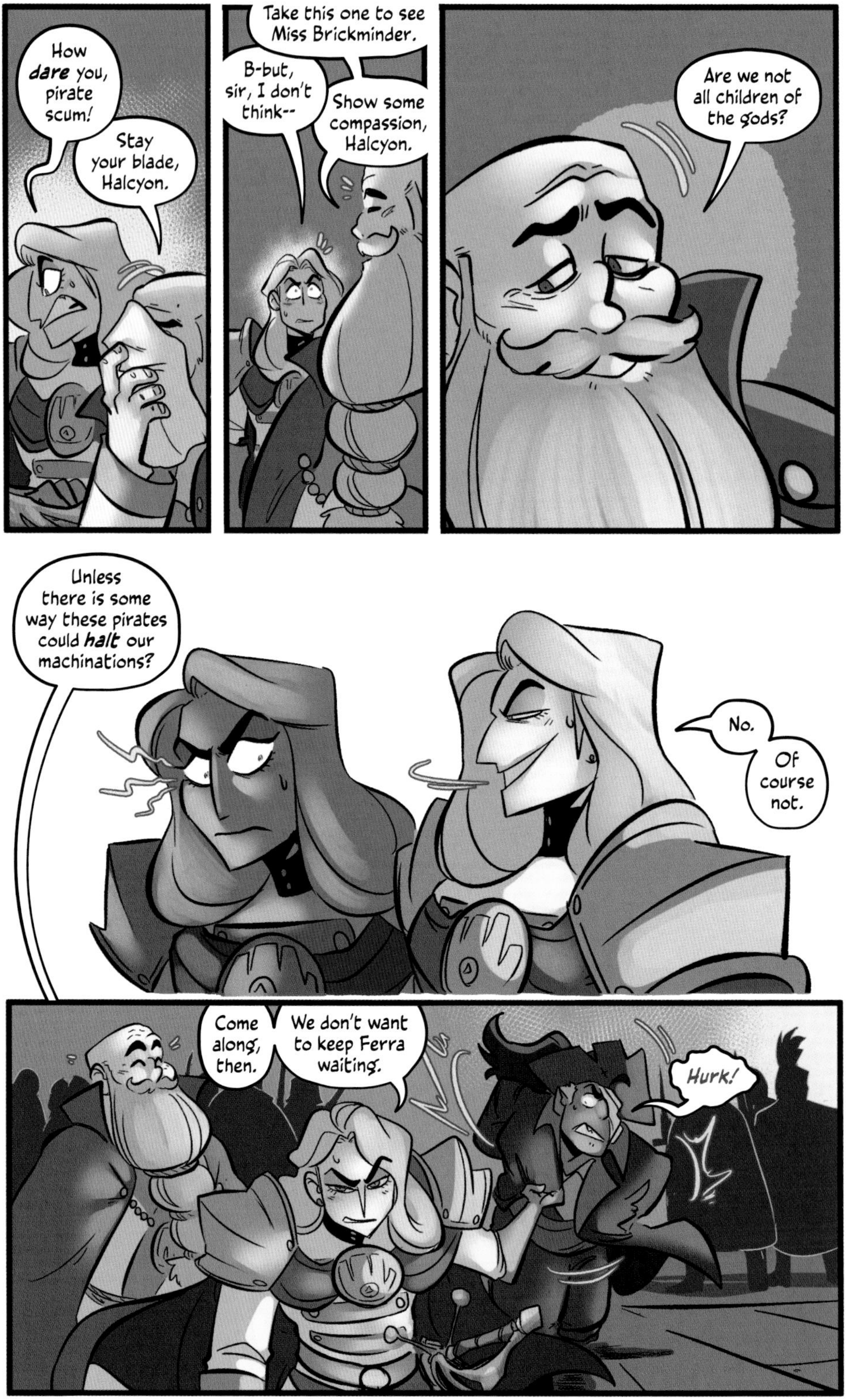
How dare you, pirate scum!
Stay your blade, Halcyon.
Take this one to see Miss Brickminder.
B-but, sir, I don't think--
Show some compassion, Halcyon.
Are we not all children of the gods?
Unless there is some way these pirates could halt our machinations?
No.
Of course not.
Come along, then.
We don't want to keep Ferra waiting.
Hurk!

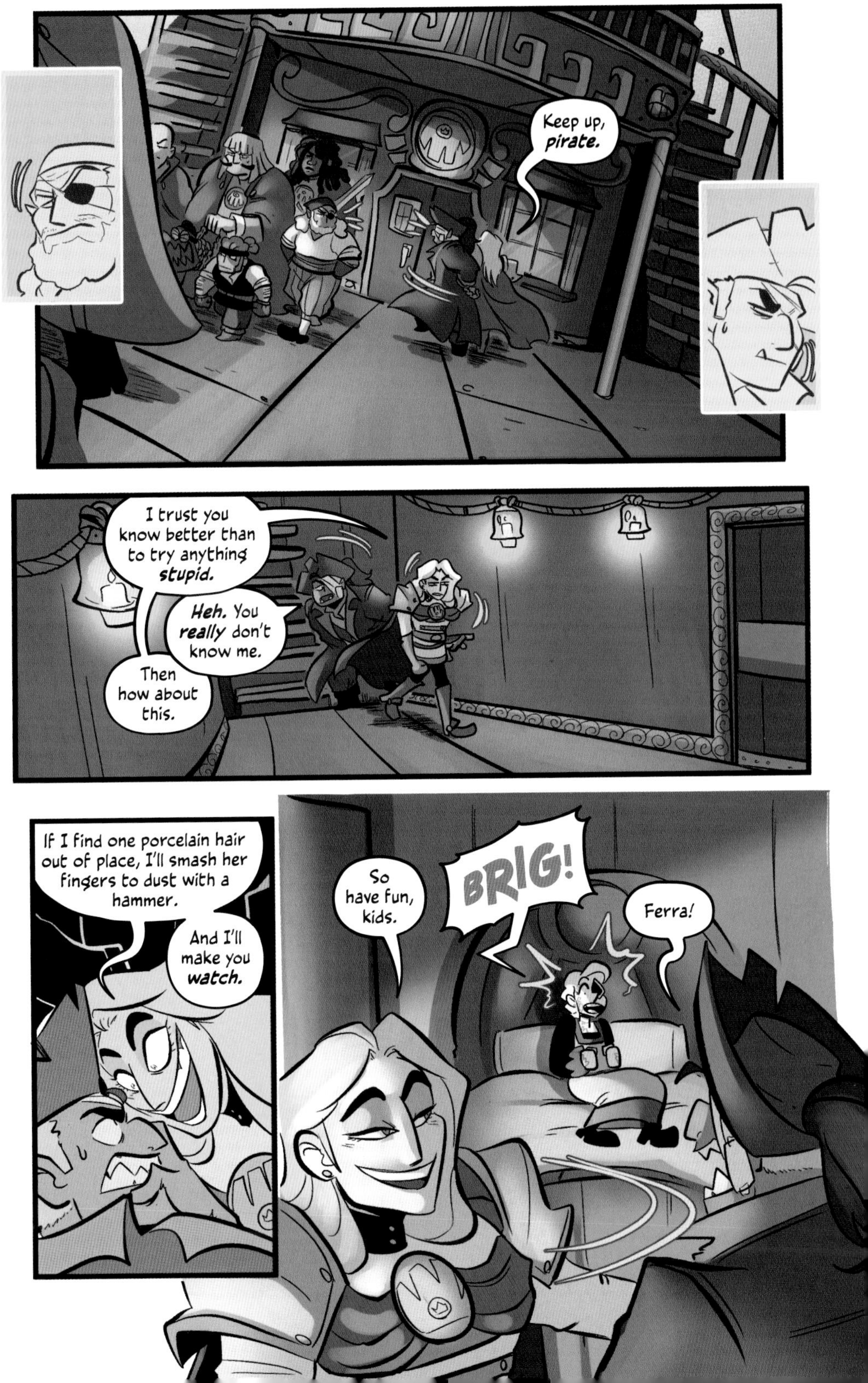
Keep up, *pirate.*
I trust you know better than to try anything *stupid.*
Heh. You *really* don't know me.
Then how about this.
If I find one porcelain hair out of place, I'll smash her fingers to dust with a hammer.
And I'll make you *watch.*
So have fun, kids.
BRIG!
Ferra!

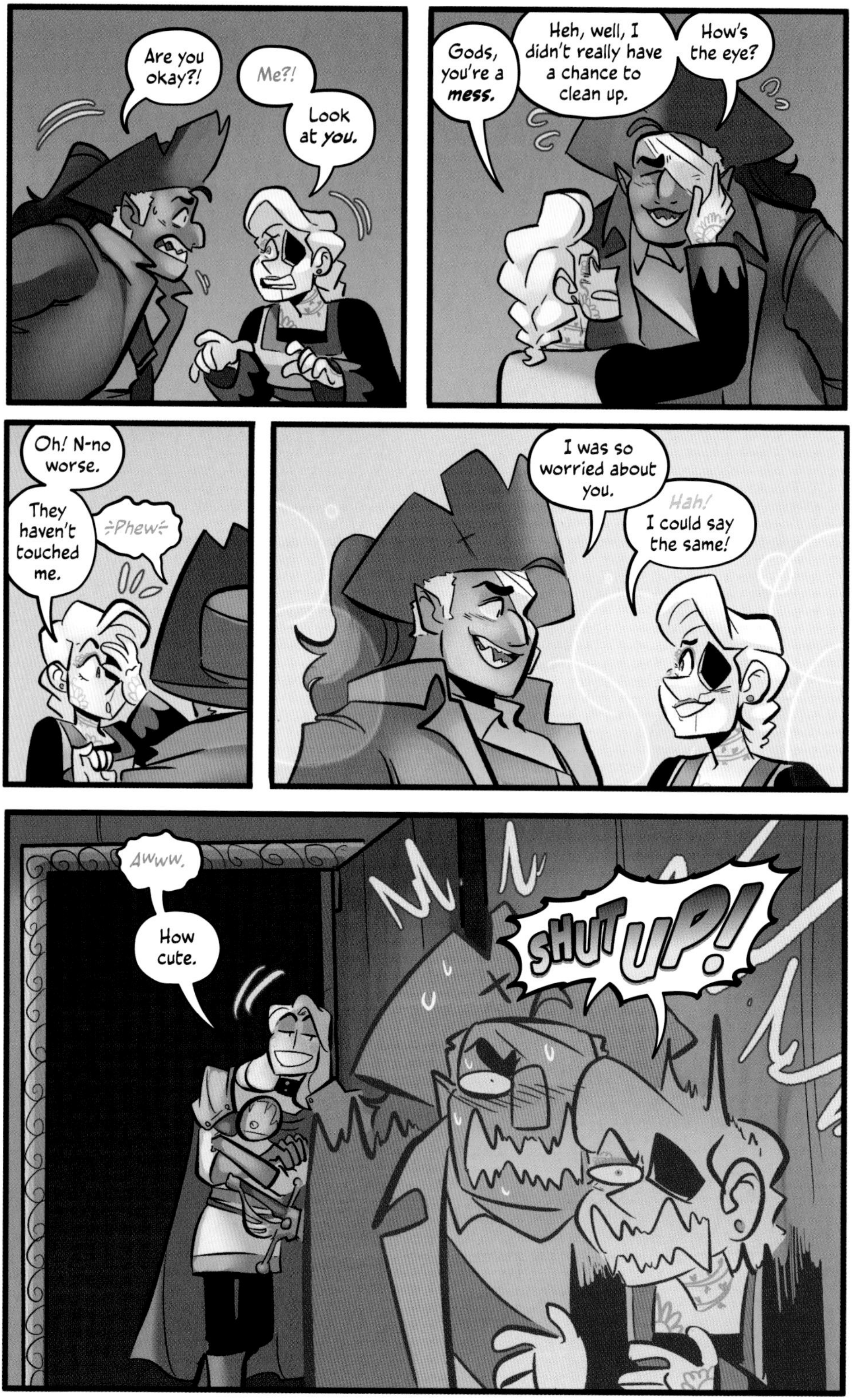
Are you okay?!
Me?!
Look at *you.*
Gods, you're a **mess.**
Heh, well, I didn't really have a chance to clean up.
How's the eye?
Oh! N-no worse.
They haven't touched me.
Phew
I was so worried about you.
Hah!
I could say the same!
Awww.
How cute.
SHUT UP!

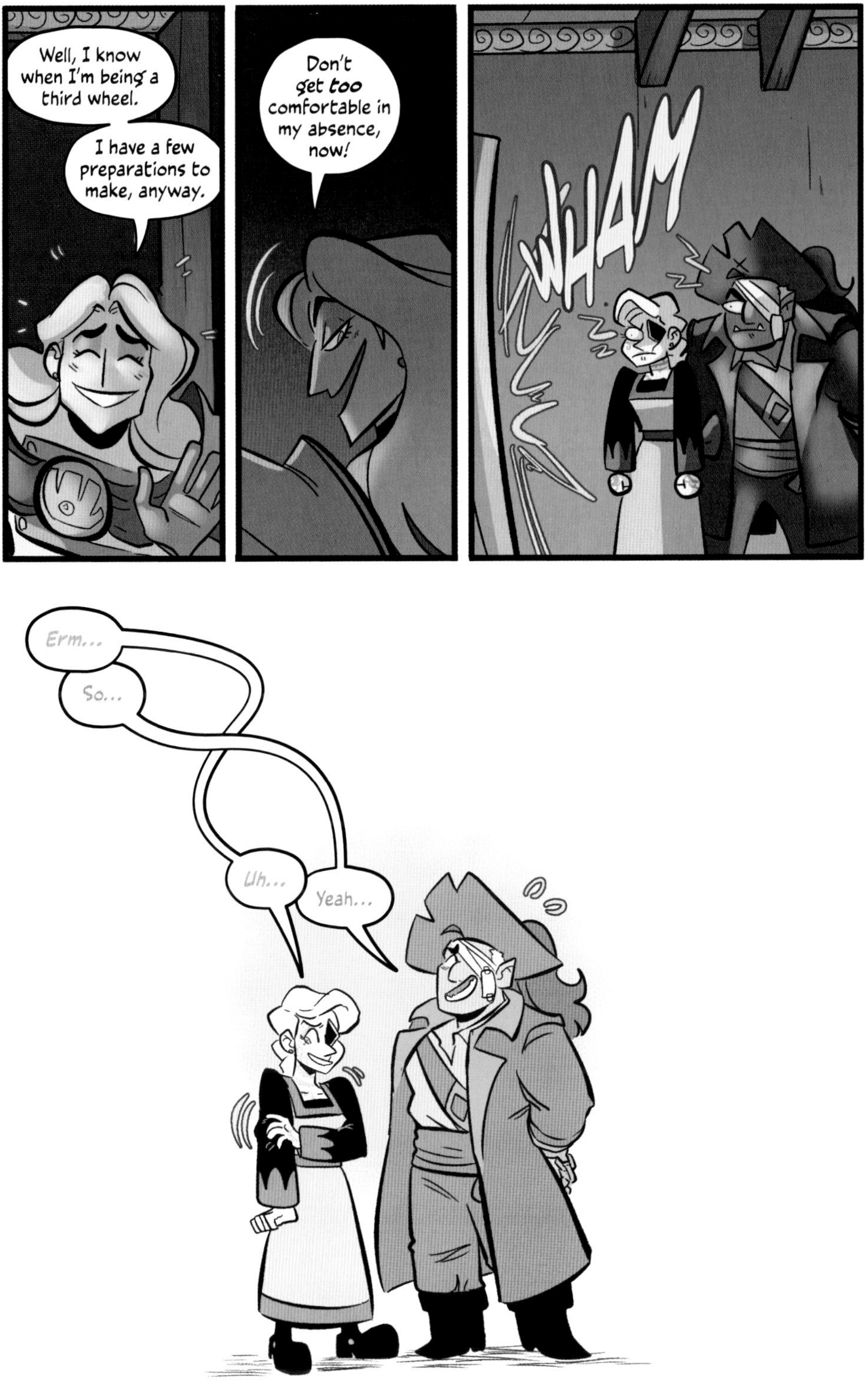
Well, I know when I'm being a third wheel.
I have a few preparations to make, anyway.
Don't get *too* comfortable in my absence, now!
WHAM
Erm...
So...
Uh...
Yeah...

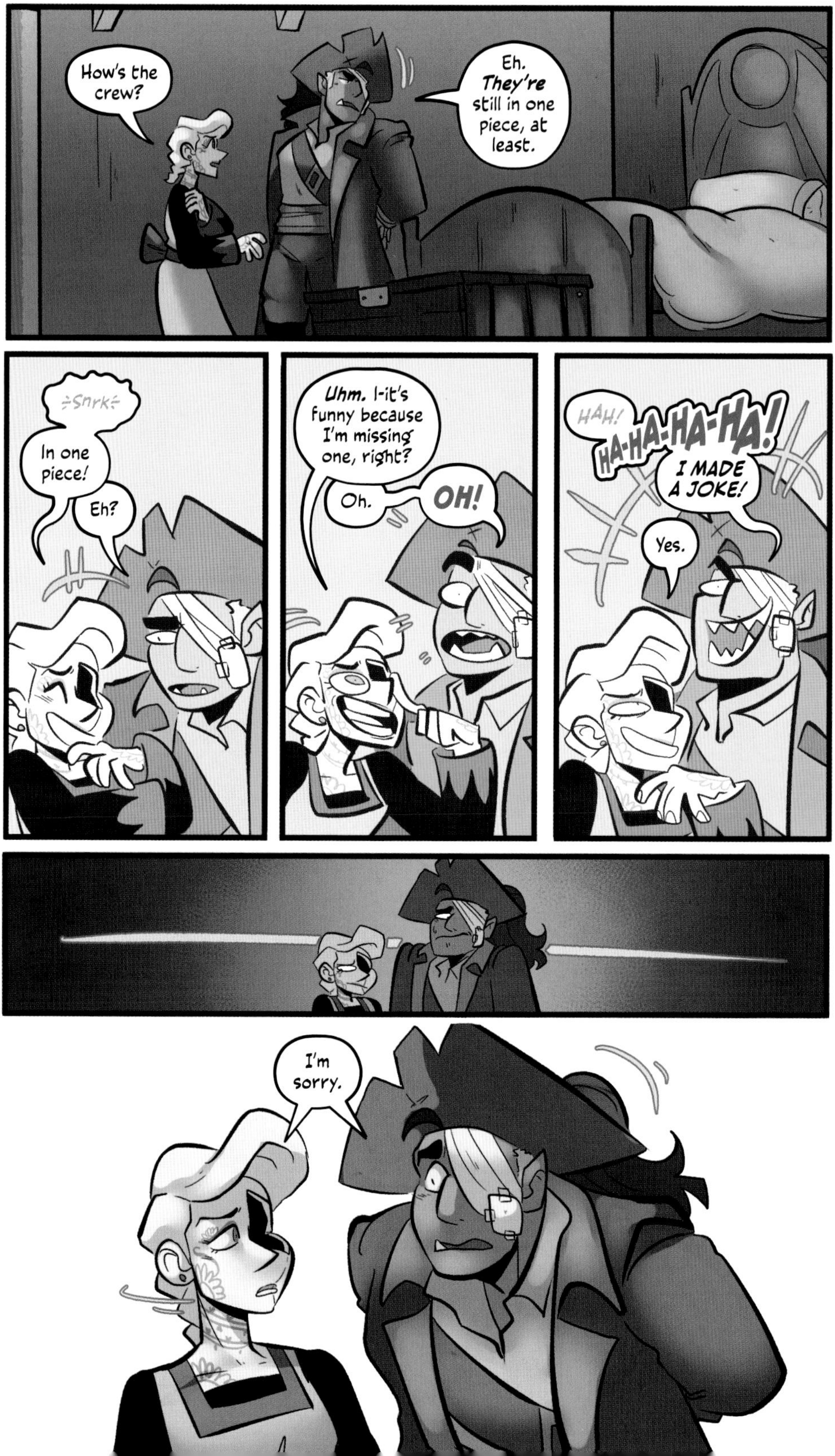
How's the crew?
Eh. They're still in one piece, at least.
Snrk
In one piece!
Eh?
Uhm. I-it's funny because I'm missing one, right?
Oh.
OH!
HAH!
HA-HA-HA-HA!
I MADE A JOKE!
Yes.
I'm sorry.

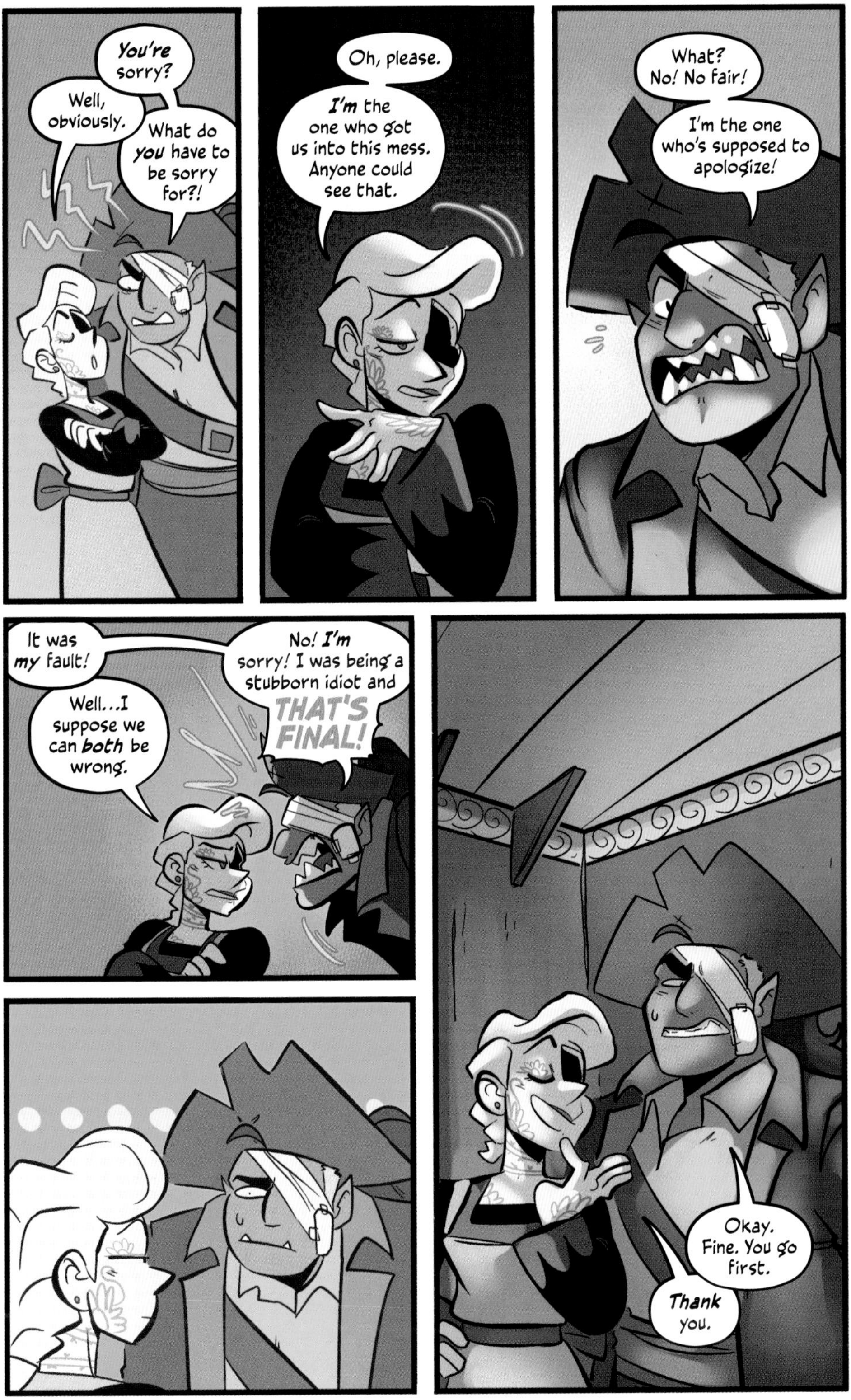

You're sorry?
Well, obviously.
What do you have to be sorry for?!
Oh, please.
I'm the one who got us into this mess. Anyone could see that.
What? No! No fair!
I'm the one who's supposed to apologize!
It was my fault!
No! I'm sorry! I was being a stubborn idiot and THAT'S FINAL!
Well...I suppose we can both be wrong.
Okay. Fine. You go first.
Thank you.

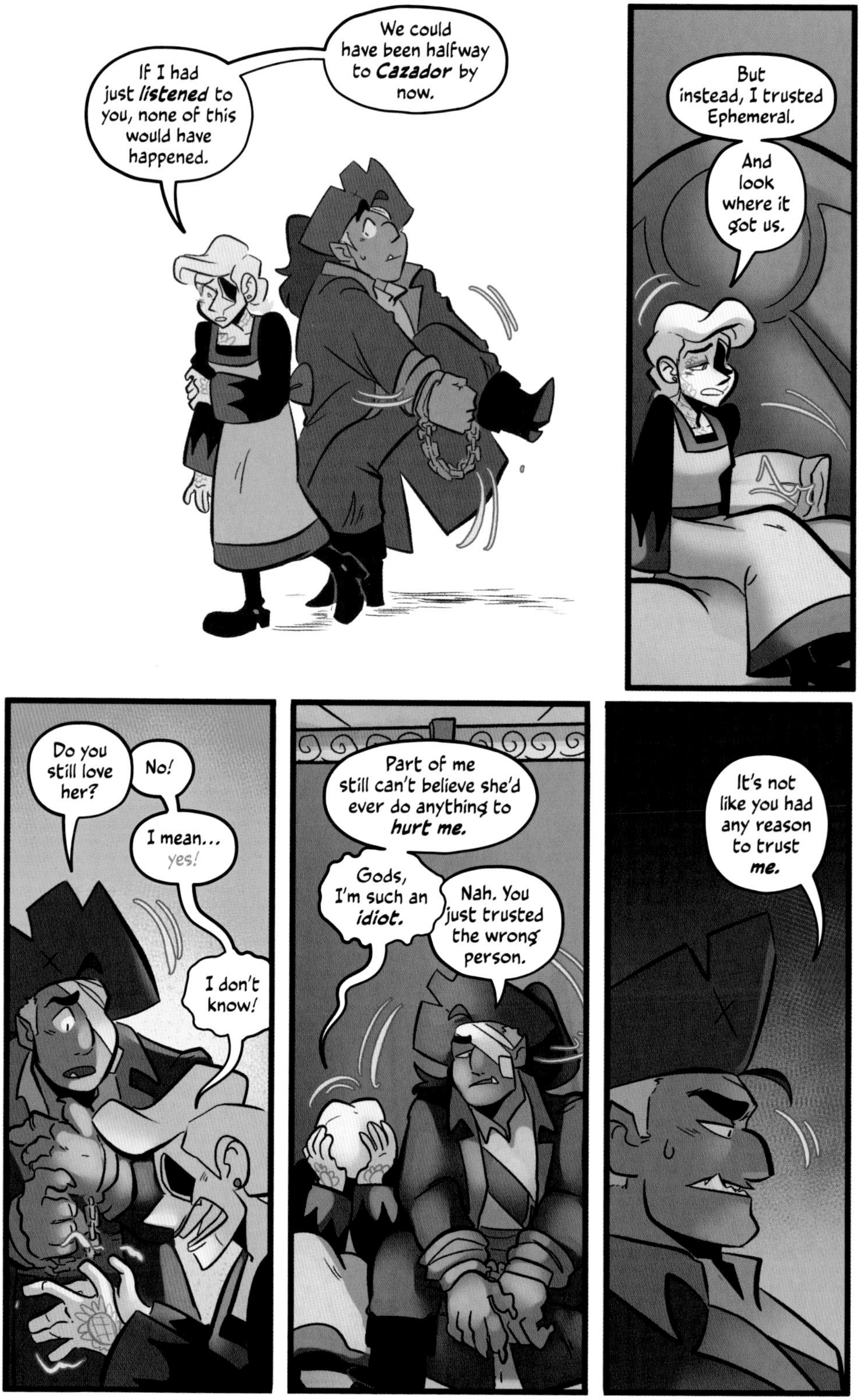
If I had just *listened* to you, none of this would have happened.
We could have been halfway to *Cazador* by now.
But instead, I trusted Ephemeral.
And look where it got us.
Do you still love her?
No!
I mean... yes!
I don't know!
Part of me still can't believe she'd ever do anything to ***hurt me.***
Gods, I'm such an ***idiot.***
Nah. You just trusted the wrong person.
It's not like you had any reason to trust ***me.***

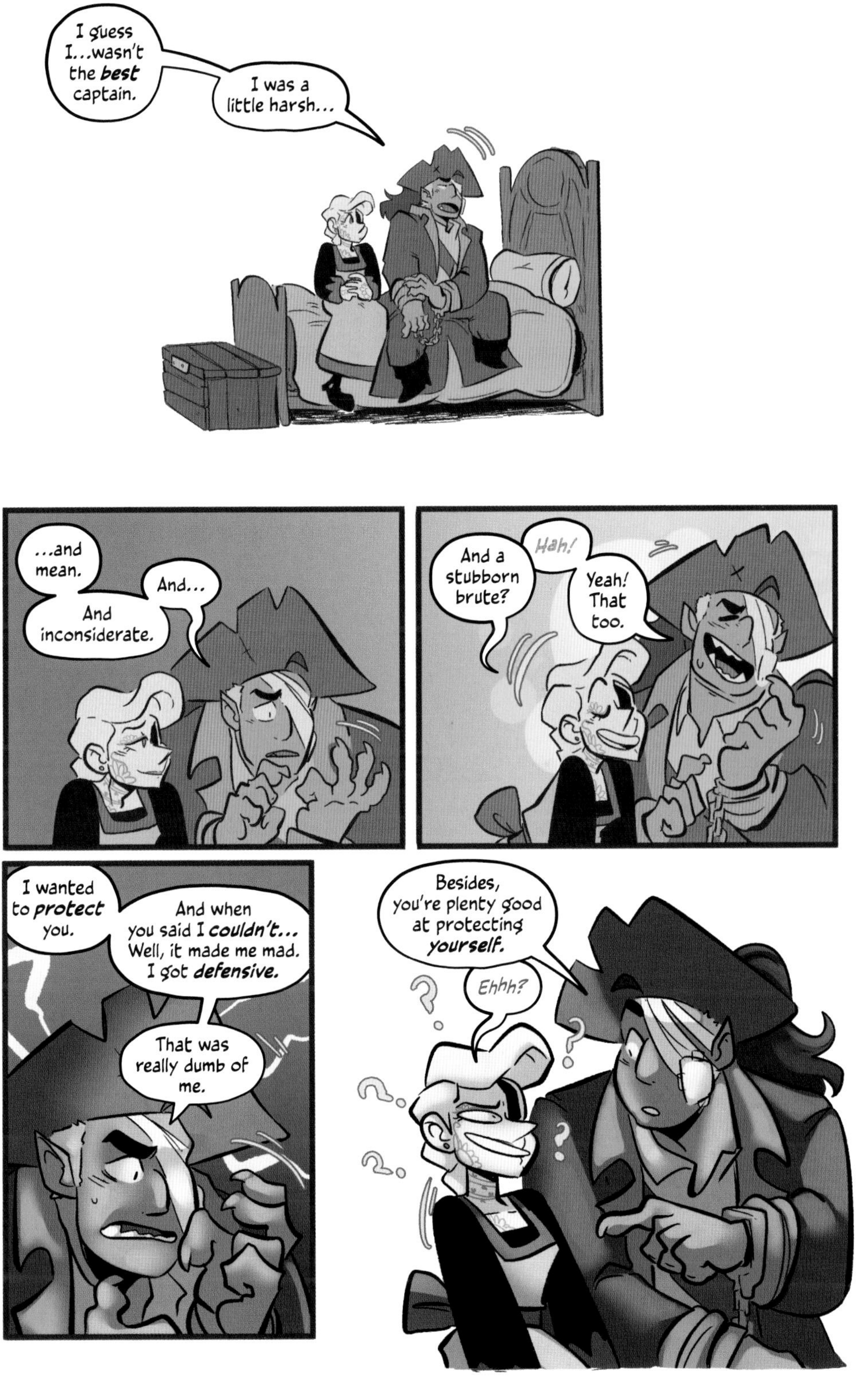

I guess I...wasn't the *best* captain.
I was a little harsh...
...and mean.
And inconsiderate.
And...
And a stubborn brute?
Hah!
Yeah! That too.
I wanted to *protect* you.
And when you said I *couldn't...* Well, it made me mad. I got *defensive.*
That was really dumb of me.
Besides, you're plenty good at protecting *yourself.*
Ehhh?

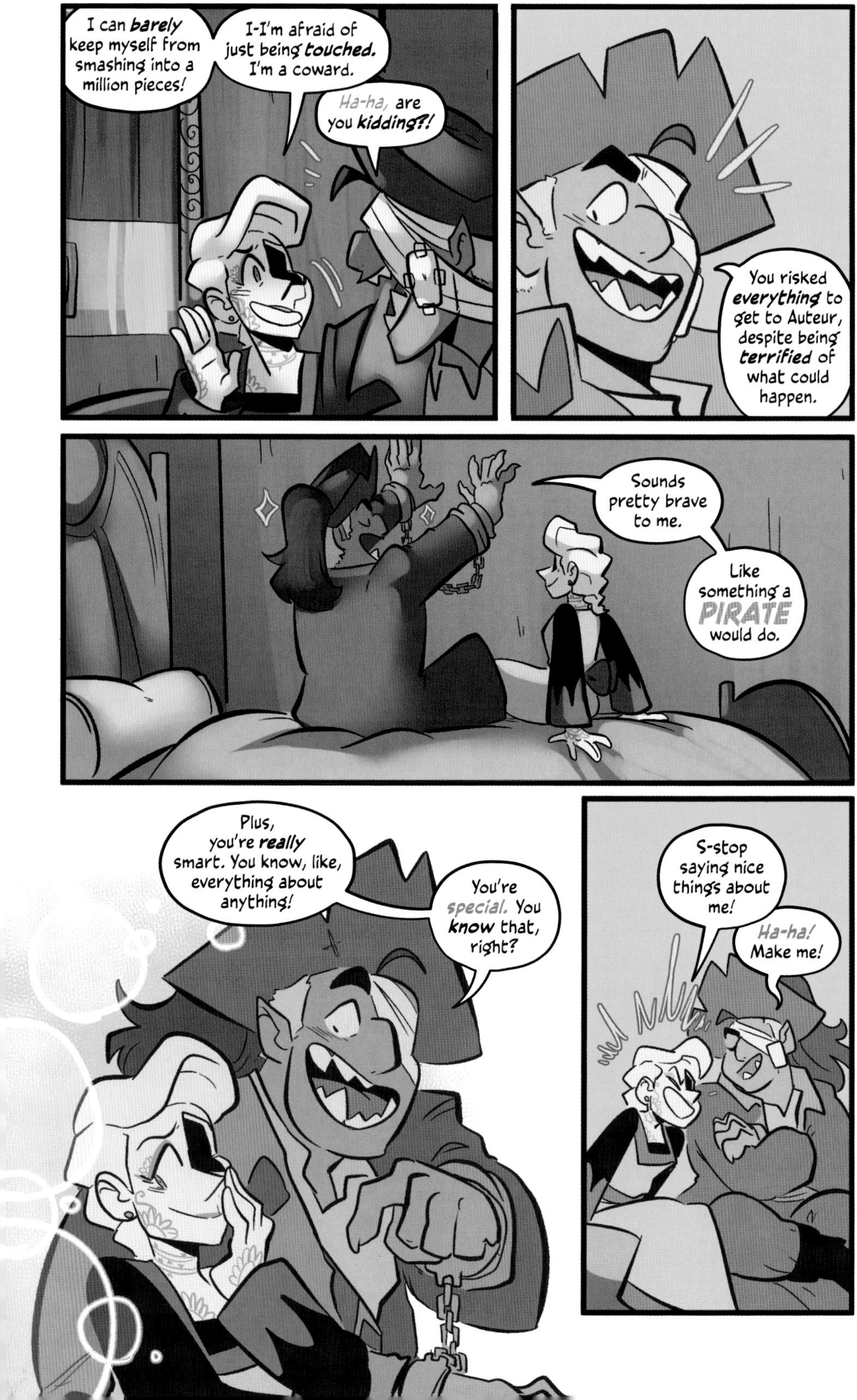
I can barely keep myself from smashing into a million pieces!
I-I'm afraid of just being touched. I'm a coward.
Ha-ha, are you kidding?!
You risked everything to get to Auteur, despite being terrified of what could happen.
Sounds pretty brave to me.
Like something a PIRATE would do.
Plus, you're really smart. You know, like, everything about anything!
You're special. You know that, right?
S-stop saying nice things about me!
Ha-ha! Make me!

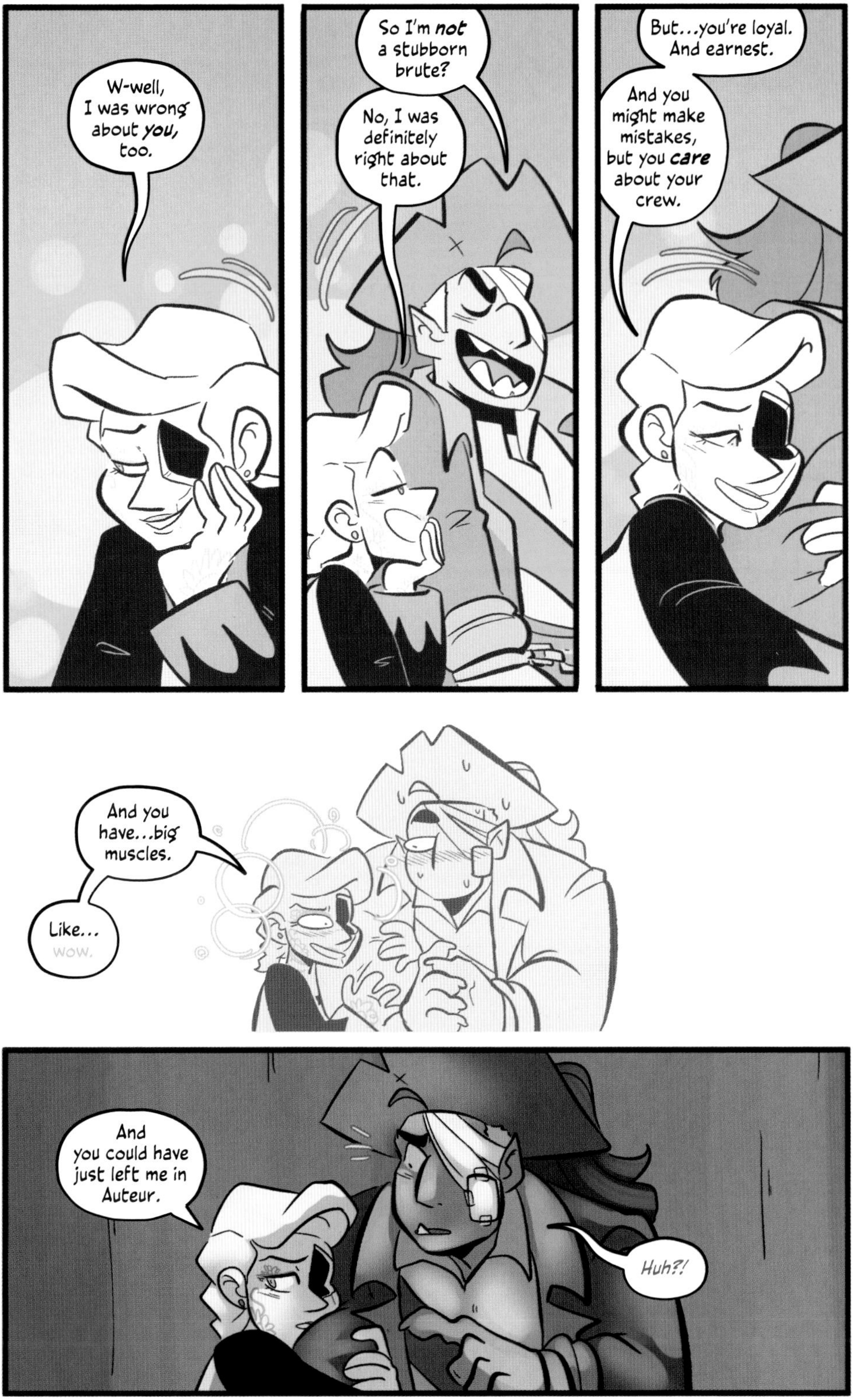
W-well, I was wrong about *you,* too.
So I'm ***not*** a stubborn brute?
No, I was definitely right about that.
But...you're loyal. And earnest.
And you might make mistakes, but you ***care*** about your crew.
And you have...big muscles.
Like... wow.
And you could have just left me in Auteur.
Huh?!

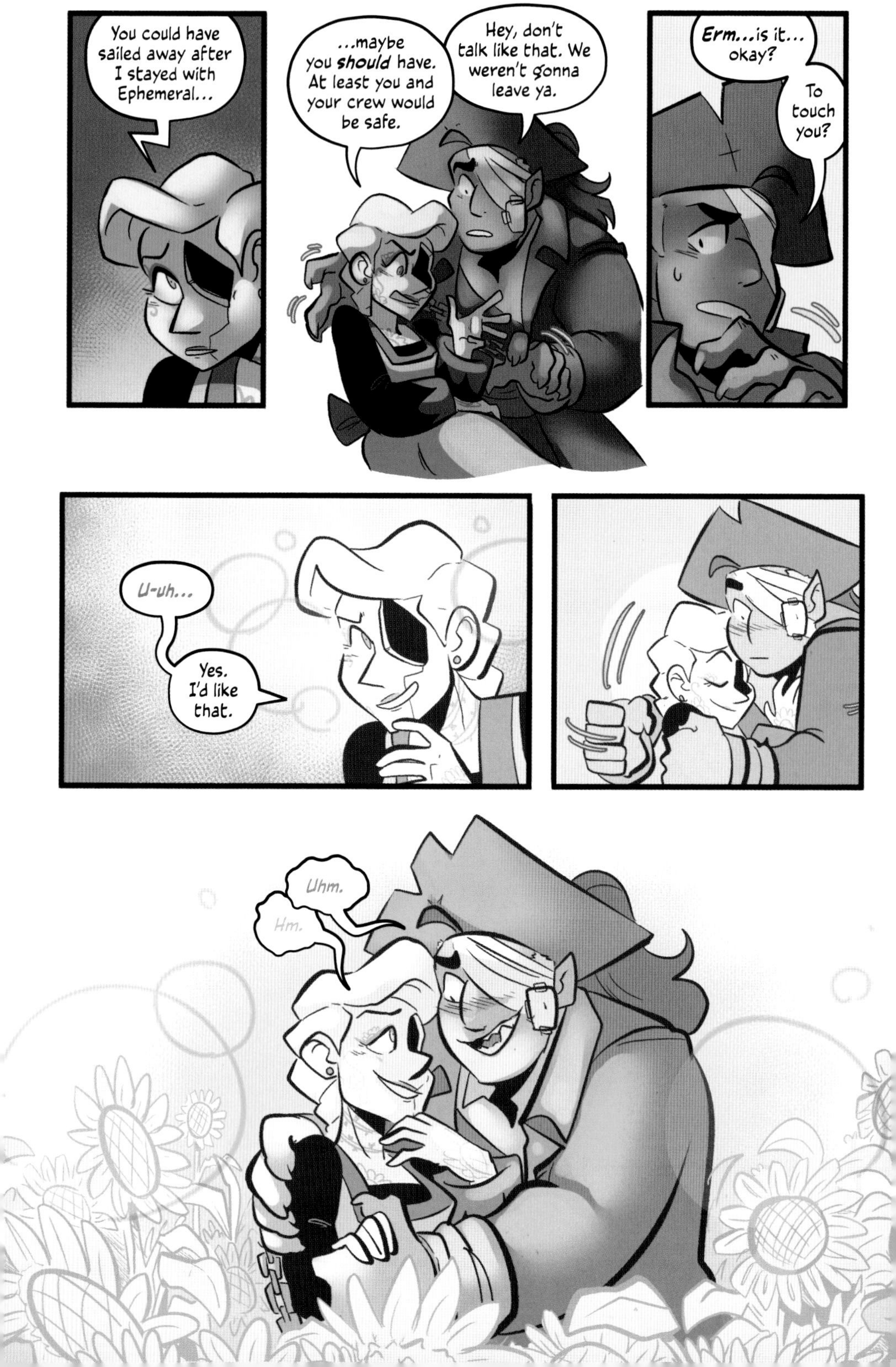
You could have sailed away after I stayed with Ephemeral...
...maybe you should have. At least you and your crew would be safe.
Hey, don't talk like that. We weren't gonna leave ya.
Erm...is it... okay?
To touch you?
U-uh...
Yes. I'd like that.
Uhm.
Hm.

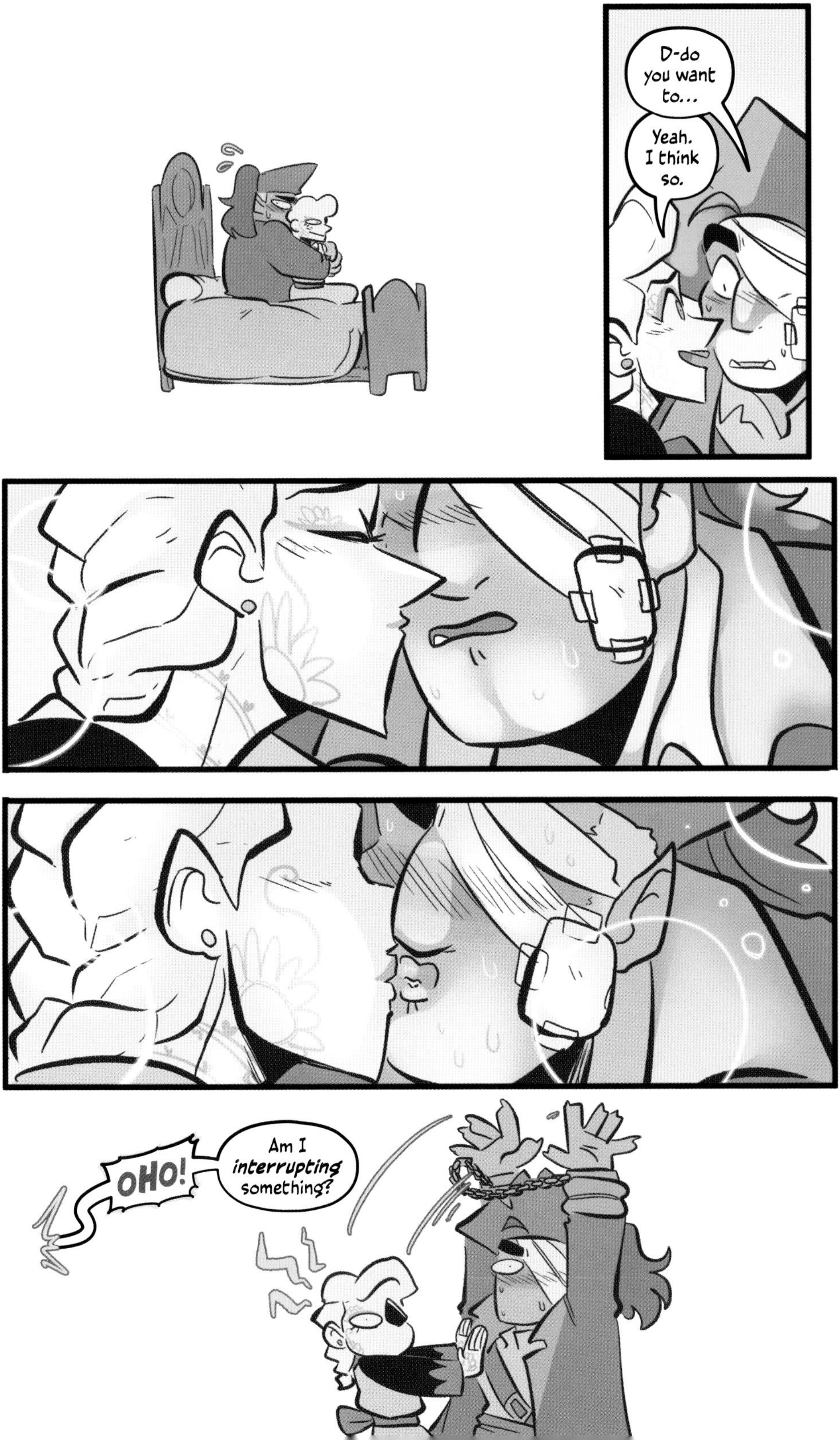
D-do you want to...
Yeah. I think so.
OHO!
Am I *interrupting* something?

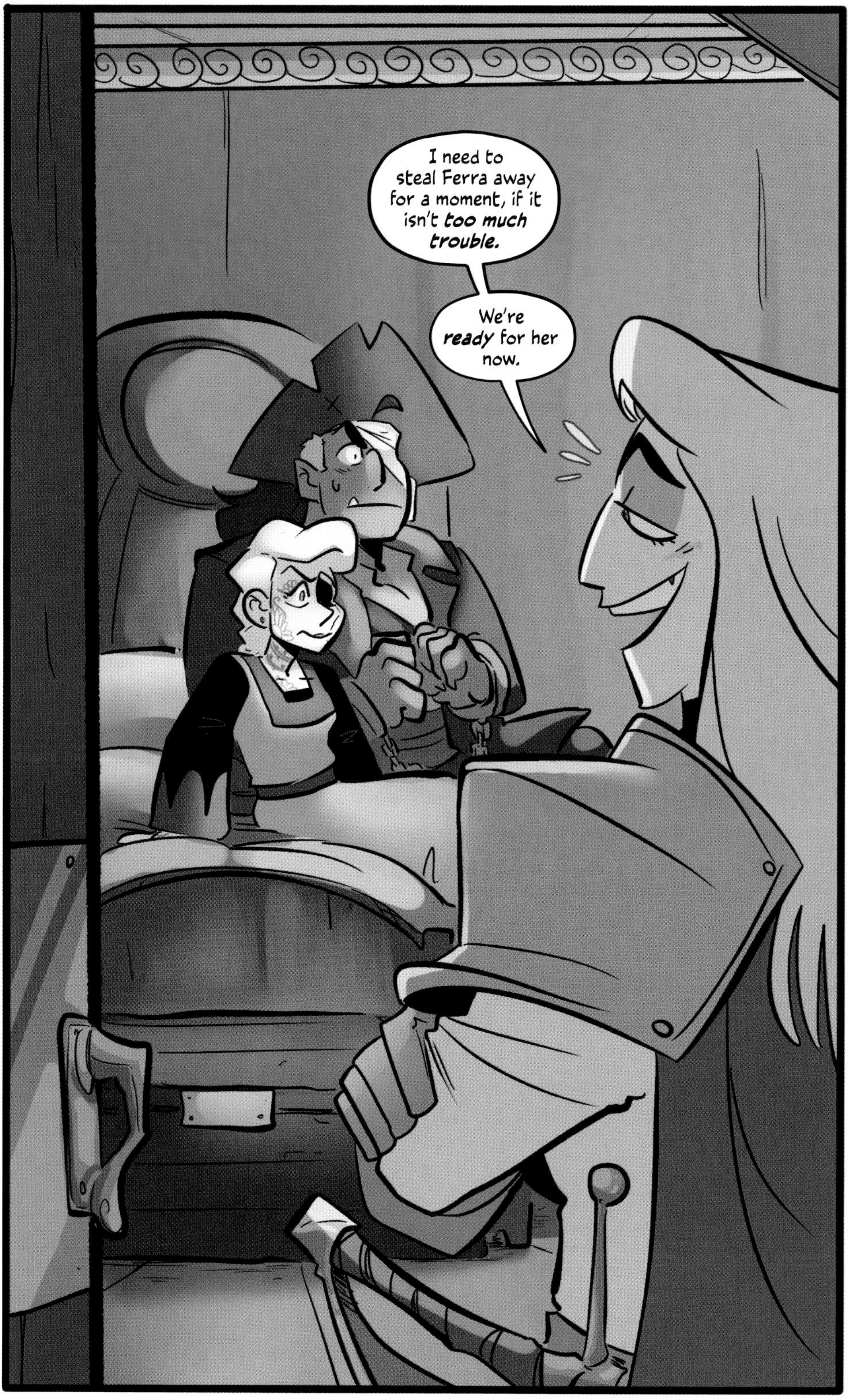
I need to steal Ferra away for a moment, if it isn't ***too much trouble.***
We're ***ready*** for her now.

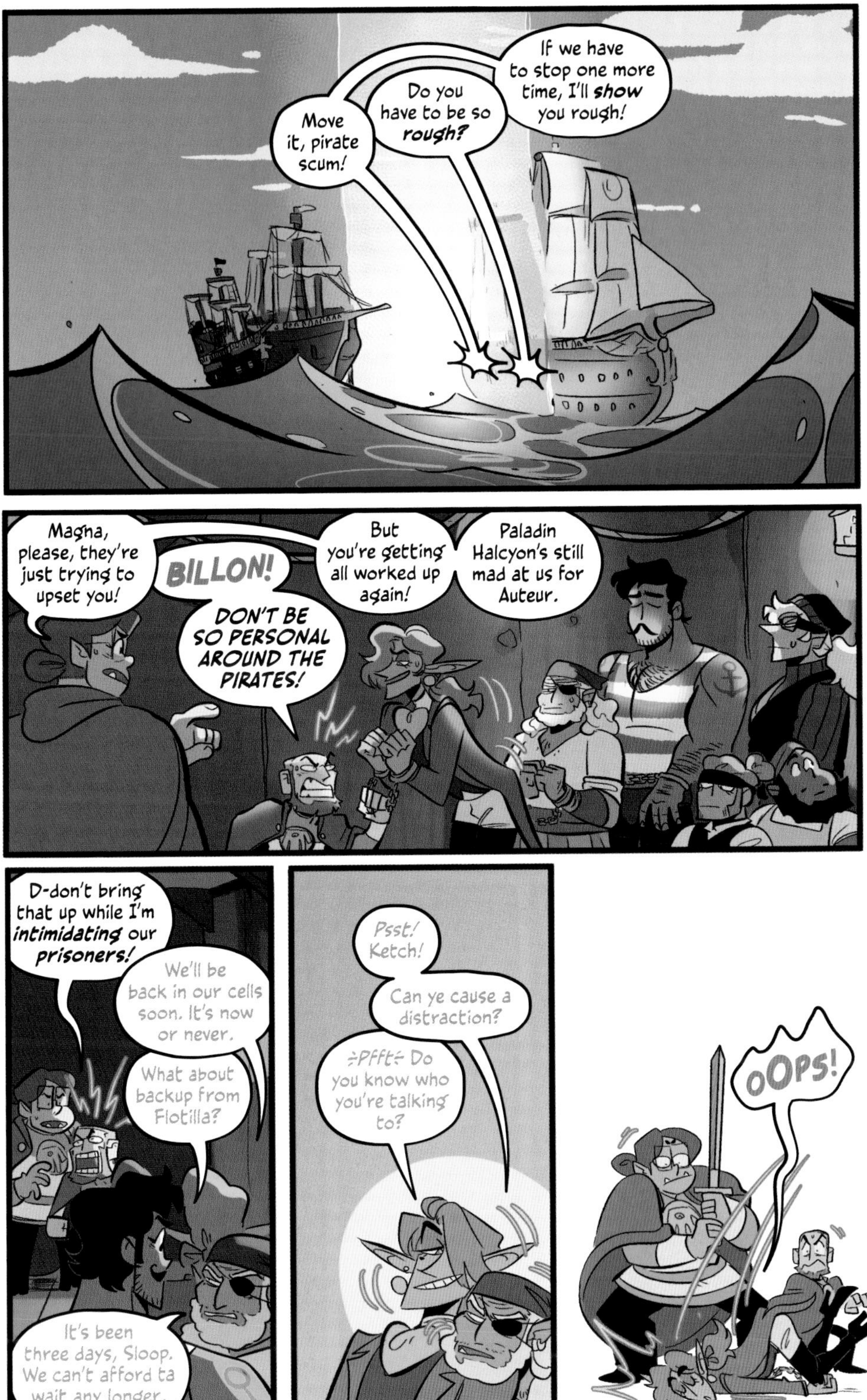
Move it, pirate scum!
Do you have to be so **rough?**
If we have to stop one more time, I'll **show** you rough!
Magna, please, they're just trying to upset you!
BILLON!
DON'T BE SO PERSONAL AROUND THE PIRATES!
But you're getting all worked up again!
Paladin Halcyon's still mad at us for Auteur.
D-don't bring that up while I'm ***intimidating*** our ***prisoners!***
We'll be back in our cells soon. It's now or never.
What about backup from Flotilla?
It's been three days, Sloop. We can't afford ta wait any longer.
Psst! Ketch!
Can ye cause a distraction?
Pfft Do you know who you're talking to?
OOPS!

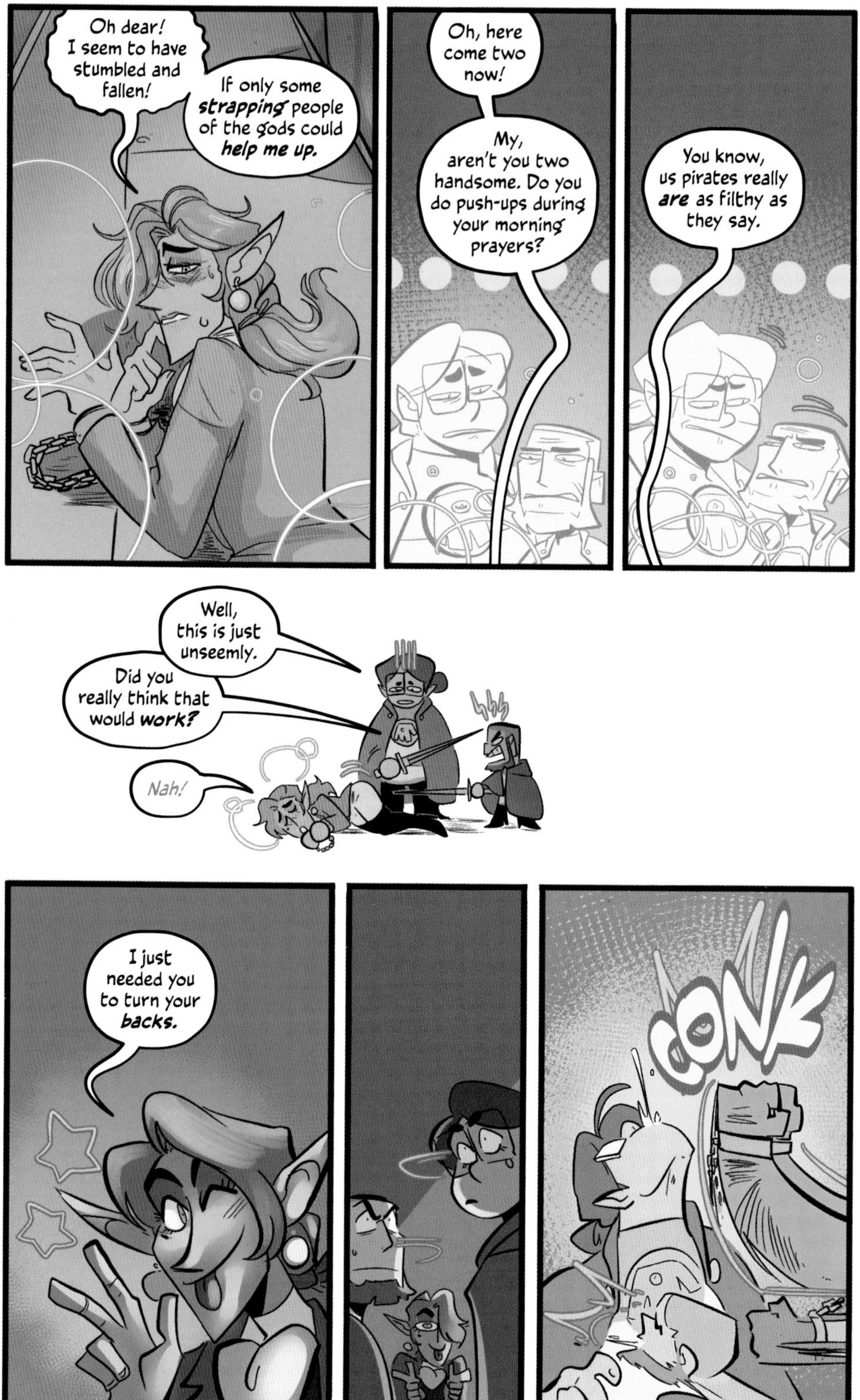
Oh dear! I seem to have stumbled and fallen!
If only some **strapping** people of the gods could **help me up.**
Oh, here come two now!
My, aren't you two handsome. Do you do push-ups during your morning prayers?
You know, us pirates really **are** as filthy as they say.
Well, this is just unseemly.
Did you really think that would **work?**
Nah!
I just needed you to turn your **backs.**
CONK

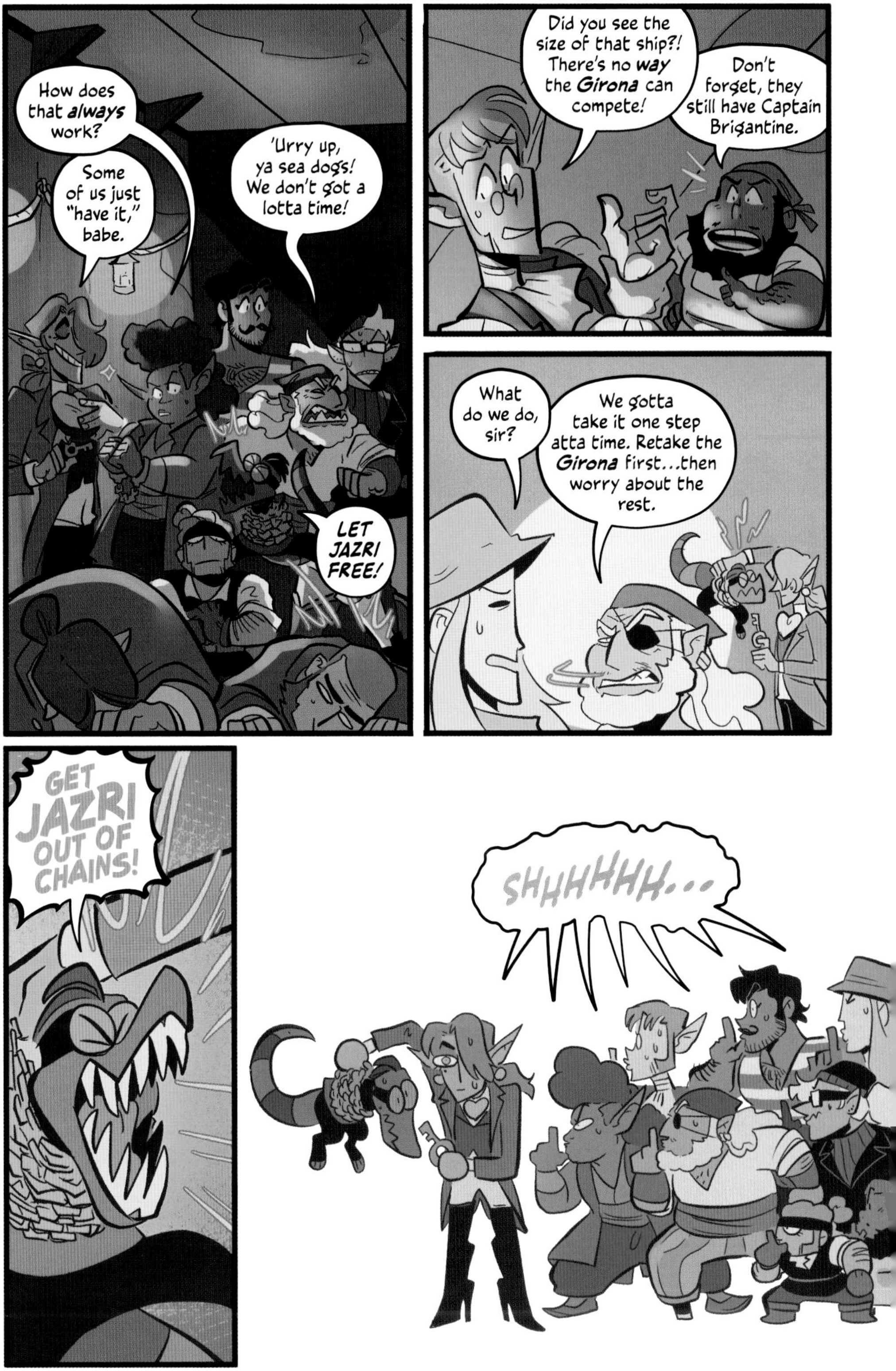
How does that always work?
Some of us just "have it," babe.
'Urry up, ya sea dogs! We don't got a lotta time!
LET JAZRI FREE!
Did you see the size of that ship?! There's no way the Girona can compete!
Don't forget, they still have Captain Brigantine.
What do we do, sir?
We gotta take it one step atta time. Retake the Girona first...then worry about the rest.
GET JAZRI OUT OF CHAINS!
SHHHHHH...

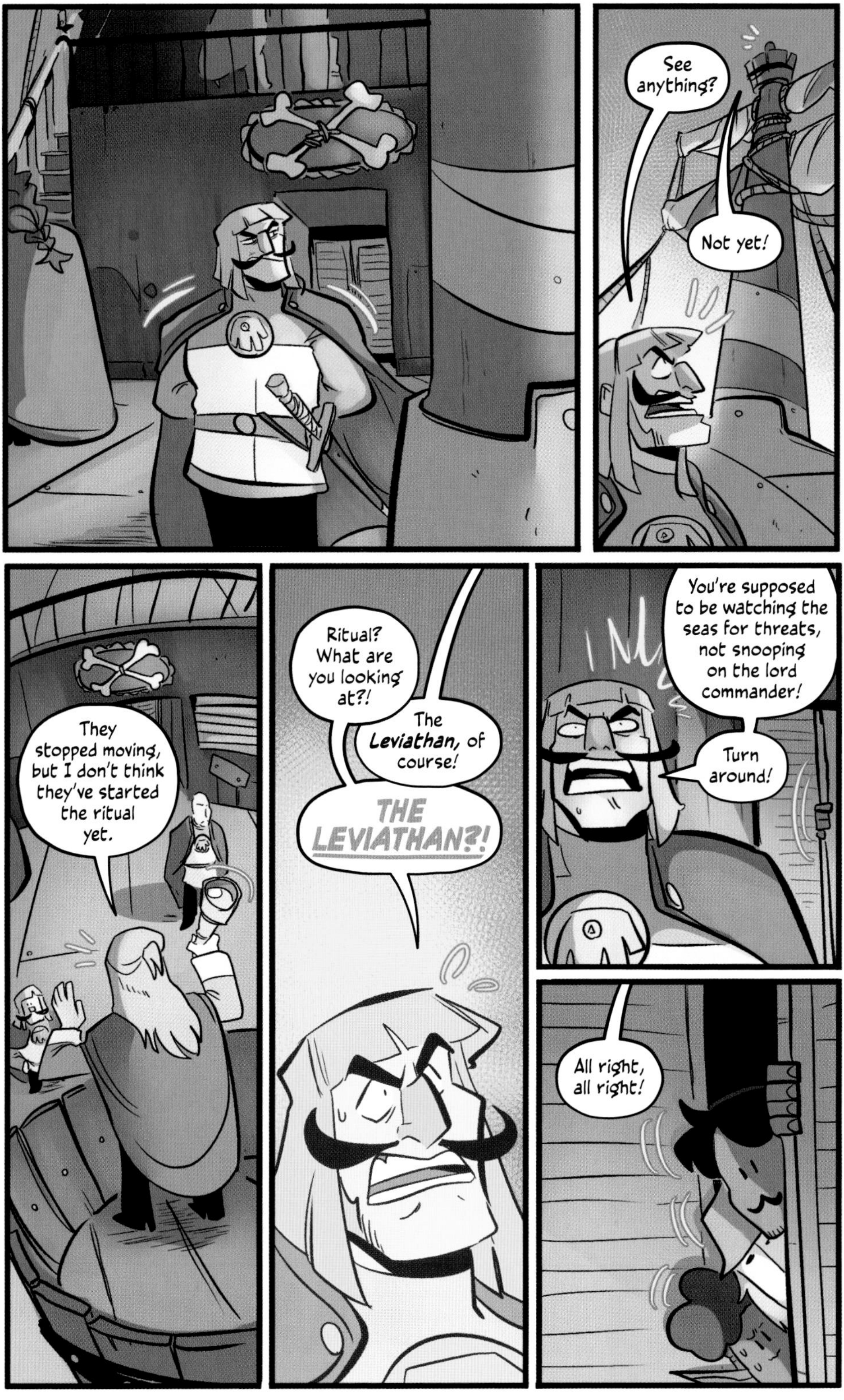
See anything?
Not yet!
They stopped moving, but I don't think they've started the ritual yet.
Ritual? What are you looking at?!
The Leviathan, of course!
THE LEVIATHAN?!
You're supposed to be watching the seas for threats, not snooping on the lord commander!
Turn around!
All right, all right!

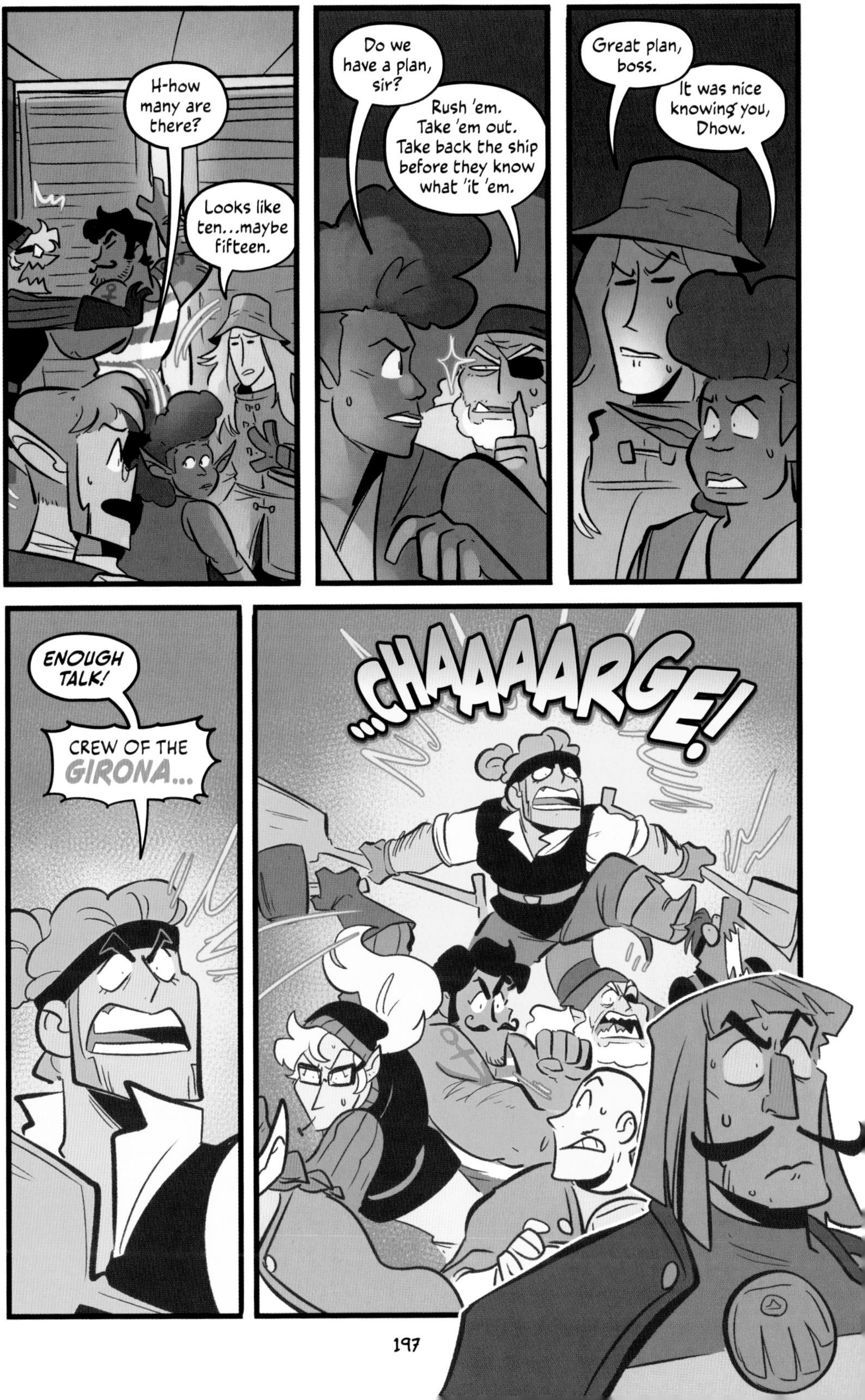
H-how many are there?
Looks like ten...maybe fifteen.
Do we have a plan, sir?
Rush 'em. Take 'em out. Take back the ship before they know what 'it 'em.
Great plan, boss.
It was nice knowing you, Dhow.
ENOUGH TALK!
CREW OF THE GIRONA...
...CHAAAARGE!

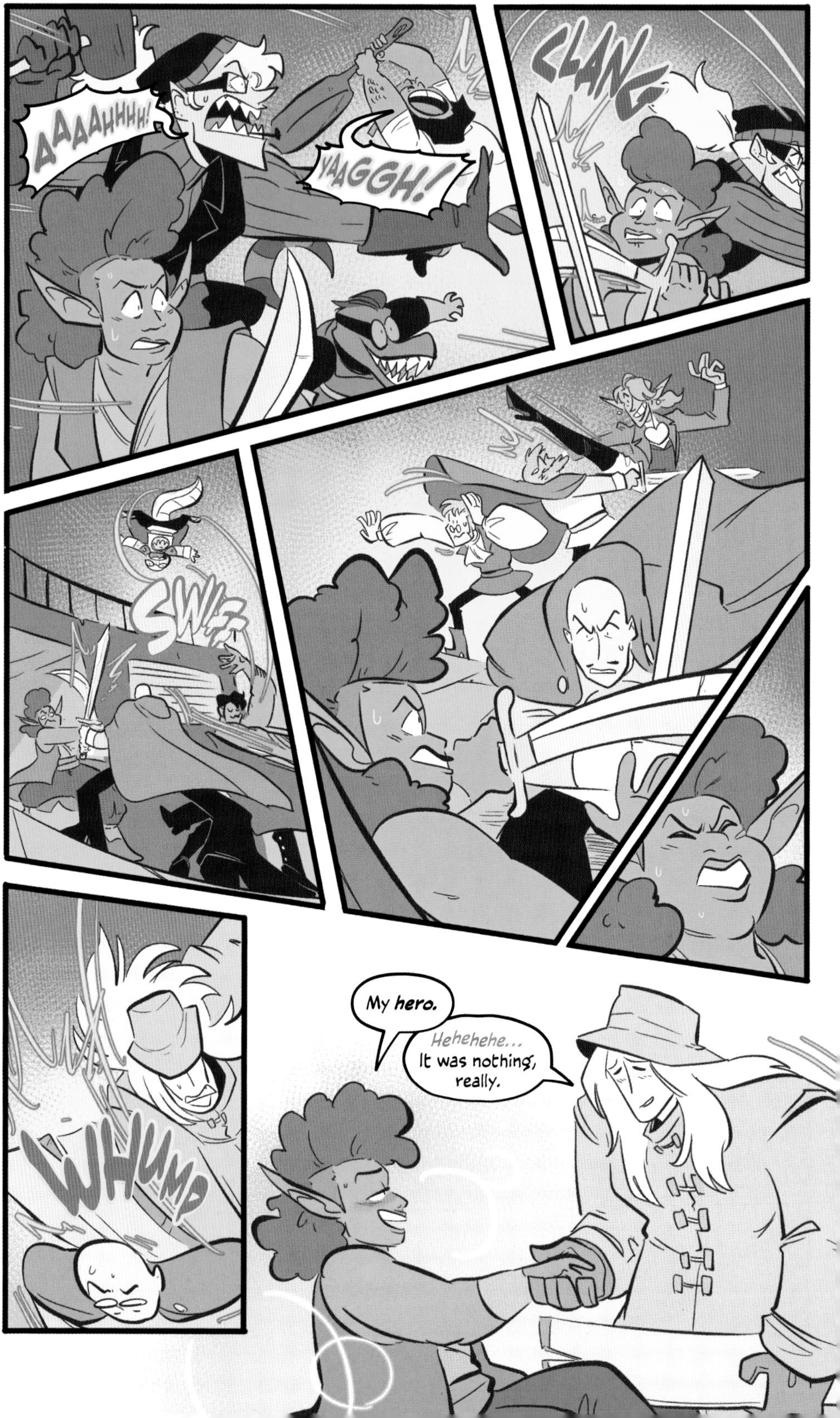
AAAAHHHH!
YAAGGH!
CLANG
SWIF
WHUMP
My hero.
Hehehehe... It was nothing, really.

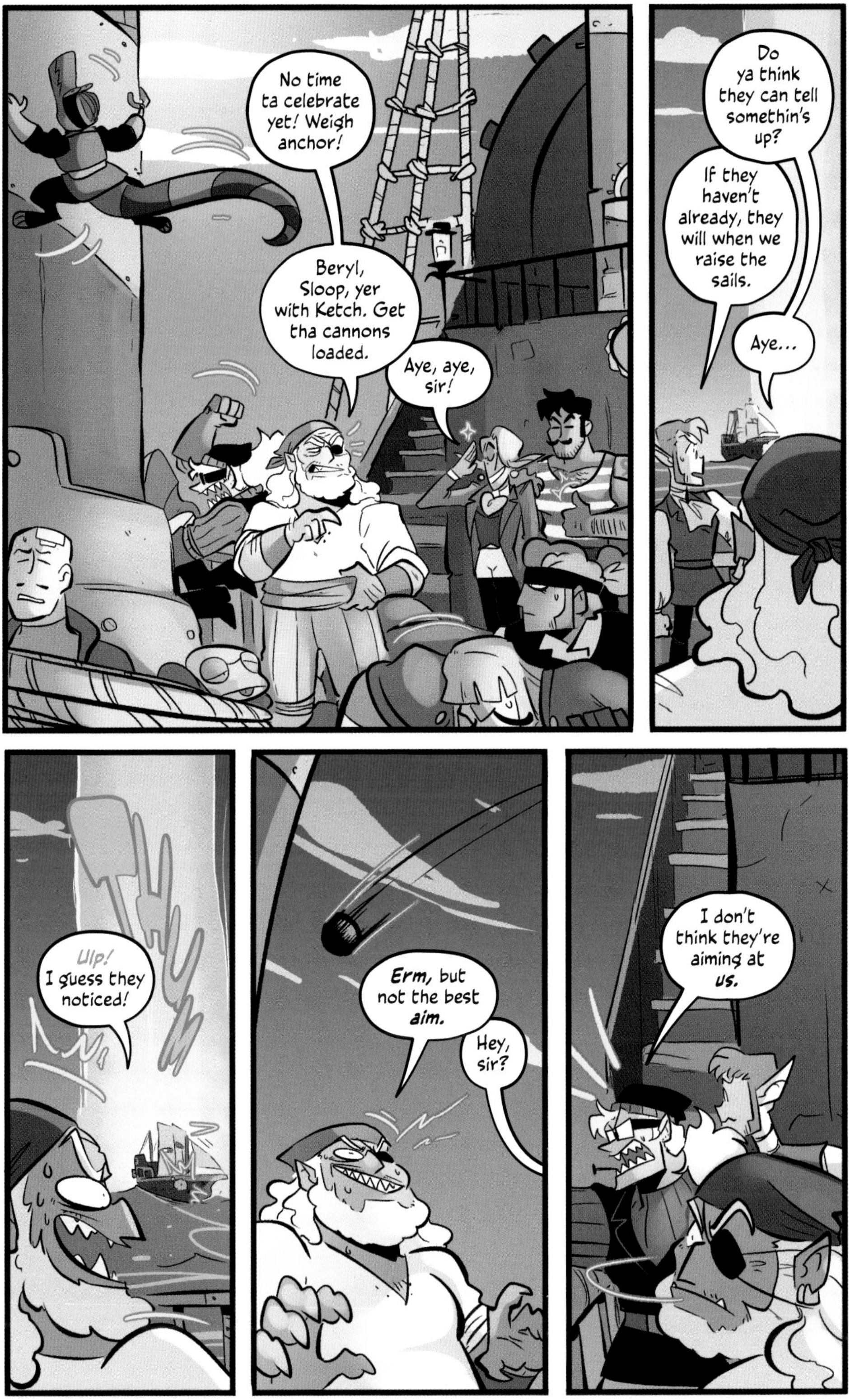
No time ta celebrate yet! Weigh anchor!
Beryl, Sloop, yer with Ketch. Get tha cannons loaded.
Aye, aye, sir!
Do ya think they can tell somethin's up?
If they haven't already, they will when we raise the sails.
Aye...
Ulp! I guess they noticed!
Erm, but not the best aim.
Hey, sir?
I don't think they're aiming at us.

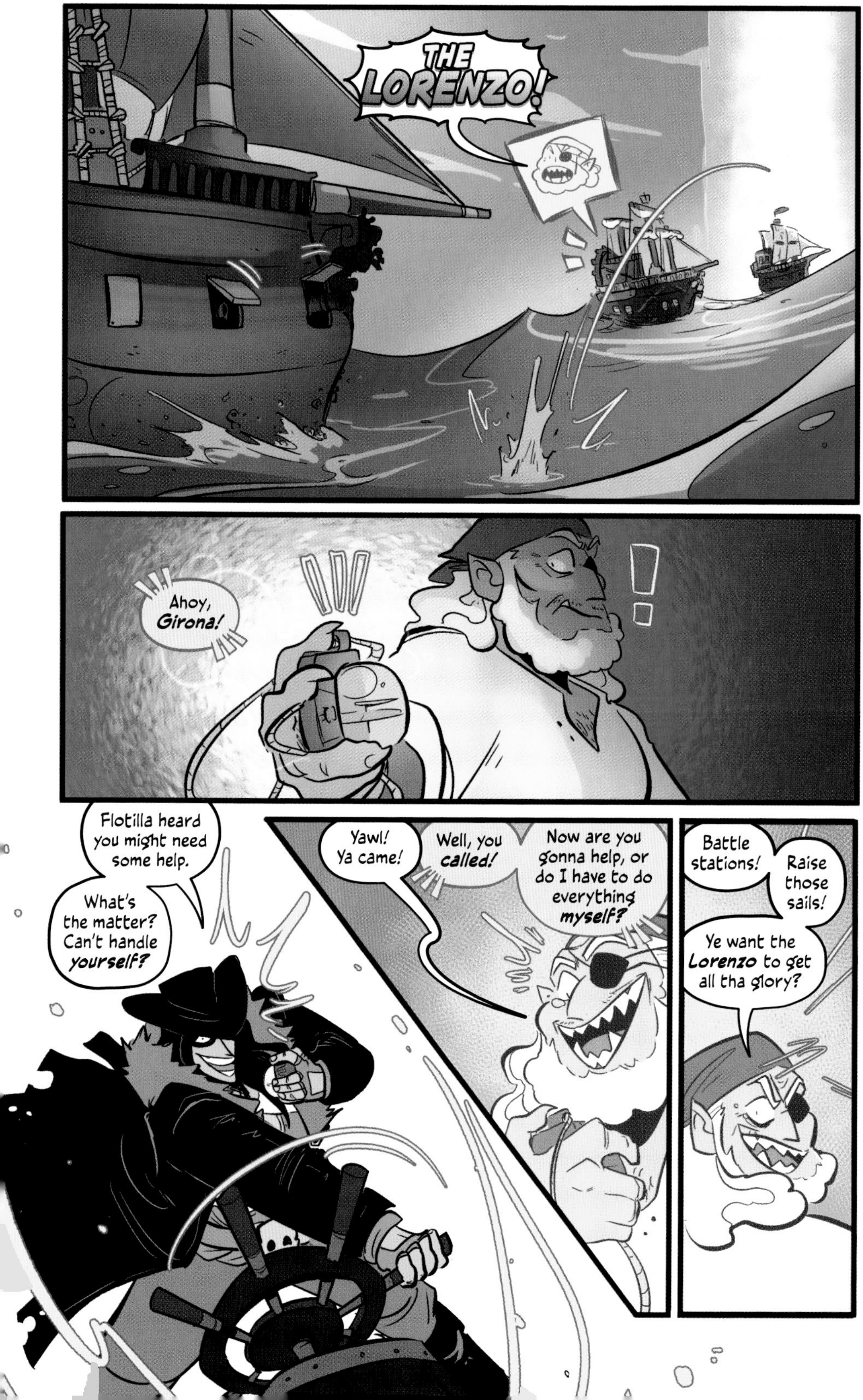
THE LORENZO!
Ahoy, Girona!
Flotilla heard you might need some help.
What's the matter? Can't handle yourself?
Yawl! Ya came!
Well, you called!
Now are you gonna help, or do I have to do everything myself?
Battle stations!
Raise those sails!
Ye want the Lorenzo to get all tha glory?

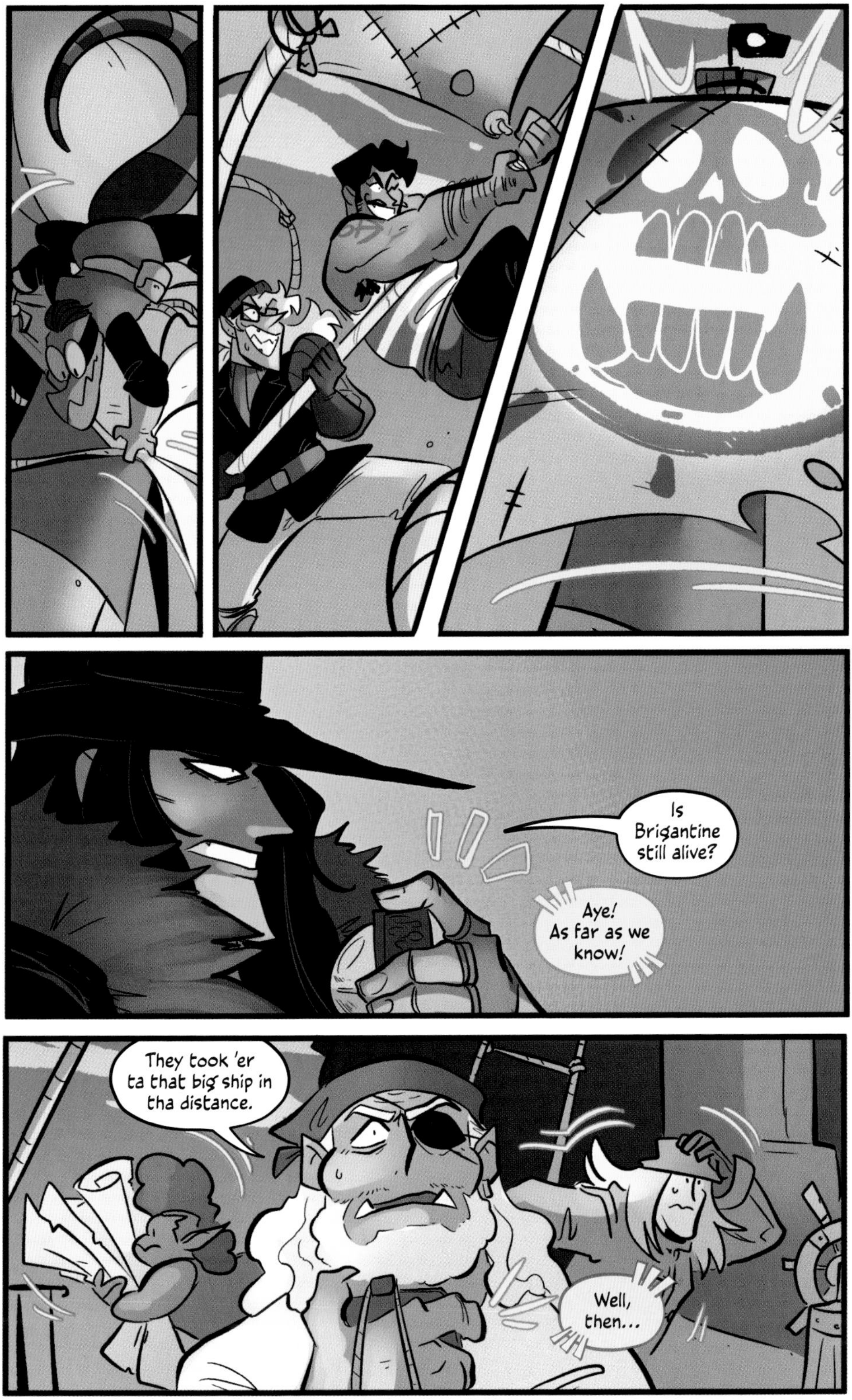
Is Brigantine still alive?
Aye! As far as we know!
They took 'er ta that big ship in tha distance.
Well, then...

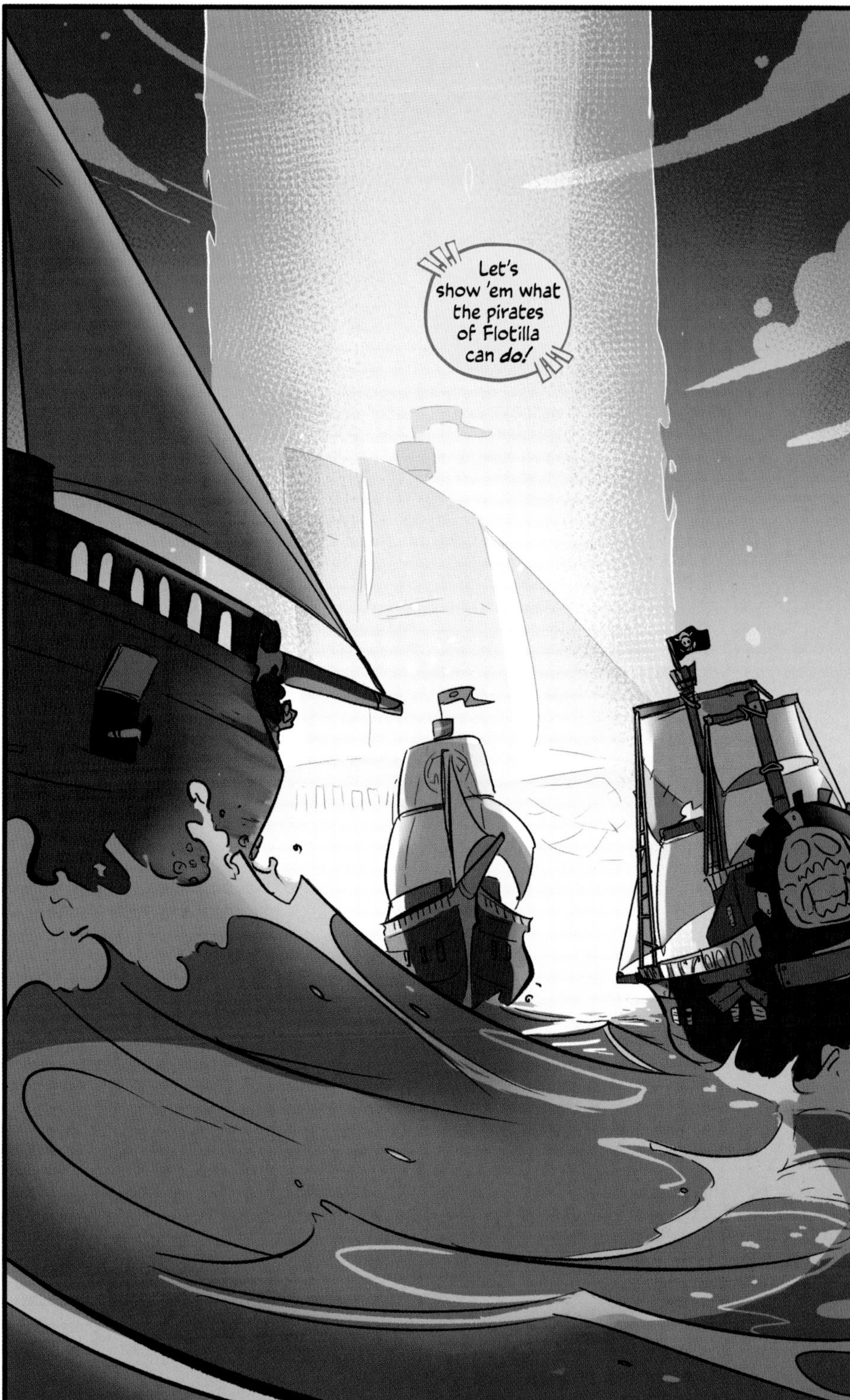
Let's show 'em what the pirates of Flotilla can *do!*

Chapter 7

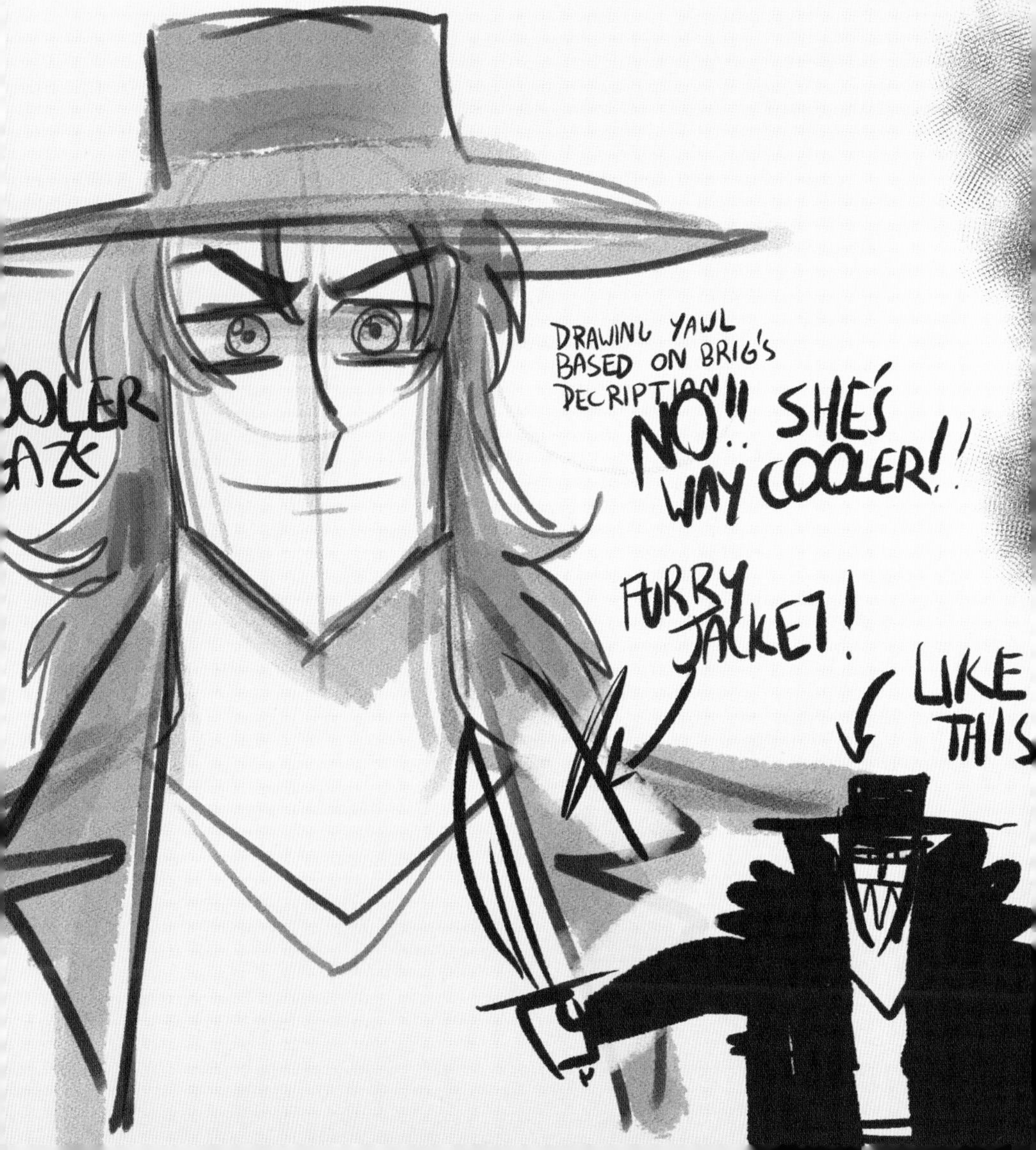
DRAWING YAWL
BASED ON BRIG'S
DECRIPTION!!
NO!! SHE'S
WAY COOLER!!
FURRY
JACKET!
LIKE
THIS

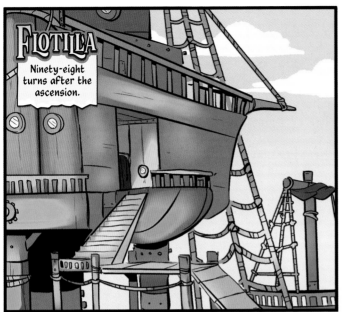

FLOTILLA

Ninety-eight turns after the ascension.

Now then...

...the Admiral's Council is in session.

That means **SHUDDUP** and wait your turn to talk.

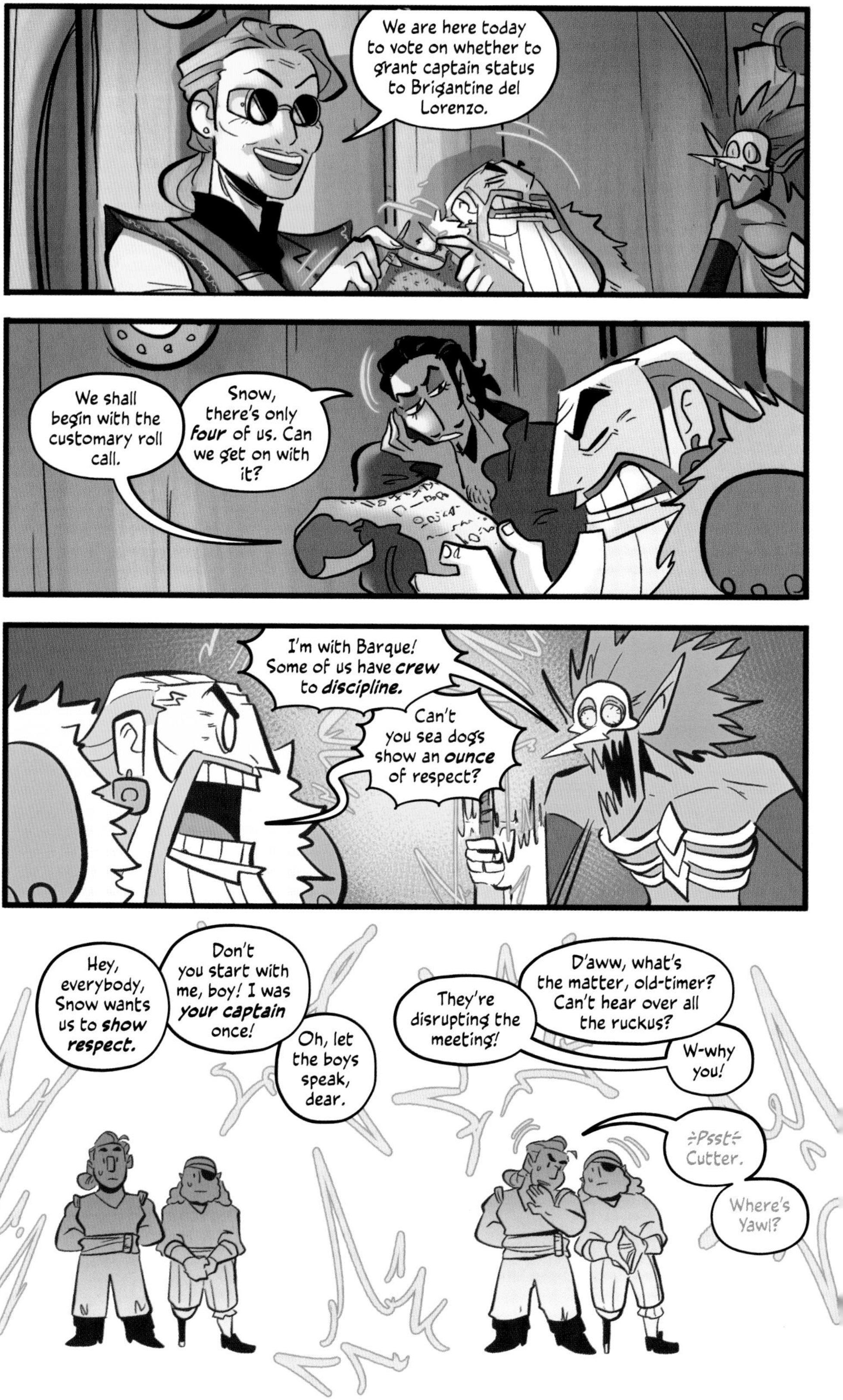
We are here today to vote on whether to grant captain status to Brigantine del Lorenzo.
We shall begin with the customary roll call.
Snow, there's only *four* of us. Can we get on with it?
I'm with Barque! Some of us have ***crew*** to ***discipline.***
Can't you sea dogs show an ***ounce*** of respect?
Hey, everybody, Snow wants us to ***show respect.***
Don't you start with me, boy! I was ***your captain*** once!
Oh, let the boys speak, dear.
They're disrupting the meeting!
D'aww, what's the matter, old-timer? Can't hear over all the ruckus?
W-why you!
Psst Cutter.
Where's Yawl?

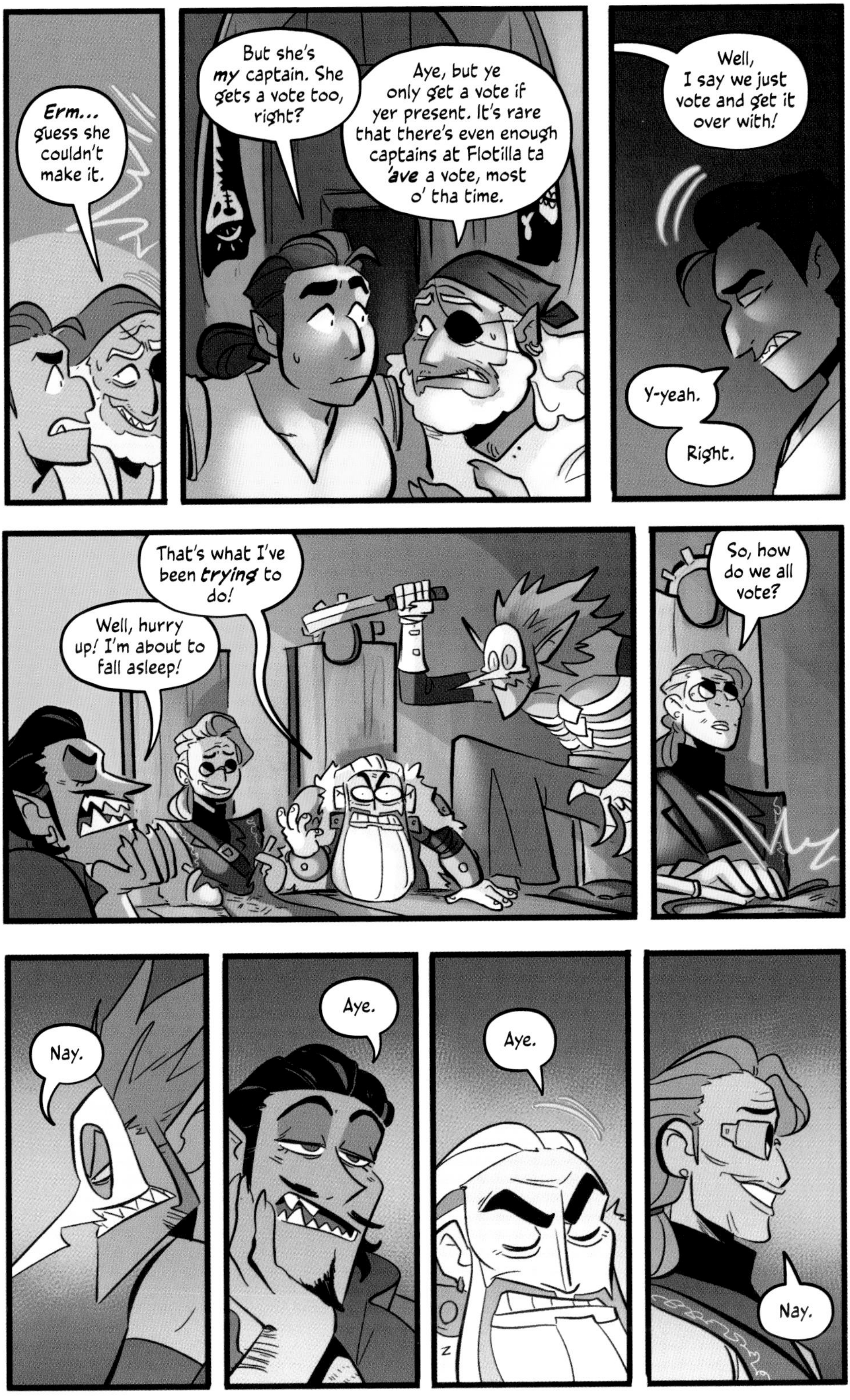
Erm... guess she couldn't make it.
But she's *my* captain. She gets a vote too, right?
Aye, but ye only get a vote if yer present. It's rare that there's even enough captains at Flotilla ta *'ave* a vote, most o' tha time.
Well, I say we just vote and get it over with!
Y-yeah.
Right.
That's what I've been *trying* to do!
Well, hurry up! I'm about to fall asleep!
So, how do we all vote?
Nay.
Aye.
Aye.
Nay.

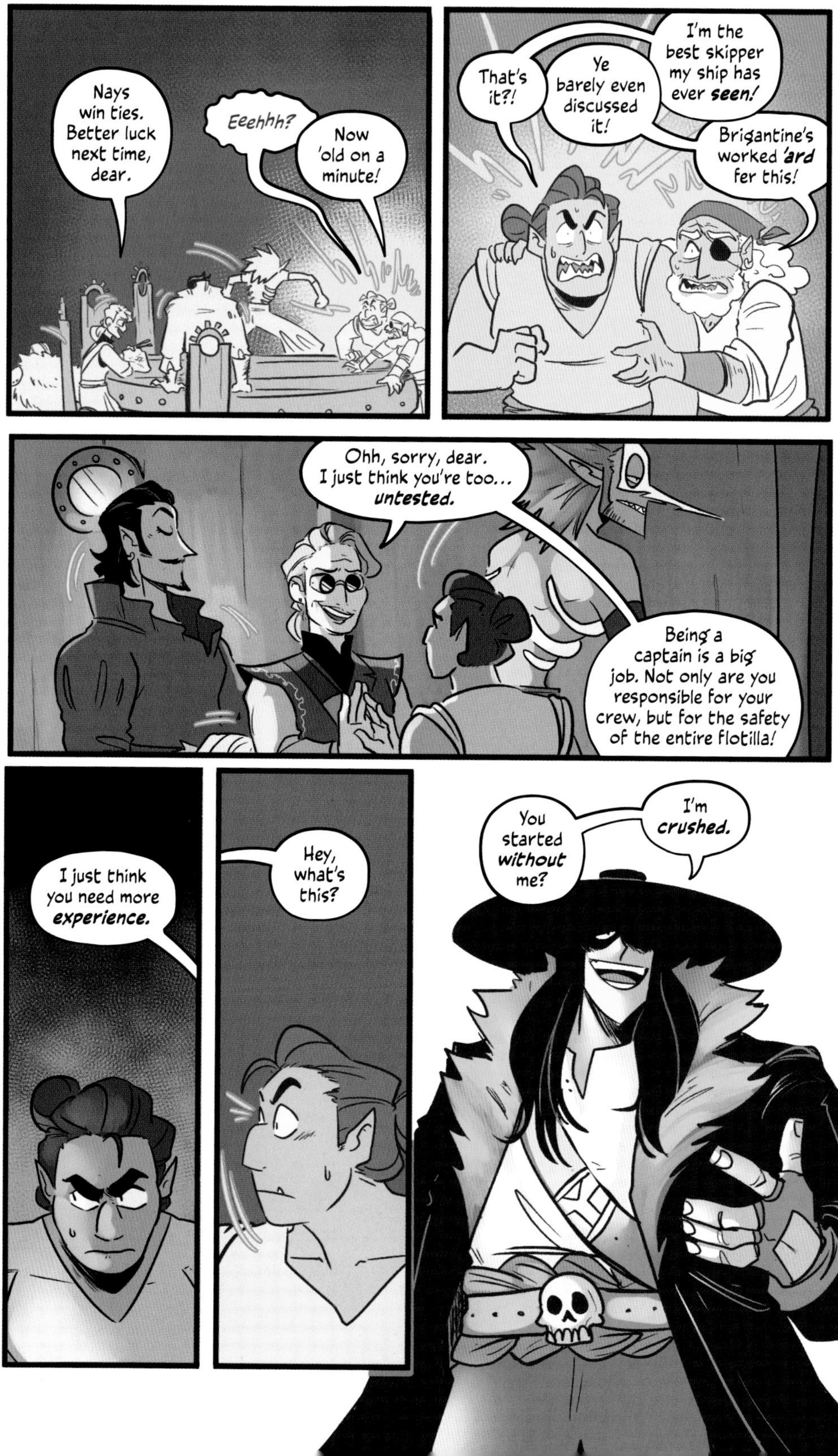
Nays win ties. Better luck next time, dear.
Eeehhh?
Now 'old on a minute!
That's it?!
Ye barely even discussed it!
I'm the best skipper my ship has ever *seen!*
Brigantine's worked *'ard* fer this!
Ohh, sorry, dear. I just think you're too... *untested.*
Being a captain is a big job. Not only are you responsible for your crew, but for the safety of the entire flotilla!
I just think you need more *experience.*
Hey, what's this?
You started *without* me?
I'm *crushed.*

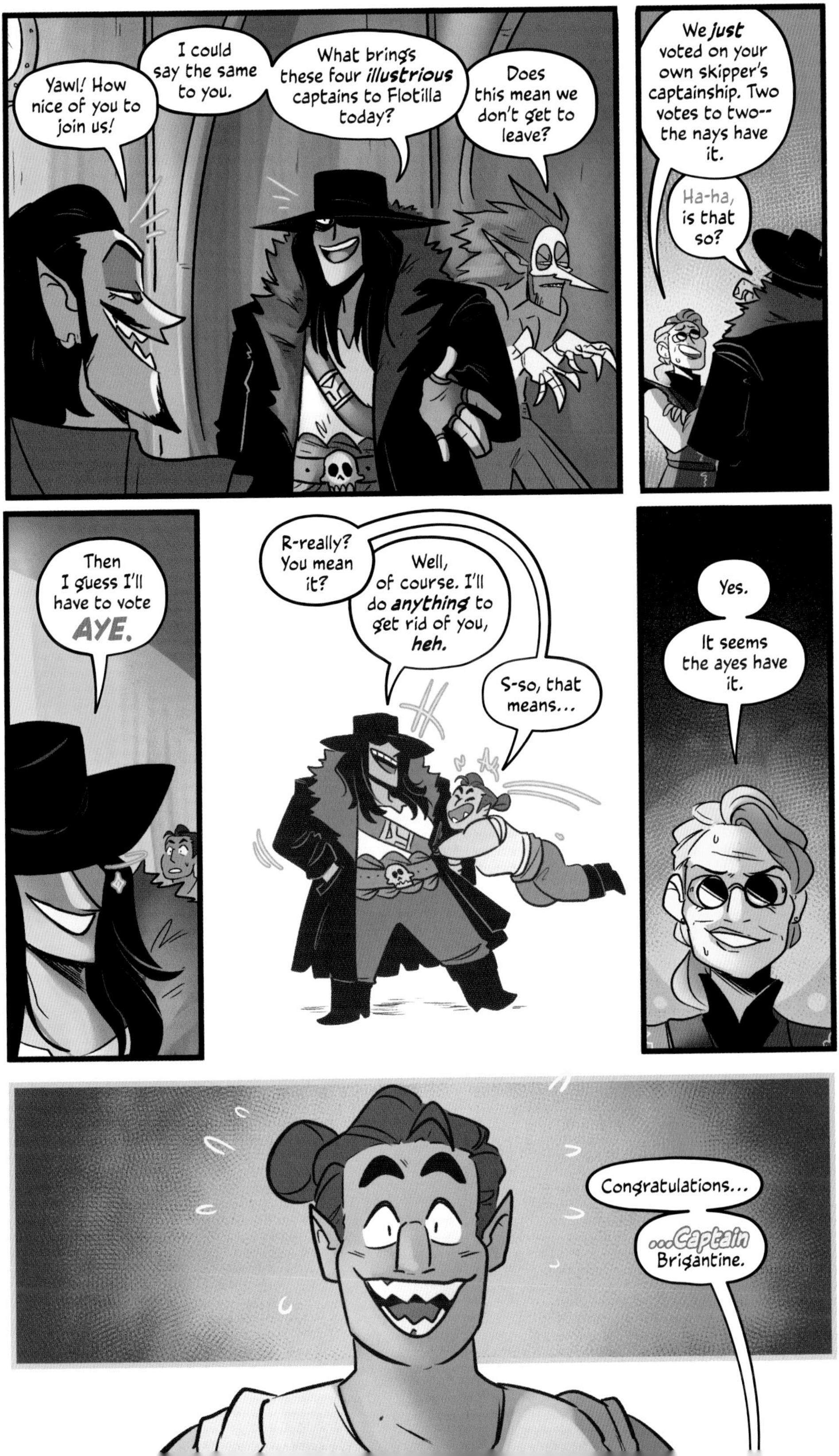

Yawl! How nice of you to join us!
I could say the same to you.
What brings these four illustrious captains to Flotilla today?
Does this mean we don't get to leave?
We just voted on your own skipper's captainship. Two votes to two-- the nays have it.
Ha-ha, is that so?
Then I guess I'll have to vote AYE.
R-really? You mean it?
Well, of course. I'll do anything to get rid of you, heh.
S-so, that means...
Yes.
It seems the ayes have it.
Congratulations...
...Captain Brigantine.

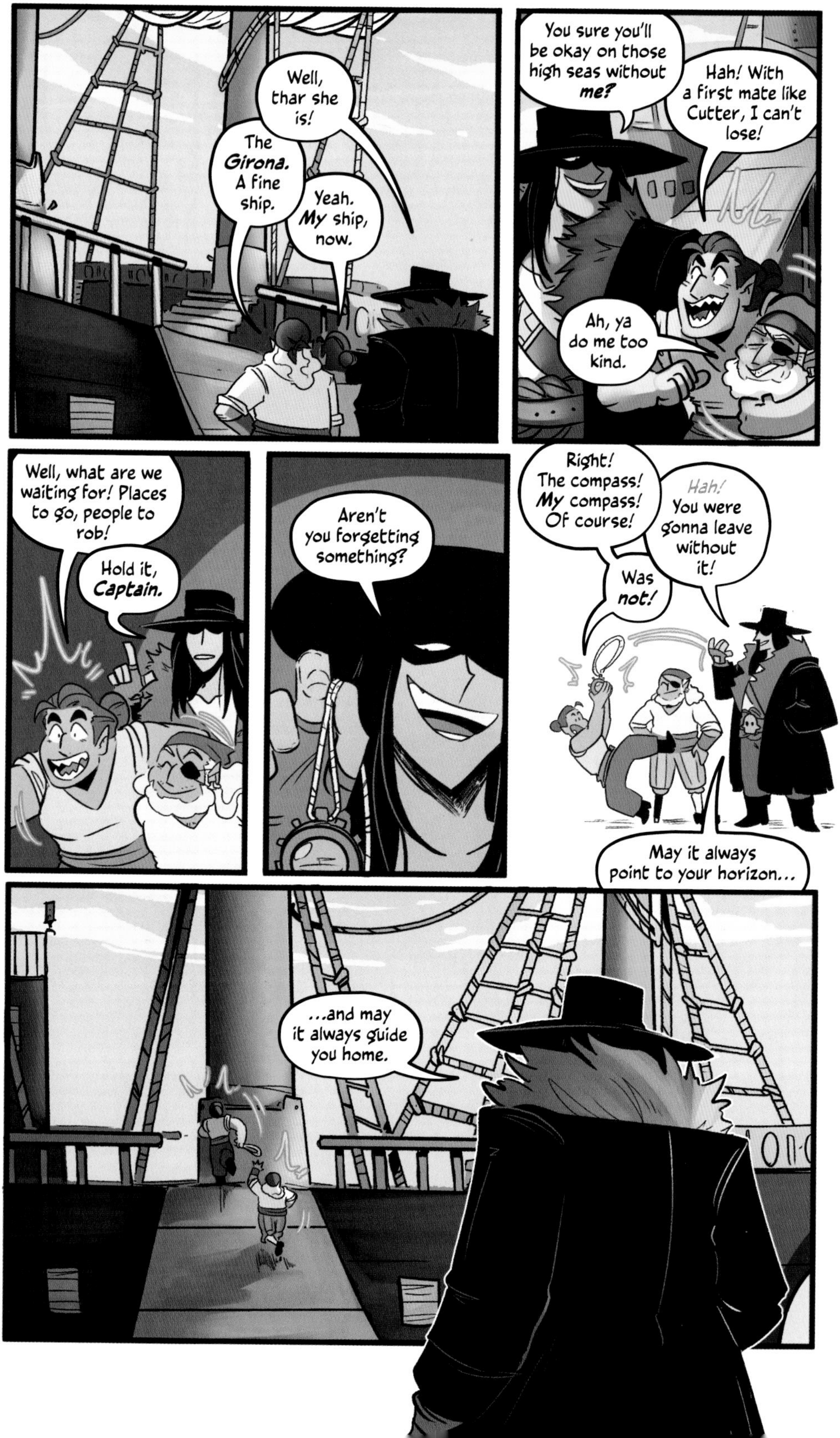
Well, thar she is!
The Girona. A fine ship.
Yeah. My ship, now.
You sure you'll be okay on those high seas without me?
Hah! With a first mate like Cutter, I can't lose!
Ah, ya do me too kind.
Well, what are we waiting for! Places to go, people to rob!
Hold it, Captain.
Aren't you forgetting something?
Right! The compass! My compass! Of course!
Hah! You were gonna leave without it!
Was not!
May it always point to your horizon...
...and may it always guide you home.

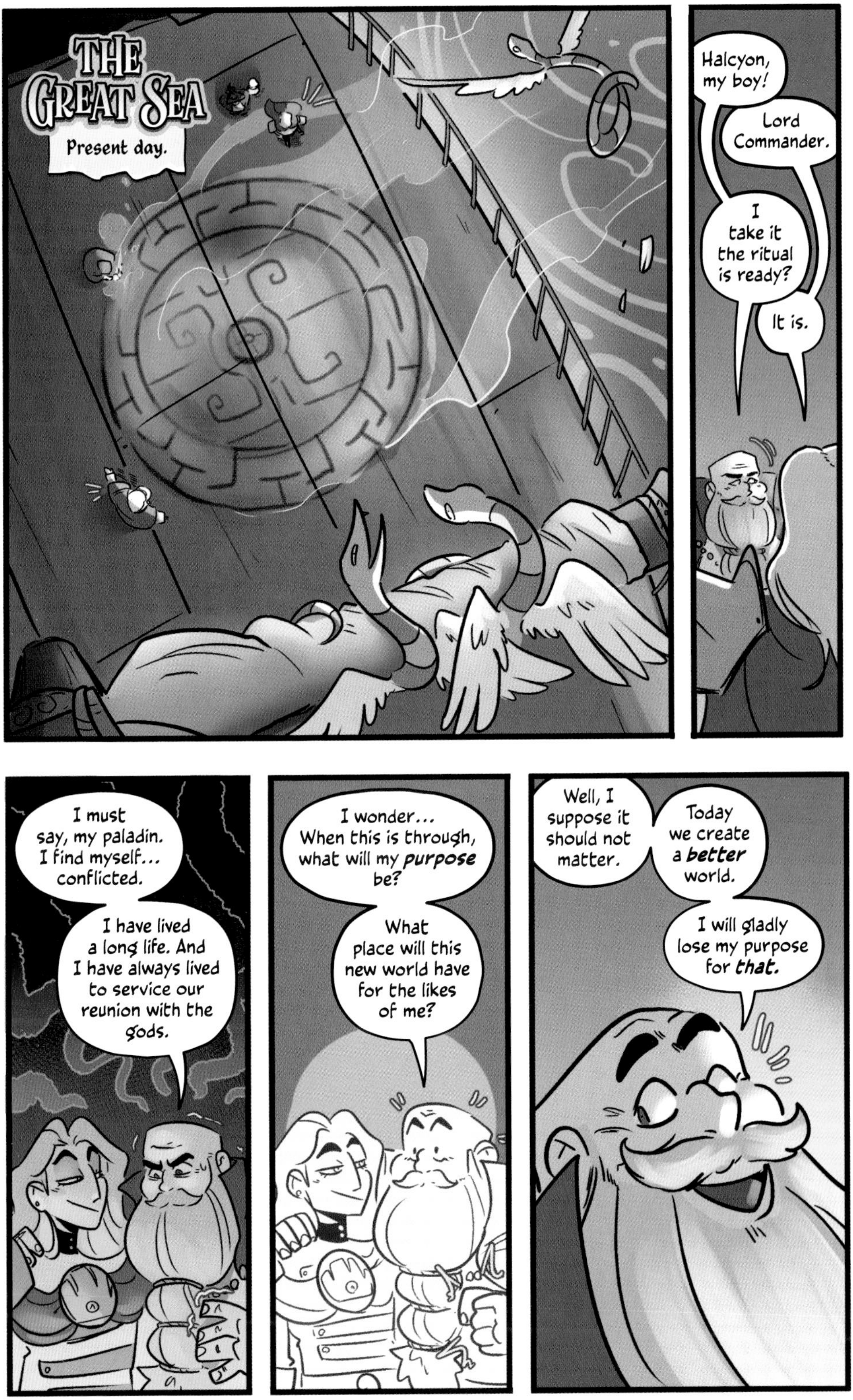
THE GREAT SEA
Present day.
Halcyon, my boy!
Lord Commander.
I take it the ritual is ready?
It is.
I must say, my paladin. I find myself... conflicted.
I have lived a long life. And I have always lived to service our reunion with the gods.
I wonder... When this is through, what will my *purpose* be?
What place will this new world have for the likes of me?
Well, I suppose it should not matter.
Today we create a *better* world.
I will gladly lose my purpose for *that.*

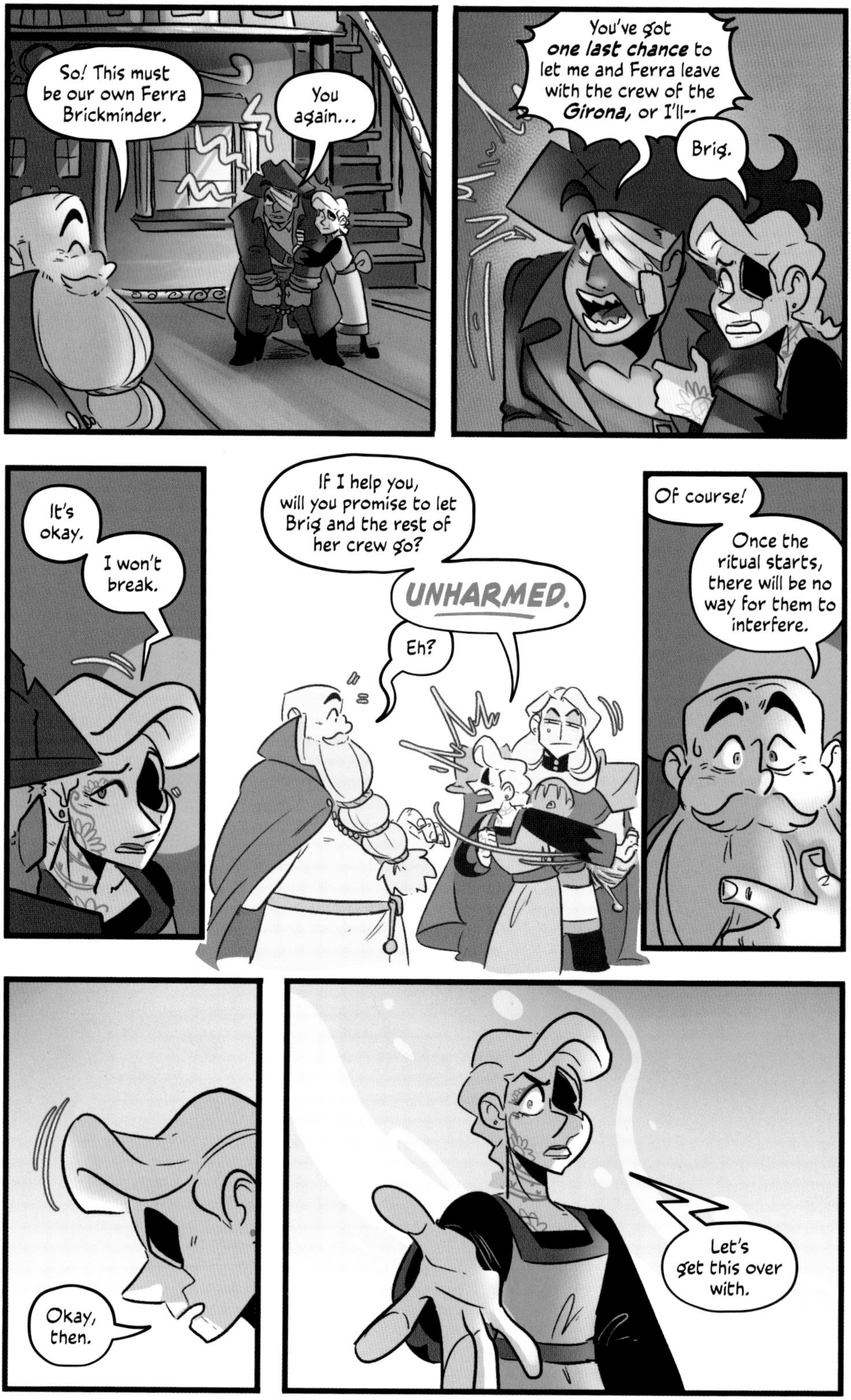
So! This must be our own Ferra Brickminder.
You again...
You've got **one last chance** to let me and Ferra leave with the crew of the *Girona*, or I'll--
Brig.
It's okay.
I won't break.
If I help you, will you promise to let Brig and the rest of her crew go?
UNHARMED.
Eh?
Of course!
Once the ritual starts, there will be no way for them to interfere.
Okay, then.
Let's get this over with.

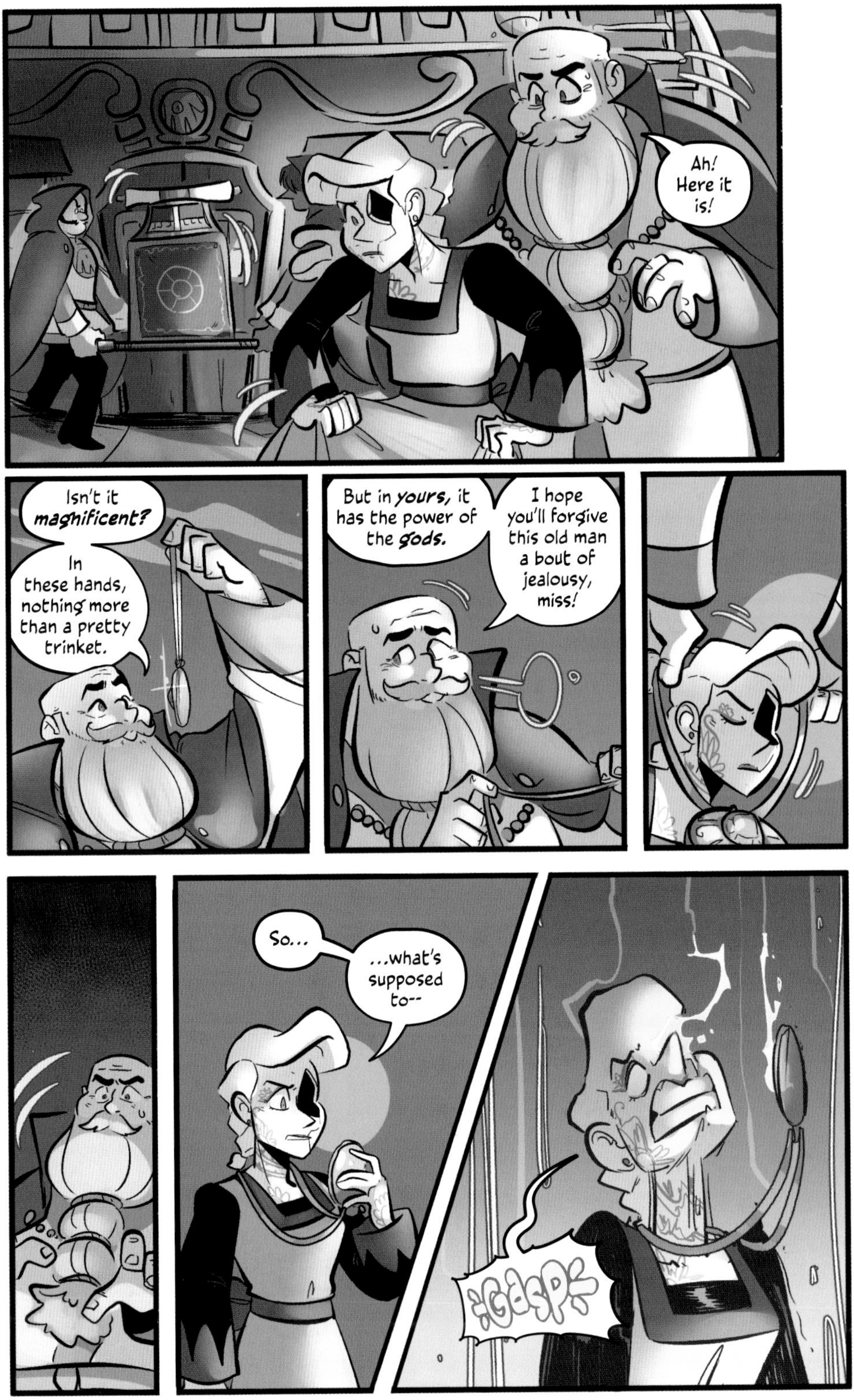
Ah! Here it is!
Isn't it *magnificent?*
In these hands, nothing more than a pretty trinket.
But in *yours,* it has the power of the *gods.*
I hope you'll forgive this old man a bout of jealousy, miss!
So...
...what's supposed to--
GASP

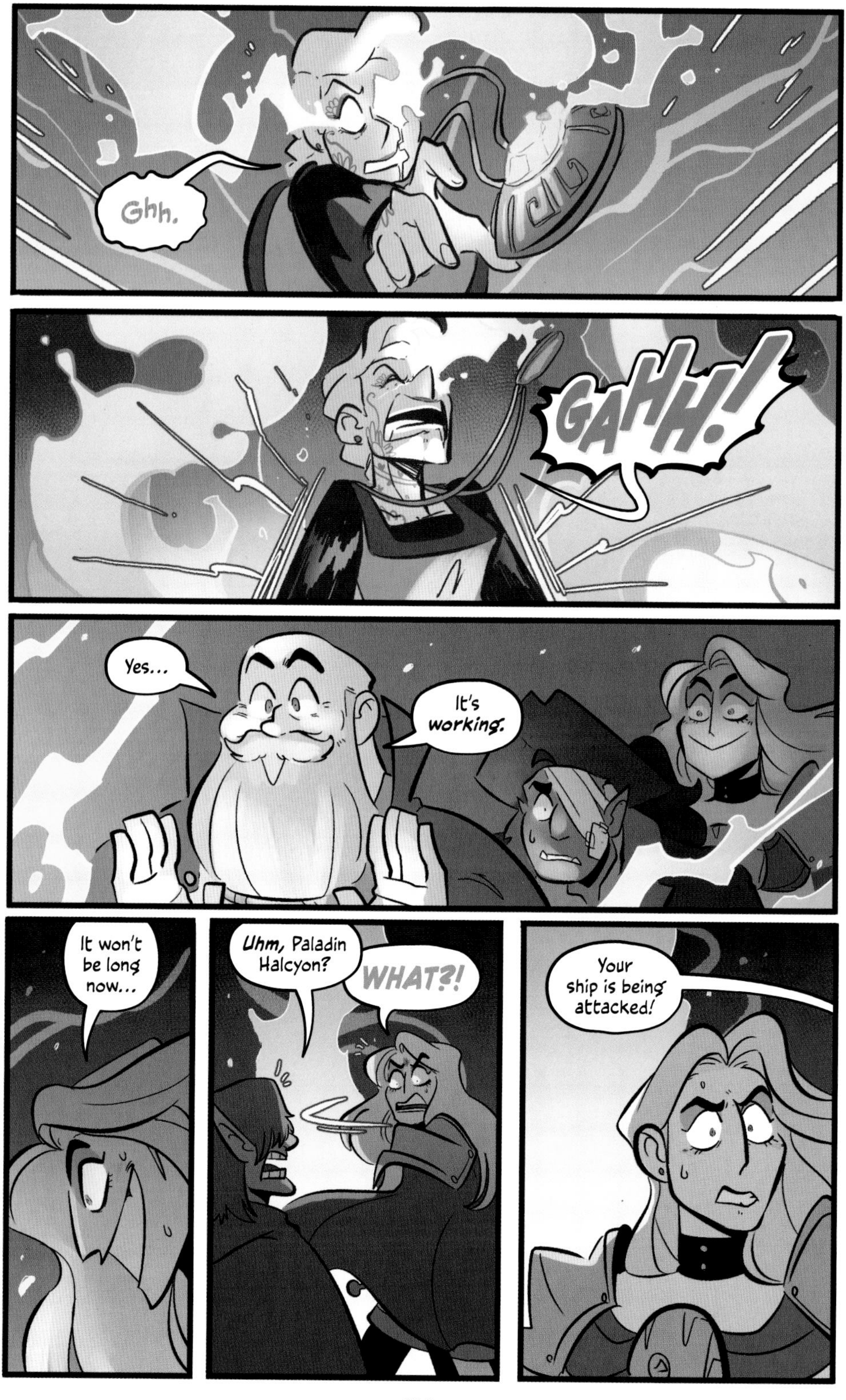
Ghh.
GAHH!
Yes...
It's *working.*
It won't be long now...
Uhm, Paladin Halcyon?
WHAT?!
Your ship is being attacked!

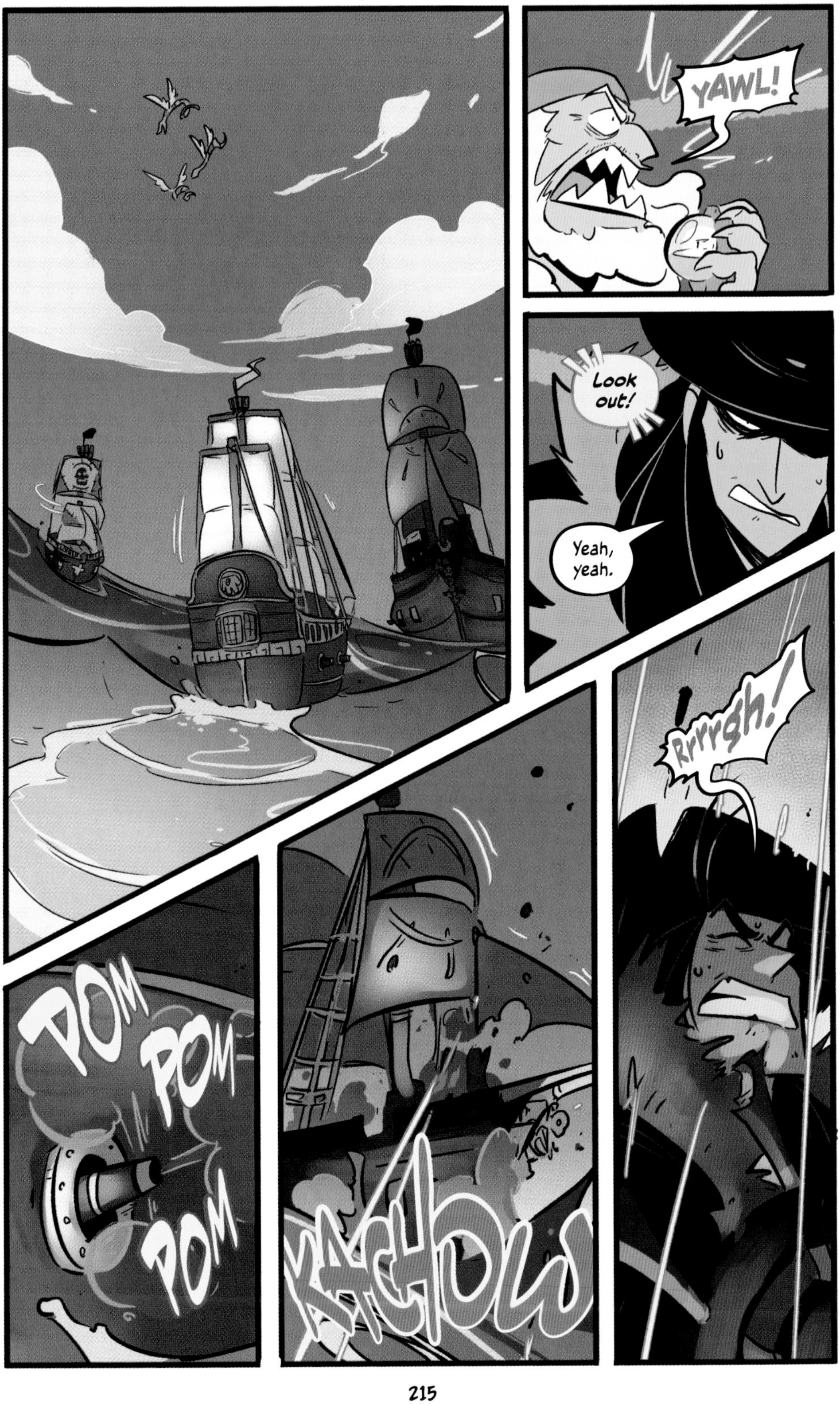
YAWL!
Look out!
Yeah, yeah.
Rrrrgh!
POM
POM
POM
POM
KACHOW

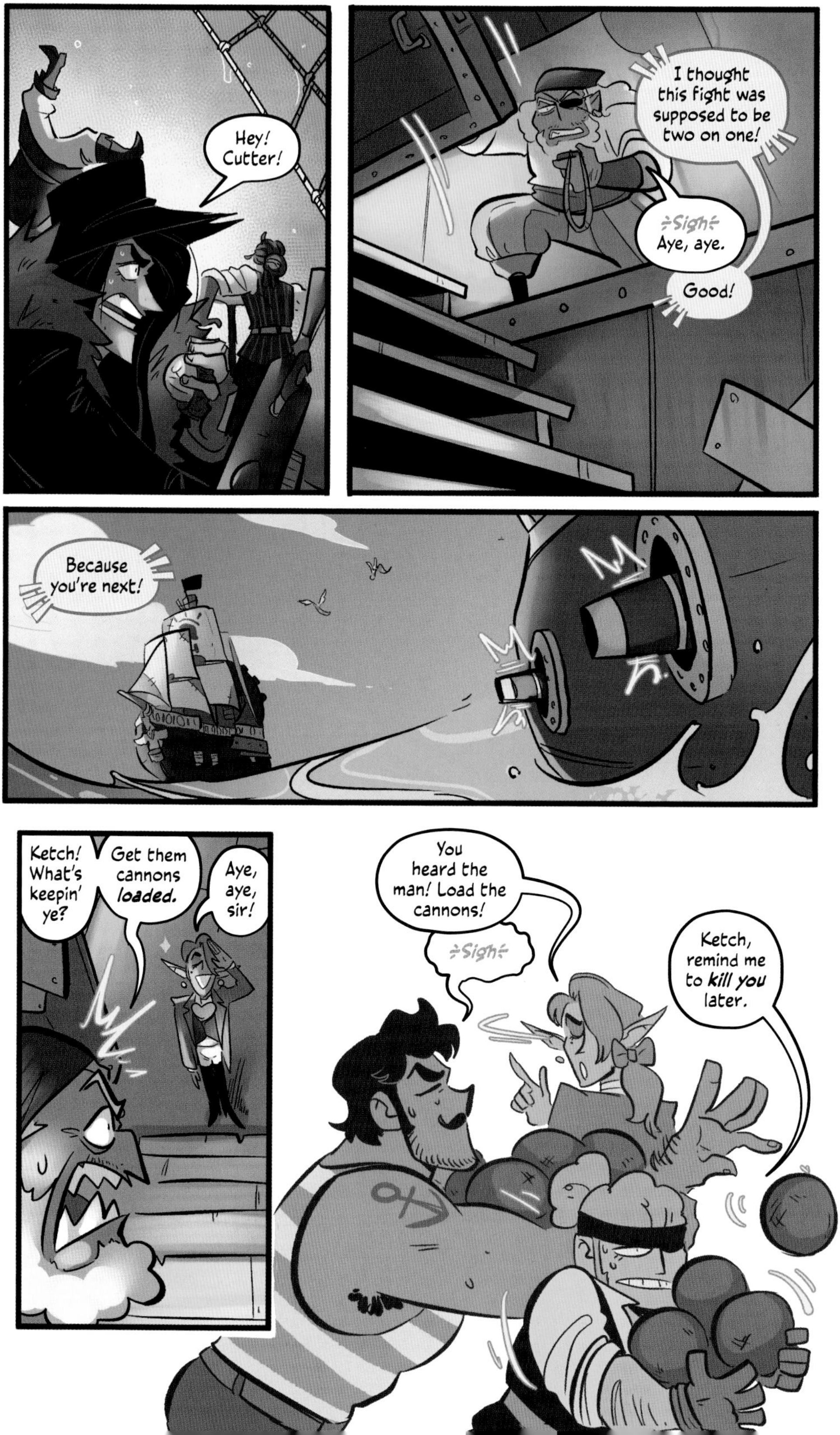
Hey! Cutter!
I thought this fight was supposed to be two on one!
Sigh
Aye, aye.
Good!
Because you're next!
Ketch! What's keepin' ye?
Get them cannons *loaded.*
Aye, aye, sir!
You heard the man! Load the cannons!
Sigh
Ketch, remind me to ***kill you*** later.

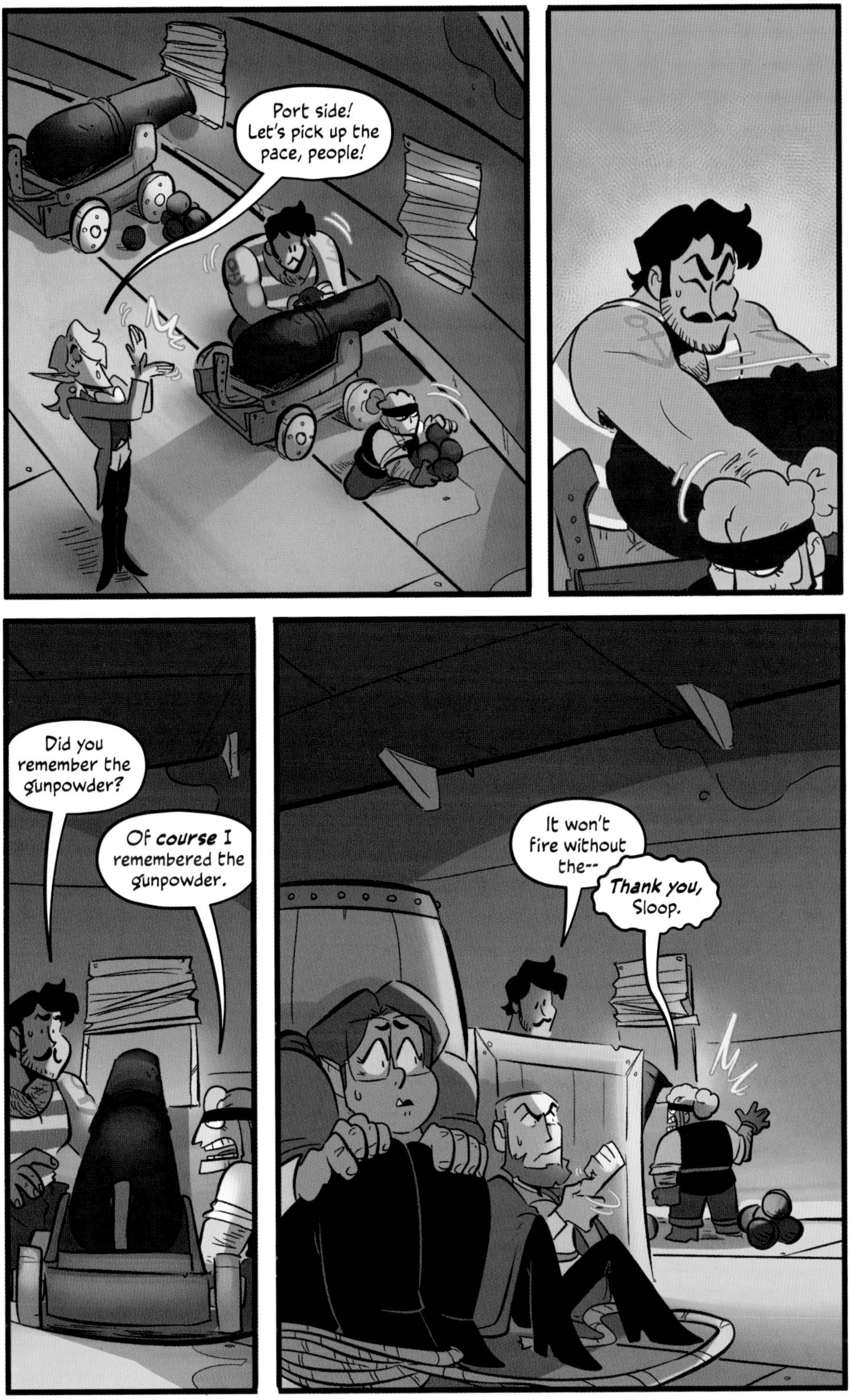
Port side!
Let's pick up the pace, people!
Did you remember the gunpowder?
Of *course* I remembered the gunpowder.
It won't fire without the--
Thank you, Sloop.

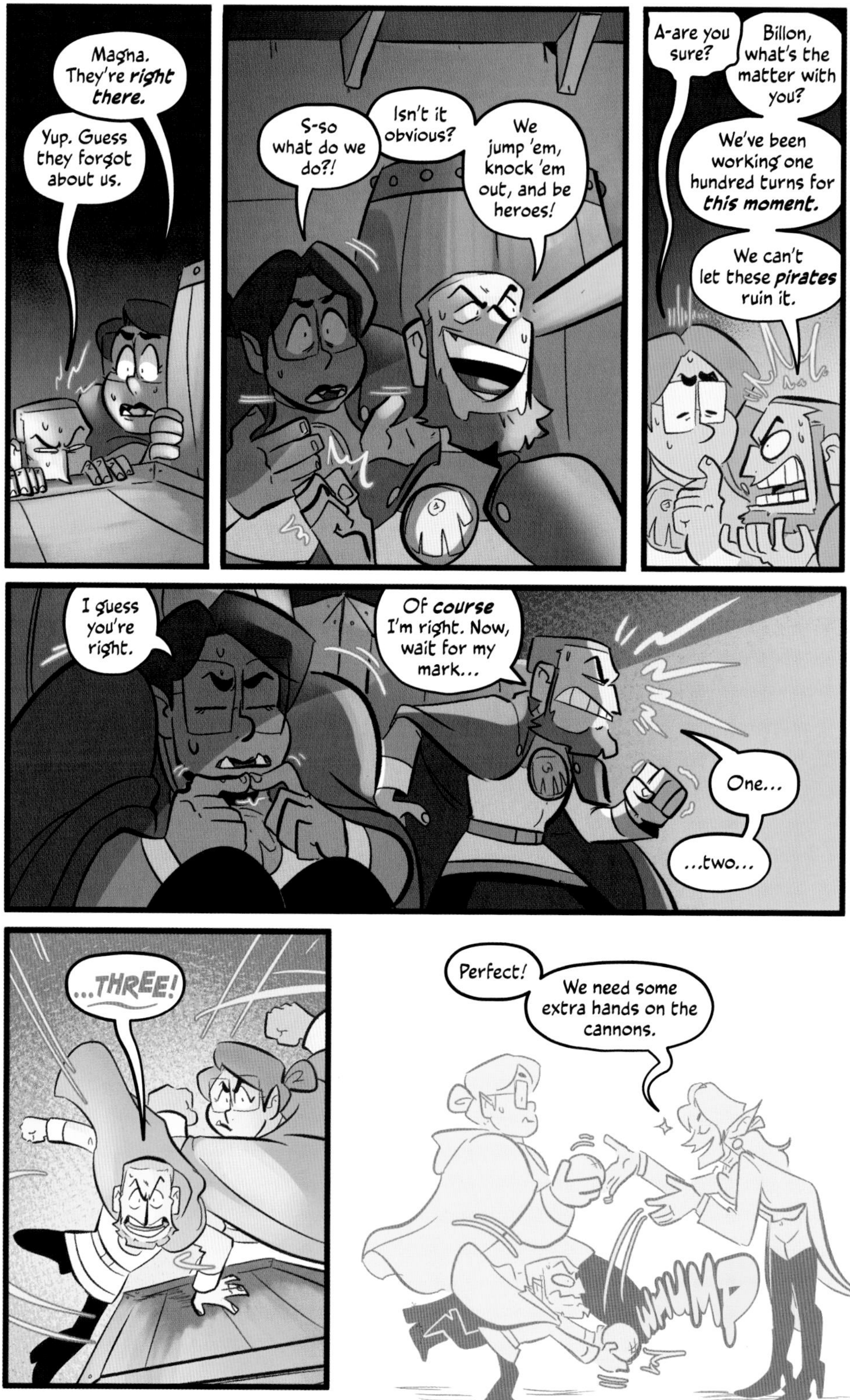
Magna. They're *right there.*
Yup. Guess they forgot about us.
S-so what do we do?!
Isn't it obvious?
We jump 'em, knock 'em out, and be heroes!
A-are you sure?
Billon, what's the matter with you?
We've been working one hundred turns for *this moment.*
We can't let these *pirates* ruin it.
I guess you're right.
Of *course* I'm right. Now, wait for my mark...
One...
...two...
...THREE!
Perfect!
We need some extra hands on the cannons.
WHUMP

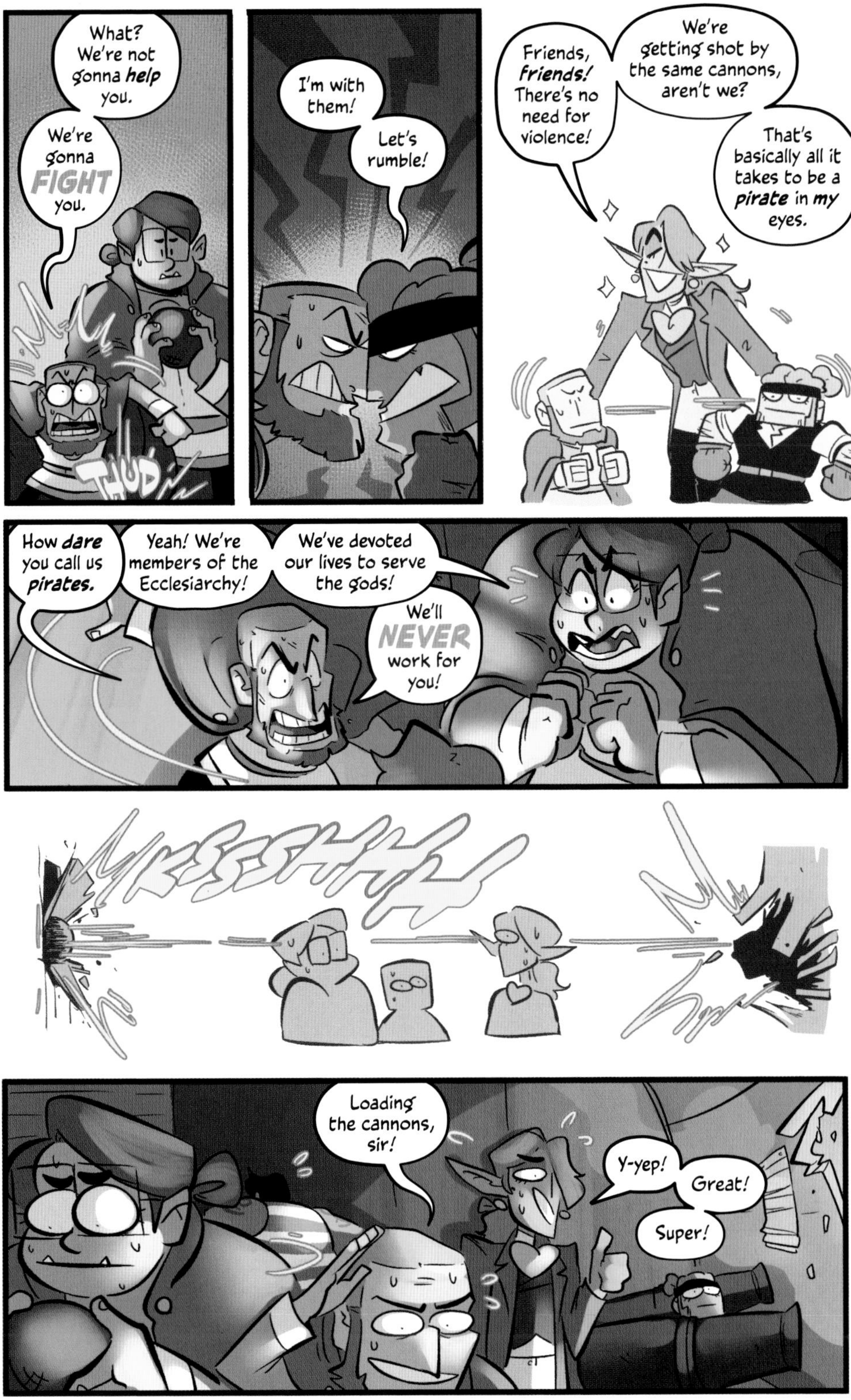
What? We're not gonna ***help*** you.
We're gonna FIGHT you.
THUD
I'm with them!
Let's rumble!
Friends, ***friends!*** There's no need for violence!
We're getting shot by the same cannons, aren't we?
That's basically all it takes to be a ***pirate*** in ***my*** eyes.
How ***dare*** you call us ***pirates.***
Yeah! We're members of the Ecclesiarchy!
We've devoted our lives to serve the gods!
We'll NEVER work for you!
KSSSHHH
Loading the cannons, sir!
Y-yep!
Great!
Super!

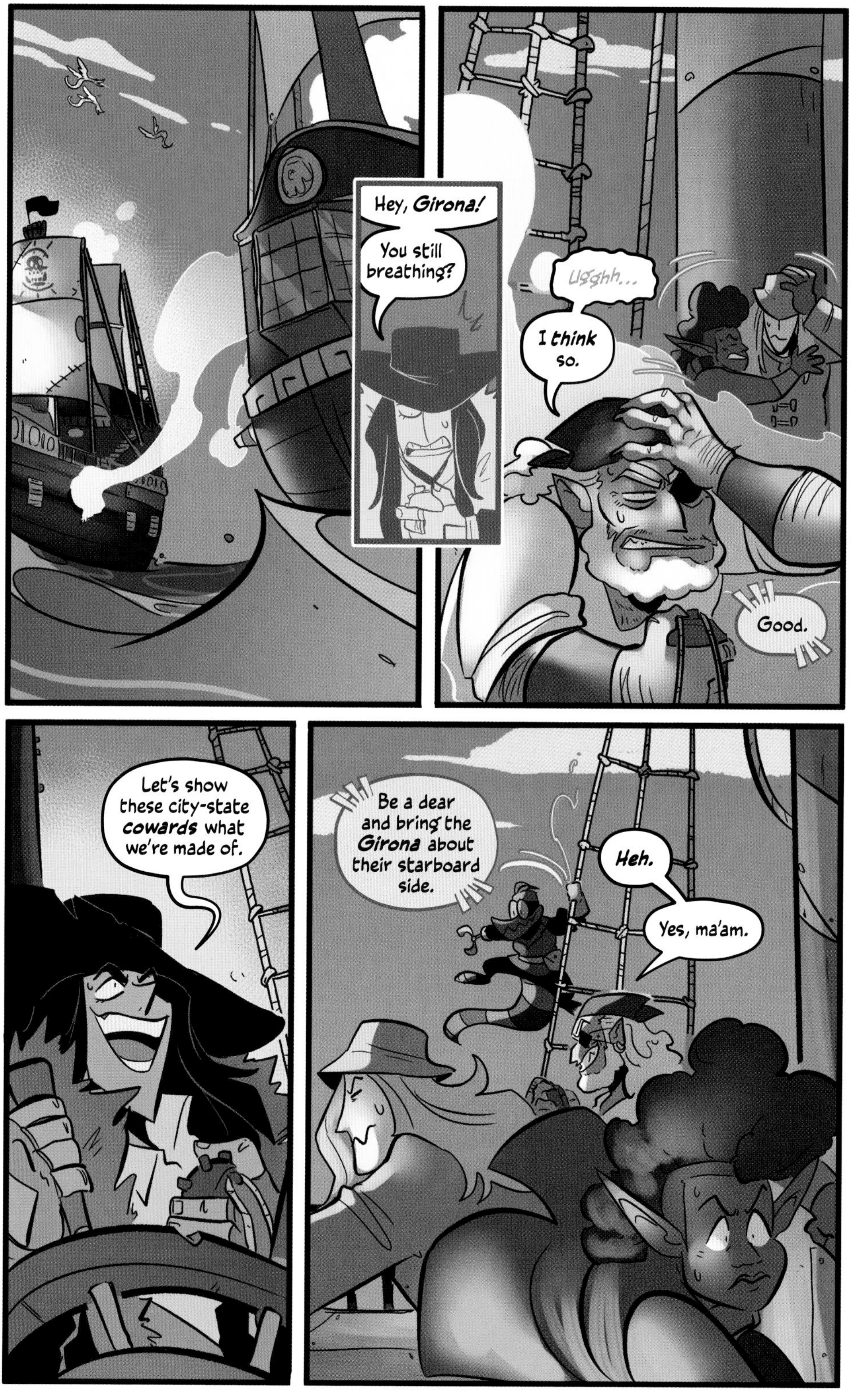

Hey, Girona!
You still breathing?
Ugghh...
I think so.
Good.
Let's show these city-state cowards what we're made of.
Be a dear and bring the Girona about their starboard side.
Heh.
Yes, ma'am.

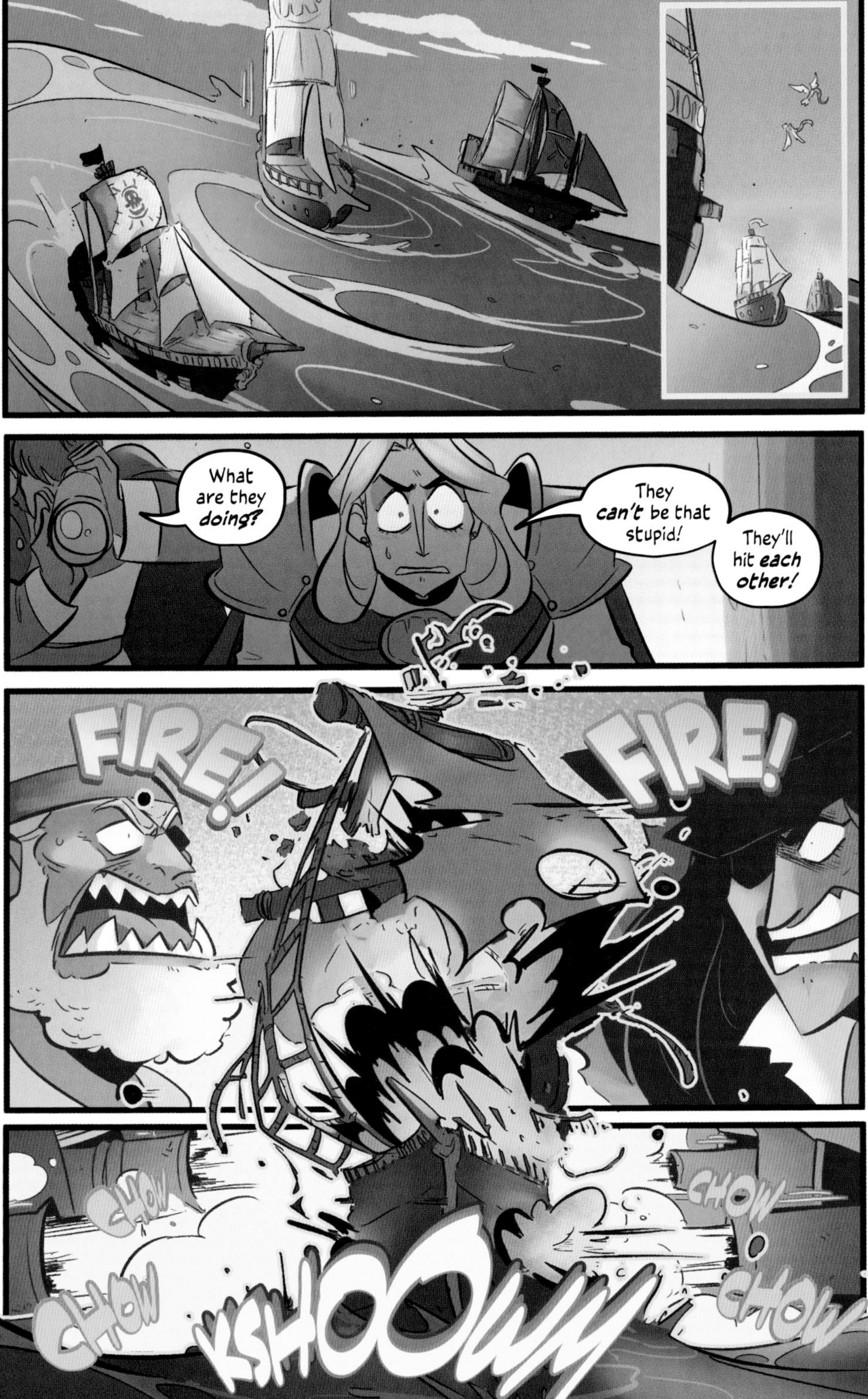

What are they *doing?*
They *can't* be that stupid!
They'll hit *each other!*
FIRE!!
FIRE!
CHOW
CHOW
CHOW
CHOW
KSHOOWM

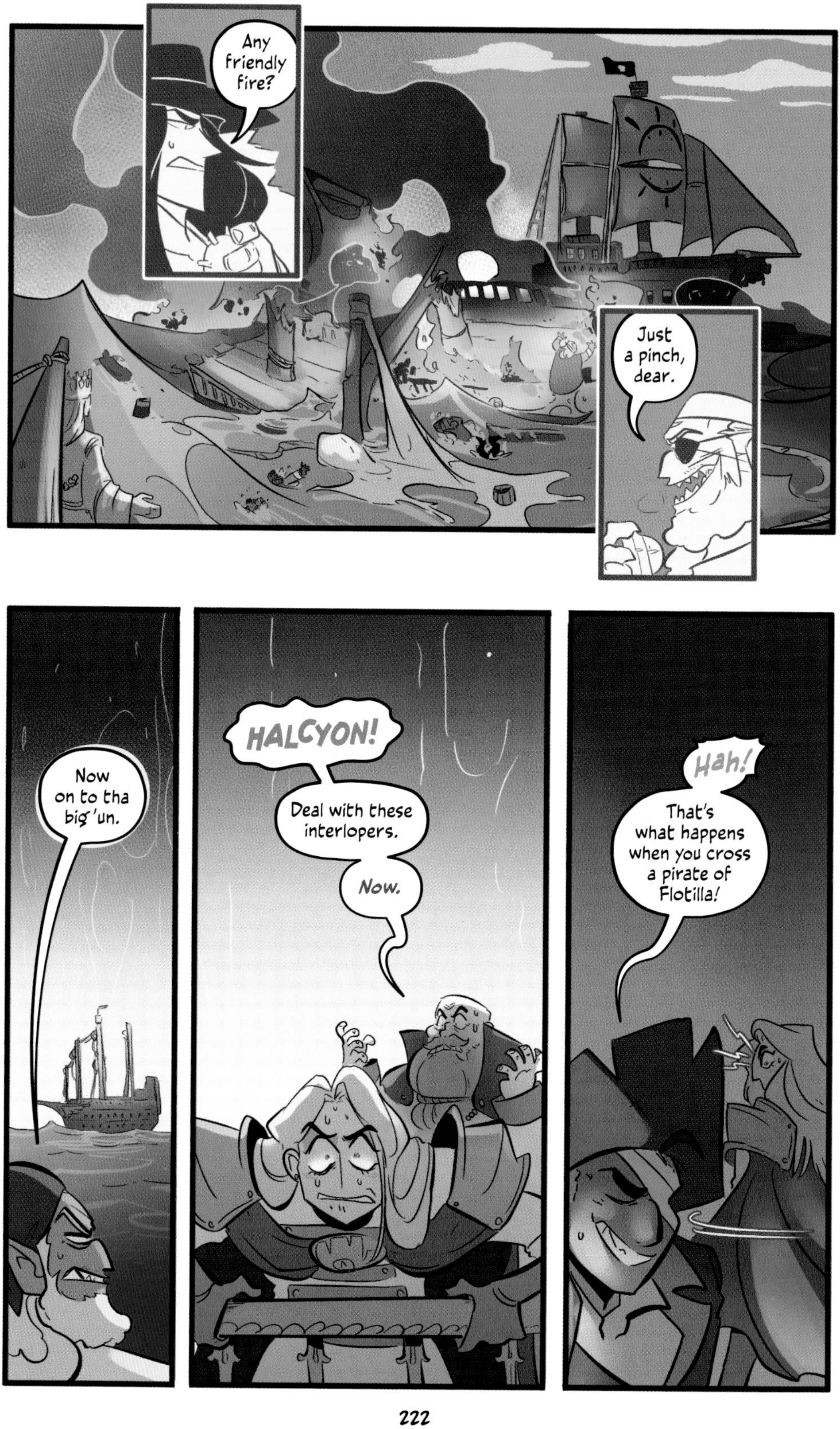
Any friendly fire?
Just a pinch, dear.
Now on to tha big 'un.
HALCYON!
Deal with these interlopers.
Now.
Hah!
That's what happens when you cross a pirate of Flotilla!

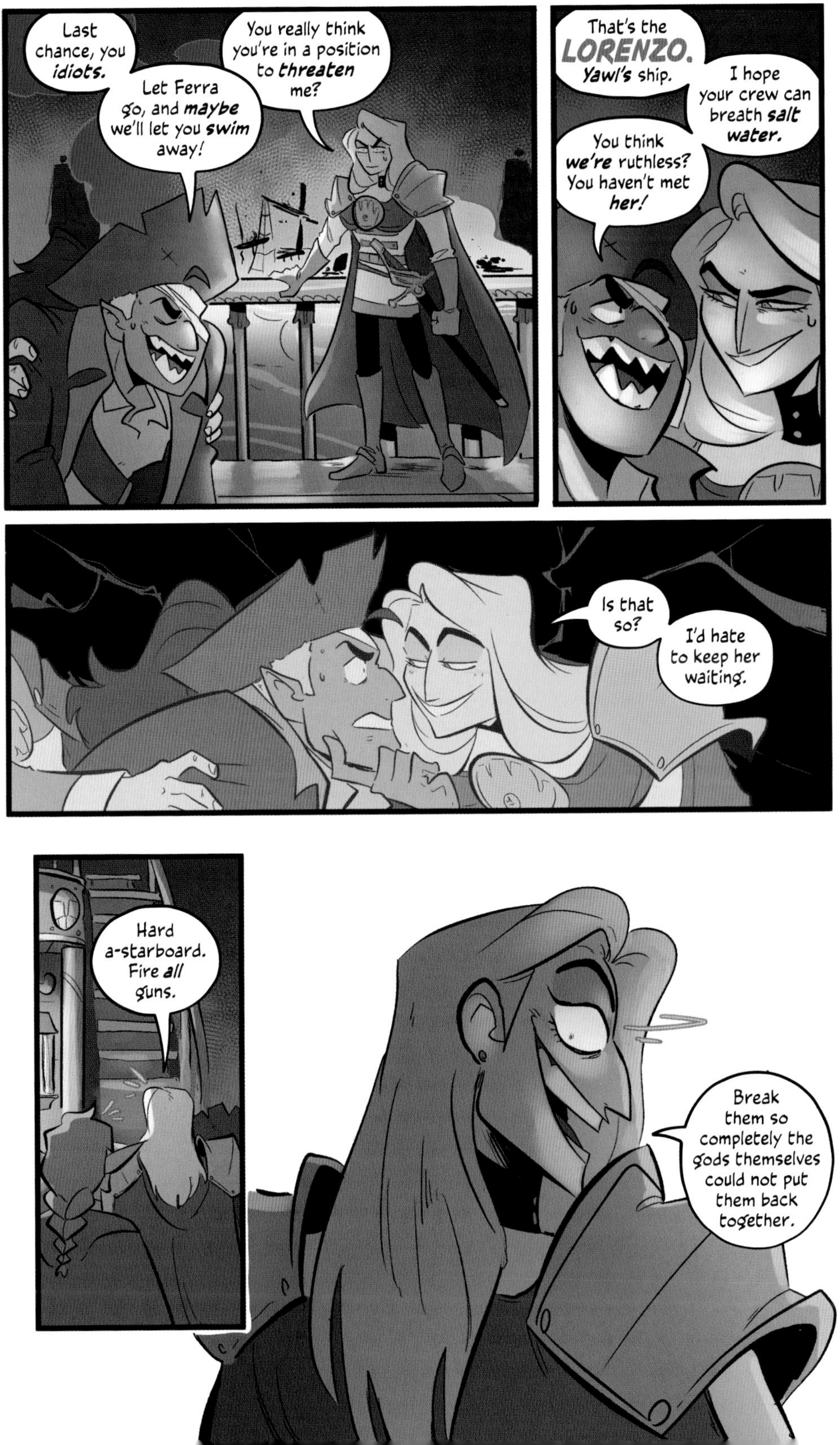
Last chance, you *idiots.*
Let Ferra go, and *maybe* we'll let you *swim* away!
You really think you're in a position to *threaten* me?
That's the LORENZO. *Yawl's* ship.
You think *we're* ruthless? You haven't met *her!*
I hope your crew can breath *salt water.*
Is that so?
I'd hate to keep her waiting.
Hard a-starboard. Fire *all* guns.
Break them so completely the gods themselves could not put them back together.

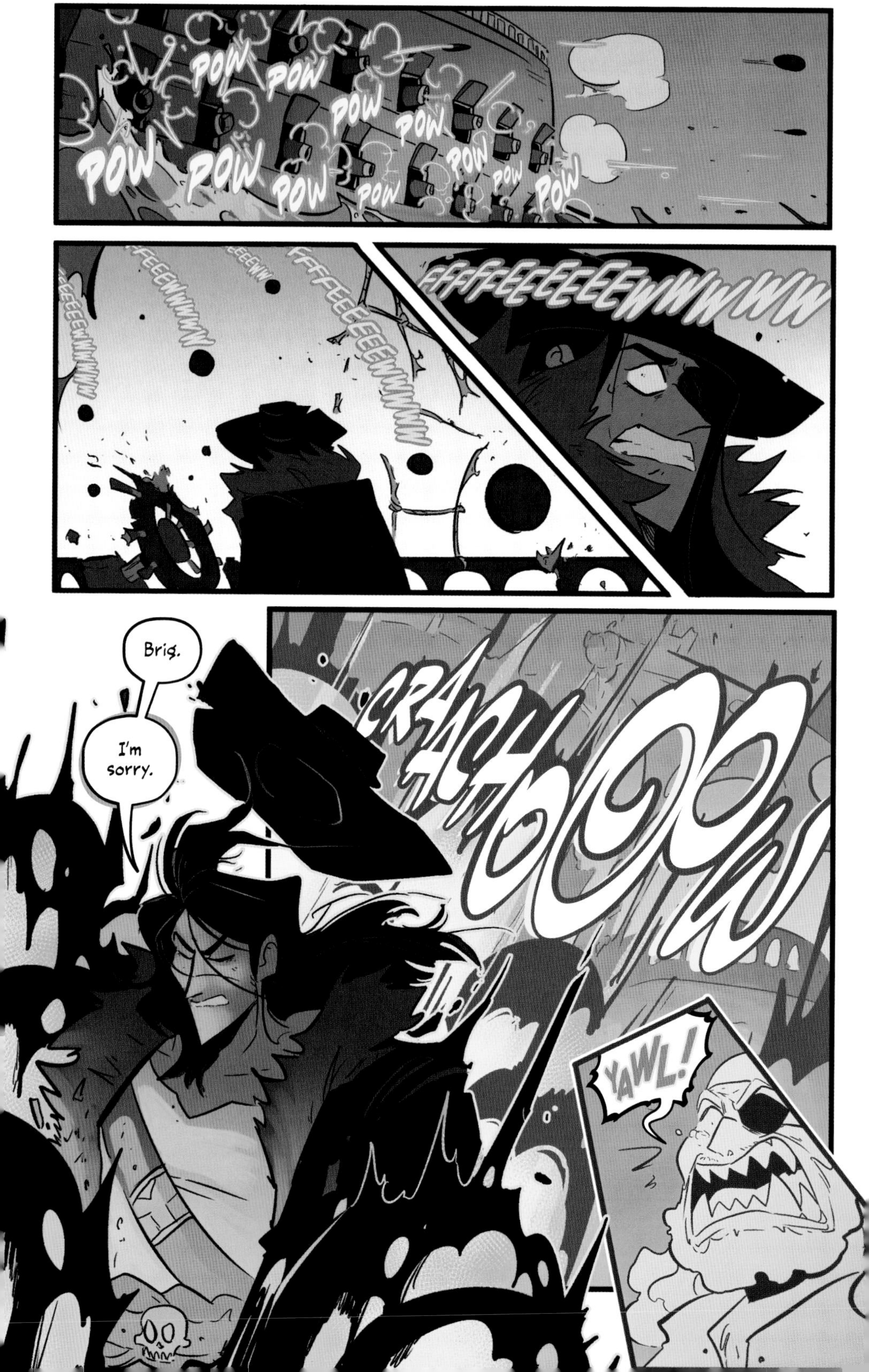
POW POW POW POW POW POW POW POW POW POW POW
FFFFEEEEEEEWWWWWW
FFFFEEEEEEEEWWWWWW
Brig.
I'm sorry.
CRASH
BOOOM
YAWL!

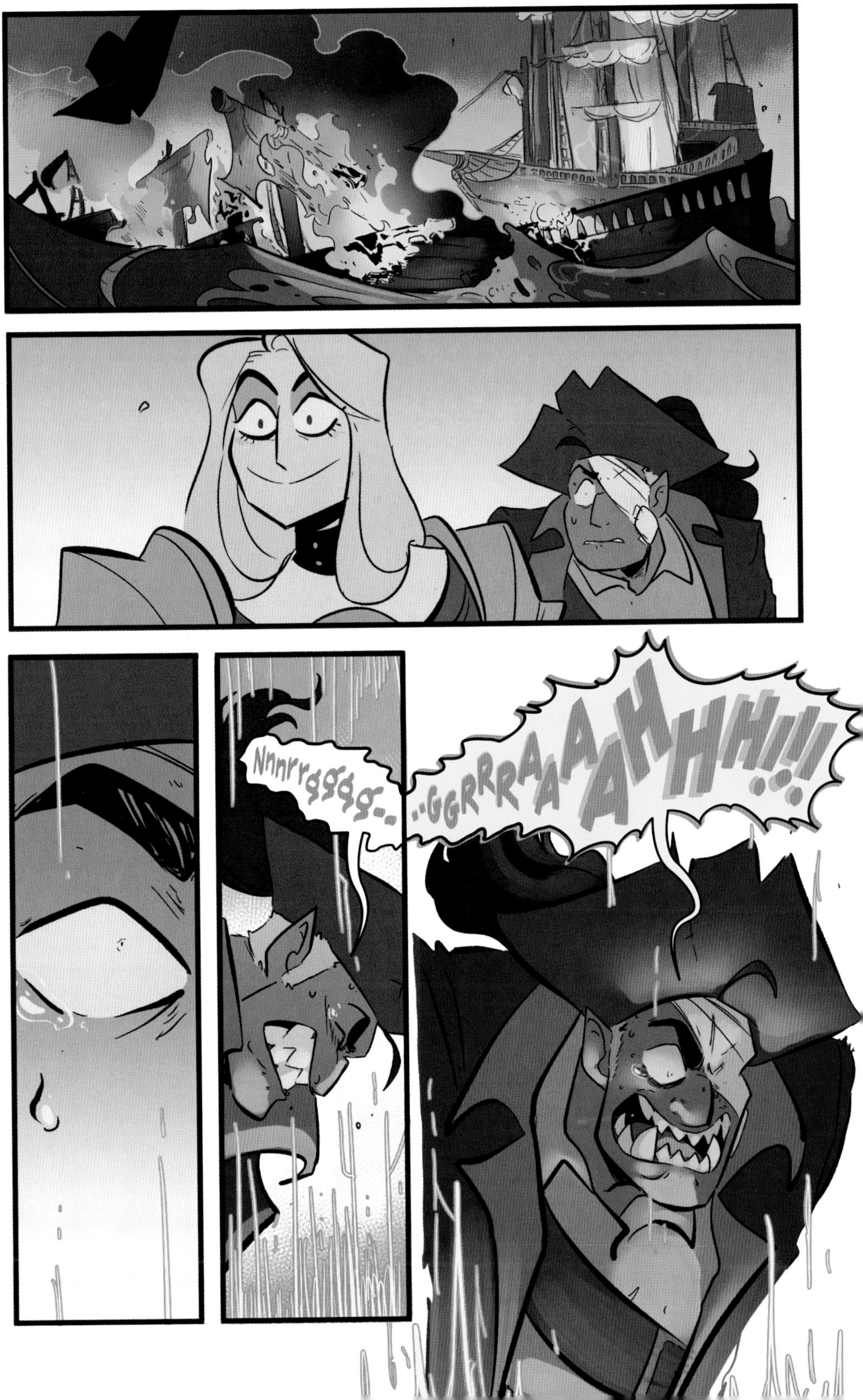
Nnnrrggg..
..GGRRRAAAAAHHH!!!

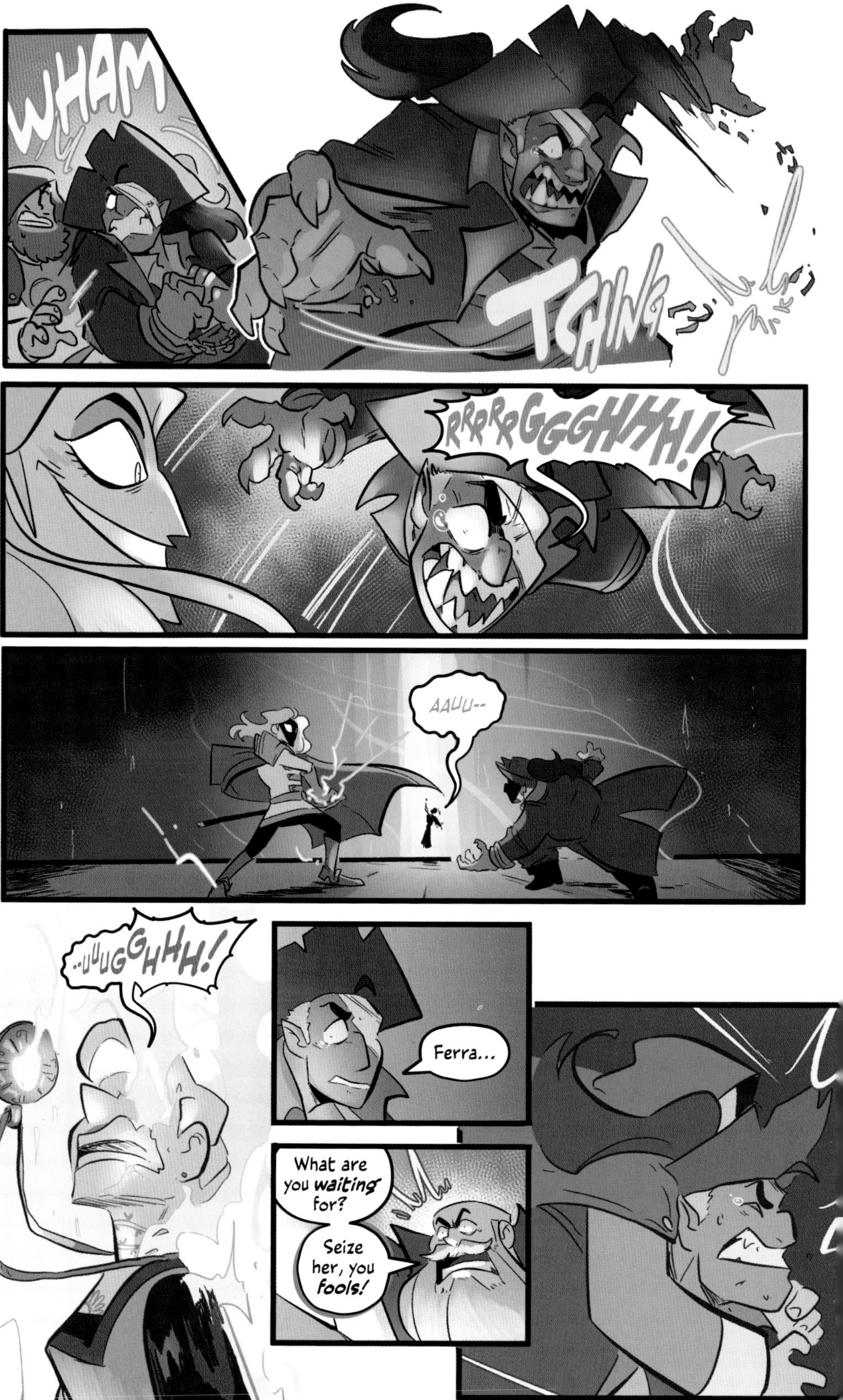
WHAM
TCHING
RRRRRGGGHHHH!
AAUU--
--UUUGGHHH!
Ferra...
What are you waiting for?
Seize her, you fools!

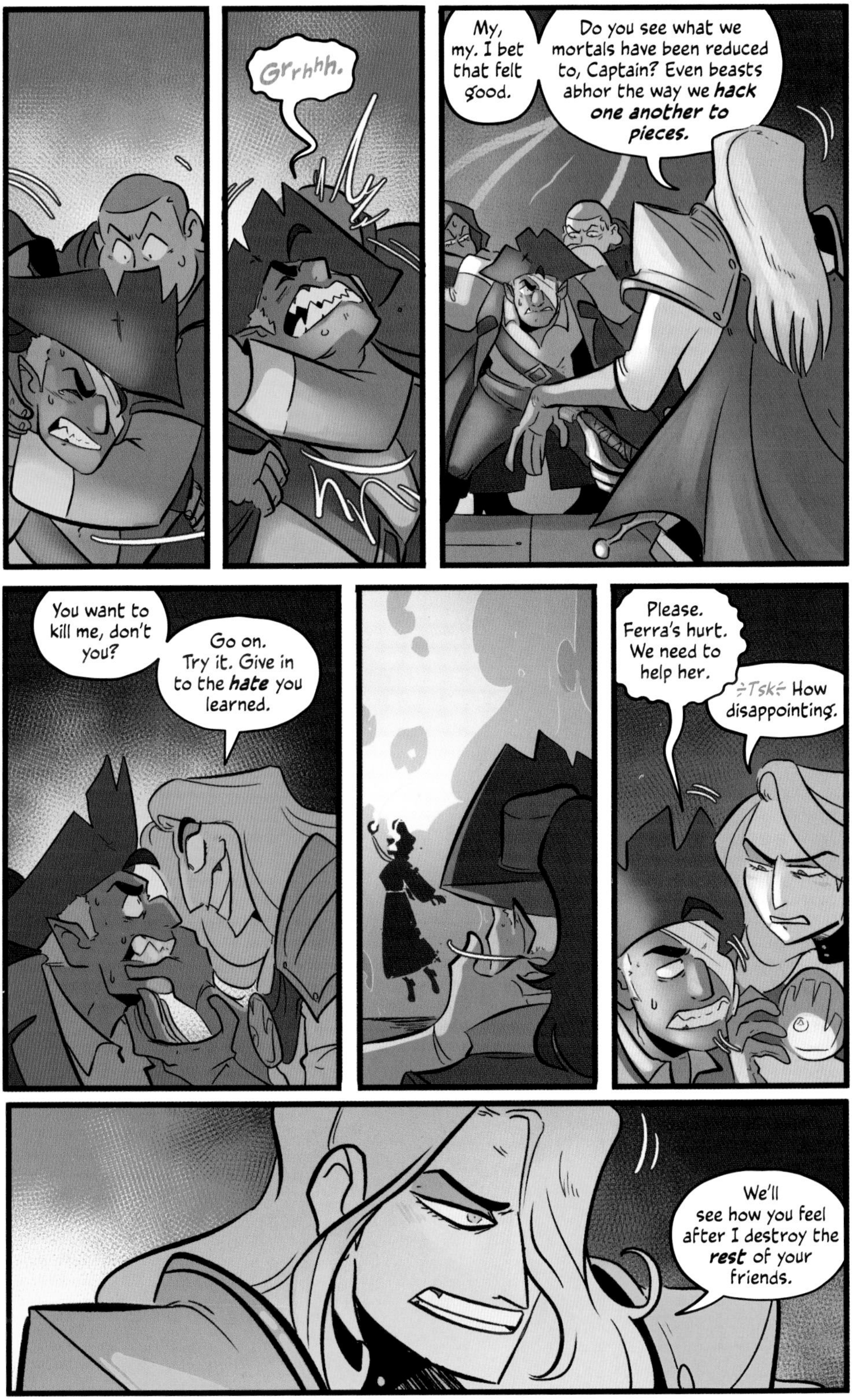
Grrhhh.
My, my. I bet that felt good.
Do you see what we mortals have been reduced to, Captain? Even beasts abhor the way we **hack one another to pieces.**
You want to kill me, don't you?
Go on. Try it. Give in to the **hate** you learned.
Please. Ferra's hurt. We need to help her.
Tsk How disappointing.
We'll see how you feel after I destroy the **rest** of your friends.

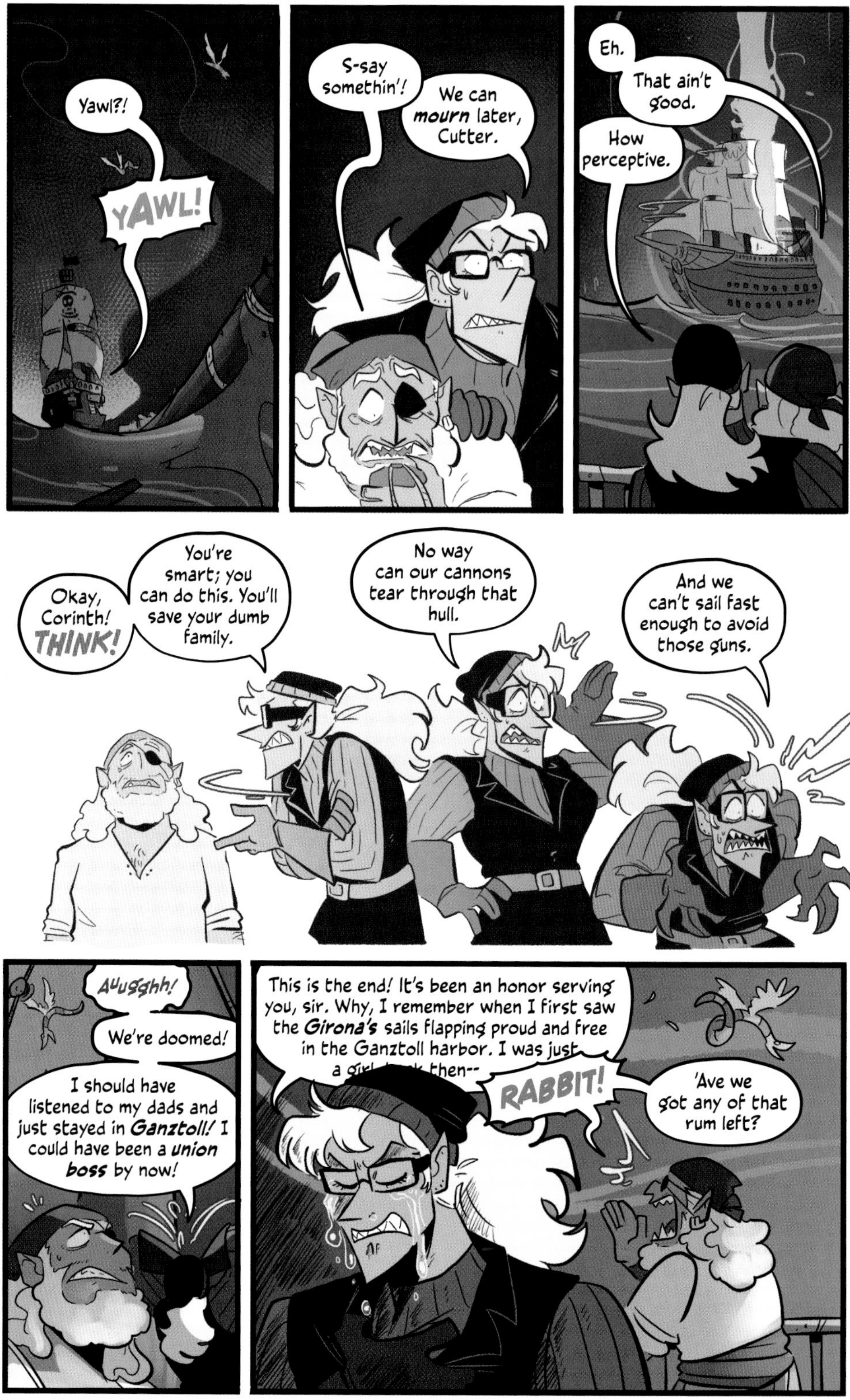

Yawl?!
YAWL!
S-say somethin'!
We can mourn later, Cutter.
Eh.
That ain't good.
How perceptive.
Okay, Corinth! THINK!
You're smart; you can do this. You'll save your dumb family.
No way can our cannons tear through that hull.
And we can't sail fast enough to avoid those guns.
Auugghh!
We're doomed!
I should have listened to my dads and just stayed in Ganztoll! I could have been a union boss by now!
This is the end! It's been an honor serving you, sir. Why, I remember when I first saw the Girona's sails flapping proud and free in the Ganztoll harbor. I was just
then--
RABBIT!
'Ave we got any of that rum left?

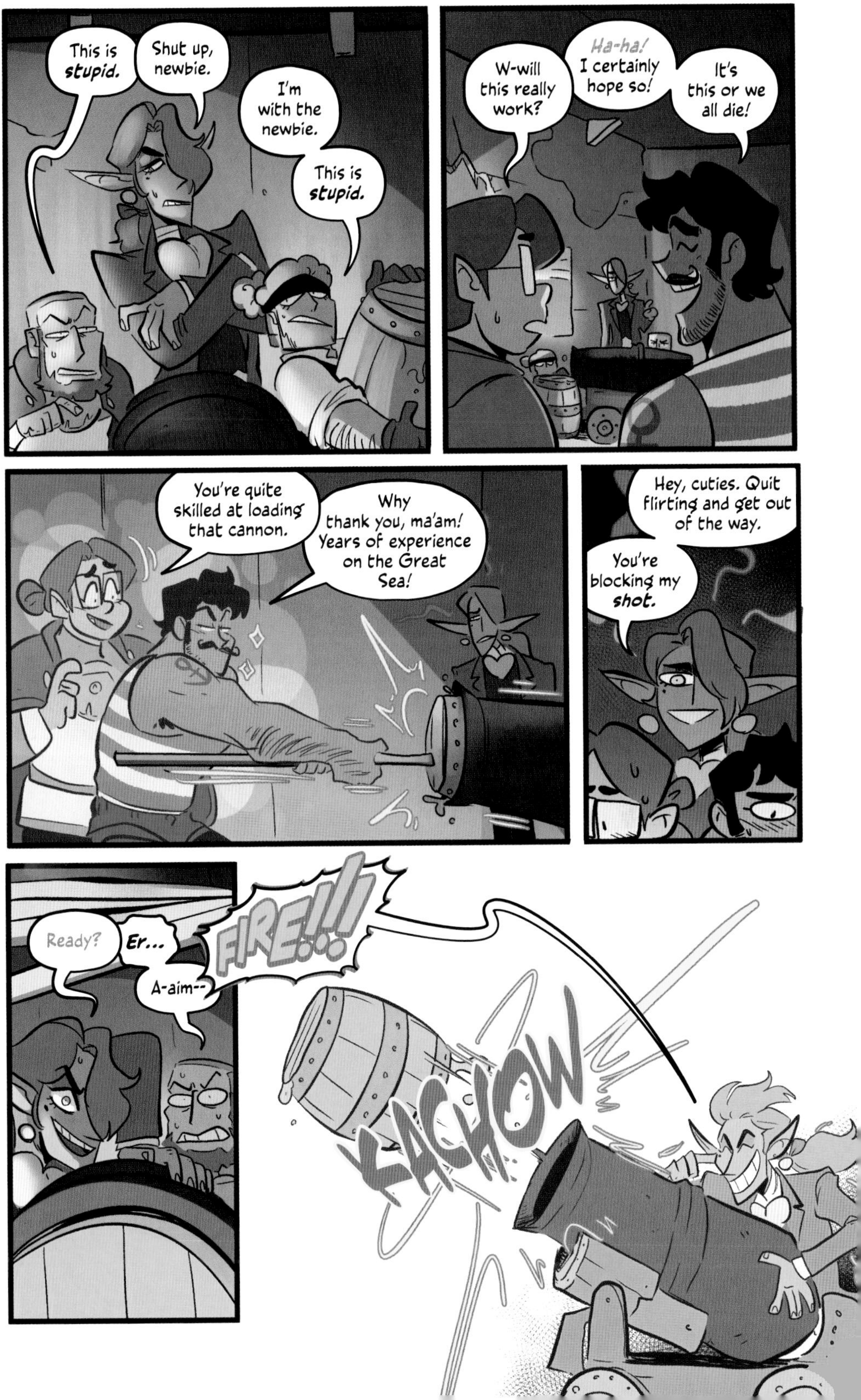
This is **stupid.**
Shut up, newbie.
I'm with the newbie.
This is **stupid.**
W-will this really work?
Ha-ha! I certainly hope so!
It's this or we all die!
You're quite skilled at loading that cannon.
Why thank you, ma'am! Years of experience on the Great Sea!
Hey, cuties. Quit flirting and get out of the way.
You're blocking my **shot.**
Ready?
Er...
A-aim--
FIRE!!!
KACHOW

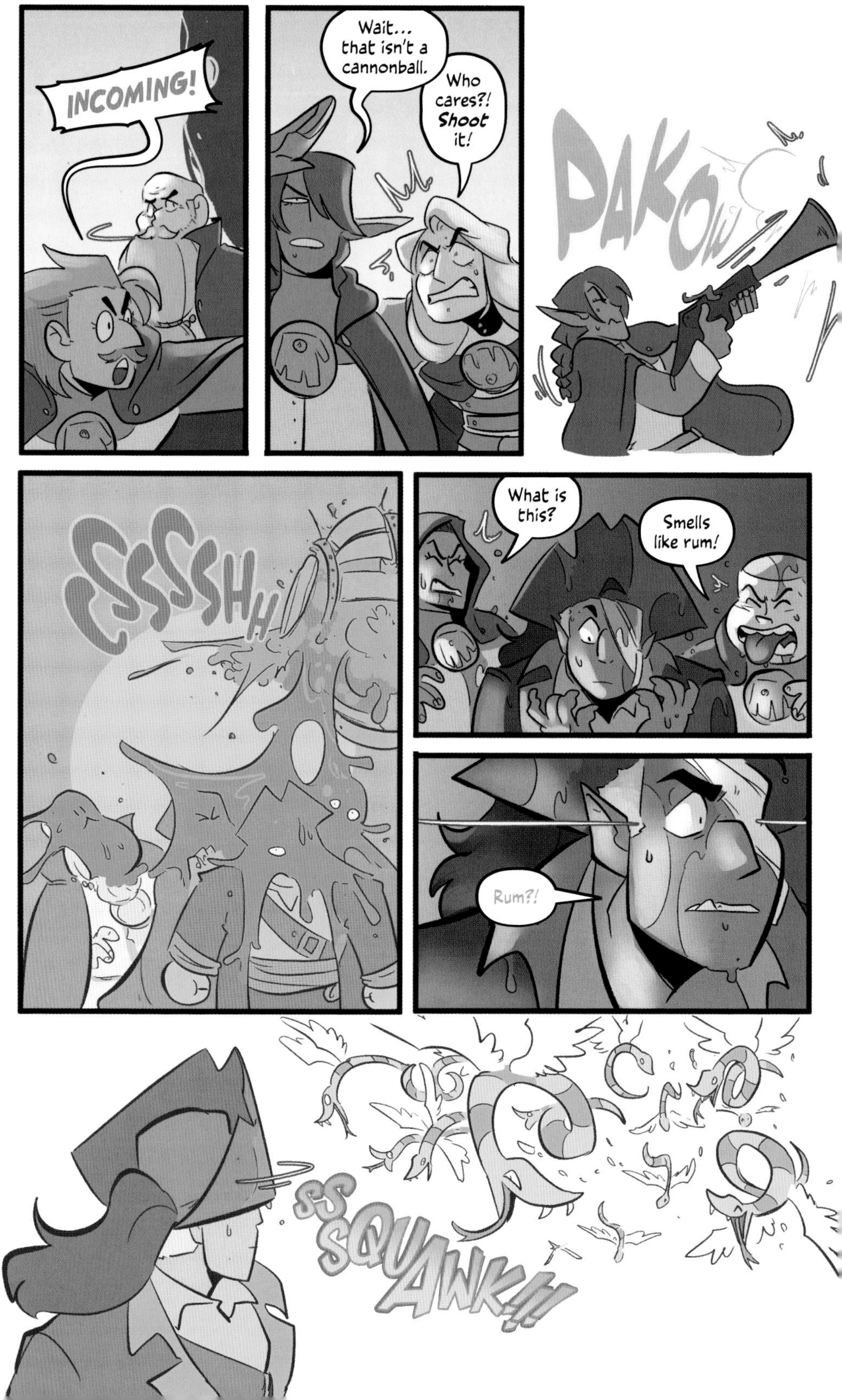
INCOMING!
Wait... that isn't a cannonball.
Who cares?! **Shoot** it!
PAKOW
SSSSHH
What is this?
Smells like rum!
Rum?!
SS SQUAWK!!!

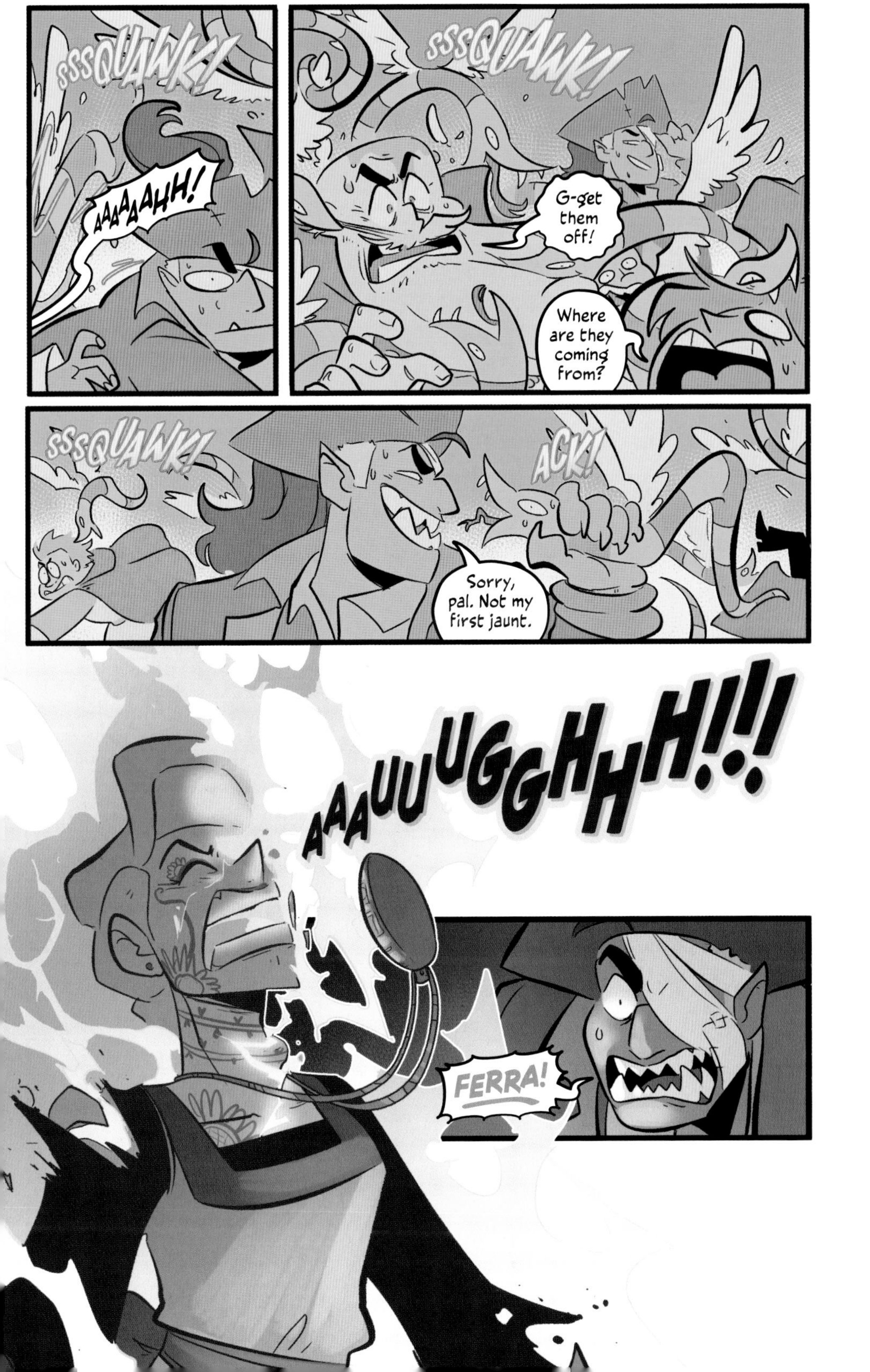
SSSQUAWK!
AAAAAHH!
SSSQUAWK!
G-get them off!
Where are they coming from?
SSSQUAWK!
ACK!
Sorry, pal. Not my first jaunt.
AAAUUUGGHHH!!!
FERRA!

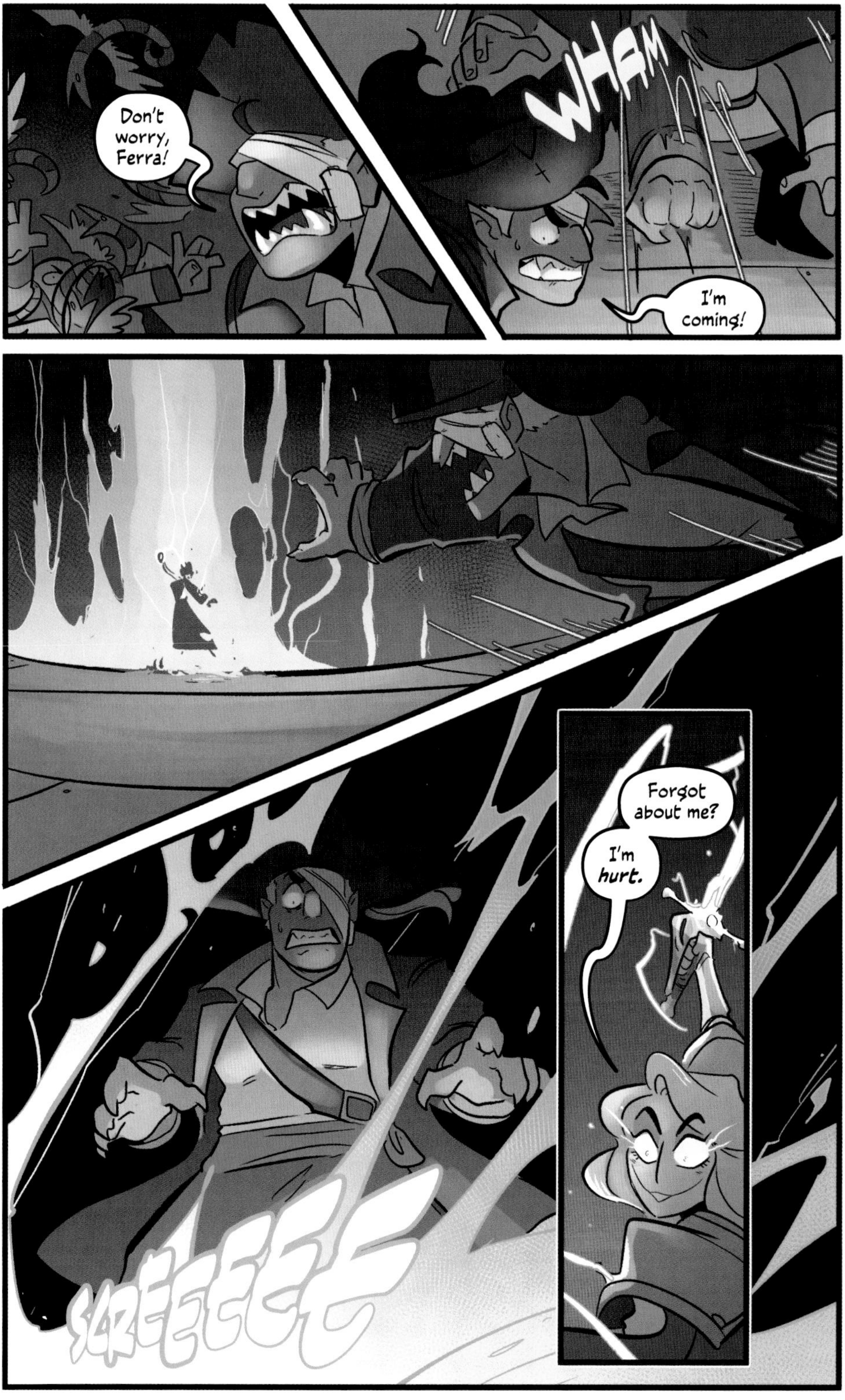
Don't worry, Ferra!
WHAM
I'm coming!
Forgot about me?
I'm *hurt.*
SCREEEEE

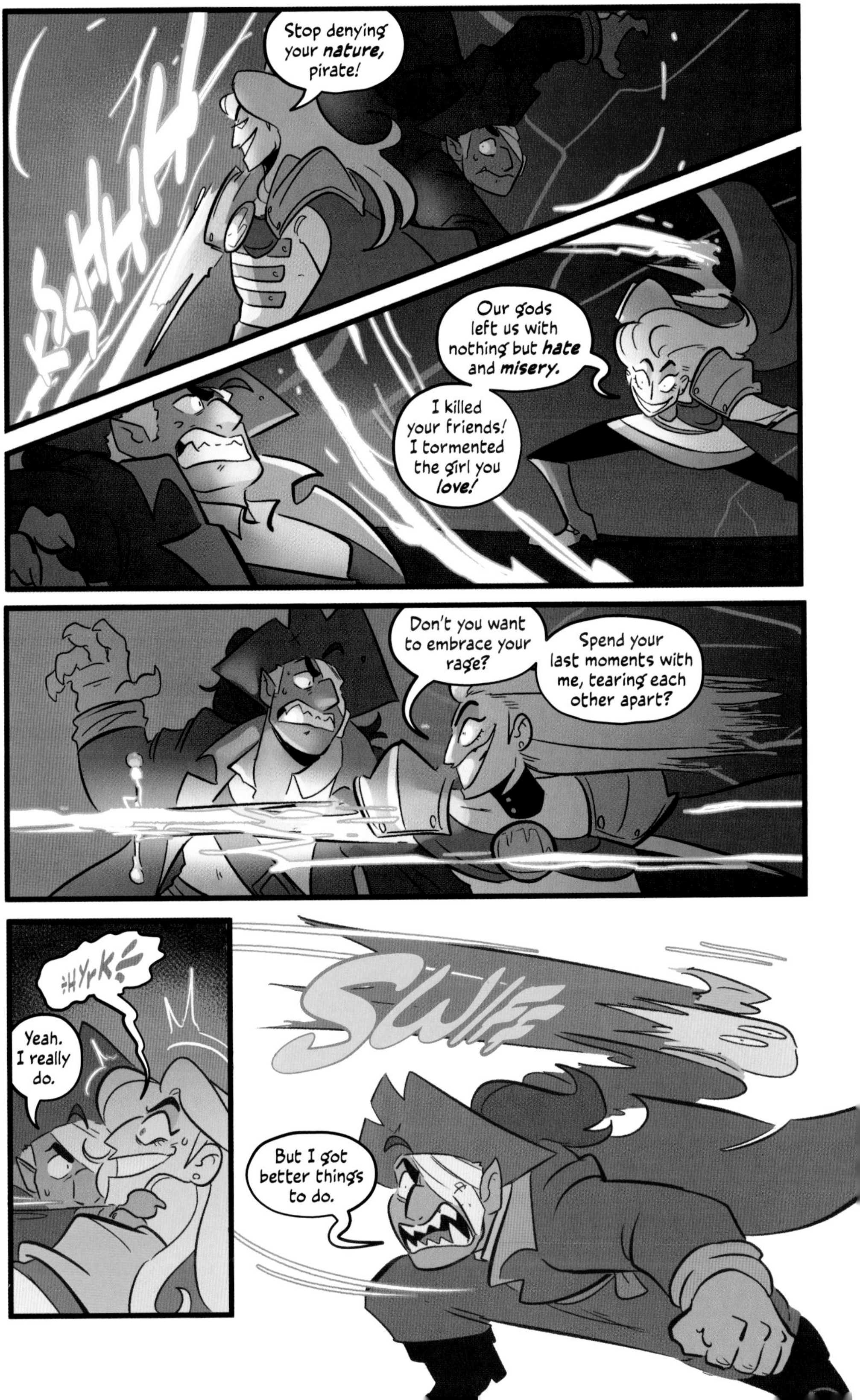
Stop denying your *nature,* pirate!
KSHHH
Our gods left us with nothing but *hate* and *misery.*
I killed your friends! I tormented the girl you *love!*
Don't you want to embrace your rage?
Spend your last moments with me, tearing each other apart?
HYRK!
Yeah. I really do.
SWIFF
But I got better things to do.

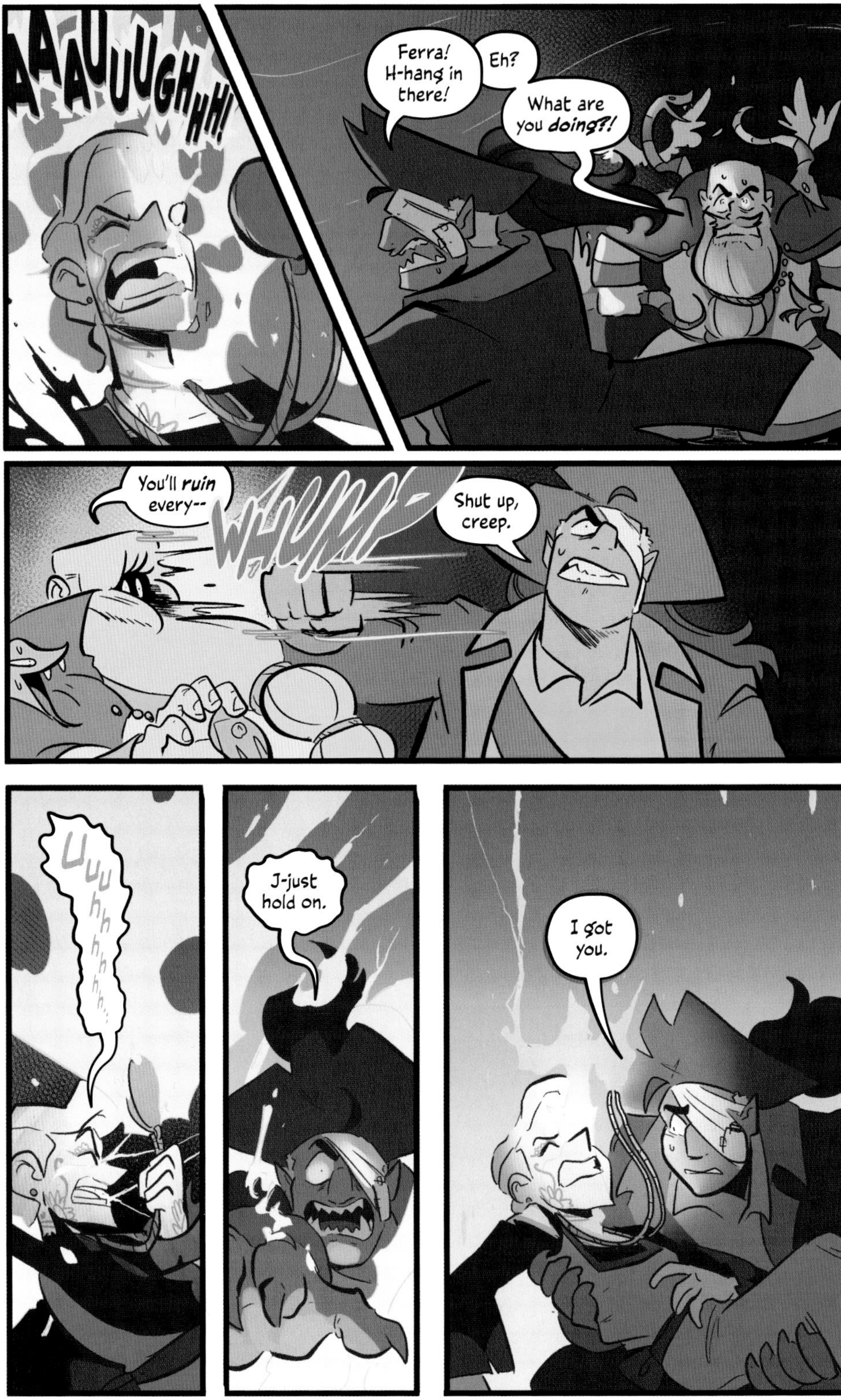
AAAUUUGHHH!
Ferra! H-hang in there!
Eh?
What are you **doing?!**
You'll **ruin** every--
WHUMP
Shut up, creep.
Uuuhhhhhh...
J-just hold on.
I got you.

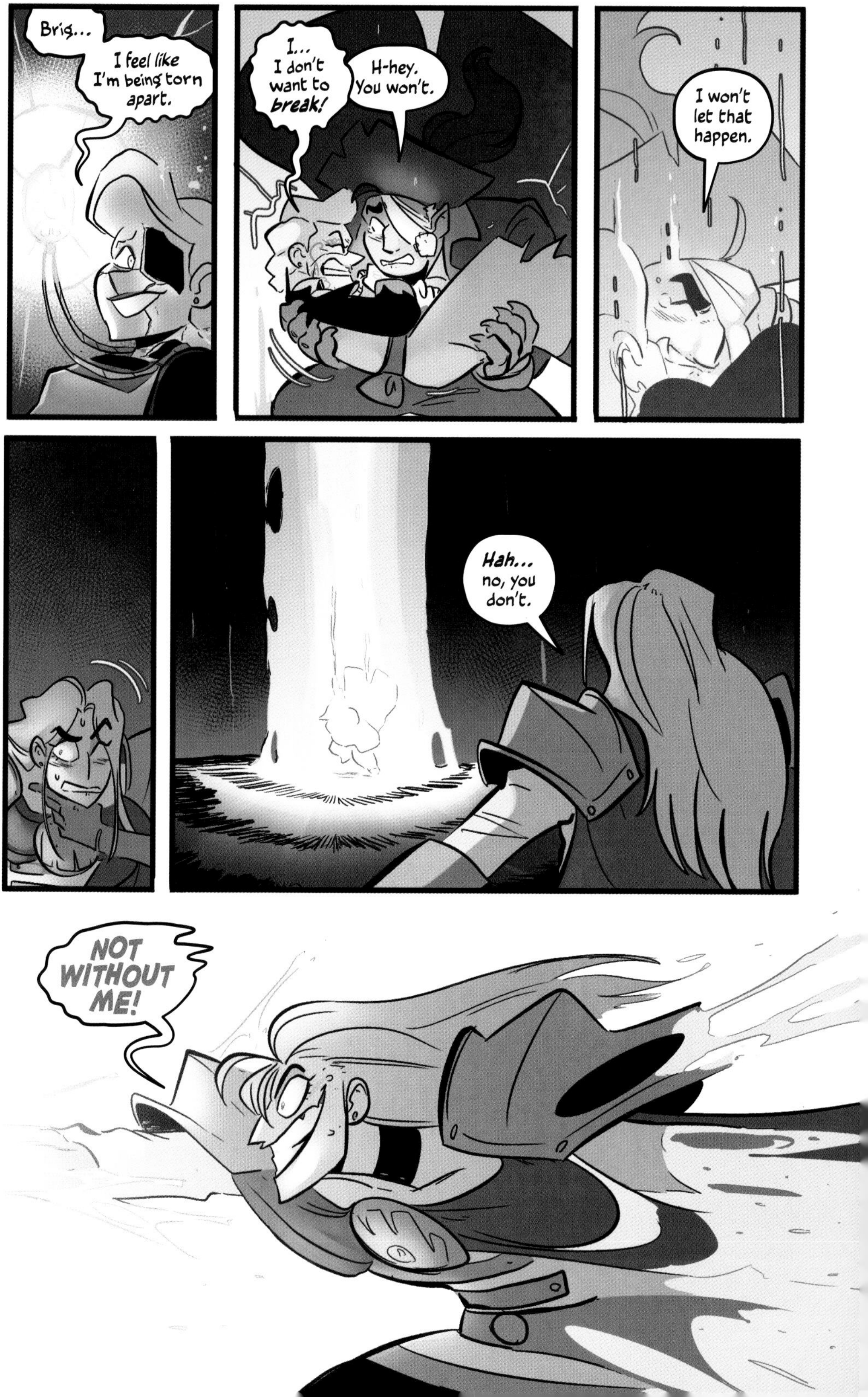
Brig...
I feel like I'm being torn apart.
I... I don't want to *break!*
H-hey. You won't.
I won't let that happen.
Hah... no, you don't.
NOT WITHOUT ME!

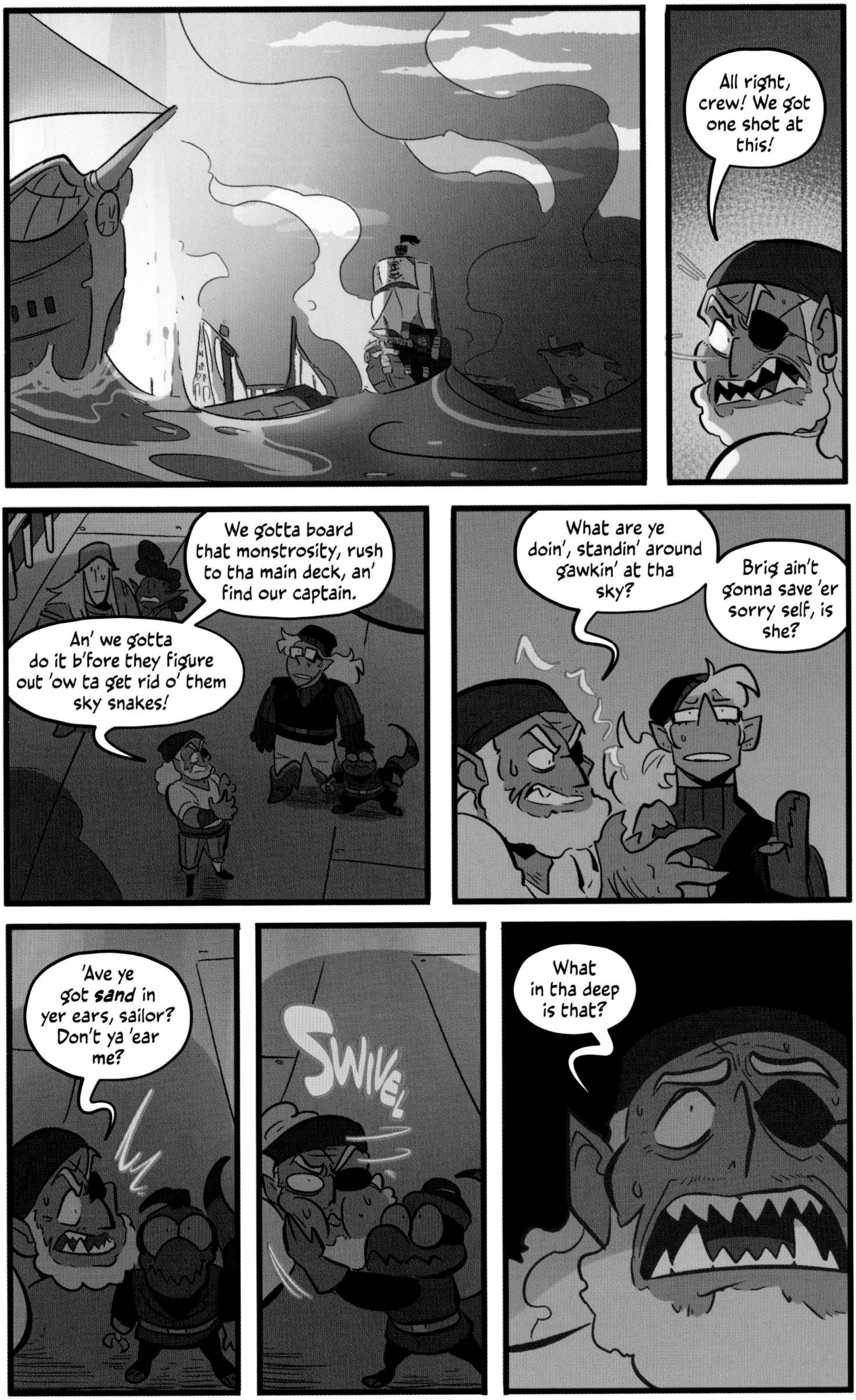
All right, crew! We got one shot at this!
We gotta board that monstrosity, rush to tha main deck, an' find our captain.
An' we gotta do it b'fore they figure out 'ow ta get rid o' them sky snakes!
What are ye doin', standin' around gawkin' at tha sky?
Brig ain't gonna save 'er sorry self, is she?
'Ave ye got **sand** in yer ears, sailor? Don't ya 'ear me?
SWIVEL
What in tha deep is that?

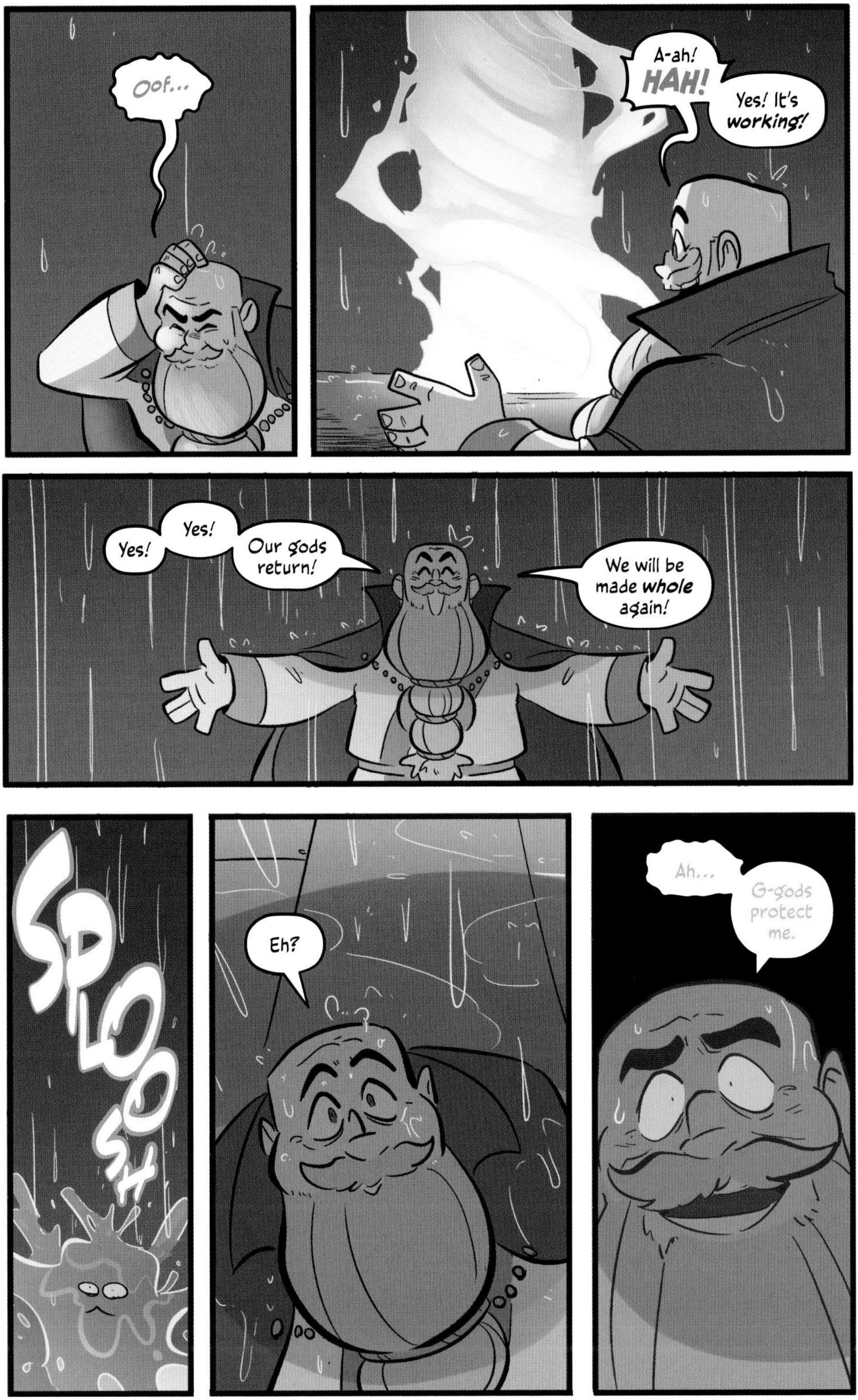
Oof...
A-ah! HAH!
Yes! It's working!
Yes!
Yes!
Our gods return!
We will be made whole again!
SPLOOSH
Eh?
Ah...
G-gods protect me.

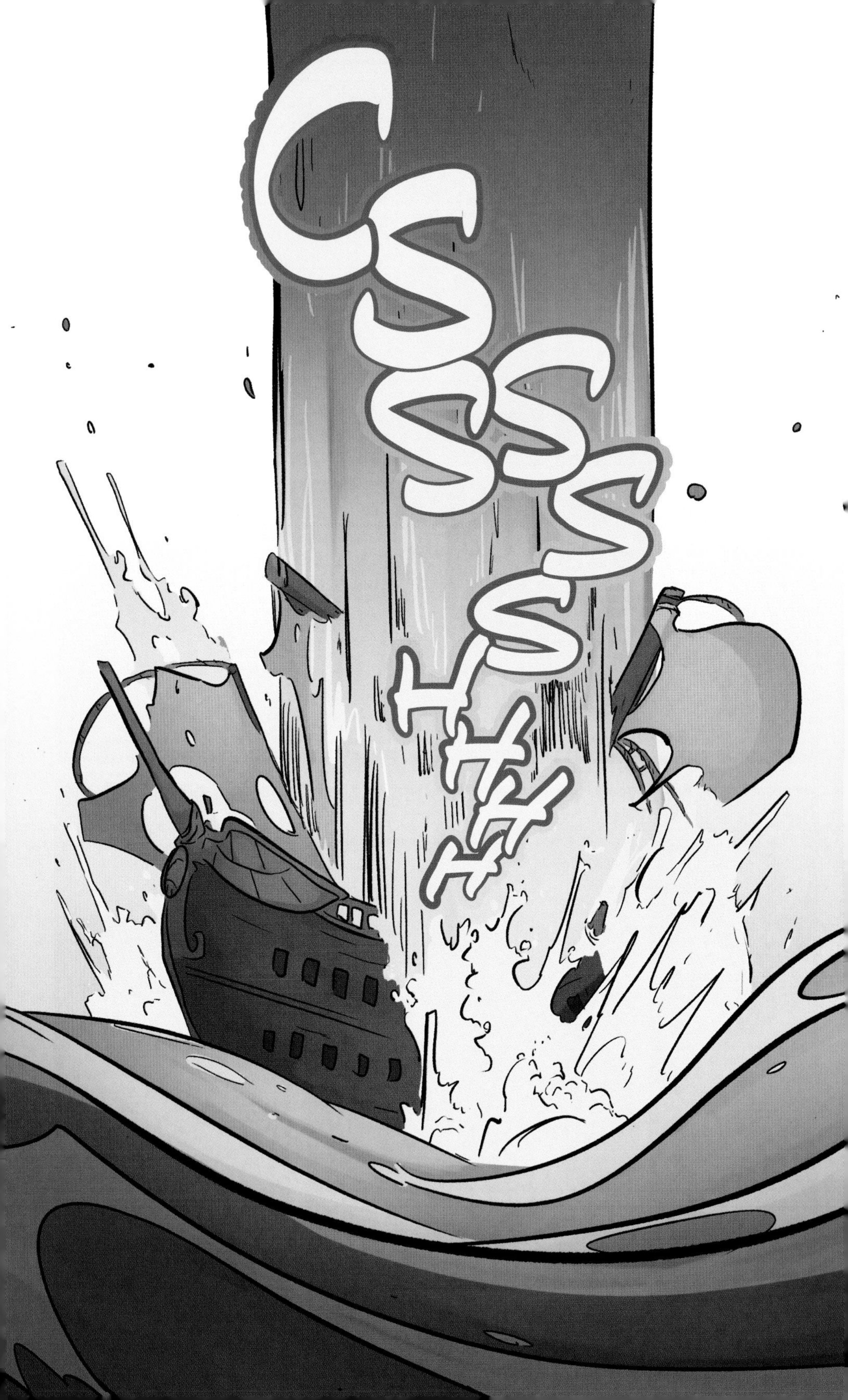
CSSSSHHHH

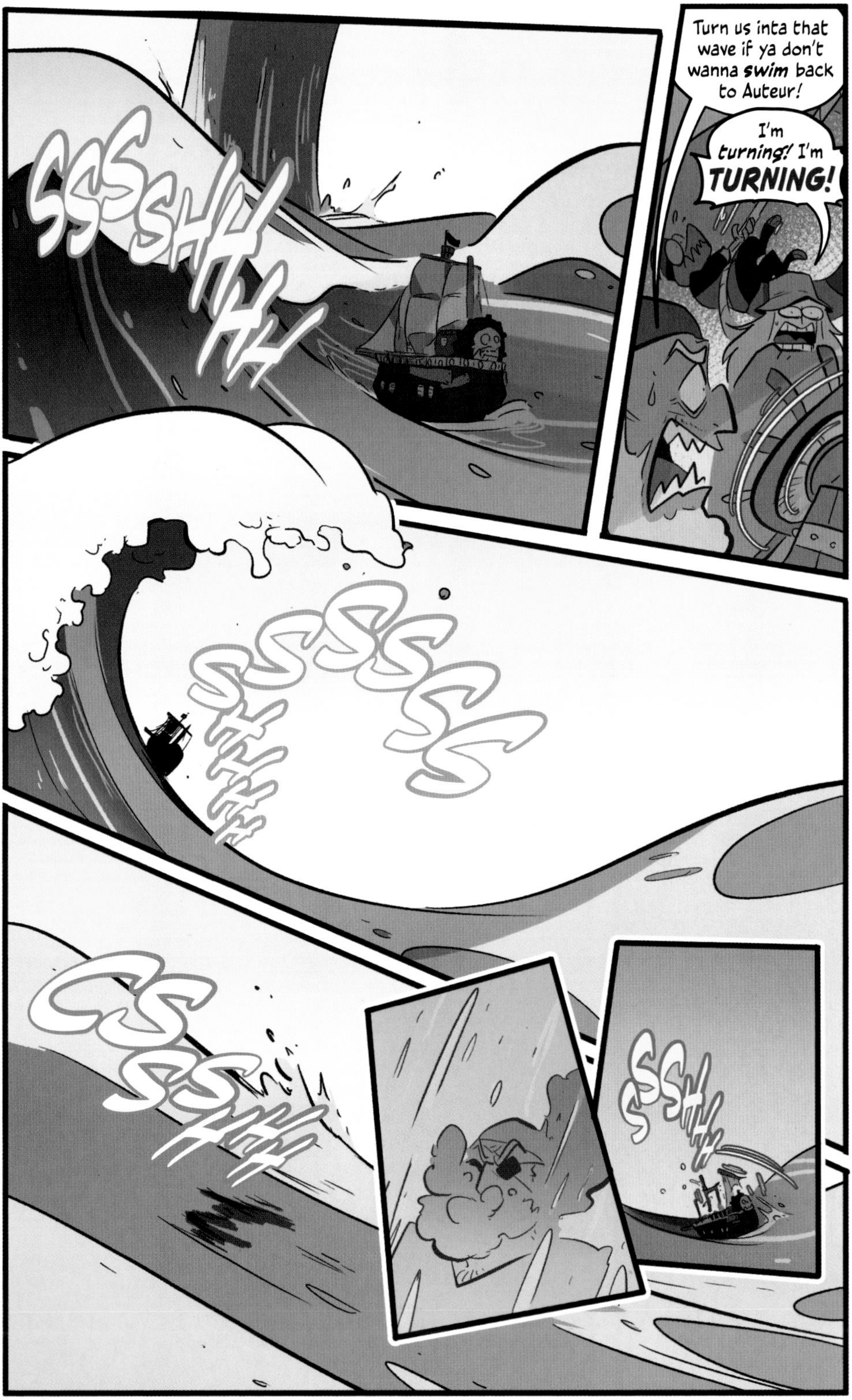
SSSSHHHHH
Turn us inta that wave if ya don't wanna swim back to Auteur!
I'm turning! I'm TURNING!
SSSSSSHHHHH
CSSSHHH
SSHHH

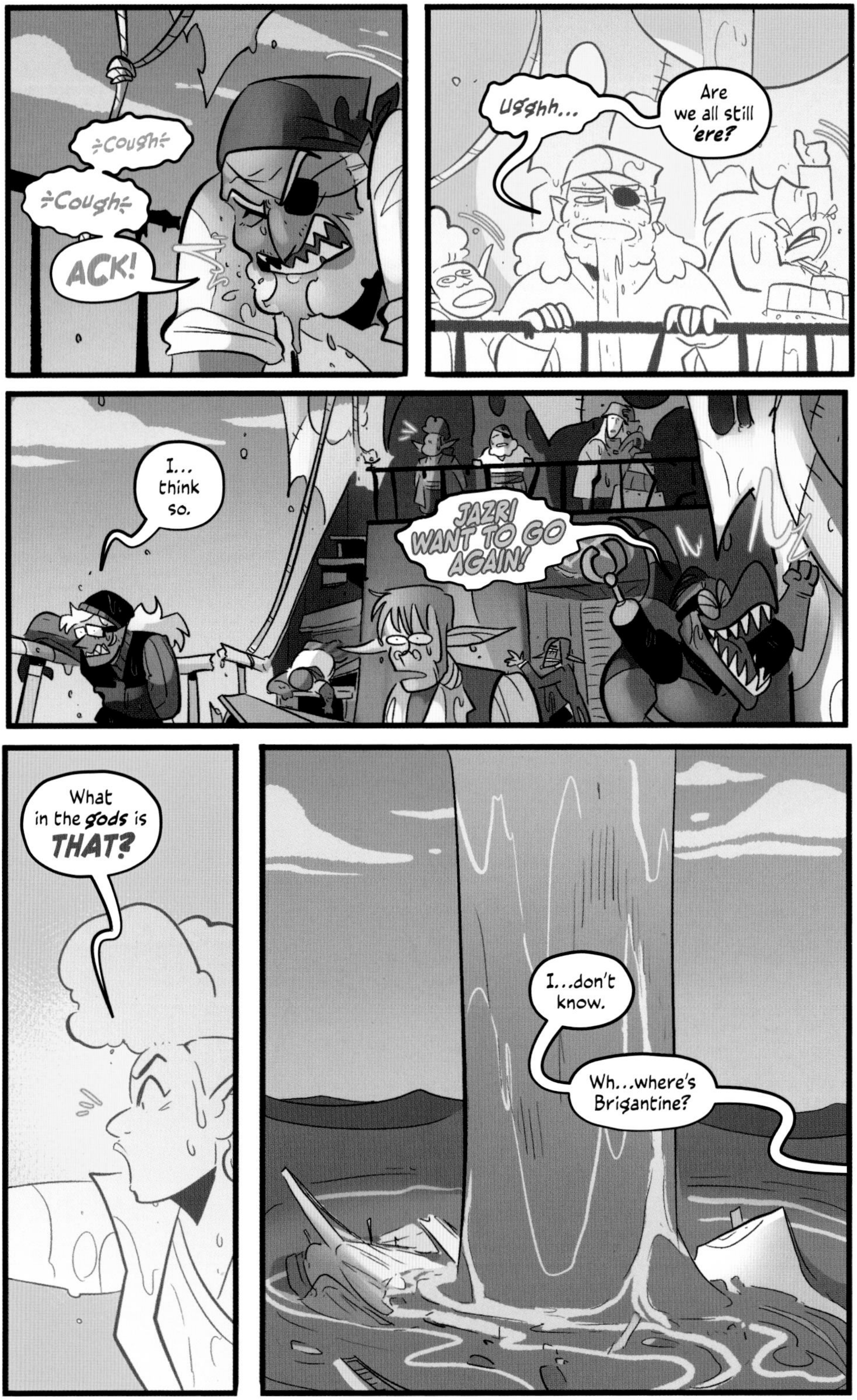

÷Cough÷
÷Cough÷
ACK!
Ugghh...
Are we all still 'ere?
I... think so.
JAZRI WANT TO GO AGAIN!
What in the *gods* is **THAT?**
I...don't know.
Wh...where's Brigantine?

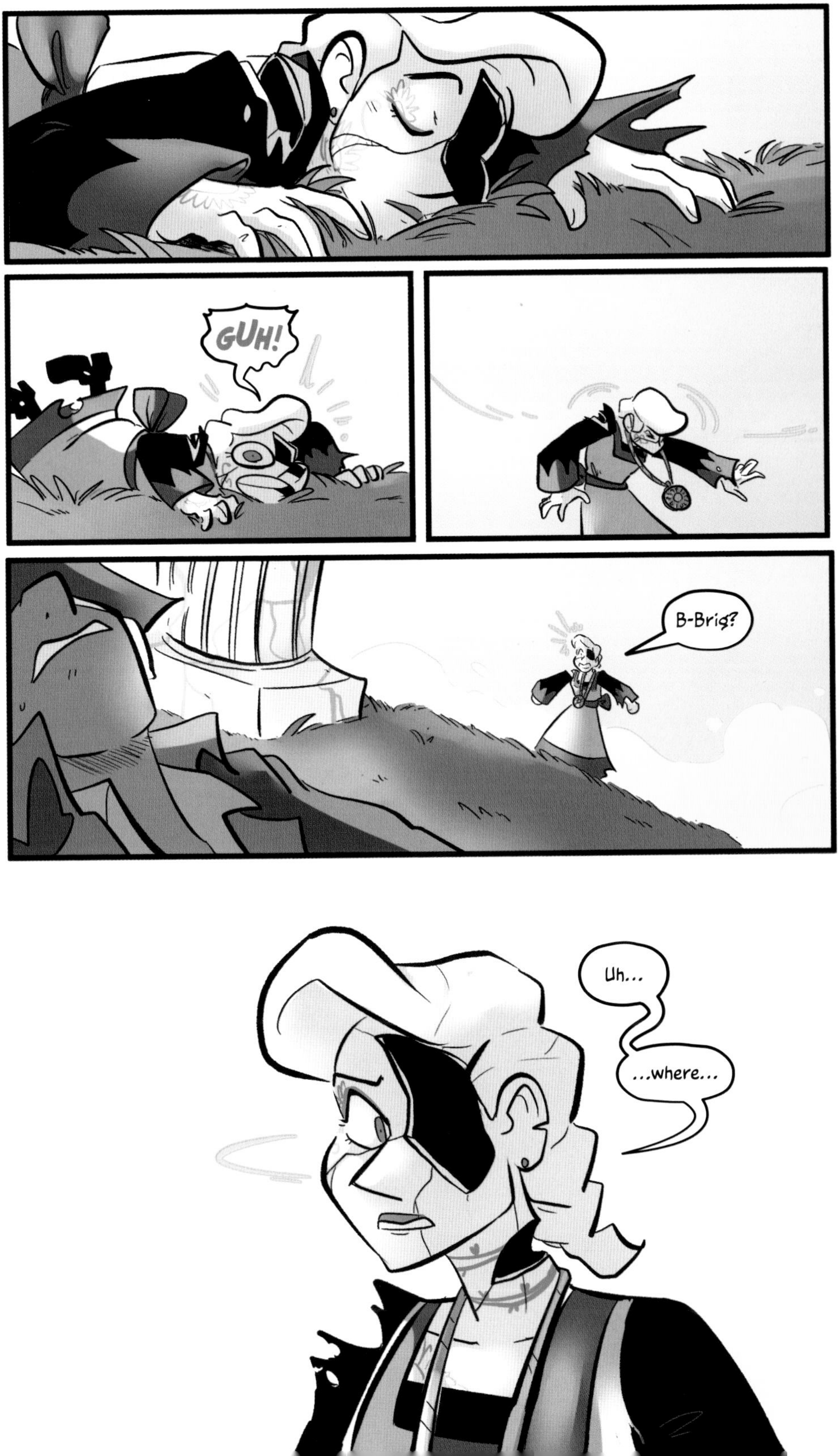
GUH!
B-Brig?
Uh...
...where...

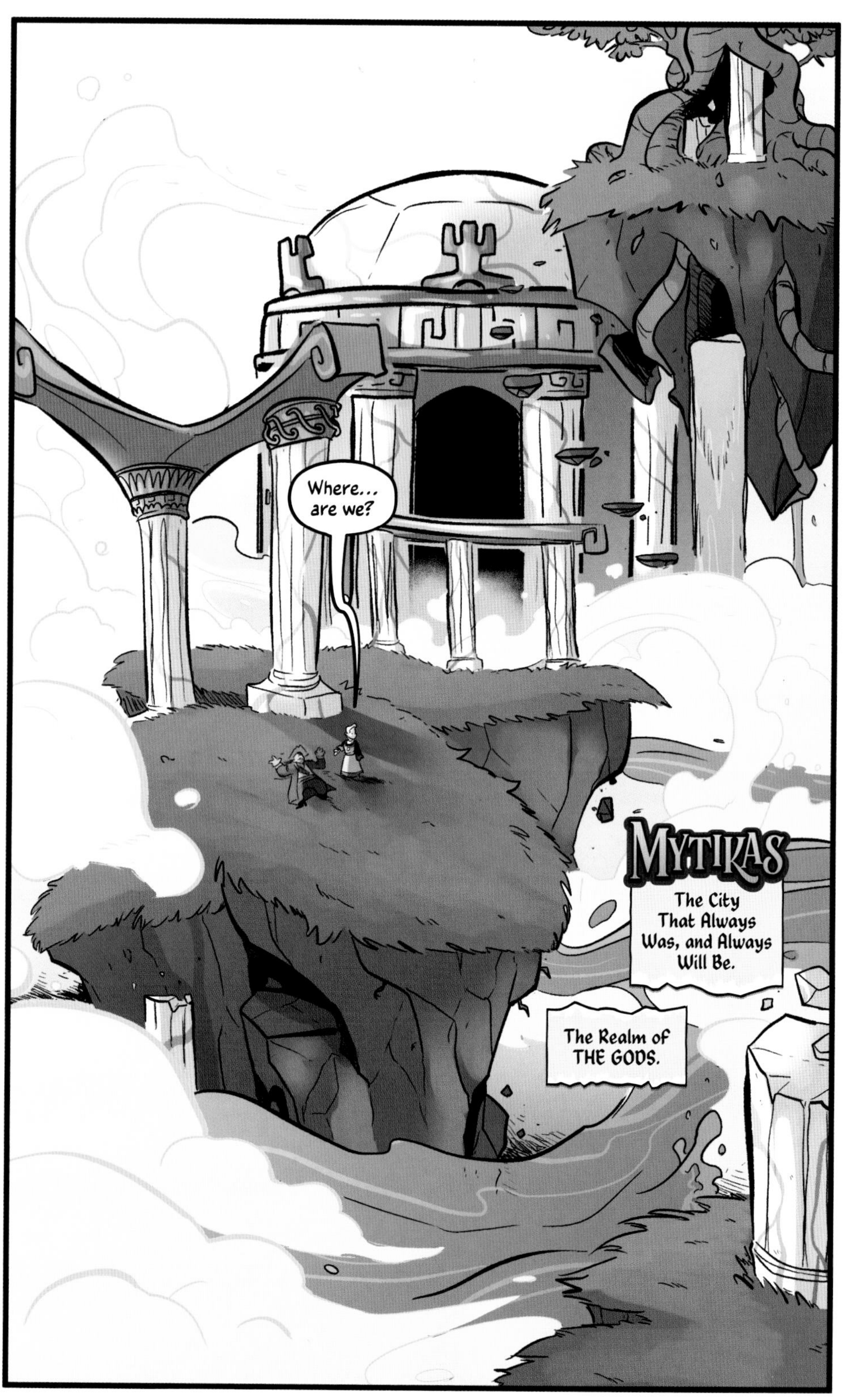
Where... are we?
MYTIKAS
The City That Always Was, and Always Will Be.
The Realm of THE GODS.

Chapter 8

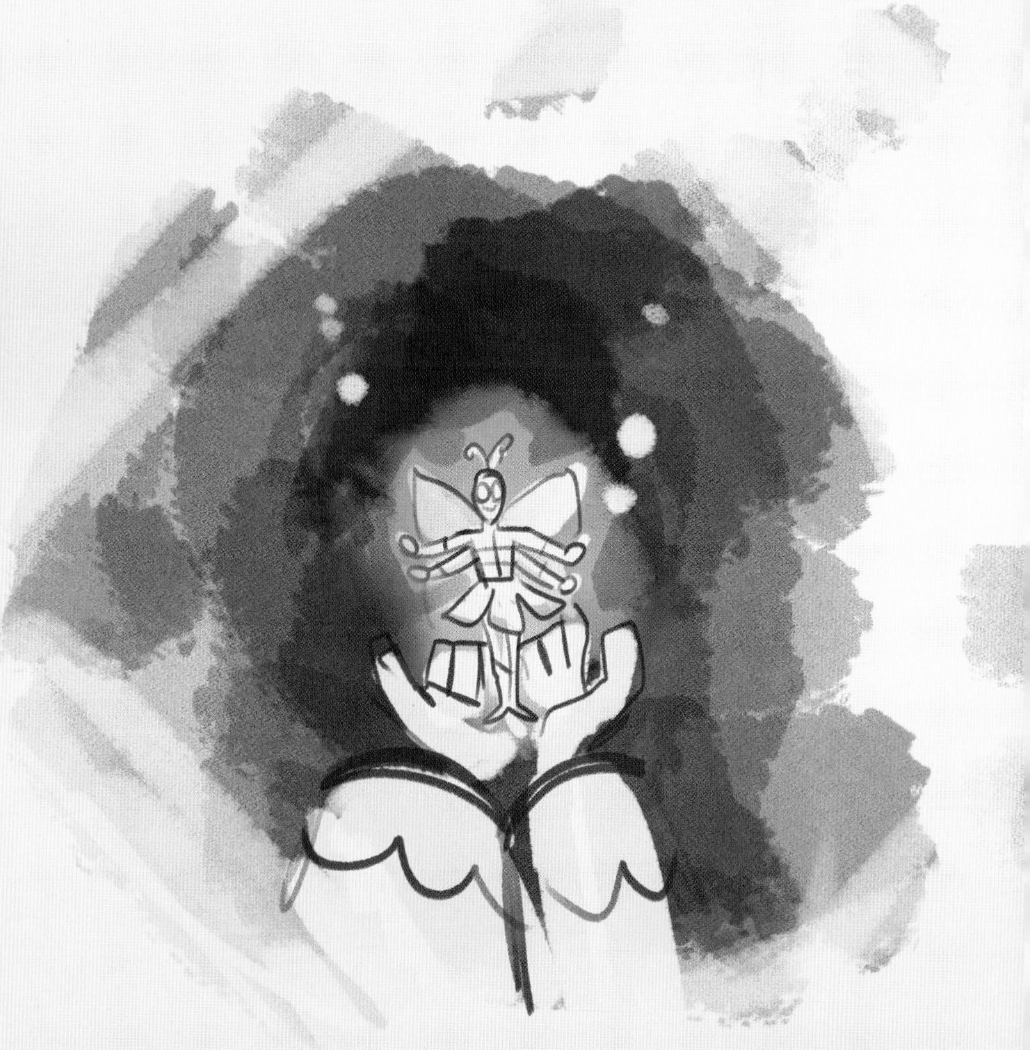

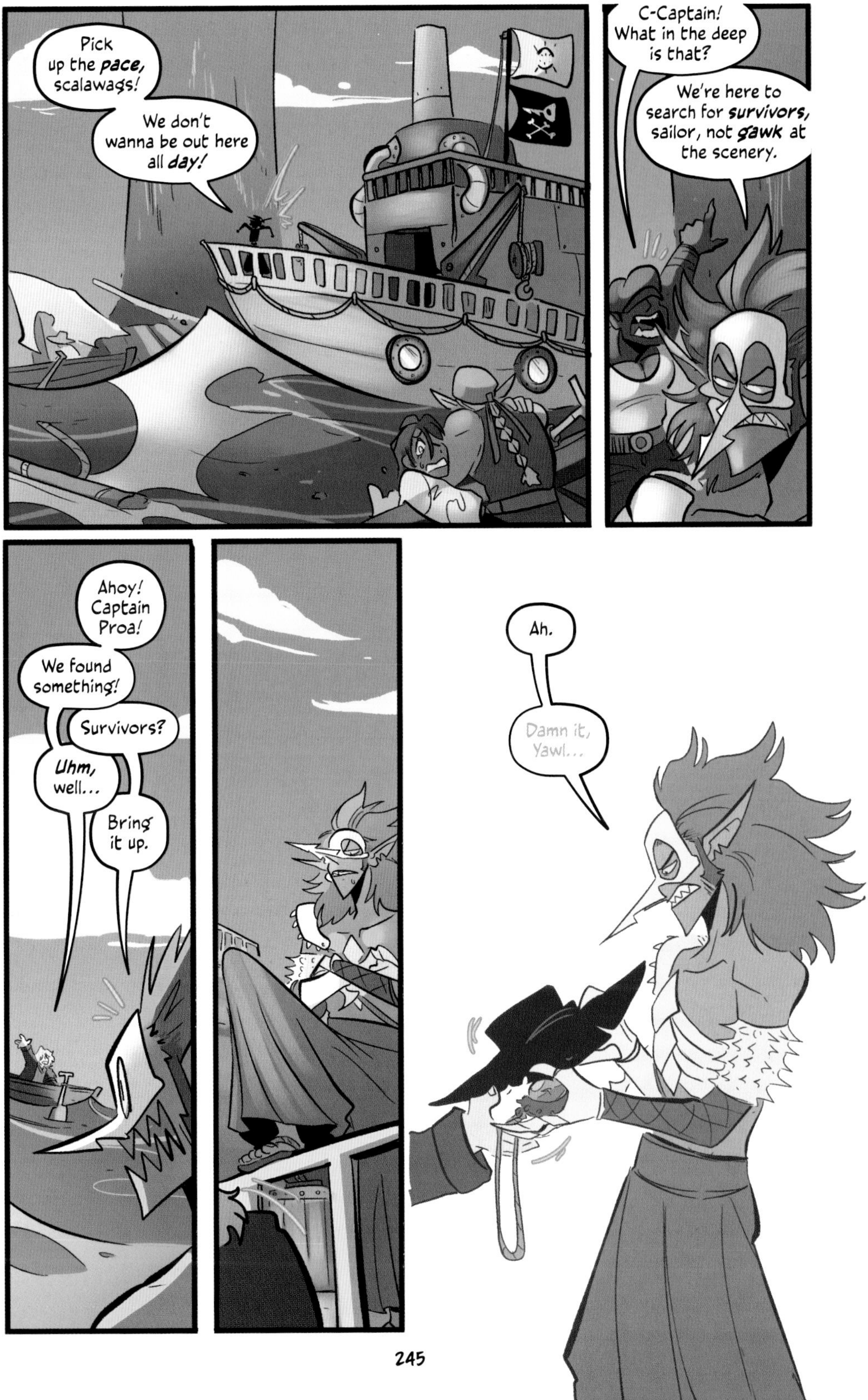

Pick up the pace, scalawags!
We don't wanna be out here all day!
C-Captain! What in the deep is that?
We're here to search for survivors, sailor, not gawk at the scenery.
Ahoy! Captain Proa!
We found something!
Survivors?
Uhm, well...
Bring it up.
Ah.
Damn it, Yawl...

Shame.

She was a good captain.

It's... not *fair*.

If she hadn't been helping those *traitors,* she--

One more word and you walk the plank.

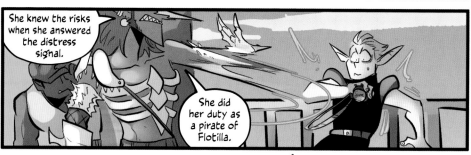

She knew the risks when she answered the distress signal.

She did her duty as a pirate of Flotilla.

Now then, the *Girona's* still out here somewhere.

We've still got *our* duty.

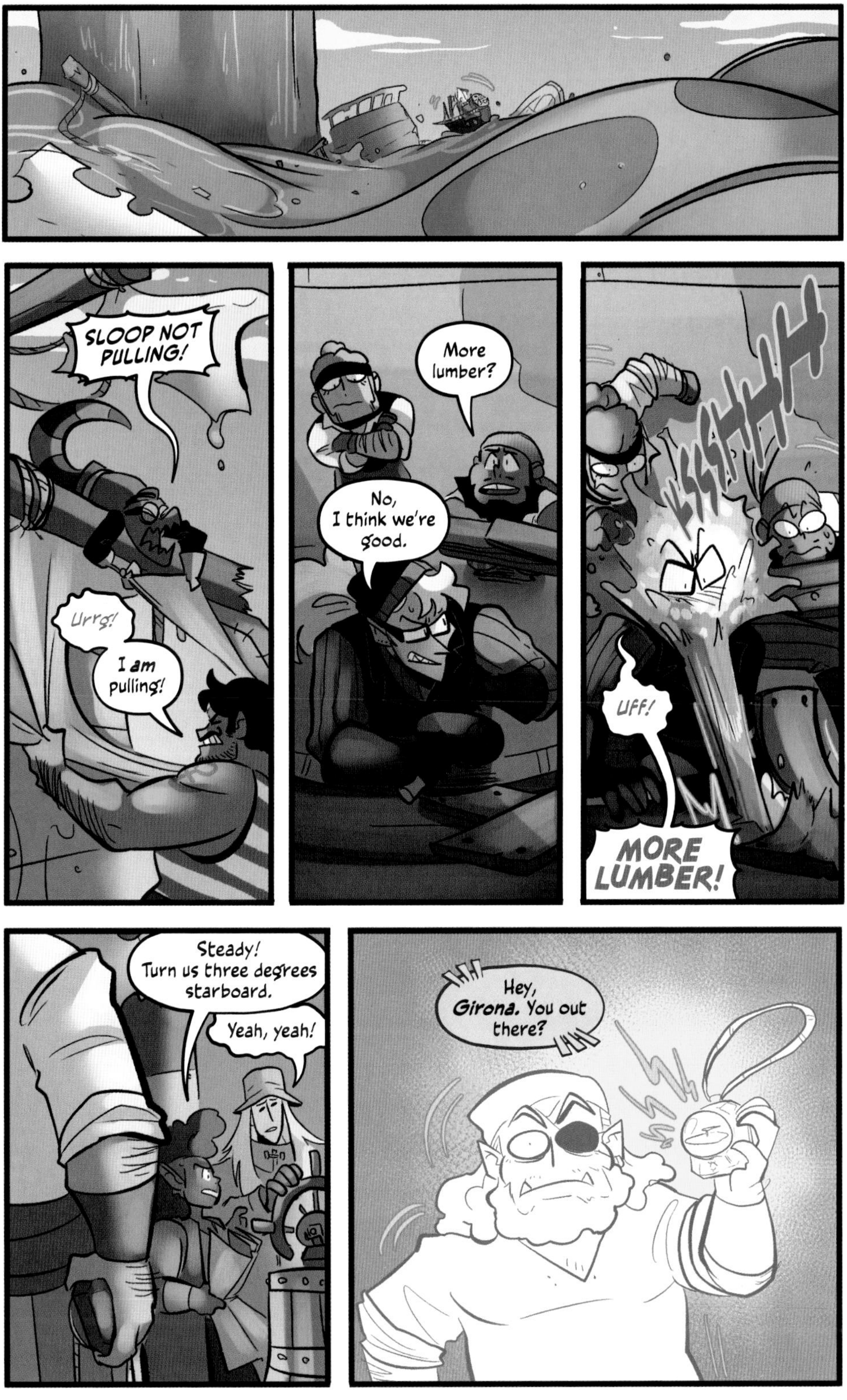
SLOOP NOT PULLING!
Urrg!
I am pulling!
More lumber?
No, I think we're good.
KSSSHHHH
UFF!
MORE LUMBER!
Steady! Turn us three degrees starboard.
Yeah, yeah!
Hey, Girona. You out there?

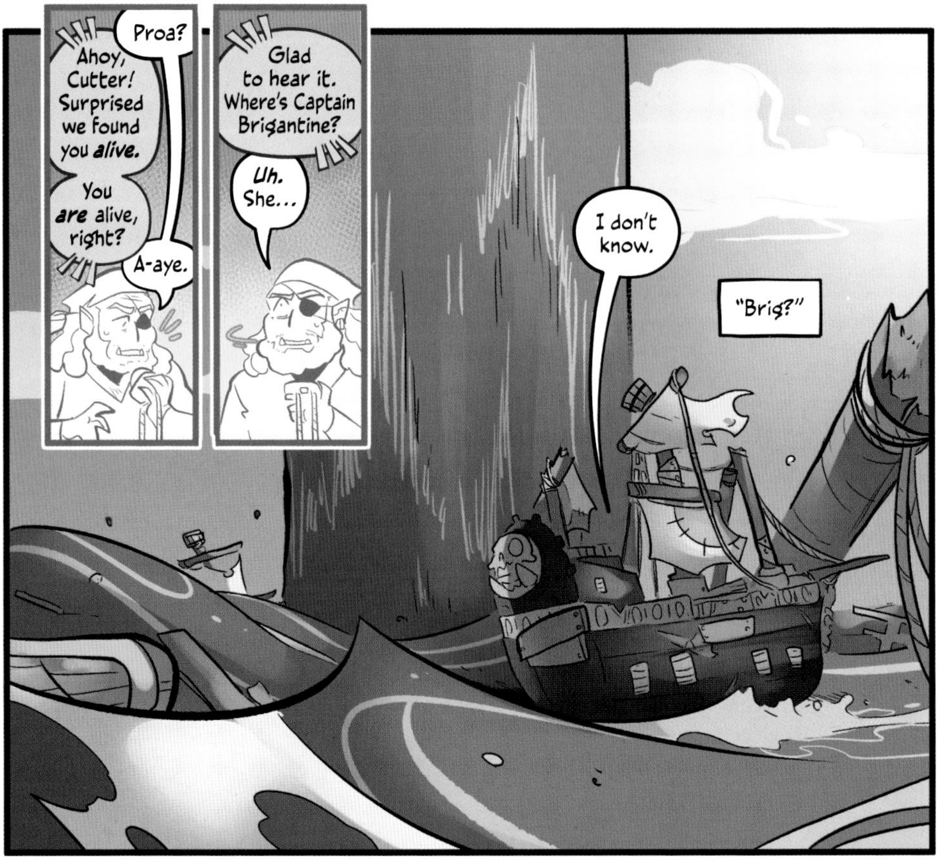
Ahoy, Cutter! Surprised we found you alive.
Proa?
You are alive, right?
A-aye.
Glad to hear it. Where's Captain Brigantine?
Uh. She...
I don't know.
"Brig?"

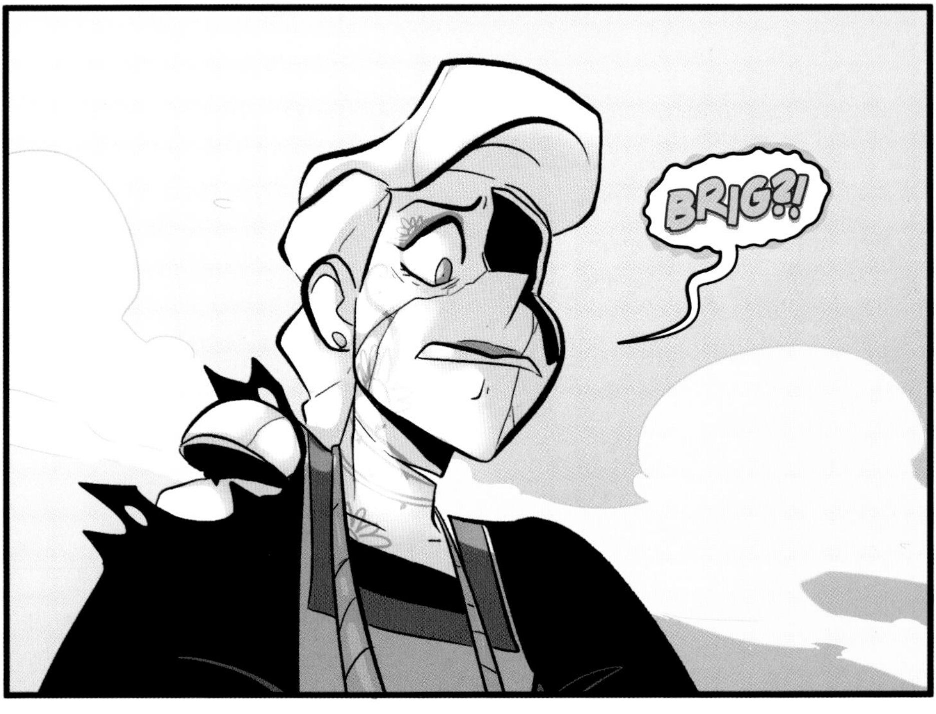
BRIG?!

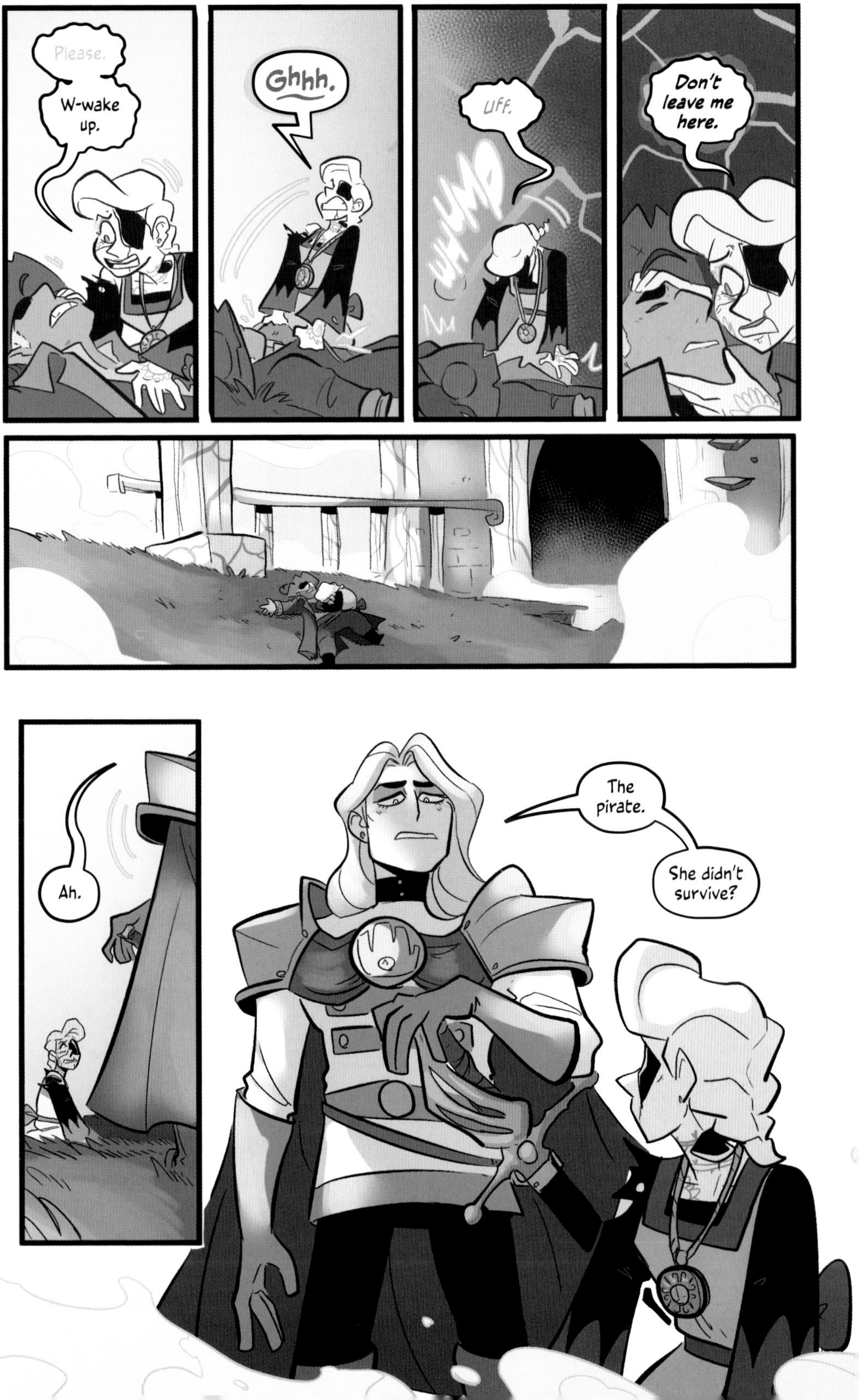
Please.
W-wake up.
Ghhh.
WHUMP
Uff.
Don't leave me here.
Ah.
The pirate.
She didn't survive?

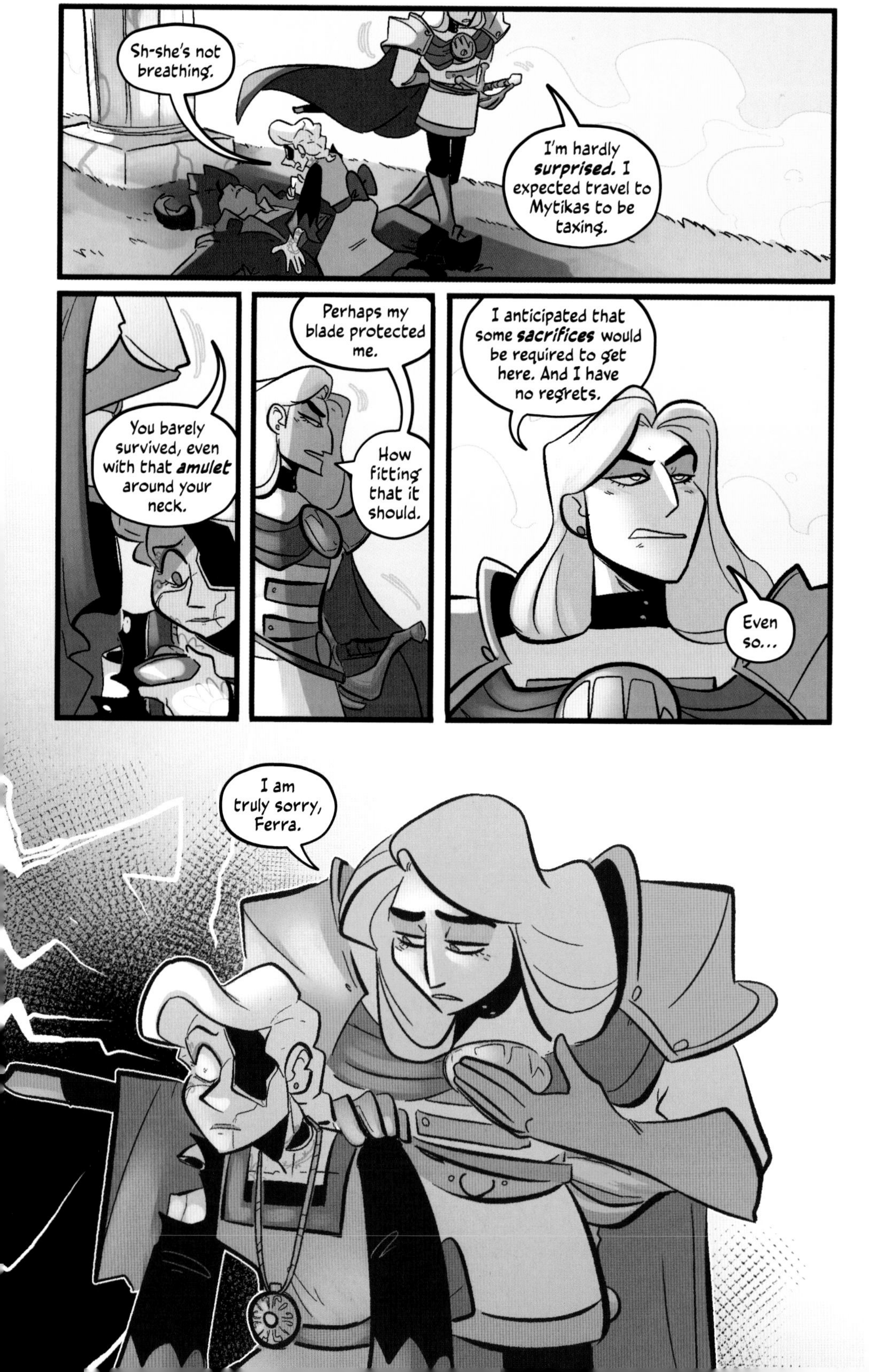
Sh-she's not breathing.
I'm hardly surprised. I expected travel to Mytikas to be taxing.
You barely survived, even with that amulet around your neck.
Perhaps my blade protected me.
How fitting that it should.
I anticipated that some sacrifices would be required to get here. And I have no regrets.
Even so...
I am truly sorry, Ferra.

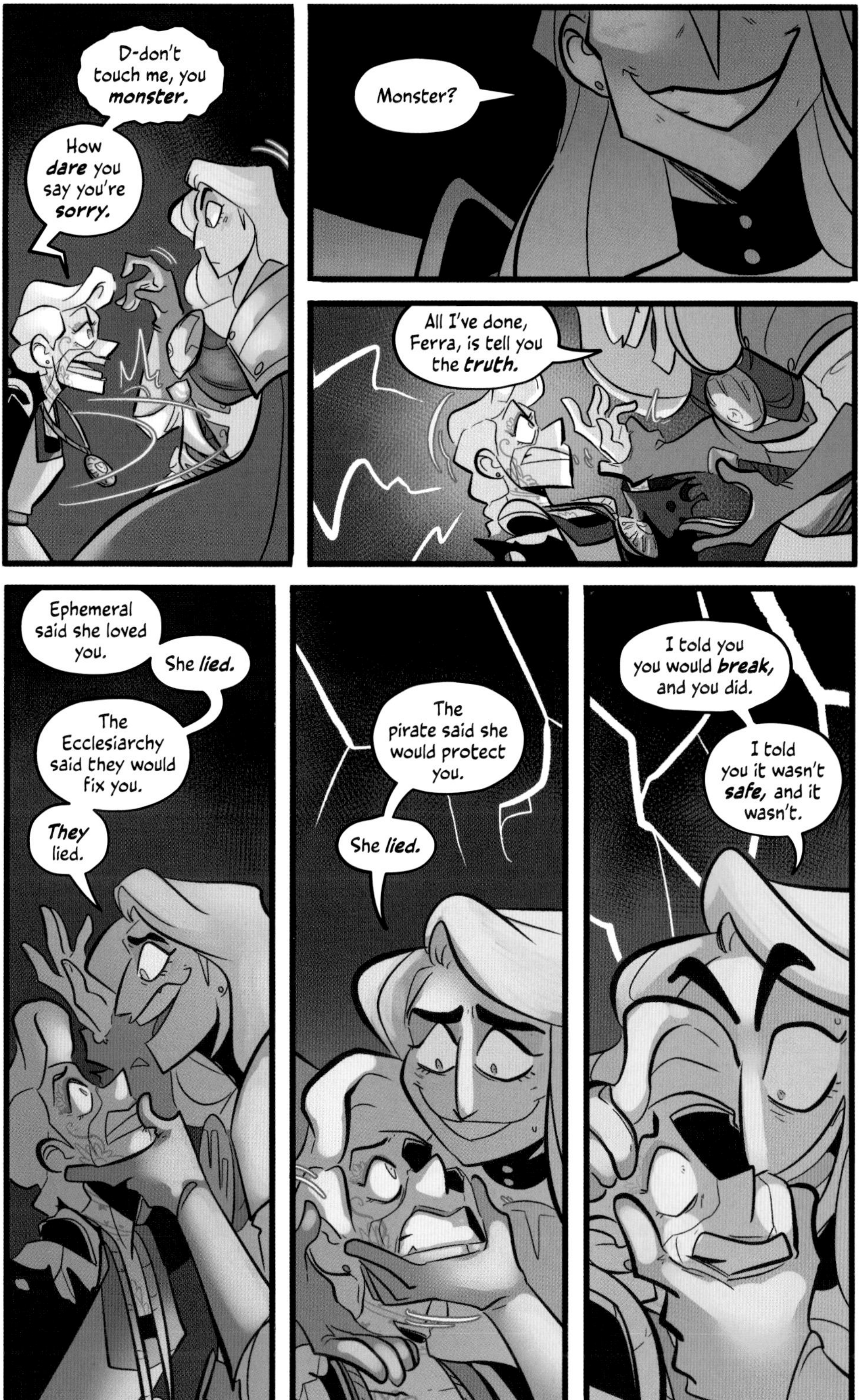
D-don't touch me, you monster.
How dare you say you're sorry.
Monster?
All I've done, Ferra, is tell you the truth.
Ephemeral said she loved you.
She lied.
The Ecclesiarchy said they would fix you.
They lied.
The pirate said she would protect you.
She lied.
I told you you would break, and you did.
I told you it wasn't safe, and it wasn't.

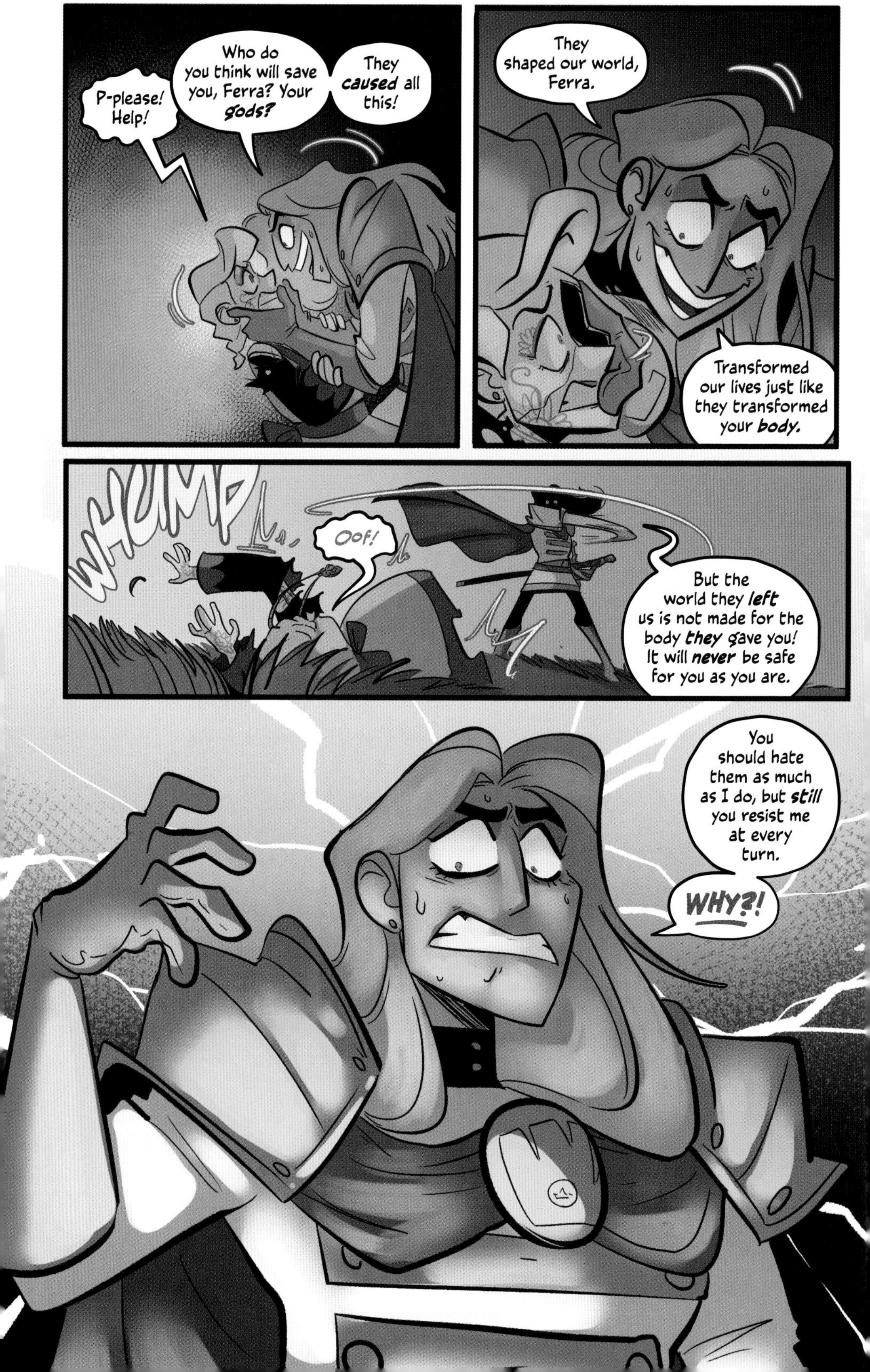

P-please! Help!
Who do you think will save you, Ferra? Your *gods?*
They *caused* all this!
They shaped our world, Ferra.
Transformed our lives just like they transformed your *body.*
WHUMP
Oof!
But the world they *left* us is not made for the body *they* gave you! It will *never* be safe for you as you are.
You should hate them as much as I do, but *still* you resist me at every turn.
WHY?!

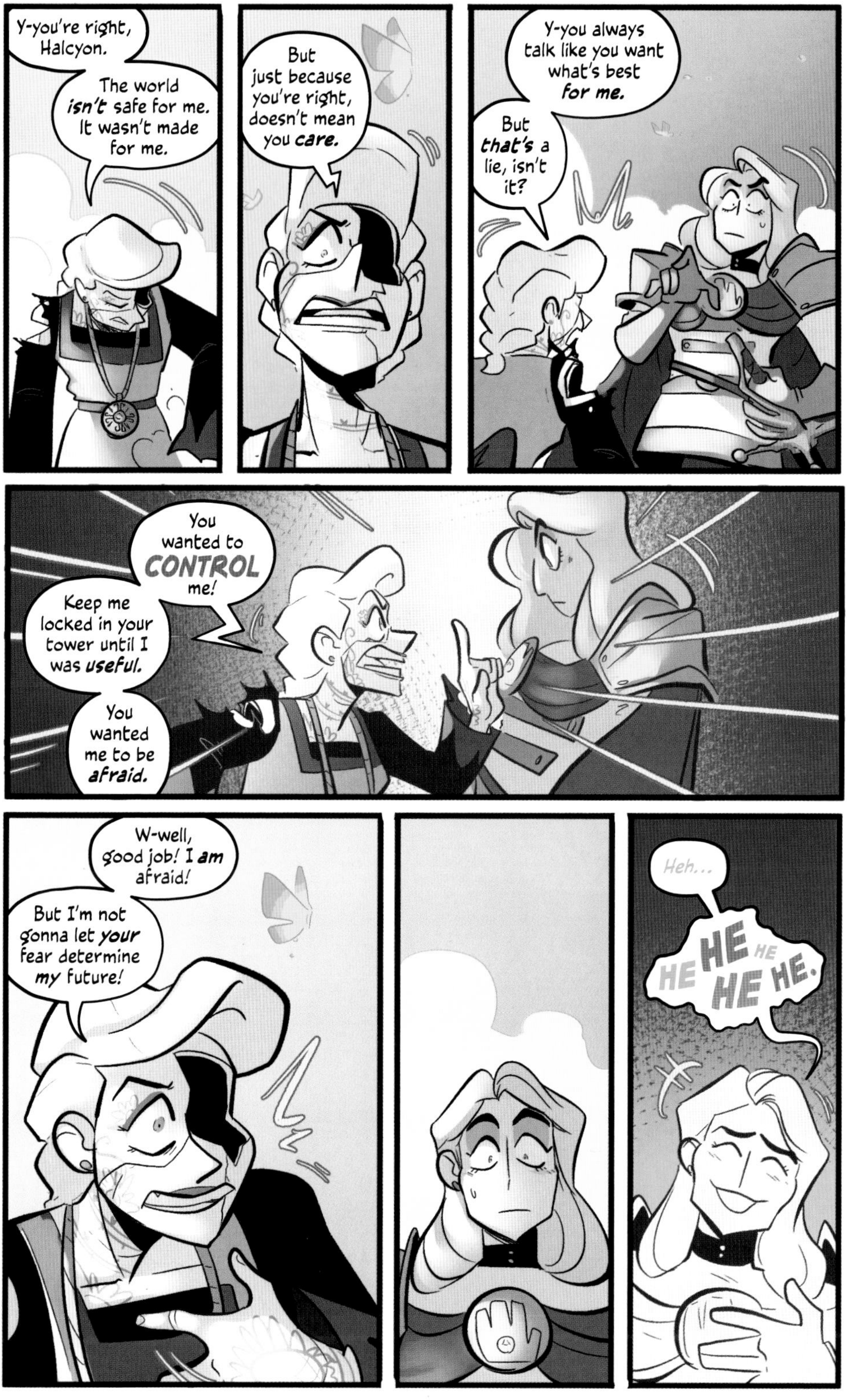
Y-you're right, Halcyon.
The world isn't safe for me. It wasn't made for me.
But just because you're right, doesn't mean you care.
Y-you always talk like you want what's best for me.
But that's a lie, isn't it?
You wanted to CONTROL me!
Keep me locked in your tower until I was useful.
You wanted me to be afraid.
W-well, good job! I am afraid!
But I'm not gonna let your fear determine my future!
Heh...
HE HE HE HE HE.

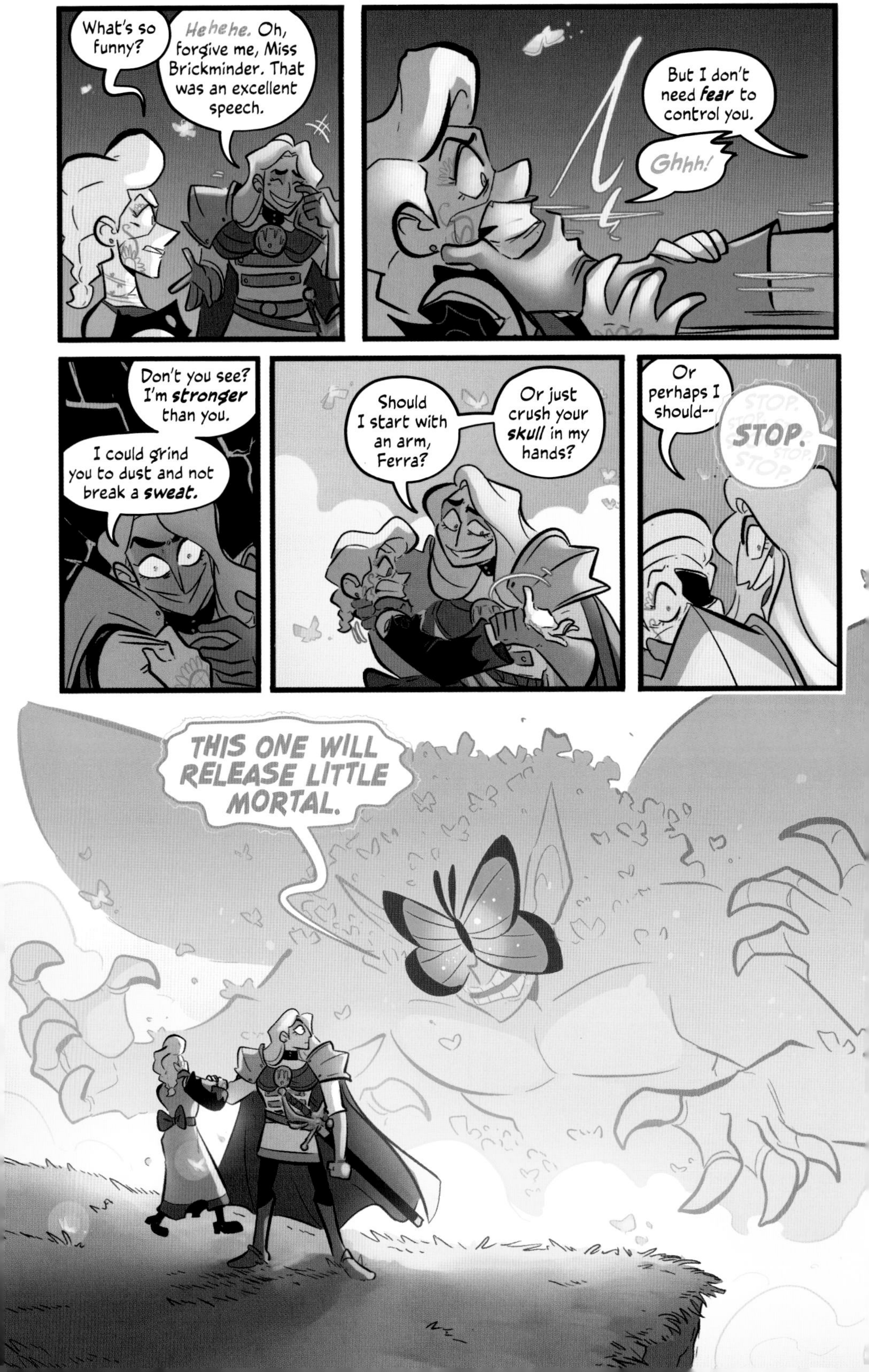
What's so funny?
Hehehe. Oh, forgive me, Miss Brickminder. That was an excellent speech.
But I don't need fear to control you.
Ghhh!
Don't you see? I'm stronger than you.
I could grind you to dust and not break a sweat.
Should I start with an arm, Ferra?
Or just crush your skull in my hands?
Or perhaps I should--
STOP. STOP. STOP. STOP. STOP.
STOP.
THIS ONE WILL RELEASE LITTLE MORTAL.

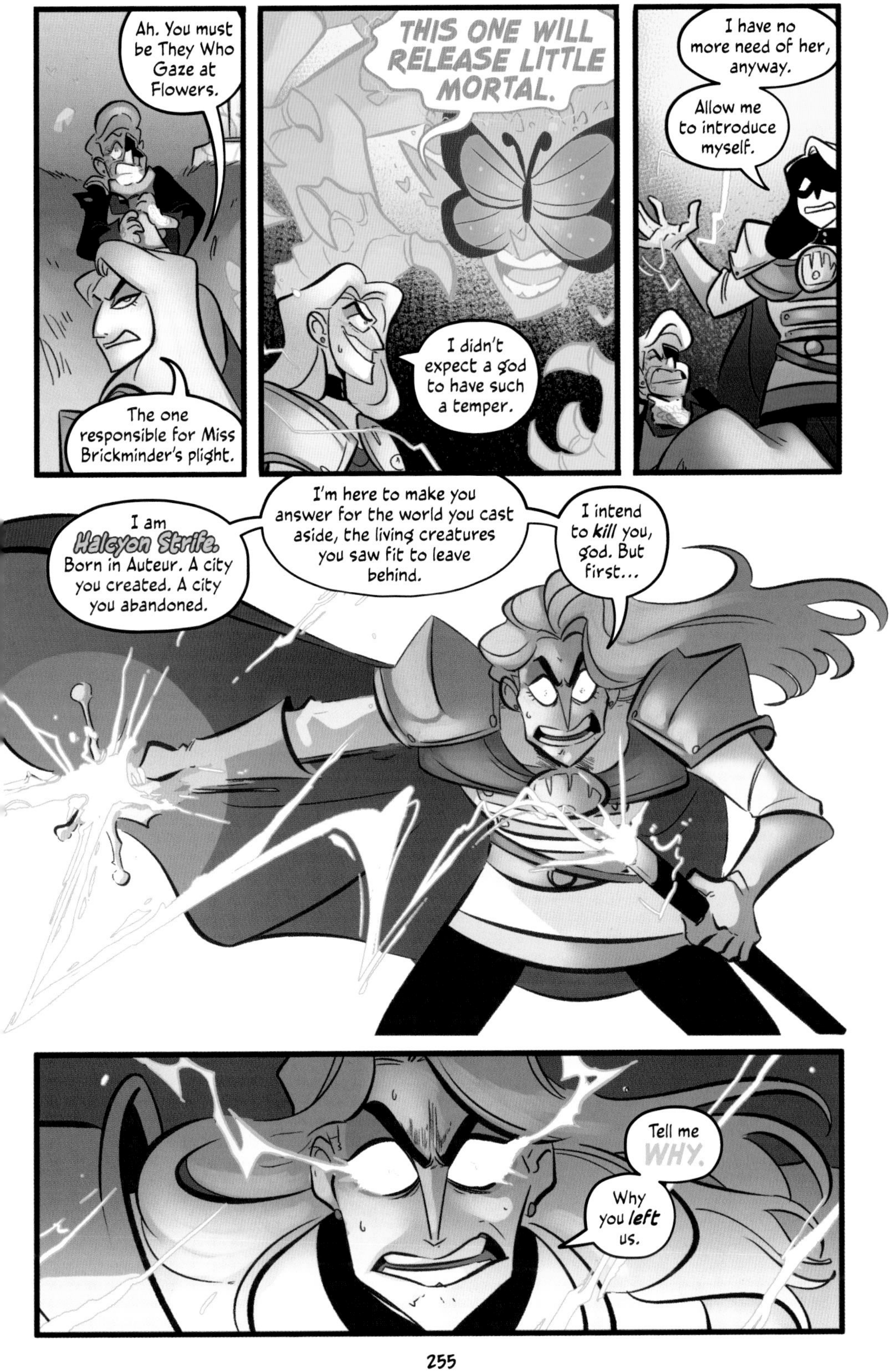
Ah. You must be They Who Gaze at Flowers.
The one responsible for Miss Brickminder's plight.
THIS ONE WILL RELEASE LITTLE MORTAL.
I didn't expect a god to have such a temper.
I have no more need of her, anyway.
Allow me to introduce myself.
I am Halcyon Strife. Born in Auteur. A city you created. A city you abandoned.
I'm here to make you answer for the world you cast aside, the living creatures you saw fit to leave behind.
I intend to kill you, god. But first...
Tell me WHY.
Why you left us.

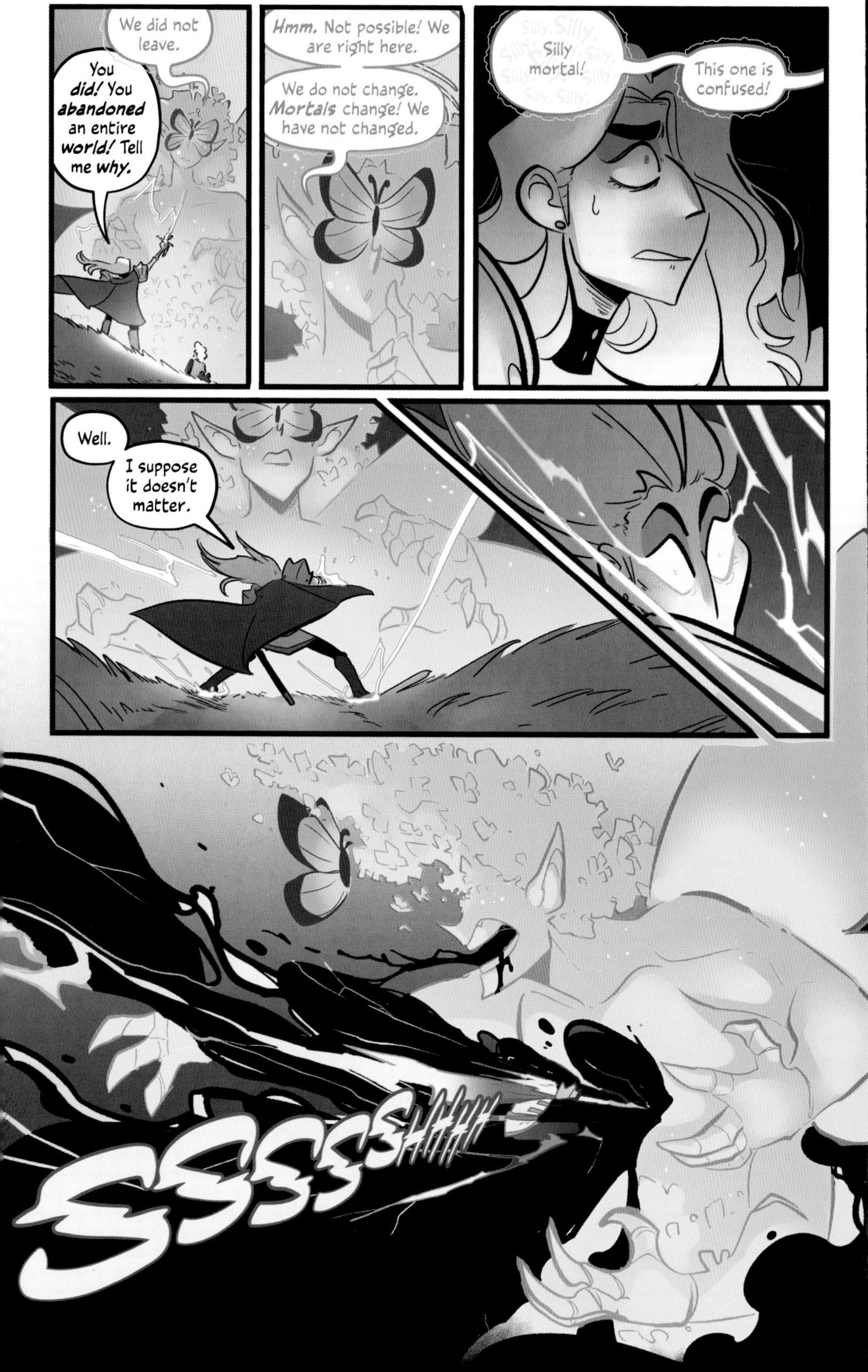
We did not leave.
You *did!* You **abandoned** an entire **world!** Tell me **why.**
Hmm. Not possible! We are right here.
We do not change. ***Mortals*** change! We have not changed.
Silly. Silly.
Silly mortal!
This one is confused!
Well.
I suppose it doesn't matter.
SSSSSHHHH

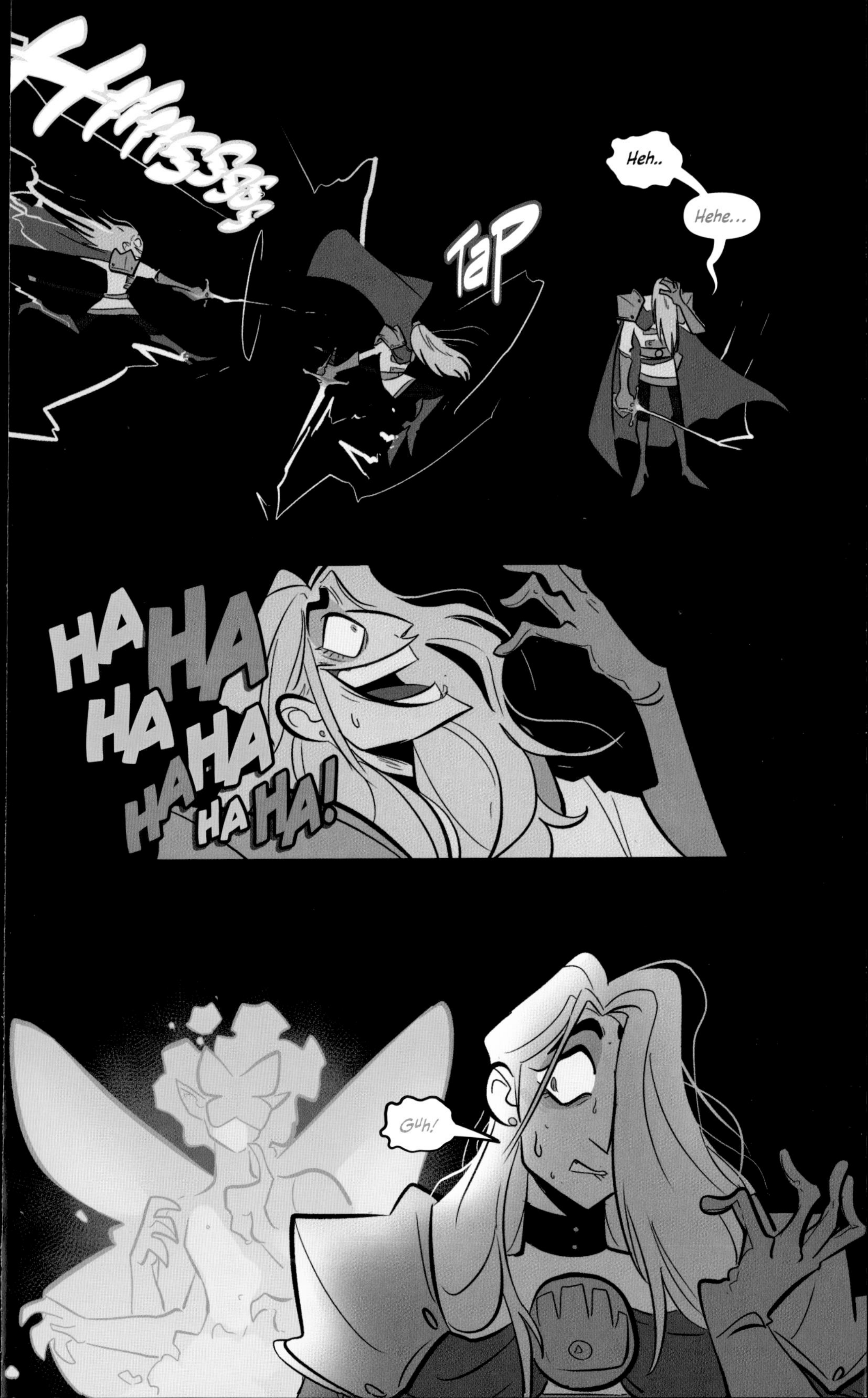
HHISSSS
TAP
Heh..
Hehe...
HAHA HAHA HAHA HAHA!
Guh!

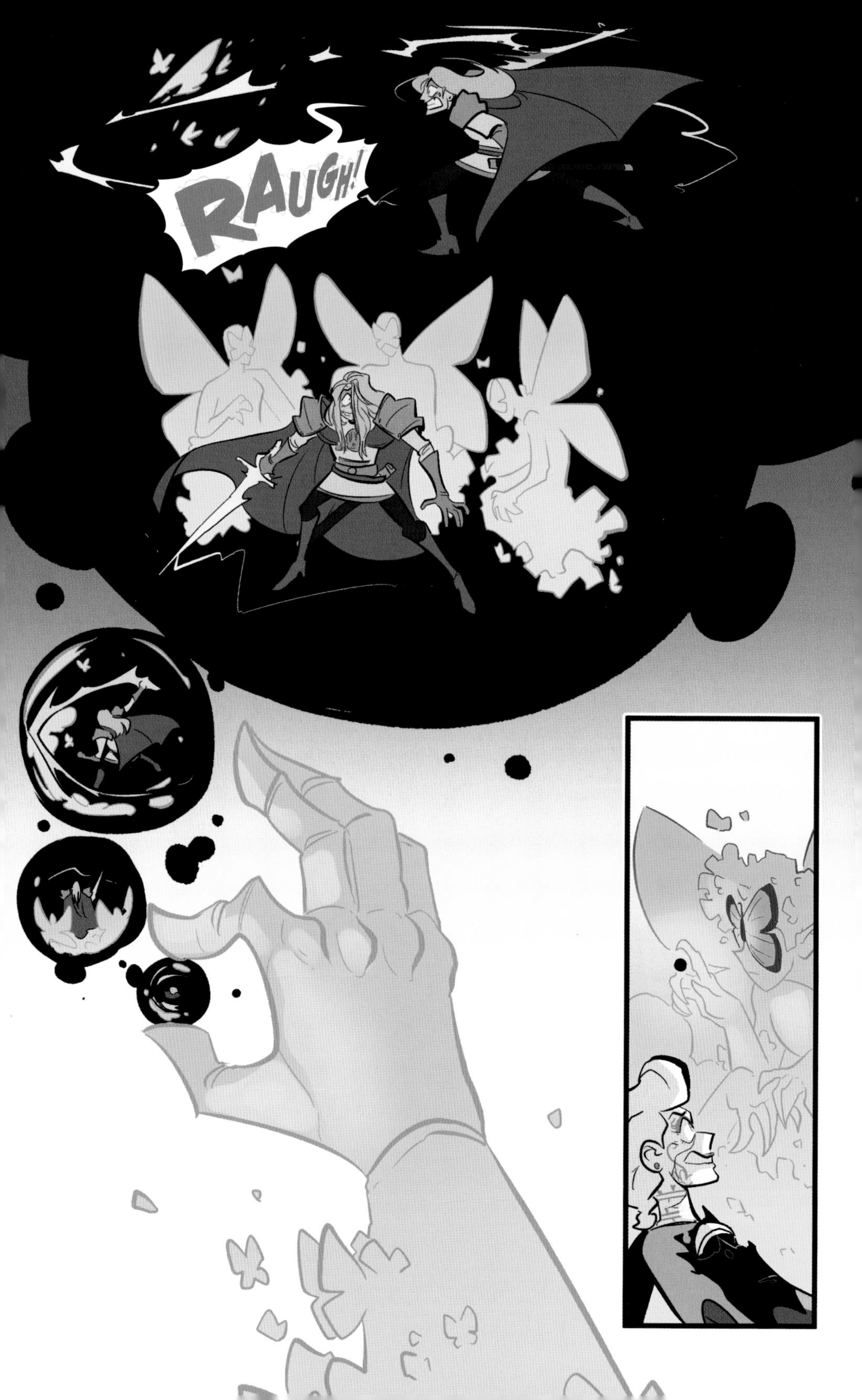
RAUGH!

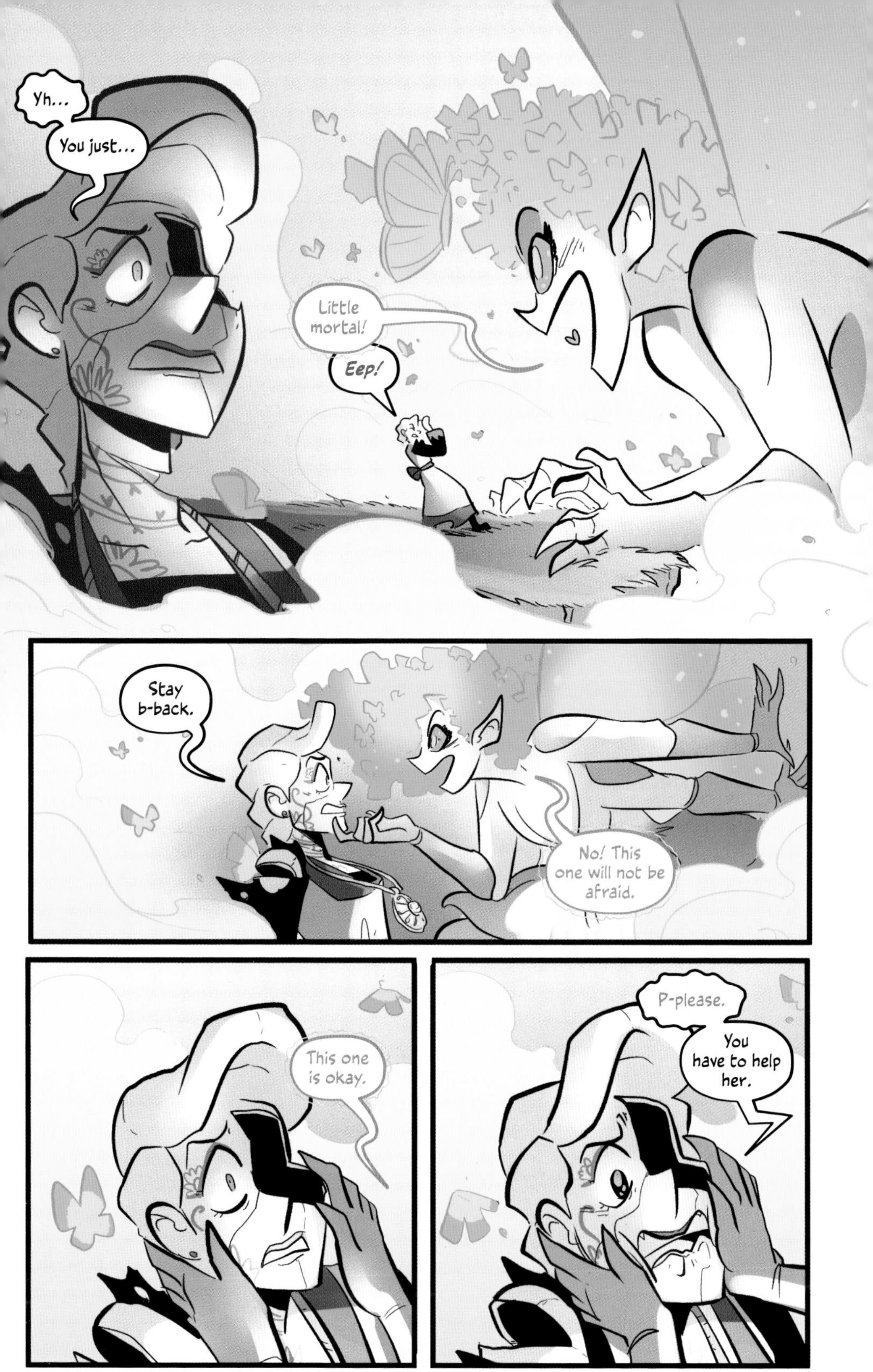

Yh...
You just...
Little mortal!
Eep!
Stay b-back.
No! This one will not be afraid.
This one is okay.
P-please.
You have to help her.

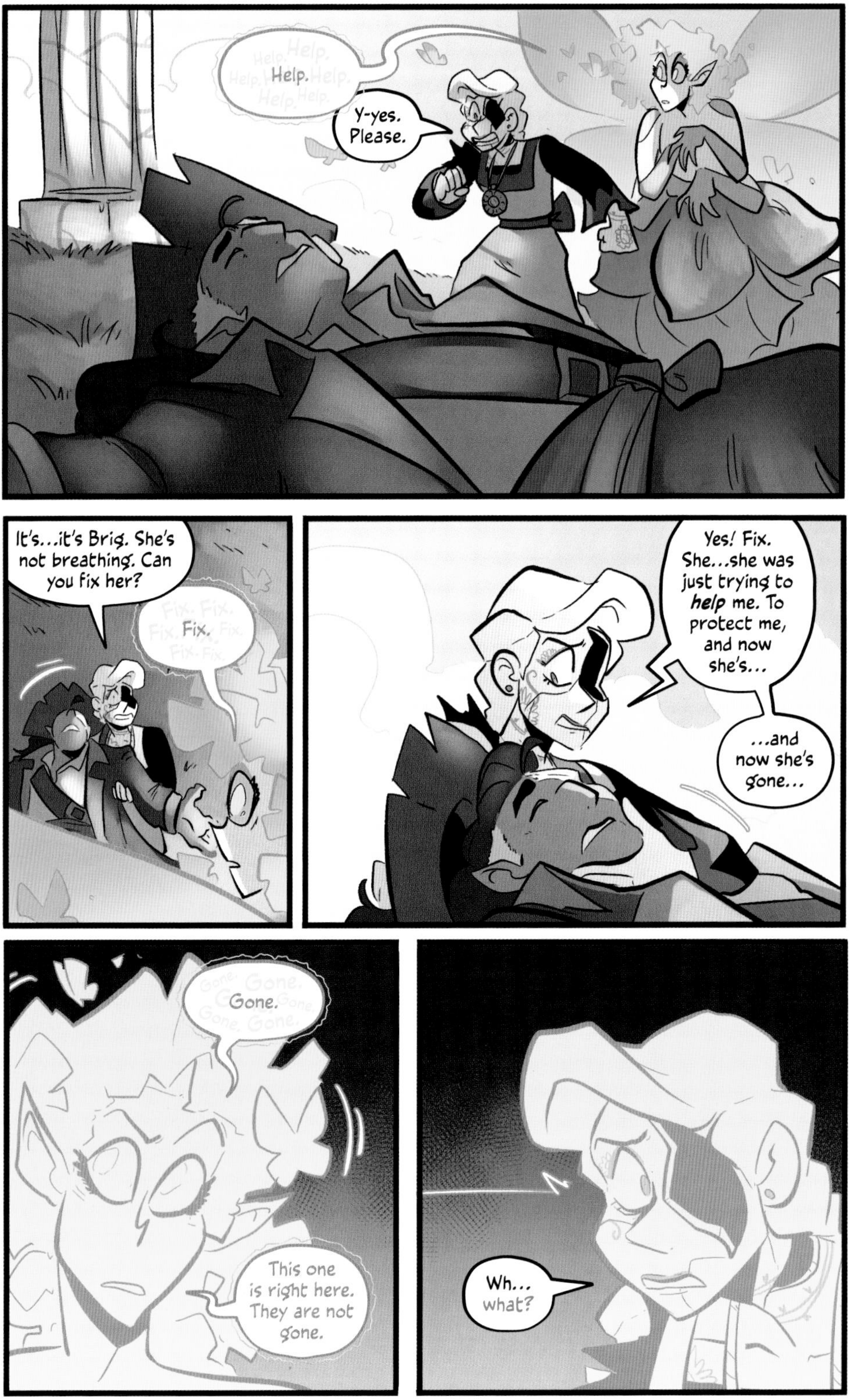
Help. Help. Help. Help. Help. Help. Help.
Y-yes. Please.
It's...it's Brig. She's not breathing. Can you fix her?
Fix. Fix. Fix. Fix. Fix. Fix. Fix.
Yes! Fix. She...she was just trying to *help* me. To protect me, and now she's...
...and now she's gone...
Gone. Gone. Gone. Gone. Gone. Gone. Gone.
This one is right here. They are not gone.
Wh... what?

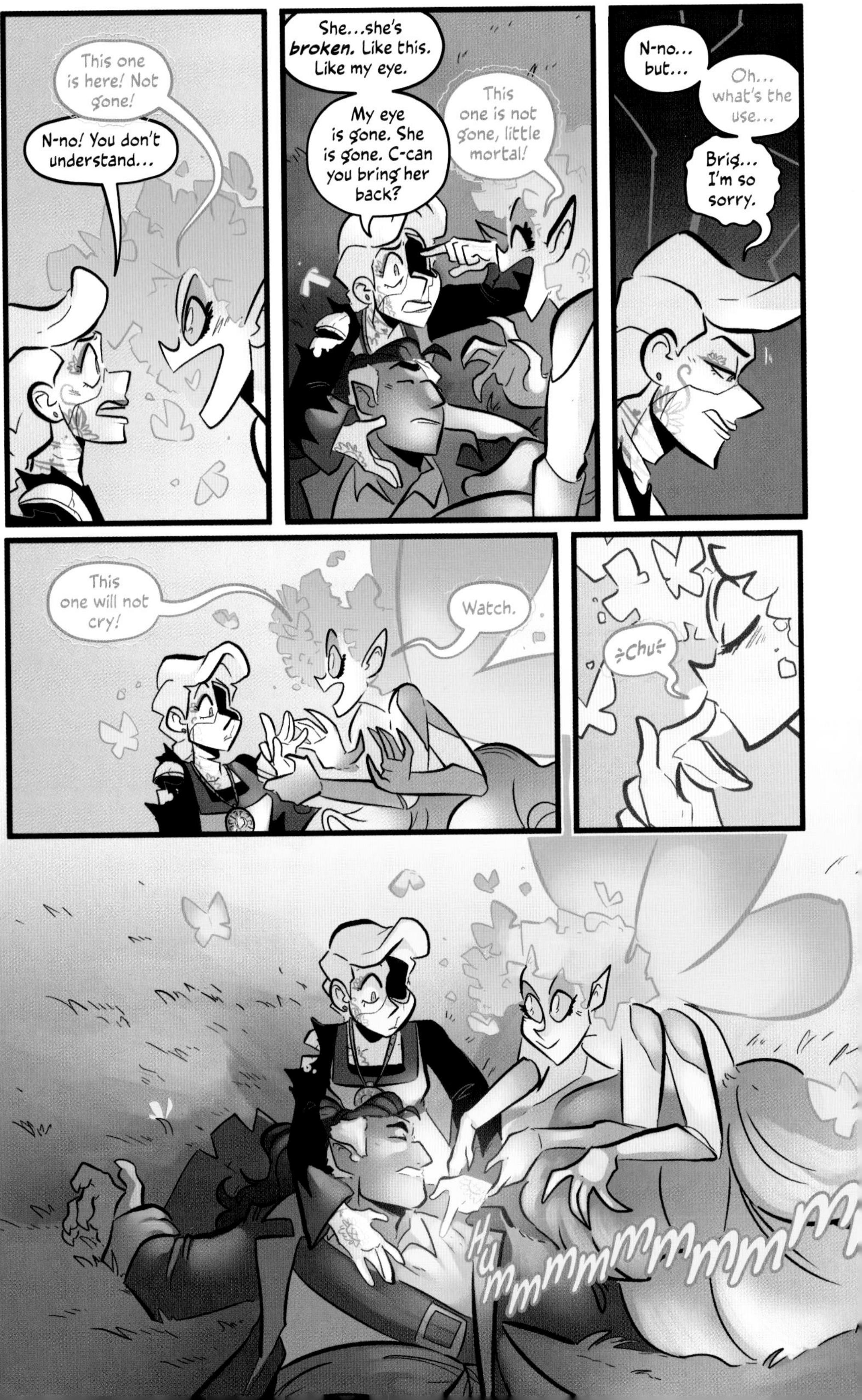
This one is here! Not gone!
N-no! You don't understand...
She...she's broken. Like this. Like my eye.
My eye is gone. She is gone. C-can you bring her back?
This one is not gone, little mortal!
N-no... but...
Oh... what's the use...
Brig... I'm so sorry.
This one will not cry!
Watch.
Chu
Hummmmmmmmmmm

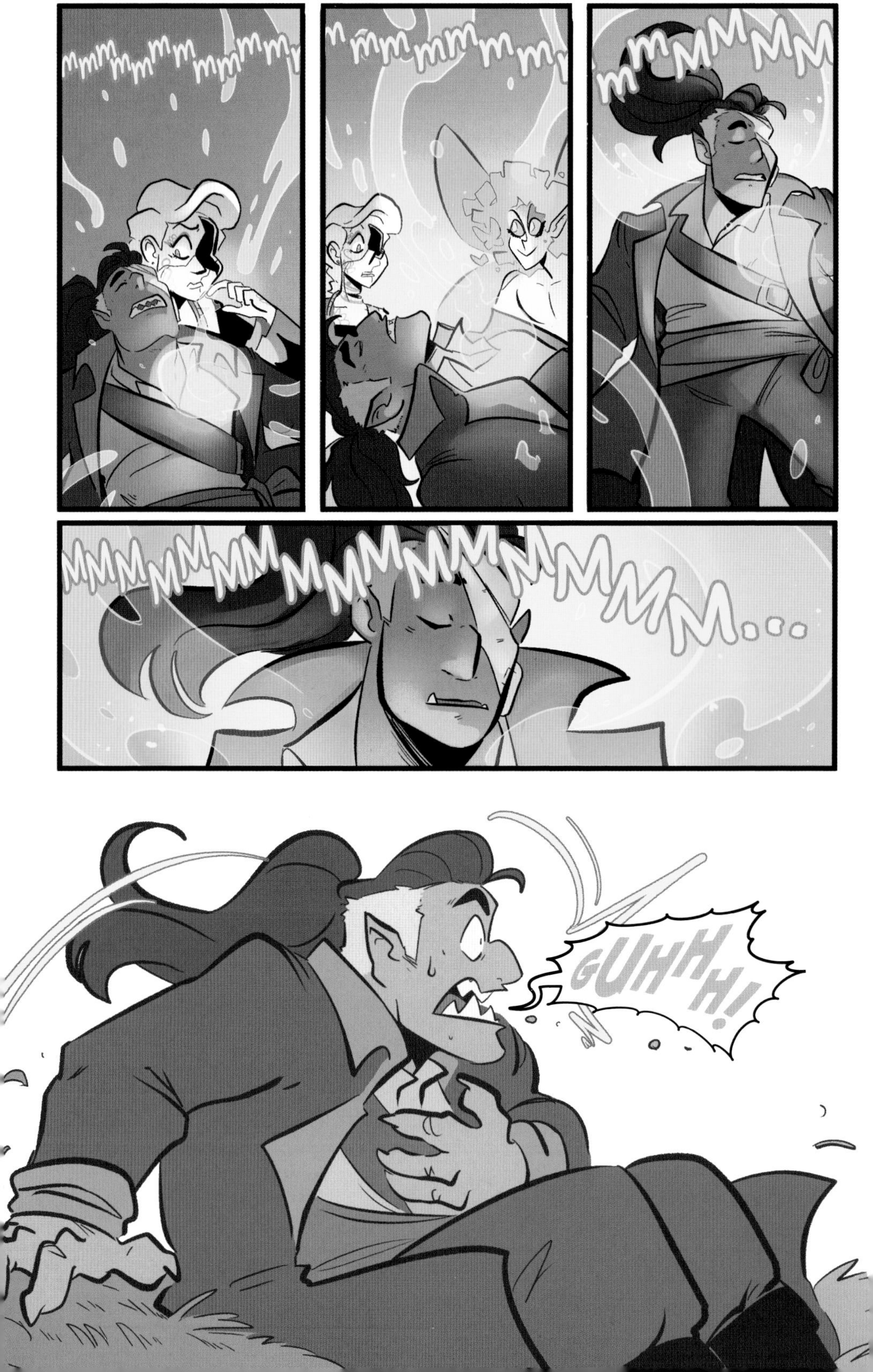
mmmmmmmmmmmm
mmmmmmmm
mmmMMMM
MMMMMMMMMMMMMMMMM...
GUHHH!

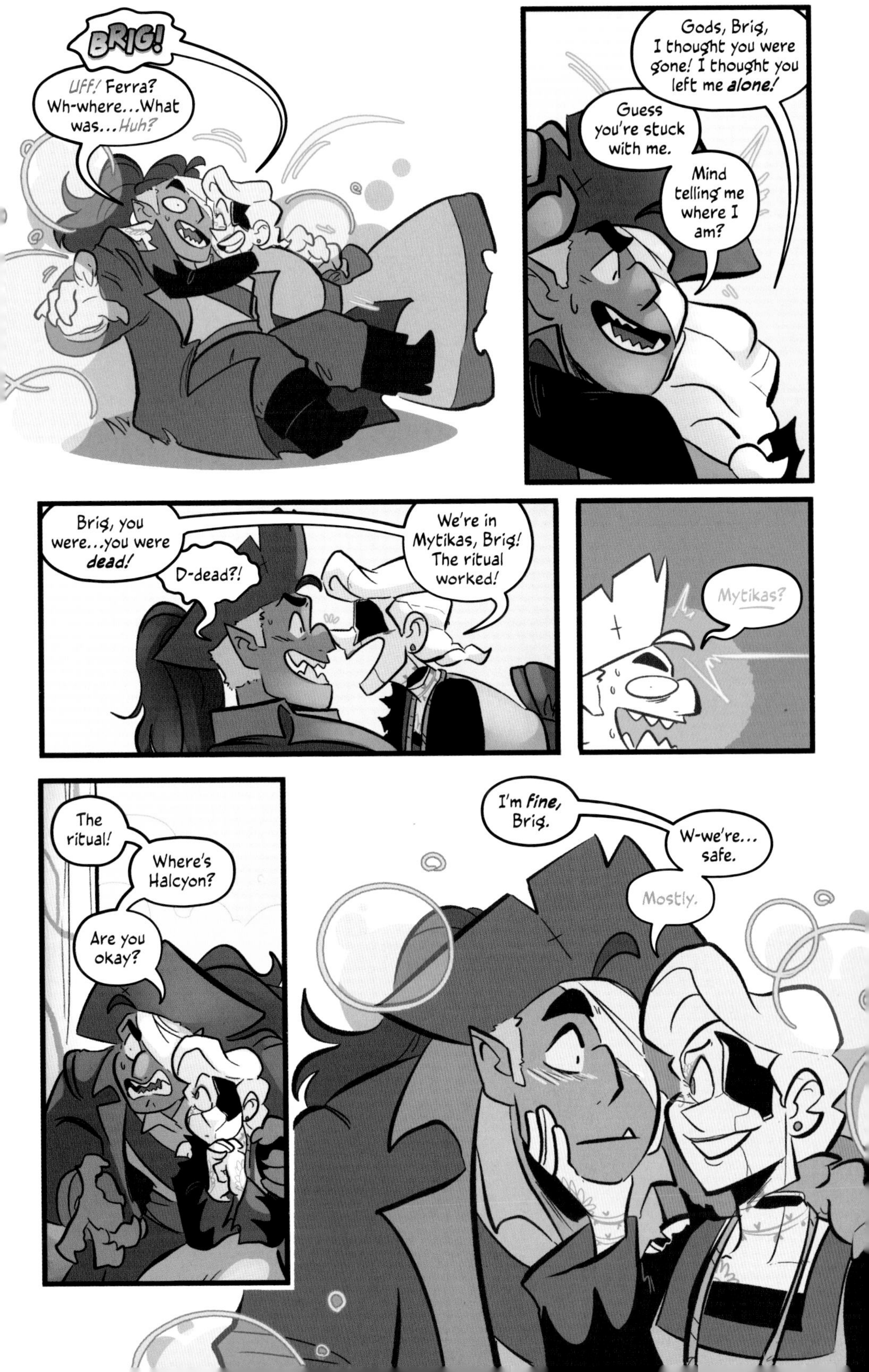
BRIG!
Uff! Ferra? Wh-where...What was...Huh?
Gods, Brig, I thought you were gone! I thought you left me *alone!*
Guess you're stuck with me.
Mind telling me where I am?
Brig, you were...you were *dead!*
D-dead?!
We're in Mytikas, Brig! The ritual worked!
Mytikas?
The ritual!
Where's Halcyon?
Are you okay?
I'm *fine,* Brig.
W-we're... safe.
Mostly.

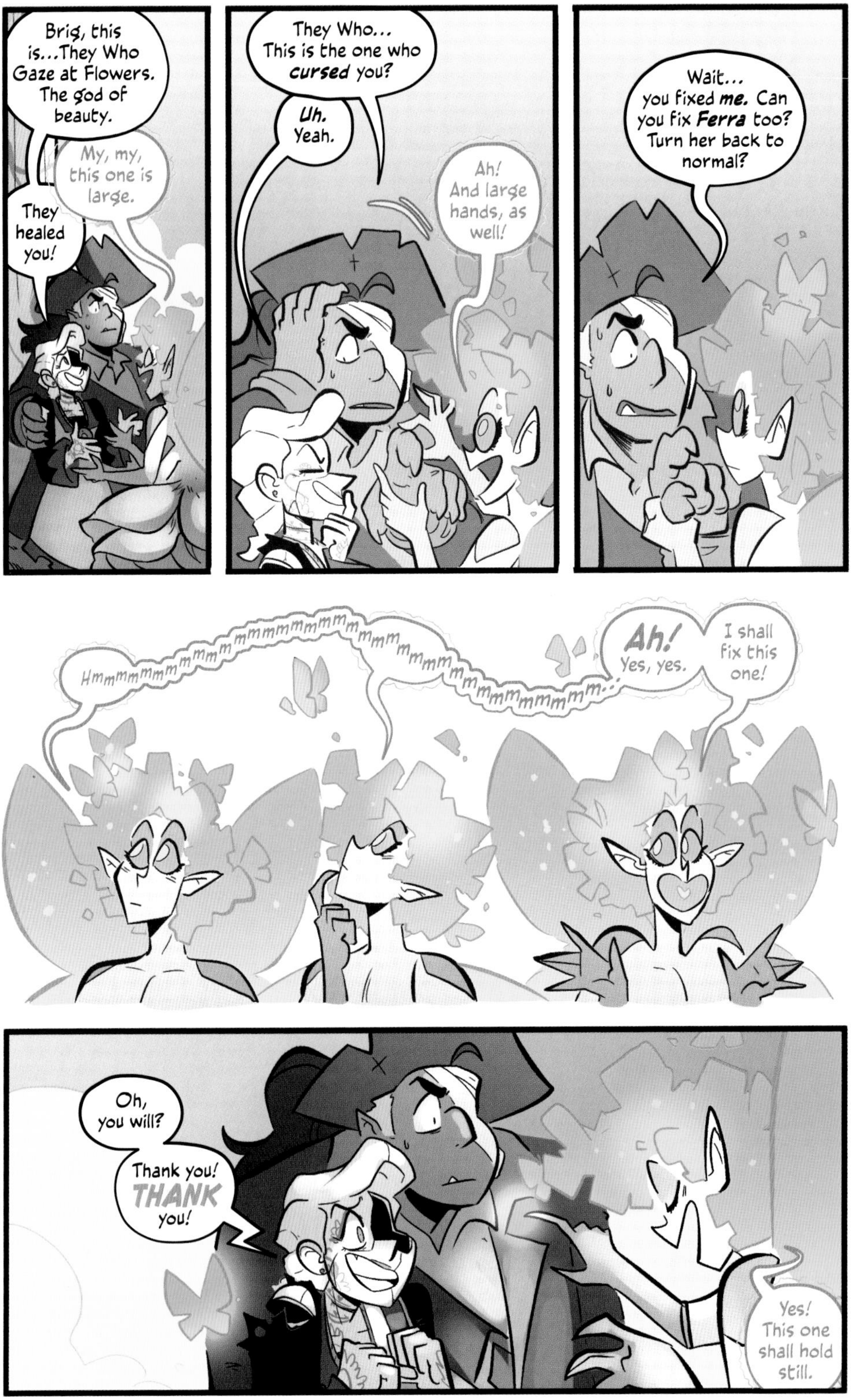
Brig, this is...They Who Gaze at Flowers. The god of beauty.
My, my, this one is large.
They healed you!
They Who... This is the one who **cursed** you?
Uh. Yeah.
Ah! And large hands, as well!
Wait... you fixed **me.** Can you fix **Ferra** too? Turn her back to normal?
Hmmmmmmmmmmmmmmmmmmmmmmmmmmmmmmmmmmmmmmmmm...
Ah! Yes, yes.
I shall fix this one!
Oh, you will?
Thank you! **THANK** you!
Yes! This one shall hold still.

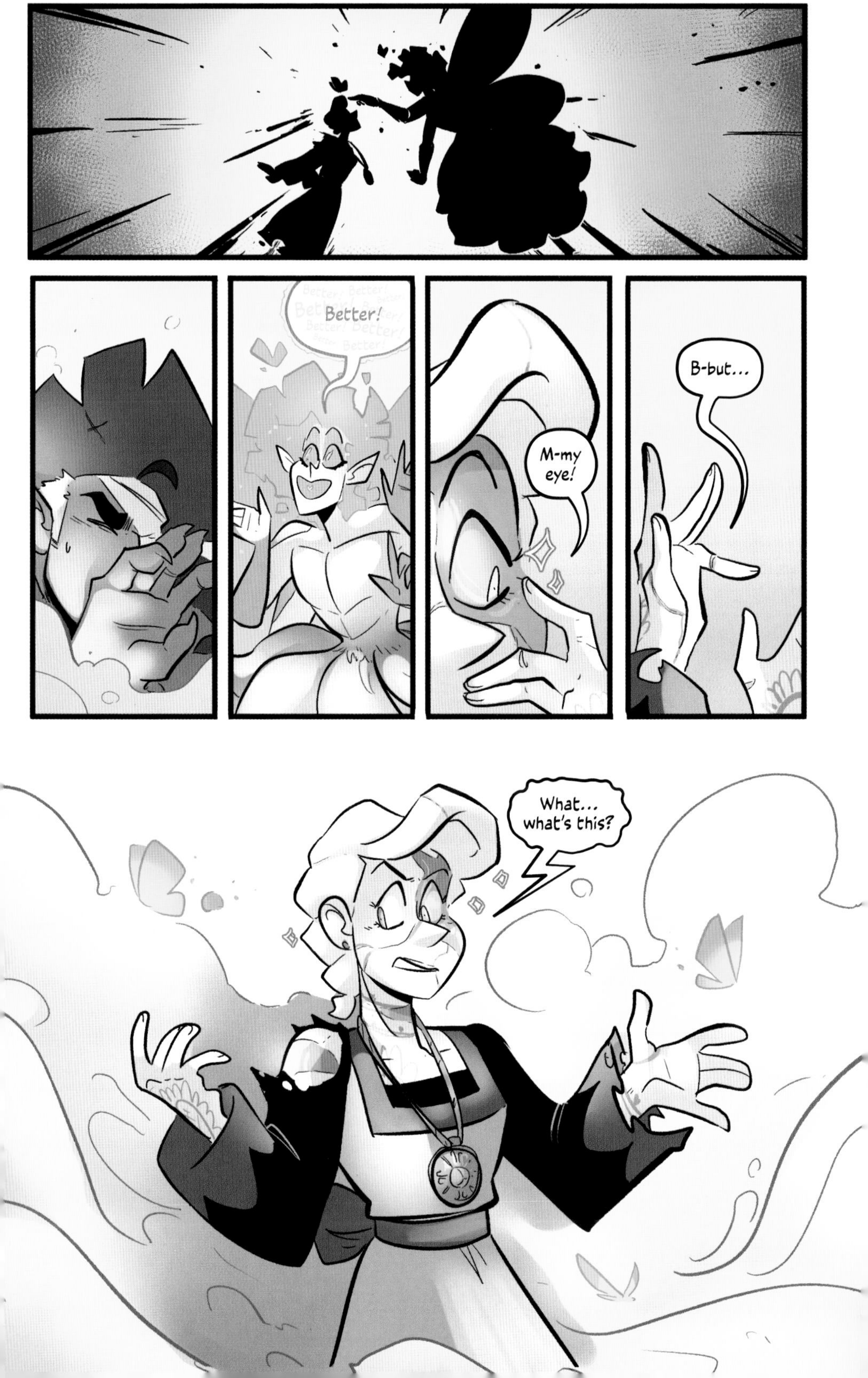
Better! Better! Better! Better! Better! Better! Better! Better! Better!
M-my eye!
B-but...
What... what's this?

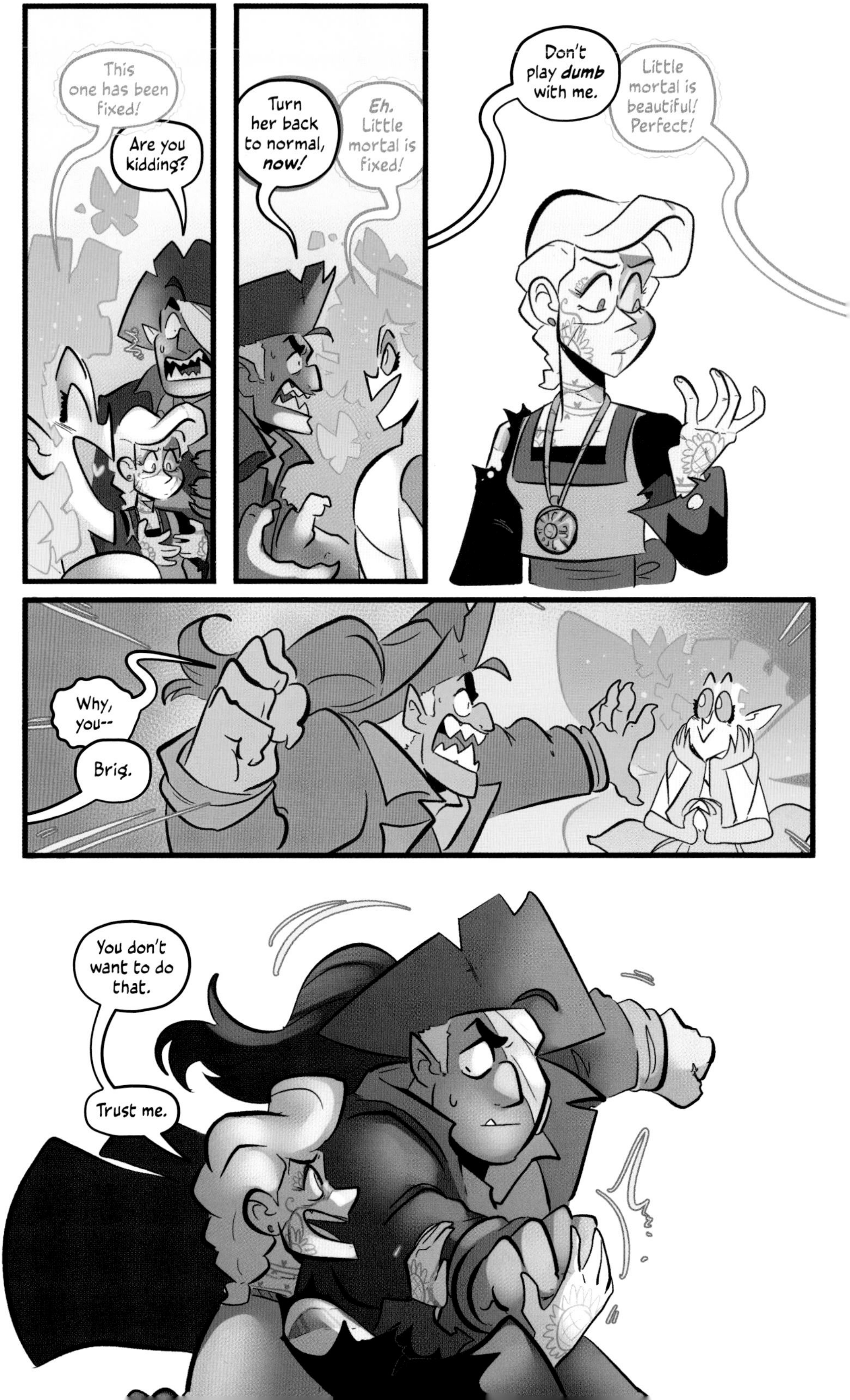
This one has been fixed!
Are you kidding?
Turn her back to normal, *now!*
Eh. Little mortal is fixed!
Don't play *dumb* with me.
Little mortal is beautiful! Perfect!
Why, you--
Brig.
You don't want to do that.
Trust me.

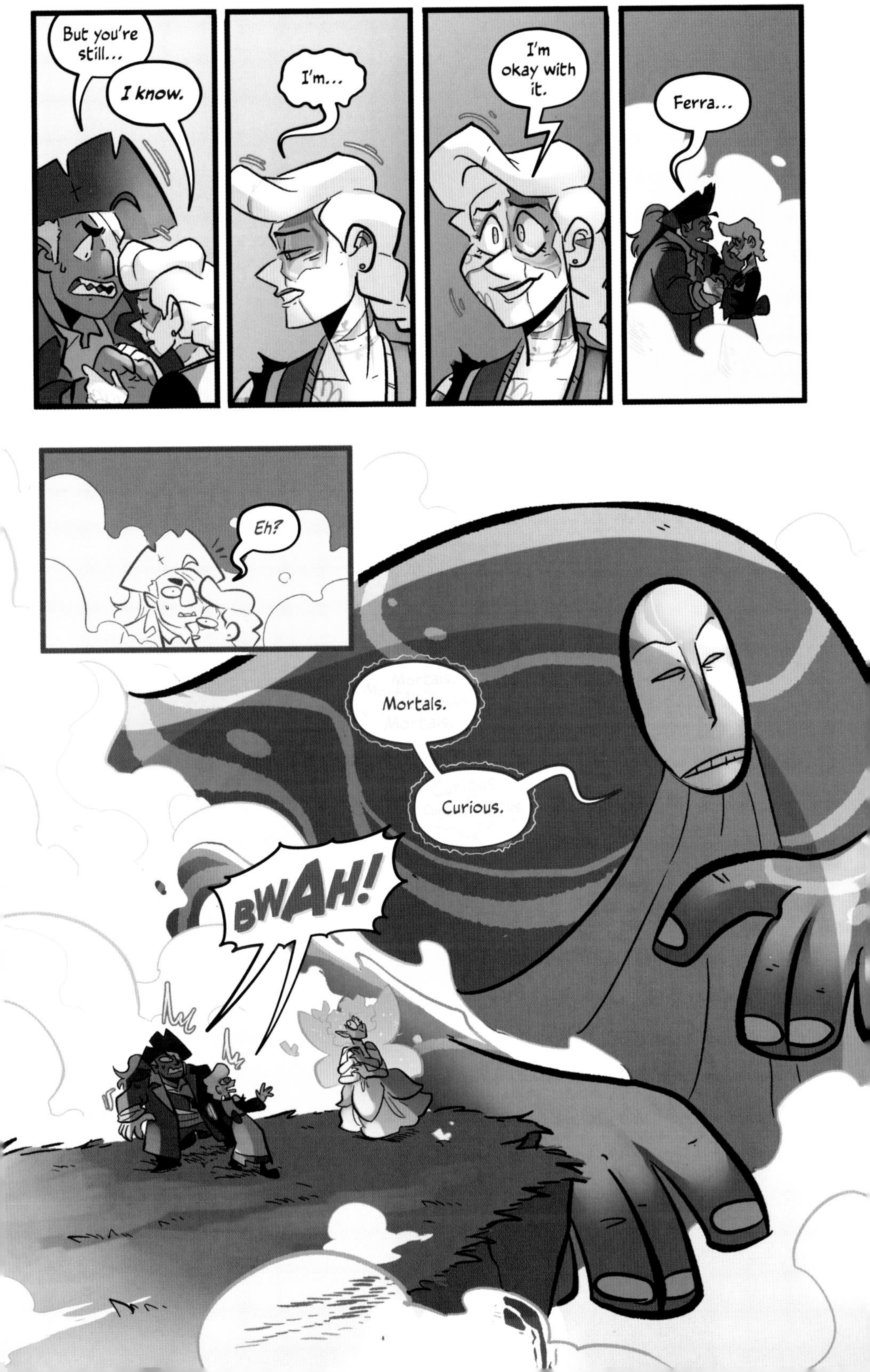

But you're still...
I know.
I'm...
I'm okay with it.
Ferra...
Eh?
Mortals.
Curious.
BWAH!

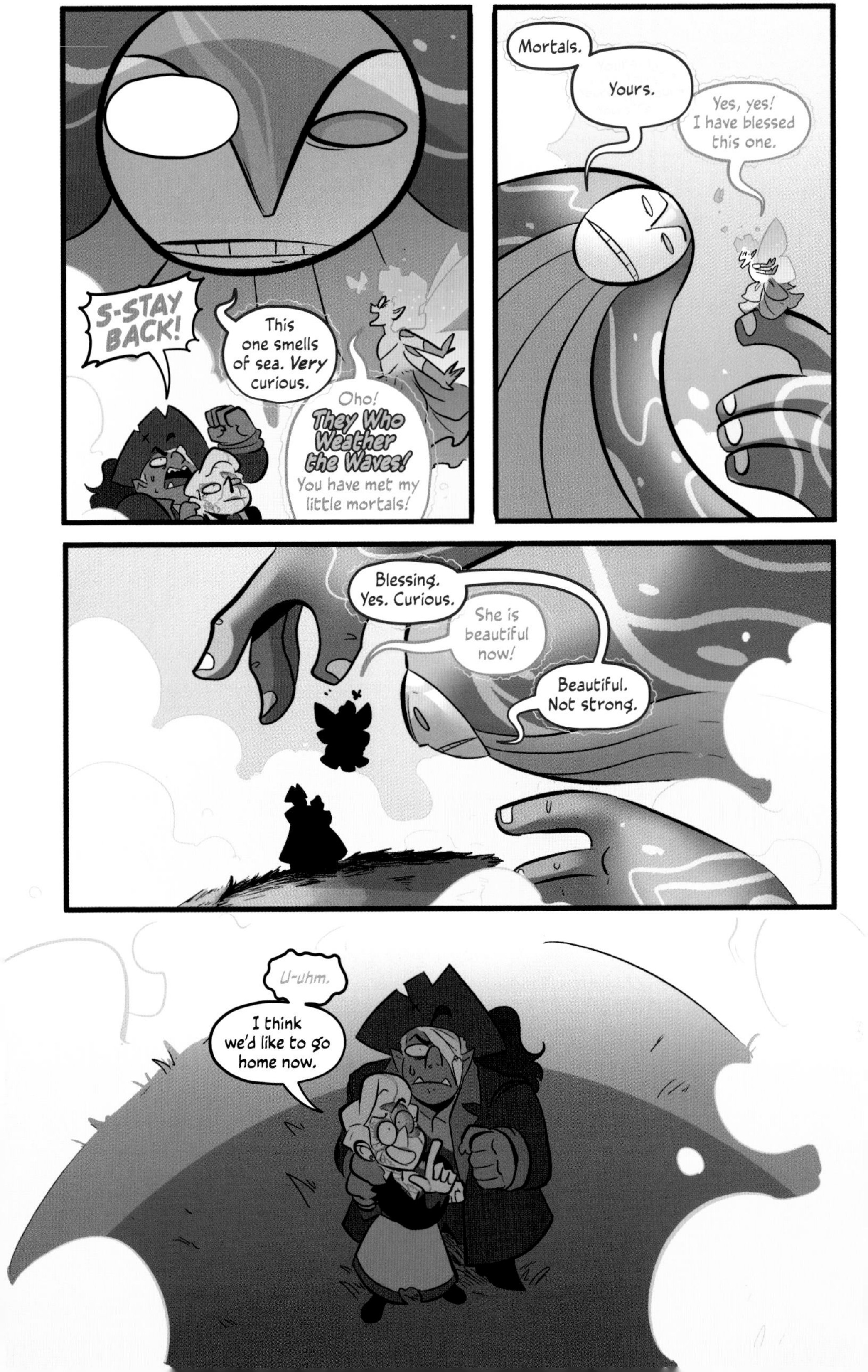

S-STAY BACK!
This one smells of sea. *Very* curious.
Oho!
They Who Weather the Waves!
You have met my little mortals!
Mortals.
Yours.
Yes, yes! I have blessed this one.
Blessing. Yes. Curious.
She is beautiful now!
Beautiful. Not strong.
U-uhm.
I think we'd like to go home now.

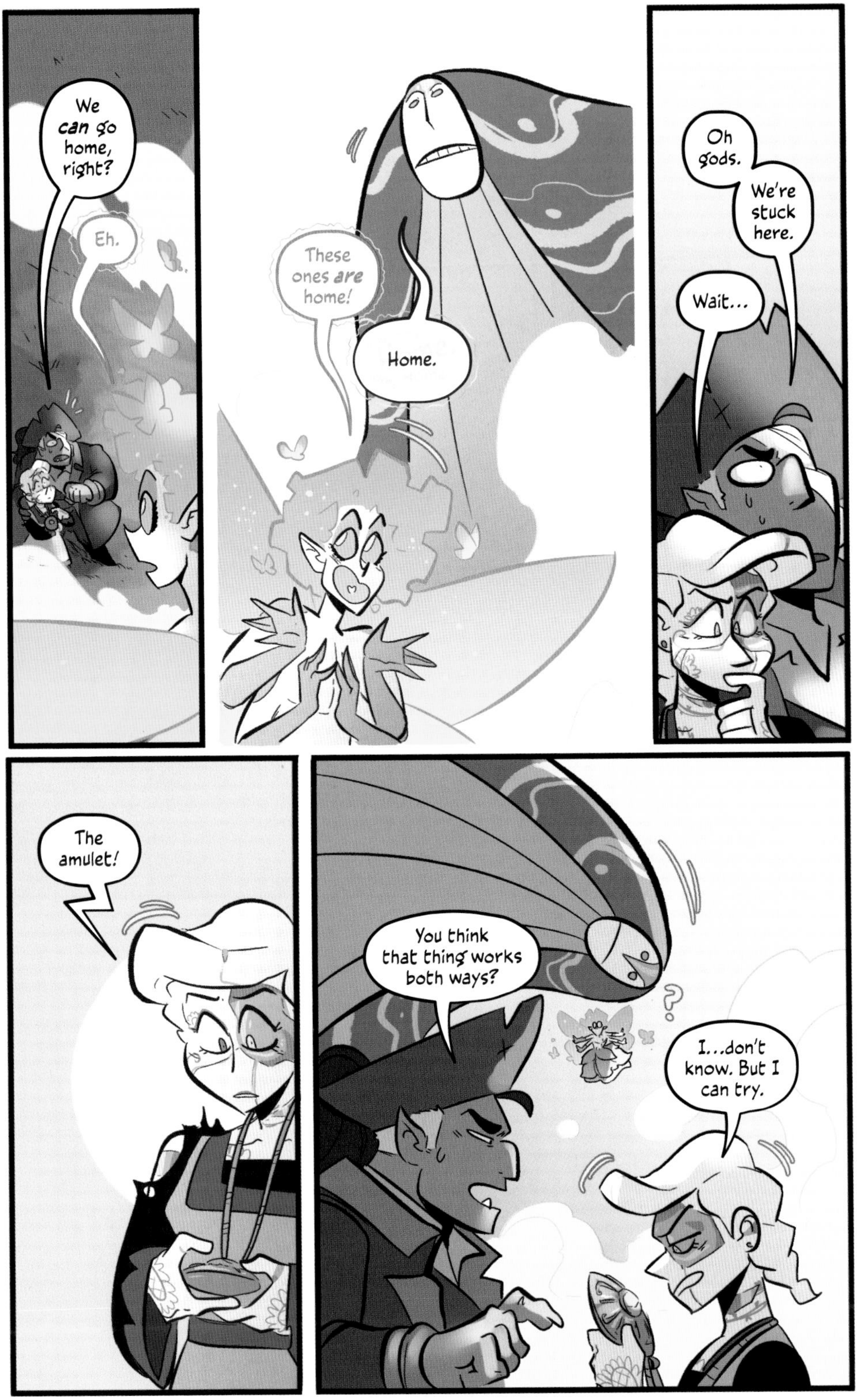
We can go home, right?
Eh.
These ones are home!
Home.
Oh gods.
We're stuck here.
Wait...
The amulet!
You think that thing works both ways?
I...don't know. But I can try.

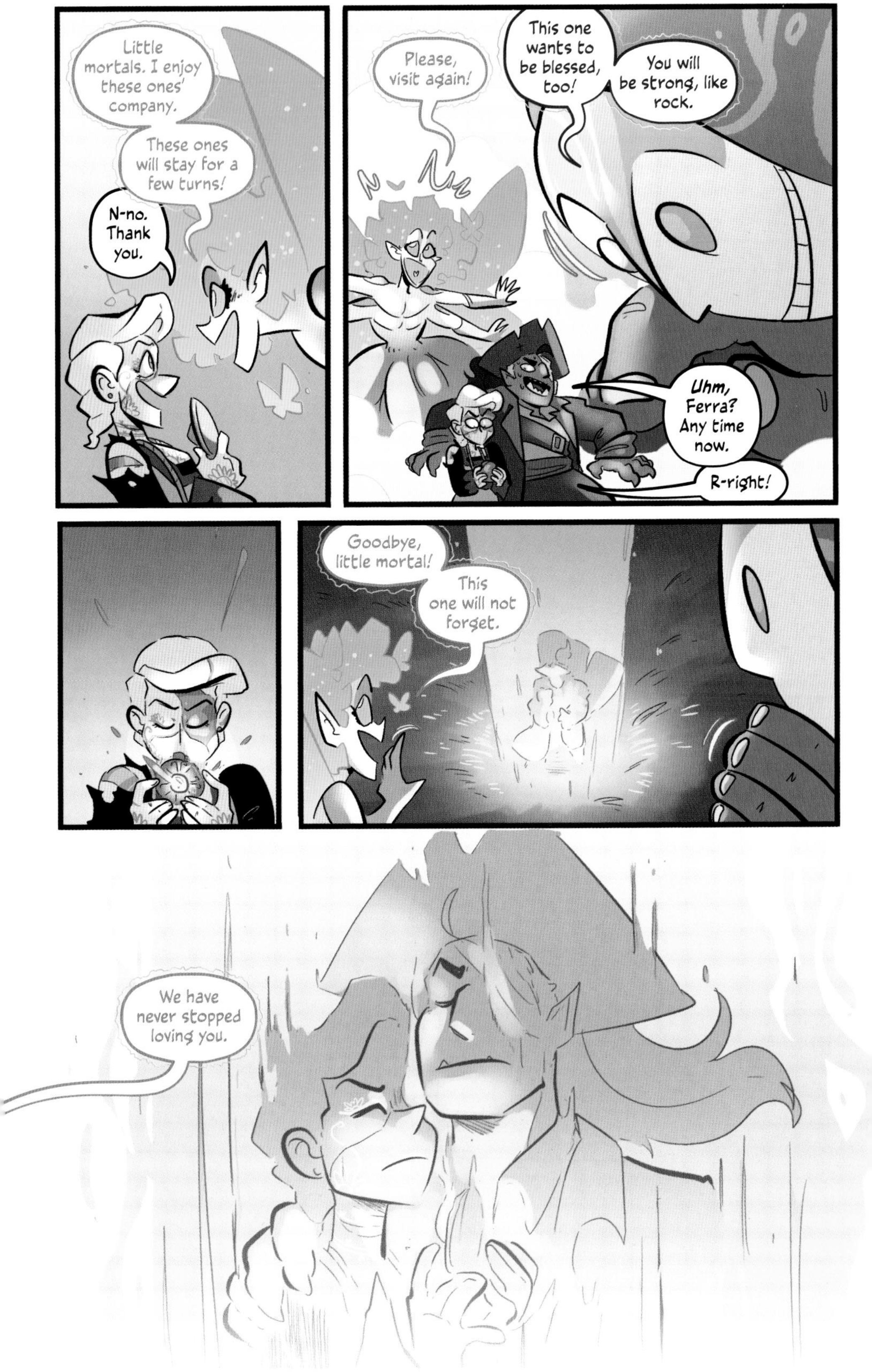
Little mortals. I enjoy these ones' company.
These ones will stay for a few turns!
N-no. Thank you.
Please, visit again!
This one wants to be blessed, too!
You will be strong, like rock.
Uhm, Ferra? Any time now.
R-right!
Goodbye, little mortal!
This one will not forget.
We have never stopped loving you.

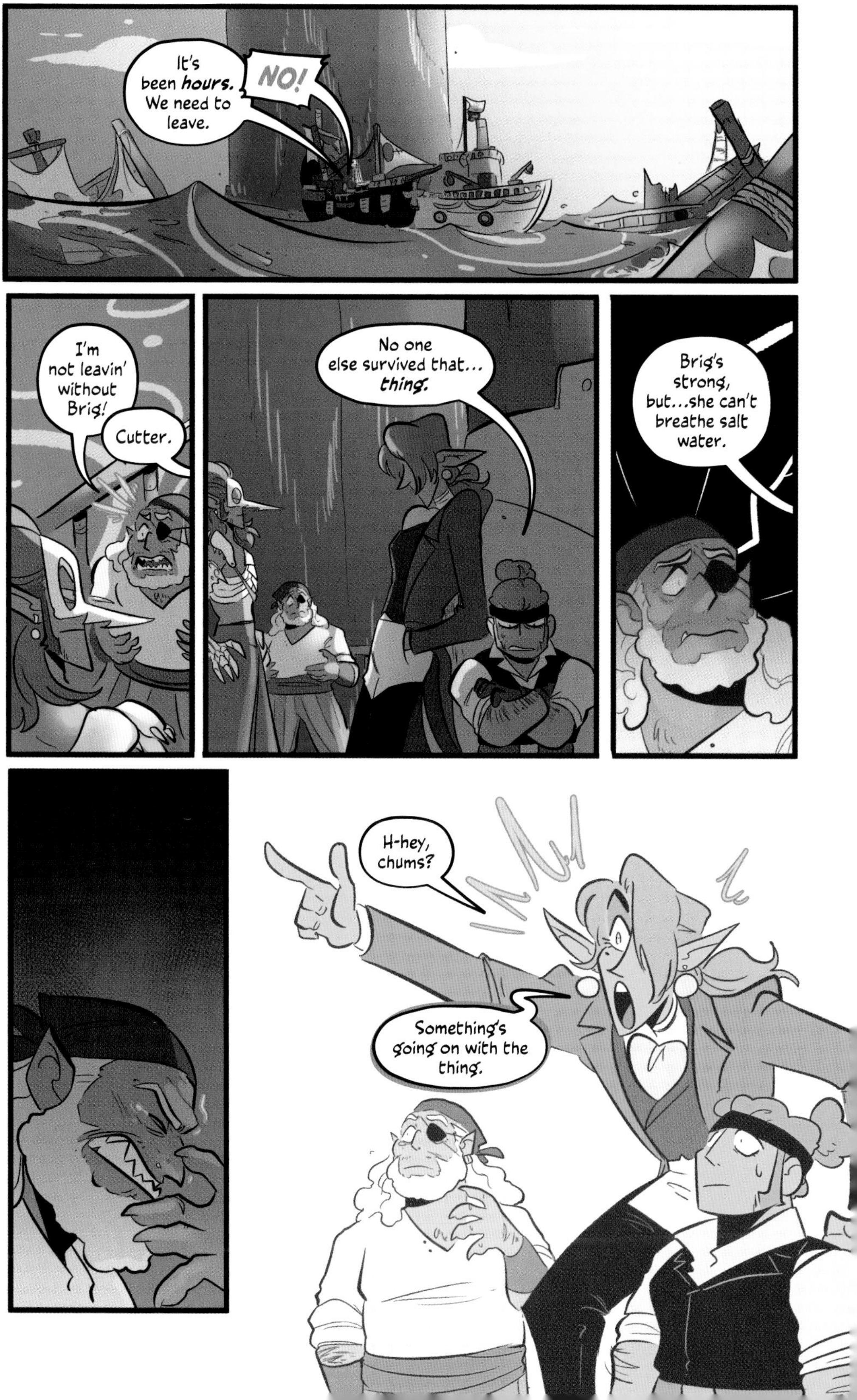
It's been *hours.* We need to leave.
NO!
I'm not leavin' without Brig!
Cutter.
No one else survived that... *thing.*
Brig's strong, but...she can't breathe salt water.
H-hey, chums?
Something's going on with the thing.

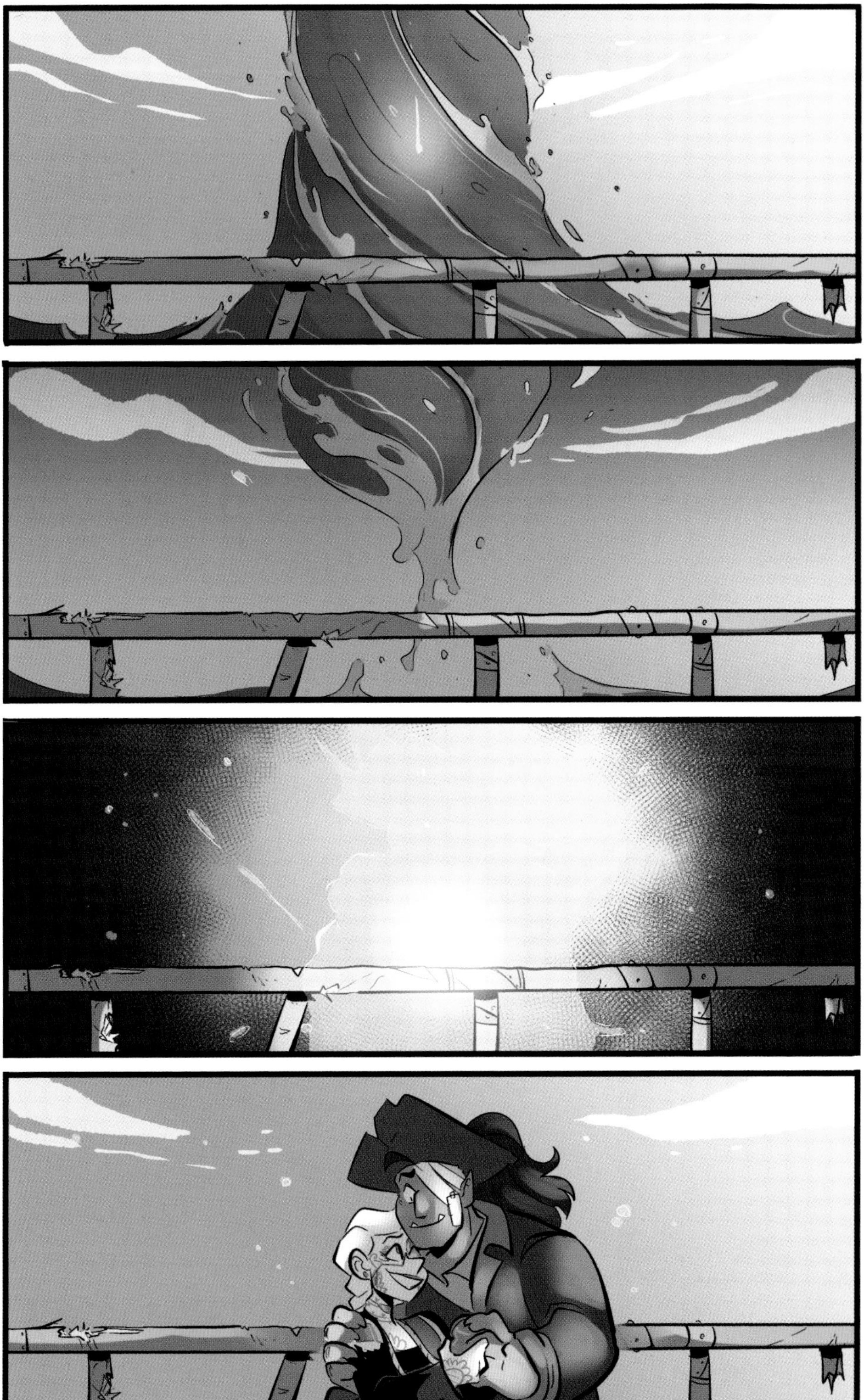

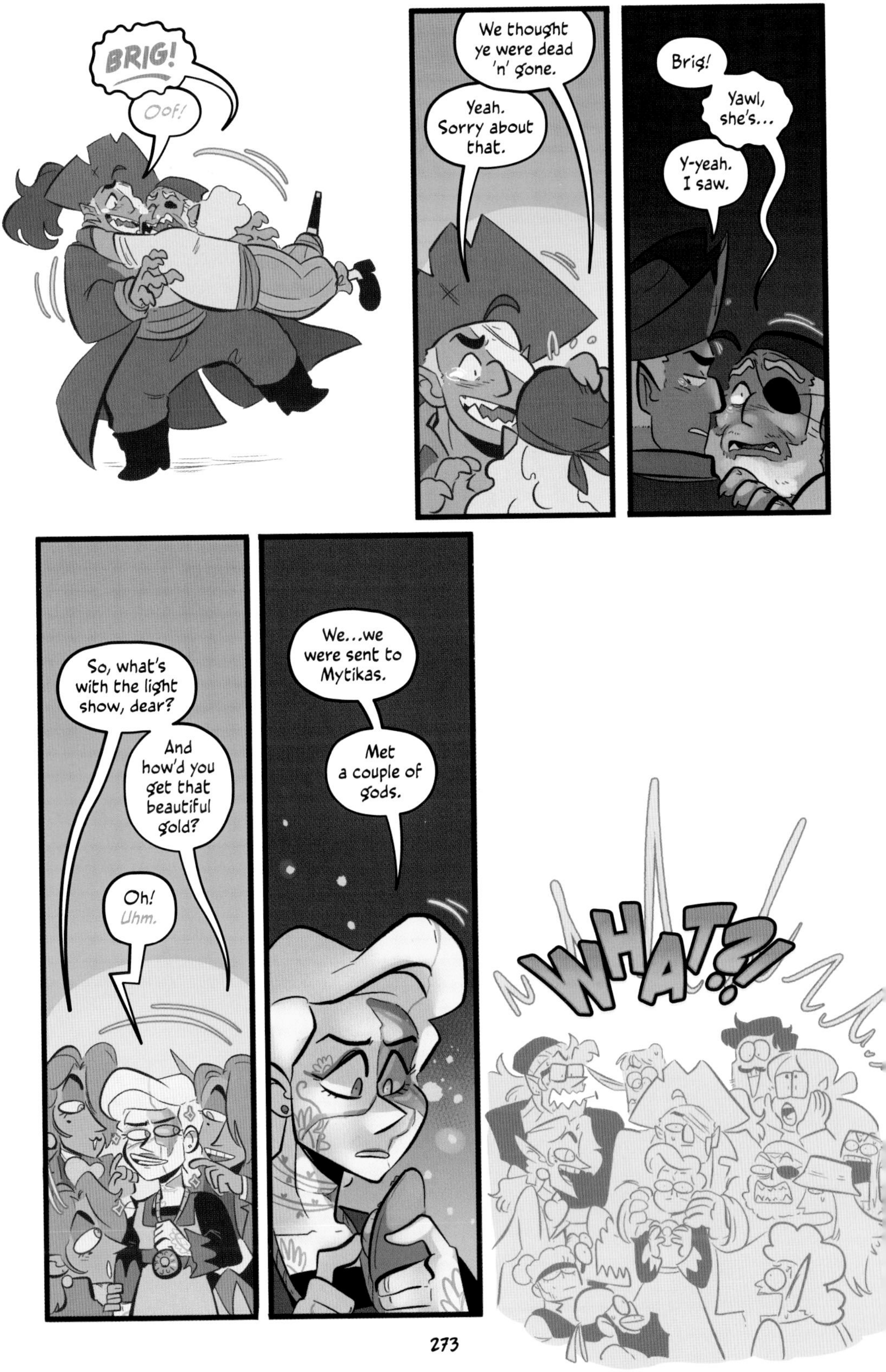
BRIG!
Oof!
We thought ye were dead 'n' gone.
Yeah. Sorry about that.
Brig!
Yawl, she's...
Y-yeah. I saw.
So, what's with the light show, dear?
And how'd you get that beautiful gold?
Oh! Uhm.
We...we were sent to Mytikas.
Met a couple of gods.
WHAT?!

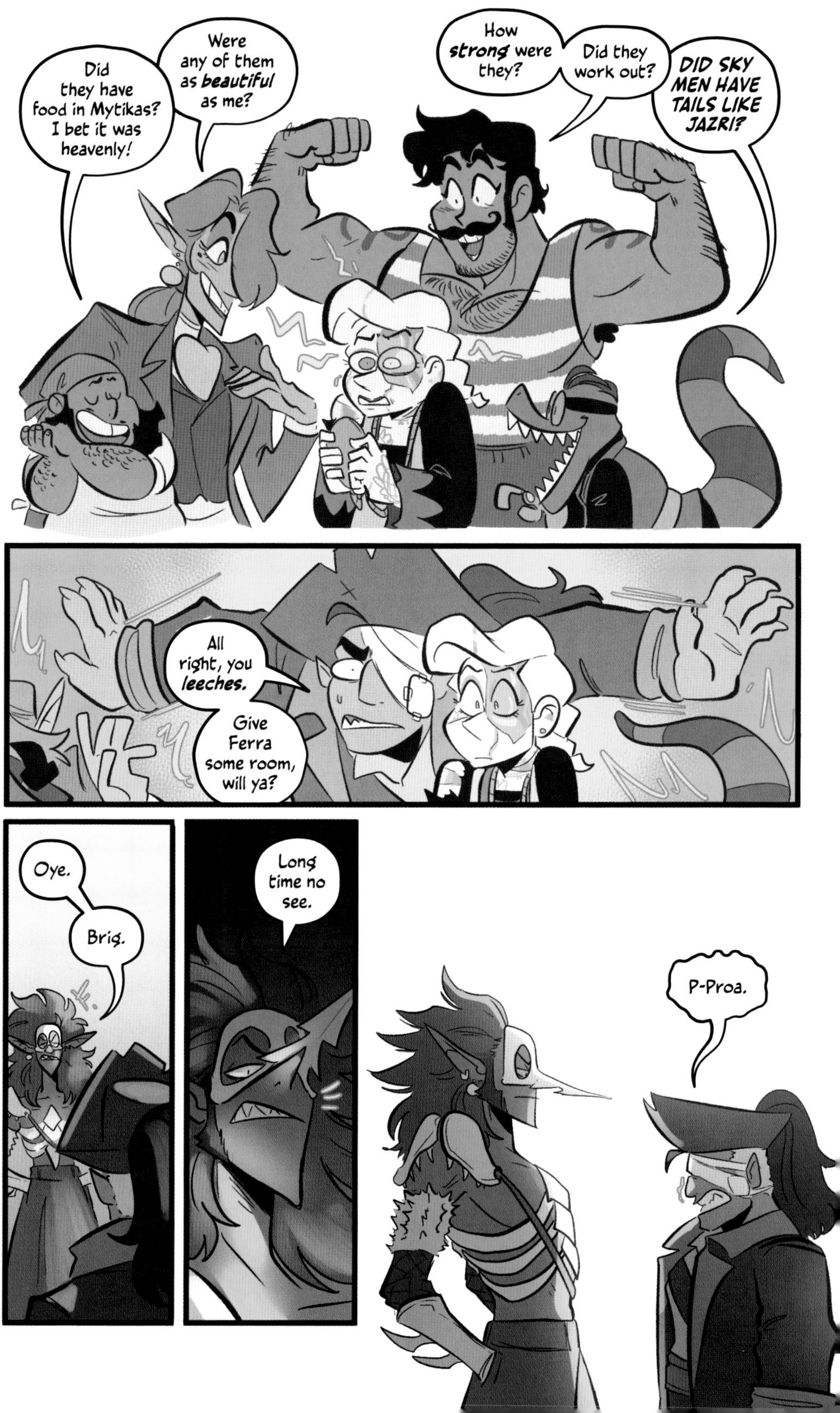
Did they have food in Mytikas? I bet it was heavenly!
Were any of them as beautiful as me?
How strong were they?
Did they work out?
DID SKY MEN HAVE TAILS LIKE JAZRI?
All right, you leeches.
Give Ferra some room, will ya?
Oye.
Brig.
Long time no see.
P-Proa.

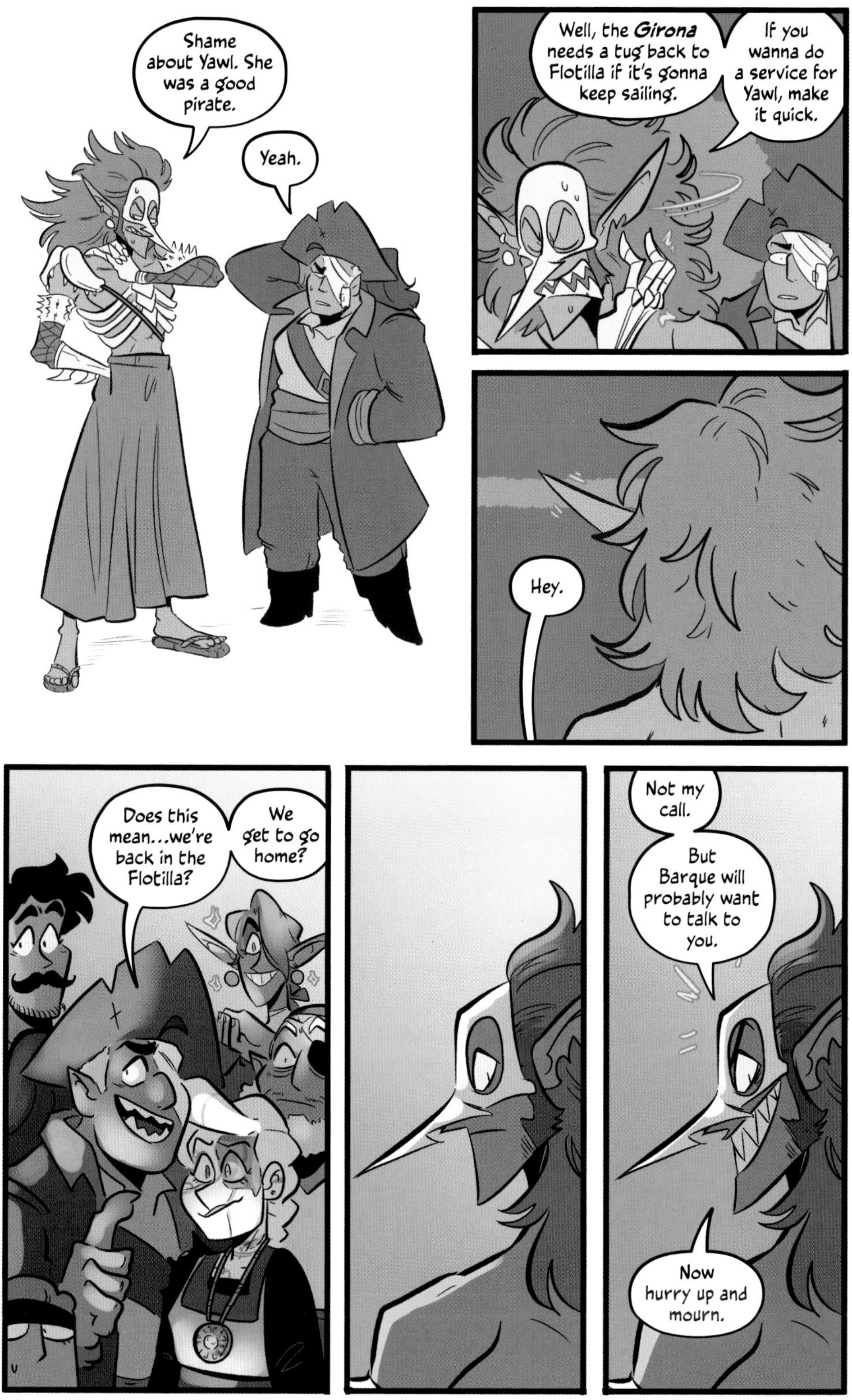
Shame about Yawl. She was a good pirate.
Yeah.
Well, the *Girona* needs a tug back to Flotilla if it's gonna keep sailing.
If you wanna do a service for Yawl, make it quick.
Hey.
Does this mean...we're back in the Flotilla?
We get to go home?
Not my call.
But Barque will probably want to talk to you.
Now hurry up and mourn.

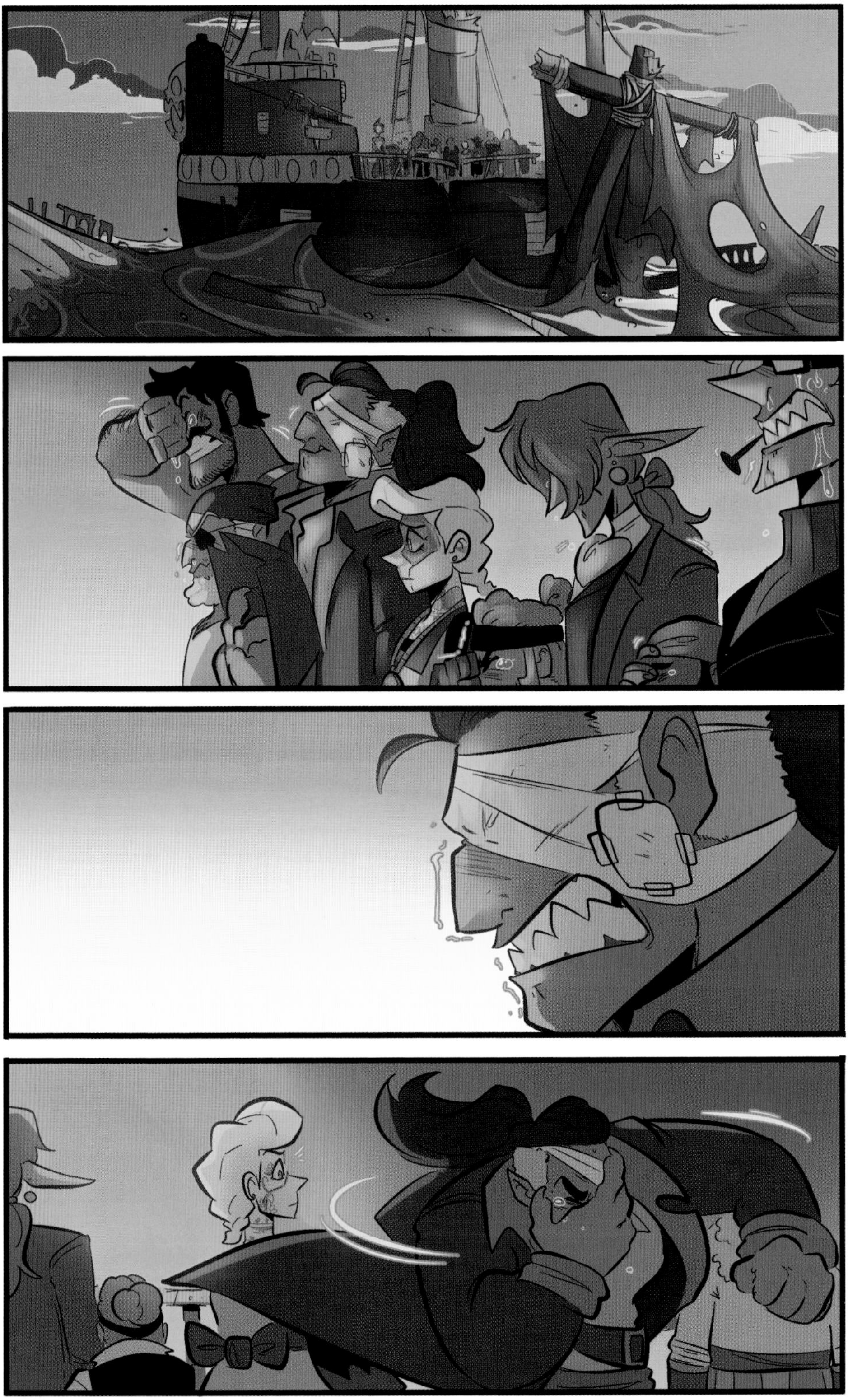

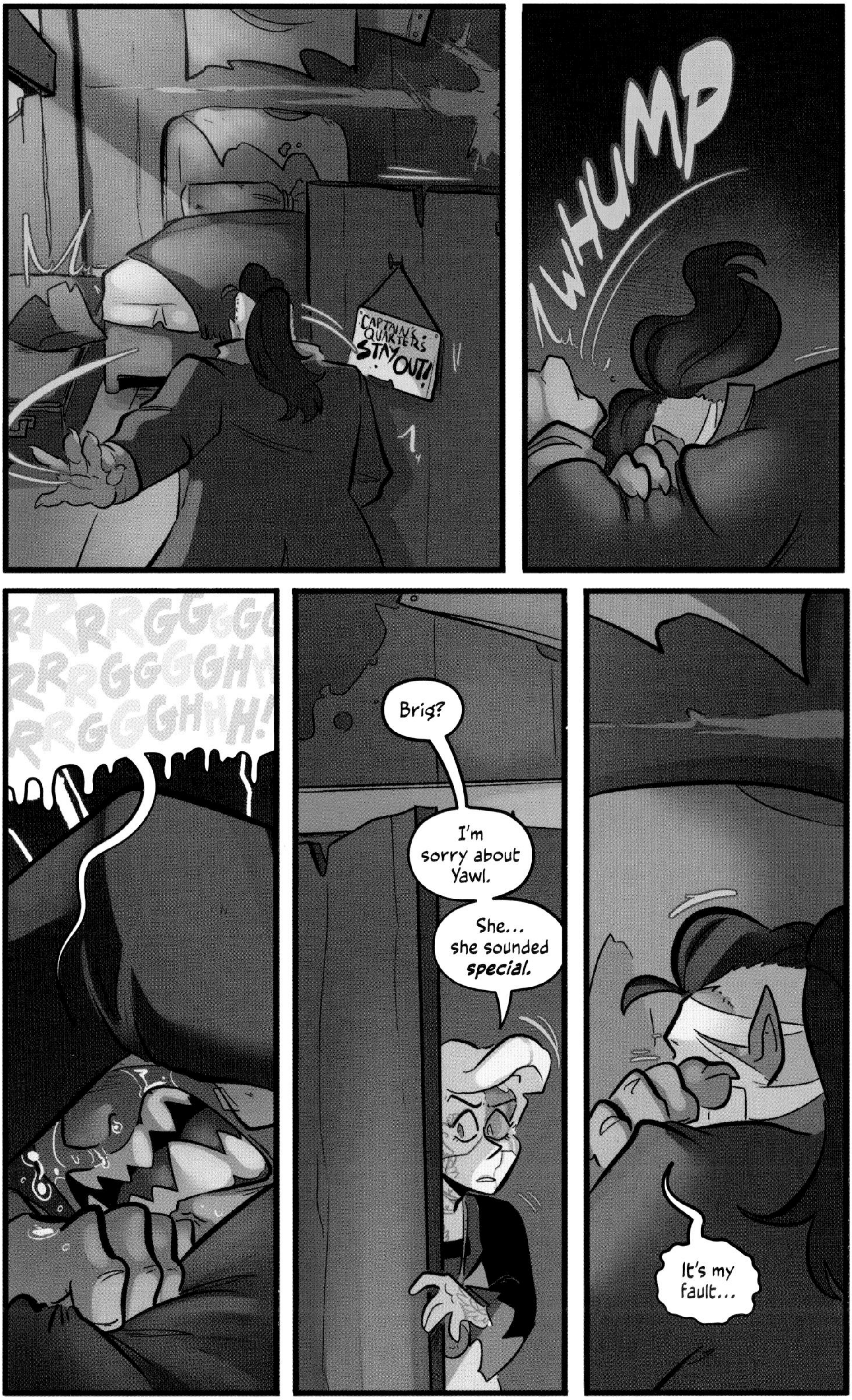
CAPTAIN'S QUARTERS STAY OUT!
WHUMP
RRRGGGGG RRRGGGGHH RRGGGGHHH!
Brig?
I'm sorry about Yawl.
She... she sounded special.
It's my fault...

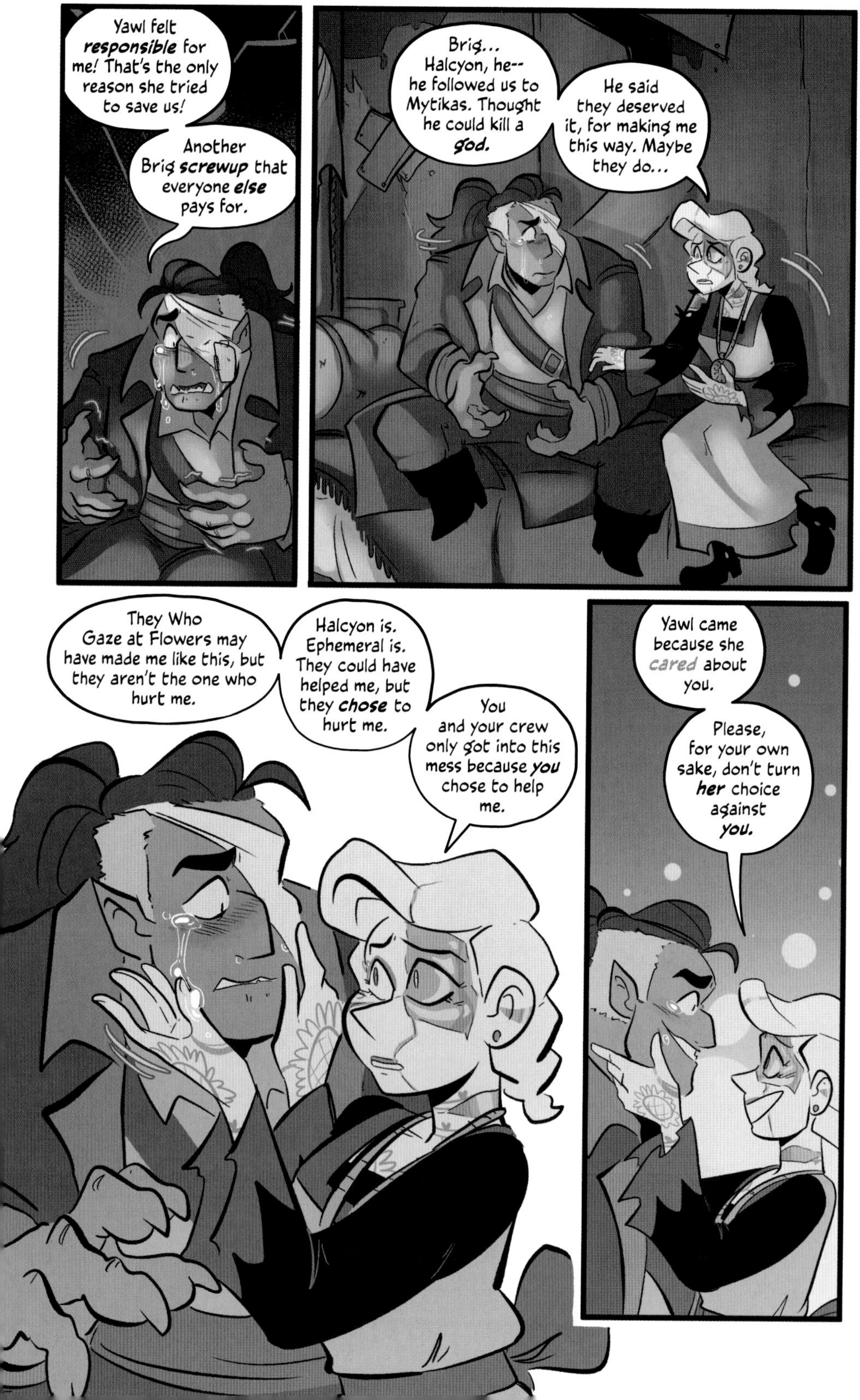

Yawl felt responsible for me! That's the only reason she tried to save us!
Another Brig screwup that everyone else pays for.
Brig... Halcyon, he-- he followed us to Mytikas. Thought he could kill a god.
He said they deserved it, for making me this way. Maybe they do...
They Who Gaze at Flowers may have made me like this, but they aren't the one who hurt me.
Halcyon is. Ephemeral is. They could have helped me, but they chose to hurt me.
You and your crew only got into this mess because you chose to help me.
Yawl came because she cared about you.
Please, for your own sake, don't turn her choice against you.

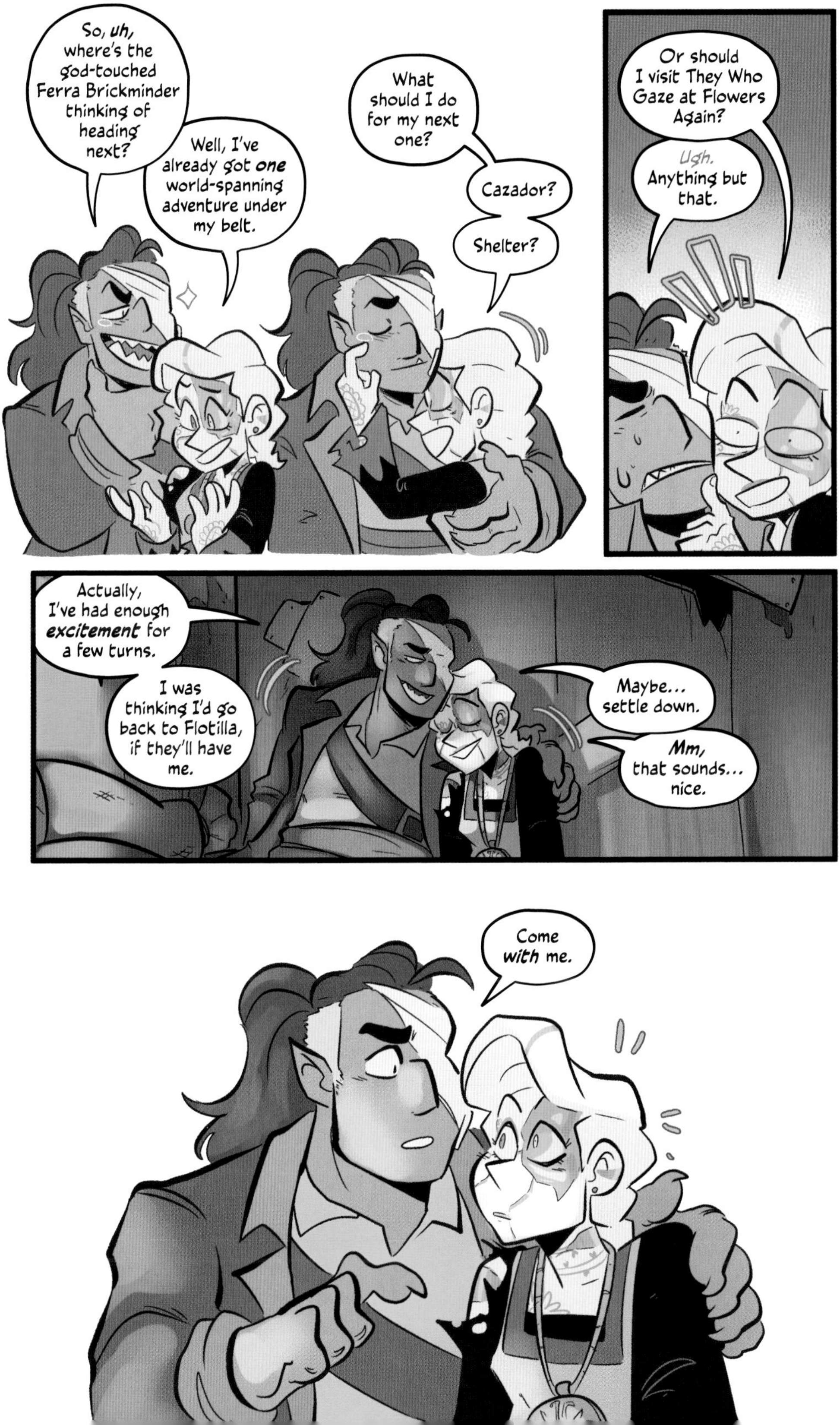

So, *uh,* where's the god-touched Ferra Brickminder thinking of heading next?
Well, I've already got ***one*** world-spanning adventure under my belt.
What should I do for my next one?
Cazador?
Shelter?
Or should I visit They Who Gaze at Flowers Again?
Ugh. Anything but that.
Actually, I've had enough ***excitement*** for a few turns.
I was thinking I'd go back to Flotilla, if they'll have me.
Maybe... settle down.
Mm, that sounds... nice.
Come ***with*** me.

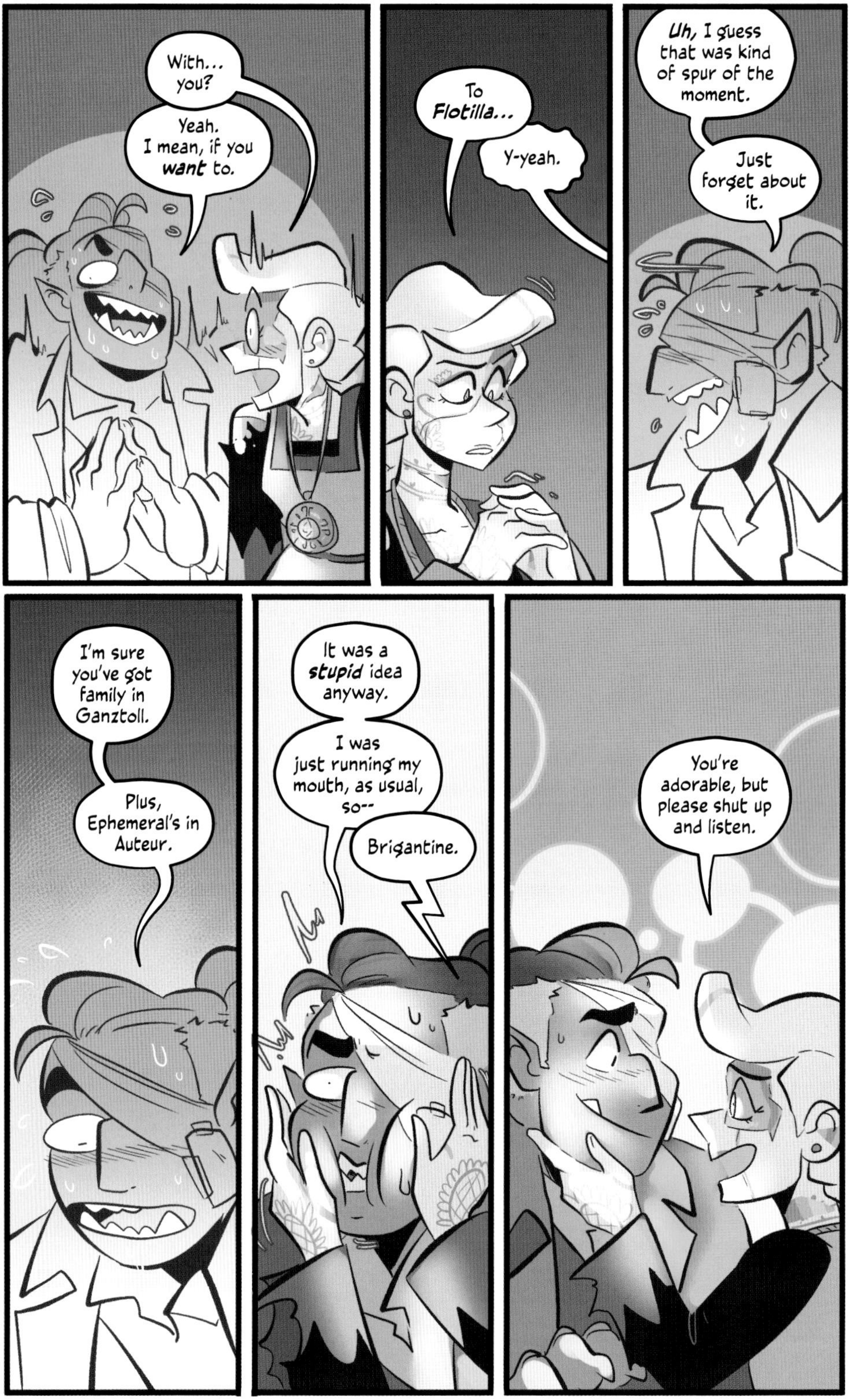
With... you?
Yeah. I mean, if you **want** to.
To **Flotilla...**
Y-yeah.
Uh, I guess that was kind of spur of the moment.
Just forget about it.
I'm sure you've got family in Ganztoll.
Plus, Ephemeral's in Auteur.
It was a **stupid** idea anyway.
I was just running my mouth, as usual, so--
Brigantine.
You're adorable, but please shut up and listen.

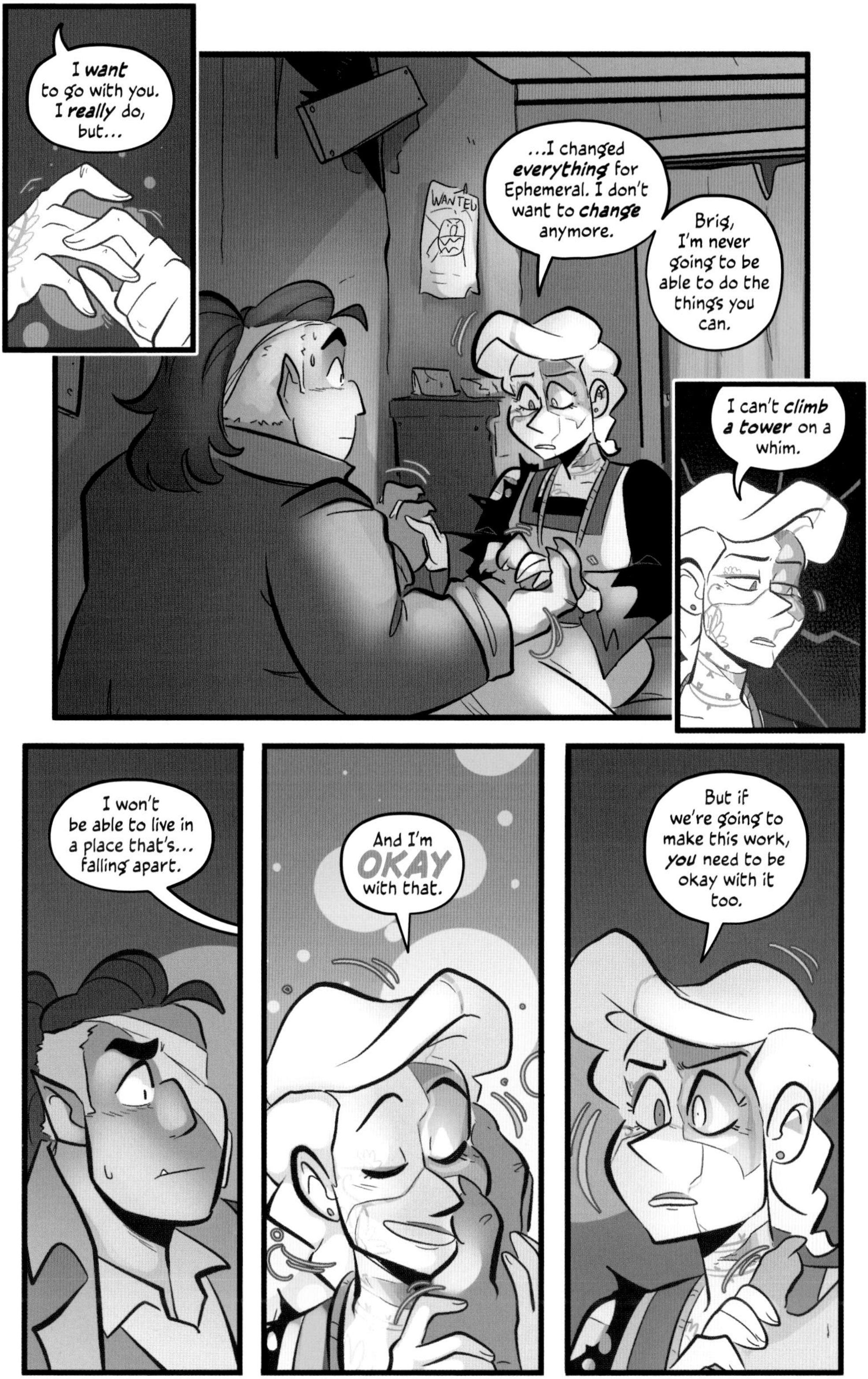
I want to go with you. I really do, but...
...I changed everything for Ephemeral. I don't want to change anymore.
WANTED
Brig, I'm never going to be able to do the things you can.
I can't climb a tower on a whim.
I won't be able to live in a place that's... falling apart.
And I'm OKAY with that.
But if we're going to make this work, you need to be okay with it too.

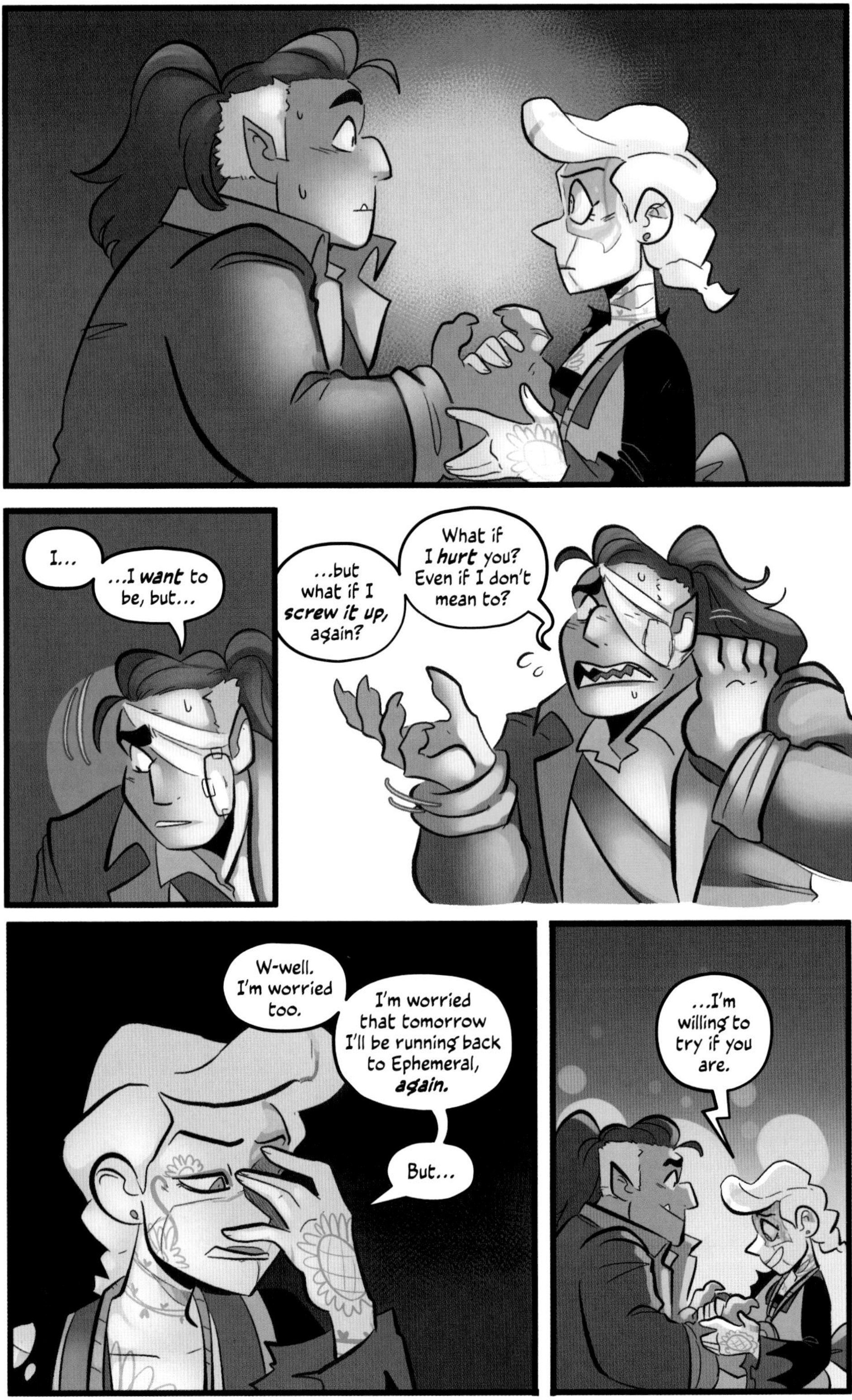
I...
...I *want* to be, but...
...but what if I *screw it up*, again?
What if I *hurt* you? Even if I don't mean to?
W-well. I'm worried too.
I'm worried that tomorrow I'll be running back to Ephemeral, *again.*
But...
...I'm willing to try if you are.

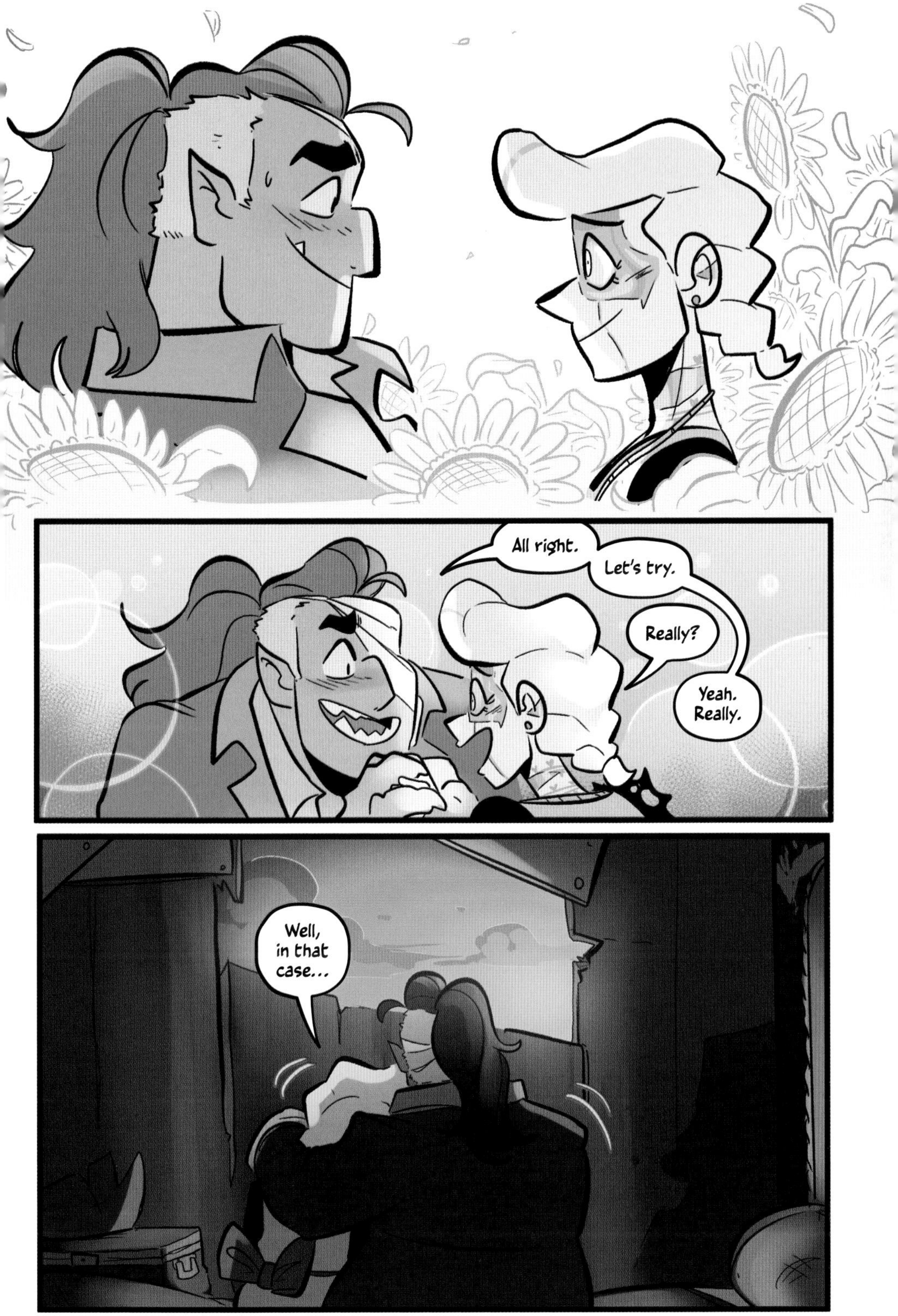
All right.
Let's try.
Really?
Yeah. Really.
Well, in that case...

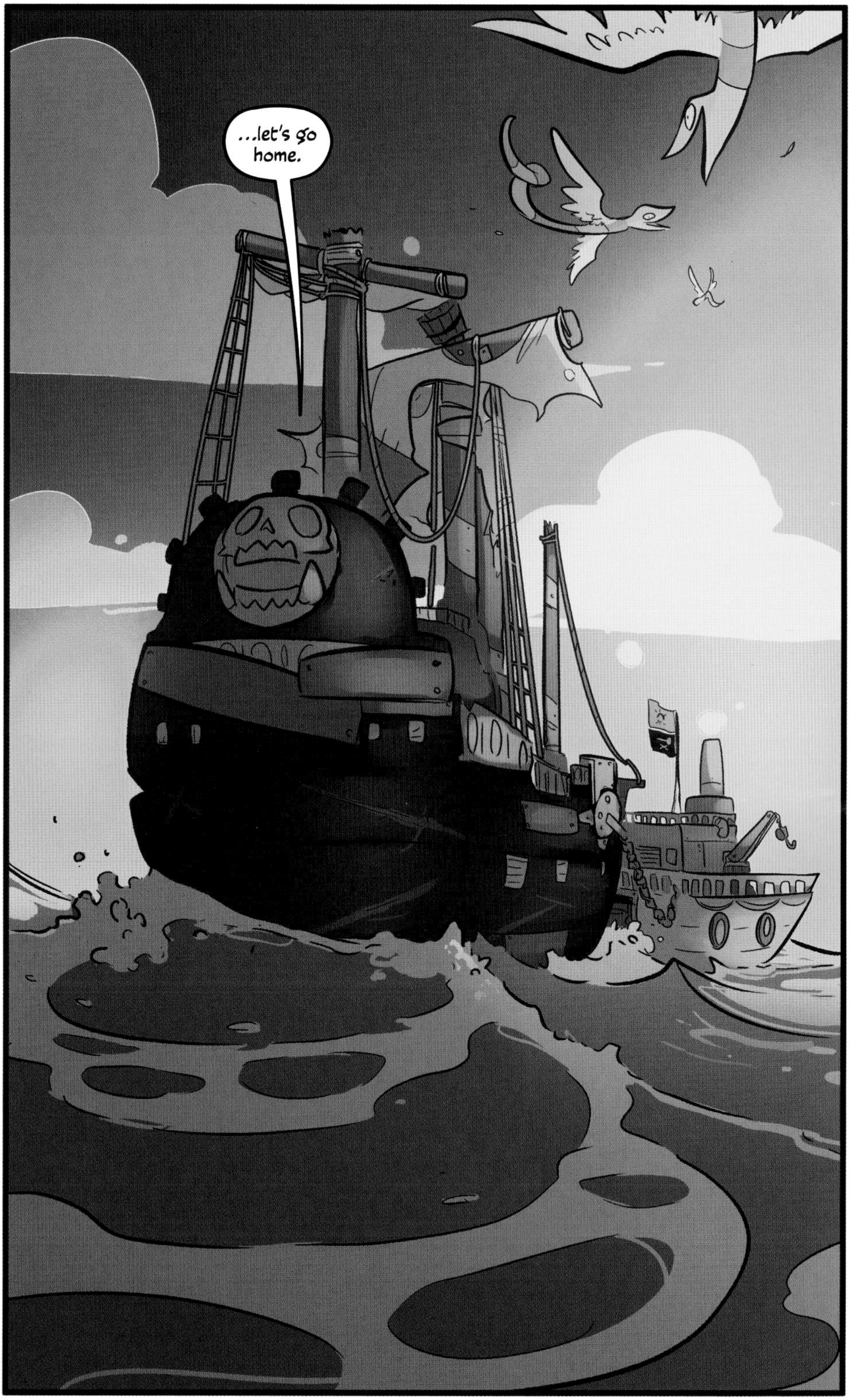
...let's go home.

Epilogue

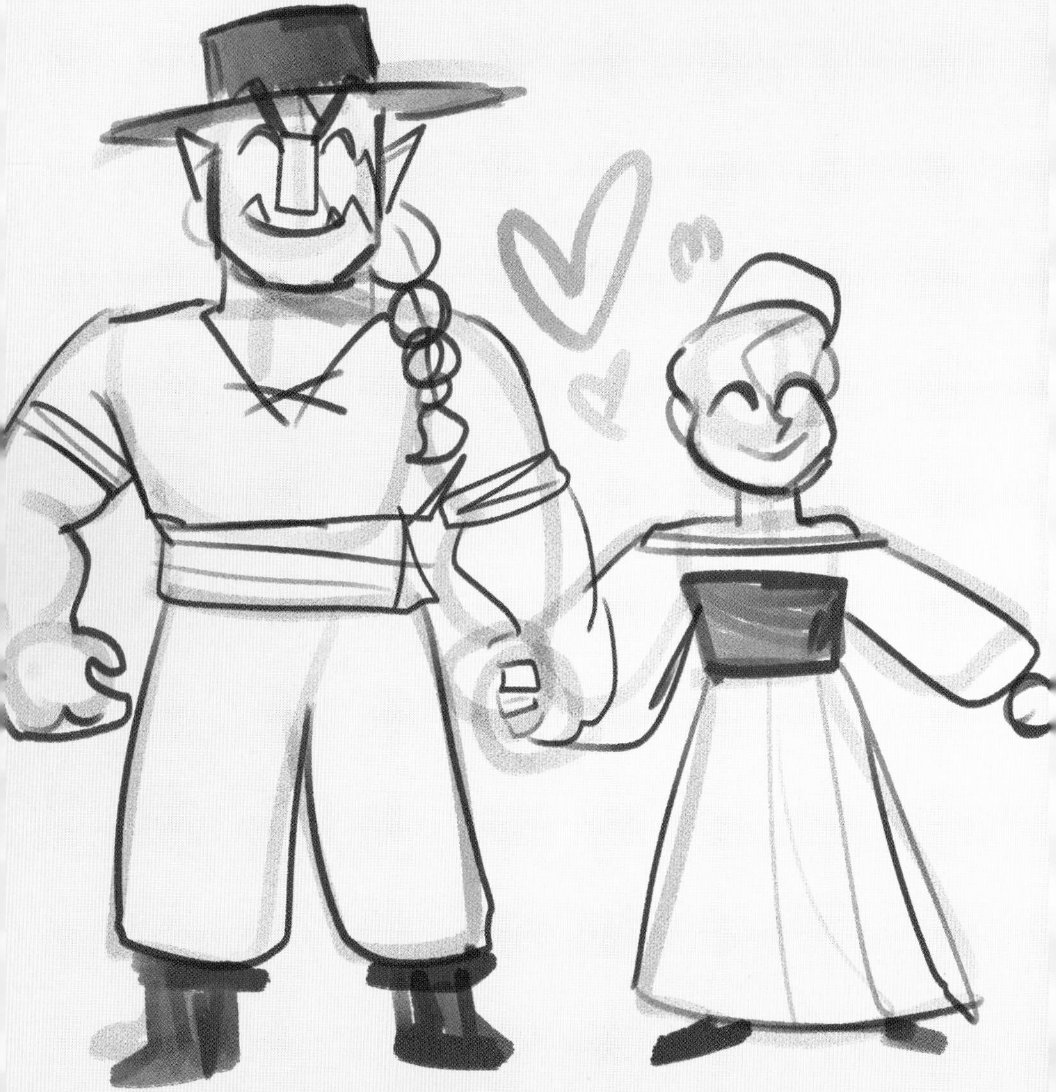

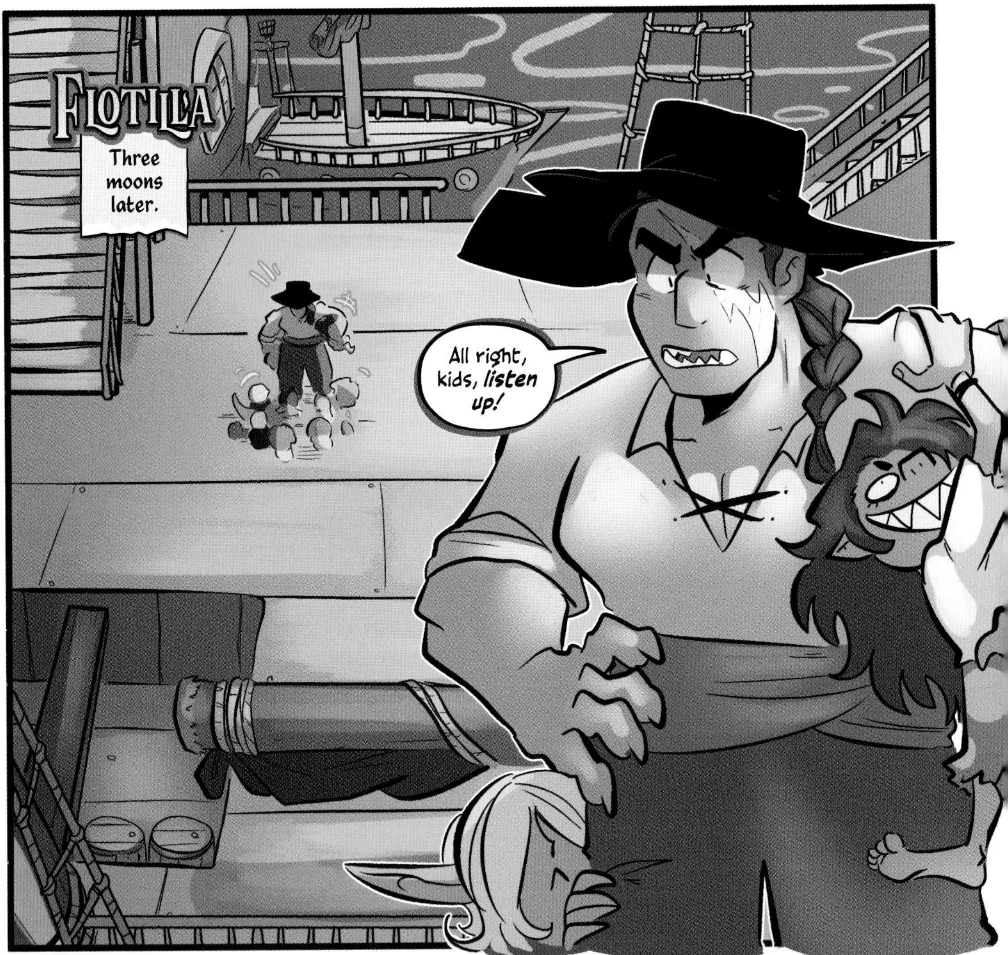
FLOTILLA
Three moons later.
All right, kids, listen up!

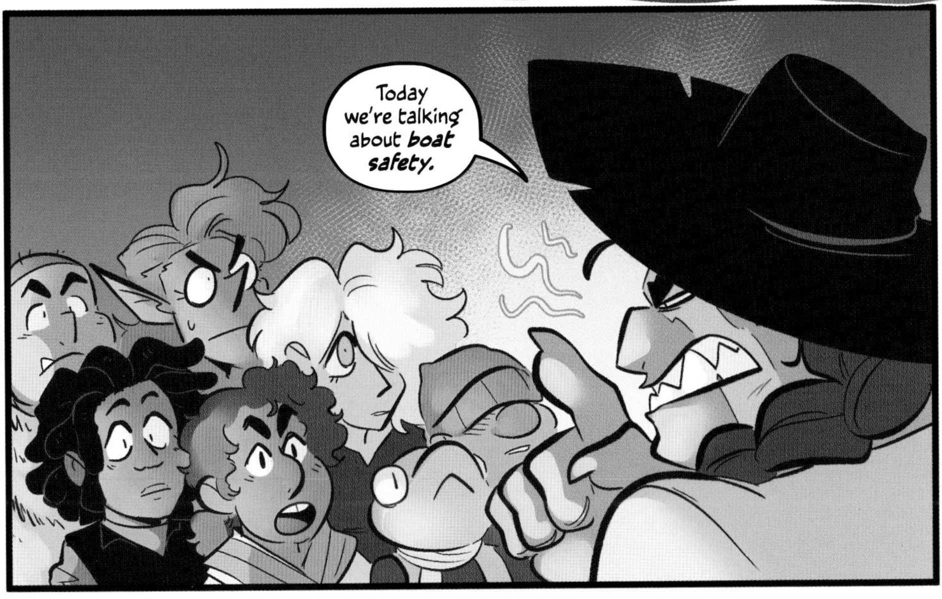
Today we're talking about boat safety.

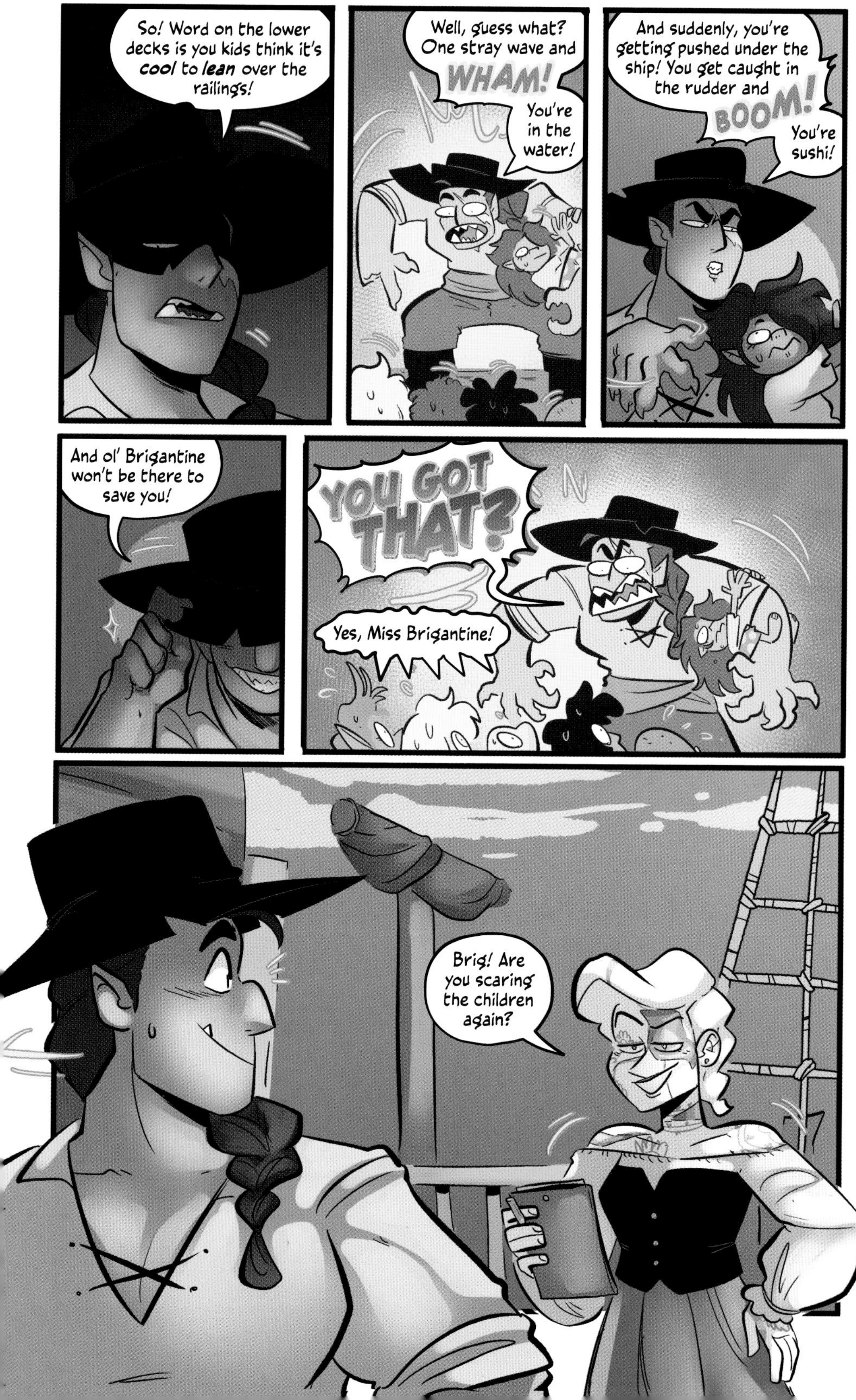
So! Word on the lower decks is you kids think it's *cool* to *lean* over the railings!
Well, guess what? One stray wave and
WHAM!
You're in the water!
And suddenly, you're getting pushed under the ship! You get caught in the rudder and
BOOM!
You're sushi!
And ol' Brigantine won't be there to save you!
YOU GOT THAT?
Yes, Miss Brigantine!
Brig! Are you scaring the children again?

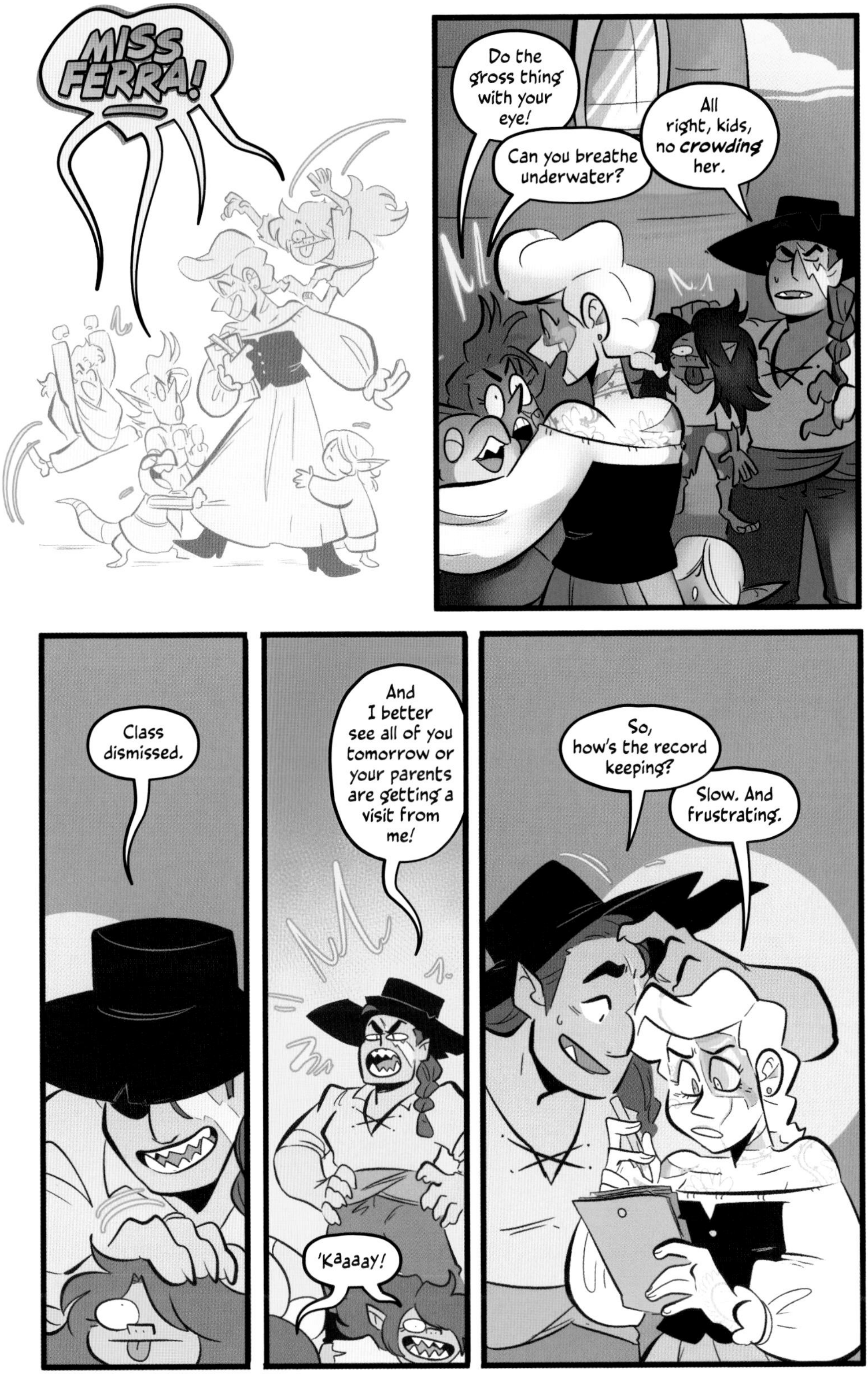
MISS FERRA!
Do the gross thing with your eye!
Can you breathe underwater?
All right, kids, no **crowding** her.
Class dismissed.
And I better see all of you tomorrow or your parents are getting a visit from me!
'Kaaaay!
So, how's the record keeping?
Slow. And frustrating.

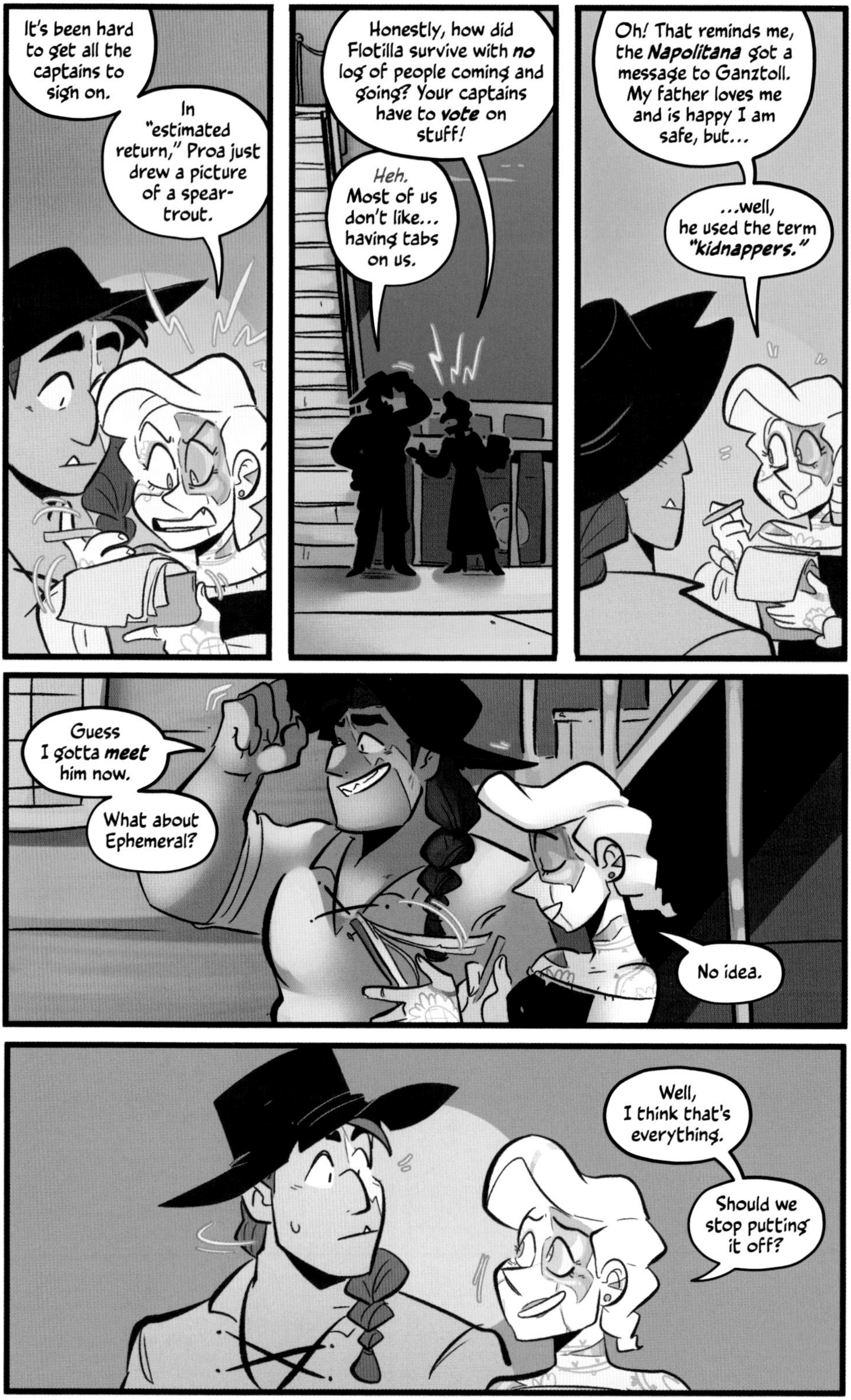
It's been hard to get all the captains to sign on.
In "estimated return," Proa just drew a picture of a spear-trout.
Honestly, how did Flotilla survive with **no** log of people coming and going? Your captains have to **vote** on stuff!
Heh. Most of us don't like... having tabs on us.
Oh! That reminds me, the ***Napolitana*** got a message to Ganztoll. My father loves me and is happy I am safe, but...
...well, he used the term ***"kidnappers."***
Guess I gotta **meet** him now.
What about Ephemeral?
No idea.
Well, I think that's everything.
Should we stop putting it off?

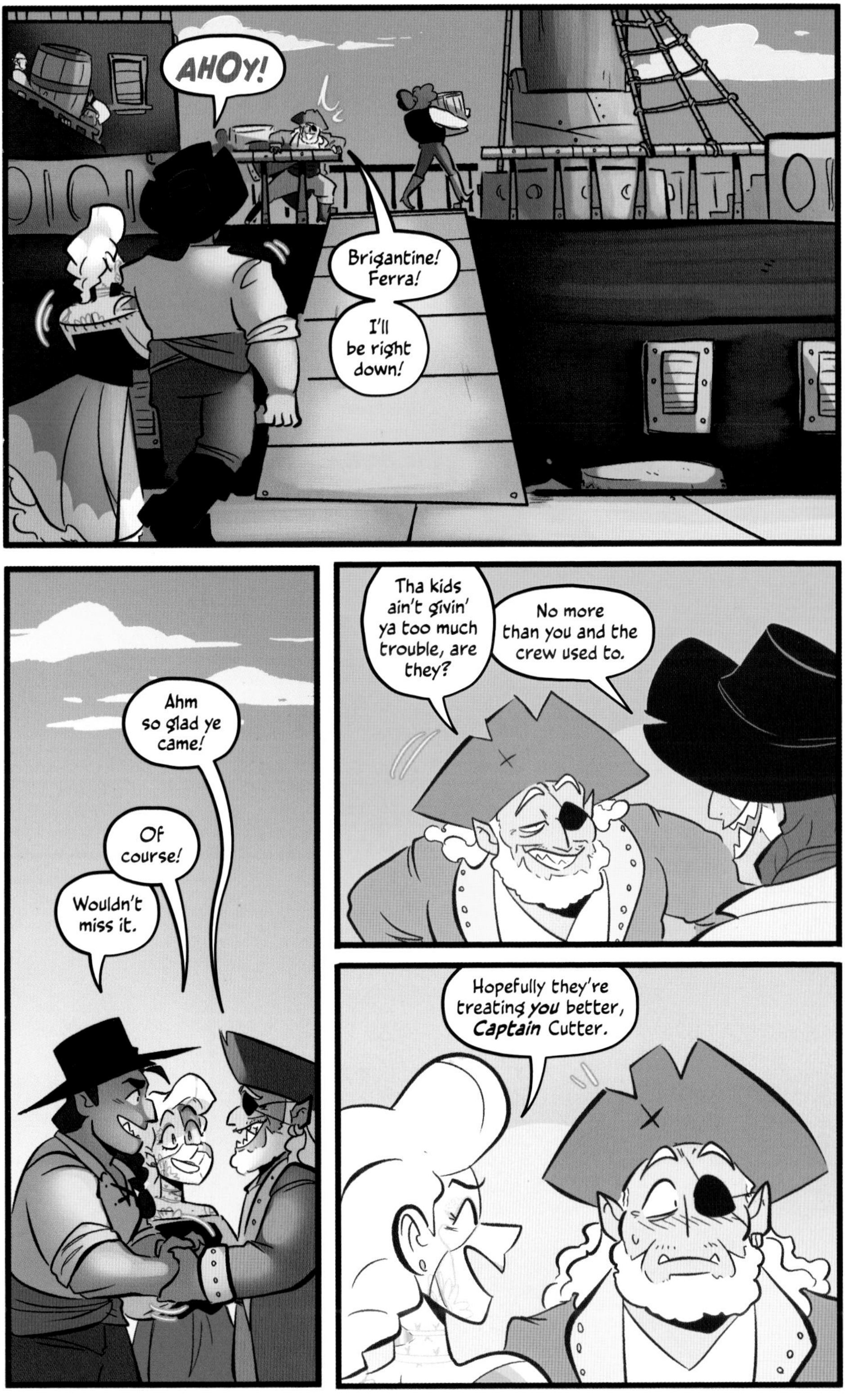
AHOY!
Brigantine! Ferra!
I'll be right down!
Ahm so glad ye came!
Of course!
Wouldn't miss it.
Tha kids ain't givin' ya too much trouble, are they?
No more than you and the crew used to.
Hopefully they're treating *you* better, ***Captain*** Cutter.

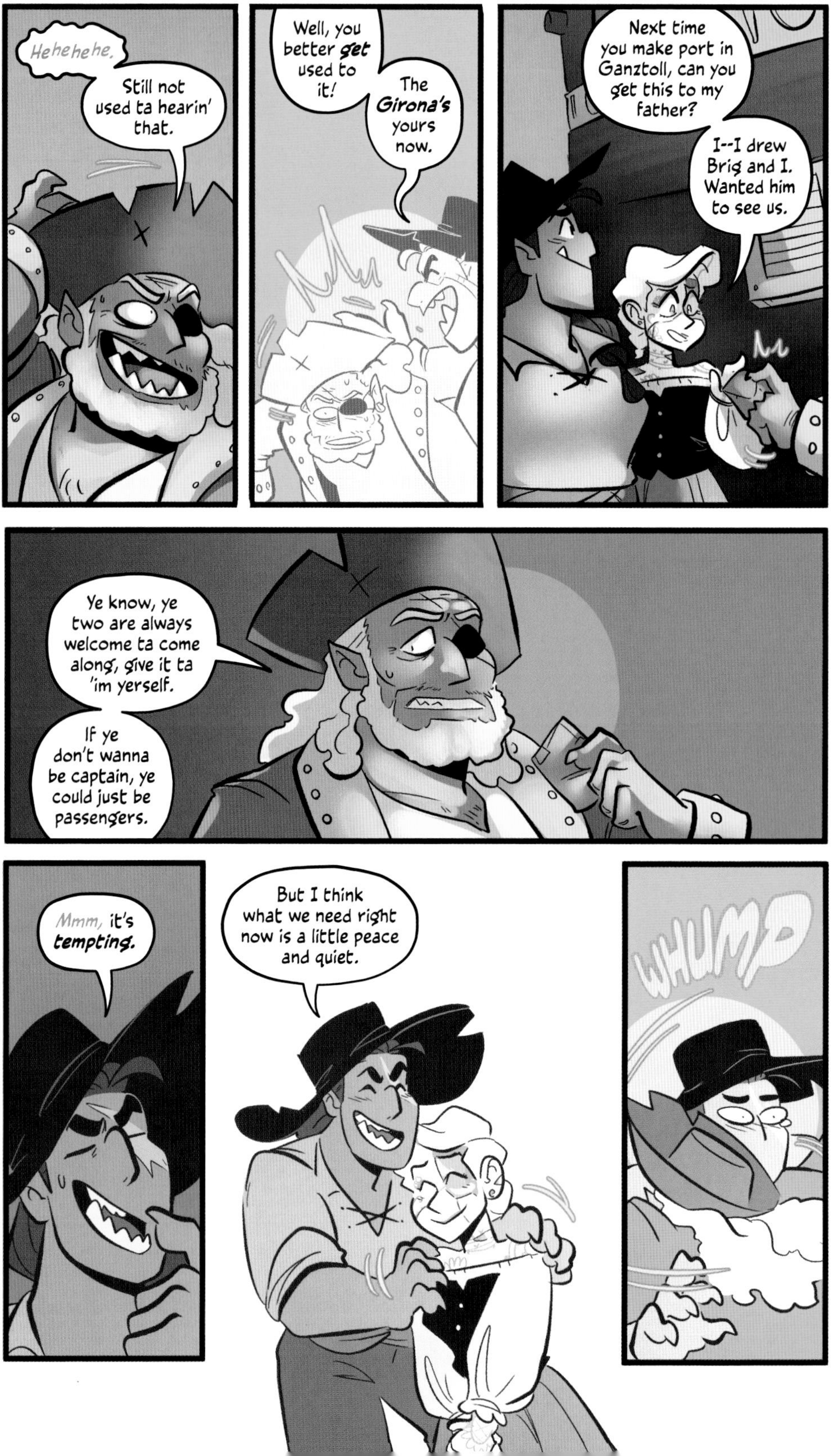
Hehehehe.
Still not used ta hearin' that.
Well, you better *get* used to it!
The *Girona's* yours now.
Next time you make port in Ganztoll, can you get this to my father?
I--I drew Brig and I. Wanted him to see us.
Ye know, ye two are always welcome ta come along, give it ta 'im yerself.
If ye don't wanna be captain, ye could just be passengers.
Mmm, it's *tempting.*
But I think what we need right now is a little peace and quiet.
WHUMP

Ahm gonna miss ye, kid.

Yeah. I'll miss you, too.

Ye better not screw this up, missy!

Uh... I don't *plan* to.

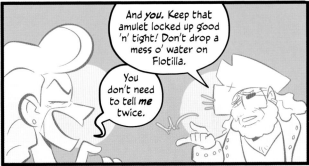

And *you*. Keep that amulet locked up good 'n' tight! Don't drop a mess o' water on Flotilla.

You don't need to tell *me* twice.

Oh, CAPTAIN!

We're ready for you!

Coming aboard?

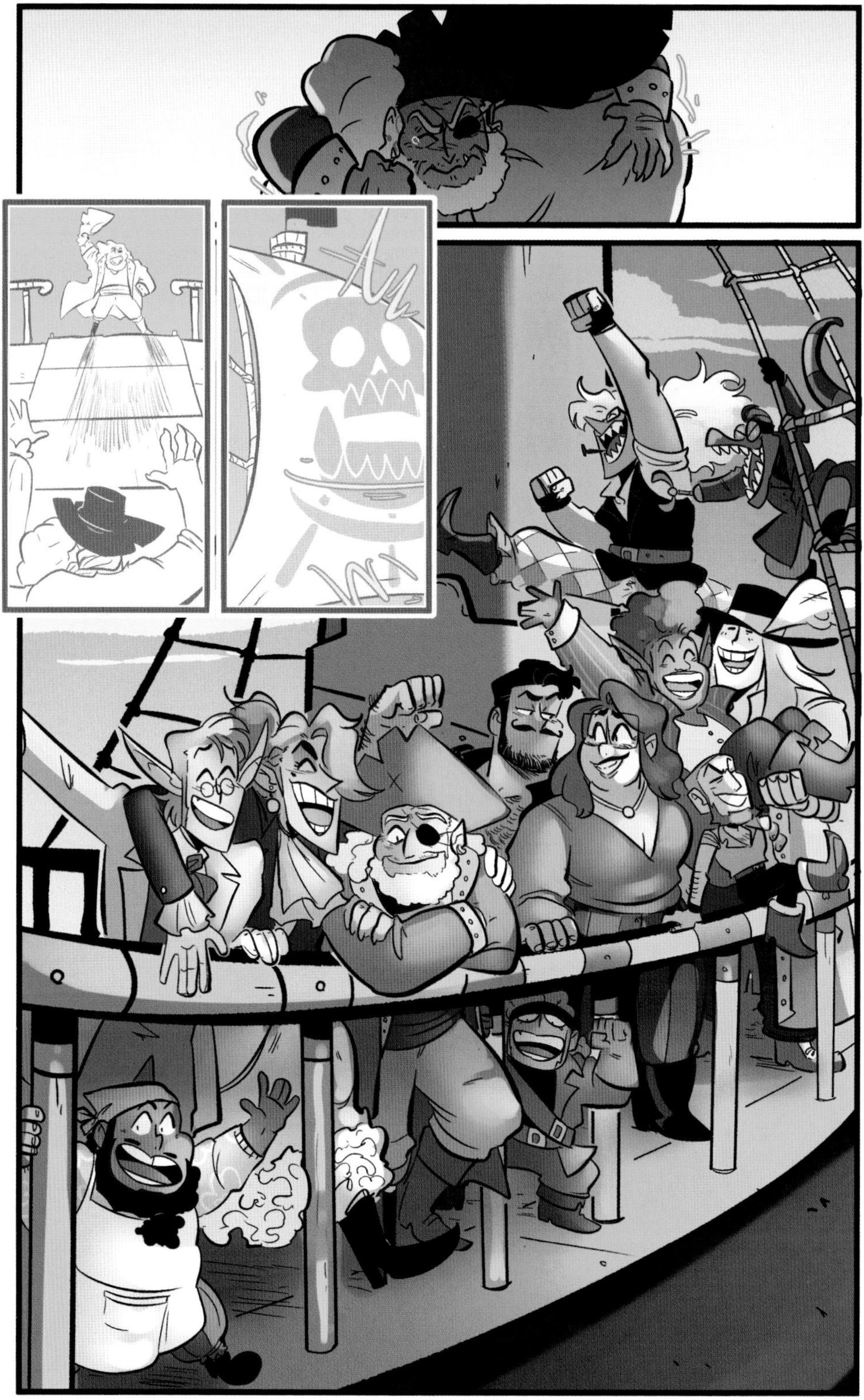

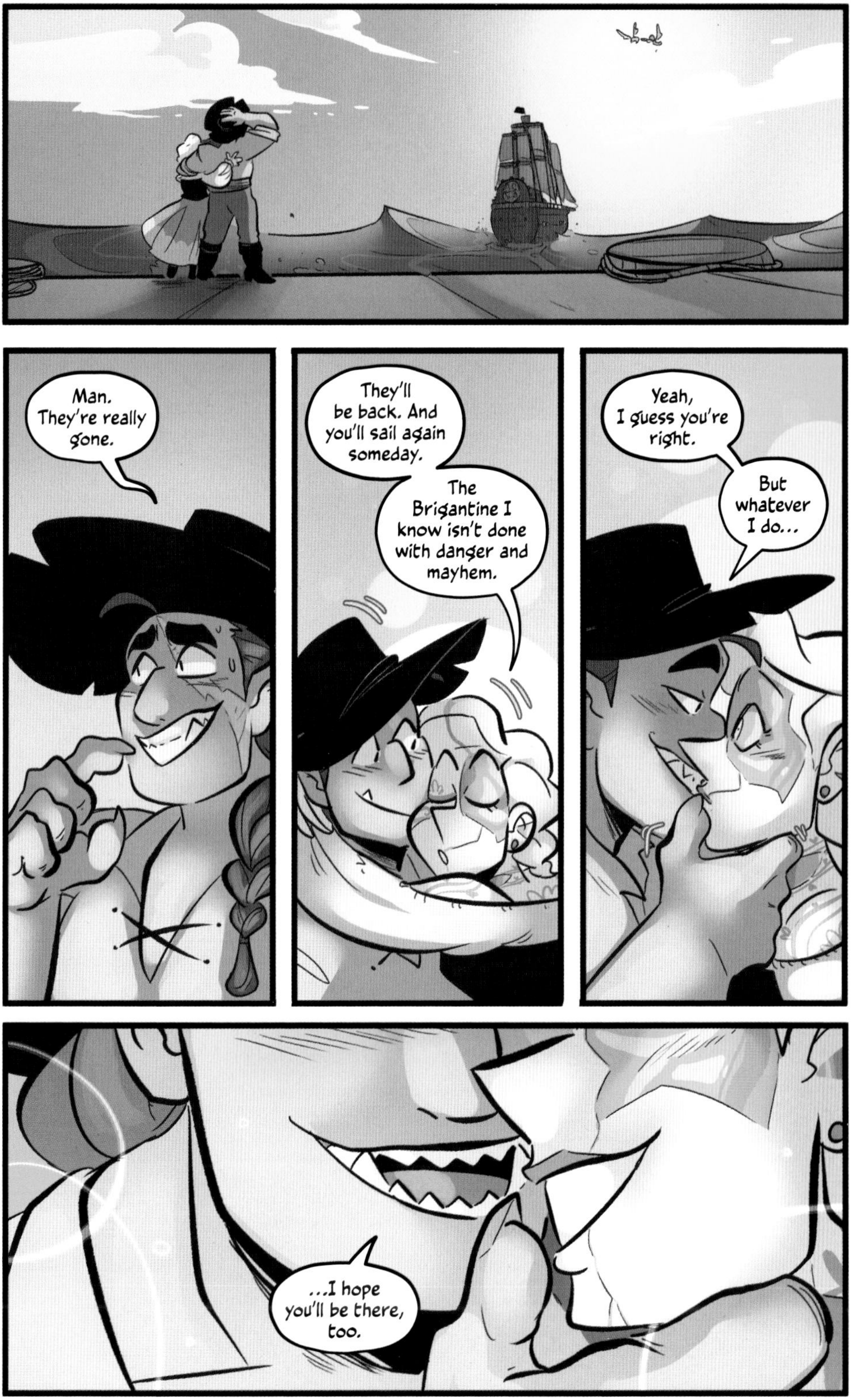
Man. They're really gone.
They'll be back. And you'll sail again someday.
The Brigantine I know isn't done with danger and mayhem.
Yeah, I guess you're right.
But whatever I do...
...I hope you'll be there, too.

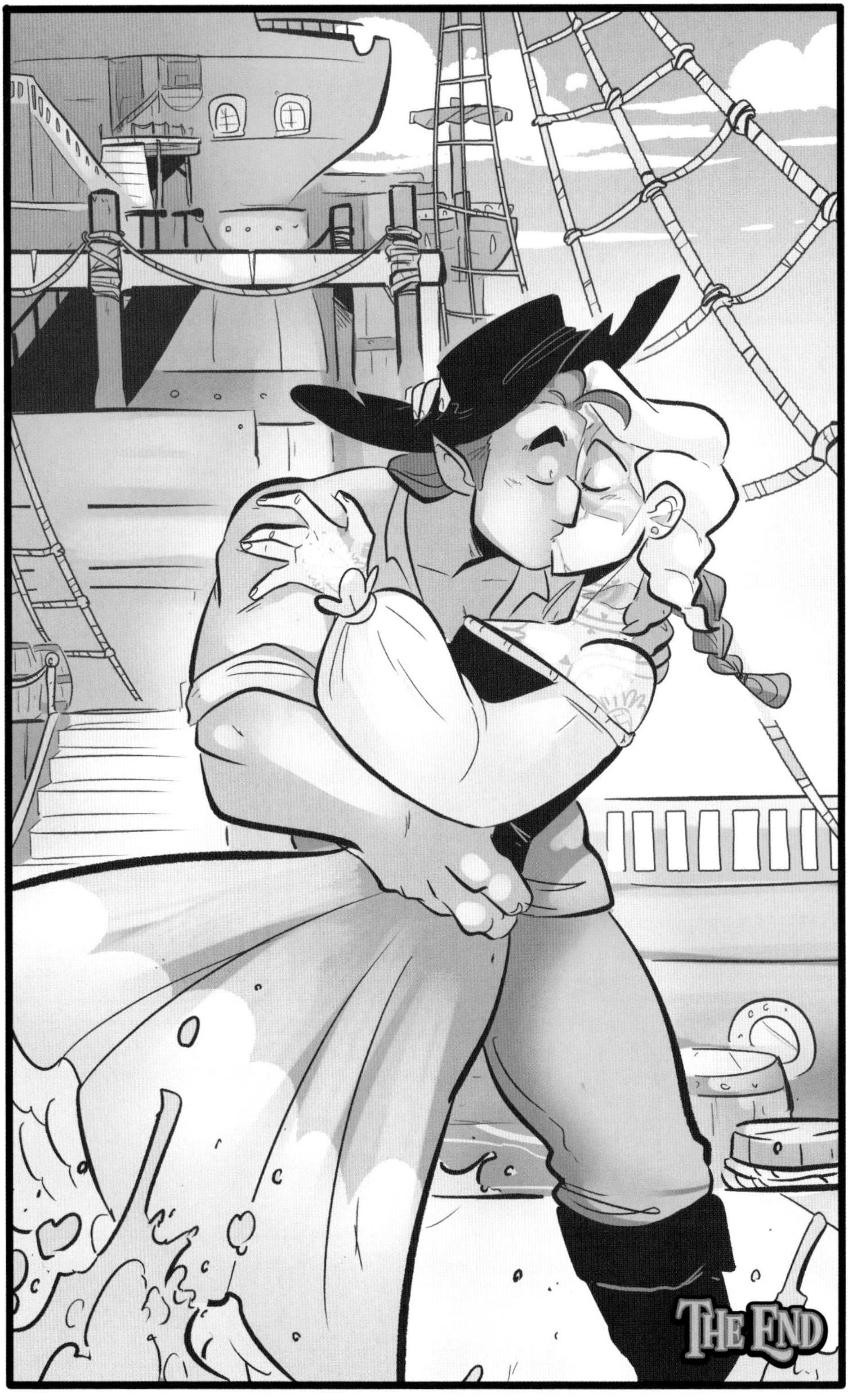
THE END

ACKNOWLEDGMENTS

Emily:

Thanks to my partners, Diane and Angie; Mom and Dad; my brother, Kevin; and all my family and friends who have constantly supported my work. Special thanks to Atla Hrafney, who edited the first chapter of this book and believed in this book when I even didn't.

NJ:

Huge thanks to my incredible partner, Tess; my mom and siblings; and my friends, all of whom have supported my passion for comics! Without them, I wouldn't have been able to make something like a career out of it.

And from both of us:

Thanks to Lucas for embarking on this book with us, Claire for having all our backs, Amanda for being our cheerleader and source of insight, the rest of the editorial team for helping this ship sail, and anyone who told us they were excited for this book!